THE
GRAVE
THIEF

THE GRAVE THIEF

BOOK THREE OF THE
TWILIGHT REIGN

TOM LLOYD

an imprint of **Prometheus Books**
Amherst, NY

Published 2009 by Pyr®, an imprint of Prometheus Books

Inquiries should be addressed to
Pyr
59 John Glenn Drive
Amherst, New York 14228–2119
VOICE: 716–691–0133, ext. 210
FAX: 716–691–0137
WWW.PYRSF.COM

13 12 11 10 09   5 4 3 2 1

Library of Congress Cataloging-in-Publication Data

Lloyd, Tom, 1979–
    The grave thief / by Tom Lloyd.
        p. cm. — (The twilight reign ; bk. 3)
    Originally published: London : Gollancz, an imprint of the Orion Publishing Group, 2008.
    ISBN 978–1–59102–780–5 (pbk. : alk. paper)
    I. Title.

PR6112.L697G73 2009
823'.92—dc22

2009020981

Printed in the United States on acid-free paper

For Fiona, with all my love

DRAMATIS PERSONÆ

Afasin, Cardinal—White-eye general of the Knights of the Temples and ruler of Mustet

Alav—Goddess of Justice, replaced Kebren during the Age of Darkness

Alterr—Goddess of the Night Sky and Greater Moon and member of the Upper Circle of the Pantheon

Amavoq—Goddess of the Forest, patron of the Yeetatchen and member of the Upper Circle of the Pantheon

Amber—Nickname of a Menin major in the Cheme Third Legion

Ankremer, Major Belir—Farlan soldier, bastard of the previous Duke of Lomin

Antern, Count Opess—Narkang nobleman and advisor to King Emin

Antil, High Priest Alos—High Priest of Shotir in the Byora quarter of the Circle City

Aracnan—Immortal wanderer of unknown origin

Ardela—Farlan devotee of the Lady in Cardinal Certinse's employ

Aryn Bwr—Battle name of the last Elven king, who led their rebellion against the Gods. His true name has been excised from history

Asenn—Goddess of Rain and Snow, daughter of Lliot

Astin—Mercenary-turned-penitent of Ushull in the Circle City

Atro—Lord of the Farlan before Lord Bahl

Ayel, High Priest Ora—High Priest of Vasle and advisor to General Afasin

Azaer—A shadow

Bahl—Lord of the Farlan tribe before Lord Isak

Belarannar—Goddess of the Earth and member of the Upper Circle of the Pantheon, once patron of the Vukotic tribe

Bern, High Priest Jopel—High Priest of Death in Tirah

Beyn, Ignas—Member of the Brotherhood

Bissen—Mage in the employ of Natai Escral, the Duchess of Byora

Bolla—Mercenary-turned-penitent of Ushull in the Circle City

Boren, Litt—Farlan forester

Borse, Sir Gliwen—Farlan nobleman from Lomin

Brandt, Commander (Brandt Toquin)—Deceased commander of the Narkang City Watch, younger brother of Suzerain Toquin

Burning Man, the—One of the Reapers, the five Aspects of Death

Cambrey Smoulder—Aspect of Ushull, local to the Circle City

Carasay, Sir Cerse—Colonel of the Palace Guard of Tirah, from the Torl suzerainty

Carel (Carelfolden), Marshal Betyn—Mentor and friend of Lord Isak, former commander of his personal guard

Celao, Lord—Litse white-eye, Chosen of Ilit and ruler of the Ismess quarter of the Circle City

Cerdin—God of Thieves

Certinse, Cardinal Varn—Farlan cleric, third son of the Tildek suzerainty, younger brother of Suzerain Tildek, Knight-Cardinal Certinse, and Duchess Lomin

Certinse, Duke Karlat—Farlan nobleman, ruler of Lomin, nephew of Suzerain Tildek

Certinse, Knight-Cardinal Horel—Commander of the Knights of the Temples, younger brother of Suzerain Tildek, Farlan by birth

Chalat—Deposed Lord of the Chetse

Chera—A little girl from Llehden

Chirialt, Dermeness—Farlan mage

Chotech, General—Chetse general of the Knights of the Temples

Citizen—see Dei, Kepra

Conjurer—Farlan mage and member of Chief Steward Lesarl's coterie of secret advisors

Coran—White-eye bodyguard of King Emin Thonal of Narkang

Corast, Petril—Farlan forester

Corerr—A junior priest from the Harlequin clans

Corlyn—The traditional name adopted by the head of the Farlan's priest branch of the Cult of Nartis

Cormeh, Scion Tew—Farlan nobleman, heir to the Cormeh suzerainty

Cuder, Sir Creyl—Knight of Narkang, founding member of the Brotherhood organisation

Dahten, Sir—Farlan nobleman, head of Suzerain Torl's hurscals

Dake, Colonel—Member of the Knights of the Temples, originally from Canar Thrit

Dancer—Farlan nobleman and member of Chief Steward Lesarl's coterie of secret advisors

Darc, Legion Chaplain—Farlan chaplain, second only to High Chaplain Mochyd

Darn, Major Ferek—Menin major in the Cheme Third Legion

Dast, Garan—Byoran government minister

Death—Chief of the Gods and head of the Upper Circle of the Pantheon

Deebek, Sergeant—Menin soldier in the Cheme Third Legion

Dei, Kepra—Landlady of the Cock's Tail Tavern in Tirah and member of the Chief Steward's coterie known as Citizen

Denn, Valo—Member of the wagon train where Isak grew up

Derager, Gavai—Wife of a Byoran wine merchant and Farlan agent

Derager, Lell—Wine merchant from Byora, a Farlan agent

Dev, General Chate—Chetse general and Commander of the Ten Thousand

Diril Halfmast—Byoran whore, an agent of Zhia Vukotic

Disten, Cardinal—Farlan cleric, once a Legion Chaplain

Doranei, Ashin—A member of the Brotherhood

Doren, Abbot—Abbot of an island monastery and High Priest of Vellern, God of Birds

Duril—Farlan forester

Dyar, Marshal Harin—Commander of the Byoran Guard

Echer, High Cardinal—Farlan cleric, leader of the cardinal branch of the Cult of Nartis

Ehla—The common name Lord Isak is permitted to use for the witch of Llehden

Eliane—The name Haipar is known by after she loses her memory

Endine, Tomal—Narkang mage in the employ of King Emin

Eraliave—Elven general who predated the Wars of the Houses; he wrote the treatise *Principles of Warfare*

Escral, Ganas, Duke of Byora—husband of Natai Escral, Duchess of Byora

Escral, Natai, Duchess of Byora—Ruler of the Byora quarter of the Circle City

Etesia—Goddess of Lust, one of the three linked Goddesses who together cover all the aspects of love

Farlan, King Deliss—The first king of the Farlan

Farlan, Prince Kasi—Farlan prince during the Great War, in whose image white-eyes were created and after whom the lesser moon was named

Farmer—Farlan landowner and member of Chief Steward Lesarl's coterie of secret advisors

Fate—Goddess of Luck, also known as the Lady

Feilin, Major—Byoran soldier, Commander of the Ruby Tower Guard

Fell, Chaplain—Cleric of Karkarn and member of Knights of the Temples, attached to the First Akell Legion

Fernal—A Demi-God living in Llehden

Fershin, Horman—Farlan wagon driver, father to Lord Isak

Firrin—A member of the Brotherhood

Fohl, Captain—Commander of the Duchess of Byora's personal guard

Foleh, Suzerain Shoqe—Farlan nobleman

Fordan, Suzerain Karad—Farlan nobleman

Foret—Farlan forester

Gesh—Litse white-eye and First Guardian of the Library of Seasons

Gort, General Jebehl—Deceased general of the Knights of the Temples

Grast, Deverk—Former Lord of the Menin

Great Wolf, the—One of the Reapers, the five Aspects of Death

Gren—Farlan forester

Grisat—Mercenary-turned-penitent of Ushull in the Circle City

Hain, Captain—Menin officer in the Cheme Third Legion

Haipar the shapeshifter—Raylin mercenary of the Deneli tribe from the Elven Waste, known as Eliane when she loses her memory

Harys—Brothel-owner in Byora, an agent of Zhia Vukotic

Headsman, the—One of the Reapers, the five Aspects of Death

Heren, Hol—Farlan forester

Heren, Jeyer—Farlan forester

Horle—A member of the Brotherhood

Ilit—God of the Wind, patron of the Litse tribe and member of the Upper Circle of the Pantheon

Ilumene—A former member of the Brotherhood

Imis, Suzerain—Farlan nobleman

Ineh—Lover of Lord Bahl before she was raped and murdered by the white-eye Lord Atro

Inoth—Goddess of the Western Seas, eldest and most powerful child of Lliot who took his place in the Upper Circle of the Pantheon

Intiss, Ginna—A merchant's wife from Tor Milist

Intiss, Harol—A merchant's son from Tor Milist

Introl, Tila—Advisor to Lord Isak, affianced to Count Vesna

Isak—Lord of the Farlan, Chosen of Nartis and Duke of Tirah

Islir, Witchfinder—Member of the Knights of the Temples, of Litse origin

Jachen, (Major Jachen Ansayl)—Commander of Lord Isak's personal guard and former mercenary

Jackdaw (Prior Corci)—Former monk of Vellern

Jackler, Sergeant—Member of the Knights of the Temples, Farlan by birth

Jato, Steward—Steward of the Tower in Byora

Jelil—Mage in the employ of the Duchess of Byora

Jerequan (The Lady at Rest)—Aspect of Amavoq

Jerrer, Emissary Peyel—Emissary from Sautin

Jesher, Cardinal—Deceased Farlan cardinal noted for his religious parables

Jesters, the—Demi-Gods and Raylin mercenaries, sons of Death

Jorinn—Maid to Queen Oterness Thonal

Kam, Jendal—Farlan forester

Kantay—Goddess of Longing, one of the linked Goddesses who together cover all the aspects of love, sometimes referred to as Queen of the Unrequited

Kass, Unmen Eso—Farlan priest of Vasle

Karkarn—God of War, patron of the Menin tribe, and member of the Upper Circle of the Pantheon

Kayel, Hener—The name used by Ilumene in the Circle City

Kebren—Deceased God of Justice, patron of the Fysthrall, died during the Last Battle

Kelet, Sir Veyan—Farlan nobleman and Ascetite

Kerek, Brother—Farlan cleric, secretary to Cardinal Certinse

Kervar, Quartermaster-General Pelay—Quartermaster-General of the Farlan Army

Kerx, Captain—Mercenary from Tor Milist in the employ of High Priest Bern

Kiallas—Litse white-eye

Kirl, Horsemistress Lay—Menin auxiliary, attached to the Cheme Third Legion

Kitar—Goddess of Harvest and Fertility, member of the Upper Circle of the Pantheon

Kiyer (of the Deluge)—Aspect of Ushull, local to the Circle City

Lady—Fate, Goddess of Luck

Lahk, General—Farlan white-eye, commander of the forces in Tirah

Larat—God of Magic & Manipulation, member of the Upper Circle of the Pantheon

Larim, Lord Shotein—Menin white-eye mage, Chosen of Larat and Lord of the Hidden Tower

Legana—Farlan devotee of the Lady, employed as an assassin and spy

Lehm, Suzerain Preter—Farlan nobleman

Leitah—Deceased Goddess of Wisdom & Learning, sister to Larat

Lesarl, Chief Steward Fordan—Principal advisor to the Lord of the Farlan

Leshi—Farlan Ascetite soldier

Leyen, Sir Arite—Principal minister to the Duchess of Byora

Lier, High Priest Ayarl—High Priest of Alterr in Byora

Lliot—Deceased God of Water, who died during the Age of Myths. His domain was divided up among his five children: Inoth, Turist, Shoso, Vasle, and Asenn

Lokan, Duke Shorin—Farlan nobleman and ruler of Merlat

Lonei, Father—Priest of Shotir in Byora

Loris, Sergeant—House guard in the Coin district of Byora

Luerce—Inhabitant of Byora and follower of Azaer

Macove, Count Perel—Farlan nobleman from Saroc and member of the Brethren of the Sacred Teachings

Malich, Cheliss—Deceased mage of Embere, father of Cordein Malich, teacher of the young Morghien. Died on the expedition to Castle Keriabral.

Malich, Cordein—Deceased necromancer from Embere

Meah, Suzerain—Farlan nobleman

Medah, Colonel—Farlan soldier, commander of a Torl light cavalry legion

Merchant—Farlan merchant and member of Chief Steward Lesarl's coterie of secret advisors

Mihn ab Netren ab Felith—Failed Harlequin, now friend of Lord Isak

Mikiss, Koden—Menin army messenger turned to vampirism by Zhia Vukotic

Minnay—Orphan from Byora, now a ward of the Duchess of Byora

Morghien—A drifter of Embere descent, known as the man of many spirits

Nai—Former manservant to the deceased necromancer Isherin Purn

Nartis—God of the Night, Storms, and Hunters. Patron of the Farlan tribe and member of the Upper Circle of the Pantheon

Nelbove, Suzerain Atar—Farlan nobleman

Nerlos, Suzerain Jai—Farlan nobleman

Nostil, Prince Velere—Aryn Bwr's heir, first owner of the Skull of Ruling, assassinated during the Great War

Nostil, Queen Valije—Aryn Bwr's queen, first owner of the Skull of Dreams, died at the Last Battle

Ortof-Greyl, Colonel Harn—Member of the Knights of the Temples

Parim, Eyl—Demagogue from Narkang in the king's employ

Parss—Aspect and son of Ushull, local to the Circle City

Peness—Mage from the Byora quarter of the Circle City

Pir, Sir Arole—Farlan nobleman, second cousin to Duke Certinse

Prayer—Farlan priest of Nartis and member of Chief Steward Lesarl's coterie of secret advisors

Rojak—Deceased minstrel originally from Embere, first among Azaer's disciples

Ruhen—The name used by Azaer as a mortal

Sailor—Farlan sailor and member of Chief Steward Lesarl's coterie of secret advisors

Salen—Deceased Menin white-eye mage, former Lord of the Hidden Tower and Chosen of the God Larat

Saljin Man, the—Daemon sent to plague the Vukotic tribe

Sants, Major—Member of the Knights of the Temples, First Akell Legion, originally from Canar Thrit

Saroc, Suzerain Fir—Farlan nobleman and member of the Brethren of the Sacred Teachings

Sebe—Member of the Brotherhood

Seliasei—Minor Aspect of Vasle that now inhabits Morghien

Selsetin, Suzerain Pelan—Farlan nobleman

Sempes, Duke Faran—Farlan nobleman and ruler of Perlir

Shael, Captain—Member of the Knights of the Temples, First Akell Legion

Sheln, Brother-Captain Tanao—Member of the Brethren of the Sacred Teachings

Sheredal, Spreader of the Frost—Aspect of Asenn

Shinir—A Farlan Ascetite agent

Shotir—God of Healing and Forgiveness

Siul, Suzerain—Farlan noble

Soldier—Farlan soldier and member of Chief Steward Lesarl's coterie of secret advisors

Soldier, the—One of the Reapers, the five Aspects of Death

Sourl, Cardinal—Ruler of the Akell quarter of the Circle City and member of the Knights of the Temples

Styrax, Lord Kastan– White-eye Lord of the Menin and Chosen of Karkarn

Styrax, Scion Kohrad—White-eye son of Lord Styrax

Tell, Lord Yanao—Former Lord of the Litse

Tebran, Scion Pannar—Farlan nobleman

Tebran, Suzerain Kehed—Farlan nobleman

Teral, Major Evor—Farlan member of the Knights of the Temples, First Akell Legion

Thonal, King Emin—King of Narkang

Thonal, Queen Oterness—Queen of Narkang

Tildek, Suzerain Esh—Deceased Farlan nobleman, elder brother of Knight-Cardinal Certinse, the dowager Duchess Lomin, and Cardinal Certinse and uncle of Duke Certinse

Tiniq—Farlan ranger and brother of General Lahk

Tol the charcoal-burner—Farlan forester and charcoal burner

Torl, Suzerain Karn—Farlan nobleman and member of the Brethren of the Sacred Teachings

Tremal, Harlo—Member of the Brotherhood

Triena—Goddess of Romantic Love and Fidelity, one of the three linked Goddesses who together cover all the aspects of love

Tsatach—God of Fire and the Sun, patron of the Chetse tribe, and member of the Upper Circle of the Pantheon

Uresh, Colonel—Menin officer, commander of the Cheme Third Legion

Ushull—Goddess of the Mountains, Aspect of Belarannar

Varner, Private—Farlan white-eye in the Tirah Palace Guard

Vasle—God of Rivers and Inland Seas

Veck, Cardinal—Farlan cleric, second only to the High Cardinal in the cult of Nartis

Veil—Member of the Brotherhood

Vellern—God of Birds

Vener, General/Cardinal Telith—Member of the Knights of the Temples and ruler of Raland

Venn (ab Teier ab Pirc)—Former Harlequin, now servant of Azaer

Veren—Deceased God of the Beasts and once member of the Upper Circle of the Pantheon, killed during the Great War

Vesna, Count Evanelial—Farlan nobleman and celebrated soldier, affianced to Tila Introl

Vrerr, Duke Sarole—Ruler of Tor Milist

Vrill, Duke Anote—White-eye Menin general

Vukotic, Prince Koezh—Ruler of the Vukotic tribe, cursed with vampirism after the Last Battle

Vukotic, Prince Vorizh—Younger brother of Koezh, cursed with vampirism after the Last Battle and subsequently driven insane

Vukotic, Princess Zhia—Youngest of the Vukotic family, cursed with vampirism after the Last Battle

Whisper—Farlan merchant and member of Chief Steward Lesarl's coterie of secret advisors

Wither Queen, the—One of the Reapers, the five Aspects of Death

Woran (Sniveling Woran)—Farlan forester

Xeliath—Yeetatchen female white-eye who has the Skull of Dreams fused to her hand

Yanai—House guard in the Coin district of Byora

Yeren, Colonel—Mercenary from Canar Thrit in the employ of Cardinal Certinse

Zaler, Lieutenant—Farlan soldier, aide to Suzerain Torl

ACKNOWLEDGMENTS

ANYONE WHO LIVES WITH A WRITER and puts up with him is a saint in my book; that Fiona manages to do so with such generosity and cheerfulness is rather humbling. Without your efforts, Fi, the book would have been all the poorer and I'd have struggled to enjoy writing it, so thank you.

Thank you also to the nice folk at Blake Friedmann who helped by accommodating my eccentricities, and my readers, Nat and Richard, yet again did sterling work pointing out all the stupid stuff I'd done. Thanks also to Nathan and Dave, for the cigarettes and philosophical musings. The last word, as always, goes to Jo Fletcher, whose efforts on my behalf go well beyond mere editing, but she does that bloody well too.

THE LAND

Xomejx

Merlat

Perlit

White
Isle

Canar
Thrit

Vanach

Tirah

Lomin

ELVEN
WASTE

Tor Milist

Scree

Helrect

Mantil

Narkang

Canar Fell

Aroth

The
CircleCity

Raland

Embere

Tor Salan

Denei

Ter Nol

Castle Keriabral

Mustet

Chotel

Sautin

ELVEN
WASTE

Vijgen

Mekray

Lochet

Verech

Cholos

Tserol

TioHe

Lenei

N

DS'05

WHAT HAS GONE BEFORE

ABBOT DOREN, head of an obscure island monastery, flees to the city of Scree with the apprentice Mayl. They are hiding from a murderous monk, Jackdaw, who has thrown in his lot with the shadow Azaer. Meanwhile King Emin of Narkang also sets out for Scree, lured by the prospect of hunting down the man who betrayed him for Azaer several years before.

Lord Isak, the new Lord of the Farlan, has left Narkang, determined to return home before news of his predecessor's death encourages rebellion. He carries with him two Crystal Skulls, given to him by a sect within the Knights of the Temples who believe him to be the Saviour of Mankind, and, imprisoned in his mind, Aryn Bwr, the last king of the Elves, who had hoped to use Isak to return to life and continue his war against the Gods.

When they reach Farlan territory, Isak's small party is ambushed by the Certinse family, which includes the new Duke of Lomin. Isak's men are badly outnumbered, but they are saved by a religious sect called the Brethren of the Sacred Teachings, led by Suzerains Torl and Saroc and Chaplain Distan, the man who uncovered the Malich conspiracy.

During the battle Carel is badly injured and Isak realises there are others whose association with him is putting them in unnecessary danger. He dispatches the failed Harlequin, Mihn, and Morghien, the man of many spirits, to the Yeetatchen homeland, to fetch Xeliath, the white-eye girl who was crippled by a stroke when Isak's fractured destiny was tied to her own. She too carries a Crystal Skull.

Isak is met by Ilumene, the man King Emin is hunting, and Ilumene, pretending still to be in the service of the king, encourages Isak's presence in Scree. Isak initially ignores him and continues home, but he knows he will have business in Scree soon enough, as it is the nearest stronghold of the White Circle, the sisterhood who tried to enslave him in Narkang.

In Scree, the vampire Zhia Vukotic continues to masquerade as a member of the White Circle and starts to develop a powerbase for herself there. She takes control of the sisterhood's recently recruited mercenary armies in anticipation of a Farlan assault, while also knowingly taking a Farlan spy, Legana, under her wing. Further south, Kastan Styrax returns to Thotel, having killed Isak's predecessor, Lord Bahl. Thanks to Azaer's warning, he manages to put down a coup within his own ranks. Styrax also comes to an agreement with the highest-ranking Chetse general, paving the way for the recruitment of Chetse legions. During the battle he is contacted by Isherin Purn, a Menin necromancer in Scree, who has sensed an artefact of immense power appearing in the city. He requests help to secure it, but Styrax, preoccupied with his injured son, resists the temptation, instead sending only a few soldiers to scout the situation in his place.

Back in Scree, the novice Mayel and his criminal cousin discover that the strange theatre group who have taken residence there are not all they appear to be—especially the minstrel who leads them, Rojak. Isak has finally reached Tirah, where he is to receive the blessing of the Farlan chief religious council, and issues a summons to all Farlan ranking noblemen, before making plans to go to Scree himself. King Emin arrives in Scree with members of the Brotherhood, his band of agents, and one, Doranei, makes accidental contact with Zhia Vukotic, who takes a shine to him. Zhia has rebuffed Rojak's advances at the theatre run by Azaer's disciples just as her brother, Koezh Vukotic, announces his presence in the city.

Kastan Styrax's soldiers arrive in Scree and are met by Nai, the necromancer's acolyte, only to be ambushed by King Emin, who has been tricked into believing one of the soldiers is Ilumene. Zhia, in her White Circle guise, arrives to keep the peace and takes Nai and two of the soldiers prisoner. By now tensions in the city are significantly raised: Siala, Scree's ruler, has declared martial law, there is an unnatural summer heatwave, and there is growing resentment towards the Gods.

Isak arrives just as the madness on the streets increases a notch. He saves Mayel from a blood-crazed mob, and a man is beaten to death for wearing what appears to be a priest's robe as he watches Ilumene forcing another man into the now-deserted Temple of Death.

Two separate armies arrives on Scree's outskirts, while inside, the White Circle appears to have lost control of its mercenary forces. The Witch of Llehden and the Demi-God Fernal arrive in Scree and encounter Isak, and working together they realise that the new theatre at the city's heart has been imbued with a spell that is increasing the tensions in the city and driving the natives to madness.

In the south, Lord Styrax has also been busy: he has double-crossed the daemon he's been dealing with for several years, freeing himself of its influence, while finding the opportunity to demonstrate his peerless martial skills to the Chetse generals—and he "accidentally" demolishes the great Temple of the Sun in Thotel, revealing the hiding place of one of the Crystal Skulls.

Back in Scree, all order has collapsed, and even well-trained soldiers are hard-pressed to walk the streets without being overwhelmed by the crazed mobs. Isak, discovering that Isherin Purn was instrumental in Lord Bahl's death, insists on attacking the Red Palace, where Siala has secreted the necromancer. He manages the attack, but is cut off from the bulk of his army by the mobs and forced into a desperate last-stand defence of the Temple Plaza, which the Knights of the Temples are trying to save from attack.

While they are fighting in the north of the city, Rojak puts the next part of his plan in motion. He sets the southern part of Scree on fire, to drive the mobs towards Isak. He ensures that Abbot Doren announces his presence in the city. And he brings King Emin and Zhia Vukotic down on himself. By this point Rojak is close to death, having tied his life to the spell he is working on the city. Rojak's troops are driven off by Koezh's undead troops, and Abbot Doren is killed by Zhia. King Emin retrieves the Crystal Skull that Abbot Doren had brought from his monastery, trying to keep it safe from Jackdaw, and finally manages to kill Rojak, though the minstrel is dying anyway.

Back on the Temple Plaza, Isak's massively outnumbered troops are pushed back until they are defending the steps of the Temple of Death. In desperation he reaches for any help he can find—and the Reapers, the five violent Aspects of Death, answer his call. They go berserk and start slaughtering the mobs just as Rojak dies and the spell is broken. Once he realises they are saved, Isak manages to stop the Aspects killing anyone else and dismisses them before accompanying the leader of his allies into the temple to give thanks—but as they do so, they're attacked by a man possessed by a daemon. Isak responds savagely, but manages to stop himself from killing the man when he recognises him as his missing father.

Several days later, while the fires in Scree slowly burn out, three of Azaer's disciples are trekking across the obliterated city. In the cellar of the abbot's house they find a woman, once a mercenary in Zhia's employ, now a helpless—pregnant—amnesiac. She is holding a book, a journal written by Zhia Vukotic's insane younger brother Vorizh, which may lead them to a prize far richer than the fabled Crystal Skull they sacrificed to get it.

CHAPTER 1

EVENING FELL WITH A WHISPER. The day's thick-falling snow had abated with the failing light and now, as the sky turned deepest blue, the air was clear and still. Venn felt the silence of the forest stretch away in every direction, disturbed only by his own laboured breath and heavy footsteps. The bite of the chill night air was savage and he urged himself on, knowing he had to reach the clearing before the cold took him. Too many travellers misjudged their journeys and succumbed. The Vukotic could keep their Saljin Man; winter was a daemon all on its own in these parts.

At last he reached the clearing and, against all common sense, stopped at its edge, staring dumbly forward. It had been years since he had last been here. The Land itself seemed to catch its breath, as if waiting for the tremors his return would bring. At last he stepped forward into the clearing, the ruin of his people hidden in his shadow.

He walked hesitantly, somewhat humbled by the grand, silent scene. Above him pink wisps of cloud catching the last of the light provided an unearthly backdrop for the place he had never expected to see again. The only sounds were his boots crunching through the snow and the occasional creak and groan of laden branches in the forest behind. He fumbled at his bearskin, trying to tug it tighter around his shoulders, but the weight of his shadow made it hard and after two attempts he gave up, leaving it open at his throat. His goal was visible now, and that was all that mattered.

The entrance to the cavern was only a hundred paces off, crowned by snow-burdened dwarf pines that covered much of these crumpled mountains. It abutted a long slow rise in the ground that continued for miles into the distance and formed one of the two crooked "legs" of what was called Old Man Mountain. There was a shrine to a God no one remembered, derelict yet still imposing, near the top. Venn remembered visiting it once, out of youthful curiosity. The God, whatever his name was, had been stooped and aged, like the bare mountain that served as his memorial. He had been no match for Ushull when the reckoning came.

Venn paused halfway to the entrance and looked back over the expanse of pine, studded by enormous cloud-oaks like nails driven part-way into the slopes, but before he could dwell on his childhood love of this view Jackdaw's wheezing broke the spell. Shaking his head, Venn turned away. He had been spared the sight of Jackdaw's twitching tattoos and scowling face that final day at least, as well as the man's incessant chatter, and for that much, Venn was glad. Once the former priest had cast the spell to bind himself within Venn's own shadow, he had learned not to waste his strength on complaints.

The cavern entrance up ahead was unchanged since he had first marched out into the Land, his swords strapped proudly to his back and his white mask hiding the man underneath. Freestanding brass braziers on either side of the enlarged cleft cast a weak light over the darkened interior and the sap of fresh spitting pine cones mingled with incense in the evening air. Each brazier stood atop an octagonal stem thicker than a man's waist, high enough that some priests had to stand on tiptoe to see over the battered edge.

They were centuries old and had suffered during those years. Venn remembered his disappointment when he had learnt the truth about the faint markings that covered the braziers. He had thought them incantations in a secret language, when instead they were only scratches, the effect of weather and time, of careless priests and gales tipping them onto the stony ground. His father had huffed and frowned at his imagination where others would have laughed.

Was that the first step on this path? he wondered. *That first loss of wonder: was that the day I saw my father as something other than an otherworldly servant of the Gods? Where once I beheld priestly robes and a half mask of obsidian shards, I found just a tired man with thinning hair and a piercing wheeze when he slept.*

"Hey—! Hey, you!"

Venn stopped walking. He didn't turn, knowing the speaker would have to walk into his line of sight. The speaker turned out to be a round-faced priest, his arms laden with logs. In his ear Venn heard an intake of breath from Jackdaw. He was invisible and near incorporeal, at least as long as he stayed in Venn's lee, and yet Jackdaw remained a coward.

Venn recognised the priest despite the smooth black porcelain that hid half his face. They were of a similar age and from the same clan, which had forced them to be something approximating friends as children. Corerr was his name, a foolish, fat little boy who'd grown up into a bewildered junior priest who'd never even lost his puppy fat in the process, a man still sent to fetch the wood for the fires in the cave, though doubtless there were younger priests to do that tiresome duty.

"Who are you? Why are you here?" Corerr called as he trotted forward to place himself between Venn and the cave entrance. Under the bearskin Venn's dyed-black clothes were just visible, clearly marking him as not belonging to any of the clans.

Venn didn't respond, preferring to wait for a grander audience. One face had already appeared at the cave entrance, his lined cheeks and lank, wispy hair illuminated by the weak light. Corerr took another step forward, peering anxiously into the gloom of Venn's snow-capped hood. In the twilight he would be able to make out that Venn wore no mask, yet he had a bloodred teardrop falling from his right eye, the same teardrop that Harlequin masks bore.

Venn kept his eyes on the cave entrance, knowing Corerr wouldn't have the courage to do anything more than look. At last another face appeared, this time that of a woman. She loomed over the first by at least half a head. Venn saw her mouth move. She was speaking softly to her companion, while never taking her eyes off Venn. He took that as his cue to abruptly move again, causing Corerr to yelp in alarm and almost fall over backwards. As Venn closed on the cave mouth he recognised the woman with eyes like polished cairngorm. Even after the long years of his absence she retained the bearing of a warrior-queen.

"Venn ab Teier? Merciful Gods, is that really you?" Corerr twittered in sudden shock and scrambled to walk alongside Venn. "Your face, your clothes—where have you been? What happened to you?"

Venn walked forward, careful to let the man's words drift over him without reacting. The other priests hadn't moved or spoken; the man was positioned slightly in the lee of one brazier, as though ready to hide behind it, and the priestess stood with hands entwined at her breast, falling naturally into the conventions of piety learned decades before. Her hair was greying and crow's feet marked the corner of her eye, but for all that she looked a younger woman, one whose heart hadn't been broken by this wilderness.

Her half mask was covered in obsidian shards, as his father's had been, but hers, crucially, also lacked the tear trails of moonstone signifying high rank. He held his breath and focused directly on her right eye, letting the glazed look fall away for the barest moment. He saw her reaction, though it was so slight he doubted she was even aware of it—only someone looking for it would have seen that flicker in the eye, but to a follower of Azaer it was enough.

Ambition in a place such as this . . . you must hate them as much as I do.

After a moment, the priestess stepped to one side and offered Venn the path into the cavern. He shuffled forward, eyes vague as he ignored the icons and prayers painted on the rough stone walls either side of the passage and started on the downward slope, breathing in the incense-laced air of his boyhood.

He continued in silence, feeling as if he were being towed by some unseen rope. So focused was he on the image he was presenting that he found himself jerking to a halt at the far end of the tunnel as it suddenly opened out into an immense space. His eyes were still glazed over, but in his peripheral vision he spotted movement in the dim light of the cavern. He listened to the priestess catching up behind. It wouldn't do to let his herald fall behind. Herald: the word reminded him of Rojak's rasping, plague-ravaged voice and those final whispered commandment of twilight's herald: *"Give them a king."*

You're right, minstrel. These people want a king—they need a king—but I am not it. I can only lead them to one worth breaking their bonds for. Is that not our master's way anyway? To show a man the path and let him choose it himself?

A large natural pillar at the centre of the cavern dominated his view; its rough sloping sides studded with glinting quartz and stained by long rusty streaks. At points on the pillar some industrious priest had hacked or drilled holes to insert wooden beams that now protruded directly out some eight feet in all directions. From those hung shallow brass braziers like those by the cave entrance, once decorated but now as battered by the years as the priests who tended them. The hum of quiet chanting and a haze of incense filled the air, bringing back more memories of his father; of long days and nights in prayer that had left him drained and exhausted when he returned home.

The cavern stretched two hundred yards from left to right of Venn's vantage point. At its widest, directly ahead of Venn, the cavern floor ran for fifty yards until reaching one of the twelve open chapels dotted around the wall. Those were dedicated to the Gods of the Upper Circle, but there were many more shrines beside these. The holy words of his people dominated the cavern from one end: foot-high characters cut into the rock with such precision only magic could have achieved it.

Even with his back to them Venn could feel their presence. Their creation had signalled the end of the Age of Darkness, the return of the Gods to the Land and to their mortal servants. Their message had enslaved the Harlequin clans and bound them to these frozen mountains. He resisted the urge to turn and look at them; his mission led him elsewhere first.

At the base of the pillar was the smallest and meanest of the cavern's shrines, little more than a trickle of water that ran down a natural channel and collected in a carved hollow. The inside of the hollow was coated in some icy substance that gave off a faint white glow. Animal symbols etched into its rim represented the Gods of the Upper Circle.

The priestess drew closer and he heard the hesitation in her footsteps. Perhaps she was wondering whether to reach out and pluck his arm, maybe even guide his elbow forward. He didn't wait for her to come to any decision but lurched off again, down the steps to the small shrine. Every visitor to the cavern would take a thimble-sized cup of polished brass and drink the ice-cold water. Legend said it had been blessed by the Gods and was the source of their remarkable abilities, but there had never been any mages among the clans and no one knew for sure.

Venn knew; his time in the Land had revealed much of its workings and he was in no doubt about what lay behind his people's abilities, yet as he knelt at the edge of the basin he felt his breath catch. With ponderous movements he took up a cup and drank. His throat tingled at the sharp chill of the water as he swallowed and began to murmur a prayer he'd not spoken in years. The prayer tasted bitter, but he knew Jackdaw needed the delay.

"*It is there.*" He caught the faint whisper in his ear. Jackdaw sounded out of breath, but Venn couldn't tell whether the man was simply drained by the exertion of his spell or if it was an effect of turning himself to shadow. "*I need only a few moments to turn the spell to our purpose.*"

Venn had to force himself not to shiver. In this form the craven mage was no figure of ridicule. As a shadow, Jackdaw reminded him disturbingly of Rojak, Azaer's most favoured disciple. Something in his voice reminded Venn that they had found no trace of Rojak's body—not even his enchanted gold chain, which should have been untouched by the flames that had obliterated the city of Scree.

He put the thought from his mind and continued the prayer. Rojak had ordered him to give his people a king, and in a few moments, Jackdaw would have added to the spell on the water, opening his people to change, to *ambition*.

Let them choose a new path. Venn thought, adding his own blessing. *Let them hope to be more than just entertainment, let them strive for something new. A king they will wish for, a newborn prince they will find.*

"*It is done,*" Jackdaw said softly in his ear. Venn gave a fractional nod of the head and spoke the final words of the prayer. He rose and turned to discover the priestess standing close by with a proprietorial air.

Here is the reward you've been seeking all these years. Do you remember the tale of Amavoq's Cup? How deeply will you drink of this poisoned chalice?

Venn looked past her as she glanced down at the basin as though expecting a miracle to be thrown into her lap. His eyes were fixed on the far wall, where the holy words of his people had been carved in the rock. All eyes were on him and sudden silence reigned in the cavern, except for the faint hiss and pop of sap in the braziers. Keeping his movements unnatural and jerky, Venn made his way to the long stretch of wall that bore the holy words and sank to his knees before them, staring up.

"Why are you here?" croaked a voice on his right.

His face blank, Venn turned to look at the stooped figure addressing him. His guard dog, the priestess, stood behind him, almost as close as Jackdaw as she staked her claim. She said nothing, but Venn could feel her poised to strike. The old man was a windspeaker, one of the revered priests whose years of service had taken them beyond prayer to a place where they could hear their God's voice on the wind. She would not challenge one so senior, but Venn knew she would pounce on anything she could to regain control of the situation. Ambition could tear down mountains.

He slowly focused upon the windspeaker. With both hands gripping a gnarled staff, the priest scowled and repeated his question.

Windspeaker, if you hear words in the rushing of air you'll see the hand of Gods in my actions. Men such as you taught me to recite the tale of the Coward's Mirror from heart. Before the end I will perform it for you, as a one final chance to avoid your own foolishness.

"I have been sent," Venn whispered eventually.

"Sent by whom?"

"The Master." Venn paused, giving them time enough to glance over at the chapel of Death where a dozen gold-leaf icons bearing His face shone in the firelight. "A bearer of tidings; of darkness past and a path to come."

Lap it up, you old bastard. Time for you to choose; hesitate here and she'll step around you. You'll fall behind and another will be remembered as the one who attended at the moment in history.

A tiny sound behind Venn told him he was right. While the old fool dithered, the warrior-priestess had no such doubts. Deceived as she was, the priestess had no fear of the future and as she strode past, a soft sigh escaped the old man's lips. Venn followed in her wake, leaving the windspeaker behind as an irrelevance.

He lowered his head in prayer, the holy words a powerful presence ahead of him. *A king for his people* was Rojak's last order to him. They would not accept any king but one they chose themselves, but Venn had learned much from the twisted minstrel. Jackdaw's magic had opened the way, and a Harlequin's skills would lead them through.

"No king to rule you, no mortal lord to command you." The last line of the holy words made the clans think they were special, that they were blessed. His contempt tasted as bitter as the prayer had.

"Listen to me well, for I am a guardian of the past," he said in a cracked and raw voice, as though he had been silent all those years since last he had visited that place. It was the Harlequin's traditional opening to their audiences.

He waited, sensing the priests gather. He felt a hand on his shoulder and Jackdaw channelling magic through him. A shudder ran through his body and continued down into the ground below. All around he heard whispers of fear and wonder as the priests felt the ground tremble beneath their feet.

"I speak to you of peace—and of a child. Flawed is our Land; imbalanced and imperfect, yet perfection must exist for us to recognise the shadow it casts. Such perfection can be found in the face of a child, for a child knows nothing of fear. Armed only with the divine gift of life their souls are unstained, their hearts unburdened.

"Let the penitent among us raise up a child to remind us of the innocence we once possessed. Let the penitent speak with the voice of a child and have no use for harsh words or boastful manner. Let the penitent see the tears of a perfect child as they repent of their sins, weeping for the loss of innocence. What greater service can there be than the service of innocence?"

In the forest, two figures shared a look, their breath cold against the snow. Shrouded against the last light of day they were nothing more than indistinct darkness, hunkered down by the broken stump of an ancient pine. One of the figures had a hand stretched out before her, a glassy, stylised skull resting in her bare palm. Her sapphire eyes flashed in the darkness.

"This is what we have come to observe?" asked the man. His voice betrayed no anger, but from his sister there was no hiding the note of scepticism.

"Every tapestry begins with a single thread. I would know the pattern he weaves while there is still time to act."

"Our time is best served unpicking threads?"

"Our time is limitless, Koezh," she replied, cocking her head as though straining to catch the last of the Harlequin's words before returning the Crystal Skull to a pouch at her waist, "and the purpose has perhaps already revealed itself."

"The child."

She inclined her head. "The fall of Scree showed Gods could be driven off, evicted from a place and a population, however temporarily that was. If the temples are emptied and the congregation turned against their Gods, those Gods are left weak and exposed."

Koezh understood. "In times of trouble folk turn to the past for comfort, and the Harlequins are the keepers of history. If those keepers begin to tell stories of a child of peace when the horns of war have sounded across the Land, the faith of the people will be not destroyed, but diverted."

Zhia smiled, and her elongated teeth shone in the twilight. "Perhaps our time has at last come."

CHAPTER 2

THE CORRIDOR LEADING TO HER PRIVATE STUDY was draughty and dark, illuminated only by the lamp she'd brought with her. Queen Oterness felt like a thief, creeping through her own palace under cover of night while sensible folk slept. It was the very early hours, not a time she was used to seeing, but ever since she had conceived, true sleep had eluded her.

And now I jump at shadows, she thought wearily, *and I fear to close my eyes no matter how many guards I have. I have become as paranoid as my husband.*

She pulled her shawl tighter and paused at the corner of the corridor where she could see in both directions. She could hear only the rain battering the shutters and spattering down the stonework onto a balcony somewhere above. The White Palace of Narkang was cold now; at last autumn had turned to winter and the chill night air coming in from the ocean made her glad of the thick shawl King Emin had given her years before.

Oterness forced a smile; the shawl was so typical of the man. It was long enough to wrap around and keep her warm, and it bore a beautiful pattern— she'd not seen the style before, but according to Emin it was typical of Aroth, from where her mother's family had originated two or three centuries ago. What made it such a typically Emin gift was not the moonstones and topazes that decorated the lilies and hummingbirds, but the fact that the design continued on the hidden knife that nudged her distended belly whenever she adjusted the shawl.

Still, it was a comforting touch, there in case someone tried to catch her when she was most vulnerable. Oterness shivered at the thought as her hand closed protectively over her belly, over the scars there. In case it happened *again*.

Her value to Emin had at first been only in her ability to influence the nation's high society, and that she had done with grace for decades. She smiled grimly to herself. The twittering matrons of Narkang's élite would be astonished at the result of any man assaulting their aristocratic queen now, since Ilumene's betrayal, for the name carved into her belly had given Oterness a terrible focus and she had learned quickly from the best of the Brotherhood.

Her stomach gave another lurch and banished all thoughts of combat, reminding her why she was up and about in the middle of the night. Every night a stomachache assailed her as soon as she lay down to sleep, and once that had settled down, then her bladder started to complain. She was trying not to let it drive her to distraction, remembering the morning sickness she thought would never end was now just a faint memory. A stomachache she could handle—she had herbs to calm it, and the solitude of her nightly walk was becoming something she quite enjoyed. Jorinn, her maid, had opened her eyes and waited for a request for aid as Oterness struggled out of bed, then snuggled back down in her cot when none had come.

Dear Gods, I never expected to be waddling like this, Oterness thought with a wry smile. *I feel like a hippo. And when I'm not lurching about like a drunken sailor, I'm sweating up a storm, just like Emin's uncle—and* Oh, Kitar's gnashing teeth! *Where is all this wind coming from? Now that I could out-fart any soldier of the Kingsguard it's a bit unfair I don't find it as amusing as they do. Not that a queen ever farts, of course* . . .

She was just a few yards from the door of her study when she heard a distant sound over the unremitting rain: the crash of the main gate and the thunder of hooves. A low tolling punctuated the night: the sound of returning royalty.

"Well, I'm here, so that must be my dear husband at last," she murmured, and manoeuvred herself around to start back towards her bedchamber. Emin would come to check on her as soon as he was off his horse. *So much for trying to get back to sleep tonight.*

As she made her way back towards the bed Oterness saw Jorinn looking up at her, catlike, from her cot. She has made it very clear that she wasn't going to be fussed over, and Jorinn would not have expected her mistress back for half an hour at least.

"Come on, my girl, up and about," the queen said briskly. "Our lord and master returns. Breathe some life back into that fire and light a lamp, then alert the kitchen staff—it sounds like the whole of the Brotherhood has just arrived back."

Jorinn hopped up and slipped her dress on over her sleeping clothes, tying her hair back with a green ribbon as she advanced on the fireplace. With practised deftness she brought the embers back to life with a small pair of brass bellows and used a twig from the kindling pile to light the lamp at the foot of the spiral stair that led up to the king's tiny private study. As she hurried towards the door she remembered herself just in time, skidded to a halt, and offered Queen Oterness a brisk curtsey. The queen waved her away with a smile and eased herself into an armchair by the fire, pulling a blanket over her legs.

Jorinn jerked open the door and gave a squawk of surprise as the king stormed in. The handmaid only just managed to avoid being knocked over. Taking one look at his face, she didn't bother waiting to be dismissed but fled, quickly pulling the door shut behind her.

Oterness tried to make out her husband's expression, but his hat was still pulled low over his face to keep off the rain. Water dripped from him as he stopped abruptly in the centre of the room. He hadn't said a word.

"Gods of the dawnlight!" Oterness cried, "Emin, what has happened?"

The king hardly seemed aware of Oterness. His eyes were focused on the floor at her feet, as if he was unable to meet hers. She threw off her blanket, panicked by his behaviour, and forced herself upright. Emin flinched and shied away when Oterness reached out to take his hand. When she wrapped her fingers about his, she realised he was bone-cold, and trembling.

"I have . . . I have—" The king's words were awkward and jagged, quite unlike his usual mode of speech, and the effort of saying those four words appeared to have exhausted him.

"Emin, come and sit by the fire," Oterness said, pulling him towards the armchair. "You're chilled to the marrow."

Emin didn't sit, but clasped her fingers tightly within his own and stared into the flames for a few moments, until a sudden shiver ran through his body.

"You're frightening me now, whatever has happened? There have been some awful rumours flying round the city—"

"They're true," he interjected sharply, "they're all true." With a sigh Emin sank down to his knees before the fire, letting his wife's hand slip from his grasp.

"All of them?" Oterness gasped. "Scree is gone? The Gods destroyed the entire city in punishment? Opess Antern told me every priest in Narkang has been acting strangely, and even the moderates are preaching that a time of punishment has come."

"The Gods took no hand in the fall of Scree," Emin whispered in a soft, tentative voice, as though he could hardly believe what he was saying. "They came too late to help anyone; too late to punish anyone—but that didn't stop their vengeance."

He took a deep breath, as if summoning his strength to speak of the terrible events. "The day after the firestorm that destroyed Scree, we spent the day recovering from the fighting and tending to the wounded. The people had gone mad; almost the whole population had become blood-crazed monsters. It was like Thistledell all over again—that village where the survivors destroyed all trace of the village's existence?—but on a citywide scale."

He ignored her gasp of horror and went on, "The next day, Lord Isak led his troops to a new encampment north of the city, abandoning his Devoted allies of the previous night. They had defended the Temple District from the mobs; a foolish last stand, and they only survived when he summoned the Gods to their aid. Somehow that boy invoked the Reapers, and their cruel claws were indiscriminate in their slaughter.

"Afterwards, Isak refused even to meet envoys from the surviving Devoted troops. They had lost all their high-ranking officers; the man in charge, Ortof-Greyl, I think he was called, was a major, their only surviving commander. He wasn't up to the task—he was like a boy alone on his father's boat and lost at sea. I think he kept expecting the Farlan to send him orders, but they never came. We sat there for a whole day, in rain that didn't stop until well into the night, doing nothing, saying nothing. No one bothered to set watches, or pray, or even to cook."

Emin raised his hand to his face and pressed his long fingers to his temple, as though trying to force out whatever was in his memory. Oterness lowered herself gingerly to kneel down beside him and pulled his hands away, holding them in her own.

"Go on," she said gently, knowing he had to finish the story.

"The following dawn I was awakened by a headache pounding away at my skull, as if Coran himself had taken his mace to it. The major felt it as well; he and the lower-ranking Devoted officers were all affected. The healers were all occupied with the badly injured, and my mages were insensate after their efforts to get us out of the city. It hurt as badly as any wound I've ever had—but it was only when one of the Devoted chaplains had something burst in his brain that we realised—"

"What was it?" Oterness breathed in horror.

"Apoplexy," Emin said, clutching his head again, "a rage beyond anything I'd ever before felt, a hatred filling me up and consuming me." He looked up, a pleading in his eyes that his wife had never before seen in two decades of marriage. "It built up throughout the day, and—*Oh Gods!*" He stopped for a moment, and then continued, the words bitter in his mouth, "My men didn't stop me. They *couldn't* stop me."

"Stop you doing what?"

"The refugees," he whispered, "there were thousands who'd not been affected by the madness, camped on the other side of the city. They had only a handful of city militiamen to protect them. Devoted officers are all ordained priests, it's a requirement of their Order, and—fool that I am—I am too. We felt the rage of the Gods running through our veins and we couldn't control it. We didn't even hesitate."

"Oh Emin, what did you do?" Oterness couldn't hide the horror in her voice even as she drew her husband closer and he sank, sobbing, into her arms.

"We killed them! We killed them all. We felt the Gods walk beside us, the Reapers, and more besides, all burning with anger I cannot begin to describe. The refugees were innocents; the militiamen just frightened fools, decent men who would not abandon the defenceless to Fate's cruelties. We left none alive. I can still hear the screams—every night I hear them, and I smell their blood upon me.

"We left the dead for the scavengers and just walked away. I . . . I don't remember much of the following days. The land around Scree was as dead as the city. We watched the smoke rising from the last of the fires as we walked to the Temple of Death where Lord Isak had made his stand, but the stink drove us away. The whole Temple Plaza was full of corpses, most as unarmed and pathetic as those we'd killed the day before. And, Gods help me, I prayed with the Devoted officers amidst the carnage, and I felt *holy*—vindicated, even. I didn't see the horror of what had been done; only satisfaction that the first step had been taken."

"First step?" she asked, trying to hide her fear.

"The first step towards a purer Land." There was pain in his voice now, and he hugged his royal bride tighter, like a frightened child. "All these years I've fought the fanatics, and now I find myself the worst among them."

"That's not true," Oterness insisted, "you are *not* the same as them; you're no coward who interprets holy words according to his own prejudice; who twists the scriptures to use them as tools they were never intended to be. The king of this nation is not such a man. The father of my child is not such a man."

"My child," Emin gasped, a flicker of life returning to his eyes as he struggled to straight himself up. "How is our child? Are you both well?"

Oterness hugged him. "We're both well, Emin, we're strong and healthy."

He stroked a reverential hand over her belly, his eyes widening in wonder as he realised how large she'd grown. "Oh my child, what is this new Land you will be born into?" he asked, his voice shaking.

"A Land yet to be determined," Oterness answered gently, "a Land that you have fought twenty years to forge, Emin, and one you cannot give up on now. I know you, better than those who work in your shadow, even Morghien. You've worked for years to contain these fanatics, and these new reports of priests demanding greater measures are just an escalation of that age-old problem. Your agents are still at work; your networks remain in place. Only yesterday Count Antern brought a letter from one of your spies, sealed with green wax."

"Green wax?" He sat up a bit straighter. Usual matters of state were sealed with red wax, matters of national security used white, and he encouraged his queen to read both, even in his absence—there might have been other women with lineage equal to that of the former Lady Oterness Bekashay, but her intellect was far beyond that of any of the other potential wives, and her help in governing his kingdom remained invaluable. But the green wax was different; it denoted messages concerned with his war with Azaer, the shadow, and that matter he was determined to spare her.

"It's up on your desk," said Oterness with a nod toward the spiral stair behind him. The pulpit-like mezzanine was shrouded in shadow, for Jorinn knew not to set foot on the stair, let alone go up, even to light the lamp on the king's desk.

Emin helped his wife into her chair before going to retrieve the letter, which was folded up so small that it could be concealed in the palm of a hand. He opened it, and read the message inside, his eyes darting towards Oterness as he finished. Without speaking he went to the bellpull by the fire and gave it a sharp tug to summon Coran, his white-eye bodyguard.

"Can't it wait? You need to eat and rest, give yourself an hour at least," Oterness said, concerned, though she knew he would ignore both his own needs and the hurt he was feeling and attend instead to the demands of his position.

But will you never let it out? Your rage at Ilumene's betrayal was buried deep, but it's still there—and now? You're asking too much of yourself, my Emin, far more than any man should.

"I will rest soon," the king replied at last, gripping the back of her chair and resting his hands on her shoulders. Coran stormed in without knocking as usual, his expression blank.

"Give this letter to Anversis Halis; tell him to draft a plan for Midsummer's Day."

"Anversis? Your uncle?" Oterness interjected with a puzzled look. "I thought he was no part of your war—doesn't he spend his days researching migration patterns?"

"True enough."

"Surely you've not found a use for his obsessions? The man is so indiscreet—you can't possibly trust him with your secrets!"

"Also true," the king sighed, "but he has applied his theories to the movements of Harlequins and this letter is the first sign of something we've feared since Thistledell."

"*We?*"

"Morghien and I. You remember when I first met him?"

Oterness nodded warily. "Something about a ghost in the library your father had sponsored, and Morghien saving you from it."

Emin scowled. "It was no ghost, it was Azaer. The shadow was unable to resist the lure of a library open to the whole population, all that knowledge, available to everyone, and it started to rewrite some of the books, changing our history. At the end of that week I had declared war against an intangible immortal, and I had a sister to bury. There is one group of people better equipped than any other to edit history, and Rojak showed us at Thistledell the power a minstrel can wield." He raised the letter before handing it to Coran. "This is a report from Helrect: a Harlequin passing through there in late summer made a mistake when telling a story!"

"A mistake?" Oterness said, surprised. "But Harlequins have perfect memories, don't they? That's the whole point." She ignored Coran as he offered the pair a perfunctory bow and hurried out.

"Exactly. And now we need to pay great attention, to see whether any other instances crop up."

The queen froze. "You said 'draft a plan for midsummer.' What sort of plan, exactly?"

Emin crouched down at her side and put a protective hand on her swollen belly. "If they have become the servants of Azaer, even unwittingly, the damage they could cause could be incalculable. In Scree, Azaer's disciples turned the citizens against the Gods—what if that happens across the whole Land? We have had so few opportunities to derail the shadow's cause, and I must not flinch now."

"You would kill them all?"

"It seems," said Emin slowly, "that there is nothing I will not do." He bowed his head, a man defeated by his own deeds.

"Fate's pity, did Scree have such an effect on everyone? Did no good come of it at all?"

The king laughed coldly. "No good?" he echoed, then the hardness faded from his face and was replaced with a look of profound sadness. "Doranei, that poor boy Doranei: he fell in love."

CHAPTER 3

Unhindered by the weak candlelight, Lord Isak looked around at the assembled faces and tried to ignore the ache at the back of his head. One scowled back, making little effort to conceal his displeasure, but Isak had grown to expect that from his Chief Steward. The young white-eye had inherited an entire nation from his predecessor, Lord Bahl, and whatever else one might say about Chief Steward Fordan Lesarl—megalomaniacal sadist being one of the more colourful terms bandied about—the man knew how to run a country.

The rest of those present were quite a handsome bunch, something that had surprised Isak the first time he'd met them, although he had never been able to pinpoint why exactly. They were divided into those staring back like cornered rabbits and those with eyes miserably downcast. He took a deep breath. The day hadn't been going well and his already bad mood had only been darkened by the persistent drizzle that worsened to a downpour every time he ventured outside.

Don't lose your temper. Isak had to keep repeating this simple message to himself: *don't lose your temper; don't turn on those you trust.* He'd seen the warning in the eyes of his friends, his advisors, especially Carel. Though he was thin now, and aged ten years or more since losing his arm in battle, Carel had always recognised better than anyone else the temper boiling within Isak. Carel had been more of a father to him than Isak's real father during the years they had lived on the wagon train, and he had been made a marshal as much for the calming effect he had on Isak as anything. He was still the person Isak trusted most.

Arranged around three tables were the nine members of Lesarl's coterie, as disparate a collection as anyone was likely to find anywhere, and not all of the Chief Steward's agents looked as if they belonged in the dusty attic of a tavern just off the bustling Crooked Tail Street. The main river docks in Tirah were only a stone's throw from the Cock's Tail, and the tavern's regular patrons were as rough and raucous as they came. The grizzled first mate sitting at one of the tables, his arms and bald head covered in tattoos and scars, looked as if he'd fit right in downstairs in the taproom; the silk-clad dandy next to him did not—but no one here was fooled by the appearance of either.

"I see you're all as delighted as Lesarl to be here," Isak said eventually.

The Lord of the Farlan was dressed almost as splendidly as Dancer, the foppish nobleman. His tunic and breeches of deep blue had swirls of silver thread and moonstones down the left side. Isak had abandoned his silver ducal circlet after a day of official functions, but everything else bar the lack of crest on his dark grey hooded robe was as custom dictated: a pristine exterior, even down to his smooth cheeks and trimmed hair, but all the finery could not disguise the muscles underneath.

"They are concerned, as am I, about the security issue," Lesarl said.

Isak acknowledged the point, and the informality. The Chief Steward had made it clear that his coterie were encouraged to speak freely and frankly, and without reference to rank.

"There are so many clandestine meetings going on every night in this city, no one is going to notice one more."

"You are hardly unremarkable," said the youngest member of the coterie, Whisper, who headed Lesarl's personal spy network. "And neither is Dancer, especially in this district."

Dancer gave her a broad smile and indicated those even more out of place than him. Prayer was a tonsured priest of Nartis, a sour-faced man in his early fifties who had sat as far as possible from the bejewelled woman called Conjurer. She in turn was making a futile effort to be inconspicuous. Isak suspected the woman was unused to this, but he knew most mages found it difficult to be comfortable in his presence. A combination of the raw skills of youth, the brute force of a white-eye, and the vast power of two Crystal Skulls would make any sane person nervous.

"Which is why there are preplanned routes for you all to get here," Isak said. "It may not be befit my position to sneak through attics and alleys all the way from Cold Halls, but anything Lesarl considers safe for himself is good enough for me."

"Not everyone has that luxury," Whisper persisted, her voice gaining a slight edge. "Prayer has to be loaded into a barrel upriver of Holy Docks; Conjurer's route takes two hours to travel and more to prepare. The shorter the notice you give, the more likely it is that the routes are compromised—even without the increased patrols of Ghosts round here to catch the interest of our enemies."

"Perhaps I didn't make myself clear," Isak replied after a pause.

Even in the dim candlelight her eyes flashed and he could see Whisper had caught the warning. She was surprisingly young for her position, no more than thirty summers, and a handsome woman. Right now she was dressed like a merchant's son, apart from the mass of wavy black hair that shadowed her face. When she'd slipped through the single attic window it had been tied back. Isak guessed she was new enough in her position to be wary, even of the rest of the coterie. Unlike the others, he suspected she'd put some thought into her attire, for he could see she was wearing nothing unusual or identifiable, not even a piece of jewellery.

"I wanted this meeting to take place," he continued, "and so it is. I know you have rules in place to protect your identities, but at the moment that's not what I'm concerned about."

There was silence. Isak inspected the faces, trying to decide who would be the key to winning over the group. Lesarl was leader, sure enough, but Isak had grown up on a wagon train and he knew full well there was always a leader among the equals. Carel had been the commander of the wagon train guards, but Valo Denn was the mercenaries' man, the one who formed their opinions and presented their arguments when necessary, the person who was just that fraction more than his peers.

So who've we got here? he wondered, managing not to jump when he got a reply from the privacy of his own head.

"Isn't it obvious?" came the scornful mutter in the corner of his mind: Aryn Bwr, last king of the Elves, or at least what remained of his tattered soul. The last king, unable to fully possess Isak's body and return to life, had been reduced to a bitter memory of former glory, while forever fearing the retribution death would bring.

To you I'm sure it is, Isak replied. *How many years were you king of your people? For the rest of us, it takes a little more thought.*

He looked around at the nine faces, men and women as different as you could find, each bound within the fabric of those communities they represented. Whisper, newly chosen by Lesarl to lead his spy networks, working hard to live up to the standard her father, the previous incumbent, had set; Dancer, marked out as a knight or a marshal by the single gold hoop in his left ear—and Isak had no doubt he was a marshal, born to the title. Perhaps it was Sailor, sitting next to Dancer, a scarred veteran with a crumpled nose. He was dressed in red, typical of his trade among the Farlan, though he was risking a flogging by eschewing the macramé knotting on his shirt that marked his ship—and made him traceable. *Confident in his ability to manipulate a superior? I wouldn't bet against it*, Isak thought.

He couldn't judge Conjurer, so affected was her manner, and Soldier looked so terrified to be sitting in the presence of his lord that it looked like he'd forgotten he was a sergeant-at-arms of twenty years' service. Merchant and Farmer couldn't meet Isak's gaze for long, so he discounted them, and he doubted any group chosen by Lesarl would follow a priest's lead.

And then there was one. So, Citizen it is, and doesn't she look a formidable bitch? I doubt she even needs that fat lump on the door downstairs to keep control of her patrons.

As if to acknowledge his conclusion, Citizen met his gaze. She showed no trace of deference as she replied to his unspoken question. "You're worried about it all," she said in a rough local accent, her gravelly voice betraying a lifetime of pipe smoking. "Not even your da's injuries are enough to take priority, though; it's the sound of the city that's got you troubled."

Citizen was a thickset woman with hair trimmed almost as short as Isak's. Her face was a mass of laughter lines, and she had a jawline to make a Chetse warrior proud. She sported three thick gold rings in each earlobe, and even in his inexperience, Isak realised it was intentional that they bore a striking resemblance to the earrings of a duke.

"Explain, please," he said politely.

She shrugged and gave a smile, more than comfortable with the attention of the whole room. "Lived in this city my whole life—I know its sounds and its moods better'n any lord. You're a white-eye, so you feel it too, though you mayn't yet have recognised it as such.

"Some days I can just hear there's an ugly mood in the city, and those days the Cock don't serve, 'cos it's those days that there's riots. The city ain't like that right now, but it's stinkin' of men crammed together like too many bulls in a field."

Citizen raised a forearm as solid as a man's calf and patted Prayer's shoulder. The priest, who was sitting on her left, ignored her and pulled his cloak tighter around his body. "Then you got the fact that all this mob are actin' even worse than the nobles, preachin' war and whippin' honest folk in the street for stupid reasons." She cocked her head at Isak. "My guess is whatever's pissed on their mood—and I hear that's the Gods bein' so angry after Scree that their priests are feelin' the effect—it's done the same for you."

"So your conclusion is that everyone's just a little bit tense?" Isak said irritably.

He had never been to the Cock's Tail before. Nor even Carel's white collar would have stopped someone taking exception to a white-eye here, but the tavern—and Kepra Dei, its formidable landlady—were renowned throughout Tirah. She was tough, and could be heartless to anyone who wasn't family; anyone working the docks knew it was asking for trouble to mess with anyone bearing the Dei name. Even her sons-in-law, big men themselves, had been glad to break with tradition and adopt the Dei name as their own. *And those three earrings aren't a joke with anyone but herself, I'll bet*, he thought. *To the rest it's a warning that round here her word's law as much as mine—maybe more so, if it came to it.*

"Tense ain't even the start of it, boy," she replied equably. "It's the confusion in the air I'm talking about: no one's agreein' with anyone else, not the nobles, not the priests, not the soldiers. What's gettin' you concerned is the chaos this city's in—can't fight a war when you're fightin' yourselves, can you? And you've got it going at every level of society—as well as within yourself."

Isak didn't reply immediately. The woman's calm expression nagged at the swirl of frustration and anger inside him. He knew she was right, but he hadn't wanted her to be quite so right. However the priests were being affected, he was too, albeit to a lesser degree thanks to the Skulls which were acting as a buffer for his mind—and that wasn't information he wanted the Land to know.

"It sounds like you've put some thought into this," he said after a moment. "You've got a suggestion for me? Your job is to advise after all, not just to state the bloody obvious."

She shrugged and broke his gaze, affecting a deference that he was sure she didn't feel. *This one really is sharp*, Isak thought. *She knows that even here—for all the informality of the coterie, and her own position within it—that it does no good to issue me with instructions.*

"Well, I can't claim to understand the trouble with the priests," she began slowly, "you've got that knowledge, not I, so I'm just goin' on guesswork—"

"Make the assumption you do," Isak said, gesturing for her to get on with it.

"Then I'd want to get rid of the distractions that are gettin' the nobles heated up," she said firmly.

"Which are?"

"Your coronation—they're here for that and they'll squabble like children until they know when they're goin' home to their families. Then there's the wondering over Lomin's dukedom. And most importantly, there's Duke Certinse."

Isak nodded his agreement. Lesarl, Tila, and Vesna had all been of one mind on the subject of the trial and execution of Duke Certinse. The man's family had too many supporters, too many dynasties tied to it for anyone's comfort and no one was sure what deals and recriminations might yet appear. Added to that, a dozen suzerains had weighed in for what appeared to be purely reasons of principle.

"And how much of the argument over foreign policy will that solve?"

"None, but at least you'll be able to *have* the argument. With one or two fewer reasons to argue, folk get less troublesome. You are Lord of the Farlan, however newly made; once folk get used to that and realise the nation's still strong you'll find the authority Lord Bahl held waitin' on the other side." Citizen paused and looked across to the far table. "Dancer, am I right in thinkin' that there's no great lobby among the nobles for Cardinal Veck's reforms?"

The nobleman gave a twitch, as though startled from reverie, and stared blankly at Citizen before replying, "True enough. Those that are listening to him are careful not to agree too loudly."

Dancer's voice was rich and mellifluous, lacking Count Vesna's deep tones but with the same rounded, measured pronunciation. Unlike Isak, Dancer had removed his cloak to reveal his formal wear underneath—much drier than Isak's own clothes as Dancer hadn't been caught in the rain.

The man ran his long, greying moustache through his fingers, a practised mannerism to develop his fussy persona that was now habit, and nodded to himself. "I can think of only one or two who'll take it seriously. The restriction on the nobility taking religious orders has thus far precluded that problem. Those who call themselves pious will follow Suzerain Torl's lead."

"Suzerain Torl is a ranking member of the Brethren of the Sacred Teachings," Isak snapped, "and since Veck's demanding to be allowed to form a religious militia to enforce whatever laws he feels like, I'm not encouraged."

"Lesarl says you've spoken to Torl about the Brethren," Dancer replied patiently. "The order's centuries old and they've never shown a desire to enforce religious law. Suzerain Torl is one of your most loyal citizens. First and foremost, he is a Farlan soldier, and that comes before everything else—his title, his dynasty, even the Dark Monks. My Lord, to treat him any other way would wound him more deeply that Eolis could—as well as digging the ground out from underneath your feet."

"And it makes him a key element in your argument over Duke Certinse's trial," Lesarl joined in suddenly from Isak's left. Pushing away from the wall he'd been leaning against, the Chief Steward walked behind the seated figures. "The Synod have strength of their own, and they know it, but they're also fully aware that ultimately no group within the Farlan can oppose the nobility. Though they are demanding to conduct Certinse's trial, for a variety of reasons, Cardinal Veck doesn't think he's ever going to succeed. All he's doing is gauging his support among the nobility. That the faultlessly devout Suzerain Torl has not voiced support for him has been noted by all interested parties."

"Prayer," Isak said, causing the man's head to snap around from Lesarl to Isak, "can you tell us any more of the current mood among the clerics? I can't help thinking that the longer Veck's demands go on, the more people are likely to be swayed by his argument."

Isak could see the priest take a breath before replying. Lesarl had described Prayer as a ruthlessly clinical thinker, so the man must be hating having his thoughts clouded by his God's rage.

"What we feel now is a residual effect of Gods becoming enraged, an echo of their emotions, if you will. It began with a murderous irrationality for the few nights following the fall of Scree, and whilst that lasted only a short time, the effects will continue." He stopped and looked around, then continued earnestly, "What you must understand is that Gods are immortal—they feel emotions, but not in the same manner as mortals; when they do, the power is remarkable—such strong feelings emanating from their God may permanently alter the minds of some of their clerics, even if the God has subsequently calmed down. I recommend you assume that the extremists will hold sway for the immediate future."

"So you and all your kind are my enemies this year?"

Isak spoke without thinking, but Prayer looked ashamed as he replied, "I fear so, my Lord, but I will not be alone in working to change that. I hope we shall prove only a minor hindrance."

An uncomfortable moment of silence stretched out into a minute, then two. Even Citizen appeared lost in her thoughts, unmindful of the muffled clatter of chairs from somewhere below them.

Isak went to the window and stared through the half-open shutter that looked out onto the street below. The early winter snows had been replaced by wet trails of rain that glistened darkly on the rooftops. There was no trace of the light white blanket that had covered the city a few days before, but

Isak could feel its touch on the air, the bite of ice on his cheek. It made him think the winter would be a cruel one.

There'll be no marching to Lomin this year, he thought distantly, the events of the previous year now ancient history, almost unreal, in his mind. *Let us hope the Elves think the same. Vesna says we hurt them badly enough last year to buy us time, but how long can that protect us?*

He looked down at the empty street below, the cobbles washed clear of the day's debris. The rain and cold hadn't stopped trade on the docks; Tirah's merchants were intent on getting as much into the city's underground cold stores before winter laid siege. For a moment he thought he caught a shape in the shadows, nothing as definite as an outline, yet enough to make Isak catch his breath.

Gods, is this still my imagination? I've seen nothing, I can sense nothing, and yet . . . and yet I have that taste in my mouth again, the one that reminds me of the Temple Plaza in Scree when I found the Reapers. He found himself nervously biting down on his lip, hard enough to draw blood. *Gods, what did I do when I summoned them?*

He shook the mood from him; it wasn't something he could afford to think about right now. His dreams had been dark enough of late, even those where Xeliath had touched his mind, for the sky had appeared darker, the blurred horizon more menacing. When she was not there he'd started to find himself on a desolate plain scoured of life. The ground was scorched and smoking, but cold to the touch. He knew there were others around, though he could see no one. The wind whipped up from the ground, trying to lift him like a kite, but he felt himself drawn downwards all the same, down to the earth which was furrowed like a fresh barrow. Every time he'd awakened from that place it had been all he could do not to curl into a ball and wrap his blankets around his body to keep the emptiness away. Strange dreams had followed him his entire life, some not even dreams, and these were as powerful as his visions of Lord Bahl's death.

Isak forced himself to turn back to the room. "So what you're saying is I should override the petitions and debates? I should make an executive ruling?" He tried to school his face so they wouldn't see his pained expression. "Lesarl said the opposite; he thinks that'll bring even greater opposition."

"And he's wrong," Citizen replied bluntly.

Isak turned to the shadowed figure of his Chief Steward, looming behind the backs of his coterie. He gave Lesarl a weak smile. "One of the annoying things about my Chief Steward is that he's acknowledged by finer minds than mine as a genius."

"I don't doubt he's right in what he said, just that he's wrong in what should be done," Citizen said firmly.

"I suppose that'll reassure both his supporters and his critics. In the last two weeks it's been suggested both that I make him the next Duke of Lomin and that I throw him in gaol for corruption. I don't know about the title, though. I'm not convinced he's got the breeding I'd want in my dukes."

"Yes, milord," Citizen said in a less than deferential tone, making it plain she had no intention of being affected by Isak's unnatural charisma. Some folk found themselves laughing along with Isak in the strangest of situations, but she was prepared for him. "Lesarl's right that it'd make you appear dictatorial, and that's a bad way to start your reign; they would've accepted it under Lord Bahl but you're still unknown to them."

"So?"

"Fuck 'em."

Isak gave a snort and turned to the rest of the coterie. Citizen's expression was blank; she wasn't joking. Only Prayer showed any reaction as he narrowed his lips further.

"Citizen's correct," Dancer joined, "in her own delightful way. The priests aren't winning themselves any friends; attendance at High Reverence is up, but only out of shame, I suspect, and that'll change as soon as folk grow tired of being reminded of their sins. I know the College of Magic has just about had enough."

"Can you blame us?" snapped Conjurer, "with fifteen suits of consorting with daemons in the past two weeks and twenty-eight charges of impropriety and impiety? The cardinals have declared war on us!"

"You tell the Archmage to exercise restraint before he fights back," Lesarl said firmly. "The last thing we need is battle-mages reacting to provocation—or any other more subtle measures of retribution. Some of your brothers rival Larat for a twisted sense of humour."

"And if the priests have a second focus of their complaints, that does the nation no great harm," Dancer agreed. "It will take a long time before people turn against the mages, they're too fearful for that. The College can instruct its members to maintain a low profile for the meantime."

"Lesarl, how soon can the trial start?"

The Chief Steward shrugged. "Four or five days. There are formalities to deal with, but the evidence is collected so the judge is ready. There are a number of ways the defence can prolong matters, but that can only last so long."

"Good, so let's announce the trial date and set up a quiet meeting with the dukes of Merlat and Perlir."

"And you'll bring along your choice for Lomin as well?"

"Yes, I want Lokan and Sempes to have a chance to object. I'm making enough enemies without consulting with the two most powerful people i—" A spark suddenly flared in his mind, stopping Isak mid-word. A trickle of magic swept the room, prickling and questing over his skin. He looked at Conjurer, but the woman showed no reaction. A shiver ran down his spine like the touch of a girl's fingertips and a voice whispered in his ear.

Isak.

Without thinking he turned back to the window. Xeliath was out there, the young brown-skinned woman who'd been tied to his fractured destiny. It looked like Morghien and Mihn had been successful in getting her to Tirah before any of the power players in this game tracked her down and killed her. Lesarl caught the movement and shot an enquiring look towards his lord. Isak nodded.

"She's here; just about to enter the city," he murmured.

It was clear from their faces that Lesarl hadn't yet shared that interesting piece of information with them. Isak managed to produce something approximating a grin as he pictured their reaction.

Heading towards the door he said, "Those of you interested in what my foreign policy is to be will be delighted to hear that I've added a new complication." He stopped as he reached the door, Lesarl on his heel, and turned back to the coterie. "There'll be a new guest at the palace tonight, a young white-eye."

"And how exactly does that affect the nation's foreign policy?" Dancer asked, voicing the question on the lips of all of the faces turned in his direction.

"Her father didn't exactly give permission for her to leave, and he's a lord, one of our not-so-friendly neighbours, the Yeetatchen."

Their protestations and questions floundered in his wake as he left the room. Outside, the narrow stair was lit only by what faint light crept up from the floor below, where a single lamp cast its light over the first-floor corridor, barely illuminating the three doors there. The two bunkroom doors were propped open; he glanced inside as he passed them and saw the usual labourers' junk in each: canvas bags, the odd oilskin coat, and a pervasive smell of sweat and mud.

At the end of the corridor a second stairway led down to the ground floor. It was a little too narrow for his massive shoulders, so he had to turn slightly sideways to get down them. Stationed at the bottom was Citizen's eldest daughter. The girl, who shared her mother's build, heard him coming and started to open the alley door on her left, giving it a shove when it stuck a little, swollen with damp and lack of use.

Isak knew she had a long knife concealed in her right sleeve, and not one just plucked from the kitchen's rack, but the blade made no appearance as she stepped out and scanned the street. The door on her right led into the tavern—Isak could hear an argument going on just the other side—but right now it was bolted shut.

Isak didn't wait for Lesarl. He pulled his hood low over his face and stepped cautiously out into the street. Citizen's daughter may have checked, but that was cold comfort: she'd neither notice nor be able to do anything about that which Isak was looking out for. Two strides took him to the corner of the building, and from there he could peer around the tavern and survey the length of the street whilst concealed in the tavern's shadow.

But it looked empty; his sharp eyes and ears caught nothing untoward beyond the occasional drip of water.

A glassy sheen had covered the cobbles as the nighttime temperature fell. The day's rain had given way to a faint mist hanging in the air, catching the yellow-tinted moonlight of high Alterr. Isak was about to move off when he caught a flash of movement out of the corner of his eye. He turned his head left, looking down the route he had intended to take home now that the streets were deserted. In the darkness, a good hundred yards off, something stood.

A crawling dread slithered down Isak's neck. No man stood there; its body was entirely black, and almost invisible in the fog, but he could guess something of the stance—it was on all fours. Visions of the Temple Plaza of Scree flooded back to him: the terrible slaughter done in the firelight, the towering figure of the Burning Man illuminating the terrified figures around him and in the distance, the humped back of the Great Wolf, stalking.

Now Isak could make out little more than a shape and a pair of burning eyes in the dark. It was untouched by the moonlight and almost hidden in the fog. Shadow upon shadow, imagination or not, the black dog did not move an inch. It simply stood there with its baleful gaze fixed upon him.

"My Lord?" Isak jumped at the voice, his heart giving a lurch until he realised it was only Lesarl standing behind him. Lesarl gave him a quizzical look.

"Look," Isak said quickly, pointing down the street, but when he looked back to where the black dog had been standing, the words died in his throat. The street was empty, and silent. Isak stared at where the creature had been, then searched all around in vain for it.

"What is it?" Lesarl said as he rounded his lord to look at where Isak was still pointing.

"I—I'm not sure," Isak admitted after a pause. "There was . . ." he stopped. "I thought I saw a ghostly dog" wasn't the sort of thing he really wanted to tell his Chief Steward. Isak hurriedly opened his senses to the Land and reached out all around. Aside from the taste of frost and mud on the air the only thing he could sense was Conjurer, in the room above, a faint flicker of magic in her body that grew as she felt his questing, but there was nothing more. Hoping that he'd be able to sense something similar to Morghien's ghosts when they touched his mind, Isak reached as far as he could, but felt nothing at all.

"There was?" Lesarl prompted quietly. The man had seen enough during Bahl's reign not to question his new lord's first instinct.

"I thought I saw something, I must have been wrong." Isak shook his head and took his hand off Eolis's hilt, where, predictably, it had drifted without him even being aware.

"My Lord, I find that a little hard to believe," Lesarl said firmly. "Your expression is not that of a man whose imagination has just played him false. So what is it that you saw?"

Isak glared at the man, but Lesarl waited patiently until the young white-eye exhaled and let the anger fade with his breath on the night air.

"What do you want me to tell you? What I thought I saw disappeared in the time it took to turn my head, and anything that can do that without me sensing where it went is a little out of your field of expertise."

"I do understand that, my Lord," Lesarl said, bowing his head, "but still I would share the burden I see in your face; no man should look so haunted—" He broke off as Isak gave a humourless snort.

"Haunted? Aye, that might just be it." He took a step closer and leaned down to look Lesarl in the eye. "I dream that death walks in my shadow. I have ever since the fall of Scree. On the edge of earshot I keep thinking I hear the footsteps of the Reapers. I feel the ground move at my feet as a grave opens before me; I remember the pain Aryn Bwr felt as he was cut down in battle, and it is so familiar to me I ache for it."

He stopped and straightened, a hard expression falling across his face. "And tonight I see a black dog with burning eyes standing in the road before me, something my mother's people believe to be a portent of death to come. Now who will share this burden with me?"

Lesarl stared up at him in alarm. For a moment Isak suddenly saw the

Chief Steward for the man he really was: beneath his calculating expression and sardonic grin, Lesarl was just a man with a mass of worry lines on his thin face and a nervous shiver enough to shake his bony body from head to toe.

"We will all share your burden, my Lord," Lesarl said after a moment, his usual calm restored. "Your advisors, my coterie, the Palace Guard, the whole tribe: if Death comes for you, He shall not find you alone."

Isak sighed. "It's good of you to say so. Something tells me otherwise, but if the future was fixed I'd already be dead, so perhaps you're right. Come on, it's time to meet the herald of our latest woes; you're going to hate her."

"A white-eye lord's daughter?" Lesarl scowled at the ground as he started off at Isak's side down the street. "I think you're right there."

CHAPTER 4

LESARL LEFT HIS LORD TO HIS THOUGHTS as they walked back through the quiet streets, winding their way through dark alleys until they had reached a better district of the city than the docks. The Chief Steward had to walk quickly to keep up with Isak's long stride, but he was glad for it, for the air was chill and his prominent nose and cheeks felt like icicles. In all his years of service to the Lord of the Farlan, he'd never got used to the cold of Tirah's nighttime streets.

It was strange to see the city so deserted. Hunter's Ride and the Palace Walk were main thoroughfares, usually only empty when snow lay thick on the ground. The tall stone buildings were dark and silent, with only the occasional pair of shutters showing a glimmer of light at the edges, night watchmen's billets and servants' quarters, for the merchants' townhouses were as dark as if they were empty, with no light seeping through the heavy drapes that hung at every window to keep in the heat.

A pair of Palace Guards loitered on Irienn Square, the semi-enclosed plaza off Hunter's Ride which was surrounded by government offices. Their sharp eyes picked out Isak by his height. They saluted, making no move to intercept them.

It wasn't long until they reached the fountain at the centre of Barbican Square, just before the looming presence of the palace walls. After the enclosed streets the open ground felt even colder, and when Isak stopped in front of the statue on the fountain, what little heat was left in Lesarl's body felt like it was bleeding away as he obediently took up his position in his master's lee.

White-eyes! They're all the same when they're brooding, Lesarl thought, suppressing a shiver as the image of Lord Bahl came to mind. *It's not taken him long to adopt that role. If I ever dreamed of ruling when I was a child, I know better now. I didn't know then that it scars in ways you could never predict; Lord Bahl once said that his soul felt worn thin, so thin it was hardly there. After Scree I think this one's the same already. Let's just hope it doesn't prove his undoing too.*

"A year, only a year," Isak rumbled from the shadow of his raised hood.

"Since you came this way for the first time?" Lesarl replied. "Almost exactly, yes, my Lord."

He left it at that, knowing that the white-eye wasn't asking for a conversation. Instead he turned his attention to the fountain itself. He passed it every day, and it struck him that he couldn't remember the last time he'd properly looked at it. It was a representation of Evaol, a minor Aspect of Vasle, God of Rivers. The scattering of coins in the fountain was likely nothing to do with her alignment, though, probably just whores hoping for a little luck.

The statue itself was of a column of water reaching up to the waist of a bare-breasted woman, who was running a fish-spine comb through her hair. Rain and wind had taken their toll on the pale stone, blurring some lines and leaving their own on the work. He resisted the urge to stamp some warmth back into his feet, but an involuntary shiver caught Isak's eye and woke him from his thoughts.

"Sorry, Lesarl, I'm keeping you out in the cold."

"My Lord, that is one of the responsibilities of the high position I enjoy," Lesarl said, keeping the reproach from his voice, though he knew he would have to explain the point yet again to his lord.

"That doesn't mean you should have to suffer because of my constant whims."

"Yes, actually, it does, my Lord," the Chief Steward said firmly. "My remit spans every suzerainty and aspect of Farlan life, unmatched power within the tribe. However good and loyal a servant you have as your Chief Steward, to fully handle the duties required of that position, he—or she— must have the capacity for cruelty and scheming. And that sort of person enjoys the position of power all too much. Lord Bahl understood it well enough to insist that I do indeed suffer his every whim." Lesarl gave a small smile. "It was only several years after I took over from my father that I realised you train a dog in a very similar way. Without blind obedience to my master I might well have started to question why it was that I was running the nation yet he wore the duke's circlet."

"So you're as much a slave to your instincts as I am?" Isak replied.

"I'm saying that those who love power are often least suited to it. Megalomania has its uses in a nation, whether anyone will admit it or not, but left unchecked, it is its own worst enemy."

"And so for the good of the nation," Isak continued, "such a person should be trained to come running when I whistle?" He grinned. "I see your point, I suppose. Maybe I should get you a collar as your badge of office."

"Yes, Master," his Chief Steward said, baring his teeth.

Isak laughed and led the way over the drawbridge. The gate was already opening, the light of a torch creeping through the widening crack. On a whim Isak turned right and headed for the guardroom, just as a Ghost in full armour stepped out. The man removed his helm when he saw Isak approaching. The white-eye stopped, recognition flourishing on his face.

"You, soldier, what's your name?"

"Me, my Lord? Ah, Private Varner, my Lord," the soldier replied quickly, his voice sounding rough, almost grating. He was careful to keep his manner deferential, but he looked apprehensive, and Lesarl remembered how Isak had described his first meeting with Lord Bahl, and the aura of power that hung around him like the heat from a roaring fire.

Isak had kept clear of the other white-eyes in the palace during the last year there. Kerin had made it clear they were a vicious, foul-mouthed lot that Isak had nothing good in common with. It was a full-time effort for the Swordmasters to keep them in check, and there was a pretty high chance that any encounter would result in a fight, which in turn would result in Isak killing a valuable soldier.

"I remember you," Isak said. "You were on duty my first night here, weren't you? You punched out my father."

"Was me, yeah, my Lord."

Isak smiled. "That was something I'd wanted to do for years. Thank you."

The white-eye blinked up at Isak in surprise. Like the rest of his kind the man was tall and powerful, but he was closer to a regular soldier in build than to Isak. It clearly fascinated Isak to see the same snowy irises and black pin-prick pupils in the eyes of another, but Lesarl saw the scrutiny was not welcome. There was no kindred spirit in those eyes, only ice.

"I'll go in this way, remind myself of simpler times," Isak said eventually. "Keep the gates open, though; we're about to have a few visitors. They're not to be delayed in any way; I want them in the duke's chambers as quickly and as quietly as possible."

"As you wish, my Lord." The man bowed low, cast a glance back at his comrade still in the guardroom, and then headed for the half-open gates.

"Come on," Isak said to Lesarl, and ducked through the small doorway into the cramped guardroom, only just missing the lintel. He turned and frowned—he had grown so much over the last year, from an outsized youth to a seven-foot-tall giant, that everything from that former life felt greatly reduced now.

Making his way to the Great Hall, Isak awkwardly acknowledged the various salutes he received. The deference was easy to accept, but he was still occasionally surprised when an entire room of strangers jumped up to salute, bow, or curtsey every single time he hoved into view.

The hall was nearly full, as it had been ever since Isak had returned with the army. Scores of those with light injuries had returned on wagons or horse-back, even walking, to avoid wintering away from their families, and many of the nobles answering their new lord's summons had chosen to billet with the Palace Guard they had once served in. Money for lodgings was tight for many of the knights and hurscals who'd travelled with their liege lords, especially when the innkeepers of the city, who had also heard Isak's summons, had cannily doubled their prices.

Lesarl had seen this as a good thing and he had instructed Kerin to make as much space as he could to accommodate anyone wearing the white. The Ghosts were the Farlan's finest soldiers, so many nobles sent their sons there for training. Almost half the men knighted on the battlefield were raised from the Palace Guard's ranks, and Lesarl was keen to encourage the return of veterans, men who'd completed their ten-year term and been recruited as hurscals by suzerains. They were men whose opinions would be respected, and it would do no one any harm to remind them of their primary loyalty, to the Legion.

Once the required personal greetings had been made to three marshals with white on their collars and a recent recruit, Scion Tebran, who was with his father, the suzerain—who, despite the stains on his tunic had obviously managed to find his mouth often enough to get roaring drunk—Isak headed through the rear door of the hall and down the long, cold corridor to the forbidding entrance to the tower, which was next to the main staircase to the private apartments.

The corridor was bedecked with mouldering flags, except for the green and gold standard of the Narkang Kingsguard, which shone bright and new. It had been presented to Lord Isak as a gesture of friendship by King Emin of Narkang after Isak had helped defend the city from a White Circle coup.

"Makes the others look decrepit, doesn't it?" Isak said, pointing to the flag.

"Should I order replacements? Some are defunct legions now, but we can have them copied without much difficulty." Lesarl stopped and turned to the flag nearest to the Great Hall. It was so old and dirty that it was hard to make out the zigzags of blue and green woven through each other down its edge, but there was enough to confirm Lesarl's judgment. "My Lord, this one is the Boarhunters, one of the oldest Tildek light cavalry legions."

"They still exist?"

"Indeed, though somewhat lacking the glory of centuries past that caused their flag to be hung here. That, if memory serves correctly, included ambushing and destroying a Tor Milist army four times their number, then blocking the main enemy force's line of retreat for two days despite terrible losses."

"The battle of Hale Hills?" Isak replied, his eyes lighting up at the memory of the heroic action.

"The very same," Lesarl said. "My Lord, perhaps it would be a gesture of peace to the people of Lomin if you officially requested a replacement flag? I can find out who the commander is; no doubt he is in the city. One of my agents mentioned that the common folk of Tildek—and Lomin too—are concerned they will be held to blame for the actions of their suzerain and the rest of the Certinse family. This might send a sign to both Tildek and Lomin that we still value them."

"Do you want to make a show of it at my investiture?"

"I would advise against that," Lesarl said, "it should belong to the people of the suzerainty, not the nobles. I will find an ennobled man to pass the request on, and that will ensure the men of the legion know of it too, not just their officers."

"Good. The investiture will be complicated enough without added theatrics," Isak growled as he started up the wide stone staircase. "Stay down here and bring Xeliath up to my chambers without letting that lot see her." He jabbed a thumb towards the Great Hall where voices were now raised in song, "She'll sleep in my bedroom—I still have my room in the Tower. I suspect the journey will have taken a toll and as the physician's at my father's bedside anyway he might as well keep an eye on her too."

"Your father's condition is unchanged?"

"There's been no change since his fever subsided, and that was a week ago. The priests of Shotir cannot heal a wound from Eolis, and the priests of Larat have been of even less use. He's in no actual danger at the moment. I'm almost tempted to blame his lack of improvement on stubbornness. Sourfaced bastard knows he'll have to bow to me if he ever gets out of that bed."

Lesarl tried to read Isak's expression as he spoke, but the white-eye gave nothing away. It was a miracle that Horman was even alive, having been possessed by a daemon and made to attack his own son in the Temple of Death.

A priest of Shotir had been found in the Devoted camp and he had accompanied them back to Tirah, nearly killing himself in the process as he kept Horman from Death's Halls.

He settled for a brief bow and a knowing look. "Perhaps your father will have noted the hours you've spent at his bedside?"

"Bloody doubt it," Isak snapped, "but either way, it's not a problem you need to be involved in." He stomped on up the stairs and turned the corner, Lesarl catching a flash of one colourless eye in the light of a torch before Isak disappeared from view.

"Of course, my Lord, as you wish," Lesarl muttered. He turned to another door which would take him to the western part of the main wing where his office nestled at the heart of several dozen others. Adjoining it were the small apartments he shared with his wife and son; his townhouse was currently rented to Suzerain Nelbove and his household.

"Perhaps I'll look in on them before going back to work," he said softly to the Land in general. "The boy might find tonight's events more interesting than sleep. We're as alike as Lord Isak and his father are. Best we don't let ourselves end up that way."

Isak acknowledged the salutes from the guardsmen sporting his dragon crest and eased open the reinforced oak door to the duke's chambers. The main room was dark, the only light coming from the fire and a single candlestick on a side table. A maid sat at the table with her elbows on it, her chin supported by her hands and her head angled towards the open doorway. He sniffed slightly and she leapt up, her mouth already opening to apologise.

"Don't worry," he said quickly, "you're not here to guard."

She curtseyed and straightened, waiting for the question he was about to ask. Isak took a moment. He couldn't remember her name; she was a friend of Tila's, the daughter of some local marshal. He knew Tila had told him—but he'd been told a lot since returning to Tirah.

"How is he?" he asked eventually.

"Still weak, my Lord." Her voice reminded him of Tila's, less melodious but with that same crisp intonation common to those of the landed gentry; it was traditional for the maids in the main wing to be drawn from the upper classes. "Your father's injuries have not opened up again, and there's still no sign of infection."

"But they're still not healing right?"

"No, my Lord." She lowered her eyes, her hands clasped tightly together over her stomach.

"The priests of Shotir came again?"

"Yes, my Lord. Only one of them was crying when he left today."

Isak forced a smile. "So they're toughening up at least." The smile faded. "I might be calling on that soon enough. He's asleep?"

She nodded.

"Good. Please light the lamps and have the kitchen send something hot up, enough for several people."

While she went about the lamps Isak looked in on his father. Horman lay on his back, his head turned towards the door. His face was half obscured by his ragged hair. He had always slept in an awkward sprawl of limbs, but now he was constrained by bandages and was lying as though fighting them. The pungent smell of sweat hung in the air, for the heavy drapes covering the window to keep in the warmth also kept the air close and stale.

Guilt slithered down Isak's spine again. Horman's left hand had been amputated at the wrist and the wound refused to heal fully. His right elbow had been repaired after a fashion, and the old injury to his knee was only marginally worse, but it was the overall effect of a daemon's possession that had taken the greatest toll on his father's health. He had wasted away in the weeks following the fall of Scree until he looked as pale and weak as a corpse. The effort required for eating proved too much for him most days and he rarely managed more than a couple of mouthfuls.

"Is this how they'll all end up?" Isak muttered, "all broken and beyond the help of healers? Maybe tonight's death omen will be the saving of my friends."

Outside the door he heard the sharp click of halberds on the stone floor: his guards were letting him know that a friend had arrived; anyone else would have warranted a verbal greeting. He shut the door to his father's room and rubbed his hands over his face to wake himself up.

"My Lord?" Tila said as she entered cautiously, Count Vesna at her elbow. Both were still in their formal clothes, although Tila had a thick woollen blanket draped over her layered grey silk dress now. She'd taken out the gold flower-head pins she'd used to put her hair up and the long dark tresses now spilled down to her waist.

"You were waiting up for me?"

"The guard on the gate let us know when you returned," Tila said, coming into the room and casting a glance towards Horman's door.

"He's fine." Isak could see she was itching to ask about where he'd been, but she understood her position within his inner circle. As Duke of Tirah, Isak's word was law, and they all had to adjust to that.

"My Lord?" Vesna echoed Tila, his eyes also fixed on the white-eye.

The maid caught the count's tone and, with a curtsey to Isak, hurried out without even waiting to catch Tila's eye. When the door was shut, Isak removed his tunic and Eolis before throwing a few more logs onto the fire.

"Isak," Vesna said, dropping the formality once they were alone, "you look troubled."

"My friend, when can you last remember me any other way?"

"Enough of that," Vesna said firmly. "What happened at your meeting?" The count was without his broadsword but his tunic was fastened up to the neck, as it had been earlier.

The white-eye paused; there was something different about the famous warrior. He thought for a moment. "You're not wearing your earrings," he commented, pointing to Vesna's left ear where the count normally wore his two gold earrings of rank. "I hope my return didn't disturb anything important?"

"No, my Lord," Vesna said in a flat voice.

"Good. She's still unmarried, you remember?"

"Yes, my Lord," Vesna replied, refusing to rise to Isak's needling.

"Isak, what's happened?" Tila asked, firmly changing the subject. "Is everything all right?"

The white-eye sat heavily into a chair facing the pair. With all the chaos of Scree's aftermath, they had yet to officially announce their betrothal. There was a grim mood throughout the city, made worse by the onset of winter. He knew they would happily forgo the state wedding offered by Lord Bahl—and by him—but neither one wanted to broach the subject until the period of mourning had finished. The Farlan had lost many soldiers, men and women, and the urns were stacked high in the Temples of Nartis. There had been no comforting words from the priests to disperse the anger and resentment which lingered like a black cloud.

"You know about my dreams," Isak said eventually. "It was a reminder of those."

"What sort of reminder?" Tila said, suddenly alarmed.

"One that made an impression. But that's not a concern for tonight—more importantly, Xeliath has entered the city."

"Xeliath? Are Morghien and Mihn with her?"

Isak shook his head. "Can't tell, but I hope so. It will be good to see Mihn again." He pictured the tidy little man with his placid expression and acrobatic skills whose failure of memory in the final test had led to his exile from the Harlequin clans. Since coming into Isak's service, Mihn's many abilities had proved invaluable, as had his undemanding friendship. *Yes, it will be good to have Mihn in my shadow again.*

"Do you want us to sit in on your first meeting?"

"This isn't an arranged marriage; we're not negotiating terms," Isak said wearily. "I'm sure they'll all want to sleep for a week—there's no urgent intelligence we need and the journey will have taken a toll on Xeliath's health."

"Should we leave?"

Isak sighed and stretched his feet out, planting the heels of his boots on a slender mahogany table that wobbled alarmingly under the weight. "Could you stay?" He stretched his neck and twisted his head to one side and then the other, trying to work out the cricks. "I don't really want to talk about tonight; I'd like to just sit with my friends and pretend the Land doesn't want me dead, at least until they arrive."

The guardsman, a lone figure on the drawbridge, took long measured steps back and forth in the quiet cold of night as he waited for life to stir in the city. It was well past midnight and the streets were silent. Alterr was hidden by cloud and Kasi had fallen below the horizon long ago. The soldier resisted the urge to turn his head and glare at the guardroom, where his watch partner was sitting in the warmth. As he reached the end of the drawbridge he started walking backwards immediately, keeping his eyes on the empty roads ahead at all times.

The fact that he was a white-eye and thus not required to walk the freezing streets keeping the peace did nothing to improve his mood. When at last he caught sight of movement in the distance, it was met with a hiss of irritation, one that increased as the horse-drawn carriage made its way up towards Barbican Square at little more than a gentle walk.

There were two figures on the driver's seat and no luggage on the roof. The coach was plain—not a nobleman then, just a merchant with money to spare. Both figures were hooded and cloaked, and hunched over against the cold, their faces hidden. If it hadn't been for Lord Isak's direct order, he would have summoned the duty squad on principle, but as it was, he stood still and patiently awaited the coach as it rumbled towards him. It stopped at the last moment, the front wheels on the very lip of the drawbridge. The passenger jumped down from his perch on the driver's seat and walked straight up to him, pushing back his hood to reveal a face he recognised.

"Fetch your watch partner and a stretcher, now, please," he ordered.

The white-eye narrowed his eyes at the foreigner barking orders at him. "Can't leave the gate unguarded," he said in response, "and last I heard, you'd been dismissed from the duke's service."

"And that would make you wrong on both counts," Mihn replied. There was no antagonism in his voice but the white-eye bristled anyway, unwilling to be ordered around by a man without position, rank, or weapon who stood more than half a foot shorter than him.

"Who's in the carriage?" he asked brusquely.

"Have you received no orders from your lord?" Mihn asked.

"I have."

"So stop arguing and take Lord Isak's guest up to him. Then take the lady to the Chief Steward and get her the gold crown she's been promised." Mihn jabbed his thumb towards the driver, who had remained hunched in her seat. Before the soldier had a chance to speak again the door of the coach opened and a man leaned out to look at them.

"What's the hold-up, soldier?"

The white-eye looked at the pair of them for a moment and decided discretion was the better part of valour. He stepped aside and waved the coach forward. The driver gave a click of the tongue and set the horses walking forward again, down into the tunnel that led underneath the barbican and into Tirah Palace. As it reached them, both men stepped up onto the coach to let it carry them through, Mihn hopping back up to the driver's seat like a mountain goat. The white-eye gave a short whistle once they'd entered the tunnel and the gate immediately started to close behind them.

Instead of stopping outside the Great Hall they took the coach around to the rear of the main wing, where there was another way up to the state apartments, a rear door that was normally kept locked and guarded. While the stretcher was being fetched the white-eye watched as Mihn and Morghien helped the last passenger out of the coach. It was obvious they didn't want his help, and they took great care to keep her face in shadow. Their precautions made no difference; as soon as he got within a few yards of her, the white-eye felt every nerve in his body quiver.

Instinctively he found his nostrils flaring, seeking her scent: she was the same as him, and more. When he lifted the stretcher the white-eye found himself taking great pains not to touch her in any way. As strong as he was, his hands trembled and his throat tightened at the power humming through her body. They started up the dark stairway and he kept his eyes on the stairs underneath him, not trusting himself to look at the hooded head inches away from him. All the way up he felt her attention on him, and a threat hanging in the air.

Isak was up and on his feet long before they reached the door to his private chambers. Vesna and Tila hovered in his wake, broad smiles on their faces at the sight of Mihn hovering beside the stretcher.

"Take her into my bedroom, then leave," Isak commanded before grabbing Mihn in a bearhug.

"It's good to see you again, my friend—but why the stretcher? Does she need a doctor?"

The smaller man smiled up at his lord and shook his head. "She's well enough, merely exhausted. The journey took a great toll, but I wouldn't want to be the one to force a doctor on her!" He looked a little thinner than the day they'd parted, but that was the only indication that the failed Harlequin had just returned from a long and gruelling journey.

Mihn embraced Tila and Vesna before following the soldiers into Isak's bedroom. The young lord gripped Morghien by the wrist as he followed them in, but the ragged-looking wanderer cut short the pleasantries. "That can wait; right now you must go and introduce yourself. We can talk while she sleeps." It looked like the journey had taken its toll on Morghien, who was tired and drawn, but his grip was as strong as ever. Isak had to remind himself that Morghien, known as the man of many spirits, was far older than he appeared—he should be permitted some trace of fatigue.

Isak patted his shoulder and went to his bedroom. The soldiers had put the stretcher onto the bed and were about to slide it from under her when Isak bustled past.

"Leave that," he said, "we can manage. The kitchen should be sending up food for my guests; check it's ready, then return to your posts."

He didn't even wait to see they'd left the room before he was leaning over the bed. He gently pushed back Xeliath's hood. The young woman blinked up at him and Isak barely managed to hide his shock. Gone was the healthy,

radiant girl he'd seen in his dreams. Instead, he saw a near parody of that
beaming beauty. Trails of sweat ran down her twitching cheek and the crumpled skin of eyebrow and eyelid drooped limp over her left eye. As well as the
permanent damage done to her body, her soft brown cheeks were flushed with
spots of colour that made him think she was feverish.

"Isak," Xeliath whispered. Her lips curled on one side and trembled on
the other. She was trying to smile. His name on her lips was tinted by the
heavy rolling sounds of the Yeetatchen dialect.

"Xeliath," he replied softly, smiling down at the wan face below him. He
eased her legs onto the bed and slid a hand under her body so he could pull
the stretcher away. Her thin limbs reminded him of a pigeon he'd shot; lying
dead in his hands, the bird had felt far too light, as though something was
missing now it lacked life.

Xeliath looked tiny, even bundled in her heavy woollen cloak. He raised
her hand and placed a courtly kiss in her palm. He folded her fingers around
it and said, "Sleep now, you need to rest. I'll bring you some soup later."

"Wait, listen," Xeliath whispered, straining to form the unfamiliar
words. Isak remembered his first meeting with her, on a featureless, rolling
field in his dreams, where she'd told him she couldn't even speak his language. That night, and every other time they'd met, she'd spoken directly
into his mind. Now, as he strained to make out each syllable from her ravaged throat, he realised Mihn must have been teaching her Farlan as they
travelled.

Her right arm fought its way free of the folds of the blanket, and Mihn
had taken a half pace forward even before she beckoned him over. Isak,
shifting slightly so that Mihn could take her hand, sensed a sudden flicker of
power from her left hand which was obscured by the cloak. He pushed it
back, and gasped when he saw the Crystal Skull fused into the palm of her
hand, her long, thin fingers clawed around it, drawn a little way into the
body of the Skull. Isak ran his finger down the side of her thumb: the skin
was fused to the Skull, so perfectly bonded there was no seam between the
two but a complete melding of materials.

Take it, cut it from her flesh, hissed a voice at the back of his mind.

Isak bit back a growl and drove the spirit of Aryn Bwr from his thoughts.
That was one blessing over the last few months: the voice had become quieter of late, cowed almost, and Aryn Bwr had been more willing to withdraw
when pushed. It was a mixed blessing, though, for it served only to increase
Isak's suspicions that it was the Reapers lurking on the edges of reality.

Again he felt a flicker of power from within the Skull. Isak withdrew his hand, an apologetic look on his face until he realised that it was not anger he felt. Xeliath was staring into space, her good eye looking past him, while erratic sparks of magic started to dance from one finger to another over the surface of the Skull. He sensed pulses of energy flowing up her arm.

"What—what's happening?" he asked softly.

"She's drifting," Mihn replied quickly. "This has happened a few times— usually after she's contacted you in her dreams. There's nothing to worry about, it's just the effect of being tied to your destiny."

"I remember," Isak said. "Her mind was almost broken when she was Chosen, when she was tied to a thousand destinies and to none, or something like that."

Mihn stroked her hand. "She still doesn't understand it fully, but it has had some sort of prophetic effect on her, perhaps like the Seer of Ghorendt— not true foresight, but glimpses of the future, though they don't make much sense. She doesn't go into a trance, or anything like that—and sometimes she hasn't even remembered it happening."

"Has she said anything that made sense to you?"

The small man shrugged. "Once she said she saw you walking around a statue of a man holding a sword to his chest, made of obsidian. A man with two shadows, one tinted with blood and one with white eyes, was watching you. Her description put me in mind of the ranger, Tiniq."

"General Lahk's brother?" Isak said in surprise. "Well, I suppose he does rather live in the shadow of his white-eye twin."

"Isak," Xeliath croaked suddenly.

The two men looked down, Mihn still with his hand wrapped around the young woman's.

"Thank you," she managed.

"For what?" Isak asked.

"For bringing me to safety, you fool," she managed, again forcing her lips into her semblance of a smile. Disengaging her hand from Mihn's, she gave the small northerner an affectionate pat on the cheek. "You are lucky to have such a loyal friend; I believe he would follow you anywhere."

Isak's face fell. "Don't say that—it might be the Dark Place he ends up visiting." He looked at Mihn, whose face was calm, the image of a man at peace in the Land. Rarely did the failed Harlequin give away much, but surely he'd have thought about what horrors he would face if he stayed at Isak's side.

How is it I'm served by a man whose qualities surpass my own so completely? Isak wondered, not for the first time.

A sharp pain in his wrist brought him back to the present. He looked down and saw Xeliath had jabbed her thumbnail into the skin, leaving a red mark. "Stupid boy," the hazel-skinned white-eye growled before switching to Yeetatchen and spitting a dozen or so angry words.

Without pausing to think, Mihn translated for Isak. "You claim I have a problem with prophecy? You, a fulcrum of history, should know better than to speak so carelessly."

Isak was stung by the admonishment in her voice. "I'm sorry," he said after a moment of silence. "All I meant was that such a thing would be too much to ask of any man, no matter how loyal."

"Too late," Xeliath replied, closing her eyes. "It is said."

Isak looked at Mihn but the man just shook his head. "We all have our parts to play."

"What if I have to ask something monstrous?" Isak asked in dismay. "You accept the burden too easily!"

"I am proud to serve you, whatever you ask of me," Mihn replied with rare openness. While he had the colouring of a Farlan, his hair and eyes even darker brown than most in Tirah, Mihn lacked the sharp, pronounced features of the tribe; his were small and neat, every edge smoothed off, every expression minimal.

"Is my part simply to ask things of others, then?" Isak said softly.

Mihn blinked. "In that, I do not envy you. I am glad I merely serve."

"Mihn, you don't even carry a proper weapon! You never wear armour, I've already asked too—"

He raised a hand to cut his lord off midsentence. "I will do what I must. You should too." He gestured towards the door. "For now, we should let Xeliath sleep."

CHAPTER 5

I<small>N THE LEE OF A TALL WAREHOUSE</small> in the southernmost district of Tirah, two men waited uneasily as midnight passed into the new day. They kept close to the building that bore a reputable clothier's name and watched the small door at the other end of the warehouse. It led to a watchman's room, that much was apparent, but as yet neither of them had any idea why a man with a Lomin accent had cornered the smaller of them three weeks before and arranged for them to be waiting here, at this time, on this night. A silver crescent each had been enough to make it clear the offer of a job was serious, but they suspected their next payment would require rather more than just their presence at a certain time and place.

They were dressed as common travellers, with only long knives at their hips despite the mystery and late hour. The Ghosts would be asking serious questions of people walking the streets armed for battle—there were so many noblemen, hurscals, and liveried soldiers in Tirah for the new duke's coronation that anyone without the protection of a title had to tread carefully.

"I don't like the look of this."

The taller of the two looked at his comrade, sighed, and reached into a pocket for his tobacco pouch. "Nothing not to like yet, Boren."

"You reckon?" Boren's sceptical look earned only a short laugh. The sound echoed back from the high brick walls surrounding them and instinctively Boren looked around to see if anyone was coming to investigate. Aside from their breath on the cold night air and Boren's eyebrows twitching, all was still.

"Now I don't say this is the best situation to be in," the other man continued, "but you just remember one thing; we've done nothing wrong. We've got few enough enemies as it is, and none this far west. We're not armed to start a fight, we've broken no law within fifty miles, and no thief announces hisself by smoking while he watches a building, so that's exactly what I'm going to do while we wait."

"Still reckon we're mad to be here without knowing a damn thing, Kam."

"Well, I like to think that's why I'm in charge," Kam replied in a muf-

fled voice as he lit his pipe. "Your friend told us to be here and that there'd
be money in it for us—isn't that enough? Unless there's something you've
not told me, you're as hard up as I am, so a bit of mystery for a bit of cash
don't bother me."

"It bugs me."

"Lots of things bug you."

Boren sniffed and scratched his straggly beard. "So you're happy that
some noble-born stranger tells me to meet him here at midnight? Hunter's
moon went down over'n hour ago and I don't see the bugger. Looks suspicious to me."

"Everything looks suspicious to you," Kam said, "but we've covered ourselves and the others'll be watching out too, so leave me to worry about this.
If I was your noble friend I'd be doing a tour of the district, checking to see
who's come with us. That means making us wait, and since we need the job
bad, let's give him time."

Boren's only response was a mutter but Kam nodded at it all the same and
took a long pull on his pipe. The shadow fell into silence once more and Kam
resumed his drifting scrutiny of the dark buildings and alleys surrounding
them. His ears were sharp; a lifetime of being a hunter in the forested
suzerainty of Siul had given him instincts he trusted. They weren't mercenaries—they didn't lead that sort of life—but their home was close enough to
the unsettled parts of the Great Forest that they learned how to fight at an
early age. Such men were normally the mainstay of the Farlan Army, but
Kam's village and those close about were all too vulnerable from Elven preda-
tion to spare anyone. Army wages weren't enough to tempt men into leaving
their homes unprotected. He lifted his head suddenly; he'd heard footsteps.

"Gentlemen, you look cold."

They whirled around. Behind them, in what had been an empty alley
when Kam had last looked, stood a man wearing a bearskin coat and thick
gloves. A wide-brimmed hat shadowed his face. The clothes were indication
enough that this was no night watchman.

"He the one?" Kam asked, keeping his eyes on the newcomer. He could
see the rapier at the man's side and was very aware of his own lack of real
weapons. Boren nodded in reply.

"I'm the one, yes," the stranger replied, "and I have someone for you to
meet." From his voice Kam realised the man was a good few years older than
he, but he wasn't taking any chances that he was so old that he'd not be quick
with his rapier. A thin blade was of little use on the battlefield, but in an

empty city street it had the reach and the speed to best most weapons. The man hadn't offered his palms in traditional greeting, not even when Kam and Boren, after a hesitant pause, did so.

"Where?" Kam asked before the small insult had time to grow.

The man pointed towards the door they were watching and started off towards it. Instinctively, Boren sidestepped to let him pass and lead the way and he inclined his head, choosing to take it as courtesy rather than precaution. At the door he gave a quick double-rap with his knuckles before turning back and gesturing to Kam and Boren to approach. They did so warily, hands by their knife hilts, watching the surrounding streets. When they reached the door the man pushed it open and stepped inside, then held it open for the pair.

Kam peered inside. There was a lamp on the table in the centre of the room, illuminating a woman clad in a long cloak, her hood still raised, seated by a small black stove, and a few stacked boxes. The warmth from the stove made him ache to go straight in, but he was careful to take a second good look round the room first. When they did enter the man lost no time in closing the door behind them.

He gestured towards the boxes. "Sit."

Kam froze at the change in the man's voice; the polite veneer had fallen away; now he was unmistakeably a nobleman used to having his orders obeyed instantly.

And what's changed? Just the woman—and a dog wants to perform well in front of its mistress. Interesting. He looked at his companion and they sank down onto the boxes as ordered. The nobleman stood at the door with his hand on his sword, and that told Kam what he needed to know. *Dog's on guard now, but who uses a nobleman as messenger boy? Maybe this wasn't such a good idea . . .*

"Jendel Kam and Litt Boren, my Lady."

"Gentlemen," the woman began, "please don't be alarmed by the theatrics." Her face was in darkness, carefully hidden from the lamp's light.

"Why not?" Kam replied gruffly, ignoring the slight shift of feet from the door. He wrinkled his scarred nose; the lady's scent mingled incongruously with stale sweat and old pipe smoke. "Don't get me wrong; I don't want trouble, but I don't like it when I can't see the face of the person I'm talking to, and that goes double when I don't know why I'm sneaking around a strange city at night."

"Perfectly understandable," she replied smoothly, but she made no move to reveal her identity. "You're here because you were given money to be here, and because you were promised a job."

"That's right enough, and so what I want to know is what sort of job this is," Kam said equably. "We're not mercenaries, nor thieves or assassins, so why come to us?"

"Because I do have a job for you, and it's one only a fool would take."

"Calling us fools?" Boren growled, until Kam put a calming hand on his friend's shoulder.

"So what sort of fool you looking for?" Kam asked.

"What use does anyone have for a fool?"

Kam resisted the urge to scowl himself. What he hated most about nobles was the way they kept their voices level, emotionless; those practised tones they used to hide whatever they were thinking. It made them sound infuriatingly arrogant, whether they intended that or not. "So what're you looking for?" he repeated.

"Men with reason enough to act the fool," she said.

"Enough of this, can you not just say it plain?"

The woman turned slightly towards the man at the door. Something passed between them, Kam had no idea what, but she slipped off her hood to reveal the face of a middle-aged woman with deep lines around her eyes. Her hair was cut short and her only concession to jewellery was a milky pearl pendent on a thick silver chain. Around her throat was tied a red ribbon of mourning.

"I hope you'll forgive me if I spend a little time gauging the sort of men I'm talking to before revealing all my secrets," she said quietly.

Kam blinked in surprise. Her voice was strained; in her reproach he detected the waver of someone so close to the end of their tether that not even years of upbringing could mask all emotion.

"That's fair," he replied quickly, "but we ain't got the advantage here. I'm guessing you know our names and where we come from and—now I don't mean to offend, just bein' honest—compared to us you're a powerful woman, so there's an unspoken threat there in that alone."

"You think I've brought you here to threaten you?"

"No, but it's there all the same." Kam raised a placating hand. "I'm just stating how I see the Land; I'm poor and you're not. If you have a job for me, there's risk involved and you're willing to pay for that, but you're not looking to be refused."

"I hope my information about you would be more accurate than that," she said, keeping her proud nose raised for a few more moments before the effort defeated her and she seemed to sag in her seat. "I acknowledge what you say as the truth, though I didn't want to go so far as describe it that way. You're right, I cannot afford for you to refuse me, and I have associates willing to retaliate if anything should happen to me." Her tired eyes flicked up again. "But I hope it will not come to that, so let me lay my offer before you: twenty gold crowns for each of you and your men, in addition to an assurance that every village they are drawn from will receive increased protection for the foreseeable future."

Kam didn't trust himself to reply immediately. The fee was immense—no one in his village could hope to earn twenty gold crowns in a year—but it was her last statement that clinched it. Whatever his objections, they would all take the job. Protection for the village was something they couldn't easily buy with gold, especially since there would be questions how they obtained so much money.

"Crowns are no use to us; commoners don't get paid in gold, only thieves," Boren pointed out, voicing one of Kam's concerns.

She smiled wryly; that was the least of the problems. "So let us say four hundred silver crescents then."

Kam nodded. "That'll do. But for that sort of money there's a good chance we all die, and money don't help my family if it's taken off my corpse."

"I will send a man to replace one in your group, a vassal of mine. You can send your man back with whatever money you wish, and my associate here will deliver whatever's left. But send any young men amongst you home; this is not a job for the young."

Again Kam heard the emotion in her voice, and he suddenly realised her words struck to the heart of the matter. *Oh Gods, could this be who I think it is?*

"Still don't want to be a corpse, rich one or not," Kam said, Boren nodding sternly alongside him.

"I understand that," the lady said, "and yet I expect many, if not all of you, to die before the job is over."

"What sort of offer is that?" spluttered Boren, looking about to rise and walk out until Kam eased his bristle-haired friend back onto his box.

"I think I understand," Kam said slowly, "but how can we trust you in this? There's no reason for you to let any of us live, or for you to contact our villages ever again once we're dead. If your friend delivers the money there's a trail back to you, and that's something you can't afford."

"How can you trust me? You can't, I suppose, but I think you know how you can believe I'll keep to my word on this." She sighed. "You've guessed who I am, and that trail you spoke of hardly matters now."

Ignoring Boren's puzzled expression, Kam thought for a while, trying to piece everything together in his mind. He controlled the sudden surge of revulsion he felt in his heart.

"With due apologies, folk aren't saying good things about you," he pointed out. "Your word might yet be worth nothing."

Not saying good things? the voice of his younger self screamed in his mind, *you fucking bitch-whore traitor, you want to drag me down with you, have my name cursed alongside yours, maybe even send me to the Dark Place to see what welcome awaits you?*

He said nothing more, but both his fists were clenched tight, as though desperately fighting the urge to pull his knife.

Poor I might be, traitor I'm damn well not . . . And yet . . .

And yet I've got a family and barely enough to feed them through the winter, and there are rumours of more Elven attacks when the summer comes. We barely survived last time; those army outriders almost caught us last winter. If it hadn't been for Boren's boy chasing after that fool dog we'd not have had any warning—

"Well, I don't know who you are," Boren said, breaking into Kam's bitter memories of the previous winter. "How about you let me know so I can be in on this deal too?"

She raised her chin and said, "I am the Dowager Duchess of Lomin."

Boren managed to cut off his hiss of surprise. Now he had to shut up. He and Kam had been friends their whole lives and Boren knew that he could trust Kam's sense better than his own temper. He folded his arms over his chest and lowered his head, a sign Kam knew well meant Boren was aware he'd regret the next words that came out his mouth.

"I'm guessing there's only one thing that you'd want from us, but I don't see how we'd break your son out of prison. There's twenty of us, and I doubt the Lord Isak is giving your son many noble privileges. If he's in the city gaol, there's more than three times our number of regular guards, and if he's in the palace cells then there's an entire legion of Ghosts in the way." Kam leaned forward, his box creaking. "I'm sorry, my Lady, but I don't see what you're expecting of us."

"You are correct that my son is being kept in squalor at the palace," she said, "but his trial will either be a civil affair, in which case it will take place at the Temple of Law on Irienn Square, or if the Synod's efforts to take over the trial prove successful, in a place yet to be designated—however, I do not believe that will happen. The man I will send to you tomorrow will bring the architectural plans for the Temple of Law, which is where I am sure my son will be transferred for the trial."

"So Duke Certinse is out the palace, but that doesn't help us. You could send us a full company of hurscals and we'd still be outnumbered by the Ghosts guarding him. So I ask again: what is it you want?"

Kam saw her lip waver briefly, and she fought to compose herself.

He's her only child, and that's the reason her promise means a damn; whatever they say about her can still be true; it doesn't change the fact that she loves her only son more'n anything else in the Land.

"What I want from you," she said in a carefully measured tone, "is whatever you can do to help. If there is a chance to break my son out, I will have men with horses waiting, and I will devote the remains of my fortune to helping you and your families. Whatever the outcome, my associate here will not be involved; he will return to Siul, where he will organise the troops to protect your villages. He will also pass on the promised payment."

"You can't really believe there's much chance of breaking your son out?" Kam asked, and immediately regretted his words as the long-threatened tears finally spilled from the duchess's eyes.

"You have no need to remind me of that," she said after a moment, regaining her composure. "But you will permit me to hope against hope? It is all I have left now." She straightened up, but made no attempt to wipe the tears from her face. "There is another service you can do him, though."

"There is?" Kam looked blank, until he remembered the only public execution he'd ever seen. "Oh, yes, I see what you mean."

"It is what I want," the duchess said in a stiff voice. "That white-eye filth intends to execute my son as a traitor. The trial will be a sham, for the conclusion is already set. I do not know what manner of execution Lord Isak intends, but I am certain there is no depravity beneath him. To speak plainly, as you desire, I say this: I will do what I can for your families, if you will do the same for mine. If all I can give to my son is his dignity in death, then I would be glad to deny Lord Isak this final cruelty after the sacking of our home, the destruction of our family name, and the death of my brother, among many other crimes.

"I chose you precisely because you are not mercenaries or assassins. I do not expect anyone to get out of there alive, and that will be their mistake: they will not be expecting anyone to act without care of the consequences. I know you have no wish to die; I believe you to be good men, honourable men. And for the sake of your families I believe you will take this terrible risk and I say to you now, if you die failing, it will not affect the payment . . ." Her voice tailed off.

Kam found himself holding his breath until she spoke again, this time with a resonance that struck at his heart.

"You are the sort of men who will risk all for your families, and in this I do not believe we are so different. I will do whatever I can to provide a diversion. And if by my own death I can offer one of you the chance to survive to see their children again, I will willingly do so."

"They say you're a mage, that you've made pacts with daemons," Boren whispered, causing Kam to jump at the sound.

The duchess shook her head, sadness in her face rather than the anger Kam would have expected. "I have no such power, and those mages in our service are now dead. I do have something that may provide the necessary distraction, but I cannot be certain how well it will work, so it may be that revealing my identity is all that I can offer. Do not trust that it will do any more than turn heads for a moment."

Kam looked at Boren, whose anger had clearly faded to nothing now, and stood.

"I'll have to discuss this with the others. When your man finds us tomorrow, you will have your answer."

"Thank you," she said, her voice sounding hollow. "Once I would have said you will be in my prayers forever, but I have none of those left. You are my final prayer—I cannot stomach any more begging of Gods who have obviously never cared for me—but perhaps the Lady will look kindly upon you and grant you luck, for one day at least."

CHAPTER 6

ASHIN DORANEI THOUGHT HARD about turning round in his seat and glaring at whoever was smoking that heavily spiced tobacco; it had been tickling the back of his throat for an hour or more and it was really starting to annoy him. After a few moments' thought he decided against it—chances were he'd just fall off his stool if he tried anything so acrobatic.

Standing up first was an option, but if he had any money he wouldn't have bet himself he'd be able to manage it.

Hah, don't bet for money no more, he said to himself, *got more fun stuff than that t'do.* He flapped weakly at his pockets for a moment. Somewhere he had a couple of wyvern claws, winnings from the last bet he'd made with his comrades.

Bastards let me kill it first, that's not agains' the rules? There're rules for us? There're rules for men like me?

"So where's the love of my life then?" said a woman from the other side of the bar.

Doranei wavered a moment before adjusting his head enough to look her in the face.

Bugger me . . . looks lot like a woman I shagged.

Doranei let his head sink down again and tightened his grip on his drink.

Prob'ly not a surprise. Janna does work here. Unless . . .

With painstakingly slowness a thought struck him and with great diffi-cultly Doranei turned his head again, this time to look down the length of the bar.

Shit. Must've forgotten to leave the Light Fingers. Why th' hell would I sit in this dump so long?

Another tankard of beer slammed down on the bar top in front of him.

Ah. Doranei's battered face skewed into a lopsided grin as he reached for the tankard. *That's why.*

"Still awake, there? Where's your Brother then, m'lovely?" the woman spoke slowly and precisely.

M'lovely. Gods I hated bein' called that—that why I stopped shagging her? A fitful burst of activity took place in Doranei's memory.

Or was it 'cos I said she smelled like a mule an' she kicked my balls up into my guts? He nodded sagely and Janna snorted in irritation.

"Still playin' the mystery then? Fine, piss on you. Let's see if you're drunk enough for me to nick one of those posh cigars you're smokin' these days."

Janna reached forward, a little hesitantly at first, until she was convinced Doranei wasn't reacting at all, at which point she gave a toothy grin and slipped a practised hand inside his tunic to retrieve a silver cigar case. "Well ain't that lovely," she said chattily. "It's got a bee on it and everythin'—" She stopped, the amusement suddenly falling from her face. "Gods, your boss give you this?"

Doranei stared down at the bar for a while, then tried to reach for his pocket. He got his hand in there on the second attempt.

Cigar case's gone. Bugger. That supposed to happen here? Someone nickin' from me in a Brotherhood pub? Bloody stupid, that.

Janna pulled out a cigar and set the case on the bar, lighting her plunder from a lamp and puffing hard until it was properly lit, then she returned the case to Doranei's pocket and set her elbows on the bar so her face was only a few inches from his.

"Now then, m'lovely, where's your boy Sebe? Next time you see 'im, tell 'im I've missed 'im and all 'is lovely scars. Gods, you should've 'eard me scream when I saw 'im bald as a fucking baby last week! Scary bloody baby, but never mind, I love 'im anyway. But I said to 'im, m'lovely, 'I've got nothin' to 'old onto,' I said, and you know 'ow much I like doin' that!" Janna gave a cackle that momentarily quietened the rest of the pub.

Janna. Girl's got good punch on her, Doranei though dreamily, lifting his beer and drinking automatically. *Poor Sebe, boy's smitten. Mind you, good punch is somethin' to respect, an' that smile lights up th' whole bloody room. She'll be a terror once he gets the guts to marry her, but she'll treat him right. Randy li'l fucker knows how to stay on her good side.*

"So what were the women in Scree like, eh?" Janna continued in a conspiratorial voice, undeterred by the lack of response. "Lookers? Bet they're an ugly lot, all black-haired Farlan bastard stock ain't they?"

"Women?" said Doranei suddenly as though only now waking from a dream.

"Fuck me, it lives," Janna chuckled. "Now that's an interesting thing, 'e don't pay a blind bloody bit of notice until I bring up the subject of skirt!"

She reached out and patted his cheek. "Doranei, m'lovely, am I to think you're finally past pining for me and 'ave got yourself a lady, or did you just meet a whore even better than me?"

Doranei took another swig of beer and let the words slowly settle into an order he could understand.

Women.

Pining.

Lady.

A vision of the three women he'd seen most often in Scree appeared in his mind: Haipar the shapeshifter, Legana, the Farlan assassin, and of course Princess Zhia Vukotic, vampire and enemy of the Gods.

"Bloody scary," he announced finally.

Janna laughed. "Fuck me, that ugly, eh?"

Doranei thought a little longer. Eventually he shook his head hard. "Not ugly, beautiful," he said once he'd regained his balance. He clutched the bar for support.

"Why's that scary, then, m'lovely?"

"Too beautiful. Too dangerous. Too—" His voice trailed off, his attention fixed upon the tankard before him.

"Piss and daemons, you do 'ave it bad, don't you? What's 'er name, then?"

Doranei focused on Janna's face. The same mess of tight brown curls, the same round face and beaming smile, a canine missing on the left side.

Janna's lovely, why didn't I stay with her? Sebe's got more sense than me. He might be scared of Janna's temper, but nothin' more. What sort of fool falls in love with a woman who bloody terrifies him?

"Secret."

"A secret? M'lovely, I've seen every bloody inch o' you from more directions than I care t'remember; you've got nothin' you need to 'ide from me."

"Can't tell."

Janna gave a snort of disappointment. "But she's the reason you're drinkin' all alone? The reason you were 'ere last night too? Fuck me, m'lovely, thought you lot worked at night?"

"Not th'only reason," Doranei muttered, a stubborn set to his jaw. Unbidden, his finger touched the small scar Zhia had left on his bottom lip, his only memento of her.

"Not the only reason," she echoed, 'aye well, I've 'eard stories about what 'appened there, so I can believe you." She took a long swig of his beer. "I'd be drinking brandy in your place if 'alf of what I 'eard went on there was true."

"All true." Doranei tugged the beer from her grip and drained it. "But we burned him. Can't forget that. Long time comin'. I burned the bastard."

"Burned him?" Janna whispered. "That's a bit personal for you, ain't it?" She gave a soft gasp. "Blood in the Dark Place, was it 'oo I think it was? That scar-'anded bastard? You burned 'im?"

Doranei felt his face twitch at the suggestion, knowing only too well who she meant. The Light Fingers was a Brotherhood pub, a safe place for the agents of the king and the city criminals they were recruited from. Janna might be just a barmaid, but she was a sharp one, and she knew most of the Brotherhood. None outside the King's Men knew the details, but it was impossible to hide the fact that Ilumene wasn't one of them any longer.

Doranei's face darkened and he shook his head slowly. "Not him, not yet. I—"

His sentence went unfinished as a hand thumped down on his shoulder. Janna gave a delighted cry and pushed her ample frame past Doranei's face as she grabbed the newcomer and planted a fat kiss on his face.

Ah, smells like a mule. I remember.

"There's my beauty," Janna cried once she'd let Sebe up for air, 'and there's even a scrap of 'air on that 'ead too." She rubbed her hand over Sebe's scalp, which sounded like sandpaper.

"Whispering sweet nothings to my girl?" said a voice in Doranei's ear. He grabbed the bar for support and levered himself around. There was a face there, indistinct and wavering for some reason.

"The fuck're you?" he muttered.

"Bloody hell, not again. Janna, got anything to sober him up?" said the blurred face. Doranei moved a little closer and it took on a little more detail. *Looks like a bloody monkey. Hah, Sebe looks like a monkey too.*

"I could kick 'im in the balls if you like," Janna said with a smirk, "woke the little bastard up a treat last time."

Someone gripped Doranei's face and turned it to the light. He growled and pulled back, lifting his tankard to his lips and trying to blow the few remaining bubbles of froth to the other side.

"So what do you reckon, boyo, a quick kicking from my girl to wake you up?"

"So what's 'is story, m'lovely?" Janna asked before Doranei could work out he was being spoken to. "Why's 'e moping about over some woman? That's not like 'im, not one bit."

"Long story," Sebe said coolly, "and not one that's going to be told here either. He said anything about her to you?"

"Nah, jus' it's a secret."

"It is, so if he's so drunk he starts to chatter, you put him out. He'll thank you in the morning."

Doranei raised his head. "Not drunk."

Something smacked into the side of his head and the bar fall sideways just before the floor hit him. He tried to take another drink, but his beer had disappeared and its loss seemed to drain his will.

He groaned slowly, then his body went limp.

"So why'd you do that?" Janna said once she'd stopped laughing.

"See the sparrow at the door?"

"That lost puppy that followed you in? 'ard to miss, m'lovely."

"I brought him here to speak to Doranei. He's been checking out the pubs down by the docks, asking for the Brotherhood."

"Tsatach's burning arse! Simple, is 'e?" Janna exclaimed.

"Desperate, more like," Sebe countered with a shrug. "Anyway, thought I'd let boyo here decide what to do with him, but now I've seen him I don't think he's sober enough."

He looked down as Doranei flailed around for a few moments before managing to sit up. It took another few seconds for him to realise he hadn't gone blind; he was just staring at the wooden facing of the bar. With an enigmatic grin, the King's Man reached up and clung onto the bar as he pulled himself approximately upright.

"Who hit me?" he murmured.

"I did," Sebe said with a sigh. "Gods, Doranei, I've never seen you this bad before."

"Sebe." Doranei blinked a few times, his head wavering forward and back as he squinted at his friend. Eventually he gave a stupid grin. "Beer?"

"Nah, got a sparrow for you to meet."

"Sparrow?"

Sebe pointed towards the door. Doranei blinked a couple of times to clear his eyes, then tried to take in the newcomer's appearance. He looked like a nobleman, but one who'd spent too many recent nights in haystacks. There were fresh scars on his gaunt face; he looked like he was starving.

The man gave a start as Doranei lurched forward and growled, "The fuck're you?"

"I—My name is Ortof-Greyl," he said quickly, as if this information alone would protect him. "Harn Ortof-Greyl." He looked at Doranei expectantly.

"Rings a bell."

Ortof-Greyl waited for Doranei to say more but the King's Man just swayed slightly and smacked his lips together, hoping Janna would take the hint.

"I was—I am a member of the Knights of the Temples," the man went on after an uncomfortable moment of silence.

"Not sure which, eh? Can see how that'd be a problem." Doranei gave the man a friendly pat on the shoulder and struggled back onto his seat. He propped himself up on his elbows. "Want a beer?"

Sebe grinned and pulled over a pair of stools, indicating Ortof-Greyl should sit between the two Brothers. Reluctantly, the man did so.

"Rank?" Doranei growled.

"Major," the man replied after a slight hesitation.

"Ordained, then." It wasn't a question, and they all knew the implications. "Where's that brandy then, woman?"

"It'll be shoved up your arse if you don't ask nicer than that, m'lovely," Janna replied sweetly.

Doranei dragged his eyes up from the bar, but her bright smile defeated whatever was passing for thought in his head. He turned to Sebe, waved a hand in Janna's general direction, and resumed his earlier position, supporting his head on his empty tankard.

With a sigh, Sebe secured a bottle and three thimble-like cups.

"Ordained," Doranei repeated in a grim voice, staring over the bar. "Bugger."

Beside him the major nodded, looking even paler than he had when he'd first entered the pub. "Some days it feels like fire in my veins. Not for much longer though," he added, "not after what I saw in that refugee camp." He knocked back his first cup of brandy before Doranei had even found his own.

"Your Order won't like that too much," Sebe said.

"The Order is fractured and lost," Ortof-Greyl replied sadly. "General Gort is dead, General Chotech is dead. I heard a week ago that General Diolis was murdered in Aroth. My group is destroyed."

"Does the Knight-Cardinal know about your plotting against him? He clearing house?" Sebe asked, leaning forward.

"I believe so; someone must have informed on us. Whatever the truth, we are in no position to deliver an army of the Devoted to Lord Isak. We've failed in our duty."

"Join the fuckin' club," Doranei growled. A sudden purpose seemed to take hold of him and he downed two shots of brandy before saying anything further.

A look at Sebe told Ortof-Greyl that he didn't know what Doranei was referring to either.

"Took a li'l trip after Scree," Doranei said while he waited for Janna to refill his cup. "Went to a monast'ry and talked to a bunch o' priests."

Sebe gave a gasp as he realised what Doranei was talking about. "Major, give us a moment please?" he said urgently.

"Fuck off, or I'll gut you like a fish!" Doranei added with a snarl, swinging wildly around towards the major and ending up just inches from his face.

Ortof-Greyl backed off quickly and retreated across the room. Janna gave Doranei a sharp clip around the head and quickly poured a beer that she took over to Ortof-Greyl, earning a grateful look from Sebe.

"So what're we going to do with him then?"

Doranei shrugged. "Don't owe 'im nothing. Send 'im home."

"As a spy? He'll need some reassurance that we're there to back him up—and what about the Knight-Cardinal clearing house? I don't like it; we're probably sending him straight to his death."

"Fuck 'em."

Sebe sighed. "Gods, boy, what's happened to you?"

"Read their history," Doranei muttered.

"And?"

"Bastards had too many secrets."

"Oh Gods."

The Brotherhood had scattered in all directions after the fall of Scree, some pursuing enemy agents, some going after Azaer's disciples. Doranei had caught up with the main part of the Farlan Army and, whilst securing an escort for his king, met the novice who had guided Abbot Doren to Scree. The young novice, Mayel, had eventually told him all about the island monastery dedicated to Vellern, God of Birds, and Jackdaw, the disciple of Azaer who'd pursued them to Scree.

"The king suspected," Doranei said, to which Sebe nodded. "Looked back an' thought we'd got the Skull too easy. Bastard minstrel could've taken it, but didn't even try. Mayel told me the Skull weren't the only magic thing they brought, there was a book too, with initials on the cover—a pair o' Vs. I got the monks to show me their book o' days. They said a Farlan knight brought the Skull, but they already had a guilty secret."

"A pair of Vs? Could still be coincidence."

Doranei gave a snort and attacked the brandy again. "Could be. Bloody ain't, though. Monastery's old, but the monks weren't the first there. They found ruins to Ilit, and a book o' days with the journal—practically shat themselves when they translated it: in the middle of the night a man came an' told Ilit's monks to hide a book."

"Let me guess," Sebe said. "That'd be a man with eyes like sapphires?" He reached for the brandy and swigged straight from the bottle.

"Bloody sapphires. Damn minstrel gave us the Skull and took a book belonging to Vorizh Vukotic, that mad blood-sucking bastard hisself. An' guess who's gotta ask 'is sister what's in it?"

"What's in it?" Sebe echoed. "What's worth giving up the Skull of Ruling for? We ain't going to like the answer to that one, are we? Might piss off Zhia that we're prying into family business too."

"More brandy, woman!"

CHAPTER 7

THOUGH HE WAS FLANKED by two squad of personal guard, Isak nevertheless found himself walking towards the massive ornate gates with his shoulders hunched. The Temple of Law was based around an enormous central hallway, almost a rival to the white marble halls of Isak's dreams, only this was teeming with life. Light filled the hall from mullioned glass windows of white and yellow, two full storeys high.

Three massive doors, peaked like the hall's main gates but without the swirling lattice of ironwork, led to courtrooms on the left, while the right wall was studded with small doorways and corridors that stretched out into a rabbit-warren of offices. Cautious faces poked out from those doorways and watched from the main stairway, and the clank of advancing armour was unable to drown out the whisper of voices and the scurry of footsteps on the marble stair.

The largest and grandest courtroom was at the furthest end of the blue-tiled hallway, opposite the main staircase and the entrance to the cells. Isak swept down the corridor like a surging tidal wave while Major Jachen, the commander of his personal guard, led an assorted party without dragon livery in his wake. The soldiers were dressed for battle, save for their helms, as tradition dictated, and each man carried a short-handled glaive, ready to swing into action at the first movement towards them. They looked threatening, and even onlookers standing well clear found themselves trying to shrink further back from them.

Flags lined the hallway: the red fox's head of Alav, Goddess of Justice alternated with the blue snake of Nartis, and Isak's own crowned emerald dragon. A crisp breeze rushed in through the open gate to greet them, gathering up the golden-tasselled flags and lifting them high. Isak felt the wind on his face and scowled as it carried the voices of the crowd in Irienn Square to him. The people had been gathering since dawn and the square was already packed when he arrived for the opening formalities of Duke Certinse's trial: the swell of flushed and furious faces had been a stark contrast to the pale young man who'd knelt in the black square at the centre of the courtroom.

Behind a line of black-and-white-liveried Palace Guard raged a mob of clerics of all colours, intermingled with the whole range of Tirah's assorted citizenry. Foremost among them all were the scarlet-edged robes worn by the Cardinal branch of the cult of Nartis, men and women of all ages and ranks. Three full cardinals were in attendance, each accompanied by a squad of liveried soldiers and three times as many novices in blue, all carrying cudgels.

Those of the Temple of Death had gone a step further—alongside the assembled priests was at least a company of grey-robed men, the novices of Death's cult. Few of the novices of Nartis were more than eighteen summers old, however, and this group were considerably older—to Isak's eyes they looked remarkably like foreign mercenaries. He didn't bother to count; there would be exactly fifty-one of them: a company of five squads and one man to lead them.

The threat was unspoken, but clearly understood. The priests were showing their hand: they had their militia already recruited, and they were daring him to become embroiled in a power struggle at a time when he had so publicly announced the need for unity.

"They underestimate you. The fever they have caught from their Gods makes them foolish." The voice was scathing.

For once, Isak had to agree with Aryn Bwr. If he had been thinking clearly, not even Cardinal Certinse would have had the arrogance to think he could face down the Lord of the Farlan and win—but therein lay the problem. They were *not* thinking clearly, and this was indeed a conflict he could ill afford.

"Send your shadow to Certinse," the last king whispered in a moment of clarity. Isak tensed for a moment, until he realised Aryn Bwr only meant Mihn. *"Have him slip into the cardinal's palace one night, and tell him that the first death in such a war will be his own. He has distanced himself from his own family to save his position, so offer him the chance to keep all he is desperate to hold onto, if only he quietens the voices of his brethren."*

"Right now I'll be happy if we get out of the square without having to kill anyone," Isak muttered, too softly for anyone else to make out, but Major Jachen still caught the sound of his voice.

"Sir?"

"Nothing, Jachen," Isak said with a dismissive wave. "Just make sure your men keep calm out there."

"They won't start swinging, my Lord, I can assure you of that—Sir Cerse has three Swordmasters out there with him to keep an eye on the guardsmen."

"Good. I think we're outnumbered."

"Not badly, my Lord," Count Vesna said with forced cheer, "and the Ghosts have faced worse on the battlefield—and let us not forget we've got a second regiment inside this building and a third covering all the surrounding streets. If they do start anything, it'll be us ending it—and you won't even have to touch your blade."

Isak turned to look at his friend, resplendent in his black silks and full-length coat adorned with gold braid. His long black hair was oiled and immaculately plaited, affording a glimpse of the knighthood tattoos he was so proud of. As well as his golden earrings of rank, Vesna wore a golden lion's head at his throat, an echo of the one on his armour, right down to the ruby in its eye.

Though the famed soldier was still in prime condition—Isak had seen him fight in Scree—he knew the count was feeling his mortality these days. Vesna looked older than when they'd first met, and his familiar roguish grin was occasionally edged with fatigue.

I hope your wedding will change that look, my friend. I don't need an old warhorse; I need a general I can depend upon, Isak thought a little sadly.

"It's a beautiful day, Vesna; let's hope none of us have to touch our blades."

The weak winter sun was already halfway behind the buildings in the east, but still it cast a pale luminescence over the white tiles of Cold Halls opposite. The Ghosts had cordoned off a square at the entrance to the Temple of Law and were holding back a crowd that appeared as fractious as when Isak had entered two hours previously. Sir Cerse, Colonel of the Palace Guard, saluted Isak from his position just within the cordoned-off area and barked an order to his men as the Lord of the Farlan walked down the two steps to the square.

The lines of Ghosts pushed into the crowds to drive a wedge through it for Isak to walk behind, but the cheering townsfolk behind the priesthood parted easily and there was no need for the extra weight. Isak was conscious of the protective ring of black-iron glaives surrounding him as he ignored the shouts ringing out from both sides.

After twenty yards Isak, towering over all his companions, spotted two figures walking onto the square from Hunter's Ride, heading straight for him: a man and a woman; the woman was hooded and anonymous while the man wore a hurscal's livery. Isak paused. Red and white checks. The colours stirred a memory, but it took him a moment to place them.

Tildek, seat of the Certinse family.

"Vesna, that's a Tildek hurscal coming towards us," he said.

Even before he'd finished speaking the count had slipped past his lord, his hand closing around the grip of his sword. Even if the man was simply looking to make a statement, they didn't want Isak involved.

"Lord Isak!" the hurscal shouted, marching ahead of his companion. Vesna too increased his speed.

Isak looked around; Jachen was ignoring the hurscal and instead scanning the crowds behind them in case this was a feint. Returning his attention to Vesna, Isak was just in time to see the man stop and fall to his knees. Vesna closed the gap as quickly as he could, but he wasn't in time to shut the man up.

"Lord Isak, you shame the tribe and Nartis!" the man called. He was young, not many years older than Isak. He had bushy eyebrows and a diagonal scar crossing his mouth where his broken front teeth were visible.

Isak could see the fervour in the man's eyes as he pulled a dagger from his belt and held it up for a moment before reversing it and driving it into his own chest. A collective gasp ran around the onlookers as a flash of pain crossed the man's face. Isak saw him sway, his hands still wrapped around the hilt of the dagger.

The hurscal's mouth fell opened and his eyes closed, but he jerked the knife out again with a breathless gasp of agony. A jet of scarlet followed it and spurted out across the paving stones at Count Vesna's feet, stopping him in his tracks. Isak felt the Land freeze around him as everyone turned to watch the hurscal. Unbidden came a memory from his year of learning swordsmanship from Carel: *a moment is all a soldier can ask for.*

He opened his mouth to shout, but before he could voice his warning, the hurscal's companion had raised something up above her head and hurled it down at the dying man's feet. Isak heard it shatter on the stones. Liquid sprayed in all directions as shards of glass flew across the ground and scores of tiny black objects bounced madly about. A dark red liquid spilled over the pale stones and a bitter taste filled Isak's mouth. For a moment he thought he tasted blood, but then the flavour turned as dry and acrid as ash. The cool air turned frosty as the hurscal pitched forward and started convulsing.

A black burst of magic filled the air as the woman backed away. Her hood had fallen back and he could see the horror on her face.

"Vesna," he roared, finding his voice at last, "*get back!* Everyone, get back!" The power in his voice broke the paralysis and people started to run from the scene.

He drew Eolis and felt a surge of magic run down the blade as the Crystal

Skull set into it pulsed with energy. Ahead of him the hurscal gave another violent jerk. The dead man's arms shot out, wrenched in an unnatural direction. Isak took a step back. A war cry came from his left and Isak watched as one of his guards threw his glaive end-over-end—

—only to have the dead hurscal pluck it clean out of the air. The taste of ash increased in Isak's mouth as he recognised the massive surge of magic swirling around the corpse.

The glaive fell to the ground as the dead hurscal's fingers splayed wide. His hands and arms distended grossly and split open like overripe fruit as grey appendages burst through the skin. From inside each arm came an angular, chitinous limb that grew in a heartbeat to the length of a man. Sharp spurs at the end slammed down into the ground as the corpse's legs erupted in similar fashion. The strange, spiky protrusions drove between the paving stones as if looking to find more secure purchase below. Slowly they flexed, and as they started to raise the torso up, it too began to swell horribly.

Screams rang out from the crowd behind, interspersed with shouts from Jachen and the Swordmasters.

As Vesna started forward, his sword raised, one limb lifted and darted out, like a probing spear, and the count, realising he didn't have the reach to get past it, quickly retreated to Isak's side.

"My Lord," he called, not taking his eyes off the creature, "we must get you away from this daemon."

Isak was transfixed in horrified fascination at what the dead hurscal was turning into. "And let *that*—whatever it is!—run amok?" he retorted, "don't be stupid!"

"This is a trap," Vesna yelled in reply, but whatever he was going to say next was cut off by a livid screeching sound which filled the air, like the voices of a thousand maddened insects.

The corpse's torso twisted violently and a long-beaked head burst out in a shower of blood, followed quickly by a solid, blockish body slick with oily blood. Two multijointed limbs hung from what might have been shoulders, so long that the clawed fingers almost brushed the ground.

The daemon's head moved and it looked around briefly before crouching a little so it could snatch up the thrown glaive. The weapon looked like a toy in its hands, especially compared with the lance-like tips of its legs that were longer than Isak was tall. The savage beak parted to reveal slender stiletto-like teeth. It had a dozen vertically slit eyes running chaotically from the midpoint of its beak back onto its grey bristling head.

As Isak watched, he could see the randomly searching eyes suddenly moving as one and snapping into focus on him. The daemon tensed and its head flicked forward, as if seeking to discover what he was.

It can see my power, he realised, *and it doesn't know what to do. But I do.*

He drew on his Crystal Skull and raised Eolis. Vesna gave a cry and staggered away as a blistering flare of crackling white flames surged about Isak's body. He had given in to Tila's urging and wore the cuirass of Siulents, his magical armour, underneath his clothes, in case of assassins, but he was painfully aware that the rest of his body was clothed only in linen and silk.

Make it hesitate, he thought, remembering Carel's training, and he increased the flow of energy.

The daemon gave a piercing shriek in response. It moved one leg forward, as if to take a step, and Isak wrapped the lightning-storm of magic around Eolis's blade and raised the sword. At the back of his mind he heard a cry, Aryn Bwr shouting out in alarm, and in the next moment he felt a presence on either side of him, twin shadows amid the storm of light, and the torrent of magic flowing through him ebbed. As the shadows surged forward heading for the daemon, Isak, shocked into inaction, stopped dead and gaped, his thoughts as frozen as his body—but it was only for a moment.

The Land snapped back into focus.

The Reapers!

He could see only their backs, but there was no need for a second look: the Soldier and the Headsman were all too recognisable. Their slaughter on the Temple Plaza in Scree would never be erased from his memory, and here in the pale light of day they looked no less terrifying: the Soldier was already swinging his bastard sword as the Headsman raised an enormous straight-bladed axe.

The daemon's head turned from one to the other, then he lunged with one long leg at the Soldier. It looked to Isak as if the Aspect of Death merely leaned to one side to avoid the blow before hacking into the daemon's leg. Ichor spewed out of the wound and over the Aspect's face and shimmering ice blue armour, but he ignored it and continued chopping at the limb.

The daemon shrieked, this time in real pain, and tried to pull itself back, but the Headsman took an almighty swing at its other front leg and buried his axe deep. The daemon sagged, dropping the glaive it had retrieved. It used its hands as props to keep itself upright while its lower limbs thrashed about wildly, trying to escape the heavy blades. It scrabbled for purchase on the paved ground, but the Reapers pursued with blow after blow. Isak watched in astonishment as the howling monstrosity retreated, spraying ichor in all directions, scattering the crowds who'd run in from Hunter's Ride to see what was causing all the noise.

As he watched, he saw a woman caught in the neck by one lance-tipped leg. She was pinned to the ground like a speared fish, though the daemon didn't appear to notice, so busy was it trying to free itself—and in the next moment the Soldier had lopped off the leg. The daemon, losing balance, fell, but the severed limb stayed upright, still piercing the woman, who was twitching uncontrollably as she died. The Headsman took advantage of his downed target and chopped down, splitting the daemon's head in two.

Isak flinched as a burst of bitter-tasting magic rushed out over the square and the daemon winked out of existence. A sudden calm descended as the Reapers stared down at the uprooted flagstones, slick with the daemon's viscous blood. The people froze where they stood, all eyes on the Aspects of Death.

A gust of wind rolled over the square; Isak flinched as the movement stirred Reapers into action. Both looked at him. The Soldier's face was half obscured by ichor-matted hair; the black eyes of the hooded Headsman all that were visible. His guts clenched as their focus became predatory and Isak remembered the Soldier's words in Scree. They wanted Aryn Bwr—how many times would he be able to deny them? He could feel their insistent tug on the magic flowing through his limbs; they were drawing energy from the Skull directly.

I will not *be forced.* He took a step back and stopped. The Reapers didn't advance; they simply watched him, the hunger plain on their faces. The only movement was the goo dripping from the Soldier's armour. Isak tightened his grip on Eolis and tried to stem the flow of energy from the Skull.

The Reapers shuddered, and Isak felt the magic buck like a mule as they fought back. The impact ran through his massive shoulders, but he refused to let go. He forced himself to take a step forward, Eolis raised, and continued his pressure to dam the energy from the Skull—and suddenly the Reapers could fight him no longer and the stream of magic vanished. Without the power it provided the Reapers were thrown backwards, fading to nothing before they hit the ground behind them.

Isak lowered his sword and gulped down air. He staggered as his wobbling knees threatened for a moment to give way. Jachen and Vesna ran up to him, shouting words it took him a moment to understand. Vesna was forced to jump back as Isak turned quickly with Eolis still drawn. His guardsmen, close behind Jachen with weapons raised, looked bewildered.

One of the Swordmasters ran straight past to where the woman who had started it all stood, apparently transfixed by the chaos she'd caused. Her hood had fallen back and Isak saw a middle-aged woman looking aghast, obviously as shocked as anyone else by what had happened. As the Swordmaster reached her she seemed to wake from her daze and raised her hands as if to plead with the man, but he didn't let her get a word out before he smashed his fist into her face. The woman flopped to the floor and went still, but the Swordmaster took no chances; his blade was at her throat within a breath, ensuring any further movement would be her last.

Isak turned to the crowd, watching in silence. A few had fallen to their knees in prayer; he could see their mouths moving, though no sound reached his ears. With an effort he sheathed his sword—

—and then stopped. Something had changed; some detail had set an alarm bell ringing in his head.

Slowly, as though through a fog, the Land came back into focus.

"Why is the gate shut?" Isak said. He took a slow step forward as realisation crept over him and he raised his voice to a bellow. "Who shut that damned gate?"

"Bind it fast, Duril!" Kam yelled, chancing a look back at the now-barred gate. Another man came for him and he swung wildly with his club. Kam missed, but Boren didn't. He caught the knight's rapier a heavy blow, sending it clattering away.

Piss and daemons, this place is still full of armed men! More feet charged down the stairs as screams came from the square outside. *Did that mad bitch know what she was doing?* Kam had caught the beginning of the chaos outside as the enormous spiderlike limbs reached up so high that he could see them, even from the back of the crowd. *Gods, I hope her friend is as good as his word,* he thought fiercely as he prepared himself for the fight ahead.

Four Ghosts charged from the guardroom at the entrance to the cells. Sir Gliwen, the Lomin knight sent by the Duchess, led Kam's companions forward, jumping over the bodies of the men they'd already taken out and rushing the soldiers, leaving Duril to finish with the gate.

The Heren brothers were watching Kam's back. "See you in the Herald's

Hall!" roared Jeyer Heren behind him. The man was relishing his chance to try his skill—and his heavy forester's axe—against the Palace Guard. He was big as a bear and fearless; he'd chopped the first soldier they'd reached nearly in two. Jeyer would buy them the time they needed. They'd said their good-byes already.

Before Kam could stop the man, Snivelling Woran raced ahead of the rest of them to attack the soldiers all by himself. The scrawny little man was drunk on adrenalin and swinging his homemade mace wildly as he reached the Ghosts, who barely slowed their charge as they ducked Woran's blows and delivered a brutal cut to his belly. Woran went down shrieking.

"Keep together," Kam yelled, knowing the rest of his men had no chance against the seasoned veterans unless they attacked en masse. He used his club to block another cut, working in tandem with Boren, giving his friend the opportunity to smash the soldier in the face. Blood splattered them all and the man went down, but it didn't distract his comrades for a moment as they savagely laid into the Siul men. Gren screamed out, a hefty blow to his shoulder almost spinning him around. He grunted as he barged into Foret, just as a glaive slashed deeply into Foret's face and he fell without a sound.

Kam quickly crouched, risking his own neck to go for the soldier's knees. It was a weak strike, but enough to unbalance the man, and Tol the charcoal-burner finished the job with his axe. They quickly killed the remaining soldiers, but not before the Ghosts had taken two more of their own.

"Move!" Kam yelled, scooping up one of the dead men's glaives and a ring of keys before heading down the corridor. The entrance to the cells was ahead, and there would be more Ghosts in the guardroom. *Keep moving, keep moving*: the words ran through his head like a mantra. They were dead men, they knew it, and they had to get to the young duke to make their deaths worth a damn.

Sir Gliwen was the first to reach the guardroom. The two remaining guards inside were standing ready, their swords gleaming in the dim lamp-light. The Lomin knight grinned and beckoned to his comrades.

Before the guards quite knew what had hit them, Tol had barrelled into them, his axe taking out a chunk of one man's arm and leaving a great splintered gash into the thick door behind as well. While the Lomin knight indulged in some vicious swordplay with the other guard, the Siul men finished off Tol's victim. It was a matter of moments before both lay dead on the floor.

Grimacing at the cut he'd received in his shoulder, Gren shoved Tol towards it to break it down before Sir Gliwen shouted to get their attention and waved the ring of heavy iron keys.

When they finally managed to get the door open, Sir Gliwen was the first man through—and seconds later he was lying dead on the floor, a grey-haired man sporting an embroidered golden eagle on his chest and brandishing a bloodied broadsword standing over him. He had leapt on Sir Gliwen as he entered the corridor, turning the knight's last-minute parry and running him through. Almost before the Lomin man had fallen, the old man was darting back to avoid Corast's swinging axe-blow.

Kam blinked in astonishment at the old man's speed. He trapped Corast's axe with his sword and lunged forward with a dagger in his left hand to skewer Corast's right shoulder. But despite his speed and undeniable skill, the numbers were against him. While Kam attacked from the right, Boren managed to clip the old man's left arm. As he recoiled, Boren smashed the glaive's weighted handle into his skull.

"Keep going," Kam panted, shoving his companions on, not allowing himself to look at the fallen. They reached a narrow staircase and found themselves ploughing into more soldiers. Someone—Kam didn't know if it was his boys or the enemy—knocked the only torch from its holder, plunging the place into sudden gloom, and cries of alarm and pain were shortly followed by the sounds of bodies crashing into each other and the clatterer of weapons falling onto stone floors. The sudden spray of sparks skittered over their heads and caught in Boren's hair. Kam ducked and struggled to stay on his feet as Boren roared in pain and flailed around, trying to extinguish the smouldering sparks, while the group barrelled on down the stair.

At last the men from Siul stumbled into the lower guardroom, trampling two black-and-white-liveried Palace Guards under their feet and finishing the job with their clubs and maces. Two more were driven back against the rear wall of the guardroom by the onrush of fight-maddened men, and with no space to swing their swords they were battered to the floor and brutally dispatched.

Kam looked around. The dimly lit guardroom was low-ceilinged, barely an inch higher than him, with grimy grey walls and the mingled stench of shit and sweat and fear thick in the air. An unlit brazier stood in one corner. The only other door in the room opened onto a narrow corridor lined with cell doors at regular intervals.

"Find the keys," he ordered as he headed towards the cells. Boren, Gren, Corast, and Tol began to search the bodies as Kam called Duke Certinse's name, looking for the correct cell. A dozen voices replied, all calling for rescue, and he started to pound on each door in turn. He finally found the right door, by listening for the only voice that sounded anything like a young duke's. He started fumbling with the unwieldy ring of rusty keys Boren had handed him.

He tugged the door open and shouted, "We've got 'im! Back up those stairs, now." He started checking the keys on the ring for one small enough to unfasten the duke's manacles, but they were all too big.

"Not that set," Certinse croaked. "Swordmaster Kerin has the key."

"Who's that?"

"He was here just a few minutes earlier; I heard him. Blue tunic with a gold eagle."

"Boren, key's on the man at the top of the stair," Kam called, and Boren grunted and disappeared. Kam took a moment to examine the man he'd given up his life for. He didn't see much to impress: Duke Certinse was smaller than he'd imagined, a slender, smooth-cheeked young man who still managed to look haughty, even when manacled to a wall.

"What's your plan from here?" he asked.

Kam shrugged. "Get out. This place is a maze—we'll find a window to slip out of and make for our horses."

"That's the extent of your plan?" The duke sounded angry.

"Stop bitching," Kam said calmly, "we're not going to get that far, not if Lord Isak's as good as they say he is."

As though in response, a flurry of shouts came from the staircase, immediately followed by the clash of swords.

"We're trapped." Kam went to the door and saw his remaining comrades gathering at the foot of the staircase, their weapons at the ready. No one spoke, not even Petril Corast, who generally had something foolish on his lips. Kam could almost see the man's two children rolling their eyes most every time Corast spoke—but they'd not be embarrassed by their da now. He was lined up with the rest, blood running freely from the wound in his shoulder. He'd transferred his axe to his left hand.

"See you in the Herald's Hall," Kam said quietly.

Beside him, Boren nodded and roughly embraced his oldest friend before joining the others. Trying to fight off that awful sinking feeling in his gut, Kam walked over to one of the dead men and pulled a pair of short-swords from his swordbelt. He returned to the cell, dropped the swords at the duke's feet, and used his axe to bash at the chains binding the young man to the wall. The links were thick and well made, and even with Kam's sharp axe blade and the strength of desperation, it took too long to sever the first chain.

He paused and pulled a vial from his pocket. It was made of thick glass and bound with wire. "Take this," he said.

Duke Certinse looked at it in confusion. "What is it?"

"Poison. You want to be sure they don't take you alive, then drink it. The swords are so you can die fighting; poison's in case you don't."

Certinse gave a grim nod, suddenly looking less of a child. He prised out the wax stopper, lifted the vial as if in silent toast, and downed the liquid. They both tried to ignore the sounds of men screaming in the guardroom as he fought back the urge to vomit up the poison.

Kam picked up his axe again, but before he could attend to the other chain, Certinse stopped him. "Arm's no good, it's not healed right." He gestured at the swords and Kam handed them up to him. He grasped one in his manacled right hand, then hefted the other in his left.

Kam nodded approval and turned to face the door. He could hear Boren's roar, and recognised Tol's nasal cry of pain over the commotion.

"Hope your mother's as good as her word," he said, raising his own glaive and stepping slightly away from Certinse to give them each room. "If she's not, I'll haunt the Dark Place itself for the pair o' you."

There was no time for a reply as the Ghosts charged in.

CHAPTER 8

HAIPAR NEEDED NO HELP TO LOOK DESPERATE. No longer the proud mercenary, the shapeshifter, the leader; the years had finally caught up with her and now she was just a broken relic. Where once she had proudly smeared ash in her hair, now there was only grey, both natural and unnatural. Her limbs, once corded with hard muscle, were now as brittle as those of a starving refugee. Only her prominent nose and brow looked almost unchanged by their trek and an all-too-brief pregnancy. Ilumene had treated her kindly on the journey south, surprising even himself. Unlike that snivelling wretch, Jackdaw, whom Ilumene had been glad to see head north with Venn, Haipar had been too fragile, too broken, to really incur Ilumene's contempt. It had been easy for the former member of the Narkang Brotherhood to restrain his vicious nature. If nothing else, King Emin had taught him the importance of self-control when on a mission.

Haipar's mind was fractured, unable to follow any thought to its conclusion, but something unconscious, primal, made her check the bundle in her arms. When she looked at the child, her own face lit up with wonder and fear. He looked back, the curl of a smile on his lips and shadows in his eyes, watching, always watching.

The crowd around her had swelled in the last hour. She had been one of the first to arrive in the big square in the city of Byora, just where the main highway led out of the quarter. Byora was the largest and most prosperous of the Circle City's four self-governed quarters that nestled around the huge shape of Blackfang Mountain.

Sipping disgustingly sweet tea from a dirty cup, Ilumene continued to watch his charge as she shielded her child from being buffeted as a sudden swell ran through the assembled beggars. They assembled there hoping—mostly in vain—for casual work of any sort. Ilumene had told Haipar to go there and there she'd gone, but she most likely had no idea why she waited there now. There was no recognition in her grey eyes, only bewilderment at a Land she no longer recognised.

The square was unremarkable save for its location on the highway between the main gate from the upper districts and its equivalent in the quarter's wall. Ilumene raised his eyes and looked at the upper districts, snug behind a high wall of stone and looking down on the rest of Byora with gentle disdain.

The huge structures that gave the Eight Towers district its name were just about visible against the low winter cloud. Flanking that, like squabbling children kept apart by a parent, were the imposing buildings of the districts of Hale and Coin. In contrast with Byora's southern neighbour, Ismess, where religious law ruled and no building could stand taller than a temple, the eight towers looked down on their neighbours, much to the ire of the priests of Hale and the merchant-princes of Coin. In the shadow of Blackfang, height was the province of the powerful, and Eight Towers made a statement to the lowborn of Byora.

Behind them loomed the mountain. Ilumene found it impossible to ignore its presence; he had been born in the coastal city of Narkang, miles from any mountains, and he was unsettled by the jagged bowl-like cliffs and the thin black spire that rose from the crater within those cliffs. He felt crowded, more than once he had found himself leaning away from Blackfang, as if it were physically oppressing him.

A sound broke his reverie and he turned to see the bobbing heads of the retinue of the Duchess of Byora, Natai Escral. The scarlet tunics of the Ruby Tower Guards were an abrupt splash of colour on such a drab day. They had been seeing to the duchess's defences, no doubt. Everyone in Byora had heard that the Menin were marching north towards Tor Salan, and if they continued on after defeating the mercenaries defending that great trading city, the Circle City was surely the next prize in Lord Styrax's sights.

"And you know you don't have anywhere near the strength Tor Salan can bring to bear," Ilumene whispered as the duchess rode closer, "despite Aracnan and the Jesters awaiting my command."

He finished his tea, glad for the warmth no matter how vile the taste, and eased his chair back a little so when the time came there would be no obstacles in his path. "Don't worry, your Grace," he murmured, "you're about to be introduced to your Saviour."

As the noblewoman's retinue reached the square, the beggars surged forward to meet them, hands outstretched for alms and a wordless keening filling the air. The shivering poor were filling the road; it was almost as if the winter wind had robbed them of any sense of danger. Haipar found herself being pushed along with the crowd. She heard a cry and looked up to see a mounted soldier bearing down on her.

"Back, back! Clear the road!" he roared, reining in at the last moment to avoid trampling the beggar in rags; he scarcely noticed the tiny bundle in her arms. It was no concern to him. The wind caught his cloak and swirled it open to reveal his pristine crimson uniform adorned with gold braiding as noticeable as the weapon at his hip. The crowd ignored his words, shrinking together to avoid the cold, moving almost as one as those at the front pressed forward.

Ilumene sat forward, watching intently. The wind had a flavour he knew, a subtle touch on his mind he recognised. Aracnan was following Ilumene's orders. The immortal would be standing at a window, somewhere within sight of the crowd, naked and holding his Crystal Skull in shivering hands. His stomach would be growling with hunger.

Ilumene pulled his own fleece-lined jacket closer as a chill seemed to rise from his bones. Aracnan had cast his own ill-humour and discomfort out into the wind to affect everyone in the square, and even though he was prepared, Ilumene felt a familiar growl of resentment. His thoughts went back to Narkang, to the king he'd once loved as a father, until he got a grip of himself and returned his attention to the crowd.

The change was immediate. Ilumene, a man well schooled in anger, sensed the shift in mood before anyone else did. His eyes were drawn to a tall man on the left-hand side of the pressing crowd who reached out to grasp the bridle of the nearest horse. The rider saw him move and reacted first, kicking the man and sending him sprawling in the dirt. The crowd, instead of retreating, surged forward. The rider cried out for help, but the words were lost as voices on both sides were raised in a wordless paean of hatred.

The cavalry remembered their training and didn't fight into the crowd. They kept their line, content with hammering down with the butts of their spears at anyone within range. Blood sprayed and men screamed, falling to the ground before being trampled. Ilumene finally rose from his seat, his sword, still sheathed, in his hand, as two squads of infantry ran around from behind the duchess's carriage.

The soldiers roared as they barrelled into the crowd, which actually moved forward to meet them before half a dozen or more beggars were smashed to the ground by soldiers' heavy shields. Ilumene tensed, his eyes on Haipar as she was pushed here and there, her arms raised to protect her child. The crowd's voice began to fail as the infantrymen drove them back, and

Haipar ducked down in fear—until suddenly she was standing alone in front of the duchess's defenders.

Ilumene was already moving when a high scream cut the air. Everyone else paused, watching as three infantrymen turned towards the woman, their weapons raised. Haipar stood still, watching her own death, while the child in her arms shrieked again.

The sound seemed to freeze everyone except Ilumene in their tracks, until the big man smashed his shoulder into the nearest soldier and knocked him to the ground. He saw a flicker of fear in the eyes of the next man as, moving with unnatural grace, he drew his sword, cut down into the soldier's knee, and moved past. The face of the third infantryman was filled with fury as he lunged at Haipar with his spear—

—but Ilumene was there. He cut down into the shaft and let his momentum carry him forward into the man. He slashed upwards, catching the man across the face. He felt blood spatter on his cheek as the soldier fell. A small man was the first to react, charging forwards with shield and spear held close together. Ilumene turned away from the spear point and let his bulk take the impact of the shield; then, slamming his elbow into the man's neck, he sent him sprawling. His sword was already rising to catch the next soldier's blow.

"Stop!" bellowed a voice behind him. "Put your weapons up!"

The soldiers came to a halt as if their feet had just been nailed to the ground. Ilumene, his head moving constantly to keep his eyes on both sets of soldiers, kept moving until he'd reached Haipar's side. Then he lowered his sword and looked at the woman whose order had stopped the soldiers. The duchess, who was standing up in her open carriage, was a middle-aged woman with a proud face. Her fur-lined hood was pushed back to expose cheeks reddened by the blustery wind. Her hair was held back by a ruby-studded circlet. At her side was, Ilumene supposed, the duke, although all he could make out was an anxious face, above which was a rather smaller circlet.

"No more killing," the duchess continued in a slightly softer tone. Ilumene waited for the soldiers to put up their weapons before doing so himself. He glanced over at Haipar. The woman had sunk to her knees, her head bowed as though sobbing—or praying. Ilumene kept his face blank, hiding his disgust at what the woman had become. She'd forgotten all her abilities, her bravery, her strength. She was worthless now, except as a wet-nurse for his Master, and that would not be for much longer. After that, her survival would depend entirely on Azaer's appetite for cruelty.

Sheathing his sword, Ilumene nodded and, as if on cue, the child let out another wail. The heartrending sound was enough to bring the duchess from her carriage. She was well known to be childless, a situation the ignorant masses blamed fairly and squarely on her meek husband.

She was as tall and solid as Haipar had been when they first found her, but otherwise she could not have been more different. Her features were small, neat, and not a single sandy brown hair was out of place. She wore earrings, spirals of gold encasing more rubies.

"What is your name?" she asked Ilumene as she pushed past her men.

"Kayel," he replied hesitantly, casting a nervous look at the soldier who'd dismounted and taken up position at her side, "Hener Kayel."

"You're not a native of the Circle City, are you?"

"No, Canar Thrit," he replied before remembering himself and adding belatedly, "your Grace." *Bugger; stupid mistake to make when I'm trying to look humble. Maybe she'll think I'm overawed.*

"You're a mercenary; signed, or looking for work?" Her manner was open, almost welcoming; clearly Ilumene had succeeded in his attempts to impress her.

He shrugged. "Was working for some merchant, escorted him to the city. Supposed to be meeting him later to talk about more, your Grace."

"Good work, is it?"

Ilumene shrugged again and lowered his eyes, waiting for her to speak again. *Good work, hah! You should have seen the flames of my last work!*

"You look like you've seen your fair share of fighting," the duchess said, looking at the rough scar on his cheek that ran to his mutilated ear.

Ilumene raised a hand to his ear and touched the scar. There were too many injuries on his forearms, even for a mercenary, but they were concealed by the long leather vambraces backed with steel links he wore—though in a moment of caprice he had wrapped twine haphazardly around the vambraces to remind him of the scars.

He shrugged, wearing a pained expression as he replied, "Been on the wrong side of a few fights, your Grace. I'm in no hurry to see many more, but I reckon I'm big enough to frighten off thieves still."

"Are you a deserter?"

Ilumene shook his head and looked at the ground as he feigned shame. "No regiment left to desert, Ma'am."

"And yet you didn't fear to step in when you saw a child in danger—one I presume you don't know, from the way you're both dressed." She looked at him musingly.

Ilumene gave a bob of the head; that was all most rulers needed in response to their questions.

The duchess turned to Haipar and placed a reassuring hand on her shoulder. A rumble of disapproval came from the soldier behind her, but she waved his concerns away. "Fohl, you're such an old woman sometimes! It's perfectly obvious she's barely strong enough to stay standing by herself." Gently she urged Haipar up and onto her feet again. "Are you hurt?" she asked.

Haipar looked bewildered for a moment, her eyes darting between the duchess and Ilumene, then she shook her head.

"And your child?" Carefully, the duchess pushed aside the fold of cloth obscuring the baby's face. Ilumene felt his breath catch at the cherubic features of Azaer's mortal form. He looked up at the duchess and twisted his mouth into an enchanting smile. Ilumene, even a few feet away, could feel the arresting power of Azaer's gaze as the duchess looked deep into his shadow-clad eyes. He shivered as he remembered the first time he had done the same thing.

"I—" The duchess sounded stunned. "Your child is beautiful."

"He's a prince," Haipar whispered. From her dull tone it was unclear if she even knew what the word meant. The sentence was learned by rote until she could not forget it, even if everything else had drained away from her mind.

The duchess nodded dumbly. After another second or two, the baby blinked and the spell was broken.

"A prince indeed. I have never seen a more beautiful child. What is his name? How old is he, six months?" the Duchess of Byora continued in a soft voice, sounding completely smitten.

Haipar shook her head and Ilumene had to restrain the urge to reach out and cuff her around the head.

"A month," she whispered. "He is called Ruhen."

"A month only?" The duchess turned with a sceptical look towards Ilumene, who just shrugged again. "I think you have lost track of time a little, my dear. Your child is older than a month."

Haipar started to shake her head again, but as she did so she caught sight of Ilumene staring at her and she faltered, frowning.

"Are you certain?" the duchess continued gently. "Well, no matter, a little confusion affects us all as we get older, I find. Come, let's get you up into my carriage, for I would not sleep myself if I left a child as beautiful as this to go hungry tonight. The streets are too cold and cruel for one so young." She forced a small laugh. "And we must not forget that one cry from his lips was enough to inspire a jaded soldier to take on an army. Just think what greatness may await Ruhen when he learns to speak!"

More than you know, bitch, Ilumene thought. *You'll regret saying that so carelessly. Once you've served your purpose, the only thing your future holds is the pleasure of me fucking you over your throne while that sap of a duke watches, bleeding out his last minutes at our feet. And then you will join him—*

"Captain Fohl, perhaps you might find a space in the guard for one who fights as well as Master Kayel? I'm sure we could offer a better wage than most merchants. He's proved his skill already." She waved a careless hand towards the fallen soldiers. One was clearly dead; the other two were still unconscious.

The captain looked less than impressed with the idea of having an unknown mercenary admitted to his troop, but he knew better than to argue with his mistress. When she had made up her mind about something, that was the end of the discussion.

"Dare say we could find a uniform to fit him," Fohl growled. He was a slim man, past forty winters, with greying blond hair and a milkiness dulling the yellow of his left eye.

"What do you say, Master Kayel?" the duchess asked. "The Ruby Tower needs more guards than most merchants, and looking scary enough to ward off thieves will serve you just as well there."

Ilumene looked at the ground and did his best to look uncomfortable. "Suppose I could manage that," he said at last, earning a scornful look from Fohl, who clearly thought his victory over the guards had been down to luck and surprise rather than skill.

Proper Litse stock, this one, Ilumene thought as he took the reins one of the cavalrymen offered him. *Yellow hair, yellow eyes, and arrogant as shit. Dare say you could find a uniform to fit me, but I think I'll take yours. Even if you had both eyes working you'd never see me coming.*

One squad of infantry was left behind to see to the injured. Ilumene kept his eyes on the road ahead, glancing only once at the crowd, where he picked out a face easily enough, a man with pinched features and scarred cheeks that spoke of childhood disease. As they trotted past, Ilumene caught a snatch of the man's voice on the wind, too faint to make out properly, but he knew the words anyway.

The cries of a child: enough to make a coward become a hero.

Legana leaned out over the polished wooden balcony and looked down at the streets. The winter wind didn't bother her; that was a small hardship when one had such luxurious lodgings. Raising her glass, she offered a general salute to the district and knocked back the last of the warmed wine.

"If only every assignment could be so comfortable," the Farlan agent sighed, brushing a rogue strand of hair from her face. "I doubt Chief Steward Lesarl would approve of me lazing about just waiting for Zhia to turn up, but there's really not a lot he can do about it, is there? So balls to him!"

She straightened up and tugged at her sleeves. Even after several months under Zhia Vukotic's determined tutelage Legana was still far from what Zhia considered a noblewoman to be; she preferred her plain leather tunic and breeches any day. Dresses were for *women*—not what Legana considered herself—but the sharp-eyed vampire would have noted an improvement in the cut of Legana's clothes all the same. The knife in her boot and short-swords on her belt remained, of course.

"But what are you doing with your time while you wait?" The woman's voice came from the room behind her.

Legana cursed; the room had been empty and she'd locked the door herself. She moved quietly to one side, grimacing as she knocked her glass off the balcony. She had her swords drawn as she turned to face the newcomer in one smooth movement.

"A little unnecessary," the woman continued, sounding amused. She took a step forward, motioning for Legana to lower her weapons. Legana felt a shiver down her arms, and they went numb. Unbidden, the weapons fell to the floor. As the woman moved closer, the weak daylight illuminated her long copper hair and her startling emerald eyes.

"Gods!" Legana breathed, for a moment stunned into stillness, then she dropped to one knee. "Lady."

"Just one of us, my dear, but you got there in the end."

Legana could feel Fate's assessing eyes on her.

"Oh, do get up, girl. Grovelling suits neither of us."

Legana obeyed, but she kept her eyes low, desperately trying to remember her childhood lessons. They'd all thought it a big joke when the temple mistress had told them the protocols for addressing their Goddess, but now Legana found herself wishing fervently that she'd paid a little more attention. Catching sight of her short-swords on the floor at her feet, she felt a pang of shame and tried to nudge them behind a drape with her toe.

"Never mind those," the Lady said. "Why don't you fetch me a glass of that wine?"

Legana surprised herself at how eagerly she complied.

"And it looks like you'll be needing another glass too," Fate called out from the balcony.

Legana looked back to see the Goddess leaning out over the balcony, looking down, and, of all things, blowing a kiss to someone shouting below. There was nothing to interest a Goddess out there; it was just a minor street in Coin, the city's financial district. There were no temples here—not even to Fate, the variously named Goddess of Luck—which was why Zhia Vukotic had wanted her to take rooms here.

Oh piss and daemons, Legana realised, *did I drop that glass on someone?* Quickly she joined her mistress on the balcony and, a little hesitantly, handed Fate her wine.

"Ah, thank you." Fate had a sly smile on her face as she sipped the wine and settled into a chair. After a moment she indicated Legana should take the other. Legana did so feeling awkward and heavy-limbed next to the Goddess, who had sat as gracefully as silk billowing on the wind. "I think you caused a young man to wet himself in the street," she said abruptly. "Did the vampire not ask you to maintain a low profile then?"

Dark Place take me, she's here about Zhia, Legana thought with a sudden sense of dread. *I'm dead—dead and damned.*

"She, ah, I—" The words faded in her throat as Fate made a dismissive gesture and Legana felt her entire body freeze; all too like a dog responding to its mistress's command.

"I'm not here about the vampire, not principally, anyway," she said after a moment.

"So why are you here then?" Legana tried not to sound curious, and afraid.

The Goddess gave a soft laugh that felt like icicles prickling down Legana's spine. "To do what I do best; to present a choice."

"A choice? For me?" Legana's startled look only amused Fate further. "Why? What sort of choice would you need to offer? I'm a devotee of your temple, I'm yours to command."

"Oh come now, you've never been the most pious of women, have you? I hardly think a divine proclamation would be appropriate."

There was no anger in Fate's voice, but Legana still trembled slightly, fighting the urge to fall to her knees. She knew that was the effect the Gods were supposed to have on mortals, but it was alarming to experience it in person. She wasn't frightened of much the Land had to offer, and she'd been trained to be a killer of the highest calibre, and yet the merest hint of a smile from her mistress sent shivers down her spine.

"I'm afraid I don't understand, my Lady."

"I do have a mission for you, that is true, but first I have a proposal." The Lady leaned forward suddenly and Legana flinched involuntarily before finding herself once again mesmerised by the unnatural emerald shine of Fate's eyes.

It reminded her of a friend who'd won a set of dice with emeralds marking out the numbers on each face. A week later he'd offered her all the money he'd won to take the dice off his hands. Few mortals would survive such luck for long.

"You were in Scree; you saw what happened there."

"I saw, but I didn't understand much of it," Legana admitted, unable to hold the Lady's gaze for long, though she found herself continually drawn back to it.

"For a time the Gods were driven out of the city; the natives turned against my kind." Fate spoke in a whisper, now no trace of a smile on her face. "It was never intended to last, that much we do know, but the precedent is, let us say, concerning us."

"And the fervour?" Legana asked timidly, unsure what reaction her question would receive. "I've heard mild-mannered priests are suddenly preaching fire-and-brimstone; that it's driven some to violence already."

"I am mindful of the situation," the Lady said, a fierce look in her eye, "but there are others whose anger is unmatched since the days of the Great War. There was hurt done to several of the Upper Circle, and they demand vengeance."

Legana shuddered. That sounded distinctly worrying. "And what would you have of me, Lady?"

"A bargain," Fate said. "The mistakes of the past should not be repeated. Our greatest failure of the Great War was to pay insufficient attention at the outset. Immortals are not suited to the mundane details of mortal life, yet I suspect that is the battleground on which we will soon be fighting."

The Goddess paused and inspected Legana's clothes, which looked even shabbier than usual when compared with Fate's dark green dress, which flowed around her in a breeze Legana couldn't detect. After a moment, she said, "What I would have you do is to join me. Normally I make little use of priests or champions, but I believe this—and more—will be required if we are not to be left behind in the coming conflicts."

"The coming conflicts? What do you mean by 'join you'?"

Fate hesitated. "We have reached the Age of Fulfilment, and I am blind to what may come to pass. There are so many possibilities, and all conflicts are as one; dark portents feed off one another. There is no single enemy to face, but a hurricane of potential to unravel, to comprehend and map. The Gods are not united. They have different goals, and will not share followers willingly—we will never again see Nartis commanding Menin armies, or Death walking the streets of a city to rally its poorest in its defence. The deeds of the Great War broke us in many ways.

"As for what I mean by joining me, I mean just that. I suspect I am the first of my kind to make such an offer but I doubt I will be the last." She produced a golden necklace, delicate, and of the finest workmanship, studded with emeralds. "We Gods need mortal agents such as we have never required before. Legana, I offer you the chance to become part of me—to share my power and act in my name."

"You want me as your Chosen?" Legana gasped. Of all the things she might have imagined, this would never have occurred to her, not for a—

"Nothing so feeble," the Lady said with a sniff. She did not yet offer the necklace to Legana, though it was plainly part of the bargain. "I intend you to be *part* of me, not my servant. I wish you to be a Mortal-Aspect. You will walk the Land with my strength and my authority.

"Place this necklace around your throat and you will become an Aspect of Fate, no longer fully mortal, but not entirely divine. I require a mortal mind to see what I cannot, a mortal body to fear what I may dismiss." She looked at Legana, something like sorrow in her eyes. "My dear, this will not be an easy decision. Such a thing has never happened before, and I cannot promise you I am certain of the effect. But I cannot wait long. I give you until dawn to make your dec—"

"There's no need," Legana said with a sudden surge of confidence. "My Lady, I accept."

Fate gave her a quizzical look, but this time Legana refused to let her gaze fall. The word "Chosen" had sent a thrill racing through her body. She had been raised by devotees of the Lady, treated with nothing but kindness; even punishment for misbehaviour had been lenient by comparison with tales she'd heard about the cruelty some novices suffered at other monasteries and temples.

The day she'd left the temple, Legana had realised the firm hand of the devotees had tempered her impetuous nature, and made her a better woman. She owed them—and her Goddess—a lot, and she would serve the Lady however she could.

And Legana was smart enough to know that this offer would never be surpassed. It was more than she'd ever dared to dream for.

"Are you so sure?" Fate said after a moment. "This is not something to be undertaken lightly, and I have no wish to bind myself to an unwilling soul."

"I'm certain," Legana said, looking her Goddess directly in the eye, her fear gone. "I have never felt I belonged, other than inside your temple—any lack of piety on my part was because I felt insignificant, not worthy of you. I'll not betray my people, or my lord, but I wish to be more than an agent of a man I barely know.

"I'll take your gift and pay the price it demands."

Fate studied the young woman, then broke into a sudden, brilliant smile. "I have indeed chosen well. Now, listen before you put the necklace on, for I suspect the sudden sense of mortality will come as an awful shock to me, and I may have to retreat to the Palace of the Gods to recover."

Legana nodded quickly, her eyes glimmering with eagerness.

"Consorting with necromancers and vampires will no longer do. Deal with your current companions, then go to my temple in Hale. You may live there; Zhia Vukotic will not come after you there."

Legana nodded again, her eyes flickering to her fallen weapons. Neither Mikiss, the vampire asleep in the next room, nor Nai, the necromancer she'd last seen the previous night, would be easy to kill, but with the strength of a Goddess what could she not achieve?

The Lady had seen Legana's eyes move to her swords. "Good; kill them both, and then look to the voices in this city. The crossroads of the West is divided into quarters, but to get through whatever is coming, it will need to stand united—and believe me, the crossroads of the West *must* survive."

The Lady spoke quickly now and handed over the necklace to Legana.

She ran her fingers over the emeralds without taking her eyes off the Lady's face.

"I suggest you start your work by killing the High Priest of Alterr here in Byora. He's a waddling little misery of a man who goes by the name of Ayarl Lier."

Legana's eyes widened. *The Gods are turning on each other now?*

"We have never been the most harmonious of entities," the Lady said with a smile, guessing correctly what Legana had been thinking. "Alterr is one of those whose rage flows unabated. She will lead us to rashness if her strength is not curtailed, and Lier has great influence, both within the court of Natai Escral and with the common folk of Hale. It is best that influence be removed. And anyway," she added with a mischievous smile, as though she had suggested nothing more than a mild prank, "Alterr is of the Upper Circle of the Pantheon, while I am not. Ambition is not limited to mortals."

Venn slowly opened his eyes, trying not to wince at the light as he focused on the figures sitting nearby. They were all young, all with the unmistakable poise of Harlequins, dressed in furs and leather, the rough clothes of the clans rather than the distinctive diamond patchwork of a Harlequin. Not their final visit to the cavern then, but not long until this fresh crop would be presented with their blades and sent out into the Land.

And they have waited for me, Venn thought with satisfaction. *It appears my newfound weakness is yet another sign of my divine mission.*

There had never been a Harlequin who had renounced the ways after years out in the Land—those who saw it as a betrayal had no idea what to do about him, and increasingly, folk of the clans were seeing him as a man who had moved beyond the usual pattern of life. The Land had reforged the finest of the Harlequins and returned him to them to usher them into the future. The otherworldly air about him, courtesy of Jackdaw, ensured those with complaints or accusations spoke them only quietly. He had asked nothing of them and had spoken no heresy; until he did their very uncertainty protected him.

His arm felt leaden as he reached out for the water bowl he kept close at hand. The cavern was a vast place of open temples and shrines, but the natural grain of rock meant there were dozens of ledges and alcoves. Venn had adopted once such ledge and spent most of his days sitting there with his back resting against the wall. He ventured outside only rarely; what little exercise he took nowadays consisted solely of walking from one shrine to the next.

There were more visitors despite the winter months, and they were there to see him, the Harlequin who had returned from the Land a changed man, so he forced himself to be awake when they came, to debate with them or preach to them.

He drank thirstily, then replaced the cup, ignoring the growl in his stomach. Jackdaw remained in his shadow, silent for sometimes days on end yet still requiring everything a normal man needed to live. The only difference was that he now drained it from Venn.

Is this how a mother feels? he wondered, his cracked lips curving into a slight smile. *A child feeds greedily from my body while I must sit here and extol the virtues of another? Master, once more I applaud your sense of humour.*

"Age is a curse we must all bear," he began, aware that the group of young men and women were all waiting eagerly for his latest teachings. *Religion: what a masterful tool. They expect wisdom, so that is what they hear.*

"The wisdom of years clouds understanding. In life there is always fear, and that leads us from truth. Given the power of speech, a newborn would provide counsel surpassing that of any king because a newborn has not known pain, not the pain of loss, nor of love, nor of hunger, nor of fear."

Beside him he felt Jackdaw stir as the former monk recognised his cue; his skills were required again. Venn raised his palms in a manner that would remind some of the icons of Shaolay, Goddess of Wisdom, that often adorned thrones. He saw the wonder in the eyes of his new disciples as a sliver of Jackdaw's magic raced through his body, subtly enhancing the God-touched image he was presenting.

"A perfect child can remind us of how we ourselves once were, before we were stained by our years in the Land; its voice can strip away the fear that clouds our judgment and take us back to that unsullied state. Such a child would calm the enraged. Such a child would give heart to a coward and cause him to fight like a God in the defence of innocence. To seek out such innocence in others, to serve a child who knows nothing of hatred; what higher calling could there be?"

CHAPTER 9

MAJOR AMBER DUCKED OUT OF HIS TENT and looked around at the Menin camp. The wind raced over the line of tents and into his face; he flinched as a piece of grit caught him in the eye. He blinked the irritant away and dabbed at his eye with the fox fur trim of his heavy black cloak. It wouldn't do to attend his lord in tears; this was not a day for the Menin to show any shred of weakness.

The sun lurked sullenly somewhere at the horizon; hiding under a thick grey blanket, as Amber himself should be doing. He pulled his cloak closer as the wind continued to nip at every exposed part of him, including his ears, left exposed by the steel half-helm he wore.

The Menin were camped in the lee of a tree-topped hill, on the western bank of a swollen river Amber didn't know the name of. He'd reached the army only two days previously, meeting it here outside the city of Tor Salan. The Menin were marching northwards; he had fled south from Scree.

"Major!" called a voice over the clatter of the camp. Amber stopped and watched as Captain Hain hurried through the mud towards him. The breast-plate and pauldrons Hain wore under his cloak, like Amber himself, made the squat captain look even bulkier than usual. Hain was carrying his helm under one arm, but as he reached Amber the major gestured pointedly at it and Hain reddened. He dropped the hood of his cloak and put the helm on, trying not to shiver as the wind whipped around him. The order had been clear: they were to look at all times like the fearless warriors everyone knew the Menin to be—and that, unfortunately, meant going armoured and appearing oblivious to hardship, no matter how cold it got, especially while they were in their lord's presence.

"Good morning, Captain." Amber raised one armoured arm for Hain to smack his vambrace against, the soldier's greeting, but he was much taller than his subordinate and found himself falling back into old habits, raising his own arm so Hain had to stretch to reach it.

Strange that only some habits are so easy to adopt again, he thought. *I've been wearing heavy armour for half of my life, and yet ever since I got back this has felt like it belongs to another man.*

"Is it a good morning?" Hain replied. With his helm on he presented the same grim grey face as Amber, although the major could see Hain's broken front tooth through the vertical slit over his mouth as he grinned. "Doesn't look like either fucking one to me."

Major Amber slapped him on the back. "I don't know, from the sound of it, it is going to be a good one for you." He led the way up the slope. He could see the backs of Lord Styrax and General Gaur as they stared out at Tor Salan through the morning mist.

"You could be right there—and for that I have you to thank, sir," Hain said buoyantly. The glyphs on his shoulder plate and helm proclaimed Hain one of the Cheme Third, Lord Styrax's favourite legion, and Amber had recommended Hain for special duties. His first job would have very public results.

"A solider makes his own luck, you know that. Anyway, I had a few spare captains—and I couldn't leave you in charge of my division—the men would've spent the summer whoring."

Hain laughed. "Happily married man, sir, don't know what you mean! Hope you're right about the day, but I ain't counting my virgins until I'm dead, as the Chetse might say."

"They say that?" Amber asked with a frown.

Hain shrugged. "Mebbe, they're an odd lot."

As they reached earshot of Lord Styrax they fell silent. Out of habit Amber scanned the figures arrayed on the rise where Lord Styrax was overseeing his latest piece of audacity, facilitated by a certain captain of the Third. General Gaur was close at his lord's side, of course, and Kohrad Styrax, the lord's son, was stationed between them and a group of men clad in fine green and blue cloaks—emissaries from Sautin and Mustet, so Amber had heard.

They were all looking anxiously at the two regiments formed up in blocks at the foot of the slope. Amber's eyes immediately went to the banners flying at the head of each block. He realised with a start that they were his own men, some two-thirds of his five-hundred-strong division. Above them all fluttered longer banners, the Fanged Skull of Lord Styrax a bloody mark against the dull sky.

That's curious. I wasn't fetched with my troops to stand guard here. Doesn't look like I'll be returning to my usual duties quite yet.

Unlike most legions, the élite Cheme Third had half again as many officers. The first division of the Third was Major Amber's command, and Major

Ferek Darn had been seconded to it after some notable deed; the result was that either could be used for special missions without crippling the command structure.

Looking past the various notables, including Amber's own commander, Colonel Uresh, standing with General Vrill and a group of grey-swathed men he guessed were part of Hain's entertainment, he saw a regiment of the Bloodsworn also assembled, still and silent. The fanatical cavalrymen were an intimidating sight, with their armour painted all in black, except for the Fanged Skull, which was bright, bloody red.

So that's the message to the emissaries then, Amber thought as he led Captain Hain around Gaur to kneel before their lord. *Inspect us as closely as you like. All you'll see is that we're every bit as big and scary as you've heard. Here's another fight we'll win without much effort. Just imagine what we could do if we tried.* Amber had seen enough of the camp to realise Lord Styrax had only part of the Third Army assembled, probably seven legions' worth of men.

As he watched, the men in grey cloaks were brought horses. They all looked short and fat to him, some almost too obese to be anywhere near a battlefield—but they all mounted with ease. General Gaur said something to them, a banner of negotiation was handed to one of them, and they galloped off towards the city.

"Gentlemen," Lord Styrax welcomed the newcomers, his voice deep and rumbling. Amber felt a flush of pride as he and Hain bowed; few career soldiers would ever be addressed in that way, this was an honour to be earned. "Captain Hain, will everything go as planned?"

"Yes, my Lord," Hain replied as they straightened up.

Lord Styrax stood the best part of a foot taller than Amber, and he was far broader, but he carried himself with a smooth grace that few large men could manage. His face was pale in the weak morning light, but it looked untouched by time or cares and was marked only by a single faint scar. Even after years of service, Amber couldn't help feeling awe as he looked upon the massive white-eye.

Again he was reminded of his drill instructor's words on his very first day of training in the army. *"If you remember nothing else of today, remember this: there's always someone better than you. However strong and quick you are, there's always someone better, so being cocky is the fastest way to get dead."*

One young recruit had nervously asked, *"What about Lord Styrax?"* Instead of cuffing the boy, as Amber might have expected, the instructor had nodded. *"Our lord is the exception to every rule; he's the one who stands above us all."*

Amber had never forgotten that moment, and the instructor's words were as true now as they were then.

"Major Amber, good to have you back—even if things didn't quite go as we'd hoped."

Lord Styrax's words jerked Amber back to the present day. "Ah, no, my Lord, not at all as planned, but I learned a lot all the same."

"Excellent. We should always be open to instruction, even old men like me." The white-eye gave Amber a brief smile before turning to the men from Sautin and Mustet. "Emissary Jerrer, High Priest Ayel, don't you agree?"

Kohrad shifted slightly to allow the two men past to converse with his father. Amber scrutinised their faces; Jerrer was obviously still trying to fathom why he'd been brought here to watch a siege, but it was impossible to tell what was going through the mind of the High Priest of Vasle. Amber had heard contradictory rumours about what was happening to the Land's priests, but nothing that made sense to him.

"What is the instruction you offer us today?" snapped High Priest Ayel. He was a tall, proud-looking man, young for his position, not yet withered by years of service. "Cardinal Afasin will not fear this display of strength, such as it is. Your army looks remarkably small for one about to lay siege to a city as rich—and as full of mercenaries—as Tor Salan."

"Hah! A city full of as much cooperation as a bag of cats," snapped Kohrad Styrax as Amber felt his own hand twitch towards his scimitar's hilt. The young white-eye appeared to be back to his normal bristling, belligerent self, a great improvement from the last time Amber had seen him, lying unconscious in Thotel, the Chetse capital . . . where the Menin had been forced to slaughter their own, that dreadful night.

"Well, Scion Styrax," Ayel continued, his eyes wide with anger, "I invite you to march on Mustet if you wish instruction in how to conduct a defence; the Knights of the Temples will be happy to provide you with an edifying lesson."

Amber felt his breath catch. *Gods, this priest is insane. You don't show you're not afraid by riling white-eyes!*

"As the seal on that scroll has been broken, I must assume you have already read my offer," said Lord Styrax without a trace of anger as his son squared up to the mage.

"I have read it, and my—"

"Do not reply yet," Styrax said sharply, cutting the high priest off before he could make too great a mistake.

Flushed with anger as he was, Ayel still hesitated in the face of Lord Styrax's glare. "Do not say something you cannot take back. You will leave today to take the offer to Cardinal Afasin."

Cardinal Afasin? Amber smiled grimly to himself. *Bastard was* General *Afasin last time I heard. Never a good sign when a white-eye gets religion. I doubt Knight-Cardinal Certinse will be much amused either. What does it say about the state of the Knights of the Temples when Afasin prefers to call himself priest rather than soldier?*

"Today?" said Emissary Jerrer. "We've been here a week—why do you release us now?" The Sautin diplomat was a nondescript man: greying, middle-aged, with weak blue eyes. His clothes were functional, not elegant, which meant he was either a lackey and sent as an insult, or he was some sort of spymaster. After a few moments of scrutiny, Amber decided on the latter; he couldn't possibly be as harmless as he looked.

"Why today?" Styrax repeated. "Because today is the day I hang my standard from the Sky Pillars."

"Today?" spat Ayel, stepping in front of his compeer. A growl from General Gaur stopped the high priest moving any closer, but he continued to speak. "You have yet to even besiege the city; it is caution alone that has made the Council of Patriarchs bar their gate!" He jabbed a scarlet-gloved finger in the direction of Tor Salan. "I have seen the Giants' Hands at work; it will take them little time to decimate your army."

Following the direction of Ayel's pointing finger, Amber looked out over the fifteen regular humps, each surrounded by heaps of rubble, that dotted the ground outside Tor Salan. From that distance they looked far from threatening, but if the Menin camp had been much closer, the threat would have been significantly clearer. He pictured Lord Styrax's fortress in the Menin homeland in his mind: even from a distance the Black Gates of Crafanc were a terrifying sight; up close they just got worse.

Lord Styrax raised a hand to stop Ayel. "I must confess I have not seen the Giants' Hands in action, but I have studied accounts carefully. Tor Salan: city of a thousand mages—and some unique defences. It must be quite a sight indeed, those great arms of brass, steel, and stone, surpassing the range and accuracy of any trebuchet—all driven by the magic of Tor Salan's mages."

"And they have more ammunition to hand than they'll need for this small force," Ayel added complacently.

"I would quake with fear," said the massive white-eye solemnly, "but I have a city to conquer. General Gaur, signal the advance."

Amber gave a start as the deep horns were sounded. He had not expected any troops to be put in the firing line. The horns were followed a moment later by the heavy thump of Menin war drums. Two teams of drummers working in unison, shirtless despite the cold weather, were clustered around the eight-foot-high drums carried by massive ox-like beasts from the Waste. He felt a shudder run through his body at the hypnotic rhythm, the insistent background to all his years of fighting.

On his left he saw Captain Hain, grinning even wider than before.

"Put that broken tooth away," Amber advised quietly as the Bloodsworn trotted off at a canter. He was unsurprised to see his own troops held position; even with Major Darn to command them it was unthinkable that he'd be excluded from their ranks in battle.

The two men looked out towards Tor Salan, straining to catch sight of movement there as the Menin cavalry regiments answered the call to advance and started out towards the city. In less than a minute there came from the city an answering call, a reply to their challenge.

"Here comes your instruction," Ayel spat. "Mark it well!"

Amber saw a flicker of irritation cross Styrax's face, a rare thing and enough to warn those who knew the white-eye lord. In the blink of an eye Lord Styrax had taken a long stride back, drawn Kobra, his broadsword, turned with blinding speed, and lunged forward, all in one smooth movement.

Captain Hain was unable to stifle a gasp at his lord's unnatural speed, but no one moved as Lord Styrax stood with his arm fully extended over the high priest's shoulder . . .

Then Ayel reeled away, clutching his head, and a girlish shriek cut the air as he fell to his knees. Amber looked at his lord's sword: there, caught between the hand-length fangs at the sword's point, was the high priest's ear, severed as cleanly as if by a surgeon.

"Kohrad," growled Lord Styrax to his son, "pick him up and explain a few things to him, would you?" A practised flick sent the ear bouncing over the scrappy tufts of grass; what little blood remained on the magical blade was swiftly and greedily absorbed by the metal.

The younger white-eye bounded forwards and grabbed Ayel by the scruff of the neck and hauled him to his feet. He proceeded to slap the man around the face until his cries of pain quietened into sobs. "That you are still alive is a gesture of goodwill towards your lord," Kohrad snarled, his face barely three inches from Ayel's, "but I promise you, if I ever see you again after you've carried our message to Afasin, I'll feed you to the minotaurs.

"Now, stand up and bear witness to what happens here today so that you may report every detail faithfully. Perhaps this will teach you about underestimating the Menin. You think we're savages because we crossed the Waste? You think we're fools, just because we're not natives of these parts?"

Amber caught some garbled words of protest, some begging, it was cut short when Kohrad smashed a mailed fist into the High Priest's gut.

"Heard of Eraliave? The Elven general? No? Some say he was even better than Aryn Bwr, because he survived to old age."

Amber could see the burning intensity in Kohrad's eyes. When Amber had left the Menin Army to travel north last summer, surgeons and mages had been trying to remove the magical armour that had been driving Kohrad insane with bloodlust. Amber had heard the experience had left Kohrad a shadow of his former self, but he saw now a spark still remained.

"In that old age, Eraliave wrote the classic treaties on warfare," Kohrad continued, hauling Ayel forward to a good vantage point. "One of his favourite saying is particularly appropriate for this current situation: 'A good general identifies his enemy's weakest point and attacks it; a genius identifies his enemy's strongest point and destroys it.'"

"The very words Lord Styrax spoke to me," whispered Hain beside Amber, "the day he gave me the assignment."

"The idea was yours?"

Hain gave a small shake of the head. "I wish I could claim it, but he led me to it by his words. Only a fool wouldn't have worked it out."

And so begin the lessons on how to think like more than a soldier, Amber thought wryly. *I remember them well! Sadly, you won't enjoy all of them quite so much.*

Any further conversation was precluded by a new sound coming from the city. There were faint stirrings of movement on each of the hills. This far away it was hard to make out any detail, but because of what he had heard of Tor Salan's defences, Amber had a good idea what was happening.

Curled up on the ground was an enormous hinged arm of steel, stone, and brass, fifty feet long. The "shoulder" of this arm was connected to a rampart of reinforced stonework, from which ran four narrow passages, like gutters. A throne-like seat of stone was set into the front, where the lead mage would sit facing the plain beyond. There were a dozen more mages in each of the channels, all feeding their power into the lead man, who focused it and used it to animate the arm. As blistering trails of magic ran up and down the arm's brass rods, so the gigantic fingers would begin to twitch, then rise and flex as the arm itself rose up into the air. Within moments it would be ready to start grabbing rocks from the piles stacked untidily around the position and lob them with uncanny accuracy into any approaching army. The Giants' hands would quickly decimate the troops; total destruction would not be far behind.

"Look; there's the first, far right," Hain whispered.

Amber saw the jerk of movement as one of the arms lifted into the air. From where they stood it looked like a stalk of corn shooting up in a field. *No*, Amber corrected himself, *nothing so meek; a dog raising its hackles, perhaps, or a porcupine its spines.*

In quick succession the other Hands rose jerkily into position. Amber couldn't begin to estimate the amount of magic required to lift such weights; he guessed every one of the mages would be stretched to their utmost limits.

As the cavalry regiments cantered towards the Giants' Hands in neat formation, the men in grey bearing their banner of negotiation had reached the halfway point. They were riding hard, as if desperate to keep ahead of the soldiers.

Let's hope the dog doesn't get nervous and snap at the first hand it sees, Amber thought.

The enormous weapons twitched as the grey men passed the range markers and continued. Several dipped, moving with remarkable speed and grace to grasp boulders and twist back into a throwing position, knuckles resting on the ground so the mages didn't have to hold the weight indefinitely.

"Come on, you bastards," breathed Hain, craning forward, "wait for your orders before firing, I don't want to have to explain *that* to Lord Styrax."

Despite himself, Amber grinned. Seconds passed and Hain's prayers were answered as the group in grey passed unharmed, no hail of enormous bits of rubble filling the sky.

The Bloodsworn and the cavalrymen were still well short of the thousand-yard marker, and they would stop before they reached it, for they were only a feint. The battle—and the siege—would be won by that handful of men in grey cloaks. Amber found himself holding his breath as the delegation reached a safe point and stopped, supposedly waiting for emissaries from the city to come out and negotiate with them one final time.

But before Tor Salan's mercenary captains could organise an official reception, the men in grey produced horns from under their cloaks and began to sound a crisp series of notes. Amber was too far away to hear the tune clearly, but he didn't need to: he'd heard the same notes as they'd marched on Thotel: Chetse army orders, played on the long horns that curled around a man's body.

The call to arms was played twice in quick succession and in the silence that followed the men threw off their cloaks. For a moment nothing happened, then the horsemen turned and advanced on the nearest Hand. The Land held its breath with Amber, waiting for the tipping point—which came in the form of a sudden flurry of activity around the Giants' Hands as the ranks of infantry defending the mages formed up in protective wedges.

"You have agents in place?" mused Emissary Jerrer, a look of dispassionate curiosity on his face. "But how to deal with so many mages? And what about the defending soldiers? You surely cannot have an army of agents."

"A handful, no more," Lord Styrax replied, never taking his eyes off the city. It was clear that there was fighting going on. In no more than a minute the main gate of Tor Salan was opening and more troops were flooding out.

"I confess you have me perplexed, my Lord," the emissary said. Amber could hear a hint of admiration in Jerrer's voice.

"It's simple, Emissary; the defenders of Tor Salan quite rightly considered their newly recruited Chetse mercenaries to be ideal for the job of defending their most important weapons."

"And they were wrong to do so?"

"Under normal circumstances, no. However, these are not normal circumstances, are they? The advance group I sent were not messengers, Emissary, but the tachrenn of the Ten Thousand, led by General Dev himself."

"The Ten Thousand?" gasped Jerrer, suddenly realising what was going on. "You allowed those Chetse soldiers to travel north to become mercenaries, ensuring enough of the Ten Thousand were among them to carry opinion? And once they see their generals under your banner, they will turn on the remaining troops, their erstwhile comrades, and slaughter the mages? But there are *hundreds* of mages out there! Lord Styrax, surely your losses will be vast?"

"Captain Hain?"

Hain flinched; he hadn't expected to be called upon to explain the plan, but when all faces turned to him he rallied and took up the explanation.

"Lord Styrax suggested to me that such an expenditure of energy as would be required for the Giants' Hands would require many rituals, and a careful bonding of power. Investigations showed that the mages are linked to each other, and thus cannot break those links quickly or easily." He cleared his throat noisily, his discomfort evident.

Amber felt a certain sympathy for the man: he'd been trained to combat; he'd not been taught how to lecture an audience of dignitaries in front of the tribe's heroes. No one was looking at him, so he gave his captain a thumb's-up sign.

Hain nodded very slightly, gave himself a metaphorical shake, and continued, "The magical energy is largely contained within the arm itself. It flows from the linked mages and is stored within the brass rods. With sufficient troops on the field the mages can be neutralised before they have started any significant defence."

"Neutralised." Jerrer looked startled by the word, as though "slaughtered" would have sounded more acceptable.

"This is war," said General Gaur in his deep, growling voice. "Unless the Patriarch of the Mosaic Council is more of a fool than our intelligence suggests, he will surrender the city and it will cost only a few hundred lives."

"But still, Tor Salan is a haven for mages—they are crucial to the city at all levels of society . . ." Jerrer's voice tailed off.

Mages were the backbone of many societies. The rest of the Land would take note of what happened in Tor Salan.

"This will serve as a lesson," Gaur replied. "To oppose Lord Styrax is folly; the extent of damage done to any city-state will be dependent on how long it takes them to accept that."

The beast-man was impassive as always. Amber had shared more than a few skins of wine with the general, but he had never been able to guess Gaur's mood from his demeanour. You could tell when the half-human was thinking, because his jaw worked constantly, pushing his long lower canines through the tangled fur on his cheeks, but beyond that Gaur surpassed even the Dharai, the Menin warrior-monks, for impassiveness.

Looking back down to the action, Amber could see only a blurred mass of movement, presumably the Chetse mercenaries cutting down their former allies. Here and there flashes of light indicated at least a handful of mages had had the time to disengage and fight back, but the magical lights were only sporadic. One by one the Giants' Hands wavered, then crashed to the ground.

The Menin cavalry had split in two, leaving a channel down the centre of the flood plain. So once they'd crippled the city's principal defences, the Chetse would simply march away, with any pursuit held at bay by the Menin cavalry.

"Captain," General Gaur called, "have our lord's horse brought up."

Hain saluted and signalled to someone and in just a few moments horses for the whole group appeared, led by an enormous grey draped in Lord Styrax's colours. The horse was fully nineteen hands, and bore a steel head covering that had long fangs hanging on each side to mimic Styrax's standard.

As they mounted up, Amber took the chance to whisper to Captain

Hain, "Are you now going to tell me how you're sure they'll surrender so quickly?"

All "special duties" carried an obligation of secrecy that transcended rank; Hain had been delighted to be forced to keep the details of his full operation a surprise for his superior. He grinned. "The Patriarch will give the order without consulting the entire council; he'll be with his most important advisors already. Once he sees his six thousand Chetse kneel to Lord Styrax he'll realise he has no choice."

"It will still be no simple task to take the city, even with this shifting of the balance."

"And so we don't want to give him time to think too hard."

"Can we force it?"

"Once we're on the way, the message will be delivered. I hear the Raylin called Aracnan was in Scree, which is why we couldn't find him for this task, but Lord Larim will manage just as well."

"Larim's already in the city?"

"The white-eye in him is looking forward to getting his hands dirty for a change!"

Amber pictured Lord Larim, the young Chosen of Larat, God of Magic, as they followed Lord Styrax out onto the plain. Larat's devotees tended to leave the killing to others; no doubt Larim would consider this mission high entertainment.

"What if the Patriarch doesn't do as he's told?"

Hain shrugged and Amber realised he'd asked a stupid question. "Then Larim will kill him and signal the attack. Wherever Lord Styrax intends to go next—west to Narkang or north to Tirah—we must control both of the great trading city-states and if Tor Salan doesn't surrender we'll inflict such destruction upon it that the Circle City will not contemplate opposing us for even a minute."

"Sautin and Mustet won't cause trouble unless we march to their doorsteps," said Amber, "and that leaves Embere and Raland, both controlled by the Devoted—and both no doubt already preparing for us."

"Exactly, sir," Hain said cheerfully, "so we'll get a fight this year after all!"

And we will build another monument to our lord with their skulls, Amber added privately.

CHAPTER 10

THE SKY WAS SLATE GREY, ANGRY. A broken mountain burned in the distance, wreathed in black coils of smoke. The freezing wind pierced his ragged clothes as he struggled to find purchase in the churned mud underfoot. He staggered on over the ruined ground, exhausted, using his bloodstained sword for balance and fighting for every step, but it made no difference. The mountain came no closer, and the darkness behind advanced relentlessly.

Collapsing to his knees, he gasped for breath and looked around. The landscaped was ruined; there were great furrows carved into the earth, and even the weeds were crushed and dead. Death was all around him, and despite an occasional discarded item—a helm here, a broken scabbard there—he saw no one else, neither alive nor dead. The broken black tooth of the mountain seemed to loom over him, unreal and untouchable.

He dug his fingers into the mud and felt it suck them down. He wrenched his hand from the dead land's grasp and tried to stand, but his legs rebelled as the darkness closed in on him. He tried to scream, but he couldn't voice his terror. He tried to lift his sword with what feeble strength he had left, but to no avail. The darkness bent over him, as insubstantial as smoke, until cold fingers grabbed him by the throat. He fell back and the mud welcomed him, burning as it drew him in, the hand at his throat pushing him inexorably down and down into the cold of the grave.

"Can I guess why you chose this place?"

Isak turned his head to where Mihn was sitting, a motionless figure silhouetted against the light creeping through the warped boards.

"Couldn't it be that I just wanted somewhere out of the way and one stable's as good as another?" Isak gestured around at the hay loft they were sitting in. Oxen shifted in the gloom below. "It's warmer than standing about in an alley, isn't it?"

"Indeed it is, but I suspect this is one stable you've been in before."

Isak shrugged. "Perhaps. Doesn't mean it's significant."

Isak doubted Mihn would be fooled. The taciturn northerner never indulged in idle chatter; he rarely initiated conversations at all, even if several months in Morghien's company had made him a little more open. Morghien had lingered in Tirah for a fortnight before the road called too loudly and he gave in to his itinerant nature. During that time Isak had seen the unspoken bond between them, similar to the one he himself had with Mihn. It was as if Mihn had forgotten what it was to have friends, but was slowly getting used to the notion again.

"I do think it significant, my Lord. You are not much of a romantic, so I doubt nostalgia is why we're here."

"Are you mocking me?"

"No, Isak, I'm concerned. Scree has changed you, in more ways than one. The witch of Llehden agrees with me, and I'm not just talking about the appearance of the Reapers in Irienn Square."

"What are you talking about then?" Isak snapped, barely remembering to keep his voice low.

The wind, a mournful moan overhead that rattled the roof of the stable, had been building throughout the day until now, past midnight, it was whipping at the city. There had been a light flurry of snow earlier that week, and Isak was sure he had felt the cold deepen as those first flakes fell.

"I'm talking about you," Mihn said patiently. "You don't joke as much as you used to. It's almost as if you have forgotten that you once used laughter to draw others to you—"

"I'm Lord of the Farlan," Isak broke in, "I shouldn't need laughter to make them obey me."

"That's not what I mean; you used to do it as naturally as breathing. Being Lord of the Farlan does not mean they will thoughtlessly follow you, only that they will obey your orders."

"Your point?"

"That you appear haunted. I've seen you glance over your shoulder, even when you're eating and your back is to the wall—and you move your chair further back than anyone else's. Yes, I noticed."

Isak looked down at the stable floor below. "What would you have me say?"

"That I am your bondsman and you trust me with your secrets."

"Of course I trust you."

"Then let me help," Mihn said calmly. "I am yours to command, whether I know the purpose behind your order or not."

"And that'll help, will it?" Isak said sourly.

"You're a white-eye, my Lord. Your nature is not to accept things meekly. That you look so unsettled leads me to believe you have not yet found a way to fight it. When you do that you'll find purpose relieves much of your anxiety."

Isak gave a soft, hollow laugh. "You could be right, but I have a few problems I can see no solutions to."

"Name them."

He looked at Mihn, almost expecting the man to be joking, but he was deadly serious.

"Okay, since you ask: first, this religious fervour that's driving everyone to madness, demanding idiocy in the place of policy. Next, since the fall of Scree I have dreamt of nothing but death, and it grows insistent." He scowled and scratched his cheek. "And there are no traces of those of Azaer's disciples who survived Scree, we still have little clue as to what the shadow's motives are, and I'm at a loss where to even begin.

"So do you have solutions for me now?"

"No, my Lord," Mihn replied gravely, "but I have advice, whatever small use it might be. You must always play to your strengths. A blacksmith will lay out those tools he possesses before starting work, and so must you."

"Have all my suzerains stand in a line?" Isak asked, a brief grin lightening his face.

"No, Isak, the tools of the man, not the duke."

"They're few enough," he said grimly, noting Mihn's use of his first name, not something he did often. "I'm a white-eye, means I've as many bad qualities as good."

"You've never hidden from those before," Mihn pointed out. "I've seen the look on your face whenever anyone mentions the battle on the Chir Plains—it's one of determination rather than embarrassment."

Isak raised a hand to stop him as they heard footsteps outside the stable door. There was a rattle as the door was pushed open and a face appeared in the gap. Vesna looked all around the stable before catching sight of Isak in the hay loft.

"Go on, quickly," Isak said to Mihn, pushing himself to his feet.

"Take the religious matter: this is an unsavoury element of society as a whole. Consider your temper, it remains volatile even now; what did you do about it?"

There was a frown on Isak's face as he stood, towering over Mihn, then he said, "I accepted that it was part of me, it was never going to go away so it needed to be shackled." He started carefully down the creaking ladder.

"Exactly; you brought it within and channelled it to a more useful end. It was either that or be eternally at war with yourself."

"You might have a point there." Isak smiled weakly. "And the other problem? My dreams of death? It seems foolish to just accept death—and something that's rather difficult to work around! Aryn Bwr tried it and look what happened to him! I'd prefer to be completely dead than a broken passenger in another's mind, even if I had the skill to achieve that."

Mihn nodded soberly. "Of course, but even there perhaps the principle remains sound? Your life is bound by prophecy and the forces driving that— without those on your heels you might not be so haunted by your own existence. There are tales of men tricking Death himself; might that free you from these burdens?" He gave a sigh and gestured to the stable floor. "On the other hand, you told me yourself that Lord Bahl's dreams were used as a weapon against him; this may be nothing more than a mage's artifice directing you down a certain path.

"However, this discussion must be continued another day, my Lord. The dukes await you."

Three more men had now entered the stable. They looked wary and stood with their hands on their swords. The Duke of Perlir was flanked by burly hurscals dressed in plain brigandines—sworn soldiers knighted for their prowess, Isak guessed, noting a swirling blue tattoo on the neck of one man. The duke could hardly have been more of a contrast to his guards. He was a slim man with a long waxed moustache, and his clothes of red, brown, and gold were fine enough for a formal ball. After a moment scanning the stable he gestured to his guards and the three of them unclipped their scabbards and knelt with sword hilts pointing towards Isak in formal greeting.

"Duke Sempes," Isak said as warmly as he could manage, "thank you for coming. Please, rise." Instead of offering his hands upturned Isak gripped the duke's arm in greeting, receiving a slightly puzzled but appreciative look.

"I thank you, my Lord. The whole of Perlir grieves for the loss of Lord Bahl; he was a greater man than many gave credit for."

"I have considerable shoes to fill, that's for certain," Isak said, but broke off as another trio entered the room, led by a white-eye bigger than General

Lahk and followed by a scowling copper-haired woman. A devotee of the
Lady, Isak realised, as the Duke of Merlat sidled in after her, his eyes darting
around nervously.

Duke Shorin Lokan, was a little older than his counterpart from Perlir,
and very different physically. He was a waddling, rather large, sickly creature,
his thinning hair scraped over his head. Chief Steward Lesarl had already
advised Isak that the duke was by no means a fool, but to Isak the man looked
as intelligent as a toad in a blue coat.

"Duke Lokan, a pleasure," he said, trying not to focus on that image.

The duke managed to get down so he was kneeling, more or less, and
tugged his rapier—plainly just ornamental—vaguely in Isak's direction.

"Every inch a lord," Lokan muttered nervously, tottering backwards as
his bodyguard gave him a hand up. "You have Lord Bahl's bearing, a reassuring sign in one so young."

"I thank you. Now, my lords, there's a back room through here where we
can sit and have a cup of wine together. I realise the surroundings are hardly
fitting to your rank, but the wine's excellent, of that I can assure you."

Without waiting for an answer, he led them past the cow stalls to a
doorway set into the back wall. Light spilled through the cracks from a pair
of large oil lamps just inside. A plain oak table sat in the centre of the room,
four chairs already set around it. Tila waited at one side, holding a tall jug in
her hands.

"You must be Lady Tila then," said Lokan as he followed the Duke of
Perlir inside.

"I am, my Lord," Tila replied with a startled look and a curtsey.

"Thought as much." Lokan huffed heavily and sank down into the chair
Isak had gestured for him to take. "My wife was cursing your name only this
morning."

"Your wife, my Lord? But I believe I have not had the pleasure . . ."

"Curious, isn't it? It's as if you had done something to upset her—but
since you have never met, I cannot see how that can be the case," Lokan said
airily, the hint of a smile on his lips. "Of course, she is younger than I, and
ten years ago was considered quite a catch—one of the most beautiful women
in the entire tribe, don't you know? No doubt it is just that your beauty
rivals her legend, nothing more. After all, it's not as if you have beaten her in
competition for anything, now, is it?"

Tila couldn't help but glance over to the door where Count Vesna was
stationed, now staring determinedly at his feet.

"Oh, well, no, of course not," she said, rallying, and curtseyed again before filling the cup he held out. "I thank you for the compliment, though I doubt I could ever rival your wife's beauty, then or now."

"Four chairs?" said Sempes, taking a seat himself opposite Lokan.

"Someone will be joining us," Isak said. "For the moment, perhaps the three of us could share a few words alone?"

Both men looked suspicious, but they nodded all the same and Tila retreated with the bodyguards. When the door banged shut, Isak sat down himself and looked carefully at the dukes.

"I know only a little of how relations were between you and Lord Bahl," he started, "but now is a time for a fresh start, whatever the problems of the past."

Isak could see the dukes knew full well he was entirely up to speed with their previous relationship with Lord Bahl; Lesarl would never have let such a meeting happen without carefully briefing his lord beforehand. But they understood the implication.

"Over the next few years we are going to find ourselves facing unprecedented—well, let's call them difficulties," Isak continued. "For that, we will need a united nation, and historically that's something the Farlan have always found difficult."

"May we speak frankly, my Lord?" Sempes said suddenly. He was sitting bolt-upright in his seat, making Isak wonder if he was wearing some sort of custom-made armour underneath his fine clothes.

"Of course." Isak ignored the unusual bluntness, taking it as caution rather than hostility.

"You want a show of support, my Lord? I appreciate the courtesy to our positions that you've shown thus far—keeping this meeting deniable if necessary, even asking for our support in the first place. I am well aware that you could force us to publicly support you at your investiture ceremony. However, a white-eye taking great pains to show such consideration? I hope you will forgive an older man's trepidation at this; I find myself wondering what it is you require our support for."

"I will," Isak said gladly. "The situation is simple, but—to speak absolutely plainly—I want you on my side because I believe there'll soon be no space for anyone but my allies." He raised a placating hand. "I don't mean that as a threat, just a statement of fact. I'll be requiring much of you over the coming years and for the Farlan to remain strong we must all accept sacrifices."

"And the support?"

"I intend to issue an edict regarding the vacant duchy, to appoint the next Duke of Lomin, rather than confirming the natural line of succession."

"You intend to deny a successor?" Duke Lokan was hunched forward in his seat, peering intently at Isak, almost as though he could divine the truth by looking hard enough.

"I do. I've brought you here to explain my reasons before publicly asking for your support. If it doesn't come as a surprise at my investiture, your reactions will send a message to the rest. If the dukes are united, every suzerain not already loyal will fall into line."

"A reasonable assessment," Sempes nodded, "but I do not see why there is a need for the denial. I hear there is some argument over succession, but your intervention should not be required once Disten's investigation is complete. Your Chief Steward will surely have told you that relations between us are not friendly; some of our conflicts have been public and because of that I will need a good reason to overlook years of hostility."

Isak nodded, well aware that the disputes between the cities of Tirah, Perlir, and Merlat had seen noble deaths on all sides. "The denial is necessary because I believe you will not find the rightful duke acceptable."

"Oh?"

"Lesarl takes an interest in such things. He alerted me and I asked Lady Tila to investigate; she spotted it immediately. If Tila only requires a single glimpse, there are others who'll not take long to follow suit. I asked her to meet with the son of the old duke's cousin, the man whose family has the best combination of claim and power. His name is Sir Arole Pir, knighted after battle by the previous duke and expected to have a great future ahead of him.

"Tila reported him to be 'a charming and extremely handsome man.'"

"Hah," grunted Lokan, a fat grin spreading across his face, "and my wife will do the same, no doubt! The whole tribe knows what sort of man Lady Tila finds attractive."

Isak grinned. "Exactly. While he might surprise us all and prove a fine duke, I suspect many might find it all a bit too convenient."

"Accidents have happened for less reason than that," Sempes added, "and even with our approval, it wouldn't be accepted by those most likely to already know the truth. The suzerains of Meah have never liked being the lesser cousins to the duke's family, and shared territories always cause a problem."

Perlir nodded in agreement. The Farlan laws on territory were strict: each duke ruled one of the four cities, but had only limited land, so they were always contained within a suzerainty. With the wealth of a city behind him, the duke often owned as much land in the suzerainty as its lord, and the Farlan were not people to share power happily.

"Suzerain Imis would be even less amused by the situation," Isak added. "His border with the Great Forest is longer than any other, so Tirah influences his decisions far more than he'd like anyway. With a puppet wearing the ducal coronet he'd feel gelded."

"Your solution?"

"Major Belir Ankremer, of the Second Lomin Infantry."

"Lomin's bastard?"

Like Major Jachen Ansayl, the commander of Isak's personal guard, who was a bastard of the Sayl suzerainty, Major Ankremer carried the name of the noble line he was fathered by, even though the old duke, as a gesture of loyalty to Bahl, had taken the name of his territory rather than using his own name, Kremer. It was a gesture his legitimate son, Duke Certinse, had carefully stepped away from too, not once but twice, eschewing both the names Lomin and Kremer in favour of his mother's family.

"You want the Farlan to be stronger, and how is that possible with a bastard soldier handed a duchy?" Lokan pointed out. "You yourself do not rely on divine mandate; you hold on to your title because of your gifts, and the Palace Guard. What's to stop Major Ankremer being even more of a puppet than Sir Arole?"

"Because he's one of the finest soldiers left in Lomin. The only command a bastard is going to get is in the infantry, because any scion, marshal, or knight will go for the cavalry, of course, a far more prestigious posting. But as a result, many of the experienced noble-born officers were wiped out last year when Lomin's cavalry was decimated. Militarily speaking, the game has changed over there, and the eastern suzerains at least respect experienced soldiers because they're usually on the front line. Lesarl tells me that Major Ankremer brings us a number of advantages, the first being that he's a fine officer. Every colonel in the region knows he's worth something; the man has no serious enemies in the army, and he does have the legions of the East behind him.

"Secondly, he is Duke Lomin's bastard, not of bastard stock, and the duke was well loved. There is apparently no truth to the rumour that Duke Certinse was not Lomin's son, but even if he is true-blooded, he didn't inherit many of his father's better qualities. Major Ankremer is the image of his father in looks *and* heart, and that buys him political capital, especially when combined with your endorsements. Crucially, he is as strong-willed as his father. Some nobles will flock to him assuming they can manipulate him; Lesarl assures me that will not work."

Isak paused for breath, and to allow the dukes time to comment.

After a few moments of thought, Sempes cleared his throat. "Let us suppose," he said slowly, "that we agree to endorse your choice, my Lord, and act the devoted subjects while you pursue your wars. All of that will cost us, and not just in reputation . . . So what are we offered in return?"

Isak tried not to scowl at the phrase "your wars," as though the two men believed there was nothing more complicated in Isak's mind than a young white-eye's yearning for conquest. "I'm sure you have a few ideas."

"I would first like to hear what new taxes will be imposed," Sempes said sharply, "and what existing agreements your Chief Steward will actually honour."

"There will be no additional taxation, but I will require troops and supplies from both of you. In particular we'll need horses, livestock, and grain, double the amount agreed under the Lower Temple Levy."

"Double?" spluttered Lokan, "my Lord, you have an unusual idea of what 'no additional taxation' means."

"The levy is not taxation; it's part of your responsibility as my subjects," Isak said, "and it is already set out in the agreement that in times of war the levy is doubled. All you are agreeing to is to encompass the spirit rather than the letter of the wording. We might not currently be at war, but we will be by the time summer comes, and we must be prepared."

"If we are discussing preparedness," Lokan replied, having composed himself quickly, "then the state of the navy must also be brought up."

"There will be no more funds made available. I agree the navy is in need of overhaul, and that's something you'll be paying for yourselves. Additional taxation of your subjects is, of course, your concern, but we can't afford to have either of you dealing with insurrection over excessive taxes. I can offer you mages from the College of Magic to help, a dedicated group for each of your cities."

"A few mages will make little difference," Lokan blustered, but Isak knew it was a generous offer. With mage assistance, work could be massively accelerated; the College of Magic was located in Tirah precisely so the Lord of the Farlan could limit their employment in other cities.

The portly Duke of Merlat drained his cup and poured another. "What I really need is the taxes on the Carfin River to be controlled, and sections dug out to allow deeper-hulled vessels to use it."

The Carfin ran from Tirah to Merlat, and was the best way to transport goods from the plains in the north, where the majority of the Farlan's food originated. Since it ran through half a dozen suzerainties, the issue of river taxes was a vastly complicated one.

"You can't have both," Isak pointed out, "but it might be possible for Lesarl to put together a proposal for the suzerains responsible, with a little encouragement from Tirah, of course."

"The herds from Merlat can at least walk," Sempes pointed out. "Remember, the tribe is dependent on my crops too. Raiding from the south is my greatest single problem. Will you give me assistance there?"

"What is it you need?"

"Southmarch."

There was a defiant look in the duke's eyes that set Isak's instincts on edge, and at the back of his mind he felt Aryn Bwr stir. The Last King had been quiet of late, cowed into near silence by the disturbing appearance of the Reapers on Irienn Square. Whatever fears Isak might have about his recurrent dreams of death, Aryn Bwr was even more terrified of the grave. There was no exaggeration when folk said that the darkest pit of Ghenna was reserved for him.

"A fortress?" The name meant nothing to Isak, and he felt a flutter of concern in his stomach. Thus far, Lesarl had prepared him for every step of the conversation, but now he was on his own. The sour look on Lokan's face told Isak that his concern was justified.

"Once a fortress, now little more than a ruin—past the end of the mountain line south of Perlir in a region called Hartoal's Steps."

"Vanach territory," Isak said, seeing in the duke's eyes that he was correct.

The border is a bottleneck between the mountains and the sea, hissed Aryn Bwr in Isak's ear. *A man who wants to defend his lands builds a fortress there; one who builds outside it wants a base for conquest.*

"Only nominally," Sempes said. "The region north of the Turnarn River has only the barest semblance of civilisation these days, hence the frequency of the raids. They're little more than savages, living in squalid chaos."

"Savages with a few decent vineyards, so I hear," Lokan commented.

Sempes turned towards his peer and said scornfully, "They have good ground, but barely a clue what to do with it. They find it easier to raid Farlan lands than to farm their own."

Isak raised a hand before Lokan could open his mouth to retort. He knew the two had disputes of their own. "These are details that can be worked out later," he said firmly. He rose and went to the door, poking his head outside to catch Tila's eye. She was talking softly with the bodyguards, but at Isak's gesture she made her apologies and hurried out.

"You expect us to take it on faith that this will all be resolved?" Sempes said, guessing that Isak was having his choice of duke summoned.

"I do. The only thing that remains is for you both to meet Major Ankremer. You need to be satisfied that he is strong enough to keep hold of the ducal circlet."

"Does he know why he's here?"

Isak shook his head. "No, he believes this is part of Cardinal Disten's investigation, but I'm confident you will both find him satisfactory, then we can tell him the good news."

The Duke of Perlir stood, his cheeks colouring. "The last three negotiations I have had with your Chief Steward ended in chaos. The man is unstable and unreasonable. I have no reason to think this one will turn out any differently, so I fail to see how I can give my approval of this bastard's legal recognition for no tangible reason—quite aside from the fact that this is a dangerous precedent to set. Bastards have never had any legal claims and now you want to hand a duchy to one?"

Isak closed the door and approached the table. There was no conciliation on his face now; he was done with being friendly. "You'll do so because I tell you to. I have instructed Lesarl to ensure a fair resolution is reached, but have no illusions; there will be Farlan deaths this year. My concern is not the delicate balance of relations within the tribe; it's surviving to see the next winter festival. I need your support most especially now that the cults have become militant, but you shouldn't expect me to worry overlong over the consequences of having you both killed."

He pulled the door open again to reveal a heavyset man of some thirty summers wearing the red and black uniform of an officer in the Lomin legions. Isak caught sight of a tangled mess of curly brown hair and a glum expression—before the surprise at seeing an enormous white-eye took over.

"Good evening, Major Belir," Isak said smoothly, guessing the man was like the commander of his own guard; Major Ansayl went by his first name, Jachen. He preferred not to use his surname.

"Ah, my Lord," the major replied in a daze before he dropped to one knee, "good evening."

"Enough of that—come in and have a drink with us."

"Us?" Ankremer repeated in confusion. He took a half step inside and saw the two dukes waiting at the table. He narrowed his eyes to make out the devices on the breast of each. Lokan's Kraken badge was as distinctive as the Perlir Reaper's Scythe. "My Lords," he said, bowing to both. Suddenly he froze, looking from the dukes to Isak and back. "Oh Gods, you're joking."

Isak clapped a hand on the man's shoulder. "'You're joking, my Lord,'" he corrected with a chuckle, "but aside from that, I'm afraid not."

CHAPTER 11

ISAK OPENED THE DOOR AND STOPPED. He could feel the hostility in the air before he had even entered his chambers. "Bickering again?" he asked.

Xeliath and Horman glared at Isak as he entered. They reclined on sofas either side of the fire, covered by thick quilts bearing Isak's emerald dragon crest. Xeliath was familiar with her condition and knew how best to make herself most comfortable, especially now her strength had returned. Horman was still not used to being disabled—his remaining hand, which Isak had broken in the Temple of Death in Scree, had not healed well, and was of less use than Xeliath's.

After a moment of irritation Xeliath's face softened and Isak felt the radiance of her smile wash over him. "How handsome you look," she said in Farlan, and Isak had to fight the urge to blush like a boy. He was impressed at her command of the language already, and it was growing stronger every day.

He had thought to stop in to check on them both before the day's business, the investiture ceremony, began, but maybe that wasn't the only reason he was here. Today the Synod would formally confirm him as Lord of the Farlan, so he was resplendent in white tunic and trousers, detailed with gold and pearls, with the crowned dragon emblazoned on his breast and echoed on his cloak. His hair was trimmed and his cheeks shaved smooth, and Tila had told him he had never looked more respectable. Isak realised it felt nice to have that remarked upon.

Gods, Isak thought wryly, *if I'm not trying to gain my father's approval, I'm trying to show off to women. I'm not even sure which is more foolish of me!*

"Don't look too pleased with yerself," Horman growled, almost as if reading his thoughts. He winced as he shifted position, but Isak was pleased to see he had more colour in his cheeks, even though he was still drawn and much too thin. "This little slut has been saying the same to every man who's been in this week. Girl was practically drooling over your noble count."

Xeliath shot Horman a filthy look, but he only laughed at her.

"Hah, don't like it when you can't bat yer eyes at a man and make him do what you what, do yer? Girl, I've put up with this one's idiocy most o' his life—white-eye charms don't do shit for me."

"Stinking peasant," Xeliath hissed in reply before switching to her own language and unleashing a stream of invective. Isak didn't need a translator to tell him the soldiers of her father's household were responsible for these terms rather than the noble ladies. The tall lacquered shutters rattled under the assault of the gusting wind, reminding Isak of when Xeliath had entered his dreams and the landscape had echoed her mood. He'd been outside earlier and the rain was lashing down with a rare fury.

"And to think Tila said I should split the two of you up," Isak snapped. "You'd both be bored to death if you didn't have each other to bitch about. I've half a mind to manacle the pair of you together."

Horman raised his arm. The ruined stump was still bandaged. "Thanks to you I'd be able to slip 'em easy enough," he grumbled.

"How long must I stay in this room?" Xeliath demanded. Her head was uncovered, which was unusual. Normally she wore a scarf, draped to cover most of her damaged left side. "I can be more use to you than keeping idiots company."

Not even Lesarl had any idea how the volatile cardinals and priests would react when they found out Isak was harbouring a member of an enemy tribe, but neither of them were keen to find out. It was a fair bet that Xeliath wouldn't back down from any form of provocation; she was a white-eye and needed no good reason to start a fight.

"I know you're bored," Isak said in a placatory voice, perching on the end of his father's sofa so he could see them both, "but it shouldn't be too much longer now. I want the investiture ceremony out of the way first—the Synod are troublesome enough at the moment, without knowing about you. Most of the suzerains will leave in a few days, and that'll help ease the pressure too. I don't want you to end up being dragged into the argument for as long as possible."

"Let them complain," Xeliath croaked. "Their dreams will become nightmares."

Isak, hearing the rasp in her voice, poured her a cup of pale tea, which she accepted gratefully. When he turned to offer his father a cup, Horman gave him a furious look and he gave up.

"Give it time," he continued. "By spring everything will have calmed down. Lesarl and I are going to deal with the priests—then you'll have no need to terrorise them."

"A purge?" Horman said sharply. "I brought you up better than to murder priests."

"Why in the name of the Dark Place would you care about that?" Isak growled before silently cursing himself. Horman had aged a decade since Isak had been Chosen. He was a broken man now, his face pinched, his body frail, and when Isak looked at his father he felt an unfamiliar clash of pity and guilt—but even now, all it took was one look from his father, one sniping comment, to provoke him. Horman could stoke Isak's temper as quickly as he always had.

"*Kill them both,*" snarled Aryn Bwr in Isak's mind. "*Cut their throats and let the whining cease; snap her fingers and tear them from the Skull. They are nothing, they are dead weight around our neck.*"

"Our *neck?*" Isak replied angrily in his mind, "*I think you forget yourself. At least they're alive, and even broken, they are greater than you.*" Out loud he was only a little less vehement. "Don't put words in my mouth, Father, you don't know me well enough for that, not anymore."

"You never gave a damn about the cults and that'll never change."

Isak sighed. "Perhaps not, but these days I can't ignore them. The path they're on leads only to civil war, they know as well as I do—and I can allow that to go only so far." He pushed himself upright. "I only came up here to see how you were faring. I see you're as happy as ever, so I'll leave you to your squabbles."

He retreated, feeling the glower of two pairs of eyes on his back, even after he'd shut the door behind him. He kept walking until he'd turned the corner and was out of sight of the guards on the door, then he stopped and pressed his forehead against the cool stone wall for a few moments. He breathed deeply and tried to massage away the headache he could feel.

"This was easier when people were just trying to kill me," he muttered. After a while he reluctantly straightened up and headed for the main stair, where he found Tila and his Chief Steward waiting for him.

"They are well, my Lord?" Tila asked as he reached them. Her face was a careful study of calmness. Lesarl's was quite the opposite: he looked as if he had a thousand thoughts running though his mind.

Isak grunted in response and glanced suspiciously at the door leading to the Great Hall. It was shut, with two of his personal guard stationed on either side, but still he felt a little trepidation. It had taken months of preparation, but now every suzerain in the nation was assembled on the other side of that door, with the exception of the two eldest, who had been unlikely to survive the journey to Tirah; their scions would stand in their place.

Isak's investiture was to be conducted by High Cardinal Echer, and the other three Farlan dukes would lead the people in swearing fealty to their new lord. It had sounded like a good idea at the time, but now Isak wasn't so sure. Would the room be large enough to comfortably contain so many powerful men?

Isak's fears were, of course, Lesarl's delight: the most powerful men of the tribe, all together in the same city. That meant deals, alliances, even friendships. The vast majority of the Farlan's economic wealth was in the hands of the nobility, and most of them would be looking to make the most of this rare gathering. For weeks now men and women from different retinues had been running in all directions, while Lesarl, like a gleeful spider, sat at the centre of this vastly complex web, the recognised master at this clandestine game. He hadn't even bothered to hide from Isak how much he was enjoying all this.

"My Lord?" Tila's voice interrupted his thoughts.

"Both well enough to be bad-tempered," Isak said, "but for the moment that's all I can ask. My father is at last on the road to recovery, but that means he's back to being a bastard. Lesarl, you have somewhere for him once he's well enough to walk? Enjoying the comforts of the palace means acknowledging I'm Lord of the Farlan every day—he can cope with the pain of his injuries, but that's beyond him."

"I have a place in mind, my Lord; one of Suzerain Tebran's stud farms needs an overseer. It'll keep your father out of the way and protected, even if he doesn't want a bodyguard."

"So let's hope he doesn't refuse just because I'm the one to offer it."

"Let me handle that, my Lord," Lesarl said with a grin. "I'm sure I can help him to make the right choice—you have more important concerns to deal with right now."

"Are you prepared for this, Isak?" Tila interrupted, friend now, rather than political advisor. "If you want a few minutes to yourself, the suzerains will wait."

Isak smiled with more confidence than he felt. "I'm ready, better we get it over with. I've been practising the spell to block sound all week, and Lesarl's going to be right beside me, so you don't have to worry."

The ducal throne had been brought from its normal position in the audience chamber and placed in the Great Hall, the only room big enough to accommodate every Farlan suzerain, duke, synod member, and city councillor, as well as the heads of the College of Magic. Without retainers, bodyguards, or advisors, they numbered close to a hundred, with twenty identifiable factions in the mix. There were several that Isak needed to speak to privately, so Dermeness Chirialt, one of the few mages Isak was sure he could trust, had taught him a simple charm to enable that.

"And you are certain that you'll be able to sense Cardinal Certinse's emotions?" Lesarl pressed. The cardinal remained the only member of that immediate family at liberty—he was a powerful man, and there was no direct evidence of treachery—but Isak had devised an alternative to having the man assassinated, albeit one they both found distasteful.

"If I can't, I'll bluff him. People know about the Crystal Skulls and he's not so stupid that he'll disbelieve whatever claims I make."

"And the High Cardinal? That frail old man has put me quite to shame when it comes to terrorising his fellow citizens," Lesarl said cheerfully. "He's targeted Suzerain Saroc particularly, and I have reports of deaths in several other suzerainties as well."

"He'll get a warning with our offer. If the offer isn't good enough for him, then your reports are obviously true and he's lost all sense of reason."

Lesarl's network of informers had been busy, and once he'd put together their information, he had ascertained that every priest driven to sudden extremism and rage came from one of six cults: the six Gods given prominence in Scree, namely, Death, Nartis, Belarannar, Karkarn, Vellern, and Vasle. It was the Gods most hurt by the actions of Azaer's disciples whose backlash of rage echoed out through the Land, infecting those bound to their spirits—the priests, who are tied when ordained—with a similar fury.

Predictably, Lesarl's reaction had been to applaud Azaer's ingenuity, rather than cry horror at what had happened. Whether by accident or design, it had provoked a reaction from the Gods, which in turn would set the common folk against them—and without the worship of the people, the Gods themselves would only grow weaker. "Inspired!" Lesarl had muttered to himself. Isak, hearing him, had grimaced.

"Having Jopel Bern whispering in the High Cardinal's ear isn't helping," Tila interrupted before he could take his Chief Steward to task.

Isak gave a curt nod. Bern, the High Priest of Death, had been as badly affected as the frail old man wearing the High Cardinal's robes. Unfortunately, at least as far as Isak was concerned, the elderly cleric showed few signs of dying, at least by natural means. Echer was clearly burning himself out with magic; he'd most likely be dead in weeks, but Bern was being more careful.

"We might have to put up with him for the time being." Isak took a deep breath and signalled the guards at the end of the corridor. "It's time; I don't want them to wait any longer."

The soldiers pulled open the doors as he reached them. As Isak entered the Great Hall, Lesarl on his heel, he was met by a gust of warm, smoky air and a buzz of voices that lessened as soon as he stepped inside. The palace looked completely different to normal: the walls were now adorned with banners of all colours, the crests of every Farlan suzerain, all dominated by a central flag three times the size of any other—Isak's crowned dragon. It was displayed behind the heavy ducal throne in the middle of the room, facing the enormous fire on the other side.

The throne was an oversized seat carved from a single enormous tree trunk. The dark wood was highly polished, and the sides were thick enough to stop an axe. The raised back was taller than a standing man. Though there were symbols of the Gods and the Farlan set into the throne in silver, gold, and jet, the overriding impression was of strength and size rather than splendour.

Isak took a moment to inspect the crowd as the assembled men turned to face him. In a ripple flowing towards the back of the room, the nobles sank to one knee, their sword hilts raised up in front of their faces. The assorted priests bowed. It was a riot of colour: the Farlan loved ceremony and ritual, and the noblemen of all ages took great pleasure in sporting the very best of their finery on occasions like this. On his left were the assorted clerics of the Farlan, with the Synod placed closest to the vacant ducal throne. Opposite them, the Dukes of Merlat and Perlir took prime position.

Beside the Duke of Perlir there was a conspicuously empty seat, and Isak could see a few people squinting around, almost as if the deceased Duke Certinse was about to make a dramatic entrance. Count Vesna, dressed in full formal regalia, stood beside the throne itself. He had not moved an inch. The silver gorget bearing Isak's crest that Vesna wore over his armour indicated that he was one of Isak's personal guard, ceremonially, at least, and that excused him bowing.

"Duke Tirah," called High Cardinal Echer in a thin, wasted voice. He scuttled over from the centre of the room and bowed a second time. Isak remembered the first time they had met, when he had presented himself humbly before the Synod. Then, Echer had been a feeble old man who had deferred to another cardinal; now, Isak could feel a thread of magic running through the man's body, easing the pains of age and lending a ghastly animation to his lined face. How long he could last like that was anyone's guess, but until Lesarl came up with something to aid nature's course, the frail old man had been transformed into a spitting, remorseless fanatic.

"The leaders of the Farlan greet you and honour you," Echer continued, "Chosen of Nartis, blessed above mortals."

Isak could see a bloody welt on his cheek, contrasting with the rest of his skin, which was so pale it was almost translucent. The toll was already showing and Isak felt a wave of revulsion at the sight. It made him think of necromancy . . . He forced himself to put such thoughts to one side and concentrate on the moment. He gave a shallow bow.

Echer advanced and grabbed the front of Isak's tunic with one skeletal hand. "Do you serve no master but your patron and Death himself?" he asked, his wavering voice at odds with the fierce light burning in his eyes.

"I serve Nartis and Death alone," Isak replied.

As soon as he had spoken, Echer tugged and they both took a step towards the throne. Lesarl had explained the tradition: the new lord was taking his place upon his throne reluctantly, each step reminding him of the heavy responsibilities of office. Isak couldn't imagine Lord Bahl going through this same process—his predecessor had become Lord of the Farlan after killing Lord Atro in a close-fought running battle that had destroyed entire streets in Tirah—and the victorious Bahl had then had to bury the love of his life, the white-eye Ineh. Isak was pretty sure any priest trying to man-handle him, ceremonially or not, would have died in a heartbeat.

Echer's next question brought Isak back to the present. "Do you declare your hatred for all daemons of Ghenna?"

"I do."

Another step. Isak felt the hum of magic through Echer and his finger-tips itched to embrace his own power. In the distant part of his mind where he had banished Aryn Bwr's spirit, he heard the dead Elven king scream and howl for murder to be done.

"Do you swear to lead the warriors of your tribe; to protect your people with strength and blood?"

A shiver ran down his spine as he remembered Bahl's words when he'd given Isak the blue hood of Nartis to wear: *"Your blood, your pain, shed for people and Gods who neither know of it nor care."*

"I do."

"Do you swear to show reverence to all Gods and follow their teachings as an example to your people?"

Make your fucking mind up, renounce or revere? "I do." *I know you'll be reminding me of that before the week is out. I wonder how many ridiculous laws he'll be asking me to enact?*

"Do you swear to show mercy to the faithful?"

"I do." *Except you, you twisted old bastard.*

"Do you swear to punish heretics and enemies of the tribe with the fury of the storm?"

"I do."

That last question took Isak up to the ducal throne. Count Vesna saluted him stiffly and held out a velvet cushion on which sat a circlet of silver and gold.

High Cardinal Echer peered up at Isak for a moment, sly glee on his crumpled face. Isak sat and Echer plucked the circlet from the cushion and held it up for everyone in the room to see.

"Isak Stormcaller," he proclaimed, "Chosen of Nartis, Duke of Tirah: the Synod of the Farlan acknowledges your claim to the title Lord of the Farlan as valid. The line of the Farlan kings has ended and we accept no majesty other than that of the Gods, yet this circlet signifies you are Lord of all Farlan. I call on all Farlan, noble and lowborn, to kneel before you and acknowledge your rule over them."

Even man in the room went on one knee and echoed, "Lord of all Farlan," even Count Vesna—although he kept his eyes raised and his sword hand ready.

A moment later, as arranged, the Dukes of Merlat and Perlir stepped out of the crowd and moved to either side of the High Cardinal. They both bowed, then the Duke of Merlat, as the elder of the two, stepped forward and knelt in front of Isak with the hilt of his sword held towards his lord. Isak touched a finger to the pommel and he withdrew as the Duke of Perlir stepped forward to repeat the formal greeting.

Finally Isak settled back on the throne and looked around the room in what he hoped was a suitably dignified manner before gesturing that everyone should get off their knees. He inclined his head to the dukes and they sat, followed shortly thereafter by the entire room.

"Duke Lokan, Duke Sempes, I thank you for the honour you do me," Isak said smoothly. "I beg a boon from you both."

The unexpected words made the High Cardinal's nose twitch with irritation, but he had enough sense left to know he could not interrupt.

"My Lord," Lokan replied smoothly, "ask it, and if it is in our powers, we shall grant it."

Isak inclined his head again. "My thanks to you both. As you are aware, there is a vacant seat here, for Lomin has no duke and there is argument over who should fill the post. I intend to appoint the son of the last Duke of Lomin as heir, to dispel this confusion. I call upon all those present to witness this— for the good of the tribe I appoint Major Belir Ankremer to the title of duke. My Lords, do you concur?"

"My Lord, I do," Lokan said, the hint of a smile on his face as muted gasps of surprise filled the air.

"My Lord," added Sempes, bowing low, "I also concur." His expression was rather grimmer, but he spoke without hesitation, and that was crucial. Neither man could have refused so public a choice, but every second they had waited would have been noted by the watching crowd.

"I thank you. Lesarl, summon Belir, Duke of Lomin."

All pretence at a respectful silence collapsed as the door opened a second time and in strode the powerfully built new duke, his black curls neatly trimmed and his uniform replaced by a crimson tunic emblazoned with the twin-towered keep of the Lomin family. As the duke approached, his face tight with nerves, Isak could see that while the clasps of his cloak bore the family crest in its entirety, the larger symbol on his chest had only one of those towers remaining, and a partially occluded moon hung above it.

Isak quickly spoke the words of the incantation he'd been practising and let a sliver of magic trickle from his fingers, sensing how the arcane words shaped the energy and gave it a sudden purpose. By the time the new Duke of Lomin had knelt at Isak's feet, the chatter of voices whispering around the room had dulled and whatever snatches of sound that crept through were garbled beyond recognition. He saw the heads of several priests and mages jerk up and stare at him, but he ignored them, even as Lesarl carefully noted who had reacted.

The Duke of Lomin also sensed the change in sounds around him and looked around as he held his hilt towards Isak.

"A spell," Isak explained. "I expect several of your peers to have things to say that'll require privacy."

"So no one else can hear us, my Lord?" he asked.

"They can hear a few garbled sounds, not individual words."

"May I ask a question then?"

Isak smiled. "You want to know why I chose you?"

"I actually wanted to know what would be expected of me, my Lord, having had this honour bestowed." Berlir spoke through pursed lips. He clearly disliked the idea of being anyone's pawn.

"I expect you to perform your duties well. I need a duke in Lomin, not a lapdog." Isak leaned forward and looked Berlir in the eye. "You were chosen because Lesarl told me you're a fine soldier, an intelligent leader, and a strong man. The coming years will be hard and cruel, and I will expect as much from you as I will every other Farlan nobleman—more perhaps, because I have chosen a warrior, something that cannot be said of your fellow dukes, Sempes and Lokan."

"I—" Berlir lowered his eyes. "Forgive me if this is blunt, my Lord, but I find it hard to accept this honour is so lightly given."

Isak grinned. "Good; if you weren't a suspicious bastard you'd be no use. Now rise and take your seat; you should enjoy these few moments of peace, for there is much to do in Lomin. There is one thing to remember, and it is crucial: it is only united that we'll survive what's coming."

The duke stood and took a half step back before a strange look crossed his face. "I don't pretend to understand your decision, but I'm a soldier, and as long as you ask me to serve the tribe, I will obey," he said, and bowed once more.

"I'm glad to hear it," Isak said with a smile. "And now step back; I believe High Cardinal Echer has a few demands."

As soon as the new duke had been greeted by Lokan and Sempes, and all the rituals observed, Chief Steward Lesarl came forward and planted himself on Isak's right, perching on a stool that had been left for that purpose. Isak had no idea who most of the men in the room were, and with Lesarl close enough to supply their names, he was also conveniently close enough to be involved in any discussion that might take place.

The High Cardinal did not forget his place in the proceedings. As the dukes had presented their sword hilts to Isak, to take if he wished, so Echer knelt and offered the oversized ring that showed Nartis's snake coiled around a sceptre. Isak thought the lapis lazuli disc looked curiously similar to Nartis's coin, which had hung from Morghien's augury chain.

I wouldn't put it past Morghien to have stolen the coins for his chain. Isak smiled inwardly, but then it faded as he thought, *How many priests will I have to kill to prevent civil war here? Enough to make my own chain?*

"High Cardinal, I thank you for your respectful greeting," Isak began, "but I hear there are some in your service who shame the Gods they profess to serve."

Echer remained kneeling as he withdrew his hand and looked up at Isak. "There are many of your citizens who shame the Gods. I cannot blame my penitents for their zeal in showing the people the error of their ways."

"Zeal is all well and good, High Cardinal, but when it takes the Palace Guard to prevent fighting on the streets of Tirah, it goes too far. I hear there are many towns where blood *has* been spilled."

"There are sinners everyone," spat Echer, "and their blood is better spilled than left to offend the Gods further."

Isak took a deep breath. There was a fervent light in Echer's eye, one that Isak longed to snuff out. He was well aware he couldn't afford to let the situation continue—it would escalate as long as there were clear lines of conflict. What passed for religious law in the Land was a garbled mix of edicts, history, and myths that required a great deal of interpretation. As yet, the High Cardinal had not put forward any clear agenda, other than the most obvious—the observance of Prayerday, censure of taverns and whorehouses—but Lesarl was convinced there was some sort of plan buried in Echer's sporadic pronouncements.

"The cults have no legal authority," Isak said firmly, "and yet your soldiers have attacked and killed in the name of the Gods. They have made summary judgments, and have carried out the punishment. In Chrien I hear a tavern was set alight and only the arrival of local watchmen stopped the arsonists from preventing anyone leaving."

"Regretful incidents," Echer said, although his face told a different story, "but they demonstrate the will of the people. No longer will they allow the law of the Gods to be broken; no longer do they wish profit to sit at the high altar. I do not condone such acts, but you ignore the will of the people at your peril. This moral decay must be stopped or the Gods themselves will be forced to demonstrate their ire."

"And how is this to be achieved?"

"I have prepared a document for your approval, my Lord." Echer glared up at Isak, as though daring the white-eye lord to deny him anything he asked for. "This document has been circulated to the suzerains attending here today, and copies are to be displayed in every temple in Tirah."

"You walk a dangerous path, High Cardinal," Lesarl said softly. The Chief Steward's face was hard now, coldly focused. "Making demands as you display your military strength could be construed as coming dangerously close to insurrection."

"My penitents are not an army, except in spirit," Echer said with an indulgent smile that sickened Isak. "We are not warriors, just men and women driven to preserve the majesty of the Gods."

Lesarl didn't try to hide the contempt in his voice. "Beating people to death in the street bears no relation to divine majesty. Providing noblemen and magistrates with armed "escorts" to get to the temple on Prayerday, keeping them prisoner for hours while your illegal courts are conducted—"

"Only a heretic would debase our piety by describing it that way," Echer interjected with a snarl.

Isak, judging he had let Lesarl stir the pot long enough, raised a hand to stop the exchange. "I will not have this argument here. Your document will give us much to think about, your Eminence. I understand you have griev-ances, and change will come, but the rule of law is in my name and mine alone. Any priest or cardinal found presiding over any form of court—anyone not a *recognised* magistrate—will be arrested. Do you understand?"

Echer hesitated, visibly thrown by the white-eye's willingness to com-promise. "Of course, my Lord, the rule of law should not be blurred," he said at last. "If there are new laws to guide the people back onto the path of piety, how could I complain who enforces them? As long as you act swiftly. You will permit me to exert authority over the cults of the Farlan, as is my right as leader of the Synod. And I trust you agree that authority extends to all affil-iated organisations?"

"You are talking about the Dark Monks—the Brethren of the Sacred Teachings?"

"Among others. We will not stand for the presence of cabals who pretend to piety yet bow to no authority."

"High Cardinal," Isak said in a level tone, "no such warnings are neces-sary between men of Nartis. Please remember your domain is of the ordained. It is *my* place to shepherd the pious majority, and I shall be vigilant in my duty."

The whole subject revolted Isak, most particularly the smug way power was exerted. He and Lesarl had rehearsed this conversation, and Isak had flown into a rage the first time as his Chief Steward had acted the High Car-dinal's part rather too effectively, twisting compliments to act as insults, describing brutality as "fatherly chastisement."

Now he continued, "In the morning I will make my own worship a public act, to serve as an example for the whole tribe to follow. I would be honoured if you joined me at the Temple of Nartis for the dawn service. I have already issued orders regarding groups like the Brethren of the Sacred Teachings—I will brook no challenge to my authority—just as I will not accept misguided folk pursuing the will of the Gods themselves."

The High Cardinal bowed his head, but not quickly enough to hide the glee spreading across his face. The sight of Isak worshipping at the Temple of Nartis under Echer's sanction would be invaluable to him. Isak just had to hope it would mollify the man long enough for Lesarl's purposes.

"My Lord is wise beyond his years and a devoted servant of his God," he murmured. "I thank Nartis for his wisdom in choosing you as Lord Bahl's successor."

Gods, do you think that's me whipped and cowering? Are you really so insane?

Isak didn't bother answering his own question. The man was utterly deluded. He had instigated many of the violent attacks that had taken place and Lesarl was afraid his madness could spark a civil war. The cults were spending their wealth carelessly to swell the ranks of their penitents and novices.

Cardinal Veck approached after the High Cardinal, but clearly had nothing further to add and he soon gave way to Cardinal Certinse, the last of the sitting cardinals of the Synod. Certinse looked drawn and pale; he had lost weight since Isak had seen him last, and his nervousness was palpable. Bloodshot eyes indicated many sleepless nights—no great surprise seeing his sister had joined his brother and nephew among the recent dead; she'd poisoned herself before summoning the daemon in Irienn Square.

Isak had no problem keeping his face stern as he reminded himself of the cardinal's crimes, at last unearthed. As he reached out to touch the cardinal's gold ring of office, he brushed the man's finger with his own and quested out, sensing what he could. The touch of Nartis was weak, barely more than an echo—and confirmation of what Lesarl had turned up.

"Look up, man! Stand up straight and show some backbone," Isak snapped. "I'm about to save your life here."

The cardinal flinched as though he'd been struck, but he did manage to lift his head and keep his terror-filled eyes raised.

"No one can hear us, but your life depends on your ability to act; understand me?"

"I—Yes, my Lord, I understand." Certinse's eyes betrayed more than a little confusion, but the man was a born politician. His nostrils flared as though finding a scent.

"Good. Now you will have to face me down as we talk; save the finger wagging for later but they must see you arguing, do you understand? Shake your head if you do."

Certinse hardly hesitated at the strange instruction before violently shaking his head. A little colour returned to his cheeks as the condemned man grasped at that glimmer of hope.

"Excellent. I'll make this quick. You're unaffected by the rage of the Gods, and I know why. Don't bother to deny it, just let it stand. I am certain this is because Nartis has been replaced by some daemon ally of Cordein Malich's. I have evidence that you were part of the Malich conspiracy from the start."

Certinse opened his mouth to argue, then thought better of it. He gave Isak a wary look. "What is it you want from me?" he asked in a small voice.

"To look bloody angry would be a start, not scared, you fucking cowardly heretic."

Isak's words had the desired effect as Certinse bristled and his face purpled with anger. "Whatever evidence that deluded maniac Disten gave you, it's false," he growled.

The bluster prompted a wolfish grin on Isak's face. He smothered it quickly. "Sorry, but no—it's real. You didn't leave much of a trail yourself, but your aides weren't so careful, and their appetites needed paying for. They stole from the bodies they were told to bury—and there's more than one alibi that depends on the deceased disappearing at sea with all his belongings."

This struck home like a physical blow. Certinse managed not to sag, but Isak saw the beaten look in his eye. He knew he'd been caught.

"Why am I here then? Why have you not arrested me?"

"Because this evidence means I own you, and much as I hate it, your past crimes mean you could be the solution to the present problem."

"I don't understand," Certinse said, sounding pathetic.

"It's simple," Isak growled, leaning forward in his seat. The sight of his massive frame looming closer sparked fear in Certinse's eyes, but any animation was better than exhausted acceptance to onlookers, Isak thought. "You have worshipped daemons and lived, and that means you are no longer bound to your God. Consequently, you are unaffected by this current rage. As much as it disgusts me, I must work with what I've got. Right now, you are the only cleric within the cults of Death or Nartis I can be certain is rational. So you will suggest you yourself are sent to conduct negotiations with Chief Steward Lesarl over the High Cardinal's new religious laws, and I must accept this insult, or lose face."

"You're just accepting this madness?" Certinse asked, aghast. "Have you read his document?"

"Right now I have no choice but to mollify the cults, or face insurrection at a time I cannot afford it—you'll be easier to mollify than Echer, because the evidence I have means you'll burn if it ever reaches a court."

"You cannot murder the High Cardinal!"

"Who said anything about murder? He's an old man using magic to keep himself strong; I'm confident he won't last long."

"And then?"

"And then your prominence in these negotiations will make you the natural successor to the position of High Cardinal. You will quell any suspicions of foul play, do your piece of screaming and shouting about moral decay, then accept a lessened set of laws—the bare minimum necessary to keep the people from fighting in the streets."

"You're making me High Cardinal," Certinse said in disbelief.

"In return for keeping control of the cults," Lesarl joined in. "You might need to have Jopel Bern forced from office, but I'm sure you could manage such a thing. Keep your house in order and you will have everything you desire: the position you have plotted to take for decades and a long life in which to enjoy it. Now, go back and tell them we quarrelled about Disten's investigation."

Isak sat back and watched the emotions play over Certinse's face. It took just a few seconds for Certinse to realise his position, then he shook his head fiercely and agreed.

Once satisfied his anger had been noted by the room, Certinse returned to report his argument to his fellow cardinals while the rest of the Synod presented themselves. Out of the corner of his eye Isak saw the frantic whispered conversation, but he managed to keep his face blank to greet each of the faces arriving in front of him.

He paid little attention to most, save for the sad-eyed Corlyn, the head of the pastoral branch of the cult who administered the rural shrines and temples. He showed no signs of being affected by his God's rage. The gentle-spirited old man had an expression of awful disappointment on his face; he knew some sort of deal had been brokered by the High Cardinal's manner and was wounded by the ease with which Isak had apparently acceded to Echer's demands.

Of the suzerains, he greeted several as warmly as he could, but his mind was elsewhere. The Corlyn's distress had turned his heart cold and made him immediately regret the deal he would have to swallow. The measures would doubtless be so drastic that even a compromise would be terrible. A voice at the back of his mind told him he'd made a hash of offering his condolences to Suzerain Torl. The ageing warrior had lost both family and hurscals to violent clashes with bands of penitents, all because he had been revealed to be a Dark Monk, one of the deeply religious Brethren of the Sacred Teachings.

Isak's only consolation was that Torl had been too distracted to take offence. He had quickly replaced the colours of his mourning: the hood he had pushed back only when greeting his lord was red, for a death in battle.

Isak's mood was further darkened by the grim news brought by Suzerain Saroc, Torl's friend and fellow member of the Brethren. Saroc was as far from the image of a Dark Monk as could be, clad as he was in silks of white, yellow, and gold, but his round face bore no trace of his customary grin as he knelt in front of Isak.

"My Lord, I hear from Tor Milist that Duke Vrerr has grown pious," he said hurriedly, his voice tight with anger. "Normally I'd applaud such a thing, but the man's a fucking cockroach who'd do anything to save his own skin. From what I hear he's made contact with someone within the cult of Death—and that's the reason they have so many novices and penitents looking like experienced mercenaries. He's terrified you're going to march south and sweep him up as you expand the border to include Helrect and whatever's left of Scree. He knows he can't fight off a full-scale assault on Tor Milist, so his mercenaries are better employed to divide us and create civil war here instead."

"How're things within your border?" Isak asked.

Saroc's scowl deepened. "Difficult. There are too many armed men in the suzerainty for my liking. They're even trying to dictate behaviour in the abbeys and monasteries. They're pressuring those not as rabid as their leaders to at least declare their public support. If it wasn't for the fact that we've standing garrisons in our towns, there'd have been serious bloodshed already."

Isak sat back and sighed. "Whatever we do, it's only a matter of time before that happens."

His Chief Steward looked worried.

Despite the weather, everyone retired outside once the ceremony was concluded. A regiment of servants waited with plentiful jugs of hot spiced wine to ward off the cold. Inside, the tables were being moved back into position and a feast laid out to honour their guests. It wasn't often the vast majority of the tribe's most powerful men were seen together in one room; Lesarl intended to keep them there as long as he could.

As evening fell, Count Vesna stood at the top of the wide stone stairs watching the noblemen and clerics as they cautiously mingled. Their faces were lit by a perimeter of torches driven into the ground. His role as Lord Isak's bodyguard was over now the ritual had been concluded, but he'd decided to forgo the festivities all the same. There were plenty of young men in the crowd below who would doubtless be interested in discussing their wives' *merits* with him—men whose pride mattered more than Vesna's much-trumpeted duelling skills. As it was, none had yet had the opportunity to provoke an argument with him so they could call him out, but in such company it was always a possibility. If that happened, he'd be needing a clear head.

It had appealed to the Chief Steward's sense of humour to use Vesna's charms as a weapon; he had bought the count's personal debts to ensure his loyalty. Vesna shook his head with a rueful smile. *I'd never have thought I'd feel too old for all that now, but it's happened nonetheless.*

Lord Isak was only a few yards from the bottom of the stairs, looking a little bewildered in such company. It was sometimes easy to forget he hadn't been brought up in these circles. He was almost kneeling so he could hear what Suzerain Ranah was saying. Ranah, an octogenarian who sat bolt-upright in his chair, was most likely telling a filthy story, judging by the looks on people's faces.

Gods, and Tila thinks I was bad, Vesna thought suddenly, remembering when he'd stayed for an evening at the suzerain's manor. *That old goat claims all three of his wives died because he wore them out.*

From time to time, Vesna could see Isak look up and direct a plaintive glance in his direction. He didn't move. Lesarl had made it very plain that Vesna was to keep clear unless there was a threat to Isak's person—and that was highly unlikely: Isak had been wound so tightly since the incarnation of the Reapers in Irienn Square that he'd likely cut any threat in slices before Vesna even had his sword draw.

"It reminds me of one of my father's hounds," Vesna said softly to Mihn, who had joined him. He indicated the group of men around Isak.

Mihn blinked, taking in the scene. He was dressed in black, as always: a tunic of tailored cotton that wouldn't catch or snag as he fought—though since returning to the palace, he had done little apart from haunting the cold corridors and ignoring offers from the guardsmen to wrestle.

"The dog had a litter of puppies," Vesna went on, "with one much smaller than the other four. The rest bullied it constantly, but my father never let me separate them: it had to find its own way. They weren't going to kill it, so it had to learn to roughhouse with the rest."

"Well, I am pretty sure Lord Isak could take the one in the chair," Mihn said, nodding towards the group.

Vesna burst out laughing for a moment before disapproving faces hushed him. "Sweet Nartis, I think that's the first time I've heard you make a joke. Morghien must have had more effect on you than I realised!"

Mihn's only reply was a shrug. Vesna looked at him for a moment, before giving up. "Still close-mouthed though, eh?"

They watched Chief Steward Lesarl doing the rounds of the various groups. From time to time he would sidle up to Lord Isak and mutter something, then he would be off again, never staying long with any one person, never allowing any real response from those he'd ambushed.

"Strike and withdraw, strike and withdraw—that is the Farlan way," Mihn said suddenly.

Vesna frowned. "I suppose so; would you have us do any different?"

Mihn shifted his steel-tipped staff from one hand to the other, still watching Isak. "It is a fine tactic, as long as you know where your enemy is. You were outmanoeuvred in Scree, however. The enemy was the one to strike and retreat—or so it appears. The Chief Steward has not had much success in tracking them down."

"So we must learn a new tactic?"

"Perhaps so," Mihn said, "though I am no general, and I do not presume to know more than you on the subject." He paused and Vesna felt a moment of indecision hang in the air. "I . . . Of late I find myself only with questions, never answers."

"What sort of questions?" He didn't need to say he sympathised with the feeling; he knew Mihn had observed it already. Tila had brought the possibility of a new sort of life to the famous rogue: real happiness, instead of fleeting pleasure. He was not far from forty summers now, and the bruises didn't fade as fast these days, but with more than half his life spent on one path, it wasn't easy to contemplate another.

Again, Mihn hesitated. "Chief among them is how I can be of use to my lord. I will not break my vow again. I will not use edged weapons in anger, even if it means my death, but I realise that makes me of less use."

"I think you help him by your presence. It calms him just to have you nearby. You've seen how hard he's finding this all"—Vesna waved at the suzerains, most trying to suck up to the new Lord of the Farlan—"and who could blame him? There's more pressure on that boy than any king could bear."

"I know. I fear it is taking its toll."

"His dreams?"

Mihn nodded again. "He does not confide in me, but I see it in his eyes—" He paused. "It's not the dreams themselves, but the fact that they might come true. He feels the presence of the Reapers in his shadow, the incarnation of violent death, and he dreams of his own death."

"Has he bound them to himself somehow?" Vesna asked, his voice dropping to a whisper. "Isak brought them into life in Scree—a place where the Gods had been driven out . . . Could he have broken their link to Lord Death by doing so?"

"And thus be to blame for intensifying the rage of the Gods?" Mihn finished his question. "I do not know. I don't think he does either, but he fears so, especially after Irienn Square."

"Then what do we do?"

"Do you remember what Morghien did for him the first time we met?"

Vesna cast his mind back to their journey to Narkang and the stranger who'd been waiting for them at the behest of Xeliath. "I remember. The spirits inside Morghien attacked Isak's mind, to prepare him for what Aryn Bwr would do."

"Exactly, Morghien prepared him. When one can see what is coming, there are only two real choices: to try and avoid it, or to accept it and be prepared."

"My vote's for avoiding death; that would be preferable here, don't you think?" Vesna's laugh sounded a little forced.

"Of course. But he has said nothing of the *manner* of his death. All we have is his past certainty that Kastan Styrax would kill him. To avoid death means killing Kastan Styrax first, and from all we've heard, that is not so simple a task."

"'The Gods made their Saviour the greatest of all men,'" Vesna said, recalling what Isak had related of his conversation with Aryn Bwr. "They made him too perfect, too strong and skilled."

"And thus, presumably, a difficult man to kill." Mihn raised his head a little and Vesna followed his gaze to the boundary of torches forced into the hard-packed earth.

"What are you saying?"

"Merely that putting the enemy off balance, doing what they do not or cannot expect, is half of the duel." He was watching a figure flanked by Palace

Guards draw closer. Lesarl stepped into the path to intercept the person—a woman, or maybe a short man, Vesna guessed. The person was wearing a thick winter cloak with the hood pulled up to shadow the face.

"You expect him to embrace his own death?" Vesna asked. "What possible preparation can there be for that? Or do you expect Isak to be able to cheat Death himself?" He sensed rather than saw Mihn tense beside him. For a moment he thought he'd taken offence at Vesna's words—until he saw the diamond-patterned clothes of the new arrival: a Harlequin, no doubt here to entertain the assembled dignitaries.

"I make no such suggestion," Mihn said in a carefully calm voice, "only that such a thing might free him from the tangled web of his destiny. It had been said of Death's throne room that no obligation or contract can follow you through those doors. What if he is tempted by such an offer? What if that is the only way to free him from those bindings?"

"That's not much in the way of freedom, is it? There's no coming back from the grave, so let's push him in the other direction, right?"

Mihn ignored Vesna's attempt to lighten the tone of the conversation. "Will we get the choice? You know as well as I do that he is going to announce a march south so he can create a buffer state to encompass Tor Milist, Helrect, and Scree; there is little else he can do if the alternative is inviting chaos and bloodshed on his own border. The Menin have taken Thotel and conquered the Chetse." He cocked his head towards Vesna as the Harlequin passed Lesarl and started up the staircase. "If you were Lord Styrax and intent on conquest, would you look west to the relatively minor states there, or north to Tor Salan and the Circle City?"

"Gods," breathed Vesna with sudden realisation. He pictured the map of the Land painted on Lesarl's office wall. "They're being drawn together?"

The Harlequin ascended the stair with a light, fluid step that Vesna recognised as very similar to Mihn's. The notion sent a slight childish thrill down his spine. He knew Mihn had been trained as a Harlequin, that greatness had been expected of him, but the air of mystery around those masked performers reached out from his childhood to enthral him once again.

The Harlequin stopped dead when it saw them and stared at Mihn for a few moments. "I will not perform while that pollutes my presence," it said in a neutral tone.

The Harlequins' sex was a closely guarded secret. Vesna recalled a story he'd heard once, of a drunkard who'd been determined to find out if the Harlequin entertaining his lord was female. It was probably nothing more than a tale spread to warn people off, but the story had described the loss of the drunk's head and limbs in what the young Vesna had thought deliciously gory detail.

"I will leave," Mihn replied after a long pause. "I would not shame my lord by driving off the entertainment."

The comment brought a slight intake of breath from behind the Harlequin's mask, but before it could reply Vesna stepped between them.

"Come on then. Both our moods need improving."

Mihn gave him a wary look, his nostrils twitching slightly, and Vesna realised the man was quivering with restrained energy. He didn't want to find out how long either could hold it before they went for their weapons.

"Some friends of mine are spending the evening in a tavern. Come on; let's join them."

Vesna directed Mihn down the other side of the staircase, away from the watching Harlequin, carefully not touching him. He'd seen Mihn fight; his reactions were almost preternaturally swift and destructive.

It was only at the bottom of the stairs that Mihn breathed again. He turned his back on the watching Harlequin. "When you say tavern—?" he began.

Vesna chuckled and dared to clap the man on the shoulder. "Yes, I mean brothel, but they serve damn fine wine, and the other'd probably do you good anyway."

He dragged Mihn towards the barbican and away from the motionless Harlequin.

"Come on, my friend," Vesna continued cheerfully, "one of the girls is rumoured to be as much of an athlete as you; it should be quite a meeting."

CHAPTER 12

MIHN AND COUNT VESNA looked a strange pair as they rode eastwards through the near-deserted streets of Tirah. The temperature had plummeted since nightfall and the cold glitter of starlight illuminated the frost on every stone and roof tile. It didn't take them long to reach Hamble Lanes, where many of Tirah's smaller merchants lived and worked. It was a far cry from the mansions of the truly wealthy, bustling during the day and pleasantly peaceful in the evening, except during the depths of winter, when, like the rest of the city, it took on a ghostly mien. It might have lacked the grandeur of the Old District south of the palace, but the shops and small workshops occupying every yard did good trade, so the buildings were large and the stone gargoyles plentiful.

Through the chimney smoke Vesna could see the coloured lights of the College of Magic shining from its five slender towers—the college eschewed the shutters and heavy curtains most used to keep the cold at bay. The chill night air had driven most people indoors already, and those few still out had hurried on by, not wanting to attract the attention of anyone on horseback.

"Do you mind if I ask you a question? A personal one, I mean?" Vesna's voice sounded unusually loud, but it elicited only a considered nod from Mihn. "I mean this out of curiosity rather than condemnation, but why stick to your vow when you're trying to find a way to serve Isak's needs? You're exceptional with that staff, but it's not the best weapon for your skills. You've served a long penance already, isn't that enough? You shouldn't suffer for the rest of your life."

"I feel it is the right thing to do."

"You say you failed your people," Vesna persisted, "and I won't presume to argue the point because I don't know your customs, but I would say the punishment is done." He reached for his tobacco pouch and began to stuff the bowl of his pipe. "I'm right in thinking you'd be able to take me if you had a sword?"

Mihn pushed back the hood of his cloak and turned to face his companion.

His face looked otherworldly in the pale moonlight, his dark eyes unreadable. "It would be closer than you think; you underestimate your own skills."

"But you'd expect to win, if we fought?"

"Barring luck, yes. You are a soldier first and foremost, while I trained as a classical duellist. If it were a formal duel my chances would be better."

"And with Eolis?"

Mihn turned back and looked down the empty street ahead of them. "Are you asking if I could kill Lord Styrax and deny Isak's dreams that way?"

"Could you?"

"Could anyone?" Mihn countered. "There is no way of knowing that until it's too late. In a duel I suspect he is unbeatable, for that is how the Gods intended him to be. I would have a better chance using an assassin's weapon, and even then, would I ever get close enough?"

"I suppose not." Vesna could hear the disappointment in his own voice and realised he had been hoping that Mihn's prodigious skills would provide the answer.

"Whatever the chances," Mihn said in a firm voice, "I will not use an edged weapon again. The more I think on it, the more I believe my duty lies with Isak himself. My failure was one of the mind or soul, not the body, and it is not my body that shall secure my atonement."

Vesna struck a sulphurous alchemist's match and put it to the filled bowl of his pipe. The shadows seemed to deepen around them in the sputtering light. They continued in silence for a while. The houses of Hamble Lanes slowly thinned as they neared the city wall.

"Did I ever tell you how my father died?" Vesna said suddenly.

"You did not."

The count drew on his pipe and exhaled. A small cloud of smoke obscured his face for a moment. "He died in a duel when I was a young man, fighting a knight twenty years younger than he over the honour of a cousin."

"That sounds a waste of life to me."

"Honour's a funny thing. Sometimes it makes demands you'd prefer it didn't."

"How sorely was the cousin's honour offended?"

"Oh, not badly, but nonetheless my father felt the boy didn't deserve a kicking for so trifling a reason." He grimaced. "A telling-off would have sufficed, so I was told."

"There was no magistrate to intervene? I was led to believe this civilised nation of yours has a tradition of law."

Vesna turned to look at Mihn. In the near darkness he couldn't tell if Mihn's words had been gentle mocking rather than condemnation.

"Unfortunately," he continued at last, "magistrates have sons too, sons they are loyal to, whatever the faults. Less a flaw of civilisation I think, than one of humanity."

"So it was an excess of pride all round that led to your father's death," Mihn said solemnly. "A great shame."

"The odd thing is that my father knew the likely outcome of a duel; he was past fifty, and he'd never been anything more than a decent swordsman."

"Yet he offered battle all the same? Because of honour."

"The boy was family; that was all that mattered to him. He used to say 'there are those you are related to who'll never be your family, and those of a different tribe you'll gladly call "brother." Never stand aside when those you consider family are assailed.'"

"So the insult could not be ignored? Bruises heal in a few weeks, death rarely so."

"Someone had to stand up for those who could not, that was how my father saw it," Vesna said sadly.

"I think I can guess the rest of the story," Mihn said, still looking straight ahead.

"Who says there's more to tell?"

"There's more."

"How do you know?" Vesna heard the wariness in his own voice. Mihn had a way of encouraging those with guilty thoughts to hear an unspoken reproach when he spoke.

"I know because I know you, and I know stories. Tales are not told without a reason. But first, I have the conclusion of the tale. Your father died, and you discovered this when you returned home from whatever trip you had been on. Had the old man waited, he would have been alive perhaps today even. A bully does not kill the father of one destined to be a hero without finding himself taken to account, and you are here to tell me the story."

Vesna found himself nodding at Mihn's words. "He was the first man I killed."

"You were away being schooled in arms? He probably only saw the child you'd once been. How many strokes did it take?"

"Three."

Mihn was silent for a while. Eventually he spoke again. "And your reason for telling me?"

Vesna sighed. "Honour can get you killed. It will if you seek to protect it often enough."

"Yet sometimes there is more to life than that—sometimes a stand must be taken in full acknowledgement of the price. Your father realised that. He wanted those he considered family to realise he valued them above his own life."

"In defence of those you consider family," Vesna continued, eyes fixed in the distance.

"I hear a question hanging in the air."

"Yes. Who do you consider family?"

In a voice so quiet that Vesna wasn't sure he heard it exactly, Mihn said, "Those I would make sacrifices for—those I would follow into the Dark Place, if need be."

The two men fell silent. Only the clatter of hooves on the cobbled street and Vesna's long puffs disturbed the quiet. Minutes passed and Vesna's thoughts had not left the conversation, but all of a sudden he heard a noise, somewhere off to the right—the scrape of a roof tile, perhaps. Both men turned immediately. Vesna slid a hand behind him to grip the crossbow hanging from his saddle.

He'd wound and cocked the weapon before leaving; night had few witnesses and some of the things lurking in the streets wouldn't be looking merely to rob him. There were gargoyles and colprys both willing to attack a human, though such attacks were rare, and bands of enraged penitents roaming the streets.

"Can you see anything?" Vesna said softly, loading a quarrel into the bow.

"No, but I doubt it'll be anything that requires that," Mihn said, cocking his head, trying to hear better. "No man would be up on the roofs tonight, not in this cold, and I can't believe any creature would attack two men on horses."

Vesna continued to stare at the silent houses, but there was no sound beyond the sound of hooves. "If you say so." He turned back to check their route, but kept the bow in his lap all the same.

The brothel they were heading for was a large fortified building set against the wall itself. It had been secured on a peacetime lease from the City Council and most likely was unaffected by the recent unrest. It was easily defended, and it catered to noble tastes, so there was money to spend on guards, quite aside from the fact that most of the patrons would have come armed.

"Are we close to Death's Gardens?" Mihn asked suddenly, pointing off to their right.

"Yes, I think so." Vesna frowned for a moment and turned in his saddle to inspect the streets running south. "Yes, they're that way, past the Poacher's Moon shrine." He pointed down one street.

Death's Gardens was the name given to a small public park owned by the cult of Death. It was less than two hundred yards long on any of its three sides. Much of it was given over to ancient cultivated yews, and in the centre was a miniature lake which, for no good reason Vesna had ever been able to fathom, contained a pair of pike that the priests of Death fed. Ehla, the witch of Llehden, and the Demi-God Fernal had scandalised the people of the city by building themselves a camp in the gardens, having both found themselves uncomfortable in the bustling confines of Tirah Palace, but the clerics of the city had thus made only a token protest at their presence. Witchcraft was no more frowned upon than magery, and the priests were more concerned about the mages, being traditional competitors, richer and not accompanied by a terrifying Demi-God.

"You want to visit the witch at this hour?"

"I am plagued by questions and I believe she understands the nature of the Land better than any other I trust with my thoughts."

"It's a bit late for social calls, isn't it?" Vesna pulled his fox-lined cape tighter about his body and suppressed a shiver. The cold prickled sharp on his face and rubbing his cheeks with the palms of his gloves only increased his discomfort.

Mihn shrugged. "She will not complain; it is her purpose in life to be there when others need her help." He nudged his horse in the right direction.

As he passed Vesna, the count saw rare uncertainty on Mihn's face and reminded himself that the failed Harlequin had been alone since being cast out of his tribe. It must be hard for him to take any sort of advice from others.

"Thank you, for bringing me out this way. I—I've not really left the Palace since returning. I think—It appears I fell out of the habit of enjoying myself quite a while ago." A flicker of embarrassment showed in Mihn's eyes.

Vesna smiled. "It's considered something of a speciality of mine, so there'll be other opportunities. Go on—but be quick; it might be her lot in life to help those who need it, but Ehla still strikes me as a bad woman to annoy and it's late enough already."

Mihn gave him a weak grin and trotted away, leaving the count sitting alone in the middle of the street.

"Here's a sorry state of affairs," Vesna muttered. "A man with my reputation, out in the cold and off to a brothel by myself. I'll probably find the rest of them stopped off somewhere else and my best chance of company tonight will be in Death's Gardens!"

Reaching the end of the road he took the right hand of a fork and, out of habit, looked all around to check for threats. Aside from the lights of the College of Magic, there were scant traces of life from the city, which was already barricaded against the pitiless winter to come. Within the walls, family life would continue as normal, he knew, but as he caught sight of one of the towers on the city wall, Vesna felt particularly aware of Mihn's absence.

So, it's not just Lord Isak who finds the man a comfort to have around, Vensa joked to himself, forcing a grin onto his face.

He left Hamble Lanes behind. In this poorer district the buildings were, perversely, larger, housing many families rather than one. The grim stone blocks were built around a courtyard, which provided winter homes for all sorts of travellers, including the wagon train Isak had once belonged to. The young white-eye wouldn't have merited a space inside during the winter; most likely he'd been sent to the stables, where he'd have to rely on livestock to provide warmth rather than a communal fire.

The clink of metal on stone woke him from his thoughts. His head snapped around and he began to scan the shadows for movement.

Damn, this is as good a place as any for an ambush. He still couldn't see anyone else abroad, but he tightened his grip on the crossbow and urged his horse into a brisk trot.

Am I imagining things? I'm sure we weren't followed from the palace. He was just about to give up and laugh at himself when a sudden scuffle of feet came from the same direction as the earlier sound. Vesna didn't wait to hear any more but slammed his spurs into the hunter's flanks and leaned low over its neck as the horse jerked forward into a gallop.

The road here was just packed dirt, but the sound of racing hooves was enough to shatter the silence. In response Vesna heard a shout from behind him. He'd been right. He urged the horse to go as faster, while trying to spot anyone ahead of him—if this was an ambush, he might not be out of the trap yet, and while he was not much of a shot from horseback, it might prove a deterrent for anyone—

He never got the chance. A blur flashed in from his left and slammed into in his horse's neck. Vesna barely had time to register it was an arrow as the horse screamed and staggered a few steps before crashing to the ground. Vesna jumped from the saddle, throwing himself clear of the falling beast. His left shoulder smashed into the ground and he sprawled heavily on his back, lights bursting in his head as it slammed backwards.

Blinking, Vesna stared up at the night sky for some few seconds, too stunned to move. From there he could see a great swathe of stars and the greater moon, Alterr, with a strip of cloud across her. As his senses returned he heard running feet and shouting: three figures closing on him fast, a large man in the centre carrying a bow.

Piss and daemons, Vesna thought, flapping at his chest for a moment before finding his sword. *Now, where's the bow?*

He looked left and right, gasping as he realised he'd cut the back of his head. The crossbow lay only a yard away, still cocked. The quarrel had fallen out of the groove, but it was beside the bow and would take only a moment to replace.

The man in the centre realised what he was doing and slowed, reaching for another arrow, but by then the three were barely twenty yards away. Vesna, dazed as he was, managed to get to one knee and level the crossbow. He pulled the trigger and saw the big man fall with a cry, then threw the now-useless weapon at the other two, who'd faltered as their comrade went down. One looked back down the road; the other hopped out of the way as the crossbow clattered over the ground towards him, his eyes widening as he looked up to see Vesna charging towards them, pulling his sword from its scabbard as he ran.

He closed the ground so quickly he'd barely freed the blade by the time he reached them. Both men carried six-foot spears, but neither looked ready to use them. Vesna smashed one man's spear aside, moving inside its reach to cut down through the man's arm, then he swung back with the pommel and smashed it across the man's face. He fell sprawling into his comrade, buying Vesna enough time to lunge like a fencer, plunging his sword into the second's heart, then withdrawing and stabbing down into the first before the second had even fallen.

He looked over at the big man. The quarrel had taken him just above the hip; he was writhing in agony and screaming rather than retrieving his weapon. Satisfied he was in no danger from that quarter, Vesna looked for the rest of the gang—

There they were, a second, significantly larger, group of men.

"Piss and daemons, I'm dead," Vesna growled.

He raised his left arm gingerly and worked his shoulder around a little. It was sore, but nothing worse.

"Weapons," he ordered himself, letting the professional soldier take over his thoughts. Five yards away was the archer, with his bow right beside him, so he grabbed a spear and went to fetch that. To give the big man something to think about Vesna kicked his hip before retrieving the bow. He realised he only had time for one shot and rushed it, the arrow skewing high of its target and barely stalling them as they ducked.

Vesna hefted his plundered spear. The men on the floor were dressed as penitents, he now saw; most likely mercenaries. *Better than zealots*, he thought as he raised the spear, *but not much.*

He waited until they were no more than a dozen paces away before hurling the spear. The lead man had been expecting it and dodged, but the man behind him was caught in the thigh and went down yelling. Without any more time Vesna transferred his broadsword to his right hand and drew his duelling dagger, moving clear of the bodies on the ground. The weapon afforded him little in terms of range but the steel guard extended down over his fist and could be used to deflect a blade.

Time to play the only card I've got left. "Do you know who I am?" he yelled at the top of his voice.

The group slowed to a trot with the lead man indicating for them to fan out around. This close he could see they wore the grey robes of the cult of Death rather than the black of penitents of Nartis.

Shit, both cults are involved, and these ones will be tougher.

They carried an assortment of swords and axes and looked like they knew how to use them. It was a strange thing to be cheered by, but warfare wasn't as sophisticated as duelling. Spearmen would have simply closed in and spitted him like a boar; these mercenaries would swing their weapons in ways he could predict and he was sure none had his skill.

"Aye, we know you, and we're goin' to kill you." It was a Farlan accent, from the north, which made it less likely they were simple mercenaries out for the highest price.

Vesna turned in a slow circle, not bothering to keep his eyes on the leader. There were twelve in total, more odds than he'd ever faced before.

One at a time, said the memory of a past weapons teacher, a man who'd taught him the value of a kick to the crotch on the first day. *Move when they don't expect, kill one and move.*

"Then you know my lord," he said, edging closer to one man in the ring. "Whatever you're being paid, we will double, treble even."

The man gave a heartless laugh. "And get me a knighthood too, I'm sure."

"It can be arranged. You'll have information we need."

"Sorry, friend, it don't work like that."

Vesna kept turning, sword extended, while the others watched him. He was moving in short sharp bursts, not fast enough to get dizzy, but at random, so his back wasn't turned to anyone for long.

"How does it work, then? You don't sound like a fanatic."

"Enough of the pleading, I'd hoped for better from—"

Vesna didn't wait for him to finish but lunged forward at the youngest of the group, the one whose eyes had been darting between the speakers. The boy yelped in surprise as Vesna dodged his axe and rammed his dagger into the boy's guts. He felt the youth's breath on his cheek as he held him in place, his eyes on the next man in the circle. He deflected a sword lunge and spun his own up and around, faster than his opponent could, his enchanted blade lighter through the air, and biting deep into the man's arm.

The man howled and dropped his sword as Vesna dragged the spitted youth in an arc to block the rest, kicking the wounded man to drive him back into a comrade.

Kill and move, yelled the voice in his head, and Vesna obeyed.

Pushing off one foot he darted out of the way of two blows, then ran forward into two hasty cuts which he caught on dagger and sword. Swerving left he stepped around one and slashed down the man's ribs. He ignored the man's screams and continued moving, *kill and move*, barely getting his sword up in time to deflect a falling axe before taking the opportunity to hammer his pommel into the next man's face.

Blood squirted down his cheek but Vesna ignored it as he kept up the momentum and pushed past the broken-nosed novice to slash at the next man's legs. The man hopped back and collided with another mercenary as Vesna rashly followed it up. A sword tip scraped over his cuirass as the man rode the impact and lunged forward himself.

Vesna felt the sword nick his arm but his training saved him as he pulled his dagger back to his chest and twisted left to pin the sword. Pushing off his left foot he cut up into the man's armpit and tore his chest open. *Kill and move.*

The pinned sword was released as the novice fell so Vesna used the guard of his dagger to flick it at the nearest novice. As that one batted the flying weapon into the ground Vesna turned, aware there were men behind. His fencer's instincts saved him again as a sword flashed forward and a line of fire cut through his ear and scraped his skull; he stepped forward past his enemy's hilt and drove his dagger into the man's side.

Moving like a dancer now, Vesna swung his sword underneath his extended left arm, and pivoted and slashed up at the next novice to reach him. Steel rang on steel as the man parried, but Vesna didn't wait to trade blows, instead using his impaled enemy as a shield. In his haste to wound the hero, the mercenary followed and was caught by a comrade's mace. As he cried out, the comrade hesitated. Vesna didn't. *Kill and move.*

The novice fell in a heap with the injured man as a roar came from somewhere behind Vesna and he turned, caught a sword stroke on his cuirass, and again stepped closer to slash at the man's hand with his dagger. Instead, he caught the sword blade, but he smashed down onto it with the dagger's guard and knocked it from his attacker's grip, then stabbed the unarmed man in the belly.

Now, as men closed in on both sides, he retreated a couple of steps to some clear ground behind where he could see all of his attackers. One man he'd driven back tried to catch him off guard, delivering a high cut as he attempted to kick Vesna off balance. Rotating sideways, Vesna caught the cut and stabbed his dagger into the man's knee in a single movement. A quick twist freed the narrow blade and he took another pace back, drawing in an enormous gasp of air as he at last remembered to breathe. The crippled man toppled over, howling in pain.

Two more advanced towards him: the leader of the group and a tall man brandishing an axe. Behind them, the man with the broken nose was shaking blood from his face, but he still carried his sword. One more was struggling up from underneath the corpse of his comrade.

Time to show off, Vesna thought, sucking in as much air as he could manage. He tossed his dagger up in the air, transferring his broadsword from right hand to left while the dagger spun through the night. Instinctively the men watched it looping lazily up. This was a duellist's trick, one that relied on sleight of hand as much as skill to succeed. Vesna swept a low cut through the air between them and the pair instinctively hesitated and lowered their weapons to follow.

Vesna grinned as he felt the dagger slap down into his right palm and he hurled it at the taller man's unguarded chest. Without arms or axe to avoid, it was an easy throw; it caught him straight in the heart. To his credit the leader didn't turn as his man gasped and staggered, but it made little difference now that he was alone. Bringing his hands together, Vesna traded two blows before nicking the man's forearm. The injury only put the leader off balance, but the next cut neatly opened his throat.

Vesna dislodged his sword with a grunt of effort and assessed the remaining enemies. *Kill and move.* The choice was easy as the man whose nose he'd broken ran forward, yelling his fury. Vesna turned the blade aside and checked him with his shoulder, almost knocking the man off his feet. The novice staggered back a step, his eyes widening with horror as Vesna's sword ripped across his gut then hacked into his neck.

Five men left, all injured. The one he'd speared first lay where he'd fallen, unmoving, so Vesna discounted him. Another had fallen to his knees, hands over his belly, and was making some sort of a mewling sound. Vesna dismissed him too; no one carried on after a sword to the gut. Of the last three, one had a ruined knee and two were standing, weapons ready, but both favouring one arm. The younger looked far from confident about using his left hand so Vesna made it easy for him. He ran forward and cut down the other two with ease before stepping clear once more.

"You," he roared, pointing at the last novice left standing, "drop that now and you'll live."

The man looked at his kneeling comrade and saw he was effectively alone. He let the weapon fall to the floor and raised his hands in surrender. In the blink of an eye the shadows behind the man boiled with activity and a figure stepped forward from the darkness. A weapon flashed, once, twice, and the two remaining novices fell, headless.

Vesna gave a cry of surprise and stumbled backwards, his sword already raised, but the newcomer only laughed, while his black robes whipped all around him like living shadows.

"Apologies, but there could be no witnesses."

"What is going on?" the count demanded. "Who are you?"

The figure stopped and sheathed his black-bladed sword with a flourish. Vesna focused, and found himself face to face with a hairless young man a little taller than he was. He had a tattoo of bloody teardrops falling from his right eye.

Oh Gods, that's no tattoo . . .

Vesna dropped to one knee, his limbs shaking from the exertion of the fight, but still obeying him. "Lord Karkarn."

The God of War surveyed the slaughter surrounding Vesna with an expression of professional satisfaction. "You fought well. I am impressed."

"Thank you, my Lord." Vesna coughed, watching the blood tears fall in horrified fascination. He knew there would be fifteen, one for each of the slain. *Piss and daemons, please let there be only fifteen.*

"Ah, how did you know, my Lord, that they were going to ambush me here?"

"I arranged it, of course," Karkarn snapped, his face shimmering in a brief moment of anger, almost as though underneath this face was another that had briefly asserted itself, the Berserker Aspect of the War God. Vesna remembered the six temples in the heart of Scree whose Gods had been worst affected by the chaos there. Karkarn was one of them.

Merciful Gods, don't let the Berserker out, he prayed silently. *I won't survive that.*

"Have I offended you, my Lord?" Vesna bowed his head as he spoke, not daring to see the reaction to his words.

"Not at all—you've pleased me. But I had to test your abilities. I was right to think that one group wouldn't be enough, too," Karkarn said dispassionately. "A good thing I brought those two together, I think."

"Ah, my Lord, you're testing me?"

"Stand up, Count Vesna," Karkarn commanded, his voice suddenly booming, resonating with the weight of centuries.

Shakily, the count did as he was ordered.

"The heresy of Scree has nicked me—no great a wound, but one I cannot ignore, and one that festers in the blood of my priests. It fell to me to defend the Gods at the Last Battle, to lead the charge that broke the enemy, and that cost me dearly. I do not intend to allow such a thing to happen ever again." There was a growl of barely restrained fury as he spoke.

Vesna nodded hurriedly to show he understood.

"Good. It is clear there are forces at work that go unnoticed by divine eyes. I need a mortal agent to protect the interests of the Gods."

Karkarn stepped forward and looked hard into Vesna's eyes. The God had iris-less eyes the colour of steel. As he breathed, Vesna recognised the fetid stench of the battlefield.

"I—I don't understand what you are asking of me. I'm no Chosen, Lord, I'm no white-eye."

"My faith in the Chosen has paled," Karkarn said, his lip curling with anger. "I intend for my agent to be more than just a warrior, I need a leader of men—a general to take the fight to our enemy."

"You want me?" Vesna asked, too dazed to think straight.

Karkarn nodded. "I want you to be my Mortal-Aspect. You will be the general and hero that all warriors need."

"Mortal-Aspect? To become part of you?" Vesna's mind was a blank as he stared at the blood-streaked face of a God he'd only ever prayed to in desperation. "But mortal?"

"To share in my power, but to remain living the life you are." From somewhere under his robe the God produced a glittering gemstone that he held up to the weak moonlight. It looked like a ruby, a tear-drop faceted shape half the length of his thumb.

"The tear of a God. Take this and keep it with you. When you accept my offer, cut your cheek with its tip."

"And then?"

Karkarn gave him a cold and terrible smile. "And then you will become part of me, both God and mortal. Do not think there will be no price for my gifts—but the rewards will be eternal."

Without waiting for a reply, Karkarn stepped backwards and was swallowed by the boiling shadows once more. Vesna blinked and stared straight ahead. The street was empty, shrouded in grim silence.

"The tear of a God?" he wondered aloud, bending to wipe his sword on the nearest corpse. He hissed with pain as he pulled the cut on the side of his head. He wiped the sword clean and sheathed it before retrieving his nicked dagger. The actions were mechanical, ingrained by so many years of habit. Once the dagger was clean Vesna gave the battered weapon an affectionate pat before stowing it away in his belt.

"The tear of a God," he repeated, wincing again. He looked at the carnage all around him. "Right now, I'd prefer a horse."

Mihn tied his horse to the wrought-iron archway that served as the entrance to the small park and walked inside. Death's Gardens backed onto an ancient shrine to Death that predated the city's principal temple. It was surrounded by a waist-high stone wall and a tall bank of laurel hedges. Once inside it was easy to feel as though one had left the city completely. In the darkness not even the city's towers were visible. Mihn struggled to make out the gravel path now the yellow light of Alterr had been covered by cloud.

The quiet crackle of a fire cut through the night and he let his ears guide him in the right direction. The witch had pitched a double-layered tent towards the far end, strung underneath three yews that had grown together to create three-quarters of an uneven dome. He set off down the path, but had gone barely a dozen paces before a deep voice spoke out from the shadows.

"It is late for callers."

Mihn recognised Fernal's growling voice. "Would I be intruding?"

"No, she will see you." Fernal stepped out from under the yew's branches and joined Mihn on the path. The massive Demi-God sniffed the air as though checking for other visitors. "She is used to being awakened." He beckoned with one hooked talon and Mihn followed without further comment. Fernal, bastard son of the God Nartis, had an air of implacability about him, one that Mihn could only aspire to. With his savage lupine face and monstrous size, he looked out of place in a city of humans, but however keen he might have been to return to his wilder home in Llehden, he appeared unperturbed by it all.

The witch was standing beside the fire when they reached her small camp. "Am I needed at the palace?" she asked as Mihn came close enough to be identifiable.

"No, I'm not here on anyone else's behalf."

She cocked her head to one side. Though visible, her face was as unreadable as Fernal's. "Then what can I do to help you, Mihn ab Netren ab Felith?"

"I came to ask what you knew about death."

"Our God, or his deeds?"

"The process as much as anything else."

She scrutinised him for a few moments before gesturing to the fireside. "Please, join me. Even under that fleece you must be cold."

Mihn did so gratefully, squatting down to warm his hands in front of the flames. Fernal picked up a small bowl and gestured at the pot hanging over the fire. "Something warm?"

"What is it?" Mihn asked as he took the bowl gratefully.

"Nettle tea," the witch of Llehden answered as she sat on a log next to Mihn. She straightened her dress so it covered her ankles properly. He knew they were of a similar age, but Mihn felt like a child in her company, the memory of their first meeting surrounded by the gentry, Llehden's forest spirits, reinforcing that feeling.

"But in this weather, who cares so long as it's hot? Now—what can I tell a man with a Harlequin's knowledge about death?"

"I—I do not rightly know," Mihn admitted after a brief pause. "I have been thinking about fate and prophecy, about the threads that bind our existence. I am not yet certain what it is I'm looking for, but I believe I need to know more about death if I am to understand my lord's fears correctly."

"Then I doubt I can help you," the witch said gently. "Your knowledge of myth and legend surpasses my own—you know the descriptions of Death's grey hall better than I, of the final judgment he delivers and of the Dark Place. I am familiar with the moments of death and birth, but not the halls of the immortals. You would need a priest of Death or a necromancer to tell you things you do not know."

"I suspect a priest would be even less likely to help me than a necromancer nowadays," Mihn said with a grim expression, "but perhaps . . ." His face became thoughtful. "Perhaps the answers are already written for those who can reach them."

The witch studied his face. "Are you talking about scripture or heretical texts? Just how much are you willing to risk?"

"You bring me to my second question. Lord Isak feels the strain of responsibility on him; he fears the hurt his position may cause those around him. Xeliath, Carel, his father—they have all been permanently damaged by their association with Isak, and that guilt runs deep. He sees me without weapons or armour, and so he fears to let me serve him."

"He is right to do so."

Mihn tried to read her expression but it was devoid of emotion. "What's that got to do with anything?" he said sharply.

"It is a consideration," Ehla replied in a calm voice. "For all his power and gifts, it does Lord Isak good to think like a normal person from time to time. Concern for his friends may prove a useful reminder that he is a man and not a God. You do remember there is no actual obligation holding you here? You could leave tonight and walk away from the death that lies in that young man's shadow."

"Says the woman far from home and camped in the freezing cold of winter." Mihn gestured to the park where the glassy sheen of frost covered everything.

She dipped her head, acknowledging his point. "I merely wish to remind you that the choice to stay is yours; that you should actually make that choice, rather than be swept along by the tide of history following him. He is a white-eye and the Chosen of Nartis; Lord Isak's presence commands those around him, so it would be easy enough to forget you still have a choice."

He shook his head. "I have not forgotten, and I choose to do what I can. I've seen the look in the eyes of those who returned from Scree. I cannot walk away."

"Very well. So what help do you need of me then?"

Mihn took a deep breath. "Last week Isak mentioned something that Aryn Bwr said to him in Scree and it stuck in my mind: 'not all steel is des-

tined to become a sword.' I will never have the power to rival his; the Gods
did not bless me in that manner, but they did bless me. Acrobatics have
always come easily to me; my skills of tracking and stealth surpass the Farlan
rangers I have met—these are abilities of subtlety that I had hoped your
witchcraft could augment."

"Would you be a thief or assassin for your lord?" Ehla asked sternly.

"I would do what my lord asks of me," he replied, "but my vow remains.
Count Vesna has already asked that of me and I will not change my mind."

"Good. I will not let my magic be infected by a murderer's deeds." Ehla
spent a while inspecting Mihn. He matched her gaze for a while, until he
noticed that Fernal was watching him equally as intently. The weight of the
Demi-God's scrutiny was harder to bear, for it crawled over his skin.

"I have watched you in your master's company; you keep close to him, as
close as a shadow—"

Fernal raised a hand to cut her off. "Be careful how you name him," he
said with a warning growl, "for a name shapes, just as it is defined by shape."

"Call a man cousin to Azaer and you open him to its influence? A sensible precaution," she conceded. "We have no idea of the shadow's power, but
if I were to augment your natural abilities somehow we should not be
thinking of you as a shadow."

"But you have an idea of what you could do?" Mihn fought the flicker of
excitement in his heart.

Ehla nodded. "It will take careful thought and preparation, but I have an
idea. A witch's magic is not based on power but insight, on working with
what already exists. You are a quiet man in manner and action, easily overlooked and skilled enough to slip through the night unnoticed. I might be
able to help a stealthy man become ghostly, to push you beyond the limits
already reached by the training of your childhood."

"How would you do it? A charm? A spell?"

"A charm you would wear, stitched into your clothing, perhaps; the
magic would have to be woven in while you were wearing it to make it
become a part of you." At last the witch showed some trace of emotion. "An
invocation to a God perhaps? Cerdin, God of Thieves? Nartis? The
Nighthunter might be a powerful ally in such a working."

"No Gods," Mihn said forcefully. "If the magic is to become part of me,
I do not wish to be linked to anything greater than me."

"Not an invocation then," she said with a nod, her attention lost in the
dancing flames of the fire, "nothing so simple. A spell that would have to be

tied to your very soul if it is to be strong enough for what Lord Isak may ask of you."

"Also dangerous," Fernal added. "Consequences will be tied to you also; it will be a binding you would not easily escape from."

"But it is possible," Mihn insisted.

Ehla took a long sip of tea and continued to stare into the fire, thinking. "It is; a spell of concealment. I have used something similar many times before, but for a ghost it will have to be painted onto your skin—no, tattooed, to bind the energy within, otherwise the efficacy is only temporary. A tattoo is part of you; it will make the spell part of you, only to be removed if the skin itself is cut away."

"How long will you need to prepare?"

Ehla wrinkled her nose. "A day to find the ingredients and tools and to make the necessary preparations. I assume the Chief Steward will be able to provide everything I need. Should I tell him why?"

"Tell him nothing, not yet."

"Very well. Tomorrow night might be rushing matters, so make it the following night."

Mihn stood, drained the tea, and handed the bowl back to Fernal with an appreciative grin. It didn't stop the chill in his bones, but it had made him feel blissful. He sighed as he felt a weight lift from his shoulders. For the first time since returning to Tirah he had a purpose. "Thank you. I will return at dusk the day after tomorrow."

CHAPTER 13

LEGANA STOPPED IN THE DARK LEE of a building and took a moment to clear the dizziness surging through her head. She tried not to massage her temple as she so desperately wanted to, knowing the movement would only draw attention. Instead, she pressed her fingers against the stone wall, glad of its cold, reassuring presence—until she realised she was pushing her fingertips right into the stone. Again she had to smother the urge to giggle like a little girl.

"I'm going to enjoy being a Goddess," Legana said softly to the night as she ran a finger over the five indentations she'd made in the granite. "Oh yes, I am."

The cool night air filled her lungs with a pleasant rush. The Lady's necklace under her clothes felt like a warm tingle on her skin. The giddiness was less frequent now, just occasional bursts of confusing and conflicting sensations as the two sides of Legana slowly became accustomed to each other: mortal and divine; outside of time, yet requiring sleep and food like she had before.

Legana had taken a fair range of narcotics in her varied life—both in rituals at the Temple of the Lady and on assignment in dens of every vice known to man—and knew nothing could compare to this. Drunk on Godhood, Legana had almost forgotten to kill Mikiss that first day as she stumbled about their shared rooms. Fortunately, the former Menin army messenger was new to his own powers and hadn't sensed the change in her in time. His moment of incomprehension had been enough for Legana to snatch up a sword and remove the vampire's head.

He barely saw me move. He still looked puzzled as he fell, she remembered, grinning to herself.

Since then Legana had been careful not to forget her mortal life, even if that was now behind her. She still had a mission, and that required preparation. It had taken more than a day for her to get a grip of her body's limitations again; now that she was connected to Fate, some of her instincts were conflicting, contrary to the requirements of a physical body. Once she had felt able again, Legana had visited Hale, the Temple District of Byora, to scout her target. She had kept clear of the Temple of the Lady, preferring to deal with matters in turn.

Legana hadn't dared to actually sit in on one of the nighttime rituals at the Temple of Alterr. Even in the smaller of the two domed chambers, the one dedicated to the lesser moon, Kasi, it was likely at least one priest would also be a mage. Under the circumstances, she couldn't afford to take the chance that someone might notice her, mark her as unusual.

She forced herself to keep walking, to remain unremarkable. Hale was never deserted, not entirely; the rhythm of prayer and ritual demanded regular attention. Few of the temples here would perform a High Reverence, but all had their daily observances and remained open for worshippers much of the day and night. A long silk cloak covered her entire body down to her ankles, rippling gently in the evening breeze. Legana had found that she could ignore the cold of winter easily enough, but the dark green cloak remained a useful way to hide swords and clothing that might be seen as out of place in Hale.

"Damn piety," Legana grumbled. "Too many witnesses during the day, and Alterr's services take place at night. Let's hope the Lady's recovered enough to smile on me now."

She reached a crossroad. On the right she could see three peaked buildings set back from the road. They were connected by slender arches, with a courtyard marked out in between them: the linked Goddesses of Love.

No doubt the priests of Triena and Kantay are tucked up in bed and trying to ignore the sounds of worship coming from their sister's temple. Legana smiled. How much easier this would have been if Ayarl Lier, her target, were the kind to take a regular trip to Etesia's temple, where the purple and red lanterns shone and lust was worshipped with enthusiasm. As it was, she'd watched the man from a distance as he walked in the street one day. His manner made it likely the young boy trailing at his heel was a catamite, so she'd dismissed the possibility.

The temple of the Moon Goddess was at the end of the road, past the linked temples, and it was dominated by the great dome of Alterr's chamber on the left. A long crescent wall with a single gate blocked the way. The top of Kasi's smaller chamber was visible on the right. In the compound behind were the half dozen buildings that comprised the more mundane part of any temple complex: dormitories, stables, and offices, for the most part.

Legana knew several of those dormitories normally given over to novices now housed penitents, the militia of choice among the priesthood, it appeared—or the piety of preference among mercenaries, depending on how one wished to look at it. Novices were usually young and bound to the temple for a certain number of years, while penitents tended to be significantly older. Penitents didn't need a formal commitment before an altar, just a robe and a tattoo on their index fingers. Before they had served the agreed period of penitence, they were tied only loosely to the temple; experience showed that many men just couldn't adapt to the rigours demanded by temple life.

She ducked through the low gate, one hand ensuring her hood still covered her copper-tinted hair, and stopped dead. A strange sensation slithered down her spine, quite unlike anything she had ever felt before. Like a faint scent on the breeze there was something unexpected within the compound. Slowly she turned to the left, where Alterr's chamber stood, a smooth-sided half dome forty yards in diameter, painted a stark white that glowed very faintly in the moonlight.

The door was shut and a pair of penitents were on guard outside. She checked the rest of the courtyard: there were no other obvious guards, but there were men loitering. Legana frowned. As inexperienced in magic as she was, something told her this wasn't a simple spell. She could feel raw energy in her veins, part of the very makeup of her Godhood, but what she felt now touched her even deeper inside.

"So what's going on in there?" she wondered aloud. Without really intending to, she took a few paces towards the chamber. The penitents stiffened, hands reaching for the spears leaning casually in the dark recesses on either side of the chamber door. They were of a similar height to her, and they looked like they both had a fair amount to be penitent about, but she reckoned even as a mere mortal she'd have been able to take them both—men always underestimated a pretty face.

"Temple's closed for a private service," one of the guards called.

Legana hardly heard him, so intent was she on the curious prickle on her skin. The sensation got no stronger as she neared the chamber and she came to an abrupt stop, suddenly realising that it was not emanating from the building at all.

"That's curious," she said quietly to herself. Just looking at the chamber had caused something to resonate inside her, like the vibration of a plucked string.

"What did you say?" the guard asked, taking a step towards her. He held his spear loosely, at the ready.

"Could it be luck?" she wondered, not paying the penitent any attention at all. At the back of her mind, realisation began to flower.

The penitent glanced at his comrade. "You understandin' her?"

"Nope. Sounds like she's talking Farlan. Looks Farlan too."

Legana frowned at the two men for a moment before realising she hadn't understood the actual words coming out of their mouths, but the meaning instead. *Another divine gift, I assume.* She thought for a moment and the local dialect came easily enough to her tongue.

"Take a step back and keep quiet. There's something bad going on in the temple." *I'm touched by the Goddess of Luck, so I think it's safe to assume my sense of timing is going to be, ah, divine, from now on.*

The first penitent opened his mouth to argue, but the words died unsaid as Legana held a sword tip to his throat, moving in the blink of an eye. A faint croak escaped his comrade's lips, but they were too astonished for anything more. They had realised no normal woman could have moved so quickly.

"I need to be in that temple right now, so take a step back," she repeated softly, "and get the fuck out of my way, or you'll find your balls shoved down your throat."

The penitents jerked back as if they were on strings. Legana lowered her sword and nodded at the door.

"Shut it behind me, please." She stepped through the doorway without pausing to look inside first. The door was slammed shut after her. The chamber was dark, sparsely lit by candles set on an iron chandelier hanging from the roof. The crescent pews were set in circular tiers, descending from above head-height at the back to knee-high around the altar. The fretwork backs of the pews and roof beams cast long shadows, but they didn't obscure the scene.

Legana slid between two pews and peered at the altar.

There were well-dressed people kneeling, their heads bowed as though in prayer. No one showed any sign of having heard her entrance. A child lay supine on the altar, twitching feebly, and blood dripped over the edges. The Lady's first thought was of a grand entrance, but Legana preferred to follow her own instinct, of caution.

A man's voice echoed out from the darkness. "You shouldn't have ignored the guards. That really was a mistake."

Legana began to wind her way down between the rows towards the altar, scanning the room as she did so. Most of the space was occupied by the pews, but she quickly became aware of movement that mimicked her own, and caught sight of flashes of a dark figure walking in the shadows, but that was enough. She couldn't place the accent—it was unlike any she'd heard before, and it sounded ancient in form. That wasn't good, old meant dangerous— and he didn't sound even apprehensive.

But they always underestimate a woman, Legana thought grimly to herself, *so let's make him walk into trouble.*

"Sorry to ruin your fun," she called out, flicking the clasp of her cloak open and letting it fall behind her. The pews were low enough now for her to vault up onto a seat with no obvious effort.

Looking down at the altar she saw there were markings on the ground, symbols written in chalk all the way around, linked by a sloppily drawn circle. They meant nothing to her, but the sight of her target, High Priest Lier, dead on the ground with his chest torn to ribbons gave her a clear idea of the intention. It was set up to look like a summoning gone wrong. The rich folk surrounding the altar had to be under some enchantment, kept alive until it was time for them to be slaughtered, providing the appropriate sound effects.

"You've ruined nothing," said the man, stepping out from a shadow opposite her. He was hairless, gaunt, and albino white, and clad in black scale-armour of a style she didn't recognise. It was the fat broadsword in his hand, its black surface prickled with elusive light like faint stars, that made her suddenly nervous. He leapt up onto a pew himself, cocked his head to one side, and smiled like a lizard at her. "My, what pretty hair you have."

Legana took a step down onto the pew in front. "You're taking enough of a risk already, aren't you?" she asked softly. "Defiling Alterr's temple and killing her high priest is dangerous enough. Do you really want to risk bringing the Lady into things too?"

His smile became a smirk. "I don't fear your mistress," he replied, reaching out towards her with his empty hand.

Legana recoiled as she felt his cold fingers close around her neck. A surge of power welled up from inside her in reaction and she felt a crackle of energy over her entire body as the warring forces strained against each other. In the next instant, it was gone.

"Strange," he said, looking puzzled but still far from worried. "Aren't you the curiosity?"

Legana didn't bother to reply. She kicked off from the pew and leapt through the air towards him, twin swords held out wide. As she flashed across the chamber, she felt the strength of a Goddess fill her—

Still a dozen feet from the murderer, she smashed into an invisible barrier, then those hands were about her throat again, only this time it was like a vice crushing down on every part of her body at once. She howled in pain as stars burst before her eyes. The swords fell from her grip as fire lanced through her veins.

"Overconfident, pretty one," the stranger snarled. With a twitch of the hand he threw her across the room and she smashed into the pews. She found herself gasping for air while colours blurred in her vision. Again she felt power suffuse her and she found herself standing upright.

She dived to one side instinctively as a crash come from where she'd been standing a moment before. She kept moving, thoughts racing through her mind, too fast to be coherent. She needed her weapons back, and she needed to move fast. It felt like the Land around her slowed as she drew on her divine half. As she raced through the pews, she pictured her swords in her mind, and they lifted themselves from the ground and began to move towards her.

But before she could get close enough to grasp them, something smashed into her side, throwing her off her feet again. This time she hit the ground shoulder-first and rolled into position to kick off the pew ahead of her. She flipped up through the air, and as she landed, she felt her swords slap against her palms. The Land appeared to hesitate again as she drove towards her attacker. He brought his sword up to meet hers, barely quick enough to parry her flurry of blows, but as they locked weapons and she kicked forward into his gut, Legana felt herself thrown backwards by some other force.

"No more!" called a voice that echoed around the room with such force the light from the candles shuddered and dimmed. Legana blinked. The Lady was standing in front of her, facing her attacker. She held a leaf-bladed spear in her hands, its golden shaft blazing in the weak light.

"Aracnan, explain yourself!"

Legana staggered back, dazzled by the light of the spear and gasping as the jewels around her neck suddenly burned with the Lady's fury.

"Explain myself?" spat Aracnan with sudden venom, sword still raised. "I don't think so."

He hand went to a pouch at his belt and he withdrew an object. White light cascaded over them all and Legana felt the walls shudder. The rumble of thunder assailed her ears as power poured from the object. She found herself screaming in fear and pain.

The air around Aracnan shuddered. "Enough of your meddling, Lady," he crowed. "Your fate awaits you."

Legana tried to turn and run, but her body would not obey. A savage stream of power from the Crystal Skull in Aracnan's hand lashed out at Fate. Legana was thrown backwards, writhing with agony as bloody slashes appeared on the Lady's body. The roar of power was all around, hammering at her ears, ringing like a gigantic bell through her head. Her screams were drowned out by the brutal energy raging around her.

The Goddess struck back with fire and spear. The light became too intense to bear as the pair fought. The roar intensified and she felt her eardrums burst, but even then the sound refused to cease. It was inside her head, battering at her skull. Legana shuddered as she felt the Lady strike and be wounded in the same moment.

She opened her eyes a fraction to see a frozen moment of violence, with blood streaming in all directions. The white light shone like a savage halo around them. The Lady turned towards her, mouth open, words forming even as she cried out. Legana felt a flame of white fire slice her face and the pain intensified throughout her body even as she was jerked backwards.

She crashed through the outer wall of the chamber, feeling nothing of it, and the blessed blackness of night swallowed her. Legana, wrapped in agony, realised she was screaming with two voices: a mortal's shriek of pain and a Goddess's death-cry. Her body spasmed as it crashed through something else and rolled to an abrupt halt.

Three words flashed across Legana's mind: *Fate help me.* Then she realised that Fate was dead, and unconsciousness claimed her.

CHAPTER 14

"WHAT DO YOU MEAN, YOU DON'T KNOW?" Natai Escral, Duchess of Byora, shouted across her breakfast table. The object of her ire, a sallow-faced marshal called Harin Dyar, shrank back under the force of her demand. Natai was sitting bolt upright, a laden fork pointed at the unusually scruffy officer.

"What use is 'I don't know'?" She was alone at the table; although a place had been laid for her husband, matters of state had got her up early, as usual.

Behind her a child started to cry: Minnay, an orphaned toddler, one of her dozen wards. She saw the haggard woman she'd named Eliane standing nearby, Ruhen content in her arms after half an hour of crawling around on the floor under Natai's supervision.

Good, I didn't disturb him, she thought with a smile. *I wouldn't want him to cry—that sound breaks my heart.*

"Ah, your Grace, Hale is effectively locked down," Dyar stammered after a few moments. "I cannot get any of my troops in to investigate."

"Locked down?" she hissed, still angry, but mindful of Ruhen's presence. "You mean you've allowed a handful of crippled old men to keep *my* soldiers from my own damn city?"

"Your Grace, we will need to use force to get into the quarter," Dyar protested, "and I do not have enough men—Hale's penitents outnumber those under my command."

"Marshal, how is it you cannot even brief me on what has happened? Why does the Byoran Guard not hold these streets?" She looked around, as if her wards—or the four nurses tending them—could provide answers where Dyar could not. The room, one of the largest in the palace, had once been a communal chamber for her grandfather's harem. It was both opulent and elegant, and Natai spent much of her leisure time there, surrounded by children.

No one spoke. The nurses all looked away, trying not to catch her eye. Eliane stared at the floor—but she rarely did much else. Since she had been saved from being trampled in Criers Square, Eliane had managed to frustrate all attempts to build up her painfully thin frame. Nor had anyone been able to coax any word of her past out of her. She claimed to have no memory of what had happened before she reached Byora, but Natai didn't believe it. Something in Eliane's eyes betrayed a damaged soul, a fear so deep it had become part of her. Despite her apparent ill health, her production of milk remained healthy and Ruhen was thriving, even while his mother wasted away. All she did was clutch that damn book, and she wailed like a daemon if anyone tried to take it from her.

"Your Grace?" called a voice.

Natai jerked her head up, looking at Dyar, before realising he and his aides were staring, astonished, at one of the soldiers at the door.

What in the name of the Gods? Who's that impudent—? Natai's thought went unfinished, for the face was familiar. He wore the crimson tunic and black trousers of her guard, but he had added what appeared to be long armoured gloves. The uniform was pristine, but the gloves, blue-sheened metal bound by a random criss-cross of twine, were battered. They triggered the memory.

Ah, Ruhen's protector, of course, Natai told herself. "Sergeant Kayel, isn't it?" she asked.

He saluted awkwardly. "Honoured you remember, ma'am."

Ma'am? I'm not some damned merchant's wife, she thought, but before she could chastise the man she found herself turning towards Eliane and the child. Ruhen was smiling up at the painted birds wheeling around the various aspects of Ilit and Vellern. The whole chamber was decorated in such a way—a lot more wholesome for innocent young children than the original paintings. She hesitated, snared by Ruhen's shining smile, and by the time she remembered herself, her anger had disappeared.

She turned back to the soldier. "You have something to add, Sergeant?"

"Yes, your Grace. I was in Hale last night. Can't tell you exactly what's going on, but I caught sight of a right mess in Alterr's temple and some young novice was chatterin' that the high priest had died."

"Lier is dead?" Natai went white. "Gods, how could that have happened? You said a mess, what sort of mess?"

Kayel grinned. "Looked like it'd been hit by a siege weapon, 'cept the wall of the greater chamber had been blown out, not inwards. Lots of armed penitents around, and a right ugly mood. Someone said something about the Lady, or a priestess of the Lady, bein' involved."

"The Lady? Could this be a feud between temples?" Natai stopped suddenly as she had a chilling thought. "A feud between Gods?"

"Perhaps, ma'am, but there's a whole lot of anger over there, and men runnin' around lookin' for someone to blame."

"What were you doing in the Temple District so late at night?" she asked, then worked it out before he replied. "Ah, a little praying at Etesia's temple?"

Kayel shifted his feet. "Spoke a few words at the Temple of Death too."

"Are you suggesting that sending troops to investigate will cause a full-scale riot?"

"I'm sayin' they looked like they were ready to start a fight given the first excuse. Might not stop at a riot either way."

"Do you have any suggestions for Marshal Dyar then?" She had meant to mock the marshal's ineffectiveness but Kayel didn't hesitate.

"Find a mage to tell you what's happened. Then when the district is open again send some men in without uniforms; see who's doin' all the talkin', who's doin' the blamin'. There's always some bastard who don't care what happened, only how to use it to their own ends."

"You really think this will escalate?"

The sergeant shrugged. "You want to take the risk? Wasn't the High Priest of Alterr tryin' to tell you how to run the city?"

Natai almost laughed at his implication until she realised he was entirely serious.

"Wouldn't be surprised if they done it themselves," Kayel added, "but my money's on you gettin' the blame whichever way."

She stared down at the breakfast she had abandoned. The Circle City was a playground of intrigue: four distinct domains and, until recently, four very different leaders. The White Circle leaders of Fortinn had fled and the quarter was now ruled by a triumvirate appointed by the three remaining leaders. It was a temporary solution suggested by the duchess herself.

The corpulent Chosen of Ilit, Lord Celao, had taken a fair amount of persuading, but at least Cardinal Sourl had had the brains to realise she was right. With bad news coming from all directions, business would be disrupted enough. They would still play their games, of course, but they all had to recognise open war over control of Fortinn would be madness.

Either of them could be behind this, Natai realised. *They both stand to benefit from religious insurrection here. Gods, they aren't working together, are they? No, that is too far-fetched. Even with their renewed piety, I can't see any alliance lasting long enough for them to execute a plan together properly.*

"Marshal, I want your full complement of troops out on the streets; concentrated on Coin, Wheel, and Breakale for the moment. Make it clear to the population that business goes on unhindered." Again the fork stabbed in his direction, emphasising her point.

The man bowed and scurried out, not trying to hide the relieved expression on his face. His two aides were on his heels. As they left, the duchess's principal minister strode in alongside the duke and she breathed a sigh of relief: at last she would hear something useful. Her husband wore a concerned expression, but Sir Arite Leyen was his usual picture of calm. He inspected the faces in the room, then bowed.

"Sir Arite, where have you been?" She raised a hand to cut off any reply. "No, I don't actually care, just tell me what you know—and it better be more than I've already heard from this sergeant or I'll damn well put him in charge of the Closed Council instead!"

A second bow was the only response to her threat; that in itself was ominous enough since Sir Arite generally managed a feeble joke in most situations. "Your Grace, I was busy in the Vier Tower with Mage Peness."

She pictured the thin-lipped mage whose round face seemed to distend when he smiled. "Peness? What does that wheedling little toad want?"

"Merely to help his sovereign," Sir Arite assured her before looking pointedly at the onlookers.

"Sergeant, help the children back to their rooms," Natai ordered.

Kayel looked startled at the command, but he hesitated for just a moment before he started to move. The children and their nurses all took one look at the hulking, scar-faced soldier and fled, even Eliane, which provoked a spark of irritation in the duchess. She'd wanted to hold Ruhen a little longer this morning, letting the stresses of rule melt away in his shadowy little eyes.

Those hypnotic eyes.

Eliane's were grey, dull; they hardly compared to the rich swirl of shadow in Ruhen's. When Natai spoke soft, adoring words he seemed to drink them in, to revel in her love for him, even as young as he was. The baby would lie quite contentedly in her arms and look at her with incredible intensity, hardly ever blinking; his stare managed to revive her in a way sleep no longer could.

She shook herself back to the present; there would be time enough for Ruhen later. "Sergeant, stay here; the rest of you leave us." Seeing Sir Arite's surprise, she added, "He was in the district last night. He's the only one who seems to know anything."

"As you wish, but my news is rather alarming."

"First of all, tell me if this was Sourl or Celao?" she said, forcing herself to regain the serene composure she was known for.

"I doubt it was either, but I wish it was both," Sir Arite said eventually. He gave the big soldier a suspicious look and Kayel stared back, unfazed. "Your Grace, I really do think it would be better if—"

"Just tell me."

At her expression he seemed to deflate a little. "Peness says that there was a vast amount of magic expended last night—a terrifying level of raw energy."

"Strong words."

"The man was frightened." He leaned forward, his voice dropping. "Peness is one of the most powerful mages in the city, and he was frightened by what he described." The words seemed to hang in the air between them until Kayel sniffed, apparently unimpressed.

"Did he say why he was so afraid?" Natai asked, ignoring the soldier.

"I—He couldn't be sure. He was being evasive, but I don't believe it was through ill will. Mages tend to have their own allegiances and an entirely different range of concerns—I believe he was worried about interfering in the business of others."

"Who would worry our most powerful mage?"

Sir Arite looked grave. "He doesn't want to make an enemy of anyone who can wield the sort of power expended in Hale last night. Whoever it was, I gather they could have levelled the entire district."

"Gods," Natai breathed, feeling a chill run down her neck.

"And that's not the only news." The knight's eyes narrowed and his voice fell to a whisper, as though his news was too terrible to be spoken in normal tones. "Whoever wielded that power—it wasn't just against the high priest. It fought a being of near-equal strength—magic such as few mortals possess—and it killed them."

A dull note of pain thrummed through her body. Every sensation was overlaid and muted by a heavy blanket of aching which weighed her down. There was a distant, unidentifiable sound ringing in her ears. As Legana drifted through the empty dream of near wakefulness she felt something missing, a hole inside her that spoke of something too terrible to remember.

An involuntary twitch in her leg suddenly brought the pain in her side back into focus, sharp and hot. Her lips parted with a gluey jerk as she moaned. The ringing in her ears became more insistent; a spiky, wet feeling that reached all around her head and dug its claws into her neck. For a while Legana lay motionless, unable to hear her own whimpers, until the pain in her side subsided a little and she chanced a look at the Land.

It was difficult to open her eyes. It felt like a long-forgotten movement that required her full force of will to achieve, and when at last she succeeded, she saw little; just a shadowy blur of yellow and the suggestion of lines that might indicate the shape of a room. Taking too deep a breath she moaned again and a spark of fear flared in her heart. The pain was an aside; what frightened her was the fact she could hear neither breath nor moan, though she could feel the air slide between her tender lips.

The blur ahead changed all of a sudden as a dark shape moved into her field of vision. It eventually resolved into the form of a man, a tonsured priest, standing over her, although the dimness remained and her head began to hurt when she tried to make out the details of his face. She saw a bearded jaw moving, but still heard nothing. In panic she tried to sit up, but a wave of dizziness broke over her and she slumped back in agony, feeling tears fall freely from her eyes in a way they had not since childhood.

The priest placed his hands on her shoulders to indicate she should keep still before gently lifting her head and putting a sodden cloth to her mouth. A few wonderfully sweet drops of water trickled into her mouth and Legana summoned all her remaining strength to swallow them. He squeezed the cloth and a little more appeared on her tongue—somehow she fought those down as well, but that was all she could manage. She sagged onto his cradling hand.

The priest nodded approvingly and put the cloth out of sight before placing a hand on her chest. His lips began to move and Legana's blurred vision swam as a warmth began to spread over her body. The sensation was alien and alarming, but something inside her recognised it as healing magic. The part of her that was touched by a Goddess screamed in fear at another God's magic, but the human side overruled it, and as she sank back into unconsciousness, the pain faded far enough into the background for sleep to claim her. A few moments later she felt nothing at all.

A steady rain was falling on Byora's granite buildings, streaking walls with dark tears and filling the gutters with a swift stream of dirty water. The Duchess of Byora ignored the patter of water on her hood and watched the rain fall for ten minutes or more instead of touching her heels to the horse's flanks and setting off down the street.

"This rain will cool tempers, don't you think, Sir Arite?" she said at last.

The blond man only gave a perfunctory nod in response. He looked more concerned by the effect the rain was having on his boots than the state of the city beyond. The duke smiled amiably at his wife, doing a reasonable job of concealing his anxiety to everyone but Natai, the person he was trying most to encourage. She returned the smile, glad of the effort he was making, however transparent. He was the only one who hadn't tried to dissuade her from this journey, the only one to look beyond his own safety and see the necessity.

This was the first time the duchess had ventured out of her palace since the news of the terrible happenings in the religious district had come in the previous morning. That there were reportedly mobs of penitents roaming the city was not her concern; she would not let them cow her. Above her the Ruby Tower looked forbidding in the overcast morning light. The stepped levels of the tower were adorned with shards of red slate, designed for the light of a summer evening. Now it merely served to highlight the grimness of the black mountain walls behind it.

"Captain Fohl?" Natai said to the commander of her guard, "lead the way, if you please."

The captain saluted, while behind him the new sergeant didn't bother to wait for the order as he started off, two squads of her guards falling in behind his horse. Natai felt a flicker of amusement at Fohl's expression when he saw the men were already moving, his Adam's apple bobbing as a rebuke went unsaid.

The captain was neatly turned out as ever, but today he looked comical to her, with his pale hair poking limply out from his gold-trimmed helm and pallid skin stretched over a weak face. Compared with the muscular bulk of Sergeant Kayel, Fohl looked fragile, almost pathetic.

It was reassuring to see Kayel at the head of her guards as they moved towards Hale. The man was a born leader—and more than a little intimidating. Natai knew that Fohl was easily offended and would have had any other sergeant whipped for the impudence Kayel showed, but even the arrogance of pure Litse blood couldn't overshadow the fact that Fohl was simply afraid of the man.

It was Prayerday morning, the day for High Reverence at the temples, and the duke and duchess had established a tradition of attending prayers at the temples of both Ushull and Death long ago. Now the eyes of the city would be watching them. The situation had not improved, and Natai knew it would take more than rain to change that—even the savage deluges that regularly scoured Byora's streets—but she refused to hide from her people.

Hale was reportedly a boiling ant's nest of activity and tension, a situation not helped by the fact that a band of penitents had decided to search two of her agents. The men had been carrying weapons, of course, and they had decided to flee rather than be arrested for impiety. A mob had stoned them to death and now their heads were on display at a crossroads Natai had to pass to reach the Temple of Death.

At her command the whole column of nobles and troops set out, Sergeant Kayel setting a brisk pace from the front with one hand resting on the hilt of his sword and his head constantly turning to scan the surrounding street. The duchess saw a range of reactions from the people they clattered past. Some scurried into their homes and barred the doors while others began to follow the soldiers behind her. Natai felt a moment of irritation; she couldn't see their faces as they followed.

"Ganas," she called to her husband, and he immediately urged his horse closer and leaned over to better hear her. His ceremonial uniform and sword echoed those of the Ruby Tower Guards—prettier, but no less functional.

"Do you think they're following just to see a fight, or are they on our side?" she asked softly.

When he shrugged she heard the clink of hidden metal. Most of her subjects assumed Ganas was simple, weak-minded even, because she ruled Byora rather than he. The Litse couldn't comprehend his lack of ambition, any more than the foolish women from the White Circle had not accepted that she didn't struggle against a husband's oppression. She was simply better at ruling than he was, and few people gave him the credit for acknowledging that and accepting it. Few men were strong enough to do such a thing. They were a good team.

"Given the choice, they'll pick us," he said in the mellifluous accent of the city, "but I doubt many will follow us into Hale. Too dangerous."

Sure enough, as they reached the religious district their escort hung back and watched nervously. There were three gates into Hale: two spanning the two largest roads from Eight Towers, where the well-off citizens lived in the shadow of the Ruby Tower, and a third in the wall separating Hale from Breakale, where the majority of the citizens lived.

The Queen's Gate was the one she commonly used on Prayerday, following the road around in a long loop to visit the temples of Ushull, Death, and Belarannar before a last quick prayer at Kitar's temple—that was her own small tradition, one that had continued long after she'd given up hoping the Goddess of Fertility would answer her prayers.

If the onlookers had been hoping for drama at the first confrontation, they were sorely disappointed. A dozen or so penitents were waiting by the gate, but Kayel completely ignored their efforts to block the path. Clearly they were hoping to get in the way and force the guards to either strike first or back down, but Kayel urged his horse on, oblivious to their presence, and the men had to jump out of the way or be trampled.

Once inside the district, Natai forced herself not to stare around at the faces watching them, but she felt a small flicker of fear when she realised how many grey-clad penitents of Death were congregated on the streets—and they weren't the only ones. Hale was a community in its own right, a small, self-contained town perched on a ledge of high ground some two-thirds of a mile across. Not all of the inhabitants were clerics, but they were all connected to the business of worship, and if Natai was being blamed for High Priest Lier's death, they would all side against her.

"Ushull, Tsatach, Nartis, Belarannar, Ilit—most of the major cults have been recruiting," Ganas commented so softly only Natai could hear. "Let us be glad the Temple of Karkarn here is too small to be of any real significance."

She nodded and kept her eyes on the road, her unease growing with every passing minute. Threatening groups of hooded figures stood and watched them from the side streets, some actually following the horses closely enough to provoke disquiet. The silence that followed her party as they continued into Hale was profound.

It reminded Natai of a dream she'd had as a child: surrounded by faceless figures as motionless as statues, the clouds racing past above them, while the leader of her tormentors, a giant swathed in white, pointed an accusing finger at her. No matter which direction she faced, she couldn't escape the weight of that gesture. Now, with the clerics and their mercenaries watching her, Natai felt a similar oppression. The journey to the Temple of Ushull was a brief one, but to Natai it seemed to take an hour or more.

Like many of Ushull's temples this one was open to the elements, but the builders had clearly tried to evoke Blackfang Mountain here, putting a thirty-foot-tall obelisk studded with crystal and obsidian shards in the middle of the oval temple, pushing up through the upper level, which in turn was supported by four great pillars that signified the quarters of the Circle City—Byora, Akell, Fortin, and Ismess. Ushull was technically an Aspect of Belarannar, and as a result, the temple was exactly a foot smaller than the Temple of Belarannar in length, width, and height.

Tradition dictated that Natai should kneel below the steady drip of the shrine dedicated to Kiyer of the Deluge first, letting water splash onto her forehead before offering a silver level and a prayer for another week without a flood.

Afterwards she would place a freshly picked flower before the shrine at the other end of the upper level, a gift to Parss, Ushull's capricious child, who casts boulders down the slopes. The last of Ushull's three Aspects had his shrine on the lower level, a squat lair made out of clay which was kept as hot as a baker's oven. There she would need to add another lump of coal to the fire to appease Cambrey Smoulder, the dormant destroyer under the mountain. That done, she would speak a prayer with one palm placed against Ushull's obelisk and leave a second silver level while Ushull's priests maintained the drone of prayer from their aisles opposite Cambrey's shrine.

Before Natai reached the temple she saw Kayel, who had gone ahead, had been stopped by a party of animated priests. There were faces watching them all around, most ominously from the temple itself, where no one was engaged in worship as far as Natai could see. The wind had been growing stronger during their journey and now it whipped across the district with an impatient ferocity, drowning out the conversation ahead. All around her Natai felt and saw a burning resentment; anger smouldered like Cambrey deep under the mountain.

Cambrey or Kiyer? she wondered as the column of troops stopped and her guards at last faced the penitents on all sides. *Cambrey grumbles and blusters, but is slow to anger; Kiyer strikes with the fury and speed of an ice cobra.*

As though in answer to her question a boom of thunder rolled over the city, the distant rumble that all Byorans had grown up listening out for. For a moment, all faces turned east, towards the mountain.

Natai shivered instinctively. Blackfang was not a flat tabletop, as most imagined, but a crazed mess of jagged rock and stagnant pools left by the rain. A storm might simply provide a soaking—or it might turn the uninhabitable wasteland of Blackfang into something entirely more frightening. When the rains were heavy enough, a torrent of water would sweep down, scouring the streets of everything as Kiyer of the Deluge claimed her sacrifices and dumped their remains in the fens a few miles past Wheel, the quarter's most westerly district.

A sudden flash of movement made her turn back. She heard Ganas grunt in surprise and stare up at the mountain with a puzzled look on his face. Captain Fohl said something, but the words were jumbled and confused. Unbidden, her horse turned away from Ganas and a sudden pressure closed about her chest and throat, squeezing the breath from her body.

Unable to move, unable to speak, Natai sat rigid and horrified as Ganas slid unceremoniously from his saddle and to the ground, one foot still hooked in the stirrup. A black-fletched arrow protruding from his back snapped as Ganas fell onto it. Natai stared down at her husband's contorted face in disbelief, paralysed by the sight as the Land exploded into movement around her.

Figures ran forward, and a hand grabbed her reins and wrenched her horse around until the beast kicked out. Men yelled and swore on all sides, swords rasped from scabbards. Captain Fohl barged his horse into hers, barely raising his shield in time as another arrow thwacked into it. She saw Sergeant Kayel draw and strike in one movement, turning back towards her before the priest's corpse had even hit the ground.

The ground started shaking, reverberating up through her horse's body and into her own. Before Natai even realised what was happening, her horse gave a shriek and staggered. Beside her, Fohl slashed down at someone just as a spear appeared from nowhere to catch him in the ribs with such force he was thrown from his saddle, crashing into her horse before he fell under its hooves.

She couldn't look down as her horse reared up. Everything lurched, and the cloud-covered sky seemed to reach out to her as Natai herself begin to fall—

Suddenly something smacked into her forearm and wrenched her forward. The sky wheeled and became a dark blur of buildings as the pressure on her arm increased, wrapped around it, and wrenched her forward. Natai felt herself crash against the ground and almost bounce up with the impact. Her arm was almost torn from its socket as whatever was hanging onto her dragged her along, her feet flailing uselessly beneath her.

She heard a grunt of exertion as she was swung up and landed heavily on something, the wind driven from her like a punch to the gut. She was lying over a saddle. Now she recognised Kayel shouting above her; short, brutal words she couldn't make out. Something clattered hard into her leg and fell away, and she felt Kayel lean over her body to hack down with his sword. There was the wet crunch of flesh and bone parting. Screams and roars came from all directions, but her eyes and ears refused to make sense of them.

Kayel's voice and the hot stink of the horse were the only things she could recognise, until suddenly the uproar was behind them and she realised they were clear; they were safe. Only then did her mind catch up and the sight of Ganas falling return, bright and vivid, and as sharp as a knife in her belly. When at last the soldier stopped and allowed her to slide from the saddle Natai didn't feel the hands trying to help her to her feet. The buzz of voices came only distantly: questions, shouts, orders, all meaningless in the face of that pain in her gut. She crumpled to her bloodied knees and puked, and again, but the agony of loss remained.

High Priest Antil paused at the doorway of his personal chamber, peering around the jamb and feeling foolish as he did so. While he was Shotir's chief cleric, the God of Healing's temple in Byora was a modest one, and his room was appropriately small. Normally a wide window covering half of the north wall provided most of the room's light, but since his patient's dramatic arrival, that was covered in sacking. There was a tiny window in the side which admitted a little pale winter sunlight, but Antil had still brought a candle.

Stop being such a fool, he chided himself, *she's your patient, for pity's sake!* The remonstrations had little effect. He still felt like he was intruding. He glanced behind him to check no priests or novices were watching him, but there was no one. People rarely came up to the top floor of the temple; they knew this was his personal space, where he could get his thoughts back in order and rest after working in the hospital below.

Antil was a middle-aged man of average height, with thinning hair and somewhat thick around the waist—a professional hazard for Priests of Shotir, those who could heal at least. Magical healing produced a fierce hunger, and only Antil's vanity had kept that in check. Unlike most of his order, his belly was a modest bulge under his yellow robes, and a tidy beard hid his fleshy neck. There was nothing he could do about the worry lines.

He forced himself to enter the chamber, and once over the threshold habit reasserted itself. She was very sensitive to light, so he walked around the bed and crouched at her side. She wasn't asleep; he could sense her wariness, like a wounded animal, and he was careful not to touch her yet. However badly hurt she might be, she was still touched by a Goddess, and he didn't want to do anything to provoke alarm in her. Instead he just sat awhile and looked at her face, fascinated by the mystery she presented.

With a tiny whimper the woman turned her head to look at him and he saw those curious eyes focus on him. They were dark green, possessing an inner light that reminded Antil of the jade ring his mother had worn until the day she died. The woman's face was bruised and covered in splinter scratches, but the swelling had already gone down. He realised she would be arrestingly beautiful once the discolouration faded.

"Well, my girl, and how do you feel this morning?" he asked gently, not expecting a response. His ability with magic was as unremarkable as he, and healing was the only skill he'd ever worked on, but his latent senses recognised enough to be worried by her. The one-sided conversation was principally for his own benefit, helping him maintain a normal train of thought so he could focus on his healing—not that he'd been able to do much yet, partly because the divine spark in her was far stronger than a priest's and resisted Shotir's workings, but also because replacing the ruined was beyond mortal skills.

Antil let a trickle of warm energy run into her body to sooth her, stroking her hand until she stopped fighting it. Once the fear was gone he pulled the blanket covering her down a little, but the mark was still there, as he'd expected.

"Damn," he said, scratching at his beard and frowning. Around her throat was a clear handprint of greyish shadow. The skin itself was not damaged, just tinted—as though an ash-covered hand had grabbed her—except it would not wash off.

"Someone's marked you," he told her, "you who have been touched by a Goddess as profoundly as one Chosen. They grabbed you and they beat you senseless. They broke your leg, a shoulder, an arm, ribs, a bone in your neck—and their very touch was enough to leave a permanent mark on your skin."

He shivered. It wasn't the only strange aspect of her neck: running his finger over it he could feel a series of lumps, for all the world like a necklace *under* her skin—and what magic he had been able to work had confirmed that was exactly what it was: a necklace she had been wearing had been driven completely into her flesh.

"That's not even the worst," he continued, looking down at the handprint thoughtfully. "We all felt it, what happened in Alterr's chamber. Every priest in Hale felt something terrible. Folk are saying a God died . . . but I wonder if it was not a Goddess?"

He found a cloth and almost mechanically began to wipe her face.

"I went to the Temple of the Lady. It's shut; the priestesses have not been seen outside the walls. Hale is in chaos, so no one else has really noticed yet, but that will change soon enough."

He removed the blanket covering her body and stared down at her body. A small wrap protected her modesty for form's sake, though the sheer number of bandages and wrappings meant almost half her total skin surface was covered. He saw to each one in turn, humming the mantras of healing as he worked. Without channelling magic they would do little, but the familiar sound was better than silence.

It was clear that she was healing supernaturally well. Antil was not so vain as to believe it was down to him. *Perhaps I helped a little*, he conceded, *but no more than that.* When he touched her tightly splinted leg the woman moaned and tried to reach out, but the effort of sitting up defeated her. She sank back down, her eyes rolling up as her lips moved fractionally. He placed his hands on her chest and channelled magic into her body, not focusing on knitting bone or flesh, which she would manage on her own, but on blanking out the pain. That at least he could manage: her mind was still human, and a mind could be fooled into ignoring pain, even if the substance of her body resisted any efforts beyond that.

After a minute he stopped to catch his breath, feeling like an old man. He'd left a small bag of willow bark pieces by her bedside. He picked it up and fumbled stiff-fingered with the tie for a moment before managing to get it open. As he did so the sacking nailed over the window fluttered under a rogue gust of wind and the movement caused him to flinch, dropping the little bag. But somehow his patient's hand had slipped off the bed, and instead of hitting the floor, the tie of the bag snagged on her fingers.

Antil looked down. Her eyes were closed, her expression one of restless sleep. There was no sign she'd even noticed what had happened.

"Good catch," Antil muttered with a puzzled frown, "or should I perhaps say lucky catch?"

He didn't know whether to wince or smile at that thought; luck was a fickle mistress—if the expression could endure after the Lady herself was dead. It would not be long before the bands of penitents began to ask earnest questions about the damage to the window. He had explained it away as a thrown fragment of stone from the explosion that had obliterated Alterr's temple, but sooner or later someone would realise that was peculiar.

"What are you in all this?" he wondered, running his fingers down her arm, feeling how hot her skin was. "If you were there with the Lady, how is it you survived and she did not? A servant cannot be stronger than the God— did she believe you important enough to save at the expense of her own life?"

Antil shivered again. The idea that an immortal would do that was ludicrous, but it was the only answer he'd come up with so far.

"My vow means I must protect the injured, even if the penitents of Death try to take you," he said, resolved to do his duty, "but if it's true the Lady saved you for a reason, you may not need that protection longer than a few days." He took the cloth and trickled a little more water onto her lips. This time they parted eagerly to accept it. "Let us hope whatever did this to you doesn't come looking, for if that happens you'll need more than my vow, I think."

Ilumene looked up at the cloudy sky and tried to discern the position of the sun. It didn't do him much good; the western horizon showed nothing more than an overall glow, but it was a more cheering sight than the east, where an ugly swell of grey crowded the jagged mountain cliffs. His instincts told him that it was not quite midmorning—after a fight, perceived time raced along, in his experience, fuelled by adrenalin and panic.

Without warning a voice spoke into his mind. *"They're coming."*

"Aracnan?" he thought after a moment of confusion. The only being to speak to him like that in the past had been Azaer and that had not happened since the fall of Scree. *"What about the storm on the mountain?"*

"They ignore it. The floods do not come with every storm, only once or twice each season, but I have done what I can to draw more power to the clouds. Kiyer of the Deluge is coming, but not before the penitents; look to your left."

Ilumene did as he was told. For a moment he saw nothing, then a jerking movement caught his eye. On the roof of a building attached to the inside of the wall he saw a small hunched shape, no bigger than a child. It was difficult to make it out clearly for the colours of its body seemed to shift, adopting the lichen-spotted hues of the wall behind.

The creature seemed to feel his gaze upon it and turned its head towards him. The curious shape to its body was suddenly revealed as a dozen sets of tiny wings down the length of its back and arms started flapping. The pattern-less flutter increased in speed until the creature's body was almost completely hidden by a blur, whereupon the flapping stopped abruptly, leaving nothing behind. Ilumene blinked in surprise. It had gone—not flown away but disappeared.

"An Aspect? They called an Aspect to incarnate here and probe our defences?"

"Exactly so," Aracnan replied. *"Your mages are on edge, they reveal themselves by their raised defences. The priests now know how many you have, and they will not fear marching on you."*

"But the deluge will cut off their escape," Ilumene said out loud, a cruel grin appearing on his face. *"Hard luck for them. Go and watch over the master until it is time to act."* He wiped the smirk from his lips and looked over at Major Feilin, who acknowledged him and trotted over.

"Sergeant Kayel?" Feilin was a decent soldier, if lacking somewhat in personal bravery. He walked with a slight limp, Ilumene noted with satisfaction. Feilin might have been in charge of the compound's defence, but Ilumene had made it clear who was top dog two days before. Feilin gave the orders still—once Ilumene decided what they were to be. His approach might not have worked on a nobleman who had arrogance and pride to contend with, but everyone in the Ruby Tower knew Major Feilin had been born to a cook and had lived his whole life in service here. The man had seen enough bullies in his life to know when he had no chance; Ilumene hadn't needed to push matters.

"Major," he said, saluting for the benefit of anyone watching, "everything in place?"

"They are, but I'm far from happy about leaving the compound open to attack—it's a big risk to take."

Ilumene had suggested the gates be left open and a fair number of the men sent out into the city. Kiyer's flood notwithstanding, Ilumene didn't want the people to feel abandoned by their secular rulers. Over the years the city's streets had been built so floodwater could be safely diverted away. He was confident the battle would follow Azaer's script and be short-lived. What was far more important was the perception people in Breakale, Wheel, and Burn would have of this day—in preparation for the day they were forced to choose sides.

"What if they slaughter the garrison?" the major asked.

"They won't," Ilumene said confidently. He looked around at the figures on the wall and congregated in the compound's yard. He'd dressed every suitable servant in uniform and set some to manning the walls while the rest were ordered to wander around looking aimless while the main complement of Ruby Tower Guards were hidden away or disguised as servants, with their weapons well hidden.

"They'll want to see the duchess's body before they do anything else. Go out there and meet them under a flag of truce and have the guards surrender.

The mercenaries they've employed will still be thinking clearly, even if the priests can't, so they will be wary. We keep clear of the gates and don't try to shut them." He pointed towards the largest group of real soldiers. "Move them to the other side of the compound, away from the gates."

"But if we let them all into the compound we'll be outnumbered," Feilin pointed out, still looking unhappy. "Surely that's why we're trying this ruse in the first place?" Like many of his fellow soldiers of Litse blood, he had pale skin and fair hair, which made him look ashen in his deep crimson uniform.

"If you don't move them, it'll be too obvious that we're ready for them—unless you've got a company of white-eyes I don't know about?" Ilumene's sharp tone was enough to provoke a look of slight fear on Feilin's face. He shifted uncomfortably, as though the bruises he still bore had started to ache again.

"No, of course not."

"Then we give them somewhere to retreat to. The gate's a bottleneck—and we might even get lucky with the floodwater."

At the mention of Kiyer's Deluge Feilin glanced nervously at the cliffs looming large behind the Ruby Tower. The thunder had abated, but the clouds above Blackfang were darker than ever.

"I think they'll stay and fight."

"Fine by me. They'll be met on three sides in that case."

"What about the mages? Surely they'll have far more than we do?"

Ilumene nodded; Major Feilin had made a good point—under any normal circumstances. They might not have anyone to rival Mage Peness, but with the assembled mages of every cult in Byora to call on they had the weight of numbers on their side.

"Peness, Jelil, and Bissen won't be able to fight them all, no," he agreed.

"So what is your plan?"

"My plan, sir?" Ilumene said with a wolfish look. "Oh no, not *my* plan, *yours*. I have just taken the liberty of anticipating your orders. The three mages are positioned in one of the eastern rooms in the tower. Most battle-mages need to be able to see their enemy to do anything really nasty."

"So what use are they going to be on the wrong side of the tower?" the major asked, bemused, still trying desperately to understand what his subordinate had in mind.

"They're going to be cowering; far enough away that the priests won't have any reason to suspect a trap." Ilumene turned and pointed at the tower. It was an enormous building, not as tall as the Tower of Semar in Tirah, but far wider. The tower was hexagonal in shape, and built in steps, the lowest being the size of a palace itself, with walls thicker than those of most castles, to support the weight of the tower above. "The Duchess Chamber," he said. "I heard it was changed, years back."

"The last duke remodelled it, what, twenty years ago, perhaps?" Feilin said, still completely mystified.

"He put in all those pillars and a hallway, so the main entrance didn't lead straight in?"

"Yes, but so what?"

"So all that work's not structural," Ilumene said. "We can bring it down—and the rest of the tower will still stand."

"But—" Feilin began before cutting himself off. "Merciful Gods!"

"Hah, they ain't showing much mercy these days, so I reckon we should return the favour," Ilumene said with feeling. "They'll have dozens of priests, all with only weak magic; an Aspect-Guide ain't as good as a mage's daemon. Maybe someone like Mage Peness has the strength and speed to do something about a roof falling in on him, but none of them will."

"And they'll be confident Peness won't oppose them," said Feilin softly.

"Aye, before they even walk through those gates they'll know whether we can match that strength or not. When they realise we can't, they'll relax. Priests ain't got a soldier's instincts; their penitents won't be able to stop them in time."

Natai blinked, suddenly awakening, and looked around. Two anxious faces stared back, the dark-haired Lady Kinna and Jeto, Natai's steward. From the look on their faces she'd been out of it for longer than she'd realised—Jeto could be as fussy as a dowager duchess at times, but Kinna was as ambitious and heartless as any Litse noblewoman.

"Your Grace?" said Lady Kinna cautiously. She'd been the only one of Natai's close circle to come straight to the Ruby Tower when she heard what had happened in Hale. *For all her youth, she's a sharp one, Ganas always said—*

The thought went no further as a spasm ran through her body. Natai felt her hand begin to tremble and had to clasp it tight with the other. *Strange. My body understands my grief when my mind cannot quite accept it.*

She looked down at her hand. One of her rings was missing a stone, and a graze three inches long ran from the knuckle beside it down the back of her hand, tracing the path of the missing gem.

It was a ruby, she recalled, *a ruby spilled with blood—who will find that? One of their mercenaries? Not a priest, their heads are raised too high now. Perhaps a pilgrim, come to pray—No; not after this. The temples will be closed until the ground is hallowed again. While these murderers live, Hale is not sacred.*

She went to the window, unable to bear the sight of the door to her chamber. Catching sight of it out of the corner of her eye was enough to make her hope her husband was about to walk through.

"Kinna, is there—?" Her voice wavered and caught, and she stopped, unable to continue. She hugged her arms around her body, ignoring the pain it provoked, the hot, heavy feeling of a badly bruised shoulder and the sharp throb where skin had been cut.

"There . . . No, your Grace," came the hesitant reply. "Nor of Sir Arite. Major Feilin has said he cannot send anyone out for information, not when we're trying to look as if we are beaten."

Natai didn't speak. That there was a battle coming didn't appear to matter. She was exhausted, her body screaming for sleep, but her mind refused.

Sergeant Kayel seems to thrive on conflict; he looks as alive now as when he was fighting my guards. Do I envy or pity him? she wondered.

Perhaps she would seek Ruhen out and lose herself in those bewitching eyes—No, she could not, for Kayel had carried her as if she were dead, up to her rooms high in the tower, careful to let others see the blood leak from her head and drip onto the stairs.

So much blood from such a small wound. A little goes a long way, isn't that what Mother was so fond of saying? A woman who'd been denied little in her life; who'd never known loss . . .

The window afforded an unparalleled view of Byora. With its back turned on the oppressive bulk of Blackfang's cliffs, the Ruby Tower looked down on the rest of the Land. Before it was spread a carpet of humanity and industry, run through by the thick veins that might soon be rushing with murky, murderous floodwaters. Rain was falling heavily on the city; Natai could not see much of Byora through the slanted slashes of water.

"Your Grace, please let me fetch you a seat," Lady Kinna urged. "You're hurt and in shock; your wounds need tending."

Natai waved the woman's protests away. The sting from her dozen small hurts wrapped her better than any bandage could. The pain took her away from the horrors of the day. Her torn and damp clothes meant nothing; changing them would change nothing.

The view had once thrilled her, as a little girl she'd been content to spend hour after hour staring out of the window at the city beyond. Now it merely echoed the numb emptiness in her stomach. What she saw was distant and blurred, not quite real.

Again her thoughts turned to Ruhen and the child's calming effect, but then she remembered Kinna, who was continually spoiling Natai's little prince, trying to steal his affections away. During every council meeting held in the Ruby Tower, at every formal court conducted in the Duchess's Chamber, the woman would find some excuse to hold Ruhen and fuss over him, running her fingers through his soft, sooty-brown hair, delighting in his every sound.

"I still cannot believe all of this," Lady Kinna said suddenly, "that the clerics would even attempt this. It beggars belief."

Natai let the woman chatter on; it was preferable to lonely silence. Gripping her hand tight enough to turn her knuckles white, Natai looked down at the open gate where she could make out the solitary figure of Major Feilin, loitering uneasily.

"They cannot believe the city will stand for it; the duke was a beloved and humble man," she went on. "The arrogance of the clerics has grown out of all proportion."

"They do not think," Natai said dully. "They have lost all reason. The temples are places of madness now; we must close them until sense returns. We will quarantine them so the people are not infected by this evil."

"A quarantine?" Lady Kinna asked. "Yes, of course, I will see it is done. The infection must be purged. The people will be glad; they are unsettled by the fury and hatred being preached."

"Better they look to Ruhen than seek answers in the temples," Natai said with sudden vehemence. "In his eyes you will find peace, in the temples there is only madness." She stopped suddenly as she saw sudden activity in the street below.

"Look, here they come."

A column of dark shapes, men huddled against the rain, trotted with surprising speed towards the main gate. A number split off and went in different directions, forming up in neat lines across the alleys and avenues that adjoined the main street.

Lady Kinna gave a tiny gasp, then straightened her shoulders. She would be strong. The duchess focused on the gate. Yes, the penitents had reached it and knocked Major Feilin down. They hadn't waited but streamed past and over him. She couldn't tell whether he lived or not; all she could do was hope that in their haste the flood of men surging into the courtyard had left him alive. Her servants, wearing the uniform of Ruby Tower Guardsmen, were gathered in a sullen, frightened clump on the right. The penitents did not hesitate but headed straight for the pretend soldiers, knocking many down and stripping their weapons with brutal efficiency. She could imagine the angry shouts and commands. They would be forced to their knees and one or two killed as an example perhaps . . .

Natai found herself holding her breath, waiting for Sergeant Kayel to appear. The mercenaries continued to stream into the courtyard, scores of men, a hundred, two hundred, all desperate to be off the rain-soaked street for fear of Ushull's savage daughter, Kiyer of the Deluge. Finally knots of robed priests followed. Though she strained to see, the tower was too high for her to make out any of the faces.

"How many of them do I know?" she murmured softly, leaning forward. "How many have laid blessings on my head?"

"Your Grace, don't stand so close to the window," Lady Kinna said with alarm. "They must not be able to recognise you."

"It is too far, they will see nothing."

"What if they use magic?"

"They don't have the strength. Peness would be able to do so, but there is not one cleric in Byora who approaches his skill."

As the soldiers continued to enter, a distant voice in Natai's head told her she should be afraid, that there were so many her guards would not be able to hold them, but the emotion would not come.

"Look," Lady Kinna said, pointing, "Materse Avenue!"

Natai followed the direction of Kinna's finger and saw the first rush of water down one of the main avenues, around the left-hand side of the compound. The soldiers still on the street abandoned all pretence of discipline and ran sloshing away from the water. One tripped and had to struggle up on his own as none of his comrades stopped to help him. In less than a minute, Natai knew, the flood would crash down the streets on either side of her compound, channelled down the four long streets of Eight Towers that had been designed to carry away the worst of the floods. Kiyer would still claim victims, she always did, but the losses would be fewer now the city had been designed to allow her passage.

Somewhere down below the message was passed to the soldiers, and the rest piled inside the compound wall. They left a respectful gap around the priests who were standing in the centre of the compound, facing the grand entrance to the tower. For a moment she couldn't see what they were looking at, until a figure lurched out towards them. Sergeant Kayel was walking none too steadily. He carried something in his hand. A club? No, a clay bottle.

Natai heard Lady Kinna gasp. *He really has no fear of these priests*, she realised. *Neither fear—nor respect.*

Kayel took a moment to return the stares he received, then lurched around and headed back inside. She knew they would follow him, and as he disappeared from view again, Natai turned for the door, throat dry and heart pounding. She ignored the urgent voice of Lady Kinna behind her. She could picture the ceiling collapsing down on their heads, snapping their withered bones like twigs, cutting off their cries like lambs in the slaughterhouse. The memory of Ganas falling, slowly, so slowly, made her stumble, but she caught herself in time and fought her way forward—down the corridor and the series of short staircases that would take her to the gallery where she could look down upon her vacant throne.

She could hear the tramp of boots starting on the stairs further down, but she went on regardless. The floors in between were the largest, with dozens of rooms each; they wouldn't reach her before the roof fell in and they raced back to find their leaders dead. With Lady Kinna following close behind, the Duchess of Byora ran through the deserted corridors to Erwillen's Landing, named by one of her ancestors out of misplaced piety for the shrine to the High Hunter, an Aspect of Vellern, he had built there—he stationed archers in it to pick off supposed assassins.

The landing, painted with garish murals, was positioned immediately above the main entrance to the Ruby Tower. Tall windows looked over the entrance and down into the Duchess Chamber. The hanging shrine was suspended from the ceiling: a wrought-iron frame from which dangled a mass of feathers, brightly coloured ribbons, and small icons bearing Erwillen's image.

As she passed, the items trembled and she stopped to look at them. The colours were faded and weak. Natai touched the nearest feather lightly and it crumbled under her finger. She stared at the ashlike remains that fell into her palm for a moment before grabbing one of the painted wooden icons and crushing it in one hand as easily as if it were paper.

"You're dead. This shrine is drained and empty. This is only the first of many in Byora," Natai promised.

Looking down into the Duchess Chamber, all she saw was her vacant throne. The fixed stone seat, large enough for a child to sit comfortably beside Byora's ruler, was set on a pedestal. There was a tall wooden frame behind, painted with the city's livery. The scene was as still as a painting—until Sergeant Kayel staggered into sight and began to follow a meandering path towards a door behind the throne. Two penitents in black-painted mail followed briskly behind. They caught him with ease, one dodging a drunkenly swung bottle as the other cracked a club over Kayel's head. The big soldier dropped to one knee with a grunt.

The Duchess of Byora felt her breath catch as the echo of footsteps came from somewhere below her. She could picture men hanging back, nervously watching the soldiers deal with Kayel before entering. The copper tang of blood appeared in her mouth and she realised she'd bitten her lip in anticipation, but before she could wipe it away a great creak rang out and the floor beneath her feet shuddered. Natai grabbed the windowsill to steady herself as the groan and crack of tortured brickwork intensified. She chanced another look down at the chamber. The two penitents were staring back in horror; even Kayel seemed momentarily frozen as the antechamber shuddered violently.

Natai froze. Kayel and the soldiers were not the only people in the chamber. She felt a scream bubble up in her throat, but fear drove the air from her lungs as a small figure toddled out from behind the throne, heading towards Kayel as something below her fell and shattered on the tiled antechamber floor. It was followed in the next moment by an almighty crash that reverberated through her body as the antechamber itself collapsed.

The violence of the shockwave drove Natai to her knees. A cloud of dust billowed out into the ducal chamber as she hauled herself forward to look out of the window again and through it she glimpsed Kayel lunging at one of the penitents. He kicked the back of the man's legs and punched him in the throat as he fell, but the second was quick and lashed out with his club, sending Kayel sprawling. Natai went white as Ruhen tottered in between them, but the penitent didn't follow up his attack.

Natai couldn't see the enigmatic smile on the child's face, but with arms held out wide for balance, Ruhen advanced towards the penitent with unsteady steps, perfectly unafraid. Natai couldn't make out the man's expression, but she felt the sudden warmth of Ruhen's beatific smile. He didn't move, not even when Sergeant Kayel pulled himself to his feet and threw his sword like a throwing knife. The tip caught the penitent in the neck and felled him.

Before the sergeant could retrieve his weapon, an invisible hand seemed to slap him backwards. Natai could just make out the astonishment on Kayel's face as a second blow threw him several yards back. Ruhen turned to follow his protector as two figures staggered into view from the ruin of the antechamber, shaking the dust from their robes and advancing unsteadily towards the child.

Fear lent strength to Natai's limbs and restored her voice. With a shriek the duchess ran for the stair, kicking off her slippers but still barely keeping from breaking her neck as she descended. When she reached the room she found the two priests standing over Ruhen. The little boy was staring up at them, completely unafraid.

One of the men saw her and took a step backwards, looking shocked. She recognised the young man, even with his face twisted in hate—he was normally to be found standing quietly in the background at the Temple of Ushull. He raised his hand and she heard a strange noise, as if something was sucking air in. A coiling stream of energy began to form around the mage.

Natai, oblivious to the danger to herself, raced towards them and threw herself in front of the child, shrieking, "You will not hurt him!"

"Filthy heretics," spat the other priest, a fat-cheeked man with white hair dressed in the distinctive scarlet robes of Karkarn. He was cradling his right arm but she could see sparks of red light dancing over his skin; he was still dangerous.

"You will all die for this crime," he said.

"*No*," said a quiet voice in her mind. She shivered and looked at the priests. She saw in their faces that they had felt it too. She turned, but Kayel was still lying on the ground.

She felt as if she were frozen to the spot, unable to move any part of her body apart from her head—and it looked like the priests were similarly stricken. Only Ruhen appeared unaffected—and he was the only one not looking around for whoever had spoken.

With a calm smile on his face and a fistful of Natai's dress bunched in his plump little hand to support himself, the little boy slowly made his way around her. He looked up at the priest of Karkarn, whose face was illuminated by the weird light of magic as he muttered an incantation. He faltered for a moment, then the hatred reasserted itself and he drew in deeply, the light intensifying.

Natai tried to reach out to Ruhen, but her limbs would not respond and all she could do was watch as the child reached out a hand and waggled his stubby little fingers towards the priest—but his little wave seemed to strike the priest like a blow and the trails of magical lights vanished. He gave a strangled squawk of shock and dropped to his knees, clutching his heart, before collapsing onto the tiled floor.

The priest of Ushull's astonished expression turned just as swiftly into a paroxysm of pain. He fell just as quickly, one hand protectively around his throat, and twitched and shook on the ground, his mouth stretched wide in a silent scream.

Ruhen was silent as he watched the two men die, though Natai thought she could hear voices whispering all around them. She flinched when the little boy turned to face her, but instead of the horror she had been expecting, Ruhen's face was just the same as ever. His cheeks dimpled suddenly as he gave her a big beaming grin and spread his arms wide, demanding to be carried.

The duchess swept him up in her arms and turned in a circle, glaring at the faces watching them until they all fled, leaving her alone with the boy in her arms and the sergeant, now groggily lifting himself up off the ground and slurring his way through a stream of invective. Natai didn't wait to thank him but, holding Ruhen tight in her arms and breathing in the sweet scent of his hair, she headed back up the stairs, not stopping until she was at the top of the Ruby Tower and the whispers were left far behind.

Venn felt his body jerk as a swirl of shadow raced past his eyes. His dry, cracked lips had stuck together, so his waking breath was more of a weak, tuneless whistle, though it was enough to attract the attention of the tall priestess sitting a few yards away. When she saw he was awake she picked up a bowl of soup that had been cooling nearby and walked over to him.

Her face had lost none of the strength he'd first noticed, before she had established herself as his nursemaid. She was a handsome woman, and her looks had not diminished under age's onslaught. She had not yet gone so far as to cast aside the half-mask set with obsidian shards, but he could sense she was close. She saw purpose in him, in every word he spoke. She would be Azaer's fiercest follower, the child's most pitiless defender.

"Even mountains fail in the course of time. Even glaciers melt away to nothing. A gradual decline is irresistible in all things."

He had abandoned the forms of instruction used by the Harlequins, for they were no longer necessary. He spoke little these days, constantly drained by the effort of keeping two hearts beating, two minds working. Jackdaw was entirely dependent on him to stay alive so Venn could not afford to waste his strength on idle talk.

The priestess knew well how hard speaking had become for him. She crouched at his side, eyes bright as she realised she would be the one to pass on this latest pronouncement. The others would have to sit at her feet and wait for her to speak, for the narcotic tingle of truth rushing through their minds.

"Even the greatest see their time end. To be a parent is to one day be eclipsed, to be shown to be in weakness, in error."

Venn heard her breath catch, a question bitten off before it could be spoken. She was close enough that he could smell the musky tang of her sweat and sour breath, even over the incense-laden air. She had been waiting for him to wake for half a day, without drinking or eating. He could smell her eagerness.

"Who then," he said slowly, his own throat dry and raw, "could chastise the Gods themselves for their failings? Where is that perfect individual, who could raise a hand and censure the very Gods who created him? When our Gods fail us, to whom must we pray for intercession in this life of woe?"

CHAPTER 15

GRISAT LOOKED AROUND AT THE MEN IN THE ROOM, who were all nervously shifting in their seats. Each one was as fearful as he. They'd ditched their penitent robes and were back in civilian garb, with mail, jerkins, and weapons wrapped in bundles so that they wouldn't look like mercenaries, let alone soldiers employed by the cult of Ushull. Grisat hadn't yet heard of any repercussions, but he knew it was coming and he had no intention of staying around to catch any of it.

He'd discussed the situation with Bolla, who had agreed with him. All the priests' leaders had died at the Ruby Tower and there was no one left of any consequence. It was time to collect the cash and walk away. Some would stay, but those he'd talked to—those he'd be able to trust now—had been of similar mind. They'd just been waiting for someone to give them a kick in the right direction.

Grisat waved away a moth, causing half the room to jump. "Piss and daemons," he growled, "yer jumpin' like frightened rabbits." He didn't tell them their reactions had made his heart leap into his throat. Fortunately, they were all so distracted, none had noticed.

"We're jus' on edge, man, tha's all. Why're you flappin' yer arms around anyway?" snapped Astin, the tall Litse with the knife scar across his nose.

Grisat pointedly ignored the man. *Damn Litse, can't keep their sodding mouths shut. Shame he's more use than the rest; a Litse won't take order from the likes of me for too long.*

He drained the pitcher of beer he'd been nursing, burped, and pushed himself upright. "Right, goin' for a piss. You lot try not t'shit yourselves when I come back."

He clapped a hand on Bolla's shoulder as he pushed past. Without his leather jerkin on, Bolla felt all bones under Grisat's palm. The lanky mercenary nodded in response and shoved his wad of numbroot to the other side of his mouth.

Grisat went out into the short dark corridor and checked left and right.

There was no one there—not surprising, since the group had taken the whole attic room of the inn. Childishly he thumped a fist against the wall as he headed for the stair, eliciting a yelp from within, and headed down to the backyard, where the stinking outhouse was located.

It was already dark outside, and cold. It hadn't felt like the sun had had much effect that day—until nightfall, when you felt the temperature plummet. Grisat shivered and breathed onto his hands, then clapped them together, trying to keep them warm. He stepped into the pitch black outhouse and edged his foot forward until he reached the gutter.

His breeches unbuttoned, Grisat pulled out his cock and sighed with relief as the hot stream began to splatter unseen over the floor around the gutter. Two seconds later, he felt the prickle of a knife tip in the back of his neck.

The stream of urine stopped almost immediately as Grisat froze. He'd seen and heard no one, so that meant someone had been waiting for him in there. Not one of his group, that was for sure.

"Aren't you glad I waited?" said a deep voice in his ear. The accent was like none he'd ever heard, overly precise, like a foreigner, and a nobleman at that. "If I'd put my knife there before you started, the opposite would have happened."

Grisat managed a gurgle in reply. This was someone completely comfortable with a weapon: that dagger hadn't moved a fraction as the man had leaned in to speak to him. He felt fingers grabbing a lock of his hair and decided not to move; he'd drunk too much to be fast enough to reach his own dagger and the unseen stranger didn't appear to be in any great rush to kill him. The dagger point withdrew for a moment—presumably for the stranger to cut off the hair—and then returned. Grisat kept as still as he could all the while.

"At least you've got the brains not to try it," the voice continued conversationally. "Who wants to take their last breath facedown in an outhouse?"

Grisat grunted. He realised the dagger had nicked him and resisted the urge to nod as well.

"Now, if your eyes aren't open at the moment open them now. Don't turn round."

Grisat blinked. At first all he could see was the darkness, which gave way to a green glow which illuminated the interior of the outhouse enough for him to be able to make out the gutter running down the centre of the room and the two thin pillars holding up the poor excuse for a roof. He looked down. His cock had withered to half the size of his thumb. Despite the cold night air he felt a warm flush of embarrassment as he waited for more instructions.

"See the light? That tells you I'm a mage, so you will know I haven't taken a lock of your hair to keep as a memento."

Grisat stiffened and felt the dagger dig a little further into his skin.

"I see you grasp the situation; good. Now, I know who you are and I know who your employer is. What I want you to do is return to the temple and act the good penitent again."

"You were sent after us?" Grisat croaked in disbelief.

"Not quite, but I want you back there all the same. The clerics have been broken, but there's still some life left in the cults, and you are going to be the one to organise unrest in the city—at my direction, of course. I intend there to be a secret war in Byora, a guerrilla resistance to Natai Escral's inevitable measures against the cults."

"Father Hiren is in charge and he hates me," Grisat began. "I don't know that he'll even take us back."

"If he doesn't, go to the Temple of Karkarn—you will need to be convincing, but at least the warrior-priests will be useful for more than just political backing."

"Why me?"

He heard a soft laugh. "One monkey is as good as any other. I choose the one who pisses highest." The dagger pushed a little deeper and Grisat gave a small yelp. "I will be keeping track of your progress—you have one week, or I shall prove just how adept a mage I am. You'll find a little hair goes a long way."

Without warning the pressure on the back of his neck was lifted and the faint green light winked out. Grisat listened to the rapid, insistent thump within his own chest for a dozen heartbeats before he turned around. He wasn't surprised to discover the outhouse empty and the yard beyond it as silent as the grave.

"Shit," he muttered as he took a step back away from the shadows and into the gutter.

"Opening at dusk, Harys? Are you practising for something?"

The broad-hipped woman gave a gasp of shock and whirled around in a flurry of green silk. Kohl outlined her pale blue eyes and her blonde hair was piled elaborately on top of her head. She stood in the centre of a room too poorly lit to betray the threadbare state of the sofas to normal eyes. A pair of teenage whores hovered at her side.

One of the girls gave a small cry of surprise when the shadows fell away to reveal two other figures in the room. At a look from Harys the whores both fled past the heavy curtain that served as a door, and Zhia caught a glimpse of the hallway, which was considerably less ornate—and less garish—than this room. She could see why the lighting was so bad in here, where the house's patrons were plied with drink whilst enjoying the talents of the singers Harys employed; with their clothes on, people had enough time to notice their surroundings.

"Mistress, I apologise—you startled me. I had not known you were even in the city," Harys gabbled as she sank into a deep curtsey and looked up at the newcomers as though squinting at the sun. "My Lord."

"We did not want to announce our presence to the city," Zhia replied. She didn't bother to add that they'd been listening to Harys's conversations for the last hour, gauging not just the state of the brothel business, but also ensuring there were no other loyalties binding the woman.

"Shall I have wine brought to the high room for you?" Harys asked.

"And food."

Harys hesitated, then started, "I have a new girl here—"

"Oh don't be such a fool, woman," Zhia snapped impatiently, "*actual* food; a meal to go with our wine. I intend to talk over supper. Now do get up and see to it, if you would."

"Of course, Mistress," Harys said hurriedly, retreating towards the doorway. She stopped and turned back. "Ah, Mistress—will you be wanting Diril there too?"

"Diril Halfmast? Gods, no; she'll put me off my supper. Send her up half an hour after the food."

Harys curtseyed again and fled.

"Mistress?" Koezh said softly from the darkness. "She isn't a White Circle agent, is she?"

"No, just devoted to me," Zhia assured him.

"And Diril Halfmast?"

Zhia gave a small shudder. "Another agent of mine here, and the Land's least successful whore—please don't remind me when we're eating."

Koezh gave a soft laugh and gestured for Zhia to lead the way. "Isn't upsetting sisters the obligation of elder brothers?"

Zhia didn't answer as she led him into the large foyer. Koezh, noticing her tugging at the hem of her cloak, did the same, mouthing the charm to turn away idle eyes. There was an ornate bar on one wall, opposite a door, and in the centre of the room an assortment of men, clerks, and young merchants in the main, sat drinking at various small tables. There were no girls mingling here; this was more tavern than brothel waiting room.

Stairs on the left of the room clearly led up to the bedrooms. A big, bald man in dark silks sat at the table nearest to it, positioned so he could see the whole room. He was fat, but not so obese as to look slow or in much need of the cudgel balanced against his chair. The wide grin on his round pink face put Koezh in mind of a carved pumpkin head.

Zhia led the way through a recessed open doorway by the bar to another, smaller staircase. They climbed two flights to a low room at the top of the building, where they found Harys busy shuttering the wide windows that occupied much of three of the walls.

"I'm sorry about the light," she said, seeing them enter. "I usually eat up here myself so I can watch the sunset."

"It won't bother us," Zhia replied, before adding with a smile, "enjoy your sunsets while you still can."

Koezh noted the pleasure that blossomed on Harys's face. *Ah, one of those.* "You always did love to be worshipped," he said to his sister in their native tongue.

A look of anxiety crossed Harys's face, but it vanished when Zhia responded as though he'd told her a joke.

"Koezh, you were always too impatient with people, even as a boy. That I have little sympathy with her wish to share our curse does not mean it cannot be useful."

"And having brothel owners in your pocket helps us how, exactly?"

"She's a fine contact, and the best source of information in this city," Zhia said, removing her cloak and settling herself in a chair with exaggerated elegance. Underneath she wore plain travelling clothes similar to her brother's, with a long skirt covering her breeches to conform to local customs. "Litse men do love their whores," she added, "and you know how indiscreet they are."

He joined her at the table, a long thin piece of mahogany so dark it was almost black.

"What was it Valije Nostil called you when she found out you were Aryn Bwr's lover? Whore of the Dawn? You've not always been too discreet yourself."

Zhia's face became stony. "I remember my brothers laughing because he was cheating on a queen with second sight. I thought I heard her laughing from beyond the grave when we faced the judgment of the Gods." She sniffed and made a dismissive gesture. "Whore of the Dawn indeed."

She turned to Harys, indicating the woman should join them. "Tell me, what is the state of the city? What has changed since I was last here?"

Harys bobbed her head and said, "Where would you like me to start, Mistress—the fall of the White Circle?"

Zhia gave a nod. "Be brief."

"People are calling it the civilised coup, but that makes it sound more dramatic than it really was," she said. "When we got news of the fall of Scree, it was clear that the White Circle no longer existed, not in any real sense. The ruling sisters fled to Tor Salan, so I heard. The rest of them just took off their shawls and walked away from their public positions. Some people panicked when they saw a division of Knights of the Temples waiting on the border, but the Duchess of Byora intervened."

"She persuaded the others easily?" Koezh interjected.

"I doubt it was easy, but Sourl and Celao aren't fools; they've both been hearing as much from the south as Natai Escral has. Everyone knows about the Menin conquest—and what's the old saying? 'Where war is found, its brothers soon shall follow'?"

"The saying refers to pestilence and famine," Zhia said pedantically, "but you've reached the correct conclusion all the same. Civil war is the last thing the Circle City needs. Its strength comes from trade, and I'm sure Tor Salan will be recruiting erstwhile members of the Chetse armies. Once the balance of power is upset, everything is up for grabs."

"Tor Salan won't be attacking anyone," Harys piped up. "Word arrived in the city a week or so ago—the Menin overran their defences in a day."

"What?" Zhia snapped, her sapphire eyes flashing in the darkness. "You didn't think to mention that first?"

"Yet more people underestimate Lord Styrax," Koezh said softly, one hand rubbing his shoulder, the site of the fatal wound the Menin lord had given him. "At least I was ahead of the pack there," he added.

"I haven't been able to work out what happened exactly," Harys said quickly. "Some say the mercenaries defending the city opened the gates to him. The other rumour is that Lord Styrax rode up to the Giants' Hands alone and created a storm that knocked them all down like stalks of wheat."

Zhia nodded gravely. "It sounds like an object lesson to the rest of us, whatever the truth might be. He identified their strength and attacked it. The man's arrogance is matched only by his ability." She leaned forward, elbows on the table, and stared fixedly at Harys. "This is not a trick question, although it might be a strange one, but you will indulge me."

"Of course, Mistress," the brothel madam said quickly, shrinking back in her seat. She looked terrified.

"Have you heard any stories recently, from whatever source, about a child?"

Koezh could hear the thump of her heartbeat quicken as she opened her mouth to reply. "A child? I don't really—" She stopped, and frowned. "The only thing I can think of is the duchess's new ward."

"She is noted for taking in orphans, no?" Zhia said, trying to encourage Harys.

"She is. I haven't paid much attention, I'm afraid, for it's talk among the young maids and my girls rather than the men who come in here. It's foolishness, for the main part; something about his cries inspiring a coward to take on the duchess's entire guard—and the Gods themselves striking down two priests during the clerics' revolt when they tried to hurt the child."

Koezh looked at his sister. "You were right."

"It was a reasonable guess," Zhia replied, looking pleased. "What we saw in Scree was the shadow at the heart of events, letting chaos unfold around it. Whatever is to come next, it will likely be centred on the Circle City or Tor Salan."

She gave an elegant shrug and flicked an errant curl of black hair away from her face. "We came here first because it was closer, not the duchess's habit of adopting strays."

"Mistress, are you saying what happened in Scree could happen here next?" Harys asked with mounting alarm.

"I doubt it," Zhia replied carelessly. She began to tap her perfectly manicured nails on the table surface, as if following a tune in her head.

Koezh waited. His sister had always tried to test his patience; her way was one of teasing people to exasperation. He pitied the poor foolish boys, like that soldier from Narkang, Doranei. Even if her affection for him was true, it would not stop the immortal from playing games with him.

And love only goes so far, Koezh thought as he pictured Doranei's face. The young man was an exceptional soldier; he'd have to be to hold the position he did, but ever since Scree, Koezh couldn't think of him as anything other than a lost puppy trailing after Zhia. *Don't think love will protect you, my boy. If this shadow can give us what we want, Zhia will not even hesitate.*

"A con artist does not perform the same trick to a crowd twice," Zhia pronounced at last. "Misdirection is the name of the game here; the shadow may be so weak either of us could swat it like a fly."

"So if the trick is repeated, King Emin would know exactly where to stick in the knife," Koezh finished for her. "So what then is the new trick? This child?"

"Presumably—we just need to work out what role it has to play. Our clues to the riddle will be in the stories folk are telling: the inspired coward, the priests struck down."

"Both stories a Harlequin might tell," Koezh added pointedly, "but I'll bet this is no quick con, not after what we saw in the north. It's too subtle, and slow."

Harys gave a hesitant cough to interrupt them. "I've remembered something else. One of the servant girls said she'd seen a leper at the gates of the Ruby Tower. The guards had driven him off, but he kept coming back every day, even though he just got driven away again. He kept saying something about begging for intercession with the Gods."

Zhia raised an eyebrow. "Accelerating the loss of faith? It cannot turn everyone against the Gods as it did in Scree, so instead it provides an alternative?"

"And then do what?" Koezh argued, "kill the child to leave them bereft of a figure of worship? That won't happen quickly, and while the Gods can be notoriously slow to react, I doubt their servants will be tardy in cutting off such a threat at the source."

"It makes a martyr of the child; that's a powerful figure when used properly." Zhia sounded far from convinced of her argument, but after watching Scree collapse in flames she had resolved she would not be outthought by anyone again.

"A martyrdom that could have all four quarters of this city-state behind it and still come to nothing. The Circle City is an important trade centre, nothing more. It isn't a power here, and it would take a decade of being led by a genius before that would substantially change. If the child had been adopted by King Emin or Knight-Cardinal Certinse, then you might have me convinced, but here there is nothing to win down that road."

Zhia nodded. "Let us hope we have time to find out what we need to know before the time comes for us to choose our side. Kastan Styrax will head this way soon, I'm certain of it." She turned back to the woman and, switching back into the local dialect, asked, "Harys, tell me how I get close to the duchess."

The woman shook her head. "I can't help you there, Mistress. I've no influence there, not at those levels."

"Who does?"

"Very few since the duke was killed. The duchess hasn't left Eight Towers this last week; some clerics have started fighting back against her measures to control them. They say warrior-priests of Karkarn have ambushed patrols all over the city for the last two weeks, and a government minister, Garan Dast, he was murdered by a Mystic of Karkarn at the Mule Gate. Even when the penitents fail, the guards are killing indiscriminately and arresting people all over the place. They're winning no friends—there have been riots, and they're getting worse."

"Who has her ear? Is it still that mincing fool Leyen?"

"No, he died in the Prayerday assassination. Perhaps Lady Kinna?"

"Lady Kinna?" Zhia repeated. "I don't recognise the name. How do I get to her?"

"I don't know, Mistress. I know nothing of the woman, other than she's apparently giving the orders on the duchess's council. They say she's pushing the others to pass an order to close the Temple of Death."

"She intends to bar the gates of Death?" Zhia said with an appreciative laugh. "I like her already. Can you get someone in her household to provide us with a lock of her hair?"

Harys frowned for a moment, then smiled a little. "Yes, I would have thought so."

"Why not just drop in and see this child yourself?" Koezh asked.

"Little steps, dear brother, always little steps when you're negotiating. We don't want to frighten the poor mite, do we?" Zhia said. Her smile showed her teeth.

CHAPTER 16

DORANEI LEANED NEARER THE LITTLE FIRE that was struggling fitfully against the breeze. The chill had begun to bite in the last half hour and he realised he was shivering even while patting out the occasional spark that hopped onto his clothes. Caution still ruled, even though they were a mile or two inside the Narkang border, hence the small fire. He risked a couple more branches, then checked around to see if they had company yet.

"Cheer up; at least it's not raining," said someone from the darkness.

Beyn's voice was unmistakable and Doranei kept on with his task of chopping up firewood as his comrade walked into view. The tall blond man hobbled his horse near Doranei's before joining him and squatting down to warm his hands. He didn't even glance at the dark shapes that had followed him but were lingering outside the circle of light. Doranei ignored them too. He knew why they were hanging back.

He grimaced. *Thank the Gods for Beyn's arrogance.*

He slipped on a glove and gingerly retrieved a lidded clay pot from the edge of the fire pit. Opening it up, he sniffed at the contents. *Good enough*, he decided; *if the rest of them want some they can damn well ask.* There was a larger pot hanging over the fire, barely bubbling yet—tomorrow night's meal, courtesy of Sebe's skill with a slingshot.

Doranei could feel Beyn's eyes on him as he bent over the pot he'd secured between his outstretched legs. The warmth of the pot itself and the first few cautious bites improved his mood to no end, but even the smile on his face didn't draw the watchers closer until Sebe trotted in from his sentry shift and squatted at Doranei's side. The wiry man pushed back his hood to reveal a lopsided grin at the prospect of hot food.

"What're you lot waiting for?" Sebe called as he retrieved a similar pot. "Want a written invitation?" He elbowed Doranei. "All the more for us, then."

Sebe's jocular familiarity seemed to decide it and five people emerged to join them around the fire. Three were members of the Brotherhood, which annoyed Doranei even more. How could his own comrades be wary around him? Why was it so hard for them to get a handle on the strange relationship he had with Zhia Vukotic?

Mind you, I've no bloody idea what's going on there myself. But they should have worked out by now that nothing's really changed. I thought we were supposed to be able to adapt to anything.

Tremal was the oldest of the three. The wiry little man had proved himself a useful addition to the Brotherhood over the last few years. He was, most obviously of all the Brotherhood, an Ascetite, and the life of a thief had honed that latent magical potential into a skill that couldn't be taught—but his catlike reactions and thieving instincts had made him permanently wary, so perhaps his reticence was just normal. Janna, Sebe's lover, always said Tremal was a few meals short of being handsome, but she'd never managed to feed the man up enough to make him worth the effort, or so she maintained.

The other two Brothers, Firrin and Horle, were both young enough to make Doranei wonder if he was getting old. They were dressed in identical brigandines. *Have to have a word about that, it's looking too much like a uniform,* he thought.

He looked at the woman with them, Hirta, who stared straight back at him. *As prickly as a hedgehog, that one—although she'll have to be if she does end up staying and joining the Brotherhood.*

Hirta was even smaller than Tremal, but she looked like she had Chetse blood in her, for she was powerful with it. She wasn't quite twenty summers, but she was already older than most when they joined up—the commander wouldn't send a woman out with them until he was sure she could cope. Most men weren't tough enough, so it was rare a woman was even put up for membership.

"Get yourselves some food," Doranei growled at last. "We'll be leaving at dawn."

"Where to?" Beyn asked.

"You're taking him to Sautin first, then Mustet," Doranei said with a nod towards the fifth member of Beyn's troupe. Eyl Parim flinched at the movement and kept his face low. The demagogue was doubtless hating life out on the open road; winter was never fun, and the Brotherhood travelled harder than most, no matter what the conditions.

Parim was something Doranei couldn't classify, somewhere between an Ascetite and a minor mage. He could use his voice to be preternaturally persuasive, and as a result, he was more used to enjoying the hospitality of rich benefactors than travelling with a band of rough-living men. Beyn had tracked him down two years ago and reminded the man of past infractions; they had been waiting since then for a real challenge for Perim's rare skills.

Never mind how little you enjoy Sautin and its enthusiastic approach to crowd control, I'd trade in a heartbeat, Doranei though sourly. His own mission was to start looking for Zhia Vukotic in the Circle City, which was presumably her nearest bolt-hole to Scree.

"Keep it quiet and keep it subtle," Doranei continued. "Sautin is the priority, so get there and start stirring up ill feeling against the Menin—and any appeasers. Once established, Beyn, you take Hirta to Mustet to lay the ground there. Once Beyn's gone on, Horle, you're calling the shots in Sautin, understand?"

"Yes, sir."

Doranei's face darkened. "Cut that out," he snapped, "we're not bloody soldiers. You answer to one man alone, remember?"

"Right, yes, sorry." Horle managed not to flush at his mistake but his embarrassment was plain to see and Sebe chuckled merrily. Doranei glowered at his Brother, but that was ignored. Sebe too had been cautious around Doranei for a bit, but now he'd taken on the role of ensuring his best friend looked like any other Brother. Doranei might be first among equals now, but he wasn't going to get the respect Ilumene had been granted—something he was profoundly grateful for.

"And you—until you stop looking like a kitten you shouldn't be laughing at anyone," Doranei said, earning himself an idle cuff around the head. Sebe'd shaved his long black hair off the previous summer and it had only just started growing back.

"Beyn, take this with you—and only to be used when absolutely necessary." He handed over a small wrapped object.

Beyn frowned at it for a moment before taking it. He disliked surprises. Inside the leather wrapping he found a large hooked claw.

Doranei felt a flicker of pleasure at the confusion on his supercilious comrade's face. "Something Endine prepared for us," he said by way of explanation.

Tomal Endine was one of King Emin's most trusted mages; while his magic wasn't particularly powerful, his knowledge and skill had few rivals in the whole of Narkang and the Three Cities.

"Is that supposed to fill me with confidence?" Beyn muttered, turning the claw over to see the sigils that had been scratched into its surface and filled with silver, the substance best suited for magic. "Are these the wyvern's claws?"

Doranei nodded. "One for you, one for me. If you're desperate to send me a message, trace it out on your arm—or any piece of bare flesh. As long as I'm carrying the other claw it'll scratch out the message on my skin."

"Sounds painful," Beyn said before a dark grin crept across his face.

"Don't even think about that," Doranei warned. The same thought had crossed his mind too. "Anything that's not urgent, you'll be getting a nice long reply, I promise."

Sebe sniffed disapprovingly. "Sounds dangerous. What if this ends up in the wrong hands—Ilumene's, for example? If tracing over the skin is enough to scratch, what happens if he pushes it into the flesh? How far would he need to go before he hits your artery? Remember the state of his hands? Bastard wouldn't even hesitate."

"It won't work like that," Doranei said, raising a hand to stop Sebe. "The claws came from our wager in Scree; the only people who can use them are those who were part of that wager. It's how Endine managed to bind the spell, so he says."

"The three of us and Coran, then?"

"That's the lot. Coran's got the remaining claw, messages go to both."

"Will we be hearing from him tonight?" Beyn asked, suddenly grave.

Doranei grimaced and felt an unexpected urge for a strong drink. He thought for a moment. Morghien had visited their agent in Tor Milist a few weeks back, and been summoned to Narkang with all haste.

"Probably not. If he's lucky he'll be there by now, but the king's too cautious; he'll wait until tomorrow evening at the earliest. I'd guess there's some preparation required and this isn't something you want to screw up."

Beyn and Sebe looked at each other; the others just looked puzzled. The king had many secrets, and not even the men of the Brotherhood got to hear them all.

"Not something I'd want to do at all," Sebe muttered. "Piss and daemons, there are some enemies you just don't want to make."

Doranei didn't reply. He was painfully aware of the hard look Beyn was giving him. *Gods, he's right too. Might be I've already made that enemy.* "Any of you got any brandy?" he asked, pulling his coat tighter around his body. "Think the night just got colder."

There was an orange smear across the eastern horizon as the fading sun dropped behind a crown of clouds. From one of the silver-capped towers of King Emin's palace Morghien had an unparalleled view of the sunset. For a minute or two he followed the progress of a local mage illuminating each of the night spheres in the wealthier streets, leaving stepping-stones of pale bluish light in her wake.

"Is it time?" called a tired voice from within the tower.

Morghien checked the sky again and turned back. "Close enough to begin."

King Emin was sat on a three-legged stool, the only seat in the room. The open arrow-slit windows meant it was freezing in there and Morghien felt a pang of sympathy for his friend, wrapped only in a white linen sheet in anticipation of the ceremony to come. He at least had his heavy leather coat and gloves to ward off the cold. Beside the stool was a bundle of clothes and a long pair of iron tongs Morghien had brought from the fireplace in his room.

The king was hunched over, hugging to his stomach a smooth, rounded object. He looked as tired as he sounded. Sleep had become a rare thing with Queen Oterness nursing a month-old son, and the touch of the Skull of Ruling only dulled the constant growl of anger at the back of his mind.

Morghien felt his fingernails dig into his palms. The Skull's reputation was not a pretty one and this close to it he could well believe the rumours. It had been made to endow Aryn Bwr's heir with the strength to rule after his father's death, but the Skull felt like a wild force to Morghien. Just being in its presence made his skin crawl, and that wasn't normal—nothing like that happened when he was with the young Lord Isak, who carried both Hunting and Protection.

Covering much of the centre of the room were two circles marked in chalk, one inside the other. Between the two Morghien had drawn the sigils of each of the Gods of the Upper Circle: Death, Karkarn, Nartis, Tsatach, Amavoq, Belarannar, Larat, Ilit, Vrest, Inoth, Kitar, and Alterr. He skirted the circles, treading carefully to avoid disrupting the chalk, and removed the augury chain from around his neck.

He pulled off the jewelled coins and placed them in turn on the corresponding sigil. The last two, the Lady and the Mortal, went into a pocket. That done, he opened a small ivory-inlaid box and withdrew a handful of dried, blackish green leaves.

"Deathsbane?" Emin said with a frown. "Is that wise?"

Morghien gave a sour bark of laughter. "Do you mean, 'Will it only antagonise him further?'" He scattered the leaves liberally between the two circles, not waiting for an answer.

"I mean that it's usually only used in necromancy, or so I understood."

Morghien shook his head. "My friend, what we are planning to do will win us no commendations for piety; deathsbane is used in necromancy because it is effective. Healers use it often in poultices and brews; they don't tell people because there's always some fool who will use any excuse to tie you to a stake, but it's not heretical."

"Very well," Emin muttered, shivering a little. "What now?"

"Now you sit in the circle, carefully."

Lifting the edges of the sheet so they did not smudge the chalk markings, Emin positioned himself by the side of the circle, squatting down to leave most of the space empty behind him. The only light in the room was a single oil lamp, turned down as low as it could go to leave just a glimmer.

Without the trappings of state, Emin looked to be a similar age to Morghien now. Emin had aged noticeably in the last year; both men had lined faces and greying whiskers now. While he retained his slender physique—all wiry strength, like a Harlequin—at that moment his majesty appeared diminished. They had first met when Emin was a carefree young man, but even then he had the bearing of a king. Now he was just a careworn, middle-aged man.

"Time to begin." Morghien crouched at the circle's edge and began to mutter words so softly they were barely sounds at all. A little magic slid from his fingertips and followed the paths of chalk around in both directions. As they met and sealed the circles Morghien felt a flash in his mind and reeled backwards as the magic barrier snapped open again.

"What happened?" Emin demanded.

Morghien took a moment to clear his wits and let the stinging in his head recede. "I—Ah, I'm not sure." He paused as he felt a stirring at the back of his mind: Seliasei, the Aspect of Vasle that inhabited his mind, was making her presence known.

"Of course," Morghien said aloud, "it's the Skull; I'm trying to contain it within the circle as well as you."

"And that is a bad thing?"

Morghien forced a smile. "The Skulls are repositories of vast power. They constantly draw in and put out energy from the Land around them. I cut off that flow with the barrier, but it was like holding back a river with a sheet of paper—the current simply tore a hole and broke the barrier."

"Are you hurt?"

"Thank you, my friend, but no. I used very little magic, just enough to seal the circle and create the binding on anything inside. Circles have a very specific prominence in the magical realm: you don't need to use a lot of power to make them effective. But the bond is inward facing. Forces entering from outside it are not subject to the same constraints."

"What do we do about it?"

He held out his hand. "Give me the Skull. It won't disrupt the ceremony outside the circles—in fact, it might make it easier."

He recommenced the ritual, sealing the circle again and then standing over the king, speaking arcane words he'd learned a century before. The Gods were traditionally at their weakest at twilight, when they would withdraw a little from the Land, so magic involving them always worked best in that halfway time. The ritual itself was simple and began with a very gentle summoning. The use of force would come later.

The memory of his first teacher in magic, the father of the infamous Cordein Malich, appeared abruptly in Morghien's mind as the soft syllables slipped from his tongue, leaving a coppery tang in their wake.

"Some see magic as a man's art, where directness and bold action will always triumph. They're the fools you need to watch for; the ones who puff themselves up like tomcats without a shred of caution. This art we borrow from Gods and daemons, creatures that could swat us like flies should they wish to. Immortals do not appreciate bluster; a little humbleness never goes amiss." He sighed as he thought, *A shame your son never appreciated your lessons, my friend.*

Morghien sensed the light grow a little dimmer. The shadows were already deep, with the lamp turned right down, but the change was enough to notice. He took a long breath.

Humble? I'm trying, master, however ill suited I am to it.

He repeated the words of summoning, holding back the flow of magic as much as he could without breaking it. He wasn't often glad of his lack of personal power, but this time it was a good thing, for a full summoning would draw an entity and drag it into the real world. With luck what he was doing was nudging it forward at a time when its reach was slightly weakened.

He nodded to Emin and the king let the sheet slip from his body, spreading it out behind him, taking great care not to let it break the circle. Now Morghien held up the lamp to reveal Emin's shadow on the sheet as he repeated the summoning, slowly, softly. If he was too insistent, the summoning might work too well; they were already running a great risk. This was by no means the first time he had performed a sundering, but King Emin's presence meant the chance of being noticed was far greater, and therein lay the danger.

The shadow on the sheet gave a slight twitch. Morghien watched it carefully. King Emin kept perfectly still, his eyes fixed on Morghien as he waited. The shadow twitched again, then turned its head to look around the room.

Excellent. He reached out and placed a hand up against the invisible barrier cast by the circle. It was intact; everything was going according to plan. At twilight the Gods withdrew a little from the Land, but a tiny fragment of their selves was imbued in each of their servants who took holy orders. King Emin had done that years ago—albeit for reasons more practical than pious. The summoning was aimed at the only part of Lord Death available to someone of Morghien's strength at twilight—that sliver within King Emin.

He turned the lamp up and watched the darkness behind Emin as it strengthened and solidified.

"I imbue," he said aloud, allowing the flow of magic to increase and run forward towards the circle. The shadow trembled. "I imbue," he repeated, summoning the image of a hammer falling in his mind. Morghien had seen a mage smith work his trade once, and had noted the directness required to weave magic into steel or silver, where the rhythm of the blows and the repetition of the words were as crucial as the strength of the wielder.

"I imbue," he said a third time, pushing out as much magic as he could while signalling to Emin. As Morghien began to speak the words for a fourth time, Emin rose smartly from his crouching position and stepped out over the circle to join Morghien on the other side. The shadow lurched forward to follow, but was caught on the edge of the circle and rebounded, shuddering, as Emin wrenched himself from its grip. It stilled to a dark stain on the linen sheet.

Morghien blew out the lamp and plunged the room into near darkness. Both men blinked to adjust their eyes.

"It worked then?" Emin said, looking at the sheet. The shadow looked like a stain of some sort. Emin thought he could make out the top of the head and one arm, but he wasn't certain.

"It appears so," Morghien said cautiously as he placed a restraining hand on his friend's arm. "Don't break the circle yet, just in case."

The two men stood watching the sheet in silence until Emin seemed to remember he was naked and started shivering again.

"Can I get dressed yet?"

Morghien nodded, his eyes not leaving the sheet. "The circle must remain until after the sun is fully down."

Emin unwrapped the bundle of clothes by the stool and quickly pulled on the breeches, then the boots. He was reaching for the shirt when Morghien suddenly stumbled sideways, as though he'd been struck in the shoulder.

"Morghien!" Emin shouted, grabbing his friend by the arm to stop him falling.

"Shit," Morghien whimpered, supporting himself on the wall with one hand, "He comes."

Emin turned towards the circle and saw the air shimmer and prickle with tiny bursts of silvery-green light. A crashing sound came from nowhere and echoed through the small tower-room, sounding like the fall of a tombstone. Both men clapped their hands to their ears, wincing, as a second crash reverberated through their bodies. In the blink of an eye a tall, cowled figure appeared in the circle. The force of his arrival knocked them both backwards, but it was Emin who recovered his wits first. He dragged Morghien down to one knee.

"You think to bind me?" Death rumbled slowly.

The eight-foot-tall God towered over them both. His body was hidden by a long robe; in one hand He held a golden sceptre. With His free hand Death stroked the invisible barrier of the circle, His emaciated bone white fingers and pitch black, pointed fingernails leaving a trail of light in the air where they scored the barrier.

"No, my Lord," Morghien gasped, flinching every time those fingers touched the barrier he'd created, "I would never presume such strength."

Death looked down at the sheet on the ground inside the circle. His face was hidden in the shadows of His cowl but Morghien felt His gaze burning like a flame.

"You presume too much." There was a growl of anger in Death's voice and Morghien felt a flicker of panic. "I see a traitor before me."

"I had no choice," Emin said, feeling the God's focus alight upon him. He chanced a look up and felt pulsing anger radiate over him, as Death's power had once burned in his veins. "What was done in Scree was an abomination, but it was done to provoke a reaction; to undo the damage it did I must be free of its influence."

"And so you betray your God," came the booming reply. "Traitors to my name are heretic and there is only one punishment for that."

"My Lord," Morghien repeated, "can you not see the damage your wrath has done?"

"I have killed unbelievers. They are of no consequence."

"The deaths are poisoning the Land against you, and Azaer exploits that."

"Azaer is a shadow, nothing more. I fear no God, no mortal—and certainly no mere shadow."

"That is what it is counting on," Emin insisted, a feeling of desperation welling up inside him. "It has made its weakness a strength. It goes unnoticed and unchecked."

"You have no need to fear the shadow," Death growled. "You need fear only me. You have walked away from the vow you took, and that makes you my enemy." It appeared to the two men watching that the figure looked off into the distance over Emin's head. "You—and your blood; perhaps my punishment should be the son you watch over at night."

"No!" Emin shouted, but before he could say any more, Morghien had plunged his hand into the pocket of his jacket.

"We are not your enemy," he roared, rising. "You are blinded by what has been done to you, and you cannot see the danger emerging from the shadows!"

"Kneel before your God," Death snarled, his voice crashing against their ears with savage force. "Kneel, or I shall strike you down and consign your soul to Ghenna."

"You will do neither," Morghien snapped, "and nor will you threaten a newborn out of pique." His fingers closed around the Skull in his pocket and a surge of energy flooded his body. "Our war is with the shadow—whether or not you see the threat, I will not let you stand in our way."

"You threaten me?" Death roared, raising his sceptre.

In response Morghien pulled the Skull from his pocket and held it in the air between the chalk circles. "You are weakened, diminished by what happened in your temple in Scree. I have felt the Reapers in Lord Isak's shadow. They are broken free of your grip and the loss has wounded you gravely. I may not have the strength to defeat you, even with this Skull, but you know the hurt it can cause you. To kill me will cost more than you can afford."

"You declare war on your God? Such foolishness shall be your damnation."

Death's reply was considerably quieter. Morghien could feel His attention fixed firmly on the Crystal Skull. For creatures of magic, fighting from within a containing circle would be like an army fighting up a mountain slope, with every step requiring huge effort. The power of one of the Crystal Skulls would be like a river running down that slope.

"I do not," Morghien said as calmly as he could with magic coursing through his body. "You are the Lord of Final Judgments and no mortal can deceive you. So I say this. I believe we serve your interests. I believe we do what must be done, and that if we fail, so will our Gods. For this reason I must threaten you, for I cannot allow even you to stop us."

"You do not lie," Death said in an emotionless voice. "As misguided as your words are, I see your belief."

Morghien pressed on, not even trying to understand the mind of a being so old and powerful. He just had to hope the God's blinding wrath was not all-consuming, that there was some sense of the divine judge left.

"Then, please accept my apology and permit us to go about our mission." He took a slow breath and played the last card he held. "At the end of the Wars of the Houses you appeared before Aryn Bwr as he was about to slaughter his defeated foes. You spoke to the fallen princes; you heard their words, and you forgave their deeds as honestly done. You prevented Aryn Bwr from wiping them out and thus healed the rift between the noble houses."

Death did not answer immediately. Morghien felt his chest tighten as the enormity of what he was doing struck home. *Bargaining a truce with Death? What am I doing?*

"You appeal for clemency? Very well, it shall be granted. I shall not destroy you or your nation for what you have done. But no more are you welcome in my temple. Your war is foolish and my servants shall give you no aid. Neither ally nor enemy, until the day of your judgment."

Both men bowed, neither trusting themselves to speak in case they disrupted the fragile balance in the air. With an effort Morghien cut the flow of magic to the circle and reached out to scuff the chalk with his hand. It was a risk, but they had to take it.

Death remained motionless. Morghien could feel the God's gaze on him, even with his head bowed low. In the next instant it was gone, and they looked up to find an empty room. The sheet lay where Emin had let it fall, but the shadow imprinted upon it had left the linen charred and crumbling. A gust of freezing wind blew in the window. A few flecks of ash skittered away over what remained of the sheet, revealing a sooty stain on the stone underneath.

"By the Dark Place," Emin whispered hoarsely, "what have we done?"

CHAPTER 17

MIHN REALISED HE WAS LURKING OUTSIDE the Chief Steward's office. He kept to the shadows and ignored the men and women who walked past—he was not exactly waiting, nor exactly hesitating . . . He was glad the palms of his hands had at last stopped stinging. His feet were another matter, but he'd already padded his boots with wool and there was very little more he could do beyond easing from one foot to the other, an occasional, small reprieve.

For the twentieth time that day he inspected his hands, squinting in the poor light. It was late evening now and most of the staff who worked here had gone home, braving the icy streets. Mihn had spent most of the day in Lord Isak's chamber, keeping an increasingly frustrated Xeliath company or sitting with Isak himself.

The white-eye wasn't a garrulous person at the best of times, but the last week had seen him turn even further inward. Now he was spending hours sitting on a ledge above his own ducal chambers, with his feet hanging over the edge and the bitter wind constantly buffeting him, watching the Land pass by. The slippery stone and treacherous swirl of winds meant he had been completely alone until Mihn had clambered out to join him.

Now it had become a strange little ritual, one that left even Lady Tila and Carel shaking their heads in incomprehension. Mihn would make his way up to the roof a while before dusk to find his lord there, a strange sort of gargoyle perched on the edge of his ledge and puffing on a pipe. Without a word Mihn would claim whatever space was left on the ledge and sit for as long as Isak was there. Isak remained silent while Mihn sang whatever songs occurred to him, from laments to lullabies.

The only response Mihn ever elicited from his lord came when he spoke the short prayer that accompanied the setting sun. Each day Isak frowned at the words and each day Mihn ignored it entirely, refusing to allow the upheaval in the cults to affect his own habits.

Without warning the office door jerked open and Mihn looked up with a guilty expression, quickly hiding his hands behind his back. Tila started out of the door, exclaiming in surprise when she saw him.

"Merciful Gods, what are you doing lurking out here?"

Mihn let her imperious gaze wash over him without reaction before he replied, "Waiting for the Chief Steward, of course."

"If he sent for a painted lady I think you might be something of a disappointment," she said, trying to elicit a smile. There was a famous pair of statues overlooking the largest of the river's docks; a man and a woman, side by side, known to the locals as Fisher and the Painted Lady. Someone had made the comment on the training ground the previous day, having seen Mihn's hands, and by the next morning it had spread throughout the palace.

"Or perhaps something rather more serious, judging by your expression," she added, giving up.

"Something rather more serious," Mihn agreed. He knew he frustrated Tila. She could be a charming girl when she wanted to be, and combined with her looks, it meant most men in the palace did exactly what she wanted. Aside from Isak, Mihn was the only man she couldn't influence, and she didn't conceal her annoyance on that front.

"You do realise one day you're going to have to trust me," she said sharply. "I spend all day as Lord Isak's representative while Lesarl runs the nation. I'm party to state secrets and yet you won't even trust me with what you had for breakfast!"

Mihn gave her an encouraging smile. "Then to make amends I will make a point to tell you that every day. This morning it was porridge. Yesterday it was also—"

"Oh shut up," she said, more amused than exasperated. "How about giving me something a little more substantive than that?"

Mihn screwed his face up in thought. "More substantive than porridge?"

"Information! Don't try your pantomime skills on me, I'm too tired." She gestured towards his hands. "What about those? Tell me about the circles."

The emotion fell from his face and his expression was blank again. "There is nothing to tell."

"Hah. It's just as well I'm too much of a lady to respond as Vesna or Carel might to that."

Mihn bobbed his head in acknowledgement. "And I am grateful for it."

"Might I at least see them?"

Her voice was softer now and Mihn hesitated, running the sounds of each word through his mind. Harlequins were trained to speak every dialect, to mimic every mood. Few were as adept at scrutinising intonation as they, and after a moment's thought he nodded. She wasn't trying to charm him now; her words contained only honesty.

He held out his left hand and let her take it and turn it palm-up. It was a strange sensation for a man who had been effectively celibate his entire life. Harlequins kept their gender a secret, and Mihn's subsequent exile had not given him much opportunity to explore or worry about such things.

Her soft fingers on his sent a tiny electric tingle up his arm. Tila, oblivious, bent low over his palm. She was taller than he, but slender, even compared to his lithe frame. Fascinated, she brushed a finger in a gentle circle over the tattoo covering most of the palm of his hand. Only his physical training stopped him twitching at the touch, but Tila still glanced up at him as though he had flinched.

"And Ehla did this for you?" she asked.

"It would have been hard to do myself," he replied, noting that she, like many of the Farlan, was uncomfortable calling the witch of Llehden by her title—despite the fact that the tribe was noted for its attachment to titles. Instead of referring to her as "the witch," they had all latched onto the name she'd provided. Fernal's words returned to him: "A name shapes, just as it comes from shape."

How true, and more people know her as Ehla—light—than her real name. But has she made herself vulnerable by allowing a name to be bestowed, or does she have a purpose in mind for what that name might change in her?

"Why an owl's head?" Tila asked, breaking his chain of thoughts.

The tattoos, on the soles of his feet as well as his palms, consisted of three concentric circles, and in the centre of each was a stylised owl's head. The two outer rings contained writing, angular Elvish runes for the inner and a stylised form of the witch's own western dialect for the other, mantras she had chanted as she tattooed his skin, imbuing his body with words of silence and stealth.

"It seemed appropriate," Mihn replied. He slid his hands from her grip and adopted a firmer tone. "I must speak to the Chief Steward now."

"What about?"

"A personal matter."

"Personal? Since when do you and he have personal business?" she said sharply. "Has something changed since last week? You normally scurry around these corridors avoiding him in case he asks you to be his principal agent."

"Scurry?" Mihn said, arching an eyebrow. It got the desired reaction and Tila laughed.

"Perhaps that was not the most appropriate word." She waved him into the room. "Come on, and I'll sit in—I'm sure Lord Isak will want to hear about whatever it is Lesarl is trying to get you to do."

Mihn acquiesced with a curt nod and followed her inside. The Chief Steward's office was a long thin room with a pair of windows at the far end. His desk, an enormous carved monstrosity inlaid with ivory, squatted in the very centre, the only piece of opulence the day-to-day ruler of the Farlan permitted himself. The long walls on either side were shelved from floor to ceiling and crammed with tied leather files. Between the windows, a pair of bookcases were placed back to back. One shelf was not full, Mihn noticed, but he guessed it was only a matter of time.

"The most accurate history of our last two hundred years," Lesarl announced when he saw Mihn looking around at the files, "if you know the way to read it. Can you guess which file is yours?"

"I expect one of the more recent ones on that bookcase behind you," Mihn said, approaching the desk. Two straight-backed armchairs were positioned next to it.

"You'd hope so, wouldn't you?" Tila commented breezily, walking around the desk to her own chair, "but it turns out our Chief Steward's paranoia knows no bounds. The numbering system allows for new files to be inserted into the system at apparent random—and I have yet to work out how to identify either the dummy files or the false documents inserted into most of the folders in case the wrong eyes do find them. I have started to get the hang of his elliptical style of notation at last, so the infrequency of names is proving less of a problem now."

Lesarl smiled at Mihn like a snake about to swallow a mouse. "It would be foolish to rely solely on the security precautions of the palace, don't you agree?"

Mihn shrugged.

"No desire for idle banter?" the Chief Steward asked. He was a thin man, with spidery limbs and a narrow, pointed face. His grin was one of the most malicious expressions Mihn had ever seen, and it was clearly one of Lesarl's favourite from a selection that might not have been as varied as a Harlequin's repertoire but was certainly as accomplished.

He stood up and said, "As the Lady Tila is quick to point out, my paranoia imposes significant demands on my time, so if you want to just sit there and stare, that's fine; you'll forgive me if I can get some work done in the meantime."

"I want some information," Mihn said.

The smile returned to Lesarl's face. "It is something I have in abundance, but you may have to be a little more specific."

"A journal—a very unusual journal, one Lord Bahl read before his death."

It was almost imperceptible, but Mihn thought he detected a very slight hesitation before the Chief Steward answered him.

"Our lord was an erudite man; you would have to be more specific."

Interesting—you know what I'm talking about, and it's a subject you don't want to discuss. Either you're not the sadist you're reputed to be, or there's something here you'd prefer didn't come to light.

"I think perhaps you know the journal," Mihn said.

"Perhaps I can make an educated guess," Lesarl replied coolly, "but what of it?"

"I want to read it—do you still have it?" Mihn ignored Tila's bewildered expression.

"You arrogant little—!" Lesarl snarled suddenly. "Are you fishing to find out if I have sold it?" He leaned forward on the desk. "I have done nothing of the sort, and nor would I—how dare you suggest such a thing?" The Chief Steward was almost shaking with anger. "I take my position here more seriously than any of you—you *children* could possibly understand. My remit is specific and to stray beyond that would mean immediate execution without trial—"

"I thought it prudent to ask," Mihn interrupted, keeping his voice quiet. "It is a sensitive subject, after all."

Lesarl looked at him, considering. His heightened colour started to dissipate and his voice was calmer when he said, "It is. The journal isn't for public consumption. Before we go any further, I would like to know why exactly you want it—in fact, how you heard of it in the first place."

"Lord Isak mentioned it in my presence," Mihn said. "As for what I want with it, I cannot tell you exactly. I seek answers—and perhaps more questions. As yet I am not entirely sure. But I am answering you honestly." *And this is the problem; I don't know exactly what I want it for. Perhaps Isak's recklessness has rubbed off on me.*

"Cannot? When this is a matter of state security?"

Out of the corner of his eye Mihn saw Tila's expression grow more intent, but she didn't interrupt. Doubtless she knew all too well that Lesarl loved to hear someone beg him for information.

"Should Lord Isak be asking why you did not destroy it?"

"Do not think to threaten me with that; bluffing doesn't work when I'm the one who can see all the cards. Anyway, if you do know what it is, you will also know that such things are not easily disposed of."

Mihn smiled grimly. "I assume you will be able to think of an appropriate favour in return for either the journal or its location." He shivered at the sudden, unequivocal delight that flourished on Lesarl's face.

"A favour, eh? Now that is an interesting prospect."

"*A favour*," Mihn warned, "no long-term arrangement."

"Frightened of commitment?" Lesarl grinned. "My mother always warned me about men like you."

"Do you accept?"

"Lesarl pursed his lips and nodded thoughtfully. "I do, but the favour comes first."

"What is it?"

"Give me a day or two; I'll need to make some preparation first."

"And you'll tell me about the journal once I've finished."

Lesarl gave him a beatific smile. "It will be discussed the very moment you return."

Two nights later Mihn found himself squatting behind a statue, trying to avoid the worst of the wind whistling up the river. Gusty spurts of rain made the exposed streets of Tirah even more unpleasant. The Irist, the city's principal waterway, was running high and dangerous this winter; and its surrounds were dark and treacherous.

A hundred yards upriver lay the Temple of Death, Mihn's destination. Like most temples, this one was adjoined by the clerical quarters and offices. The temple was built like an enormous cross marking the location of buried treasure on a map. It occupied a large stretch of prime waterfront and had converted the buildings on either side of the temple itself to more secular activities or rented them out to merchants.

This ensured there was sufficient wealth to properly welcome their unusually large crop of penitents, while many of the actual temple staff—devotees, priests, and novices—had been moved further south. Only the principal residence of the High Priest remained; a modestly sized palace that nestled in the crook of two arms of the temple cross and retained the fine river views lost by those less devoted to their God. It meant there were fewer people around to catch Mihn when he did finally leave the statue's shadow to break in.

He had eschewed his staff in favour of a pair of fighting sticks, more easily stowed on his back and better for use indoors. Aside from those and the rope-and-grapple currently tied around his waist, he also carried a small porcelain vase with a lid screwed on tight and bound with wire, a flask of moonshine the Palace Guards had named *bastard*, and a black cloth hood from which trailed a plait of horsehair.

Showing a breathtaking lack of loyalty, Lesarl had suggested that last so that if Mihn were seen, his build, coupled with the plait, would lead observers to direct any possible blame towards the Temple of the Lady and her devotees. The Chief Steward hadn't been impressed that his agents there had recently ignored his orders; he was quite happy for any potential problems to land on the temple's doorstep rather than his own.

Mihn had skirted the perimeter earlier and had a fair idea of where the guards would be stationed. Even while taking care not to be seen—he was, after all, suspiciously foreign looking, as Isak was always quick to point out—he'd made an extra effort to keep clear of the patrolling penitents. The crucial detail of the mission was to avoid being detected; Lesarl's other available agents were better at murder than subtlety, hence his current position.

But as was often the case, subtle also meant convoluted. Lesarl had been vague on the details of what would happen when Mihn unbound the wire and removed the vase lid, but he did at least suggest that Mihn beat a swift retreat and make his escape in the ensuing confusion.

Mihn slid off the oilskin he'd been wearing, kicked off his boots, and set off through the darkness. Immediately he felt a change, an altering of his perceptions of the Land. He couldn't hear his own footsteps against the drumming of the rain falling on the cobblestones, and yet only an occasional discordant drop fell on his shoulders. The pain from his tattoos had been replaced with a warm tingle as he walked from one shadow to the next. It was disconcerting at first, but it wasn't long before Mihn was enjoying the sensation. It was not comforting, nor even comfortable, but it sparked inside him a thrill like he'd experienced when his father first taught him to track and stalk: the excitement of a predator hunting.

Mihn had mastered the art with such remarkable speed that his father had known years before time that his son was easily agile and deft enough to be trained as a Harlequin. Now he had the witch's magic, which enhanced his skills even further, beyond any normal human talent.

The cold was painful on his toes but he blocked out the discomfort and focused instead on his journey. The first patrol loomed out of the darkness and Mihn veered closer to the warehouse . . . their gazes washed over him without registering. *In darkness it is less shape that betrays the prey than movement.* The spell woven into his skin did not mask what he was—the magic required for that was beyond the witch's abilities—but it did hide his actions. Wearing black in the shadows, Mihn could have stood still in a shadow half the distance from the two sodden penitents without being spotted.

As their heads turned to check the other direction, Mihn broke from the shadow and continued on his journey with swift, silent strides. He smiled underneath his hood as he saw the high priest's palace up ahead. The tattoos had done everything Mihn had asked from the witch. Now it was time to see what trouble a ghost with a mission could stir up.

The palace was not a building designed to prevent intruders, and the increased security of the past month was founded upon complacency. Reaching the end of the warehouses Mihn took a few moments to check one last time. There were guards at the temple entrance of course, as Death's house must remain always open, but the palace of the high priest had only a single patrolling penitent doing slow circuits. Mihn waited for the man to stray into a blind spot where he would be out of sight of the outer guards, then raced soundlessly up behind him and used one fighting stick to deliver a hard blow to the back of his head.

He dragged the unconscious guard into the shadows and pulled out the moonshine. He poured most of it into the man's mouth and massaged his throat until he swallowed. If he did wake up again he'd have twice the headache. Then Mihn spilled a liberal amount down the penitent's robe and dabbed a bit of the man's blood on the wall nearby.

Bastard was well known and popular with the more serious drinkers, being a fast road to blackouts and near-comatose sleep. Lesarl's informants had told him the priests had restricted supply within the compound, so the most likely question to be asked here was why the guard hadn't shared with his mates. If he woke to tell a different story, it would just as likely be viewed as weaselling out of a charge, rather than the truth.

That done, Mihn checked there were no patrols in sight before he took a run at the nearest wall; momentum carried him to the raised ground-floor windowsill. The bite of icy-cold stone made Mihn hiss softly as he dragged himself up to on the ledge, but he didn't intend using his grapple on such a clear, silent night unless absolutely necessary. The ceilings of the ground-floor rooms were at least twenty feet high, grand enough for receiving important guests but with the added bonus that the windows went up almost to the ceiling.

Once he was upright, supporting himself on the window embrasure, Mihn could see the sigils scratched into the thin panes of glass that would amplify the sound of breaking glass, and it was fair to assume that there would be more on the thick oak frame to do something similar if the whole window was broken or removed.

Carefully, Mihn turned himself around so that he was facing out towards the street. Ancient Tirah was a magical sight with its spired halls and imposing towers illuminated by Alterr's light. Tirah in the middle of a winter rainstorm was something else again: a miserable city of hateful streets and uncaring, lofty arrogance.

A city of snobs, looking disdainfully down on everyone else—especially everyone who has business outside on a night like this, Mihn thought with rare petulance as he watched a patrol wander past in the distance, not even bothering to look up at the palace. His fingers and toes were starting to ache with the cold, and they complained further as he flexed them to keep the blood flowing.

But then again, I've spent more nights like this outside than I can remember, and everywhere looks pretty awful when it's raining.

The life of a wanderer had taught Mihn one thing above all else; bitterness would kill him if he let it. As an automatic reaction he argued the point in his mind, aware that complaint would poison his mood and allow mistakes he couldn't afford.

Gods, I'd almost forgotten what it was like at home; the freezing rain coming down off the northern coast that felt like it could strip the flesh from your bones. Slowly a smile forced its way onto his lips. *And Pirail in the Elven Waste—how stupid to forget to leave that place before winter set in . . . damn wind didn't seem so awful in summer.*

He shook his fingers out. *Time to go.* He put flattened palms against the the wall on either side of the window, braced, and lifted himself up until he could do the same with his feet.

And Tio He, he continued in his head to distract himself from the pain of the stone's freezing, rough surface on his skin as he edged his hands upwards and repeated the movement. *Air so thick and heavy you could almost take a bite out of it.*

He manoeuvred one hand under the lintel and wedged the fingers of his right hand in the crack above it so he could pull his feet up further, ignoring the screaming complaints from his fingers as they took so much of his body-weight. He wasted no time in pushing himself clear of the window and up, grabbing the windowsill of the first floor with his left hand.

Mihn gave a quiet grunt as he got his forearm onto the windowsill and pulled himself up until he could twist and sit down. *Ter Nol*, he thought as he filled his lungs with air and flexed his hands again, this time checking for cuts as much as keeping the circulation going. *Perhaps I could go back to Ter Nol and enjoy the view for a few years. Summer and autumn both, some of the most beautiful evenings I've ever seen were while I was sitting on Narwhale Dock. I'm sure after a year or two I'd hardly even notice the smell.*

He stood on the windowsill and leaned out to check the window above him. The second floor was a fair way off. He pulled a pair of what looked like broken daggers from a leg pocket. They each had a fat inch or so of metal, liked hooked blades, and were designed for climbing rather than fighting. Reaching above the lintel he stabbed one between the stones and pulled it gingerly, gradually letting it take his weight. The blade was strong enough, but he felt his wrist wobble slightly—the blade didn't have enough purchase. Sighing, he jerked the dagger out of the mortar and slipped them both back into the pocket.

"Grapple it is then," he whispered, his lips brushing against the stone of the wall as he leaned to the right to gauge the distance. "Let's hope they didn't bother securing every window in the whole damn building."

The double-headed hook was securely bound to his back, but even with numb fingers Mihn managed to free it quickly. He hadn't wanted to use the grapple, but the distance was short enough to the next windowsill that he was confident it wouldn't be too obvious except to anyone already watching, and if that were the case, he already had a problem. Within a minute he was crouched in the shadow of the second-floor window and smiling at the pristine surface of each pane of glass.

He stowed the grapple carefully before removing the lead around one pane with his knife so he could ease out the glass and slide a hand inside to open the bolt. Soon he was standing in a barely furnished office, thanking the accuracy of Lesarl's information as he put the windowpane back and redrew the heavy curtain against the winter air. As an afterthought he dried as much of his body as he could on the inside of curtain—it would dry long before anyone might check, and it was certainly safer than leaving damp footprints in the corridor.

He left the room and ventured out into the corridor, taking a moment to place himself on the map he'd memorised then setting off left for the servants' stair. He went up two flights and quickly found the high priest's bedroom, which, together with the man's vast private office, occupied half the floor.

The ornate patterned curtains that hung over the three doorways to the room had been drawn back from the middle entrance which, by tradition, lacked a door, in imitation of the temple. This was where High Priest Bern received formal petitions. Mihn stepped silently through and checked his surroundings. The single oil lamp hanging in the corridor gave only a little light, enough to reveal the bare outlines, but that was sufficient for him to make out the shelves against the walls, and only a desk and a couple of chairs standing in the centre of an otherwise clear floor.

On the right was another doorway, which led to the high priest's bedroom. Mihn guessed it would be locked, despite the weak security he'd encountered thus far, but he didn't bother trying it—he didn't need to. He pulled a sheaf of papers from inside his shirt and scattered them around the desk, then unstrapped the jar and set it on the floor.

Above him was a long beam running the length of the room, almost as wide as his body and certainly big enough to perch on while he watched events unfold—he was pretty sure anyone entering the room soon wasn't going to be bothered about looking up, and he had the witch's spell if they did. He carefully unknotted the wire holding the jar's lid on. The jar itself was little bigger than a flattened palm, and twice the thickness. It had a dark green swirling pattern on it that Mihn didn't recognise. Once the lid was dislodged he didn't wait around but launched himself off Jopel Bern's desk. He grabbed the beam above and quietly swung himself up until he was lying flat along it. Then he kept very still and watched the jar.

It did precisely nothing. One heartbeat stretched into five, then ten. Mihn realised he'd been holding his breath and let it out softly . . . and as he did so a dull green glow began to build around the mouth of the jar. Without warning it rose in the air and expanded into a cloud larger than a man before coalescing into a figure.

Merciful Gods, let the witch's magic work here too, he prayed as he gripped the beam tighter.

The daemon was the size and approximate form of a large man, and naked, with irregular clumps of spines like a mangy porcupine. While its left hand was relatively normal—if you ignored the overlong fingers and claws—

the right was much larger, with two stubby, fingerlike protrusions from which extended a spray of long, thick spines.

As Mihn watched the daemon twisted its body left and right. It had no neck on which to turn its flattened head, but it did have an assortment of eyes to cover most angles. For a moment he wondered why it was turning—until he heard a snuffling sound and saw the hanging flap of skin on its face twitch up and jerk first in one direction, then the next.

Realising what it was doing, Mihn readied himself to leap from the beam the moment he saw the quill-arm rise. The daemon continued to look around, sniffing the air with increasing vigour, taking a step forward towards the neatly stacked shelves on the opposite wall. It continued by fits and starts, following a scent Mihn couldn't fathom, until it reached a corner shelf.

The daemon sniffed hard, grabbed the end book, and flung the entire row of files and books onto the floor, then gave a growl and swept something else aside—a wooden panel, Mihn guessed, from the way it clattered to the floor—and peered at the wall.

Mihn couldn't see what it was looking at, but whatever it had found didn't worry the daemon. Nor, it appeared, did the sound of a muffled voice from the high priest's bedroom. With a heavy, rolling sound that might have been a chuckle, the daemon reached out and wiped its hand against the wall before reaching into a recess and pulling out a thick book. In the faint green-tinted light of magic playing around the daemon, Mihn saw the corners of the book gleam.

Silver, most likely; it's a grimoire—but what's a priest doing with a grimoire? Only mages bother compiling a book of spells.

The daemon turned back, hefting the large book in one hand with an appreciative grunt. Though he couldn't see its mouth, or even if it had a mouth beneath that strange, oversized nose, Mihn could tell it was pleased: it had found what it had been looking for.

There were more noises from the bedroom now, and the daemon raised its lethal right arm. Looking up, it caught sight of Mihn, perched on the beam. The flaps of its nose rose towards him.

"The one who is to be protected," the daemon rasped as if through a throat made of sandpaper. "He should not have worried. I smell power on you. You belong to one greater than I." It raised the book. "The writings of Cordein Malich; the account of his obligations and the scent of his soul. Tell the other I am satisfied."

In the next moment the bedroom door was flung open and High Priest

Bern emerged like a ghost in a billowing nightgown, his walking stick raised threateningly. The daemon moved forward almost lazily and flicked its spiny hand out to impale the high priest in the chest. Bern gave a wheeze of pain as the spines ripped right through his body and emerged out his back, spraying blood over the wall behind. The daemon gave another laugh and turned its body towards Mihn, the gleam of two of its eyes bright in the darkened room.

"The other requested mayhem to aid your escape." It reached out and dabbed a finger to the blood pouring out of the high priest's wounds before licking it clean. "Mayhem will be a pleasure."

CHAPTER 18

HE WATCHED THE DAWN BREAK, the weak rays puncturing the cloud. Something in him recoiled from the light, but he faced it down, as he had every morning for years. The feeble winter sun was still strong enough to sting his eyes at first, if he'd been awake all night glorying in the darkness.

Despite the rain and thick stone walls, he could still smell them from his vantage point, still hear their breath and feel the hot pulse of blood in their veins. Sometimes the smell was too insistent, making sleep impossible, and on those nights he would find himself a dark corner as far from others as possible. Even the foul winter nights of driving rain and biting wind wouldn't affect him; the discomfort was barely noticeable against the warm hunger simmering inside.

With the dawn came voices, movement, animal calls; the bark of dogs and crow of cockerels. He managed to smile. Another night survived. Another night of sitting there watching the sleeping city, waiting for life to be breathed back into the streets. Another night where he did nothing. The sunlight crept over his skin and drove the feelings away, driving the darkness back down into the pit of his soul.

It was getting harder every year, but recently it had become much worse. He felt a tear on his cheek and gently wiped it off with one finger, holding the tiny drop of water up for inspection before tasting it delicately with his tongue. He spat it out immediately and felt the shame well up.

He pursed his lips. The dawn was here now and he was safe. *One night at a time*, that's all he needed to remember, even though it was harder and he was feeling the need much more strongly. Though it had threatened to boil over many times, he'd managed to resist. He'd managed without the voice in the shadows for years, and he could survive this absence. He had to; to do otherwise was unthinkable.

I will not become a monster, I will not permit it.

Despite his brave words, he knew it was not so simple. Battle could not frighten him; violence and death were just happenings around him, but succumbing to his need was a terrifying prospect, one he could not even afford to contemplate.

Gods, last night was bad, so bad. I almost didn't make it to the dawn.

Gods? The word meant nothing to him now: it was a habit, a meaningless curse. The Gods had never listened to his prayers; the Gods were not interested in him. When he had been at his lowest ebb, holding the corpse of that dog in his hands, his teeth clenched so hard his jaw had ached for days, had it been the Gods who answered him? No, the soothing voice from the darkness had been no God—Gods came in triumph and shining light, not unseen in the shadows.

And yet his prayers had been answered, for the hunger had subsided as the voice spoke to him and sustained him. Why it had suddenly stopped, after more than a year of whispers and soft laughter, the only true marker of the weeks passing, he had no idea, nor how long it would be until he heard it again—a week, a month? He'd come to rely on that voice, and then it had gone away with no explanation or warning, leaving just a sense of loss that nagged almost as hard as the thirst inside.

"I will be strong, the shadow will come again," he said softly, his resolve strong again. He stood and walked into the street where the new day was breaking.

From the rooftop above him a head turned to watch him go.

Curious, thought Mihn, leaning out as far as he could until the other had walked out of sight, *most curious. Something to add to your file. Lesarl will be pleased.*

Lesarl smiled down at his young son's sleeping face and eased the door closed. It was early, only a hint of dawn in the sky when he'd risen to get a few hours' head start on the rest of the city. There was a musty smell about the house, faintly overlaid by stale sweat, the scent he had come to associate with the hours before the household started its day, before the bread was set to baking and the bustle of city life intruded.

This morning he could also smell the dampness in the air after the night's rain. From his dressing room window he could see the city was still quiet after the downpour. One great puddle filled the street outside, leaving barely enough room for the two guards standing at his gate. They were half perched on the low wall, their backs pressed against the railing.

He walked towards the breakfast room. He loved the chamber despite its unsuitability, the five tall, rain-streaked windows ensuring the room was always chilly. A lamp sat on the table beside a steaming bowl of porridge. It did little to dispel the gloom, but it would be enough for browsing through the morning report his secretary had sent over. Withered grey-brown foliage left a skeletal trail across the lower parts of the windows, not dead, just waiting for the summer sun to return.

Noticing he was missing his usual rosehip tea, Lesarl went to call a servant, but as he reached the door something darted out from the shadows and he gasped as he felt something hard pressed against his windpipe. Without thinking he grabbed for the stiletto he always carried, but his attacker was quicker and smashed an elbow into his bicep so hard the arm went numb. Whatever was at his neck pressed a little harder.

"Give me one good reason not to break your neck," hissed a voice in his ear.

"My endearing smile?" Lesarl croaked as best he could.

"Not going to be enough," Mihn said, emphasising his point by shaking the taller man like a rat. "The daemon and I had a quick chat before it left with Malich's journal."

"Don't tell me that was the one you were after?"

"No more games," Mihn said quietly.

"Very well," he managed, "check my morning reports."

Mihn turned them both so he could see the pile of papers on the table. There was indeed something substantial there amongst them. He released Lesarl and shoved the man back into the room.

The Chief Steward gave a cough and rubbed a hand over his throat as Mihn went to the table. "High Priest Bern had the original," he explained in a hoarse voice, "and until the fall of Scree that wasn't a problem—I hadn't even considered that entrusting a necromancer's writings to the High Priest of Death might prove a problem."

Mihn picked up the journal and opened it, scanning a few pages to verify that it was the translation prepared at Lord Bahl's request. He shut it and retied the leather fastenings. "Enjoy your porridge," he said with a scowl as he headed for the door.

Lesarl paused as Mihn disappeared from view. "Don't tell me the cook oversalted it again?" he called. There was no reply.

Cardinal Certinse didn't bother looking up when he heard the door to his office crash open. There was only one man who'd barge in unannounced and it would take more than a withering look to dissuade the man once known as Colonel Yeren. The eye-patched bastard had a reputation to match Count Vesna's, and he took every opportunity to remind the cardinals that the title they'd given him was just a technicality.

"Senior Penitent Yeren. And am I to assume you have a matter of theology you feel we must discuss without delay?"

"Yah, something like that," the broad-shouldered mercenary replied as he deposited himself in one of the chairs facing the desk.

"Please, take a seat," Certinse murmured, eyes still fixed on the report in front of him as he finished the last few lines. He restrained the urge to bring the page closer, despite the ache behind his eyes that now appeared if he read much while tired. Better not to show any weakness in front of a bully like Yeren, whether he was in your employ or not.

As last he finished and put the report aside. He looked at the soldier over bridged fingers. He and Yeren were of an age, but there any similarities ended. Yeren was a heavyset native of Canar Thrit, and had more white hairs than Certinse, and more than his fair share of scars too. He had reportedly bought himself out of the army early on in his military career, before being court-martialled on charges of corruption, although not soon enough to avoid losing an eye in battle. He'd spent the next ten years as a Carastar, one of the bands of bandits sanctioned by Vanach to patrol the border with Canar Thrit, tasked with *dissuading* anyone fleeing religious rule so they could keep that borderland conflict ticking over without allowing it to explode into open warfare.

"Do you have news for me?"

"That I do," Yeren said with a scowl. "There's one hell of a mess at Holy Dock—damn thing tore a hole in the wall of Bern's palace. Whole bloody flock of crows runnin' round wringing their hands and blamin' each other."

Certinse ignored the "crows" reference, although the black-robed priests of Death might not have appreciated it, and restrained the urge to ask what flattering reference the mercenaries used for the priests of Nartis. "Did you manage to speak to your friend?"

Yeren knew most of the mercenaries employed by both cults, of course; they had all served together in Tor Milist.

He nodded. "No sign of nothin' 'cept a guard who claims he got blind-sided that night."

"And did he?"

"Doubt it, he won't be the first flogged for drinkin' on duty. Still, it's damned convenient for the Chief Steward and I wouldn't put it past the bastard, but Kerx says he checked the whole building as soon as possible and all the doors were still bolted from the inside and there are charms on all the lower windows, so unless Lesarl's got an agent who can fly I don't see how he could've done it. Patrols're in constant movement in the streets round the temple; they'd've seen someone carrying a fifty-foot ladder."

"Your conclusion?"

Yeren sighed. "That Chief Steward Lesarl is more intelligent than Captain Kerx."

"A week-old rabbit is more intelligent than Kerx," Certinse said drily, "but you're right, coincidence is a stretch. All that remains to discuss is what we do about it."

"What do you mean?" Yeren said in surprise. He crossed his legs, revealing for a moment the leather breeches he wore before tugging his penitent's robe straight to cover them.

Certinse smiled inwardly. *Lucky for them it's winter and an extra layer is welcome. In summer they actually might have to forgo their fighting clothes.* "I mean: our goal is not civil war; we don't need evidence that this was a setup to provoke a conflict. But that doesn't need to be the only result."

"Why not? You've got 'em runnin' scared," Yeren said, gesticulating as he spoke. "They agreed wholesale to the High Cardinal's reforms. If you ask me, whatever happened in Scree broke Lord Isak's spirit—"

"I do not pay you to think," Certinse snapped, "and of that I am glad when your skills at it are so poor. Do you think we would be in such a secure position if Lord Isak was so easily swayed, considering it is the Chief Steward whispering in his ear?"

He reached for the bellpull and gave it a tug to summon his secretary, a weak-chinned little man whose father had named him Kerek, clearly hoping he'd sired a great warrior, rather than the cautious cleric he'd grown into.

The secretary hurried in and, blinking first at Yeren, bowed to Certinse. "Yes, your Eminence?"

"Prepare a letter to High Cardinal Echer. I advise we distance ourselves from the unfortunate late High Priest Bern, and that we should encourage the investigation be concluded swiftly and quietly. I want it to imply we know more than we're going to tell on the subject."

"Won't that make him suspicious?" Yeren interjected, failing to pay attention to Certinse's hard look. "They'll be looking to see who else might have been in league with daemons. You Farlan find conspiracies far more entertaining than the truth."

"Firstly," Certinse replied with exaggerated patience, "they will be looking for conspirators within the cult of Death, not outside it. Bern would be unlikely to take his heresy out of his domain. Secondly, Echer is so far gone he's barely even aware when it's Prayerday. Now that his proposals have been accepted the man's as happy as . . . well, as happy as an utterly deranged man can be. Kerek, do you think there's an appropriate term?"

"Ecstatic, perhaps, sir?"

Certinse nodded. "The right hint of fervour, certainly. Anyway, Echer is content to occupy his time devising more strictures to impose on the Farlan people. Fortunately for the Farlan people, he sends them to me for my contribution now that he sees me as his champion and I have in my employ several talented, albeit argumentative, theologians to help refine the text."

"Meaning you let him argue with them all day, leaving you to run the cult?"

Certinse inclined his head. "For a soldier you're not so great a fool."

Yeren managed to not allow himself to be baited. "That won't work forever."

"I know. Kerek, have you seen your friend Ardela recently?"

"I have, your Eminence," Kerek replied with a bow that wasn't fast enough to hide his smile.

"You should write to her, ask her to put her debating skills to use. Perhaps afterwards you could go and see her, just to ensure she is well. It must be a trying time for her; I hear shocking news about her mistress. Invite Yeren along too, perhaps?"

"Mistress?" Yeren said sharply as Kerek bowed again and retreated out of the room. "That wouldn't be the Lady, would it? Rumour has it that she's dead, murdered in one of her own temples."

"I wouldn't know the details, I'm afraid, but I too hear she is dead." Certinse watched Yeren's face as the soldier fitted the pieces together. A devotee of the Lady. The irritant that was High Cardinal Echer. *Honestly Yeren, it's not that difficultt, is it? Or are you just trying to believe better of a man of the cloth?*

"Piss and daemons!"

Certinse smiled. "Not quite."

"Your secretary didn't even bat an eyelid," Yeren protested. "What sort of bloody life do you clerics lead?" The man actually looked outraged, as though he had been a paradigm of goodness throughout years of bloody civil war in Tor Milist.

Bat an eyelid? The man barely did that when I told him to renounce his God and worship a daemon-prince; I doubt he's going to care about murder. It hardly interests him unless he gets to participate.

"The cut and thrust of clerical debate can be most wounding," Certinse agreed. "He will set up a meeting with Ardela after she has presented her argument to the High Cardinal. Perhaps you should take a squad with you to meet her. As with many of those with copper hair she can be somewhat fiery; perhaps it is something in the dye?"

Appetites that need paying for. Certinse recalled Lord Isak's words all too clearly. *Damn you, Ardela! Your sloppiness has put me in the Chief Steward's pocket for the rest of my life, and that's the sort of mistake you don't get away with. I almost wish the daemon-prince had not been killed by whatever it was that managed the feat. I would be pleased to send your soul to him, but I'll have to settle with just killing you.*

"Somewhat fiery?" Yeren echoed, "I doubt she'll be comin' along quietly, either."

"The sad realities of life," Certinse agreed as he returned to his report.

CHAPTER 19

A COLD WIND WHIPPED ACROSS HIS BODY, slapping his cheek with fingers of ice. He kept his head low and watched his feet rise and fall to the tune of tortured muscle. His feet were bare, always bare, his clothes ragged and torn. Eolis in his hand tugged him forward, dragging him towards the broken-tooth mountain that filled the horizon. He could smell the mud and burning on the wind, so unlike the furnace of Scree, yet similar for the upwelling of horror it provoked within him.

He stopped and looked at the shadows lying thick on the ground. The sun was absent from a grim grey sky yet the shadows were tangible for their blackness. They began to shift and writhe under his gaze and he staggered a few steps back, seeing sudden movement everywhere he looked. The shadows thrashed and kicked, rising a little then falling back to earth. He felt eyes on him and realised the shadows were not monsters or daemons coming to life. They were much worse.

Faces from all parts of his life, blood-splattered and screaming, enemies he'd barely seen before he'd killed them, butchered friends: they all stared at him from every direction. It was a field of the dead; those slain by his own hand lying in great heaps alongside those who had died because of his order.

He turned to run, unable to face their eyes and their cries any longer, but there were more behind him, and standing over those, five figures watching him from his shadow.

"What do you want?" he moaned, sinking to his knees. He felt the cold in his numb hands and feet, draining what little life remained.

"*We wait*," was the only reply he received.

One of the figures stepped closer and bent down so it could look him in the face. The pitiless grey ice of her eyes made him cry out with pain, but the sound was dulled and muted in her presence. Her dress was once of a rich pale blue cloth, now torn and ragged like his own. A small, withered bunch of flowers hung loose from her fingers.

"*We wait for release,*" she whispered in his ear, each syllable like the last breath of a dying man. *"We wait for our lord to claim you. Can you hear his foot-steps yet? Can you feel his hounds draw closer?"*

"Isak," the voice called as a hand nudged his shoulder.

He flinched. The hand was as hot as a furnace on his skin after the pervading chill of the dream. He squinted up at the figure standing over him, his head feeling muzzy and heavy. Xeliath held out her wasted hand towards him. She looked far stronger now than when she'd arrived. Being a stranger in a strange land had forced her to become stronger, and even crippled, she was a white-eye, with more than enough stubborn resilience to rise to the challenge. Invited guest or not, many Farlan would simply see a Yeetatchen, an enemy—but after her weeks of recuperation Isak guessed Xeliath would relish the coming fight.

"Careful where you point that thing," he growled, scowling at the Crystal Skull fused to her palm. Their relationship was still a little strange, neither one really sure what it was, despite the occasional visits Xeliath still made to his dreams, which were sufficiently unreal to allow an easy veneer of closeness.

She didn't reply other than to hook over a chair with her crutch and sit down with a contented sigh. Isak took a moment to look at the fierce brown-skinned girl he'd stolen away from her people. Her figure was hardly visible under the layers of thick woollen dress she wore, but her hair—longer now than when she'd first arrived—fell loose about her ears. It had been threaded with ribbons, brown, purple, and yellow, and a golden charm of Amavoq, patron of her tribe, was at her throat.

"It is a feast day for my people," she explained, seeing his gaze, "so we all wear the colours of Jerequan, the Lady at Rest and—Well, we eat like a bear does for winter!"

"Jerequan is a bear?"

"An Aspect of Vrest, yes." She stopped and looked closer at his face. "Are you hungover, or are your dreams still bad?"

Isak attempted a smile. "How do you feel about a bit of both?"

"Typical man! Drink away your problems and forget the rest of the Land." She leaned back, her chestnut-coloured nose wrinkling in distaste.

Isak looked puzzled until he noticed his mouth tasted like a mouse had crawled in and died while he was asleep. He was pushing himself upright when he suddenly remembered where he was.

"How did you get in here?" he demanded. He was sleeping in the room where he'd spent his first night in Tirah Palace, halfway up the Tower of Semar, and it was unique, as far as he knew, in that it had no staircase. Instead there was a well or chimney, running through the centre of the tower, and a spell engraved onto the wall at its base to lift people up on a flurry of spectral wings.

Xeliath grinned, suddenly looking like the girl she was rather than the time-ravaged crone her stroke often made her seem. She gestured towards the circular hole in the floor on her left. "Lady Tila was helping me with my hair when she mentioned that the tower had obeyed your command your first night here."

"But I'm Chosen of Nartis," Isak protested, "it's *supposed* to accept me."

"Hah! Anything some fool Farlan can do, I do better," she declared, raising her twisted left arm. "The tower knew what was good for it and obeyed me."

"Betrayed by my own tower?" Isak muttered. "Somehow that doesn't surprise me."

"That often happens after much wine. Were you hiding here to drink, or just to sleep?"

He shrugged. "Didn't feel much like getting a lecture on drink from anyone, least of all you."

"I never get like this when I drink," she replied scornfully.

"I know," Isak said with a smirk. "I've seen how you get! Makes me nervous to go to sleep when you're like that."

She looked him up and down critically, and Isak tried to pull his clothes to order, his shirt having somehow twisted around his body while he slept. "It is better that I'm drunk. Anyway, most men would be happy to be allowed to sleep at the same time."

Isak gave up. "Not complaining, just saying I should be allowed to drink in peace if I want. Makes me feel better—and it doesn't kill anyone, which, frankly, is better than anything else I've done as Lord of the Farlan."

He looked around for the wine jar he'd been drinking from and found it on its side by the bed. There was enough left to swill around his mouth to get rid of the worst of the sour taste his dreams had left there. "If you want to know what happened to the Land that makes a devotee of the Lady go mad and kill the High Cardinal—well, I'll tell you: it was me. I'm what happened; I'm the stone in the path of history, the start of all the shit that's happening around here."

Xeliath shook her head, the ribbons dancing like butterfly tails. "The death of the Lady wasn't your fault, nor the rage of the Gods. Whatever you did to the Reapers, you couldn't have predicted it—I doubt even Azaer's disciples did, and they planned most of it."

Isak looked down. "Then why do I still feel guilty?"

To his surprise, the fierce-eyed Yeetatchen white-eye laughed, not mockingly, but affectionately.

"Because you are human, you fool! Whatever the Gods—or anyone—asks of you, they cannot take away your humanity. The Gods made you that way, and anyone who argues otherwise will have to explain themselves to me.

"It doesn't matter that your purpose might be impossible," she added fiercely, her Yeetatchen accent growing more noticeable with her vehemence, "or already fulfilled. That is the fault of others, not you. They filled your dreams with prophecy and destiny. They gave you power, and forgot a white-eye is still human, no matter how great a weapon."

"So here I am—a saviour without a cause who can't even use drink to hide from his dreams of death?" Isak hadn't meant that to sound as abjectly pathetic as it came out, but Xeliath's face fell all the same.

"How often?"

"The dreams?" he sighed and shook his head. "Not often. Rare enough to be a shock when they do come; not so rare that I look forward to going to sleep."

"Have you seen the hound again?"

"No, and for that at least I'm glad." He grimaced again and rubbed his palms over his face. There was a tingle in his cheek where the single ring he wore—a tube of silver bearing his dragon crest, a replacement for the one he'd given to Commander Brandt's son back in Narkang—had caught it. "What bell is it?" he asked as he began to tug on his boots.

"Past the fifth," Xeliath replied, waiting until he had finished before reaching out her good arm to him. When he took it she hauled herself upright and together they entered the dark circle in the centre of the room. "I prefer to walk the palace at night when there are not so many faces to stare."

"You walk the palace alone?"

"When I wish. I am always pleased to have Mihn's company, and sometimes Lady Tila or Count Vesna accompany me, but I will not have a nurse."

"Are you sure? I'd be happier with someone watching your back."

"I am not so slow—it would take more than a soldier with a grudge," she said, adding with a grin, "and unlike you, I have no dreams of death!"

Before Isak could reply her twisted left hand gave a jerk and the storm of wings enveloped them, raging ghostly and near silent, but preventing conversation until they cleared. Isak blinked and let the shape of the lower chamber resolve in the gloom.

It was as cold as an ice store, and the only light was the faint glow of magic emanating from the sigils and spells chalked on the wall. There were two separate spells, one keeping the high and slender tower standing through even the winter storms, the second to carry people up the tower.

Dermeness Chirialt, a mage from the College of Magic, had gladly taken upon himself Isak's magical education, though his speciality was the production of armour; the price for his help was that Isak help him with his own research. One of the first tasks he'd set the young lord was to translate each of these runes, letting the syllables flow through his mind until he gained a sense of their shape and power.

He passed a hand over them as they passed, remembering those lessons, then asked Xeliath, "Where do you want to walk?"

"Walk?" she replied as she hobbled through the doorway towards the Great Hall. "Tonight I want to ride."

"There's a heavy ground frost again. It won't be safe."

She rounded on him, her expression changed all of a sudden. "Safe? I tell you something: guess how many times I have longed for the death you hide from? The months I lay in bed unable to move at all, only to find if I could move, still I was manacled to it because they thought I was a prophet?" Her accent became thicker the angrier she got.

"The pain, the loss of my beauty and strength! Pretend your future was tied to another's like a dog, as twisted as your broken body. Not safe? You entered Scree with just a bodyguard, was that safe? I will not again ride well, but I *will* ride. If I risk death to avoid white faces staring, I choose it."

She turned back towards the Great Hall, adding under her breath, "It is the only choice I have left. Everything else is decided by a saviour who cannot even save himself."

Isak watched her go, not trusting himself to reply. His hands had tightened into fists with the effort of keeping silent, but the next voice to echo down the corridor was Xeliath's, snapping at a servant on duty in the Great Hall, demanding a horse.

"Bloody white-eyes, eh?" said a voice to Isak's right. He turned and saw Carel standing halfway up the wide stone staircase that led up to the state apartments. His former mentor wore a long green overcoat with a white collar as befitted his status as a former Palace Guard, his left sleeve was pinned back, while his right hand held a silver-headed cane. Carel claimed his balance was still a little off since Isak had performed a battlefield amputation on his right arm, but the Duke of Tirah wasn't convinced.

Tila had confirmed his guess that duels could only be demanded of those in the habit of wearing a sword, and Carel, having passed his sabre, Arugin, on to Major Jachen, was now officially a pensioned retainer of Lord Isak's. The net result was that he could pretty well be as rude as he liked to any nobleman, and any demand for apology in the form of a duel would have to be offered to Lord Isak instead. Of course, if Isak judged his friend correctly, any illegal attack on Carel's person would see the former élite guardsman thumb a catch on his cane and suddenly regain the balance of forty years' superb swordsmanship.

"Reminding you of anything, old man?"

"No, not at all," Carel replied breezily. "You were much worse."

"Were?" Isak said sourly. "You heard her; I'm now a Saviour who can't even save himself. At the moment I'm inclined to think that might be worse than a petulant child."

"So a petulant child might claim, but I know which one I'd prefer to share a pipe with out in the moonlight." Carel gestured towards the Great Hall and they walked in side by side. The servant now tending the fire still had a shocked look on her face, the result of Xeliath's passing. It took a moment of panic before she remembered to curtsey to Isak as the three rangers sitting at a table rose and bowed.

Once out on the moonlit training ground, Isak took Carel's proffered tobacco pouch and thumbed a wad of tobacco into his pipe. He lit it and took a deep breath of the warm smoke before passing it over.

"I cringe every time I hear the word 'Saviour.'"

Carel nodded, his face partly obscured by the shadow of hair made silvery in Alterr's light. "Don't surprise me, that's a bastard term to live up to no matter who you are."

"I never realised how powerful the word was, the hold it takes on some folk."

"Ah, folk are dumb as mules, you know that," Carel declared carelessly, gesturing to the other side of the training ground where they could just make out a flurry of activity at the stables. "Sometimes as stubborn too."

The sky was dark. It was well past midnight, and all they could see ahead was the moonlight catching the frost on the many peaked roofs of the palace.

"Whether a saviour is needed or not, that don't matter to some. We're mortal, whatever tribe or colour." The veteran shrugged, the stump that was all that remained of his left arm nudging Isak's sleeve. "'Frail mortals, weak and fearful'—isn't that what it says in the Devotionals, the one to Lord Death? That's what we are, my boy, frail and weak. We don't lead perfect lives and deep down every one of us knows we could be better, as people, and as servants of the Gods. Who then wouldn't want a saviour to be the light showing us the way?"

"And they look to me?" Isak shook his head in disbelief. "Because at some point years ago the Gods feared Aryn Bwr's revenge, only to have their tool twisted awry? I'm no example."

"Ah but you are, like it or not," Carel said firmly. The man handed back the pipe then knocked the head of his cane against Isak's massive thigh. "Whatever playing was done with your destiny, it made others see a leader in those oversized boots of yours."

"And what about me?" Isak countered, rounding on the veteran and ducking his head so he could look the smaller man in the eye. "Who do I look to when I run out of answers? I'll tell you now I've got sod-all clue how to deal with the fact that I can feel my own death creeping up behind me, let alone whatever games Azaer is playing. So do I look to Kastan Styrax, perhaps the only man in this Land more trouble than I am? The man I feel in my bones is going to kill me?"

"No need to take that tone with me," Carel said sternly, "I ain't saying I've got all the answers." He jabbed his cane against Isak's chest and after an angry moment the white-eye stepped back. "I'm just out here for a smoke," Carel continued with an approving grin as he watched Isak swallow his temper, "and who'm I to say what manner your salvation might come in?"

Isak hesitated as Carel's words seemed to rush through his body. "Salvation? Gods, is that what I'm looking for?" Suddenly aware of the swirling winds up above him, the energy and power coursing through the darkness, he felt the cold of night fall away. Some instinct kicked into action, sending a tremble through his veins and clearing the last remaining vestiges of alcohol from his body. In its place was a sensation he couldn't place, almost like a trickle of energy waiting to be shaped into magic.

"Don't know what you're looking for," Carel said, oblivious to what has happening to Isak as he watched Xeliath struggle into a saddle and set out at a walk for the open space of the training ground, a terrified groom at her side. "Think Mihn's the better man to ask about salvation, even if he's getting a little strange of late too. You seen those tattoos of his? I'd never call the man a savage, no matter where he's from, but he's starting to look it with those arcane symbols tattooed onto his skin."

"There must be a purpose to it," Isak said distantly, prompting a snort from Carel.

"Purpose to everything, so the priests say, but sometimes you got to wonder."

Oh too true, my friend, Isak thought, staring blankly into the black sky, *and wonder I do. Death and salvation, now they're strange companions in any discussion. But if the strands of life and destiny are woven together, what happens if I grab one and give it a tug? If nothing works as intended around me, what would happen if I faced death head-on?*

"I think Mihn knows more than he's letting on," Isak said finally.

"If he does, he's got good reason, I'd say. That man is as loyal as they come; don't you worry about him."

"I'm worried *for* him."

"Ah, now that's foolish talk. You're Lord of the Farlan; it's your duty to ask difficult things of others. It's Mihn's responsibility what he gives to your cause, though; his choice, and one that's gladly made."

Isak was silent for a moment. "So what's your advice for me then? Like it or not, you're the one I look to for answers."

"Don't make fun," Carel growled irritably.

"I'm not, I swear." Isak clapped him on the shoulder. "All my life you've been the only one I could turn to. I'm not expecting answers to all my problems, but your advice has guided me this far. If nothing else, it's a comfort to hear, and these days I'll take any comfort I can get."

Carel looked suspicious for a moment, then shrugged, hearing no mocking from the boy he'd instilled with a soldier's sense of humour. "Not sure there's much more I can teach you, but you're slow, so I'll repeat some of it and see if it sticks this time." He grinned briefly before turning back towards the Great Hall, but not fast enough to hide his face as it became grave once more.

"A soldier can't let fear rule his life," Carel said. "Fear tells you you're still alive. Without it you'll be dead damn quick, that I promise, but if it's fear guiding your horse you're riding straight to the ivory gates."

My host of fears, all waiting in my shadow, Isak thought. *I think you're right, I've been letting fear play my hand for me, so perhaps it is time that changed.*

Isak turned back towards the warmth of the Great Hall and draped an arm over Carel's shoulder. "It's good to have you back."

The old soldier chuckled as they headed back. "I'm sure it is; you never did bother to buy your own tobacco. At least give me the damn pipe back, you oversized fool."

Vesna didn't hear the discreet knock on his apartment door. Slumped in a chair before the fire, he had even forgotten the bandaged wound on his head that nagged constantly. His focus was entirely occupied with the bloodred gem he turned over and over in his hands, feeling the slick surface of the cut faces and watching the light glitter through the stone. He'd never seen a stone like it, but for all its beauty it made him more fearful than anything else. For days now he'd spent hours, after everyone else had retired, sitting and staring at the stone. Questions ran through his head, but any answers just slipped off those glassily smooth facets and vanished.

The knock came again, this time louder. Vesna gave a start and sat up, his heart racing as he looked around the room in confusion before realising it was someone at the door. He hauled himself up, tucking the gem into a pocket before he called for the person to come in.

Tila came in, her hair falling loosely about her shoulders and a worried look on her face. She had wrapped a thick blanket around herself.

"Damn. Sorry," he started, "it's late isn't it?"

Tila nodded. No doubt he didn't look quite at his best, bandaged up and with bags under his eyes from lack of sleep.

"I'd hoped you had just fallen asleep," she started, "but I saw the light under the door."

Vesna crossed over to her and took Tila in his arms. He hugged her close and dropped a kiss on the top of her head. "I'm sorry," he started. "I meant to come to say goodnight, but I hadn't realised how late it was. My mind's all fogged at the moment—this damn cut." Even in Scree, Vesna had made a point of going to say goodnight to Tila at her bedroom door, and that had continued even after she had moved into Isak's rooms to keep Xeliath company as much as to help her.

"Is it still hurting?" she asked, immediately concerned. "Do we need to get the healer back up here?"

"No, no," Vesna said, dismissing the matter with a wave of the hand, "the stitches need time, nothing more."

"Then what else is it?" she persisted. "You've had injuries before—did they always make you act so strangely?"

"I—" Vesna faltered, disarmed by the look on his betrothed's face and admitting, "No, this isn't normal."

"Then tell me what the matter is." Tila urged him back to his chair and knelt beside it, keeping hold of one of his hands in hers. "We're to be married in a few weeks; is that the problem? Just a case of nerves?"

Vesna saw in her eyes she didn't believe that for a moment and he didn't even try agreeing. He sighed, realising the time had come. "No, that's not it, believe me. That is something I could not have happen soon enough." He squeezed her hand.

"Well?"

"The night I was ambushed," he started, then paused. "Tila, there's something I didn't tell you about that night."

"You were going to that brothel for more than just drink?" she said, trying to smile.

"Gods, no!" he exclaimed with a grimace. "I wish that were all. No, I meant during the attack. Something happened afterwards, and I've been thinking about it for days, trying to work out what to do."

"So tell me. There's nothing that could change things between us." Seeing Vesna wince as she said that, Tila continued sharply, "Evanelial Vesna, do you think I'm stupid? You've been a professional soldier for twenty years, and I am well aware what that entails, the demands it makes of you. As for the rest, I know you've performed services at Lesarl's com—"

"What?" Vesna spluttered, "he told you?"

"In a fashion. Oh, don't look so shocked, I'm working alongside the man on a daily basis and I have put a fair amount of thought into marrying you. Did you think that meant I've spent weeks wondering how to do my hair?" Her voice softened. "My father asked me about a dowry and I didn't have to look very hard to gain an idea of the debts your father left you; there's no way you would have been able to service those debts and pay the College of Magic for your armour."

"Did you read my file? Do you want me to tell you?"

Tila ran a hand down his cheek. "No, dearest, I know you; I know the extent of what you would do for the tribe already. I don't need to ask. However unsavoury your reputation might be, no one has ever bothered to claim you gloried or delighted in death. What you did in the past for the good of the tribe is not my place to ask."

Vesna looked stunned at how easily she'd dismissed the matter. "Are you sure?" He remembered all too well the look on Tila's face when Isak had announced rather casually that he'd murdered a man the previous evening. "That's quite a turnaround since Count Vilan's death."

"Vilan? I'm not saying I like murder, or that I approve of it, but I don't believe you would ever talk about it the way Lord Isak did then." She shivered. "His callous streak still catches me off guard from time to time, but I forgave him that, just as I forgave you your reputation. Do you think I was impressed when Lesarl intentionally left a note from the Keymaster of the Heraldic Library where he knew I'd find it? The note was to confirm that Lord Bahl would approve our marriage if such a thing might occur."

"The Keymaster of the Heraldic Library?" Vesna wondered aloud. His confusion increased when Tila's expression darkened.

"Keeper of the family trees," she said in a cold voice. "Apparently it was not only Sir Arole Pir who Lesarl considered it necessary to confirm his true parentage."

Vesna opened his mouth to speak but Tila held up a finger to stop him, her face thunderous. "Trust me; you do not want to continue that conversation any further. It will not end well for you. Just be glad the marriage is still going to happen."

He nodded dumbly. Suddenly the cut to his head didn't hurt now. It was overshadowed by the cold sensation of dread in his belly.

"Now, tell me about the night you were attacked," Tila said, perching on the arm of his chair and staring intently at him.

Vesna couldn't meet the force of her stare for long, but he knew not to drag the silence out and began to relate the last few moments of that fight and his conversation with the God of War.

After he had finished, Tila was silent. He chanced a look at her, but could read nothing from her expression as she stared into the fire, digesting the implications of what he'd said.

"This is what you had to tell me before we married. An offer of immortality from the God of War. I can see the dilemma." Her voice was cool, clinical.

Vesna's dread continued to mount as she left the words hanging in the air. His mouth went suddenly dry.

Abruptly, she stood up and turned to face him. "My beloved, you are an utter fool."

The count's mouth dropped open. That wasn't the response he'd been expecting.

"I can see the train of your thoughts now: We are in troubled times, my lord needs a general he can trust; I cannot shake my doubts. What value has there been in all these years of fighting? Have I made a difference? Here I am, a scarred man getting past his prime with nothing but a flawed reputation to show for it. Could this be my chance to do something more worthwhile, to prove to myself that this life and talent weren't wasted? Could this give me the strength I think I've lost, replace the innocence that died on one or other of a hundred battlefields?"

Vesna was frozen to his seat, unable to move as the hare turned on the hound. To hear his thoughts spoken aloud undermined his resolve entirely and he sat helpless as Tila continued, her face still unreadable, her voice giving just as little away.

"And so to the real problem, the words that have been running around your head for days: how can I refuse a God when he offers everything I've hoped for? But how then could I then still marry Tila?" She took a step forwards and Vesna felt himself lean away instinctively, sensing her growing anger.

"Well, my love," she growled, "as our great and currently steaming-drunk lord would put it: 'I couldn't give a damn, you don't get the choice.'" She took a deep breath, as though daring Vesna to interrupt before she had finished.

"Do you hear me? No choice whatsoever. Whatever argument you had worked out, don't you dare even voice it because I will clout you round the head. Whatever idiotic ideas of nobility and sacrifice you might have for even suggesting such a thing—and dear Gods if you deny that. I swear to Kantay I'll claw your eyes out with my nails for being half the man I think you are."

He heard her voice waver there, but only for a moment as Tila bit back the threatening tears and continued, "None of you damned soldiers have got the brains of a mayfly, so don't ever try to argue with me; your job is to obey and that's the way it's going to continue. Do you honestly think I'm going to meekly submit? Curtsey and be on my way?

"The look on your face shows that you can't be trusted with thinking, so here's what's going to happen. We are going to be married, as planned, and after that you might, on occasion, be permitted to think for yourself over the next few years, but that will only happen with my permission until you prove to me you're not the iron-brained grunt you've just demonstrated here today.

"And by the way, no you don't get a choice in that either. I love you and I know you love me too, so there's nothing to discuss. I'm going to marry you to save you from your own idiocy. Whether you accept Karkarn's offer is something to be decided later, but Mortal-Aspect, immortal, whatever you become, you'll be a married one.

"And if you thought for a moment that I couldn't make you marry me, then just you wait, and you'll find out what a campaign truly looks like. I'll make your life a bloody misery in a whole host of ways you've never even considered, and the longer you squirm, the more allies I'll draw into the fight, starting with Isak, the Chief Steward, Xeliath, the witch of Llehden, Mihn, and even the entire Palace Guard if necessary. You'll be outflanked, alone, and crying for mercy by the time I'm finished, so be a good boy and just do what you're told."

Tila took a long breath.

Vesna tried to do likewise, but found himself still paralysed. Without warning, she stepped forward and kissed him on the forehead before heading back towards the door. As she opened it, she called over her shoulder, "Now, get some sleep and just think about what you almost did."

CHAPTER 20

HIGH PRIEST ANTIL WAITED until the sound of footsteps receded. He was standing in a tiny, dimly lit corridor, looking down the cramped spiral stair, holding his breath as he strained to hear anything below. Out of habit he mouthed a silent prayer to Shotir. Hale had become a frightening place of late, and even if the God of Healing heard his servant's prayer, Antil still feared for his charge's safety. There were limits, it seemed, even to a God's blessing. Next time there might be no priest of Death to stop penitents searching the temple.

Fortunately for Legana, the only way to reach the consecrated hospital, kitchen, and dormitories that occupied most of the temple's space was through the shrine room. Thus far, the soldiers had balked at marching through, but Antil didn't expect that to last much longer. Since the Ruby Tower massacre there was a whisper of betrayal on the wind and the remaining militants were looking for anyone to blame.

Antil scratched his neck before abruptly pulling his hand away again. It was a nervous habit of his and these days he was sporting a patch of permanently raw skin there. The stairway remained dead quiet; the temple's priests were all busy as the hospital room remained full despite their best efforts. Legena's presence was a secret Antil had divulged to only one other, an amiable junior priest known as Fat Lonei, and for safety's sake Antil intended to keep it that way.

Father Lonei was entirely lacking in magic; his obesity was purely a product of gluttony. He had been banished as a danger from the hospital room, but he was a good worker in the kitchen and had been Antil's faithful helper for years. For all Lonei's simple nature, Antil knew he could trust the man to have relieved the priest attending the shrine downstairs and checked the way was clear.

Antil retreated to his room. It was as dim as the corridor, yet Legana still squinted when she looked in the direction of the window. Her eyesight was terribly poor now—she was trapped in a blur of grey, barely able to make out shapes or colour. She reacted mainly to movement, and now she flinched as he crossed the room towards her, her hands moving within the folds of the robe he'd given her.

"It's only me," he said softly as he stopped and slowly waved his right arm in front of his face. He wasn't sure how well she could hear him, so he kept the movement going until he saw her nod in acknowledgement. Despite his best efforts, Legana had managed to find at least one of her long daggers and he had no intention of startling a woman who could move as fast as she did, half blind or not.

The shadowy handprint on her throat remained and Antil was sure her voice was ruined beyond repair, but the rest of her body had healed supernaturally quickly, considering the broken bones and inevitable internal damage.

Legana gave a raspy whisper and fumbled for the slate he'd found for her. On the slate she scribbled three words. —*It is time.*

"Give Lonei a few more minutes; we're in no rush," Antil said in reply.

—*We go now*, she wrote and started to manoeuvre herself off the bed.

Antil reached out automatically to help her, but she pushed him away. She was as tall as him, and while she lacked his build, she was stronger, however unsteady at times. Her grey- and copper-streaked hair was inexpertly cropped short by Antil; he'd tied it back out of her face, but once she was standing she pulled the scraps of ribbon out so her hair fell over her face, partly concealing her startling eyes. Her face had recovered now, and except for the mark on her throat, her skin was perfect, unblemished by cuts or bruises.

"Why now?" he asked with a pantomime shrug.

—*Twilight.*

Antil frowned and repeated his gesture. "You fear the Gods are hunting you?"

She cocked her head to one side for a moment, straining to catch his words before realising his meaning and shaking her head. With her sleeve she erased the word on the slate.

—*Distraction. I feel it, like a spiderweb moving.*

Spiderweb? Antil wondered. *Gods, what sort of spider walks Hale that she can feel it?*

There was obviously no point arguing; her mind was made up, so he walked ahead of her to pull the door open. He reached out a hand for Legana to take and reluctantly she did—he could see she hated to be reliant on someone else. Her shining green eyes wide open, she shuffled along the wooden floor until they reached the stair, sliding her free hand along the wall.

The robe Antil had given her was a little short, enough to stop her tripping over the hem as easily. Antil was often called away to tend those unable to leave their homes, so with luck, no one would bother a priest and novice of Shotir.

The pair encountered no one until they reached the shrine room where Fat Lonei hovered, peering anxiously around the yellow-painted door.

"Father, I can see soldiers," he hissed when he noticed them.

Antil gestured for Legana to stay and hurried to Lonei's side. "What're they doing?"

Lonei shook his head, fear showing in his eyes. Antil stepped past him into the street, noting they were far from alone: monks, novices, priests, and laymen—everyone he could see was staring down the street at a company of Ruby Tower Guards, marching past the crossroads in two neat columns, followed by a less orderly band wearing the grey-and-white of the Byoran Guard that served in Hale.

As Antil watched he saw more than a few people taking flight at the sight of the soldiers. Shotir's temple hadn't been the only one called upon to deal with the victims of the troops' savage reclamation of control. But far from matters calming down, the violence was escalating, with the activities of the previous night as shocking as anything Antil had heard of in peacetime. Some of the Byoran Guard had vented their anger at the Temple of Etesia, then moved on to Triena and Kantay as well. They had dragged priests and novices of both genders out into the courtyard between the linked temples and raped one after the other, butchering any who put up a fight. All except one of the eunuchs had been killed; the lucky—if you could call it that—survivor had been bound to one of the temple archways with the entrails of Etesia's high priestess. The soldiers had cut off one of her breasts and jammed it in the eunuch's mouth, cutting off a finger every time he spat it out. Antil had heard the brutal story in silence, only the greyness of his skin betraying his horror.

And now it looked as if it was starting again.

"Where are they going, Father?" Lonei asked anxiously.

"I don't know," Antil replied, his sense of foreboding growing. He looked up at the sky. "Whatever they intend, they're doing it at twilight, when the Gods rest."

The breeze tugged at his yellow robes, like a child urging him on, and brought the scent of burnt spices from the Temple of Tsatach upwind of them. The fires were still burning there, but he saw none of the usual bustle on the sacred ground itself.

"So the Gods cannot see what they do?" Lonei almost gibbered at the thought. "Are they going to desecrate another temple?"

Antil scowled. "I don't know—but whatever they plan will lead to more deaths—of that I'm sure."

Following the troops of the Byoran Guard were two carts, each piled high with wood. As the carts jerked and bounced over the stony ground, a long plank slipped from the back of one and crashed to the ground.

"It looks like they're going to build a barricade. I wonder where?"

He felt the touch of a hand on his back and flinched until he realised it was Legana standing behind him. Her eyes were screwed up, though in truth it was anything but bright.

"Yes, it is time to leave," he said.

He thanked Lonei and ushered him back inside, promising to return as soon as he could and warning him again to say only that he was visiting the sick.

Legana walked with him in silence through the open streets of Hale, not objecting to the firm grip he maintained on her arm. When he looked at her face Antil felt more and more confused: that the girl was terrified at her vulnerability was plain, but there was also an air of wonder about her—as the breeze touched her cheek or as a horse passed by close enough that she could feel the vibrations of its falling hooves. Following Hale's gentle downward slope the pair eventually came to the Pigeon Gate leading into Breakale. There was only one guard on the gate, a young man with long dirty hair and pinched cheeks. His face brightened when he saw inside Legana's raised hood, but when he realised her eyes were almost entirely closed he scowled in disgust.

"Permit," he announced in a flat voice.

"Excuse me?" said Antil, confused.

The youth held out a hand. "Permit," he repeated, his eyes dull and unblinking like a fish.

"I need a permit to leave Hale?"

"You're a priest, ain't you?"

"When was this law passed?" Antil asked in dismay.

"Three days ago. Proclamation was put up all over the bloody place." The guard took a pace forward. "You ain't going nowhere without a permit." He carried a halberd, which he leaned on as he peered at Antil.

"I'm sorry," Antil said, keeping his voice gentle. "I've been attending to patients for the last few days. How do I get one? I need to get this woman back to her family in Breakale."

A lopsided smile crept onto the guard's face. "Well then, we can't have you failing in your duty, can we?" he declared and jabbed a thumb towards the small guardhouse set into the stone wall. "Take the young lady in there and I'll sort you out."

Antil laid a protective hand on Legana's arm. "No, I think perhaps we should just return to the temple."

"Oh you reckon, do you? Well how about I decide you're traitors? Maybe saw you running from the Ruby Tower after all your mates got killed?"

"No!" Antil said, his voice betraying his fear.

The guard lowered his pike head to shoulder height. "Then get in the guardroom and we'll see about that permit," he growled.

Flustered, Antil allowed himself to be herded into a dark room thick with the smell of tobacco and sweat. Aside from a weapons rack on the far wall, the only furniture was a square table and a pair of stools. As soon as he was inside the guard gave him a rough shove and sent him stumbling over one of the stools onto the floor.

"Just you stay there," the young guard warned, setting his pike against one wall but patting the pommel of his currently sheathed short-sword as he gave Antil a meaningful look.

As the priest started to climb to his feet the guard kicked the door shut with his heel and shoved Legana back against the table. Legana gasped in shock as the guard ran his hand up her body and closed about her right breast. He hardly saw her left hand move as she grabbed his wrist between thumb and forefinger, twisting it away effortlessly. The guard gave a strangled yelp as something snapped, but his scream was cut off when Legana pulled her dagger from her sleeve and slammed it into the guard's throat so hard she pinned him to the wall. She kept her hand on the blade for a moment before gripping his jaw and pulling the knife out again. The corpse fell to the floor and she bent over it to wipe her blade clean on his uniform.

Antil hadn't had time to react at all, so fast had Legana moved. Now she turned to him, her eyes wide again and her hands reaching, hands out like those of a lost child. She opened her mouth wide enough to scream, but only a dry croak came. Antil looked down at the guard, then, his mouth too dry to speak, and gave a jerky wave to attract Legana's attention. She fumbled for the slate hanging from her belt and wrote: —*Wine merchant. Beristole.*

"The Beristole?" Antil wondered aloud. "I know where that is—off the main highway to Wheel—but I'm going to take you to a friend's, where you'll be safe."

The smile fell from Legana's face. —*Friend*, she added to the slate, rapping it with two quick taps to emphasise her point.

He didn't bother arguing. Legana, even as near death as a person could be and still remain conscious, had proved to be as stubborn as a mule. "Very well, the Beristole it is."

Her smile returned.

The streets in Breakale were narrower than in Hale, the buildings taller and more regular. They found a walking rhythm soon enough, shuffling along with their eyes fixed on the ground ahead. For the main part passersby gave the pair pitying looks, but from time to time Antil found himself jostled; fear of being caught stopped him from commenting. The first woman to do it had continued without even a glance back as Antil stumbled and only Legana's strength had stopped him from falling in a sprawl into the street.

It didn't take him long to realise that the anger emanating from the temples, in both sermons and proclamations, was reaping the only crop it deserved. The fact that he wore the yellow robes of Shotir, God of Healing and Forgiveness, seemed to make no difference.

Can I blame them? Antil wondered as he was elbowed in the ribs by a man whose face was bruised yellow and purple all down one cheek. *Where were my exhortations for calm? When Death's priests were baying for the blood of sinners, my objections were too softly spoken.*

The wind picked up as the sun dropped to the horizon and light from windows started to glow into the street. When they paused at a crossroads for Antil to recall the way he felt suddenly exposed. Since becoming high priest he had left Hale only rarely, and then usually for Eight Towers; calls for ministration from Wheel and Burn—the ramshackle shantytowns of workshops, tanneries, and every other sort of physical labour—were attended by younger priests. Even before the recent tensions, these had not been safe places for a high priest to walk without escort.

He looked around, getting his bearings. Left would take him into the heart of Wheel, bisected by the two swift rivers that drove many of the district's waterwheels. Beyond were the miles of cultivated fields running towards the treacherous fens. In the place of temples and statues the buildings in Wheel tended to be haylofts, waterwheels, and warehouses.

Burn, to the right, was a cramped and squalid imitation of Breakale. It straddled a deep fissure in the ground from which, every year or so, a great gout of gas and flame would erupt, killing anyone up to a hundred yards downslope. The hot springs dotting the area meant folk had to pretty much ignore the danger.

Criminals ran both districts. Byora's rulers had long ago realised that as long as poverty remained rife there, their control would only ever be tenuous. An unofficial but well-known accommodation had proved cheaper and easier for all involved.

Legana gave his arm a tug as he stood still, the urgency plain on her face.

There was a statue in the centre of the crossroads around which the crowds hurried, presumably representing a God or Aspect since its arms and head had been broken off and filth smeared down one side. That wasn't why he'd stopped.

"The sun's going down," he explained. "I can't remember exactly how far the Beristole is, but I know the Byoran Guard don't go there after dark."

She checked her dagger in the long sleeve of her robe before dragging him forward once more.

"Yet here we go, perhaps to our deaths," Antil said under his breath before moving ahead of Legana to guide her to the safer part of the road, away from the carts and horses. As he did so he felt a body thump into his back and he crashed first to his knees, his hand slipping from Legana's, then fell face-first onto the cobbled ground, too quickly to even cry out before his head struck the stones.

"Whoa, sorry about that, Father," said a man behind him. Antil moaned as a jolt of pain ran up his arm from his already cold hand.

Before he knew what was happening a pair of hands had gripped him under the arms and lifted him upright. Antil winced, letting the man take most of his weight, his feet wobbling underneath him.

"You hurt, Father?" asked the man, a dark blur wavering in front of his face until Antil blinked and the details resolved into a youngish face, rounded features, and tufts of black hair poking out from under the hood of his cape. He didn't sound like a local, and from the scars on his face, Antil guessed he was a mercenary of some sort, but the man was grinning like a monkey and sounded genuinely apologetic.

"I—No, I am fine, I think," he said, touching a finger to his temple and not finding anything hurting too badly there. "Thank you," he added, rather belatedly.

"Ah don't worry about it," the man said, making a show of dusting Antil down, though it was apparent from the smell that dust was the least of his problems. "Should've been watching where I was going."

"Death's bony cock," growled a voice behind the man. The grin fell from the man's face and he looked over his shoulder at the speaker.

"Steady on, boyo, man's a high priest," he remonstrated, but his companion paid no attention. He was staring at Legana. Her hood had slipped a little and she stood in the emerging moonlight like a ghost, her skin pale and her eyes unfocused.

The first man squinted at her for a moment. "Shitting fuck," he breathed, frozen with surprise. His companion shoved him out of the way and grabbed Antil by the collar, hard enough to make the priest cry out.

"You better pray to Shotir that you weren't the one to do that do her," he hissed, pushing his face into Antil's. He was not as scarred, but he was more heavily built and looked just as well used to violence. Antil picked out a small tattoo, on his earlobe of all places. "If you were, you're in more trouble than you could possibly imagine."

"Got some strange luck on you, Father," muttered the first man, "running into us like that. Pissed off the Lady recently?"

Fat Lonei did not like the Land outside Hale. Whenever he was asked to travel elsewhere in the city, he was obedient and mindful of his vows. He performed his task as best he could, then scampered back to Hale, his heart pounding nervously until he was once again in familiar streets. He was a foundling, and had been nicknamed Fat Lonei in his fourth year in the temple, less out of malice—he was an amiable child and hard to dislike—more a statement of fact. He had never given anyone the impression he was unhappy with the name; it was simply who he was. His was a life of humble wants. Had the Gods themselves offered to make his every dream come true, Fat Lonei would have wondered what they wanted to hear from him.

He had been watching High Priest Antil head off down the street with the strange blind woman on his arm when he was suddenly struck by the notion that events of importance were afoot. A braver man would have followed the high priest and his charge to ensure they reached their destination safely, but one moment of imagining himself doing that was enough to make him realise that would leave him, Fat Lonei, out in the open, all alone. The chaos and bustle of Breakale frightened him and even the image of people lurching and shouting and barging brought the prickle of sweat to his brow. He saw himself surrounded by darkness, looking big and bright and obvious in his yellow priestly robe, while the filthy masses edged closer, baying for the blood of priests. No, that he could not do, but there was another option and this he embraced with the relief of a man who'd found a way around his conscience.

Scuttling from shadow to shadow, hanging well back, Fat Lonei followed the column of soldiers through the streets of Hale. The locals, clerics and laymen alike, scattered like frightened rabbits in the face of their advance. He heard the authoritative voices of the sergeants breaking the evening quiet, calling pointless orders, keeping their lines in order—anything to impose their presence on the cowed district.

Only when a halt was called did Fat Lonei realise their destination was the black needle-tipped dome of the Temple of Death, but not even seeing the carts brought clattering to the head of the column made him guess their purpose. He crept closer, careful to ensure that there were others nearer than him to provide ready targets, should the soldiers turn.

He saw the troops fan out, their weapons at the ready. A band of men, Byoran Guard, jumped to work when a big sergeant with a cruel face shouted. Lonei saw he was dressed as a Ruby Tower Guard, though he was, unusually, a foreigner, set apart not just by his tanned face but also by the strange elbow-length gauntlets he wore that seemed to wink slivers of bluish reflected light.

He heard cries of dismay emanate from inside the temple, swiftly echoed by many of those watching from a safe distance. Entreaties, angry shouts, and the wail of young novices accompanied the bustle around the open entrances of Death's temple, the traditional three arches leading into the main temple. When the big sergeant climbed to the top step and bellowed at his men to work harder, Lonei realised the Byoran Guards had been dragging their feet once they'd collected the wood from the carts. Perhaps they'd not properly understood the order correctly.

The sergeant struck someone about the ear and knocked him down: there was no mistake. Tools were produced, wood lifted up, and the first of Death's open gates was quickly blocked. Lonei felt his breath catch; he'd never seen or heard of such a thing before. Barring Death's gates? That was such a blasphemy he could not even conceive of it . . . the priest of Shotir sank to his knees like a puppet with the strings cut. Those around him stared in disbelief and horror, as shocked as Fat Lonei.

"By the order of the duchess," the sergeant bellowed at the top of his voice, waving a piece of parchment to the crowd assembled just out of reach of his cordon of Ruby Tower Guards, "the Temple of Death is closed until the traitors within the cults are brought to justice. Any violation of this decree will bring summary punishment."

It was a ridiculous decree, most likely impossible to enforce without leaving a garrison, yet even Lonei realised its effectiveness as the strength drained from his limbs. The Temple of Death was the heart of Hale, the house of the Chief of the Gods—this was a punch to the gut for all of them and it drove the wind from all those witnessing it. An insult and injury: Death's house defiled, Death's honour spat upon by a handful of soldiers.

An old woman, a priestess of Death, mounted the steps howling with grief. The sergeant turned at her high shrieks but motioned his troops to stay back. Each step was leaden as the priestess wove a path towards the sergeant, screaming curses at him between her heaving sobs. The sergeant laughed and reached out one hand to hold her off as she tried in vain to claw out his eyes, her fury impotent against his size and strength.

Lonei bowed his head, praying for Death to answer the insult. He didn't see the crossbow bolts flash towards the soldiers, but he looked up when the screams became more urgent and people started to flee in all directions. Through the scattering crowd he could see two of the Byoran Guard on the ground, one lying still, the other writhing and crying out. He looked around and caught sight of a handful of men with crossbows fleeing down the street, the brown robes of Ushull's priests flapping wildly as they ran.

Angry yells came from the ring of soldiers and some men started off down the street before being called back. As they turned Lonei saw a man suddenly burst forward through the cordon, long scimitars in each hand. The man was wearing a bronze-edged robe of bright, bloody red. He was short but extremely wide, and his head was shaved. The angry shouts turned into cries of alarm as he cut across the nearest man's face and spun gracefully away, slashing at the next as he moved in behind the troops.

Lonei gave a gasp: he was watching a Mystic of Karkarn. The God of War had always attracted penitents, and some of those found a deeper truth in the combat skills they had learned, honing their prowess with prayer and fanatical dedication.

The line of soldiers crumpled inward as the mystic's long shining swords, flashing like bolts of lightning, tore through the unprepared men. The big sergeant gave a furious shout, drew his own weapon, and jumped down the steps to the street. The mystic turned neatly away from a falling man to meet the new threat with a flurry of blows, but somehow the foreign soldier parried them all and managed to plant a heavy kick in the cleric's side.

The shaven-headed priest reeled, riding a blow that would have knocked a weaker man flying, but he was given no time to recover. He twisted to deflect an outthrust pike behind him, then raised a leg clear of a blade sweeping towards his shin before driving the point of his curved weapon into his attacker's throat.

The distraction of the troops proved enough for the big sergeant to make up the ground and he chopped through the priest's right hand with one savage blow. Momentum carried him close enough to hammer the pommel of his sword into the mystic's cheek and he was already falling back from the force of the blow as the sergeant rammed his sword deep into the mystic's stomach.

A hush descended. Lonei saw a spasm of agony cross the mystic's face as he fell to his knees, spitted on the long sword. The sergeant lifted the hilt up, forcing the mystic to open his mouth in a silent scream as he yanked the sword out. The mystic fell as the sergeant turned away, leaving the dying man to twitch his last.

He turned his malevolent gaze to those watching. "Arrest them all, every one you can take," he roared.

In the torchlight he looked like a raging daemon, a cruel grin on his scarred face. Lonei whimpered as he looked at the prone figure of the old priestess lying on the steps. The soldiers ran to obey their commander, but Lonei was frozen to the spot. He didn't see the troops run past him, nor the gap-toothed man who barely checked his stride to smack his pike handle into Lonei's head. *A flash of light, a screech of pain* . . . Lonei felt himself fall into blackness where there was only the face of a daemon in a scarlet uniform.

CHAPTER 21

IN THE CITY OF TOR MILIST, in a grand house redolent of neglect, a woman stood with her hands clasped, staring at her unexpected visitor. Gian Intiss presided over her late husband's household like a duchess, but not even pride and determination were enough to keep everything together. Civil war left its mark on every building, just as it scarred the families within. Everywhere Gian looked she saw reminders of their failing fortunes: the cracked paintwork, the warped boards, the broken trap in the yard. Even when she closed her eyes it was all around her: the distant bang of a shutter in the wind, its latch broken; a gust of wind through the broken window pane . . .

The day's cost felt like a punch to the gut, but though the ledgers had nothing but bad news, she had had no choice: Harol's birthday marked his entry into adulthood, and as such it required a celebration worthy of a merchant's firstborn. Without it, both competitors and creditors would start to ask questions, questions Gian couldn't answer.

She stood at the kitchen door, barely listening to the clatter of preparation going on behind her as she looked down the hall that was the heart of the house. White mourning drapes still hung from the beams and around the other three doorways and what decorations they had added were barely noticeable in comparison. The hall presently held more than fifty people, adults standing in knots of four or five while children raced around them squealing in delight. A nursemaid squatted on the ground next to the small playpen containing half a dozen toddlers who were crashing Harol's old wooden toys against each other and delighting in the noise.

At the other end of the hall a slim figure faced away from her, standing perfectly still and looking at nothing as far as she could tell. The noise from the room washed over it as though it was just a ghost, belonging to another place and time. The Harlequin had removed only its bearskin and pack when it arrived. It was still wearing a long sword on each hip, as it had when it arrived and announced it would entertain her guests. Tunic and breeches were a patchwork of multicoloured diamond shapes, each one no longer than her middle finger. Brown boots covered its legs, a white porcelain mask its face. The hair visible from behind was so dark it was almost black, and long enough to be tucked inside the Harlequin's collar.

Gian shivered. She knew she should be grateful and give thanks to the Gods for its presence, for it added to the veneer of continued wealth, but there was something about its manner that made her nervous.

"You've got that look on your face again," said a voice beside her. Harol slipped an arm around her waist and gave his mother a kiss on her cheek. "You're worrying."

"It feels like I'm always worrying about something," she sighed, giving her waifish eldest son a tight squeeze. "But if I don't, who will?"

They had always been close, and Gian had never understood why father and son had found so little common ground between them. She and her bear-like husband had been as close as could be, and she adored her son, but something had always set the pair at odds with each other.

"You should eat something then," Harol said, gesturing at the platters of food that had been laid out on the long oak table. He was wearing his new velvet tunic and Gian realised the thick sleeves she'd given it did nothing at all to hide his skinny, boyish arms. "Try the honeyed pork, it's delicious."

"You're the one who needs building up," she replied, giving him a weak smile and patting her stomach. "The last thing I need to do is eat more. A fatter belly and more worry lines: that's all I'll get from this party!"

"What is there for you to worry about?"

"That Harlequin," she started, but stopped. "I don't know, it's just—"

"Harlequins are always a bit odd, aren't they? You offered it meat and wine when it arrived, didn't you?" Since his father's death, earnest young Harol had taken a sudden interest in protocol and etiquette, as if he thought he had to become master of the household immediately. He had begun to affect a strangely formal manner in front of guests.

Gian nodded. "But it refused the Harlequin's covenant and said it would only take bread, only drink water."

"Why?"

She sighed heavily again. "I don't really know. It said it would make no further covenants until it found innocence? What did it mean by that?"

Harol made a dismissive sound and stuck his tongue out at the Harlequin's turned back. While his figure was every bit as slim and androgynous as a Harlequin's, Harol's face was always animated—when he wasn't telling himself to act grave and adult.

His cheeks were flushed, no doubt with wine as much as excitement at the day. Celebration had become a rare thing in Tor Milist over the last decade; even the end to the slow, drawn-out civil war had been met with uncertainty and apprehension. They knew Duke Vrerr's moods and methods too well to shout for joy.

"Listen to me well, for I am a guardian of the past," the Harlequin said in a sudden loud voice, still facing away from the room.

The voices died to nothing almost immediately. Even the smaller children sensed the change in atmosphere and ceased their raucous play. Several crept forward to where their parents stood and sat at their feet, all heads turned towards the speaker.

Without warning the Harlequin turned to face the room. Gian felt her hand tighten as its masked face swept the room, the bloody teardrop on its cheek alarmingly bright. One of the smaller children whimpered at the sight, but she could see the others were enraptured.

"In the city of Aineer in the years when the Gods were unquestioned throughout the Land, there was born a Yeetatchen girl by the name of Jerrath. Aineer was a city of faithful piety in those years, content in its fortunes and far removed from the city it was to become—the city that Lliot, God of the Seas, destroyed for the behaviour of its citizens."

A mutter ran around the room. Gian saw the face of a friend of hers tighten and become stern. Far from stopping, the rumours had been exacerbated by the sudden change in the priesthood. Folk said Scree had been destroyed by the Gods, obliterated in a firestorm while the cowled head of Death looked down from the clouds, His laughter like thunder.

She frowned as a grim quiet fell over her guests. *Why remind people of that? Why stir up more anger and resentment?* she wondered. Tor Milist had been spared major violence, but there were reports of skirmishes, religious executions, and arbitrary punishments coming into the city from every direction.

"Jerrath was the perfect daughter," the Harlequin continued, "cheerful about her chores and humble in her manner. From an early age she took to walking the streets each morning to visit each of the city's main temples."

The Harlequin's voice was strong and clear, somehow unmuffled by the thin porcelain mask it wore. It stood perfectly still, hands clasped in front. "Ever courteous, Jerrath became a popular sight on the morning streets. As the years passed all of Aineer came to know her face and love her. When she neared womanhood, however, no suits of marriage were offered by the rich men of the city despite her beauty. It was clear to all that Jerrath was too good for a mortal life and was destined to join the priesthood."

The Harlequin's voice softened. "One Prayerday morning, the High Priest of Nartis passed his counterpart in Tsatach's service and they fell into conversation. Both looked decidedly pleased, and each enquired why the other was so happy. The answer given by the Night Hunter's servant was quickly echoed by the other: "There is only a week until Jerrath comes of age and joins my temple."

"Both priests looked at each other in astonishment before realising that the Jerrath they knew as a faithful and devoted servant of their God was just as devoted to all of the Gods of Aineer. Quickly they gathered all of the senior priests of the city and, unable to agree amongst themselves, went to the house of Jerrath's father to demand a decision from the girl herself."

Gian felt a tingle run down her spine. She hadn't heard a Harlequin tell a tale since childhood, but even as a careworn mother of three, she felt the spell of its words just as strongly, every syllable teasing the nerves down her neck like a lover's caress.

"The humble Jerrath could make no such decision. She became frightened as the gaggle of clerics shouted their demands at her, for she had never realised she would one day have to prefer one God above the others. It fell to Jerrath's father to hush the mob, whereupon Jerrath begged him to make the choice on her behalf. Her father thought for a long time, frightened by the decision he was to make.

"Knowing only too well that Jerrath was beloved of the city, he saw the avarice of the priests who might benefit. Jerrath's popularity would bring the citizens of Aineer flocking to whichever temple she served; the God of that temple would become first among the Gods of Aineer. He feared his decision would give that high priest sway over the entire population.

"The longer he delayed his decision the angrier the priests became.

"Soon he could no longer stand the clamour as more shouting clerics gathered outside the house to add their voices to the debate. He called for silence and was ignored. Twice more he cried for quiet and each time they continued to shout. Eventually Jerrath's father pounded on the table with a leg of lamb, freshly slaughtered and being prepared for their evening meal, and blood flew over the whole crowd. Only then was there quiet.

"In a loud voice Jerrath's father declared he could not choose one God over another, so he would leave it in the hands of the Gods themselves to decide. Upon hearing this, all assembled understood what he meant by this,

for Aineer was a city that loved competition and wagers as much as the child
they were fighting over. The temple coffers were filled by taxes upon these
both activities and offerings from competitors.

"Jerrath's father declared that on his daughter's birthday a race would be
held in the streets of Aineer. The priests of each temple were to carry the
statue of their God from one temple to the next, following the path Jerrath
took each morning. The first to reach the Temple of Alterr on the far side of
the city would be declared the winner."

The Harlequin paused and took stock of its audience, standing in rapt
attention. Gian followed its gaze around the room; only she moved; her guests
and servants alike were statue-still, as though frozen by some ancient spell.

"The day of the race," it continued, starting straight at Gian, who felt a
sudden cold chill, "the whole city lined the route before the first rays of dawn
touched the rooftops. Bets were laid and a feast prepared for the winner, but a
surprise awaited them all as the sun crept into view. Drawn by the fervent
prayers of their servants, the Gods themselves stood in the bright morning light
outside the house of Jerrath's father, surrounded by the priests of their temples.

"Jerrath's father walked out of his house to start the race and the blood
drained from his face. Before him were the eight most prominent Gods in the
city, as tall as houses and terrifying to behold: Tsatach, with his great flame-
bladed axe and fat copper bands on his arms; the Queen of the Gods in robes
of red and orange—she whose true name is accursed for the pity she demonstrated during the Great War—and beside her stood proud Larat in his patchwork cloak of every colour in the Land. Behind them were Veren, God of the
Beasts, alongside his winged brother, Vellern; then the sister-Goddesses of
Love, Triena and Etesia, whose purple ribbons danced in the air; and grey-
faced Kebren, God of Justice, with his huge brass scales across his shoulders.

"The Gods were silent, all watching Jerrath's father as he stood in the
doorway of his house, shaking with fear, until Jerrath herself squeezed past
him and bowed to each God in turn, prompting him to follow suit.

"With the Gods themselves thus arrayed on his doorstep Jerrath's father
announced that the priests should not carry a statue of their God on a litter
but the God itself. The crowd watching cheered his words immediately and
in the face of such enthusiasm the Gods agreed. They lined up as best they
could in the street, and each of the Gods sat upon a litter with a dozen of their
strongest priests carrying them.

"With a great roar from the crowd the priests started off towards the first
of the temples—all but Kebren's servants, who, try as they might, could not

manage to stagger more than a few steps under the weight of their God's enormous brass scales. All twelve priests fell to the ground, exhausted. As hesitant laughter rang out from the crowd, Kebren gave a roar of fury to silence the voices and disappeared in a clap of thunder.

"And seven remained."

Gian frowned. She had heard this story only once, years before, but it sounded strange to her ears. "That's not how it happened," she muttered. "The Gods suggested the race themselves, I'm sure of it, and Kebren did not fly into a rage."

In the hushed room her voice carried and a number of people turned to glare at her. Gian almost gasped at the furious faces turned in her direction.

"What do you know, were you there?" growled one.

"I've heard this story before," Gian whispered.

"You think your memory better than a Harlequin's?" hissed Peira, her favourite aunt. The old woman's face was contorted with spite. "Everyone knows what the Gods are like; of course they were angry."

"But I'm sure—"

"Shut up," said burly Vorren, her cousin, as his fat fingers flexed and closed tight into a threatening fist. "Stop defending them."

Gian raised her hands, trying to placate him, but Vorren immediately bristled at the gesture. She lowered them hurriedly and looked down, feeling the anger in the room like a fire blazing. She bunched her sleeves in her fists, trying to stop her hands shaking as they all stared at her. The moment lingered, her fear deepened—and then the Harlequin spoke again, resuming the story and defusing the suddenly choking atmosphere.

"Seven, the remaining Gods numbered, and seven sought to turn events to their advantage. As they reached the first temple, that of Kebren, the Queen of the Gods realised her feeble priests would not last much longer, so old and infirm were they. She adopted the form of her chosen creature, the phoenix, intent on carrying both litter and priests in her claws, only to have the conflagration of her outstretched wings burn the priests to cinders.

"Seeing this attempt at treachery, Vellern gave his bearers wings of red and blue plumage, but without hands to carry the litter they left their God behind. Both Triena and Etesia stopped by the wayside to charm a watching company of knights and have them carry both priestesses and litter, but the soldiers started to fight amongst themselves for the honour and blocked the street.

"Veren, Lord of the Beasts, imitated his brother, Vellern, and changed the legs of his priests to those of powerful stags. They raced ahead of the others and had the next temple in sight when their hooves became entangled in a drain gutter, quite unable to move. Tsatach bestowed upon his priests the strength of the Chetse heroes that were first among his followers, but so sure were they of their superior strength that once they had outdistanced the rest they stopped to drink at a tavern. There, as the Chetse, Tsatach's chosen people, are wont to do, the priests quickly started trying to impress their lord with feats of drinking—but of course the God outdid them all, leaving them drunk on the ground.

"The last of the Gods in the race, Larat, stopped his priests as soon as he saw the others begin to fail. Realising that pride would be their undoing, he did nothing to his priests and instead turned the litter into a chariot. A golden whip appeared in his hand and the traces ensnared his priests like striking snakes. With a crack of the whip he set off again, laughing as hard as the crowd lining the street while his priests yelped and howled."

The Harlequin's voiced dropped until it was low and mournful. "And so it was Larat who won the race, Lord of Cruelty and Manipulation, and the last sight of Jerrath afforded to her father was the sight of her trailing after Larat, the golden whip caught around her neck, as he dragged her away for fifty years of service."

That's not right, Gian thought, biting her lip hard enough to make it bleed so she would not speak the words aloud again. *That is not the tale I heard.*

She looked around the room and saw tight faces and angry expressions, but more than a few of her guests were nodding at the Harlequin's words, as though recognising a great truth. Careful not to draw attention to herself Gian slipped the bronze charm to Kitar hanging around her neck inside her dress, away from the eyes of her guests.

"*Merciful Gods, what has happened to them all?*" she whispered.

CHAPTER 22

DORANEI LEANED FORWARD, HIS EYES ON LEGANA. The woman gave no sign of noticing him; she was looking around the room like a blind woman, instinctively turning at each small sound. At her side was the priest, Antil, fussing over her like a lover.

The thought stopped Doranei in his tracks. A bitter bubble of laughter welled up in his throat and he had to cover it with a cough.

Oh you poor bastard if you've fallen for her, he thought. *Martyrs to our own hearts, we are.*

The room was lit only by a single candle, at the priest's urging. Doranei had to strain his eyes to see what Legana had written on the slate.

— *Where am I?*

"Somewhere safe," Sebe replied from the doorway, "we ain't taking you to your wine merchant tonight."

They were in a private room over the safest-looking tavern he'd been able to find. There were three sets of bunks fixed to the wall, four stools, and a table too light to barricade the door with. The landlord had taken one look at the four of them and doubled his standard rate. It was money they could ill afford to spend, but Doranei knew they had to get off the street as quickly as possible. If worse came to worst, he could always steal more. A childhood among criminals had many benefits.

"Tell us what happened," Doranei interjected. "What's that on your throat?"

Legana made no response other than to turn to the priest. Antil wilted under the combined glare of the three killers. Like most priests of Shotir, Doranei noticed, the man had worry lines on his face and more fat than muscle under his robe—and right now he found himself in a different Land to the one he normally inhabited. Most likely he was ready to collapse in nervous exhaustion.

"I found her in my bedchamber," Antil began, colouring at the sound Sebe made from his position at the door. They'd rigged a tripwire as the bottom to catch anyone charging in, but Sebe was standing guard all the same.

"She had been thrown through the window when the Temple of Alterr exploded."

Doranei blinked "It did what now?"

"You haven't heard about that?"

"Not that it had bloody exploded!" Doranei said with a disbelieving laugh. "We've only been here a couple of days, just enough to hear about the Clerics' Rebellion and general chaos. Someone mentioned a damaged temple, but nothing as drastic as that." He looked at Sebe, who nodded in agreement.

"I don't really know much more, other than whatever Legana met in there was powerful enough to kill a Goddess—and to break half the bones in Legana's body as an afterthought."

"Goddess? Which one?"

"The Lady," he said sadly.

Both men gasped in shock. Nothing had prepared them for that. Doranei assumed the rumours meant a minor Aspect—but the Lady was almost within the Upper Circle!

"So Legana lived while a major Goddess died?" He didn't bother to hide his scepticism; something about this didn't make sense.

The pale-skinned woman nodded.

"But how? I've seen you fight—and you're damn good—but when a Goddess dies nothing mortal gets out of the room alive. Come to think of it, if you broke so many bones, how are you walking around?"

"Ah," Antil piped up, "I helped there a little—but she was touched by the Lady, and a residue of that power remains."

"But she's just a devotee!"

"Oh." The priest shut his mouth with a snap and looked down.

"What?" Doranei demanded irritably.

Legana gave him a predatory smile. Her sight was still vague and unfocused, but she was following the sound of his voice well enough. For the first time since they'd bumped into her she looked like the woman he'd known in Scree, controlled and confident. Doranei had found it so unnerving to see her walk to the tavern with uncertain, jerky steps that he had eventually moved ahead to scout the road so he didn't have to watch. The fiery-tempered Farlan agent and he had never been friends exactly, but he'd admired her powerful grace and purpose. To see a peer so vulnerable and damaged left his hands trembling, his throat burning for a drink.

Legana scribbled on her piece of slate and held it up to him.

—*Mortal-Aspect.*

"Piss and daemons," Doranei breathed, ignoring the high priest's expression. "I never even heard of—Merciful Death! And Fate's dead? Does that make you—?" He let out a sigh of relief when Legana shook her head.

"What about Ostia?" he asked awkwardly, his fear mounting. *Oh Gods, please no, don't let it have been Zhia who did this.*

Again Legana shook her head, but her expression became grave. She wrote again on the board.

—*Talk alone.*

It took a little persuading to get Antil to leave her side, but once they were alone Doranei dragged his stool close beside Legana so he could see the slate.

—*Aracnan*, she wrote.

Doranei frowned. He knew the name, and the reputation, but he hadn't expected to hear it in this context. "Do you know why?"

She shook her head, her grey-and-coppery tresses falling over her eyes.

"Can you guess? What was he doing in the temple? You must have walked in at just the wrong time—I had no idea Aracnan was so powerful that he could kill a God at all, but not even Death would choose lightly to fight the Lady."

—*Pretend ritual, summoning.*

"Pretend?" Doranei scratched the stubble on his cheek as he thought. "Making it look like a priest was summoning a daemon? Doesn't matter whether you believe it or not, it stirs up trouble. Either one more reason to consider the clerics enemies, or confirmation that someone's trying to discredit them."

—*Who profits?*

Doranei shrugged. "Depends what the priest was like, what position he held in the city."

—*Powerful, ear of the duchess.*

"Could be bloody anyone then; might be trying to replace him as an influence, undermine the duchess, damage the reputation of the cults within the city—or could be something entirely personal for all we know."

—*Azaer?*

He scowled and wiped the name out with his sleeve. "Hope not. Gives the shadow far greater scope if one of its followers is strong enough to kill a God." Doranei looked around, checking the room once again for mirrors, relieved that he hadn't missed any.

—*Why are you here?*

"To find you, in a manner of speaking."

—Zhia?

"The king sent me," he said hurriedly. "I need to speak to her on his behalf."

—Not here yet.

Doranei looked Legana full in the face, and only then did he realise her eyes had changed colour. Where they had once been the normal Farlan deep brown, now they were a brilliant dark green, deep pools in which a man could lose himself. It wasn't the only change in her appearance, just the one that most obviously marked her as linked to Fate. How had she described herself, Mortal-Aspect? He'd never heard of such a thing, and most likely that was a bad sign. When the Gods were involved, change would surely come only under the most extreme of circumstances.

Legana was as beautiful as ever, but now her alabaster skin, seamed hair, and green eyes made her look strangely terrifying. And now he was close enough to notice a series of lumps at the base of her throat where the shadowy handprint was, almost like a necklace underneath the skin.

"Gods, what happened there?" he breathed. Without thinking he reached out to touch the bumps, only to have Legana flinch away. Red-faced, he started muttering his apologies.

—My business, she wrote.

"Of course, sorry." He shook his head at his own foolishness. "Do you mind—? I'm sorry, but I've just realised I don't know who I'm talking to anymore. Are you an agent of the Gods? Of Lord Isak, still? How do you know Zhia isn't in the city? You cannot still be standing in her shadow after becoming Mortal-Aspect of the Lady?"

Her shoulders fell and she looked at the ground for a few heartbeats, her expression unreadable, until she wrote on the slate. *—Alone now.*

"What about Lord Isak?"

—Need to send message.

Doranei nodded. "Sebe can do that for you—he can take it to your wine merchant at least. What do you need to tell him?"

—News of Menin, Aracnan, lost contact Zhia, injured.

"Where is Zhia?"

—Following.

"You don't know where she's been?"

Legana shrugged, the movement causing her to wince in pain. Her head sagged forward a little and Doranei realised she was trembling as the hand holding the chalk wavered uncertainly.

He gently took the slate from her and said softly, "You're exhausted. You need to sleep."

She didn't respond at first and he repeated himself, louder. This time she gestured her agreement and allowed him to help her up. Without complaint from the former assassin, Doranei slipped an arm around her waist and half carried her to one of the beds. She managed to slide herself back until she was leaning against the wall and she sat there, breathing hard, while Doranei fetched her slate and arranged a blanket over her.

He risked a smile. "What a change! You'd have broken my arm if I'd done that in Scree."

—*Still can.*

"I'll take your word for that," Doranei said, sitting on the side of her bed. He felt suddenly feeble, like a heartsick old man. "I didn't expect any of this when I signed up."

Legana watched him, motionless for a moment before writing her reply. —*Poor baby.*

Doranei frowned at her. There was more than a spark of the old Legana left, that prickly, savage woman he'd met in Scree. As she wrote on the slate the strokes were quick, merciless slashes across the surface. —*You are not broken.*

He could see the anger radiating out from those emerald eyes, stripping away the scars on his soul. "Gods, woman," he muttered angrily, "no wonder people think you're a pitiless bitch." He stood, but as he started to walk away he remembering something. "Business then; how do I find Zhia?"

Legana didn't reply beyond closing her eyes but Doranei, now irritated, gave her a rough nudge on the leg, then another. The third time she opened her eyes again and glared at him, but he stood resolute until she reached for her slate.

—*Coin, Rose Fountain Square, blue door.*

"She's there?"

A shake of the head.

Doranei thought for a moment. "She's expecting you to be there, with her vampire friend—what was his name, Mikiss? Did you kill him?"

A nod.

"So Zhia will probably be able to tell you're not there, which will make her suspicious. So I need to pay someone to watch the house and give her a message when she snatches them."

Now he had an idea of what he was going to do next, Doranei felt some of the weight lift. He headed for the door. "I'm off to check out this house first. You've got some strange sort of luck around your shoulders for us to run into you like we did, so maybe it'll rub off on me enough to last the evening. If you flutter your eyelashes at Sebe while I'm out, he'll probably take that message for you."

As he closed the door behind him he heard something thud into it and turned to see the tip of a knife blade protruding through the wood. He grinned and went downstairs to fetch the other men.

Outside it was dark and quiet. The streets were close to empty, the night-time chill more than enough to drive most people inside. He checked his weapons out of instinct. There were enough armed men on the streets that he didn't think he'd look out of the ordinary to a patrol, and looking a soft target was almost as good an idea as borrowing the high priest's robe.

Overhead the clear sky was a dark blue, fading to black towards the western horizon where a spray of stars were visible. The Hunter's Moon was at its height ahead of him, its pale light inviting him on. Below that were the tiers of the city, the wealthier districts looking down on the rest from the mountain side while the concave cliff of Blackfang itself towered over all of them, a sheer black wall of jagged teeth. He touched the sword grip under his coat and hurried on.

He's visited the city before and found his way to the Rose Fountain without difficulty. Getting into the district hadn't proved a problem; fortunately Zhia, true to form, had chosen rooms in an unremarkable corner of the quarter, a good area but far from any likely excitement. As he'd passed the gates to Eight Towers, he had seen the guards there, Ruby Tower soldiers as well as the Byoran Guard.

In Coin too the streets had an armed presence, but they were not restricting movement. Most were liveried private companies employed by the district's bankers, and their instructions were to make their presence known and to discourage any potential excitement. Doranei knew they'd be no trouble unless he started taking an interest in the wrong house.

Where the road widened to bulge around the Rose Fountain stood three tall stone-faced buildings: a pair of silversmiths and what he guessed was a lending house occupying the ground floors. On the other side were the more expensive homes, half hidden by elms and eight-foot-high stone walls.

Doranei slowed his pace as he reached the fountain and fumbled for a copper coin—a house, they called them in Byora, but it looked like any other copper piece he'd ever used. There were two men watching idly, standing guard at the side of an open gate that led into a courtyard. Most importantly for Doranei's purposes, they stood like men who were bored, leaning on their halberds with glazed expressions. Rather than watch from the shadows, a risky idea when there were guards posted everywhere, he might as well hide in plain sight.

"Need all the luck I can get these days," he called to the guards, gesturing towards the fountain.

"Din't you 'ear?" one replied. "Luck's in short supply these days." He was the younger of the two, the best part of ten winters younger than Doranei.

Doranei cocked his head. "Hear what?"

"They say the Lady's no more," the guard replied in a smug voice. "Bloody Gods bin arguin' among thesselves and she got killed. That's luck fer you—bad luck, hey?"

"Shit, really?" Doranei took a step towards them, his face a picture of shock. The guard grinned, pleased to have had such a dramatic effect while his older comrade watched them in taciturn silence.

"Aye, that's what they're sayin'. Where you bin that you've not 'eard nuffin?"

"Riding on the slowest bloody wagon train I ever seen," Doranei sniffed. "Haven't heard nothing 'cept mules and drivers farting for weeks." He patted his coat theatrically. "There were benefits though, I'll tell you." He pulled out a battered leather case from a coat pocket. "Convoy carried tobacco for the main part—you can be damn sure I'm gonna make friends with any man transporting a hundred boxes of cigars!"

Doranei gave a hopeful little look at the guards, then through the archway. "Got a fire going anywhere?"

The younger guard's grin became wider. "Got a spare coupla them cigars?"

"Hah, didn't say I wanted a smoke that bad," Doranei replied good-naturedly, watching the older guard carefully. The man was scrutinising his every movement, he'd be suspicious of any excess generosity. "These things cost half a day's work each." He paused. "Tell you what though, maybe you could do me a favour as trade."

"You walk careful now," the older guard rumbled suddenly. "It's a cold night an' I'm in no mood to smack someone around, but we got a job to do here, so you want to watch what you say next."

"Nothing like that; I'm no thief," Doranei protested, holding his hands out. "I was asked to do something by the wagon master, but the man's a fucking criminal and I wouldn't trust him further than I could throw the grease-haired bastard. I never been to Byora before, don't know whether what he's asked is going to make me money or get my throat cut."

Doranei could see the man weighing up the situation. He waited; the eagerness on the younger guard's face was plain, so he'd let the older one work it out for himself.

"Fine," the guard said eventually, hefting his weapon to point it at Doranei. "Yanai, you go get that daft girl to fetch you a taper from the kitchen." He nodded to Doranei. "You try anything stupid while he's gone and you'll get this right through you, understand?"

He smiled and nodded, ignoring the impulse to step back, out of range of the halberd, while Yanai scampered off.

"Name's Kirer," he said conversationally. "You?"

Sergeant Loris," the older man replied.

Ah, one of those, Doranei thought. *Insists on his rank even though he's just a fucking guard. And Loris? Good Litse name that one, but his looks don't back it up.* The guard had a thick face and small features: thin lips and small hooded eyes. *All cheeks and forehead, this one, like a child's head that got inflated.*

"So, Sarge," Doranei continued, maintaining a harmless grin, "know the city well, d'you?"

"Well enough," he grunted.

"So what would you say to this job I've been offered? I'm to buy two bags of Queen's Favour—whatever in Ghenna's name that is—from a house near here. I talked one of his drivers into a good deal and he reckoned I could do it twice."

"Queen's Favour? I've heard of it," Loris said cautiously. "It's a herb, gathered from the mountain slopes."

"So it's just a medicine? No problem then—"

Loris grinned at Doranei's naïveté. "Not exactly 'no problem,' son. Witches and whores use it to kill babies in the womb, get rid of the unwanted. Gathering or buying Queen's Favour is banned, so he better be paying you well for the risk you're taking."

Yanai returned carefully carrying a smouldering taper. Doranei handed them each a cigar, cut off the tip of his with his knife, and lit up. "Man's been sent to buy Queen's Favour," Loris said to his colleague. He rested his halberd against his shoulder and bit off the tip of his cigar and spat it out. He brought the taper to it and drew deeply until it was glowing, then raised it in a toast and gave Doranei an appreciative nod. "Good smoke, this. Thanks, friend."

"Queen's Favour, eh? Bad game that one," said Yanai, trying to copy the deft way Doranei had prepared his smoke. "So what're you doing 'ere?"

"This is where I was sent to buy it." Doranei indicated the blue door Legana had told him about.

"Nah, not in Coin," Yanai said with a laugh. "You wanna go to Burn for that shit. These parts is respectable; a man don't last long peddlin' Queen's Favour 'ere."

"This is where he sent me," Doranei insisted. "Said to ask for Nai the Mage, funny-looking man with odd-sized feet."

Neither name nor description elicited anything from either man.

"Mage, eh?" Loris puffed out his cheeks. "Didn't realise it had a use in magic too."

"'ere, reckon thass why that bloody kid was 'anging round 'ere'?" Yanai said to Loris suddenly. "Some brat checkin' out the square coupla times a night for the last week now," he explained to Doranei. "Could be watchin' out fer customers mebbe, or pr'aps be in the pay of one o' the Burn gangs that sells Queen's Favour and don't like the competition."

"And tonight?"

"Came past, mebbe an hour ago? Don't 'ang around long when we're 'ere, she knows she'll get a beatin' if we grab her. Just 'ad a look up the windows on that side and carried on past."

Doranei nodded. The inhabitants of Coin wouldn't appreciate a potential thief being allowed to case the houses here, but the guards weren't going to waste too much time catching a girl if they didn't think she was going to cause a problem. "Be back tonight?"

"Fair chance—you c'n only be sure she'll be 'ere at sunset though, she's always through round 'bout then."

Might be worth my while to catch her then, even if you two can't be bothered, Doranei thought, drawing long on his cigar.

Tobacco was a spy's friend. King Emin had told him that, years back. He didn't much care for the habit himself, but he recognised its importance and smoked just enough to ensure he didn't look out of place with pipe or cigar. Soldiers were the same the Land over: simple men, more often than not, with too much time on their hands. They'd rarely refuse the offer of a smoke and once their guard was down they'd gossip worse than any knitting circle.

The King's Men of Narkang didn't have to play court games; King Emin had aristocrats to do that. The information Doranei got came from footmen, guards and kitchen hands. He'd spent half a year when he was twelve winters getting slapped from one end of The Light Feathers' kitchen to the other and that experience had served him well countless times since. As Sebe put it, make friends with a cook who doesn't know anything useful and you still get a meal for your trouble.

Monkey-faced little bugger will do anything for food, he added to himself, smiling inwardly.

He raised the cigar in a sort of half salute to the two guards. "Right, I best be clearing off. Don't want people to think I'm messing in anything illegal, don't sound like the regiments have much sense of humour these days."

"Aye, you're right enough there," Loris agreed. "Glad we're well out of it over here. The city's going to shit so fast Kiyer herself can't wash the streets fast enough. Take the bastard's money and find yourself a pretty young tart for the night instead. You clear out of sight and he won't bother doing much about it, and the regiments will care about as much as a magistrate."

Doranei grinned. "You could be right there. I left my stuff with the wagon master, but six quarters will sort that out with change to spare. Teach him for being a crap judge of character."

He made his excuses and left; the guards didn't mind—talking to a passing stranger to ensure he wasn't going to cause trouble was one thing, gossiping for too long smacked of shirking duty. Doranei made his way back to a crossroads he'd scouted out earlier: anyone coming from Burn would pass this junction, even if they were taking an oblique route. He didn't think he'd need much luck to identify the young girl Yanai had been talking about, but he would need to avoid a scene—she was certain to be armed, with so many bored soldiers and mercenaries on the streets.

"She comes only after sunset," he mused as he watched the glistening frost on the rooftops. "Looking for Mikiss or Nai, or Zhia herself? Can't be an informant for the duchess or she'd be watching the door all day too."

He was leaning against the trunk of an ancient creeper that covered a high courtyard wall and reached up the wall of the adjoining house to the rooftop. Though leafless, the ragged mess of tangled stems made a curtain dense enough to make Doranei near invisible as he waited.

At the end of the wall, on the corner of the main street, a dozen or so long strips of white ribbon tied to the creeper fluttered in the brisk evening breeze—small offerings to Sheredal, Spreader of the Frost, he guessed. The owner of the house was probably elderly, and with this chill wind the ground in winter would very quickly become icy, a real threat to the elderly and infirm. However good High Priest Antil and his portly band of healers might be, a bad fall could easily be fatal. From what Doranei had seen on his travels ribbons on a wall was as close to a shrine as Sheredal ever got, and the only image he had even seen of Asenn's gentle Aspect was part of a carved frieze in Narkang. King Emin had commissioned it: a strange collection of minor Gods and Aspects that summed up the king's whimsical nature perfectly; the image of Sheredal was a bent old woman with jagged, spiky hair and long, crooked fingers. She had looked sad and lonely, stuck between more noble Gods, but as far as Doranei knew, she was entirely the product of the artist's mind.

But that doesn't matter, not now. That's how half of Narkang imagines the Spreader of the Frost these days. I think he commissioned the piece to give some of us a lesson in the power of belief.

Doranei's vigil didn't last long. None of the few passersby noticed him standing there. He spotted a hunched figure trudging up the road, bundled up in a tatty sheepskin coat made for someone much larger, and realised immediately this was the girl the Yanai had spoken of.

He'd taken the precaution of filling a pocket with small stones earlier. He flung one at the girl as she reached the centre of the square and it thwacked harmlessly against the coat, stopping her dead, just as he'd intended. She looked around in puzzlement. The street was empty in both directions, and she had been so intent on watching where she was going that she'd not seen him emerge from the ivy to throw the stone.

"Sorry," he called, assuming most thieves and murderers in Byora didn't start by apologising to their victims. She turned towards the sound and peered forward. He took a step out into the street and waved.

"What you do that for?" she asked angrily. Her voice was high and rough, and even with Doranei's imperfect command of the dialect he could tell she was from the poorest part of the city. She sounded younger than her height implied.

"So you wouldn't take fright."

The girl checked behind her in case someone was creeping up on her, but she was still alone, other than the strange man now talking to her. She tensed, ready to run.

"What you want then?"

"One thing first," he said, holding up a hand to stop her questions. "My aim's good with stones, better with a knife."

"So?"

"So," he said, trying to sound as unthreatening as possible, "I've got less friendly ways of stopping you in the street." As he spoke he produced a knife from his sleeve and spun it in his fingers so it was ready to throw.

The girl froze, about to run, but Doranei knew she didn't want to turn her back on him. "There's guards in the next street and they'll come runnin' if I scream."

"Yeah, I've met them. One old, one young. Neither think much of you, and you better believe I can take them both."

"What you want?" She was clearly confused. Doranei had threatened her, but he hadn't yet taken a step closer. He wasn't so close that he could be certain of hitting her, or catching her on foot, but she knew that'd be a dangerous gamble to take.

"To talk to someone."

"Can't afford a whore?"

Doranei laughed. "You remind me of a woman I know. Her mouth's got her in trouble all her life; if she weren't one of the toughest bitches I ever met she'd have died years back." He sniffed. "Point is, you keep talking like that and you better be trained to kill as well as her, get me?"

The girl hesitated, then gave a quick nod.

"I can't hear you."

"Yes, sir," she replied in a sullen voice.

"Good. Now just listen. I don't care about you, and you'll get in no trouble for talking to me. You were going to Rose Fountain Square to check one of the buildings there again—any movement, any lights showing, that sort of thing—just like you've been ordered to."

A longer pause, then another nod.

"Good, least you're not lying to me. Now, I'm guessing you work for someone in Burn or Wheel, right? You'll be taking me back with you. I think they want to talk to me."

"She won't like it," the girl answered, "she's gotta bad temper on her. Most likely she'll get Vasca to break our heads."

"Who's Vasca?"

"Doorman."

"Brothel? Tavern?"

"Both."

Doranei put the knife away. "He wouldn't get a punch in," he said confidently, taking a step towards her.

"Now who got too big a mouth?" she demanded.

He shrugged. "Doesn't matter if you believe me. He's no friend of mine and if I have to break his face to talk to whoever wants that door watched, that's fine by me." He clapped his hands together with forced jollity then pulled his cloak tight around his body. "It's getting pretty cold out here though, so if you want to argue further let's do it walking in the right direction."

"What's in it for me?" she demanded, holding her ground as he began to head towards her.

"You'll get a silver level for your trouble, how about that?"

"Up front."

"Piss on you," he snapped, stopping a sword length away from her. "You'll get a copper house if it'll stop you whining and nothing more till I meet your boss."

She didn't argue the point. He could still hurt her if he wanted. "Fine, this way," she said sulkily.

He fell in beside her, one of his longer strides to two of her brisk little steps. After half a minute she cleared her throat and spat the phlegm on a doorstep. "So where's that copper then?"

"Gods, your name isn't Legana, is it?"

She made a disgusted sound and skipped two paces ahead of him, forcing Doranei to catch her up. "Gimme the coin and you find out."

Doranei was surprised at the size of the tavern. It had clearly once been a warehouse, with staff quarters on one side and the owner's round the back. Fat pitch-blackened beams melted into the gloom of night, leaving panels of whitewashed brick appearing to hover in the air. Silhouetted against a thin veil of moonlit cloud were two stone gargoyles, hunched on the corners of the tavern front and peering down at the entrance.

There was a sudden break in the cramped streets past the tavern—the fissure the locals called Cambrey's Tongue. The smooth ripple of scorched black earth, the only undeveloped ground in Burn, extended a good hundred yards downslope. Doranei had only ever seen it in spring, when the seeds that drifted down from the mountain burst into rare and lovely wildflowers.

To Doranei's surprise the girl didn't break and run for the door, shouting for Vasca, but walked in, bold as brass, through the double-width oak door.

She was pulling off her coat before she'd even crossed the threshold. Walking to the bar she cast a meaningful glance back at Doranei for the benefit of the fat man propping it up.

The mood in the room changed immediately as Vasca heaved himself up off his elbows and started forward. Doranei flexed the fingers of his left hand under his cloak and tightened them into a fist. He stepped forward to meet the big man as he unhooked a club from his belt.

Vasca wasted no time in swinging at Doranei's ear, hard enough to crack the Narkang man's skull, but Doranei checked his stride and jerked his head back just in time. After that, Vasca barely saw him move.

Grabbing the doorman's wrist, Doranei pulled him off balance and swung a low punch up into the man's exposed ribs. When his steel-backed gloves connected Vasca gave a piglike grunt of pain, but Doranei hadn't finished. He tugged Vasca round and smashed a knee into his kidneys. The doorman's legs turned to jelly but Doranei was already swinging back around and a loud crack rang around the tavern as his right forearm smashed across Vasca's nose. The man fell to the floor.

Doranei spun around on instinct, bringing his sword up, just in case anyone had slipped behind him, but everyone in the room was frozen to their seats, staring aghast. He lowered his sword a little. There was a table of soldiers by the left-hand side wall.

"A little dramatic, don't you think?" said a voice to his left. "I don't recall you being much of a fan of the theatre."

Doranei nearly dropped his sword when he saw who'd spoken: sitting at a table of his own in the corner, lounging like an idle young nobleman, was Prince Koezh Vukotic. The vampire was the only person not drinking out of a clay pot, and Doranei found himself hoping it was just red wine he could see though the cut glass.

Koezh was dressed in anonymous grey travelling clothes, his only jewellery a gold signet ring on a chain around his neck. There was an indulgent smile on the vampire's lips, but Doranei had grown used to being mocked by members of that family. If Vorizh Vukotic had turned up and laughed at the state of his boots, Doranei was pretty sure he'd just sigh and shake his head, refusing to rise to the bait. Almost sure, anyway.

He sheathed his sword and stepped around the supine Vasca, who gave an involuntary snort as the blood began to run up his nose, then whined like a beaten dog at the pain. Doranei looked at his young guide, who flinched away when he pointed towards the kegs behind the bar, and walked to join the ruler of the Vukotic tribe. Koezh's eyes flickered momentarily around the room and their audience obediently turned their attention elsewhere. By the time Koezh invited him to sit, the conversations at every table had resumed.

Doranei pulled the chair out and sat, not bothering to remove his cloak. He doubted it would be long before Koezh dismissed him and he would have to leave like a dog with its tail between its legs. They sat facing each other in silence. After a half dozen heartbeats a pewter tankard of beer was placed in front of Doranei. Divested of her outdoor clothes, Doranei saw her guide was a fragile-looking little thing with auburn curls and a thin face. Twelve winters, no more, he judged. In Koezh's presence her face was expressionless, her demeanour muted.

Good thing too; no matter how bad your attitude is you'd have to be a fool not to sense his power.

"Aren't you going to say something?" Koezh said once the girl had gone. "A delight to see you again? I've missed you? That jacket really brings out your eyes?"

"Don't even know what to call you," Doranei muttered, wondering what exactly he'd got himself into. Koezh had tolerated him, but nothing more than that—and Doranei was horribly aware that he was the only person in the city not under Koezh's control who knew his identity. Added to that was his mission: to pry into the secrets of Vorizh, Koezh's younger brother.

"How about Osten?" Koezh replied with a smile, "I'm sure my sister would approve. Shall we get our business out of the way before we start reminiscing?"

"Business?"

Koezh leaned forward and Doranei felt his entire body tense involuntarily.

"You are not drinking your beer," the vampire pointed out, indicating the tankard. He spoke the local dialect in a precise, slightly stilted manner, a blend of thick Menin consonants and elongated Litse vowels. Doranei might be more fluent than Koezh, but in comparison he sounded like a dockworker.

The King's Man coughed, trying to smother a nervous laugh. Koezh was not a particularly large man, but there was an aura surrounding him, and that filled Doranei with dread. The sapphire eyes didn't blink as he reached for the beer and took a long swig. A second reduced the tankard to half full and finally calmed his jangling nerves. *Shame there isn't a shot of brandy in this*, he thought.

"Business then," he said for the second time that evening, wiping his mouth on his sleeve. "Want to tell me what you're doing here?"

"Not really," Koezh smiled. "You?"

"Perhaps."

The smile widened a shade further than Doranei would have liked. "Progress, then."

"I was looking for your sister." Doranei said cautiously.

"That is not your reason for being here. As much as I would like to dismiss you as a foolish little boy, you have not tracked her down to play the lovesick puppy."

"Is she here?"

"In the city," Koezh conceded, "but busy this evening. Shall I pass on a message?"

"I have questions I need ask of her."

"She is a little old for romantic gestures."

Doranei hiccoughed at the thought and needed another gulp of beer before he continued, "You remind me of King Emin."

"Does that mean you will perform tricks at my command?"

Doranei's eyes narrowed as Koezh's voice hardened. "Is that what you think of me?"

"Only that you are more brittle and grim now than on that magical night we shared at the theatre." Koezh leaned back in his chair, one elbow propped on the armrest while sipping his wine delicately. "Keep your temper under wraps, puppy," he said lazily.

Good point, Doranei thought, *wrong person to get into a pissing contest with. I should have left as soon as I saw he was alone here.*

"I'm sorry. Today has been a little strange."

Koezh looked at him enquiringly. "Stranger than the usual company you keep? Do tell."

Doranei thought of the half-blind Farlan woman with a shadow's handprint on her throat and a God's blood in her veins. *Mortal-Aspect of a dead Goddess. I don't want to know what would happen if they met.* "I cannot, not yet."

"Then tell me what you want to ask my sister."

Doranei hesitated. He knew perfectly well that whilst they may have been allies of sorts in Scree, that meant nothing now. The Vukotic family were enemies of the Gods and nothing would ever change that, just as no amount of good works would bring them redemption.

"I wanted to ask about your brother."

"Vorizh?" Koezh sounded genuinely surprised for a moment there. "What do you want with him?"

"We've heard a rumour," Doranei said hesitantly, "of a journal belonging to him."

Koezh took another sip of wine, all the while looking at Doranei through narrowed eyes. "A journal? You remember my brother is quite mad, don't you?"

"We do. And that is why I've come to ask why someone might want to read it."

Koezh pursed his lips. "All sorts of fools—we are a somewhat notable family, after all."

"Do you know of this journal?" Doranei suddenly felt the air grow cold around him, the shadows lengthen.

"No. But I will tell you this," Koezh said softly, his dark eyes gleaming. "Be careful when you pry into the past. The Great War saw horrors you cannot even comprehend. Some secrets are best forgotten." He leaned forward. "You have finished your beer—it is time you left."

CHAPTER 23

"**H**E'S ON HIS WAY."

"What? Are you certain?" Certinse looked up, the papers piled on his desk immediately forgotten.

Senior Penitent Yeren nodded absentmindedly as he wandered over to the drinks cabinet, scratching the stubble on his cheek. "Mebbe hasn't left yet, but he's accepted the invite." He gave the fat brass door handle an experimental tug and smiled as the door opened.

I shouldn't have left the damn thing unlocked, Certinse thought, taking another sip of Fayl whisky and rolling it around his mouth. Yeren pulled out a decanter of wine and held it up to the light, wrinkling his nose at what he saw. *The brute even knows what he's looking for.*

Reaching further into the recesses of the deep wooden cabinet he found a rather smaller decanter. This time the pitch black liquid received a nod of approval. Yeren plucked a glass from the top shelf.

"That's a goblet," Certinse said. "The blackwine glasses are on the far left."

"Yep," Yeren said, setting the decanter down so he could remove the stopper, "but they're tiny."

Certinse rounded the desk with rare speed and removed the goblet from his hand, replacing it with a far smaller one shaped like an opening tulip.

"I don't care. Blackwine isn't for quaffing, or whatever it is your sort do. It is to be savoured," Certinse said firmly. To his surprise the mercenary didn't argue and filled the glass he'd been handed before raising it in toast.

"How did you find out?" Certinse pressed.

"My men are better couriers than any wet-behind-the-ears novice. Most clerical correspondence goes though us nowadays."

"Haven't they noticed you're reading the messages?"

Yeren laughed. "Your lot are bloody stupid, didn't you know that? They know nothing of secrecy. If they declare war on Lord Isak, the Chief Steward will have them for breakfast."

"A good thing too," Certinse pointed out, refilling his own glass, "but before you make too many claims to competence, might I remind you that Ardela ended up not dead, but in the Chief Steward's custody? Lucky for you I managed to make a bargain with Lesarl to deal with her quickly." He sighed and sat back on the edge of his desk, pondering the news Yeren had brought for a while. "Every member of the Synod thinks he should be the leader of a glorious religious crusade," he said eventually. "I'm amazed they managed to agree in council that he should be invited—whatever his religious status, he's still from another tribe."

"Well they did, and he is," Yeren announced, unperturbed. "You don't want him?"

"Use your brain, man; can you imagine what will happen?"

Yeren grinned. Certinse could smell the alcohol on his breath—not blackwine, but some sort of rough moonshine the soldiers brewed. *Gods, he probably can't even taste the blackwine. He's just drinking it to annoy me—and to show he does know what the good stuff is.*

"Would be quite a sight if you ask me," Yeren said.

"And afterwards?"

The mercenary's face fell slightly. "I see your point."

"He is coming to Tirah."

"Are you certain?"

"Of course, you damn fool." Certinse's voice rose to a high whine. "The Synod has approved it and invited him openly."

"Can you not persuade the Synod to change its mind?" Prayer kept his voice to the barest whisper. He believed they were alone in the vaults beneath the Temple of Nartis, but voices carried far in the dim underground passages. Though the vaults were home to room after room of records and religious texts, there were few scholars willing to come here these days. While the newly raised High Cardinal Certinse had blunted the savagery of his predecessor's Morality Tribunals, it hadn't stopped half a dozen different sorts of purges being enacted. Some were cross-cult; most were simply unfathomable.

"They are suspicious of me as it is. The Morality Tribunals haven't turned out the way they intended and they're looking for someone to blame—and the tribunals were *my* success!" Certinse spat the last word as though it burned his mouth to say.

Prayer could imagine the look on the High Cardinal's face, though he was unable to see it because he'd positioned himself round a corner in an attempt to keep his identity secret. He had left the High Cardinal instructions for how to contact him in an emergency, never really believing it would come to that. Lesarl preferred his coterie to keep a pace back from events, listening and gathering information rather than actively acting like spies.

"What are they saying about the deaths of Bern and the last High Cardinal?"

They know Lesarl was behind Bern's death—Gods, even a child of five summers could work that one out—but they can't work out how to officially blame him yet. As for High Cardinal Echer, they're confused; the death of the Lady has thrown them. They don't know what to think there. They know Lesarl uses devotees, but Ardela has never been on the roster. Because she has always been a clerical bodyguard that means she's come from their own camp."

"They have accepted your evidence?"

"Yes, and for that reason they don't want to hear any more of it. If Lesarl announces he has captured and executed her immediately they will breathe a sign of relief. None of them trust each other. Just don't let her surface where she'll be recognised, and keep her from coming after me. I've got enough problems without her pursuing a vendetta."

"You cannot stop him?" Prayer said, getting back to the matter in hand. He heard the swish of robes against the stone wall and imagined Certinse shaking his head violently.

"Lesarl must find a way."

"He must," Prayer agreed. "We don't want to have to rebuild Cornerstone Market again, do we?"

Dancer stamped his feet on the paved floor in a vain attempt to get some warmth back into them. He winced as the unyielding leather pushed down on his toes and once again tried to work out a better way to meet his employer clandestinely. Cold Halls had been abandoned as a ducal palace, and failed as any other sort of private residence every time someone tried to make it their home. Though it was undoubtedly grand, Cold Halls lived up to its name. Dancer didn't know whether it was because of a quirk of architecture, an underground river, or supernatural forces, but by the time Chief Steward Lesarl turned up he wouldn't be able to feel his own face.

Dressed in the uniform of a Palace Guard—courtesy of a guardsman only too happy to lend it out while he sat in a coffeehouse with his feet up in front of a fire—Dancer lurked just inside the stable-side door of Cold Halls and waited. From time to time clerks would hurry through the door, stamping the snow off their boots, and head off to their office without even a glance at the soldier guarding very little in the dim hallway.

After the best part of an hour Dancer heard neat little footsteps patter down the corridor towards him. He remained at attention until he was sure the Chief Steward was alone. When at last Dancer did turn to face his employer he realised the man was even paler than usual, a rare sign of strain.

"You look ridiculous," Lesarl grumbled.

Dancer bit back a comment about the way Lesarl's coat hung on his spindly frame. "He's coming."

"The High Cardinal can't stop it? What damn use is the man then?"

"It's out of his hands, as you well know," Dancer said firmly. The Chief Steward's mood had been foul of late, but Dancer didn't have the luxury of time to coax him round from whatever bee was in his breeches. "We need to find a way to stop it."

Lesarl nodded. "I spoke to Whisper earlier, but she had pressing business and couldn't wait for you."

"Gods, I never expected this when Lord Bahl offered the man sanctuary. He was supposed to be a boon for the tribe! Have you come to a conclusion?"

The question prompted a scowl. Despite everything, Dancer had to keep himself from laughing; Lesarl, the hunched, glowering minister stalking the corridors of Cold Halls reminded Dancer of a play he'd seen some years back, portraying King Deliss Farlan, father of the first white-eye, Kasi Farlan, as a scheming tyrant degenerating into syphilis-induced madness. The actor had somehow managed to capture the essence of Lesarl in his portrayal, much to the amusement of most of the city.

"A conclusion of sorts," Lesarl said eventually. "Far from one I like however—it's a bad sign when even the theory leaves a bitter taste in one's mouth. How I will persuade Lord Isak I cannot even begin to imagine."

"You can't kill him?"

"If we could manage that," snapped Lesarl, "there wouldn't be a problem in the first place!"

"But how do we deflect his attention?"

The clatter of something falling echoed down the corridor and Lesarl held up a hand to silence his companion. It was a full minute before he continued, "I have received a letter from Duke Lomin. The man is keeping a careful distance from Lord Isak, as you might expect, but he's a loyal soldier all the same. He gave me advance warning of this. The only way we can deflect this is to offer the fanatics something they would prefer, and sooner or later, for fanatics, that comes down to a sacrifice of some sort."

"I don't follow."

Lesarl shook his head, lips pursed in anger. *"Bloated beasts of hatred and petty jealousy; a murderer for a sire and fool for a shepherd,"* he said, more to himself than Dancer.

The nobleman frowned, recognising the words but taking a moment to place them. When he did, the enormity of Lesarl's decision took his breath away. The words were a playwright's; spoken by the last great Litse lord, Yanao Tell, when he was told Deverk Grast had mustered the entire Menin tribe.

"How?" Dancer croaked.

"You must persuade Suzerain Torl to gather his Brethren and make a declaration."

"Torl?" Dancer said. "You want the Dark Monks involved?"

"Hardly." Lesarl paced the stone-paved floor. "But they are the only way. Tell Torl you are speaking with my authority. I cannot go myself—Lord Isak cannot be seen to be involved. The declaration must come from an independent group."

Without waiting for a reply Lesarl turned back the way he'd come.

Dancer listened to the sound of his footsteps even after the man had turned the corner. Even when he could no longer hear Lesarl, Dancer found himself unwilling to leave his post. The chill in the air no longer mattered. It had paled in comparison to the emptiness in his stomach.

I'll just stand here a little longer. Just a few more minutes, and then I'll go and ask the finest man I know to commit suicide. Just a little while longer.

Isak sat up suddenly, drawing in a deep breath, as if he'd suddenly come up from under water. He looked around, blinking in momentary surprise. It was a rare thing for him to be so absorbed in a book that his senses withdrew from the Land around him.

The palace library was still and silent aside from the lazy crackle of the fire opposite. Isak sat facing the fire—and the door—at the huge partners' desk that stood in the very centre of the room: a nearly square block of red-tinged wood and gleaming brass fittings. The room was softly lit by a heavy-based lamp sitting in the middle of the desk and the brass oil lamps on the ends of the bookshelves which extended from three walls into the room.

Most of the palace must have turned in for the night, Isak guessed, though something must have started him out of his reverie. "Probably Tila, slamming doors again," he muttered. His eyes drifted longingly towards the massive padded armchairs flanking the fireplace. There was something irresistible about a comfortable chair beside the fire—but he'd be curled up like a cat and asleep before he'd turned a page.

He stretched and was about to return to his book when the door opened. Isak relaxed when he saw Mihn enter.

"The Chief Steward is looking for you, my Lord," Mihn said, his voice indicating that Lesarl was right behind him.

"And the last place he expected to find me was the library, no doubt," Isak said with a smile. His eyes narrowed. "What's that on your neck?"

Mihn's hand flew to his neck, where a dark mark was visible over his collar. "Nothing of importance, my Lord."

"I don't believe you. Very little of what you do is unimportant." He pointed at Mihn's neck. "Show me."

"Yes, do show us," said Lesarl as he walked through the door.

"Lesarl, give us a moment, please." The Chief Steward's eyes glittered at the command, but he bowed and retreated without a word. Isak was very protective of his unusual bodyguard; now that Lesarl had accepted Mihn would never be an agent of his he avoided conflict on the subject.

"It is just another tattoo," Mihn replied once Lesarl had shut the door behind him, a flicker of discomfort in his eyes.

"Like the ones on your hands?"

"Exactly, my Lord."

"Tattoos of what exactly?" Isak urged.

"Leaf patterns, nothing more." Mihn walked up to the desk and turned his head to look at the book Isak had been reading.

"*Last Days of Darkness*," Isak said. "Stories from the end of the Age of Darkness."

"Your reading tastes have become somewhat morbid of late," Mihn noted.

"You're the one who started me on that path," Isak protested. "You told me to accept everything about myself, including my dreams of death! If I am to accept something I must understand it better. I—" Isak hesitated. "I'm not entirely sure what I'm looking for, but I need to know what the dreams mean."

"Then I suggest you try Cardinal Jesher's collection of parables, most specifically the one entitled 'The Moneylender.' It is the story of a money-lender who dies, but is so obsessed by his trade that his spirit visits his debtors after he is dead, trying to collect what he was owed."

Isak thought for a moment. "Sounds like you've just ruined the story for me, but I'll give it a try, I suppose."

Mihn smiled. "Jesher was a theologian of great note in his time, and his parables are characterised by the depth of his insight. You will find his work instructive on the subject of death—you might also try a Menin play called *The Stargas*. The Menin style of declamation may amuse you, and the char-acter of the Prophet Dirik is beautifully written, however inaccurate."

"I think I've heard of that one. Doesn't he pray for death each morning?"

Mihn's eyebrows rose. "I'm impressed, my Lord. Dirik prayed for death, for then he would be relieved of the burden of prophecy."

The white-eye grinned. "Don't be impressed; I just remember Tila saying I make her say a prayer for Dirik some mornings. I didn't understand the reference so I made her explain it." He slammed a palm down on the desktop. "Damn you! I almost forgot what I'd kept you here for!"

"The Chief Steward is waiting," Mihn reminded him.

Isak gave an exasperated grunt. "Fine; you win. But tell me what the tat-toos are about. You don't need to show me, just tell me. I'll trust what you say."

Mihn didn't react immediately. His almond eyes thinned a shade and dropped momentarily to his palms. "Very well, my Lord," he began slowly. "You expressed a concern over my safety, thus I have asked the witch to tattoo my arms with rowan and hazel leaves. Both types of wood are used to protect against a variety of supernatural influences. She used sap from the plants in the ink and placed charms of protection on each leaf. Her magic is not pow-erful, but I am not a man of power—I believe her subtlety will complement my own skills to keep me as safe as any man could hope to be."

"Rowan and hazel, eh? Very well, thank you." He looked down at the desk and after a moment flipped the book shut. "That's enough reading for one evening, I think. Go and help Xeliath. She'll probably be on her way down to the training ground by now, even though there's bloody snow on the ground. I'll join you once I've finished with Lesarl."

The Chief Steward's face bore a permanent frown these days and today was no exception, Isak saw. Tila told him how hard Lesarl was working these days, barely getting three hours of sleep on a good night, and spending large parts of his days riding from one part of the city to another.

Every other day the clerics would think up some new problem—refusing to acknowledge the authority of magistrates, or judges, or the Palace Guard—and only Lesarl's swift intervention had prevented anything worse than minor bloodshed on Tirah's streets. To make matters worse, Sword-master Kerin had died of the injury he'd taken at the Temple of Law and the Ghosts were unwilling to back down from any confrontation. On top of that, he had fifteen lawsuits over the new religious decrees going through the courts, plus the aftermath of Isak's investiture, where he had brokered and signed more deals among the nobility than in the whole previous two years.

"You have news?" Isak asked, indicating they should sit by the fire.

Lesarl sank gratefully into the armchair's embrace. "Unfortunately, I do."

"That bad?"

"My Lord, I do not know how long we can continue in this way," Lesarl admitted. "We have bands of penitents attempting to restrict what little food that comes into the city, and violent clashes on a daily basis. I've needed troops to clear courtrooms and prevent the Morality Tribunals from trying civil and criminal cases . . ." He sighed and pinched the bridge of his nose, screwing his eyes up tight for a moment. "Just today a priestess of Vasle set up her own independent court and she's passing sentences of drowning, and I have just had confirmation that a warehouse owned by the cult of Death is being used as a makeshift gaol for people who've publicly opposed their troops. I could go on—"

"Anything I can do?"

Lesarl shook his head. "I don't want to give anyone the satisfaction of your personal intervention, and where there's fighting there's always the chance someone will try to assassinate you." He sighed and reached his hands out towards the fire. "If you die we have civil war, if you're injured we still need to conduct the purge we've been trying to avoid for weeks now."

"So your news concerns something different?"

"Yes, my Lord. Your guest in Lomin has apparently become less than sat-isfied with incursions into the Great Forest. After the fall of Scree he started taking religious matters seriously."

"Oh Gods," Isak groaned. "I think I can guess what's coming next."

Lesarl's face was grim. "The cults have invited him to Tirah; they're looking for a figurehead and my agent in Lomin tells me he is obsessed with the liberation of his people. His physical appetites have apparently waned since the high summer, presumably triggered by the fall of Scree, and instead he is starting to see himself as some sort of mystic, a spiritual leader as much as a soldier. I hardly need tell you of all people what a terrible combination that makes."

"Can we not stop him coming?"

Lesarl shook his head. "I can't have the offer withdrawn without killing more priests to give Certinse the moderates he needs on the Synod—and we'd need to lose too many. We cannot expect to reason with him any more than we can be confident of killing him on the way. If Sir Kelet and a team of rangers were in place already I would have chosen that path—even he would not survive a poisoned arrow—but as it is they won't be able to negotiate the cults' patrols in time."

Isak found himself picking at the chair as he thought. "So the alternatives are?"

"Allow him to come here and see massive bloodshed on the streets, or deflect him."

"Have they asked him to lead a revolt?" Isak said in surprise.

"No, my Lord, but you are white-eyes and these are fraught times. With the two of you in the city, you will fight—I guarantee it. With armies at your sides, the destruction in the city will be extensive."

"Your expression tells me I'm not going to like the other choice much either."

"No." Lesarl was quiet a moment while he stared into the fire.

Isak felt trepidation flood his body.

"My Lord," Lesarl began hesitantly, "this is the only viable course of action I can recommend. I don't want you to think too long about it because the longer you do so the more terrible it will seem."

"Understood, now tell me."

"Suzerain Torl is a devoted servant; he will realise the necessity. We need him to persuade the Dark Monks to go south, drawing every fanatic in their wake. I cannot entirely predict the end result, except to say that where religious fervour is concerned the usual rules of war, diplomacy, and common sense do not apply."

"You're talking about a crusade?" Isak said, feeling the enormity of his words like a millstone on his shoulders.

"Yes, my Lord. To avoid civil war here in Tirah, the Brethren of the Sacred Teachings must announce a holy war against the Menin—to be joined by the whole spectrum of murderers, madmen, and self-serving opportunist bastards in our priesthood when we circulate the rumour that Lord Styrax has consorted with daemons." He sighed. "And they will ask Lord Chalat, Chosen of the God Tsatach and deposed Lord of the Chetse, to lead them."

CHAPTER 24

IT WAS COLD in the Duchess Chamber of the Ruby Tower. Dropping the antechamber onto Byora's clerics had opened the room to the winter wind gusting through the large double doors. The small group of petitioners trooped in under the beady eye of Jato, Steward of the Tower, mindful of the positions they had been assigned. Luerce was almost last, lacking both wealth and a title, but that position gave him time to observe the others. Timing was everything, and Luerce was well used to gauging a crowd.

He was a slight man, pale and thin boned as most Litse were, but folk described his face as washed out rather than porcelain, the more usual description for those of that tribe. It was an easy face to see weakness in, and few doubted it when that was what was displayed. Azaer hadn't had to show him the value of weakness; he already knew it.

The group on either side of the door included workmen, and a fat man in a drooping velvet hat. While some repaired minor damage to the plaster, others watched as the fat man painted on the newly whitewashed wall, tracing faint lines with sooty water. Luerce couldn't quite resolve the shapes into anything recognisable, but still it made him want to smile: he was painting shadows where once images of the Gods had been. The destruction of the antechamber had revealed enormous murals of Death and Ushull. The duchess had fallen into a rage at the sight of them and demanded both be whitewashed within the hour.

Now the duchess sat on her throne, with little Ruhen on her left, in the shadow of Sergeant Kayel. As Luerce stared at Ruhen, scarcely able to believe what he saw, the duchess said something to the boy and brought him round to sit beside her. Ruhen, apparently five winters of age and the picture of innocence, smiled up at the duchess as she bent to place a kiss on his brown curls. At the side of the room a grey-haired woman watched, bewildered— the child's mother, Luerce remembered. She was little more than skin and bone, and she looked broken, lost. He could see nothing more than a glimmer of recognition in her eyes, and it obviously wasn't enough for her to take exception to the duchess's motherly attentions to her son.

Then Ruhen looked up and stared straight at Luerce, and he felt that electric tingle down his spine. As his master fixed his gaze upon him, the sounds of shuffling feet and hurried whispers withered to nothing.

"Gods below," Luerce breathed. The woman ahead of him turned and gave him a puzzled look, but he was so lost in the swirl of shadow in his mind that he hardly noticed.

Careful to keep the thought to himself, he recalled, *I was there that day in the square when the duchess took you in, just a matter of months ago, no more, and look how you have grown.*

"Where is Lady Kinna?" the duchess called, fingers idly stroking Ruhen's hair as though the boy were a pet.

Steward Jeto cleared his throat. "Ah, she sends her apologies, your Grace. She came down with an ailment, an illness of the throat, two days past; she has been unable to leave her bed since."

"Have my doctors been sent to attend her?"

"They have consulted with Lady Kinna's doctor, a woman from Helrect, so I am told. Your doctor is satisfied that she is receiving good care. They tell me a few days' rest will see Lady Kinna better than ever."

Jeto finished his statement with a nervous cough. The fussy little sexagenarian had jet black hair and a prominent nose, both of which contrived to make him look rather like a crow amongst pigeons. Black hair was rare in Byora, and Jeto lacked the height and thick bones of the Menin. Luerce was a small man himself, but he felt sure he could snap Jeto's neck like a twig if it became necessary.

"Very well, let us begin," the duchess announced, holding Ruhen close.

Steward Jeto bowed ceremoniously and brought the first petitioner forward, a tall woman of similar age to the duchess—and her rival in wealth, if the jewellery with which she was adorned was anything to go by. Indeed, the duchess greeted the woman almost as a friend as Jeto began to outline the suit. Luerce let the words drone on without listening. He had a task to complete, but he could not risk interrupting a woman as powerful as this one clearly was.

Luerce had been apprenticed to a chandler from an early age, but he had not found the trade to his liking, despite being a good worker and popular with the customers. People were his greatest skill, making friends and connections as much as ferreting out their secrets. The old master had not lasted long after Luerce had married his daughter.

Now he left his wife to run the chandlery; so many foreigners passed through Byora that there were always opportunities for a man with a quick mind and glib tongue. His illicit living had been even more profitable than the chandlery, but he'd thought the fun had come to an end the day he tried to con a man with scarred hands and a quicker mind than his own. He'd spent the next few days confined to bed while the swelling subsided, and during those uncomfortable sleepless nights the shadows had spoken to him.

Since then Luerce had been waiting for the day he was needed, all the while extending his contacts within the city and smiling sympathetically at stories of hauntings and unfortunate accidents among his rivals.

The second petitioner was a waddling mage in robes that had once been very fine. Luerce bided his time, unwilling to steal a mage's thunder. The third was a meek-looking merchant whose fortunes had seen better days, judging by the state of his clothes. With a mournful wail Luerce slipped through the lines and past the merchant, falling to his knees well short of the point where Ilumene would have to give him a second beating.

"Your Grace," Luerce moaned, "I beg your forgiveness but I cannot wait any longer! I am cursed; cursed by a vengeful priest of Death. My daughter lies at home, one foot inside Death's Gates because of his spite and no healer can help her."

He felt the crowd behind him shift, alarmed at the mention of a curse. The guards on either side started to move closer before Ilumene raised a hand to stop them. He had already stepped forward, putting himself between Ruhen and Luerce, as a bodyguard should, and now he peered at Luerce as though trying to see whether he was mad, or simply desperate. He was great actor, Luerce thought.

"Why do you come to me?" the duchess asked sternly, not at all cowed by the mention of a curse. "I have no dealings with the priesthood." She spat the last word out and Luerce cringed. "I suggest you find a mage to undo the curse, or some witch to fashion a charm for you."

"I have tried," howled Luerce as the tears began to come, "and none have been able to break its spell. First my wife sickened and died, then, as a black dog crossed his path in the street, my brother's heart gave out." He gave a choking sob. "You Grace, most blessed lady of Byora, I beg your intercession, I beg help—"

"Enough," the duchess snapped, "I cannot . . ." Her voice tailed off as Ruhen slipped from beside her on the throne. "Ruhen dearest, sit back up here," she began.

The little boy shook his head solemnly. When she opened her mouth to speak again he held up a hand to her and the words died in her throat. With the room transfixed, Ruhen reached out and ran his little fingers through her sandy hair. When the little boy turned around, Luerce saw he had a single hair in his fingers. With an expression of total concentration Ruhen walked towards Luerce, apparently oblivious to the intake of breath from the crowd behind.

Awestruck, Luerce stayed where he was, as if frozen by Ruhen's unblinking eyes. "Little prince," Luerce whispered, his voice carrying around the silent room, "I am a sinner, but I did not deserve this curse. I swear it."

Behind Ruhen he saw the duchess, sitting bolt upright, unmoving, gripping the armrests of her throne, her knuckles white. Beside her, Ilumene's expression reflected her concern.

Ruhen ignored them all and kept his eyes firmly on Luerce. Without even thinking about it he slowly raised his hand and the child stopped before it, studying the dirty fingernails and raw skin. Eventually Ruhen reached out and tied the hair about Luerce's index finger, the movements painstakingly slow.

"Go home," he piped, his childish voice quite unlike when Azaer had spoken to Luerce, but with the same electric effect.

He kept still until Ruhen broke eye contact and went toddling back to rejoin the duchess. Luerce pushed himself upright, staggering a moment before turning to look at those behind him. They were standing in stunned silence until he stumbled towards them and they parted to allow him out through the half-open doors and into the grey daylight.

"The touch of the innocent," the mage said in a hushed voice. "They say the pure can cast out sin and daemons, so why not curses too?"

"He begged intercession," breathed someone within the crowd.

"And intercession he received," the duchess finished, looking down at the child beside her. Ruhen smiled up at her and she felt herself enveloped in warmth.

Venn stirred, drifting slowly towards wakefulness. His head felt heavy, his chest tight. The smell of incense tickled his nostrils and he came awake with a twitch and a cough. He turned his head and felt the greasy, sweat-soaked cushion against his ear.

I cannot continue like this. I am dying here, he realised, reaching out for the cup of water by his bed.

Someone put the cup in his hand and helped him lift it to his lips. He blinked and slowly focused on the face before him—not the priestess, but a young woman, a Harlequin, one soon to walk out into the Land. He recognised her; she had sat at his feet often these past few . . . weeks? Months? He was no longer sure. Her name eluded him too, but much did, for up to an hour after awakening. He'd once been a great athlete, but he had had to become used to being a broken old man while Jackdaw lived in his shadow.

"We have come to say goodbye," she said softly as he drank.

"You are blessed now and sent out into the Land?" he croaked, his throat raw.

She shook her head. "No, Master. We go to seek the child, the innocent, the prince of your tales."

I have you, Venn realised, *only just in time. You choose your king, and when you find him you will cast off your masks and march under his banner.*

"You believe the Land is in need of intercession?"

She nodded urgently.

"Then I should come with you," Venn said, struggling to rise.

She helped him up, her face a picture of concern. "Master, you are very weak."

"Have faith, sister. When I start on the journey to find our little prince, faith will restore me." The words were barely out of his mouth before he realised his mistake—it was far too early for him to leave. His desperation to be rid of Jackdaw had made him rash, he had not reached enough Harlequins yet. His impatience could be the undoing of everything.

"We are ready to leave whenever you are, Master," she said, indicating half a dozen other young Harlequins standing close by.

"Then slip my swords upon my back," Venn intoned, echoing the words of a heroic tale they would all recognise, "and let us go wherever our master leads."

"No," said a sharp voice behind her: the priestess. She looked weary, but her voice was still full of authority. "There's still too much snow; a journey will kill him."

The young Harlequin glared. "The worst has passed already."

The priestess walked up to the young woman and looked down at her. "He is too weak; you must wait for the thaw."

"We shall carry him. 'The strong shall bear the weak on their backs, letting the weak guide them, for it is they who see the safest path,'" quoted the Harlequin.

Venn winced at the smugness of her piety, though he was fascinated to see how they interpreted his words to their own ends.

"And his weakness shows you the path, child," the priestess replied triumphantly. "His weakness shows you that such a journey should not be undertaken until the spring."

Spring? Can I last that long with Jackdaw in my shadow? Venn wondered. *It could be the equinox before the snow recedes this far nor*—he stopped dead. *The Equinox Festival, when more Harlequins gather then than at any other time.*

He gave a weak cough and interrupted, saying, "Priestess, you are correct. My weakness tells us we should wait, that there is preaching yet to be done. We shall stay until the Equinox Festival and when we have celebrated with our kin, we shall go." He paused, breathing heavily.

When he'd caught his breath, he added, "And you will come with us, Priestess, to minister to those of the clans who join our quest." *And we'll need to bring as much water from the pool as we can—those Harlequins we meet on the journey will challenge my authority unless I can get them to receive her blessing first.*

The priestess bowed low. "You do me great honour, Master," she said, her eyes brightening at the prospect.

I will give you everything you have always wanted, Venn thought as he allowed himself to be helped back to bed. *You should read your scriptures a little more carefully, priestess. Such a thing has ever been a curse.*

CHAPTER 25

As EVENING FELL OVER BYORA a gusty wind brought stinging sheets of rain. Two men crouched in the lee of a chimney stack, their waxed-cloth coats held protectively over their heads, and peered over the edge of the rooftop at the street below.

"What do you think?" Sebe said, his voice almost drowned out by the falling rain. He nudged Doranei forward, making room for him next to the warm side of the chimney, but Doranei ignored him. His focus was solely on the man he was watching through the ground-floor window of the house opposite. Despite the rain the shutter was open enough for anyone to have a good view of the street.

"He ain't there for his health," Doranei said eventually. "They're taking shifts at that window, not so obvious about it that you'd notice if you weren't really looking."

"But there's no doubt, is there? Shit. So what do we do about it?"

"Our job." Doranei looked his fellow King's Man in the face and Sebe nodded reluctantly. "They're not innocents sent to watch a door. They're the enemy. Those boys might not be great at surveillance, but they're not complete amateurs either."

Sebe led the way back, crouching until they reached the rear of the building. They dropped down into the small backyard and were heading for the alley that ran behind it when they were startled by a cough.

Doranei turned to see a man standing under an awning outside the next-door house, a filleting knife in one hand, a half-skinned rabbit in the other. The man was grey haired but far from decrepit and he showed no fear as the two men turned towards him. He raised his knife as he reached for a second, but Doranei shook his head at the movement.

"Just passing through," he said firmly, opening his coat enough to show the man his weapons—a pair of slim long-knives, as well as his sword and axe. They were not the weapons of a thief.

"There'll be trouble?" the man asked in a thick accent, setting his knife down to acknowledge it wasn't a fight he wanted any part of.

"No," said Doranei, "we're gone."

The man looked relieved as Doranei headed out of the yard. The rain was keeping most people off the streets and they were clear to find a safe route to the back of the watchers' house. It took them a while before they were satisfied they would be able to get in without any fuss, but Doranei was feeling increasingly apprehensive. The house being watched was the base for the Narkang agent in Byora, a contact used only by a very select group. King Emin's intelligence network was small, and everyone knew not to take any risks unless directly ordered to; that anyone knew about this safe house was a worrying development.

The house backed onto another, and a path ran down the side of each to the gardens. The gate to the first didn't budge but the second opened without a problem. With rain and the dark keeping folk inside, they thought it a reasonable risk to walk in, hop one fence, and then the next. Once in the watchers' yard Doranei and Sebe didn't need to break stride; the rear door was unlocked and Doranei, a long-knife in one hand, pushed it open to find a blond man leaning over a stove. Before he'd finished turning at the sound of the door opening, Doranei had lunged at the man and sliced his throat open. The man flailed about, knocking a pan off the stove which crashed to the tiled floor before Doranei could stop it. Doranei caught the man and lowered him to the floor, wiped his knife, and followed Sebe, who had nipped past him.

"What'd ya drop now?" called a voice from the front room as Sebe reached the doorway. Sebe exploded forward, and Doranei, waiting at the door, heard the loud rap of steel on skull, followed swiftly by some rapid thumps and the sound of a man falling.

He peered in and saw Sebe astride a prone man, his blade positioned under the man's throat, and moved on to check the other rooms on that floor. As expected, they were empty, as were the upstairs rooms when he checked them. In seconds he was back down the stairs.

In the front room he found Sebe had arranged the man's hands behind his back so he could kneel on them, pinning him facedown. Sebe wasn't a heavy man but it was an awkward position, and the prisoner would have no hope of stopping Sebe from cutting his throat. Doranei stabbed his own long-knife into the wooden floor right by the prisoner's head and squatted down next to him.

"Your friend's dead," he said in a matter-of-fact way, "so you want to avoid going the same way, you answer quick and true and you don't bullshit me, right?"

There was a slight grunt from the man, who was more concerned about keeping his head up.

"The knife stays there," Doranei said, "and the longer you take over your answers the harder you're going to find it to stay in that position."

A second grunt: Doranei took that as understanding and continued, "Good boy. Who do you work for?"

"Duchess," the man wheezed. There was a cut on his temple where Sebe had hit him, not hard enough to crack his skull but enough to put a man off balance. A steady trickle of blood was coming from the cut but Doranei guessed he couldn't even feel the sting yet. His blue eyes were wide with fear and Doranei saw he wasn't anyone special, certainly not part of Doranei's own violent world. That was good news; he might think he had a chance at survival if Doranei looked happy enough with his answers.

"You're watching Forty-Two, door with the eagle's head knocker?"

Another grunt.

"Why?"

"Don't know," was the hoarse reply. The man's face was white now; Doranei could see his jaw trembling with the effort of keeping it up. "Not told."

"Free his left hand," he said to Sebe, and their prisoner gave a gasp of relief as he wedged an elbow under his body. "If any like us entered you were to send a message? You Ruby Tower Guards?"

"Byoran Guard, special corps. Anyone goes in, we send a message to the tower."

"Who gave you the orders?"

"My captain, but message was to go to the new sergeant at the tower."

"Name?"

"Kayel, big foreign bastard, they say, never met him."

"Big bastard?" Doranei wondered, sharing a look with Sebe, who was clearly thinking the same thing. There were few people who'd know who the Narkang agent was in any given city, and how to put a watch on him, but the traitorous golden boy of the unit was certainly one.

"This sergeant, what's his full name? What's he look like?"

"Hener Kayel, I think. Never met him but I heard he boasts a lion mauled him—took half his ear as he killed it. They're all scared of him, kill you soon as look at you they says."

Doranei didn't speak for a moment, casting back in his mind to the day Coran, King Emin's white-eye bodyguard, had staggered back to the palace, his knee ruined and Ilumene's dagger still lodged in his ribs. Coran had managed only a glancing blow; Ilumene had done more damage himself when he'd sliced off the bit of his ear that was tattooed with the Brotherhood's mark. He sent it to the palace two days later so King Emin would be certain that he still lived.

"There's no doubt then," Doranei said at last, sheathing his dagger as he rose. "Time to call for help."

Without looking down he stepped over the man's legs and headed back the way they'd come. After one quick jerk, Sebe followed him.

Legana woke with a start as her narrow bed shuddered. She looked around for a moment, the memory of a sound lingering in her ears, until she realised it had been made by the heavy front door below her room slamming shut. It was dark, and no light crept around the curtain, so she must have slept past nightfall. Legana felt for the chair beside her bed and found her clothes. She dressed as quickly as she could, and finish off by wrapping herself in a long shawl of coppery silk that the wine merchant's wife had gifted her with. Legana couldn't appreciate its colour now, but everyone in the room had gone silent when she put it on, and that told her enough.

Collecting her slate and chalk, Legana unbolted the door and went out into the darkened corridor. She barely needed the support of the walking stick the wine merchant had lent her. It had been old and blackened—his father had used it for thirty years—yet when she touched it, the tarnish had disappeared, revealing the stick's beautifully patterned silver head.

Legana paused to tuck the slate under one arm and allow her eyes to get used to the light coming up the stairs. They were still sensitive, colours washed out to grey, but much of the fuzziness had gone and now she could see the corridor almost as clearly as anyone else. It was for comfort that she ran her fingers along the wall as she headed for the stairway that led downstairs.

She still felt fragile, but instinct told her that her healing was done. Her hearing was diminished and her voice remained a ruin, but she was far stronger than a man now, and vastly more resilient—the occasional bouts of poor balance and her tendency to move slowly and carefully were ingrained, and she would have to learn to live around them.

The building was split into three parts. Business was conducted in the large hallway at the front. It looked more like a storeroom than a shop front. Legana headed there first, knowing Lell Derager, the wine merchant who was

Byora's Farlan agent, didn't conduct business after dark. The slamming of the door was almost certain to have been those fools from Narkang returning.

As she reached the bottom of the stair Legana found Derager and his wife, Gavai, standing at the entrance to his cramped office. At the sound of her feet the rotund man turned and spread his arms in a welcoming gesture, remembering that Legana found the nuance of facial expressions difficult to make out.

"Legana, do you feel better after your nap?" he said in a booming voice.

She nodded, not bothering to write on the slate. Lell wasn't the sort of man to mind. He was courteous to the point of sparking Legana's suspicious nature, and did everything for her himself, rather than call for a servant. He wasn't old—less than forty summers—but his muttonchops and beard made it hard to judge his age. He was far more ebullient than his wife, who was ten years his senior, but they were both considerate, caring hosts—and the least likely spies Legana could imagine, which had presumably been the former Whisper's logic.

"Your friends have returned," Gavai advised her. "They're just drying off. Let us go into the family room and wait for them." She offered her arm to Legana. After a moment's hesitation she took it and allowed herself to be led to the second-largest room in the house. She had precious little actual experience of how a daughter should be treated, but Legana was beginning to imagine it was something like this.

An inordinately wide bog-oak dining table dominated the room, but large though it was, there was at least a ten-foot clearance on either side. A candelabrum hung from the main beam of the low ceiling above the table. On the left, a mismatched assortment of chairs were arranged almost at random around the fire. Gavai directed Legana to one facing away from the flickering flames and placed herself beside the former Farlan assassin. Lell followed them in and ushered his teenage son towards the kitchen, saying something Legana didn't catch.

By the time Lell returned, goblets of wine in each hand, Doranei and Sebe had joined them and gratefully accepted the offer of a drink. Doranei tossed back the wine in one gulp, which didn't surprise Legana until Sebe followed suit swiftly.

As Lell picked up the brass wine jug to refill their glasses, Legana scribbled on her slate, —Bad news? She thought she detected a scowl on Doranei's face, and that was confirmed by the grim tone of his voice.

"Looks like you were right," he said reluctantly. "Azaer's disciples are here."

"You're certain?" Lell said, before adding, "well, of course you are. No one wears that face unless they're sure. How did you find out?"

"Our agent here is being watched by men reporting to the Ruby Tower," Sebe answered for Doranei as he made headway on the drink. "It's a tighter network than yours, and almost certain not to be casually picked up. We interrogated one of the watchers. They're to report any visitors to a new sergeant in the Ruby Tower Guard."

—*Duchess and Azaer?* asked Legana.

Doranei shook his head. "I doubt it, but the description of the sergeant was easy enough to recognise. If he's here, then the rest of Azaer's disciples probably are too. I don't think they have the strength to divide their forces now; Scree, especially the loss of Rojak, will have drained their resources considerably."

"Which means either Aracnan's murder of High Priest Lier is coincidence or it's a sign that he's under Azaer's command," Lell said, glancing at his wife. "Getting Lier out of the way makes the duchess more easily influenced, as well as fuelling the conflict between Eight Towers and Hale."

"And this is not a business of coincidences," Gavai finished for her husband. The pair might not have ever been at the sharp end of spycraft where Legana and the King's Men lived, but they were under no illusions about what they were involved with.

"I know enough to report to my king," Doranei said, staring straight at Legana, "but what are you going to do?"

Legana didn't respond immediately. As everyone turned to look at her, she kept her eyes on Doranei. He didn't understand what had happened to her—she didn't understand it herself yet—but he himself, perhaps without knowing it, was not just a pawn in the game; he was a man who could call Lord Isak friend and Zhia Vukotic something more. Of all of them, he was the only one who could understand the twilight world she now inhabited. Her hand went to the line of bumps around her neck, a regular curve just above the collarbones. She couldn't feel the shadow mark that overlaid half of the emeralds under her skin. She couldn't see her own eyes, though she knew they were different. And the changes didn't stop there. There was a fire in her blood, like she'd always imagined magic to be like: a tiny prickle that could erupt into the fury of a furnace at a moment's notice.

Do I call myself Farlan any longer? Can I? I accepted the Lady's kinship but she's dead now,—I feel the part of her inside me is dead,—but what about the other Gods? Are they my kin now, or am I just Raylin, a being of power but with no allegiance?

Finally she wrote hesitantly, —*I do not know to whom I now kneel.*

Gavai whispered the words aloud as Legana wrote. She placed a sympathetic hand on Legana's arm, but withdrew it when she flinched.

The only place I've ever belonged is the Temple of the Lady, Legana realised as she wiped the slate clean. *Whatever spark of divinity that remains, is that enough to sustain the temples, or will they just end up as killers for hire? We were halfway there already.*

"I understand your problem," Doranei said, interrupting her thoughts, "but we could use your help. You once called us allies; could that not continue? Even if only out of a common enemy?"

—*He is too strong for me*, she wrote.

"Gods! I'm not asking you to take Aracnan down." Doranei shook his head firmly to emphasise the point though he was speaking loudly enough for her to hear him. "Information will be our greatest weapon; information provided by someone with insight we cannot get elsewhere."

—*They would sense me if I spied on the duchess.*

"Then let us find another way." He paused. "You do want revenge, don't you?"

Legana didn't reply. For herself she felt nothing, just the emptiness in her gut that had once been the divine touch of the Lady. But then she remembered that night in the temple; the brutality that had broken her body, and the sight of the Lady, skin flayed and scorched as she turned away from Aracnan.

Why did she save me and not herself? Even if she couldn't save herself, why save me? Who gives up in a fight even if they're outmatched? Legana felt her hand tense at the memory of Fate's dying expression. *The Goddess didn't think like that. The creed says we are her daughters, and a mother does not abandon her daughters.*

—*I want revenge.* The image of Fate was clear and painful in her memory, the emerald green of the Lady's eyes shining out from the darkness of the grave.

—*But not enough to abandon my sisters*, she added, holding the slate out to Doranei for emphasis.

"Of course. I understand," he told her. "King Emin always spoke in fond terms of the Lady. If there is help Narkang can provide you, just ask."

"Before all that," Lell interrupted, "I need to send a bird to Tirah. Lord Isak needs this information."

—*I will tell him.*

"Can you reach him directly?"

She shrugged. Her divinity was so new to her that she hadn't had much chance to explore its potential; she'd been sleeping mostly, recovering her strength, not testing its limits. It was also risky—Lord Isak was also new to power, and he might react without thinking. The prospect made Legana's hands tremble, but she had made up her mind: her loyalty was to her cult and her sisters, but she had spent years fighting for the Lord of the Farlan, and she had respected Lord Bahl, and that meant she had to extend that to Bahl's heir. That in turn meant telling him to his face that she was no longer in his employ.

—*I will find him*, she wrote with crisp, certain strokes.

King Emin looked up at the massive man at his side: Coran, his bodyguard, was staring silently down at him, his face grave. Behind them Emin could hear the shutters rattle and shudder under a storm's assault.

"Well?" Emin turned in his seat to look at the white-eye. There were only two other men in the gentlemen's club, a retired captain of the Watch who was snoring softly in a corner, and Count Antern, who stood at the back of the room frowning down at a stack of reports. The king used the club as a front for various activities, and many of the members had been involved in those activities at one time or another. Coran would normally be happy to speak in front of either of those present.

Coran pushed up the left sleeve of his tunic. "I'm going to cut that damn mage's balls off," he said fiercely, and turned so King Emin could see the inner forearm.

"We can't blame Endine for his successes, can we?" Emin replied in a slightly forced way. It was clear to all that a weight had been lifted from him after his sundering, but the process had taken its toll.

Coran gave him an old-fashioned look as a trickle of blood ran down his fingers and dripped onto the carpet. "I think I'll find a way."

Emin peered at the bloodied skin. "Just be glad he used the Brotherhood's shorthand, my friend! 'Enemy sighted, Ilumene and others, purpose unknown, request orders,'" he read aloud. "Curious he doesn't specify what others—important enough to mention but not name."

"Ilumene will be in charge, whoever else is there," Coran growled, the reason for his dark mood now apparent. Ilumene had escaped him twice now, and Coran took such things to heart.

"No doubt, but I think it more likely Doranei has identified a new disciple, one we've yet to assign a shorthand symbol to." Emin stood and looked at Count Antern on the other side of the room, who had looked up when Coran started speaking. He had heard the message.

"Antern, please fetch Sir Creyl and Morghien," the king asked, and his first minister hurried away. Emin walked over and nudged the dozing man.

"Captain, time for you to go home to your wife," Emin said gently.

The white-whiskered man twitched a few times before he opened one eye. "Eh?"

"Bugger off home," Coran said.

"Bugger off yourself," the captain replied in a gravely voice. "She don't want me there, not since Brandt died defending your palace." His skin was creased like old, worn leather, and his white beard had grown rather patchily where there were scars. He was past sixty now, and losing the bulk that had kept him alive in many a street fight. When Coran didn't reply he gave a sigh and began to heave himself upright. The white-eye reached forward and took most of his weight until he was standing.

"I dreamed I was young again," the captain complained to Emin, "chasing a man through Queen's Square with all the gladness of youth."

The king smiled. "You were a growling old bear when we first met and I doubt it was any different twenty years before that."

The captain laughed and began to walk stiffly towards the door. "Hah— and you were the most arrogant man I ever met," he said. He added softly, "Still haven't come good on your promise though. I'll never forgive you if I don't live long enough to hear the shadow's dead."

"I'll do my best, my friend," Emin said as he watched him hobble out.

As the old officer passed them, Morghien and Sir Creyl, Commander of the Brotherhood, nodded respectfully. Once the door was shut, all was business again.

"Gentlemen, Doranei has sighted Ilumene in the Circle City," King Emin announced. "Suggestions?"

"Don't let anger get the better of you," Sir Creyl said. He was a heavyset man dressed in the functional clothes of a hurscal. His arresting pale blue eyes had more than once been mistaken for white, though Creyl was a calm man who was entirely out of place on a battlefield.

"Thank you, the point has already been made."

"What was the message?" Morghien asked, walking past Emin and settling himself into the chair just vacated by the captain. He stared at the fire, watching the flames dance in the occasional gusts of wind down the chimney.

Emin repeated it.

Since the ritual in the tower they had barely spoken. The wanderer looked even more strung out than usual. He had moved into one of the club's guestrooms and spent as much time in the Light Fingers as Doranei had before his latest mission. "Another ruse?" Morghien said eventually.

"Bit close to playing the same trick twice, isn't it?"

"Double bluff, then. I wouldn't expect the shadow to be so stupid, and the bastard knows it."

"We need to know how the information was come by," Sir Creyl said. "Last time it was thrown in our faces for their purposes. What if they have allowed Doranei to discover this?"

"The point stands either way," Emin sighed. "Come on; you've all thought about our next step; what are your suggestions?"

"Watch your own backyard," Morghien said before the others could speak. "If it's drawing your attention to the Circle City, then maybe it's got something planned for Narkang again."

"Pah! The city's locked tighter than even the Brotherhood knows," Count Antern said dismissively. "The shadow wouldn't bother trying."

"I trust Doranei," Sir Creyl said slowly. "He's watching for ruses; he's learned the lessons of Scree."

"Your man's burned out," Antern countered. "There's no mention of Zhia Vukotic at all—and that's why he was sent there in the first place."

"I trust him," Creyl repeated, "he knows what he's doing and he's not burned out. If Doranei has passed that message on, he came to this properly and this isn't a trap—unless the ruse is so fantastically clever every one of us would have been taken in."

"So?" King Emin enquired, pulling a cigar from his tunic and lighting it with a taper. He offered the leather case to Morghien, but the man of many spirits waved it away.

"So we act," Creyl said firmly. "If Doranei's looking for orders, that means he can't manage it himself. I suggest I put together a kill team, mages and Brothers, and send it to the Circle City. We don't worry about the condition of the city or relations with them; we make a big mess and leave it for someone else to clear it up."

Antern gave a sharp nod. "Grossly unsubtle, something I doubt will be either expected or anticipated. I've had intel that envoys from Mustet and Sautin have travelled to Thotel. If they agree on a treaty with Lord Styrax, he'll be free to move north towards Tor Salan, the Circle City, then Embere. Everything south of the Farlan sphere of influence will be open to him, so we have no need to protect our good relations with the Circle City: we'll tear a hole in the city and get out quickly. It's our last chance to act there before we find ourselves looking over the border at the Menin Army."

"And then we have a whole new set of problems," Coran added.

"Surely we must try to discover what Ilumene is doing there?" Morghien asked, "or are we just going to throw away years of covert surveillance in favour of revenge?"

King Emin was quiet for a moment, watching the thin trail of smoke from his cigar. "This is not about revenge, my friend. I've made that mistake already. We'll take this chance to damage Azaer's disciples, and prepare for the next stage, for we all know there will be one." He tossed the barely started cigar into the fire, his lips pursed as though the taste had suddenly revolted him. "It will hide behind the Menin conquest so we must ensure that, when it does act, we are there waiting."

The last few rain drops hissed into the fires Ehla had set around Mihn. He sat cross-legged, trying to ignore the creeping damp soaking up from the ground, and despite the fires he shivered. It was relatively mild for winter, but under the cloak he wore no shirt and his lean frame had no fat to keep him warm.

"The spells are working well," Fernal said from his position under a tree. His midnight blue fur merged seamlessly with the shadows and Mihn could barely see anything of the Demi-God beyond his yellow-tinted eyes and fangs. "They masked your approach—unless you were overshadowed by Xeliath's presence."

"What did it say?" Xeliath demanded from her seat just inside Ehla's tent, bristling at the sound of her name in a language she couldn't understand.

"*He*," Mihn replied calmly, "said he could not sense me as we came, but that might have been down to your presence."

"Hah," the girl scoffed in Farlan so Fernal could understand, "got eyes only for me, have you, Hairy? Too blue for my tastes, so keep yourself under control."

Fernal growled softly at Xeliath, prompting laughter.

"*Xeliath*," the witch said, speaking into everyone's minds, "*you are here as a guest; behave like one. Someone of your strength should know better.*"

The young woman scowled, but said nothing. She wrapped her hands as best she could around the tea Fernal had given her a few minutes before. From beyond the ring of firelight the monstrous son of Nartis fixed his unblinking stare on Xeliath: she might be a fraction of his size, but with the Crystal Skull fused to her palm she had the advantage.

The witch stepped out from her tent and stood at Xeliath's side. "Mihn ab Netren ab Felith, a third request you would have of me. It is said that to ask of a witch a third time is to give away a piece of your soul."

"So it is said," Mihn replied solemnly. He had spent the day fasting and preparing for what was to come. Hours meditating in the small Temple of Nartis at the palace had brushed aside the clutter of everyday thoughts and deepened his certainty that this path was the right one. "The price of power is to wield it," he said in a level tone, "I cannot turn away from a path that must be taken, not when I am the one best suited to walk it."

The witch took a step closer, peering down at him like a hunting hawk. "And the price you will pay?" Her voice was dry and harsh, as remorseless as the north wind.

"I will pay what I must."

"Brave words for now."

Another step forward. Behind her, Xeliath pulled herself upright and fell in behind the witch. She looked like more of a white-eye now, with that same intent, predatory expression Mihn had seen on Isak's face so many times.

"Two services I have performed for you, grave thief; the third permits me to name a terrible price. Silence I have given you, the unseen glide of a ghost-owl. Protection I have given you, the leaves of rowan and hazel on your skin."

"Grave thief," whispered Xeliath from beside the witch, her face alight with savage delight, her eyes gleaming.

"More you have asked from me," the witch continued, her voice growing in strength. Mihn felt the sound all around him, shaking through his bones. "And a claim on your soul is mine, to do with as I wish. That claim I offer to another; to the grave, to the wild wind, to the called storm."

The words struck Mihn like hammer blows, the force of each one echoing through his mind with the finality of nails in a coffin.

"It is given," he whispered, feeling an empty pit open up in his stomach. "Whatever is asked shall be done. Whatever cannot be asked of another will be done. Whatever should not be asked of another, it will be done."

The witch took one more step to come within arm's reach of the sitting man. She bent down to look him in the eye. Her pale, proud face had never before looked so terrible.

"To be led through darkness one needs more than light." She reached behind herself and took Xeliath's hand as she grabbed Mihn's throat. He made no move to resist the witch as her nails dug in deep and drew blood.

With his blood on her hand the witch lowered it and placed her palm on Mihn's chest. He felt it warm to the touch as the wind suddenly whipped up and began to swirl all around them, tearing through the trees as Xeliath drew hard on the torrent of energy at her disposal.

"In darkness you will find my price," the witch cried. "In darkness you will weep for master and mistress as cruel as the ice of their eyes. In darkness you will find both a path and a leash on your soul."

The warmth of her hand intensified and Mihn gasped as leaves tore past his face and the ground shuddered. Distantly he heard a sound, a moan from the son of Nartis, but he had no mind for anything but the pain as a lance of flame seemed to run through his chest and a white-hot light filled his eyes. He screamed, and his cry mingled on the wind with the witch's animal shriek.

The Land fell away, only to abruptly return as Xeliath broke the flow of magic. Mihn was thrown backwards to sprawl on the ground, curling into a fetal ball as his howls became whimpers.

"It is done," Xeliath said, uncaring of the writhing man on the floor, "and it has attracted someone's attention; I sense them closing on the wind."

Mihn gave a cough which shook his whole body and sent a final burning tingle racing down his limbs. Fernal raced from the shadows and helped Mihn to sit upright. Mihn groaned, the echo of pain still strong. Once he was upright once more he noticed the smell of burnt flesh rising from his chest. He squinted down, his eyes blurred with rain and tears.

"It is done," Fernal repeated.

Mihn frowned, unable to see properly. With an unsteady finger he poked at his chest until he found the right spot and was rewarded with a hot stinging from the red patch of skin on his sternum. Bright against his painfully white skin was a circle containing a rune, one he knew well.

"Is it finished?" he asked drunkenly, looking up at the witch.

There was sorrow in her eyes, so profound it frightened Mihn as much as the pitiless expression she had worn only moments before. "No, grave thief, it is far from over."

"Shit." He sank back into Fernal's arms and unconsciousness embraced him.

The grey sky surged and roiled with distant fury. On top of a small hill stood the broken stub of a tower, just one storey high, rising from a sea of gorse. Xeliath occupied a grand throne on what was now the roof, the shattered walls affording her an unhindered view. The gale that lashed around the edges of the tower failed to ruffle her silk shirt or riding breeches as it whistled ferociously over the scarred stone.

The Yeetatchen girl was lost in thought as she scowled at the gorse. She wasn't afraid, just puzzled. This was her Land, the dreamscape shaped by her mind, and she feared no one here—but she had never before been approached so tentatively here.

She flexed the fingers of her left hand, feeling the duel sensation of a palm both unencumbered and still fused to the Crystal Skull. With a thought she clothed her body in glittering armour of crystal and a short-handled glaive appeared in her hand, like those carried by the Ghosts, but carved from ivory.

"You will have no need of that," called a woman from behind her.

Xeliath blinked, and the entire Land seemed to spin around her while she remained still. The woman, a copper-haired Farlan, staggered and almost fell before she found her balance once more. She was putting her weight on a silver-headed walking stick, moving as if she was injured; even in this dream-state she looked not entirely whole.

Is this a ruse, or does she lack the strength to appear as she wishes? The Yeetatchen could not help but glance at her own left arm, now perfect and straight. *Vanity perhaps, but the Land owes me that at the very least.*

"Who are you?" Xeliath said, her voice cutting the wind like a sword through smoke. "What do you want with me?"

"You are Xeliath?" the woman asked. She pushed her hair away from her face and Xeliath saw a black handprint on her throat. "My name is Legana." The wind tore at her long emerald cloak.

The white-eye reached out with her senses and her puzzlement increased. "What are you?" she wondered. "Your face says Farlan and your hair says a devotee of the Lady—so why do you smell of Godhood?"

Legana took a step forward. The wind assailing her abruptly stopped. "I am the Mortal-Aspect of the Lady, but once I was an agent of the Farlan. I wish to speak to Lord Isak, to give my final report before I leave his service."

"Why should I believe you?" Xeliath asked.

"I am in your power," Legana said simply. "Here, I am at your mercy. Lord Isak knows me, he will recognise me, but I am not strong enough to reach him directly."

"Do you wear your true face?" Xeliath mused. An unexpected gust of wind slapped past Legana, making her flinch. When she looked up again her face was unchanged, but Xeliath could now see a curved line of bumps running around her neck.

"This is my true face. I lack the strength to hide it from you," Legana said, before adding in a bitter voice, "if I did I would certainly remove from my neck the mark of the man who broke me and killed my Goddess."

Xeliath let go of her glaive. The weapon fell slowly and disappeared just before it hit the ground. In its place a small table appeared, bearing a crystal decanter and two glasses. "I have summoned him," Xeliath announced. "A drink while we wait? It's not real, of course, but who cares?"

The two women spent the next few minutes in silence, carefully scrutinising each other. In this dreamscape Xeliath was unaffected by the paralysis of the real world, and while Legana's beauty was undiminished, her sinuous athleticism had been replaced by that ethereal quality possessed by all Gods.

When Isak arrived, his peevish expression at the rags he found himself wearing vanished quickly, and he looked both women up and down, not trying to hide his appreciative grin. Only when Xeliath gave him a distinctly unfriendly look, accompanied by a distant rumble of thunder, did the Lord of the Farlan step forward, his palms upturned in greeting.

"Legana," he acknowledged as she returned the gesture, "you're changed since last I saw you."

"There have been many changes, Lord Isak." She inclined her head, to concede the point rather than show deference. "I come to give you my final report."

"Final?" He shot a look at Xeliath, who was now lying on her side on a green upholstered sofa, watching the pair of them like a cat. "You wish to leave my service?"

"I have left your service," she corrected. "My allegiance is no longer to the Farlan."

"Are we enemies instead?" His voice was cautious rather than hostile, but, apparently unbidden, Eolis appeared in his hand.

"Not unless you wish it, my Lord," she said carefully. "I am not so changed that I have forgotten my past."

"Sod it, then," Isak replied, trying to look casual. "I've got enough enemies. Let's hear your report."

"In brief, to begin with. You know the Lady is dead?" He voice was impassive.

He nodded, but said nothing.

"It was Aracnan who killed her, and almost killed me too—I discovered him staging a situation to make it look like a high priest had been sacrificing to a daemon."

She paused as Isak's expression soured all of a sudden, his ever-ready glower appearing even as he motioned for her to continue. "I encountered two King's Men from Narkang in Byora, and we have good reason to believe Aracnan is acting under the orders of Azaer, and that other disciples of the shadow have infiltrated the Duchess of Byora's inner circle."

"High priests playing with daemons? The bastard will be pleased to hear whose tactics he's borrowed," Isak muttered. "Do you have any clues as to what the shadow intends?"

"No, and I am in no condition to find out more."

"How easily did you find all this out?" Xeliath interrupted. "Isak, you said yourself that Scree was a setup from the start—so why would this situation in Byora be any different?"

Legana hesitated before answering. "I was lucky to survive the attack— I barely did," she admitted in a quiet voice. "I had only been the Lady's Mortal-Aspect for a few days before she sent me to the temple where I found Aracnan. She stepped in to save me, realising too late that he was too strong even for her."

"Too strong for a Goddess in a straight fight?" Isak marvelled, disbelieving. "I hadn't realised."

Xeliath made an angry sound. "Is any mortal? Is any *immortal*—except for the Gods of the Upper Circle and the princes of the Dark Place?"

"What are you saying?"

"That you're a slow-witted wagon brat!" she exclaimed fiercely. "Aracnan could not be so powerful by himself; he is only a Demi-God. If he was powerful enough to kill the Lady in a straight fight, then why has he not ascended to the Pantheon?"

"Karkarn's horn," breathed Legana as realisation struck her.

"What?" Isak looked at each of them, bewildered. "What the fuck are you both—? Ah. Oh."

"Exactly. We know one of Azaer's disciples has a Crystal Skull in his possession," Xeliath said, flexing the fingers of her left hand.

"Legana, you should leave the Circle City as swiftly as possible," Isak said. "Your existence is a loose end he'll be keen to tie up. But first tell me why you don't think it's a trap."

"In Scree they did not try to control events, but let them play out as they spiralled out of control. If the duchess is under Azaer's control, then they are being more direct, building on Scree's destruction. There's no madness tearing the city apart this time, but a careful drawing of battle lines between powers."

"But if that's true, what's to stop me marching the entire Farlan Army south and pounding Byora to dust? The road is clear, and Tor Milist would not dare hinder me—even united, the Circle City could not hope to win if I attacked. It could be a ruse," he insisted, "tempting me to act preemptively."

Legana thought through what Isak was saying, then her eyes widened. "Because Azaer will not be alone! Byora is awash with rumours from Tor Salan; the Menin have taken the city and are preparing to move north. The Circle City is weaker than it has been in decades. Lord Styrax can pick the cities off at his leisure. They will be crucial if he is going to take Raland and Embere."

Isak swore. "They'll reach the Circle City long before we could ever hope to. Did the shadow engineer that, or just anticipate it?"

"Whichever is true, you cannot attack Azaer without coming into conflict with the Menin."

The white-eye lord gave an unexpected laugh, sounding world-weary and full of bitterness despite his youth.

"And so my deeds come back to haunt me. Avoiding conflict may not be possible, I'm afraid—tomorrow morning I give an official farewell to an army under Suzerain Torl's command!" Isak looked away for a moment, his face grave. "At my urging, the Brethren of the Sacred Teachings and the newly militant cults of the Farlan have declared a crusade against Lord Styrax. No prizes for guessing where those armies will meet."

CHAPTER 26

S UZERAIN TORL AND HIS TROOPS left Tirah on the first fine morning of the year in Tirah. After weeks of winter misery, the citizens needed no more encouragement than a little sun to fill the streets, however uneasy they were at the sight of unfamiliar uniforms. Mihn stood at his lord's side on a raised stone platform in Bloodletters Square, on the southern edge of the city, watching the troops assemble in the crisp early-morning air.

Only now did Mihn appreciate how sapping to the spirit the weeks of constant rain and gales had been. He felt a weight lift from his shoulders as he felt the morning sun on his skin. People filled the massive square, pressing against each other and against the buildings, to watch the army marching out of the city, and Mihn could see his own smile reflected on everyone's face. The appearance of Tsatach's eye appeared to have done more to diffuse tensions in the city than all of Chief Steward Lesarl's efforts. Even the buildings themselves looked more cheerful as the sun lightened the grey stone and glittered on windowpanes.

"How much longer?" growled Lord Isak. He shifted his feet impatiently and his eyes roved over the bustle before him.

"Not long, my Lord," Mihn replied with excessive cheerfulness. "Just try to enjoy the sun while it's here."

"Do I look like I'm enjoying the fucking sun?"

"Not really, but it never hurts to try."

Mihn's broad smile only made Isak's frown deepen. He'd been unable to sleep further after the meeting in Xeliath's dreamscape and he'd been in a foul mood from the moment he left the Tower—it was only because Mihn knew how volatile his temper was that made him so sure the three palace servants would not really be dismissed for this morning's transgressions, and nor would Count Vesna's title be stripped from him because of an argument over a spoon.

"Never hurts to try?" growled Isak. "It feels like a badger's nesting in my head and this sun really isn't helping." Isak looked past Mihn to the edge of the large square pedestal they were standing on to watch the troops assembling. "I could backhand you right off this thing, you know?" he added.

Mihn shrugged and turned back to the sun. "Perhaps. I'm not sure you're that much quicker than I am, though, not at the moment."

Isak leaned down so his head was nearly level with Mihn's. "Think you're so clever? After what you did last night, I don't have to catch you, do I?" The massive white-eye slipped his right hand inside his tunic and smirked coldly. Before Mihn worked out what his lord was talking about, Isak jabbed his thumbnail into the scar on his chest hard enough to break the skin and the smaller man yelped as he felt the same pain.

"Ah, Gods on high!" Mihn gasped as Isak, teeth bared, twisted his thumb in the cut.

"Like that, do you?"

"Shit, ow! No!" Mihn clamped his hand over his own chest, feeling the echo of Isak's scratch magnified by the fact his burn was still blackened and raw.

"Take back what you just said about enjoying the sun?"

"Gods, you're spiteful!" Mihn hissed, moaning as Isak gave another twist of the thumb. "Ow! Yes, yes, I take it back!"

Isak bared his teeth in a mockery of a grin and lowered his hand. "Good, now shut up and enjoy the view."

Mihn winced as the pressure was lifted from his burn and the pain subsided to a hot throbbing. He straightened up, ignoring the puzzled faces of Isak's personal guard who were surrounding the stone block.

"At least I managed to put a smile on your face before you have to speak to the priests," he muttered, turning away from the irritable thug and to the troop formations ahead.

On the north side of Bloodletters Square was the shrine to Nartis, the only part of the square still serving the purpose for which it had been built. All the grand buildings surrounding it had been extensively converted over the years, and most now housed workers' families. Four thirty-foot-square platforms the height of a white-eye dominated the square itself. They occupied most of the northeastern corner, leaving space for several thousand men to be formed up on the remaining ground.

During the reign of Lord Atro, Lord Bahl's predecessor, a wealthy nobleman had planned a grand temple complex to overlook the southern gate to the city. The nobleman had died before his plan had come to fruition, and his son had immediately put a stop to the project which would have ruined his family, but the land had already been cleared around the gate and work on the largest of the temples had started. Because space within the city walls was at a premium, Lord Atio's Chief Steward had bought the square soon after, laughingly dubbed it Bloodletters Square, and installed the city's principal cattle market there.

As Mihn watched, officers began to give orders and the masses coalesced into discrete blocks of troops. He could see Isak's personal guard were nervous —and with good reason; a significant portion of the religious troops in the city were assembling just ahead of them. Whilst there had been no signs of hostility from the mercenaries, Mihn was well aware how quickly such situations could turn. Soldiers were trained to fight, and one of the first lessons was this: the slowest man to respond was usually the one who died. It was a small step from that to anticipating the enemy and drawing first blood yourself.

"Sometimes I wonder if I'm Farlan at all," Isak said abruptly. "Their capacity for hypocrisy knows no limits."

Mihn turned to him, his eyebrows raised.

Isak pressed fingers into the bridge of his nose to ease his headache and began to explain. "After weeks of what was virtually civil war, during which the laws of civil, military, and cult domains were infringed so comprehensively it's impossible to pick out each individual violation, the clerics still have the gall to pretend their penitents are new to all this." He pointed at the orderly ranks. "That they can pretend to have reorganised thousands of men into coherent military units overnight—well, it amazes me, and not least because there's been not a word of objection. Suddenly everything's back to normal, all traditions are scrupulously adhered to, and the cults formally request my blessing on their crusade, acting as meek as lambs now they think they've got what they want."

"Did you expect anything different?"

Isak sighed. "You're an actor, and I can understand you being able to adopt a role easily, but to see it on such a mass scale—these rabid zealots, all suddenly smiling and polite—it disturbs me. Folk shouldn't be able to change so easily."

He pointed to the fringes, where the Brethren of the Sacred Teachings divisions where already assembled and waiting to salute their lord before they left. There were two horsemen not in rank; the functional uniform of the Dark Monks disguised their identity, but Mihn knew the knights were Suzerain Torl and Brother-Captain Sheln.

"Those two are talking to Legion Chaplain Darc, and have been for the last twenty minutes. That bastard's personally hanged six of their comrades in the last few weeks, and yet there they are, making small talk. I'd have cut him in half by now, but I'm a white-eye—we don't civilise easily."

Mihn looked at him. "You don't react in the same way to crisis the way normal folk do either. For everyone else, custom and protocol cushion the blow. It gives them time to accept and rationalise what has happened, and the greater the upheaval, the more easily they accept the established structure. It may not last for long, but it doesn't have to. What sets men apart from beasts is the ability to learn, to adapt."

"And so they suddenly accept my blessing on their crusade?" Isak said, nonplussed.

"Tradition papers over the cracks in society. When an army leaves Tirah, it should do so under the flag or blessing of the Chosen. The zealots are too delighted with the growing size of their army to care about challenging tradition right now."

Isak glared in disgust. "Why should they care? They get to tyrannise those they think aren't sufficiently godly." He pointed again, this time to the opposite corner of the square. "Look: men in the uniform of the bloody Knights of the Temples, at least a division of them, and under a runesword standard big enough for a legion. The law hasn't changed overnight, Lord Bahl's edicts on the Devoted haven't disappeared, but today they're allowed to gather under arms because we're all dressed in our finest for a parade. It would be considered . . ." Isak hesitated, groping for the right word for a moment, "it would be *impolite* to arrest them right now." He shook his head. "I'll never understand rich people."

Before Mihn could reply, loud voices rang out over the hubbub and they looked up to see a procession of carriages clattering into the square. Six heralds dressed in a livery of white, blue, and red rode ahead, standing in their stirrups and bellowing at the soldiers to clear a path. Each held a fluttering banner, like a suzerain's hurscal.

"Those banners have the snake of Nartis on them," Isak said, narrowing his eyes, "but those knights don't look like penitents to me."

"The Cardinal Paladins," Mihn supplied, almost without thinking. "I remember Chief Steward Lesarl talking about them; he was amused that the Synod had resurrected the regiment that once protected them. It's made up of devout knights, and the cream of the mercenaries they employ."

He hesitated and lowered his voice. "My Lord? Speaking of Lesarl—My Lord, where are your advisors? This is a ceremonial occasion, however false the sentiments, and—"

"They're busy," Isak said abruptly, shutting his jaw with a snap. He stared off into the distance for a few heartbeats, then turned back. There was a rare look of concern on his face. "I ordered them to stay away. The reason we came early was because I needed to think."

"Do you wish me to——?" Mihn began before Isak waved the suggestion away.

"No, not at all. You don't disrupt my train of thought. If anything, you've helped. Did Xeliath not tell you about last night?"

Mihn looked down. "I wasn't in much mood to listen, I'm afraid. I hadn't realised how draining the ritual was going to be. By the time Xeliath, ah, *returned* to herself, I was asleep."

Isak put a hand on the small man's shoulder. "Of course. I'll give you the brief version." He rubbed a hand over his stubble and Mihn suddenly realised his mood was not just because of a poor night's sleep—and whatever was bothering him was serious enough to make his eyes look haunted. "I pretty much grew up on a soldier's potted wisdom; you know that, right?"

Mihn nodded. "Of course—but Carel's no fool, and it's not led you far wrong, has it?"

"Last time I asked him, the old bugger said he had nothing more to tell me." Isak gave a sour laugh at the notion that there was nothing more for him to learn. "He just repeated something he's said before to me, "if it's fear guiding your horse you're riding straight to the ivory gates"—but I guess I ignored it the first time he said it. I didn't think it applied to a white-eye. But now—now I realise it's the answer I've been looking for, the one I think you've been nudging me towards for weeks."

"What was the news?" Mihn asked quietly, keeping an eye on the cardinals' carriages. They had stopped in the centre of the square. The cardinals would, of course, want to inspect their troops—and show they were in no great hurry for Isak's approval.

"Lord Styrax has moved north faster than we could have possibly imagined; he's taken Tor Salan and will be at the gates of the Circle City soon, in days perhaps. For years—*years*—I dreamed of Lord Bahl's death; and for the last few I always woke in the certainty that the same man would one day kill me. The man who's marching this way."

"That means nothing," Mihn protested. "Whether the dreams are true or not, the Circle City is a long way from Tirah. It would take one order to have Tor Milist under your direct control, and that gives us miles of open ground to exploit our advantage: the cavalry. However good a warrior Lord Styrax is, he cannot win a battle all by himself—and the Farlan cavalry is the finest in the Land."

"I agree, so isn't it ironic that I'm sending a chunk of my army chasing after him? This isn't something I can stop without inciting civil war, and if I don't give them support I'm throwing away valuable troops."

Mihn looked puzzled. "What are you saying?"

Isak pulled a rolled parchment from inside his tunic. "This is Special Order Seven, one of Lesarl's preprepared contingency plans. You want to know where my advisors are? They're off enacting my orders. This order puts the Farlan nation into a state of war."

"You're marching south?" Mihn gaped at him. "But why?"

"Because I will have to, and that you know better than you're making out, my friend." There was no accusation in Isak's expression, just a know-ingness more suited to Carel's careworn face. "You said a few weeks ago that I was haunted by prophecies and other forces that have shaped my life. You told me to accept and work around them, to turn them to purpose, just as I have tried to turn the zealotry of the cults to my gain. You know I can't continue to submit to fear, and if I let my dreams dictate my actions, I will die like Lord Bahl, alone and haunted—and faithful bondsman that you are, you're trying to prepare your own contingency plan."

Mihn opened his mouth to argue but shut it again when he saw the look in Isak's eye. The Chosen of Nartis was in no mood to be contradicted, especially when he knew he was right.

"I will go south because I believe I must. My goal is not to meet Lord Styrax on the field but to buy enough time to get into Byora. Lesarl's agent Legana—well, former agent—she told me that Azaer's disciples are controlling the Duchess of Byora, that the next step of their plan will be enacted there."

The white-eye paused and checked to see if the cardinals were close enough for his attention yet. He looked at Mihn once more and thumped his fist against his chest. Mihn felt the echo though the rune linking them.

"At the very thought of going I feel fear; a cold, tight band around my heart. That isn't something I'm used to and it terrifies me, but it also tells me Legana's right: Azaer knows I am a danger—I am strong enough to kills Gods, so a shadow would be no great feat. It has survived so far by being unknown, but now it is my enemy it must use the threat of Lord Styrax to ward me off."

"It has underestimated a white-eye's aggression then," Mihn muttered.

Isak shook his head. "Not really. We are born to fight, but we're also born to survive, no matter what. That means we'll fight with every ounce of strength, but a glorious death holds no interest." His voice became more urgent. "You know that, don't you? Nothing of this has been by accident; it is all by design. My dreams have imbued this fear of Styrax into every fibre of my body.

"Meeting him face to face I'll feel like the frightened little boy I have always been in my dreams. Even at my best, I've been one of the Chosen for only a year. Lord Styrax has ruled the Menin for several hundred. He's beaten Koezh Vukotic in a fair fight, and he killed the last Lord of the Menin with a plain sword! In a straight fight against Lord Styrax, I will die, and that I know with a certainty I cannot even explain. And I don't need to tell someone as skilled as you to tell me what happens when you are certain of failure even before the first blow is struck."

Mihn didn't speak. He was stunned by Isak's honesty—this raw openness wasn't part of Isak's personality, or the military world he lived in. Somewhere in the distance he heard a cough and realised the cardinals were nearing their position, but he couldn't yet tear his eyes away from the young warrior before him.

Isak forced a smile on his face and clapped a hand on Mihn's shoulder. He sagged under the weight as Isak pulled him closer to whisper, "I think I've guessed what your contingency plan is—let us hope it never comes to that. I'm not sure what frightens me more."

Mihn nodded dumbly. For a moment he saw complete understanding in his lord's eyes, and an acceptance that was chilling to behold.

Then the shroud of politics descended and by the time Isak turned to greet High Cardinal Certinse, the welcoming smile on his face looked almost natural.

Certinse himself looked harried and drawn, not showing the same pleasure as his colleagues at the prospect of riding at the head of a crusade.

"Your Eminence," Isak called, "I have excellent news." He raised the parchment. "This is Special Order Seven."

The day passed swiftly, and Isak watched the chaos he had sparked throughout the city with a vague, sour smile. Mihn kept to his lord's shadow and watched him carefully. By the end of the day he still wasn't sure if that displayed amusement was a politician's ruse or—more worryingly, Mihn thought—what Isak thought he should be feeling, and so displayed as a mask, hiding the fear and emptiness within.

Sunset found the pair of them back at Tirah Palace, perched on Isak's high ledge in the chill evening air and watching the activity on the training ground below. Isak had sent two legions of City spearmen with Suzerain Torl and promised more to follow. He'd also given Torl seven written orders, with instructions to hand them out to every suzerain he came into contact with. The results would be seven of the nearest suzerains joining him within days, accompanied by whatever troops they could muster at short notice; Lesarl estimated that would add some three thousand men to Torl's division of Dark Monks. There were six thousand mercenaries already signed up under a variety of cult flags.

Another division of Dark Monks waited in Saroc's suzerainty, which would take the initial total to ten thousand fighting men. Depending on how long he waited before following them, Isak would bring anything from five to twenty thousand men—and that could treble once word of his Special Order spread. With a few weeks' notice the second-string troops would be mobilised, and that was another fifty thousand men, half of them cavalry and already trained, before they had even to begin recruiting civilians. There was a very good reason why the Farlan was the most powerful nation in the Land and, as Mihn realised during the day, the tribe's military men were keen to remind the rest of the land of that fact.

"With a full mobilisation, you could beat the Menin," Mihn commented once he'd finished the prayer to the setting sun.

Isak made a noncommittal sound. "His victories have been swift and easy so far because his enemies underestimated him; I don't intend to do that."

"You're going to offer Styrax a chance for peace?"

"A full mobilisation would mean he's massively outnumbered, it's true, but reports from Tor Salan say he's turned the Ten Thousand to his service. If he has time to raise troops in Tor Salan and all the Chetse cities, our advantage is reduced. Narkang will stand with us, but they're not ready for full-scale war. If we have to fight, best we are better prepared and fighting on ground of our choosing—"

"Are we ready? If you send too many of the standing legions south, who will protect our other borders? You do remember the Elven invasion last winter? If you take the bulk of Lomin's troops to the Circle City, the Elven scryers will discover it soon enough. Will Duke Lomin even permit his troops to leave?"

"I've spoken to Lomin already, through those mages I met with earlier. He will provide troops; I've promised him support of another kind."

Mihn hesitated. Isak's shoulders had dropped slightly as he spoke, as though there was yet another burden weighting them down. "What sort of support?" he asked in an apprehensive whisper.

"Something only I can offer." Isak leaned backwards and rolled his massive frame off the ledge and onto the small walkway that encircled the palace's main wing. "It's something I must do now, even though it may backfire." He sounded a little unsure of what he was about to do, which was unlike him.

Mihn was worried. "Isak, shouldn't you rest first?"

"No, twilight's the best time—if you want to stay, keep quiet and don't interrupt."

Mihn agreed and Isak opened his fleece-lined white cloak and held up one of his Crystal Skulls. Eolis was belted to his waist, and the other Skull was in its usual position, fused to the sword's hilt. Isak was wearing a formal red tunic braided with gold thread underneath the cloak, looking like he'd just stepped out from a banquet.

"Don't be coy, bitch," Isak muttered, staring into the smooth, dead face of the Skull.

Mihn felt his hand tighten on his staff as the hairs prickled down his neck. Suddenly he couldn't feel the cold night air; a greasy sensation crawled over his exposed flesh instead, as light as a butterfly's touch. He twitched involuntarily and it receded a shade, as an unnatural wind began to whip up from the roof.

"Don't make me draw you out," Isak snarled. "You won't enjoy that at all."

Mihn froze. *Oh Gods, please tell me you're not—*

The thought died unfinished as a greenish flicker raced around the rooftop like a lightning bolt. The wind tugged at the corners of Isak's cloak and traced fleeting images of green in the air around the Farlan lord.

A stench of putrefaction and decay came from nowhere, causing Mihn to reel. He covered his mouth, trying not to retch, and flinched as he felt a flash of movement like a rap of the knuckles on the inside of his ribs. When he looked up she was there, as beautiful as a shard of blue ice and just as cold, the terrible face of Death's most savage Aspect: the Wither Queen.

Mihn's stomach gave a lurch, out of terror as much as the rancid smell. She took a step towards him, all the tenderness of a conscienceless murderer in her eyes, reaching out to him with fingernails like jagged icicles—

"I didn't summon you here for that," Isak snarled behind her, making the Wither Queen snap her head around.

Mihn gasped as his heart began to beat once again.

"Why do you call me?" the Wither Queen intoned in a rasping voice. Her limbs were so thin that her bones were plainly visible. In a ragged dress of grey-blue she looked like a corpse come to life. Her matted black hair was seamed with grey, and on her head she wore a tarnished filigree crown set with unfinished gems. Long scabs marked her deathly white skin; everything about her spoke of ruin and decay.

"I have an offer."

She made a sound like a choking man's last breath. Mihn guessed it was a laugh.

"The Reapers do not bargain with mortals, we only hear their pleas." She took a step forward, her fingers flexing slowly, as though preparing to make a grab at him.

The raised Skull pulsed with bright white light, stopping her in her tracks. "I'm a busy man," Isak warned, his voice thick and husky with barely restrained aggression. "I don't have time for your bluster. You know what this is and you know what I can do with it, so I suggest you listen."

The Wither Queen continued to watch Isak like a hawk, her fingers constantly in movement, but she didn't refute his words.

After a moment, he continued, "You are Aspects of Death, temporarily beyond His reach, but Aspects nonetheless. Furthermore, you are only one of five. I offer you the chance to become the greatest of the Reapers."

"You would worship me?" she said mockingly.

"Not only I, but members of my tribe too."

"Empty promises."

"Be careful who you call a liar. I can always kill you and make a similar offer to your brothers."

Mihn saw the look on Isak's face and realised he was half hoping he'd have the excuse to do just that. He was making no effort to hide his revulsion at the Goddess of Disease.

"What is the price of this worship?" she asked.

"The price is that you scour the forest east of Lomin for a hundred miles; that you take no man, woman, or child, but you ensure no Elf walks those parts and survives. I must have the troops that protect the east."

"What you ask exceeds my power," the Aspect hissed.

"This afternoon I ordered a temple to your glory to be constructed in

Lomin, and shrines built in every town of those parts. The last day of the Festival of Swords shall be your praiseday, when all will worship you for the protection you extend." Isak hesitated, licking his lips nervously.

Mihn felt renewed fear. *There's more? What else is he offering her? Is that not enough?*

"If you pledge to protect the Farlan throughout the Great Forest, and hunt down our enemies, I swear that for the rest of my days I shall further your name—the temples funded, the shrines maintained, the people reminded of your plagues."

"The rest of your days?"

Mihn could hear the hunger in her voice, a sickening anticipation for what could be hundreds of years of service. How powerful would she be by then? What sort of Goddess would they be serving? Would there truly be only one Reaper?

"For the rest of my days," Isak confirmed. "Your service must continue as long as there are prayers spoken in your temple in Lomin, and my life is forfeit if I break this vow."

"There must be a covenant," the Wither Queen insisted. "This bargain must be sealed." She reached her hand out to Isak—

—and before he even knew what was happening, Mihn found himself shouting, "No! Don't touch her skin!"

Isak hadn't moved. There was a cold set to his face that Mihn had rarely seen. "Don't worry," he said, never taking his eyes off the Wither Queen, "I saw what she did in Scree. I'll not forget the faces of the men she touched." With a flourish he drew Eolis.

The Wither Queen cringed, keening softly but Isak ignored her. "A covenant is required," he whispered. He touched the edge of his sword to the index finger of his left hand, where the skin was as white as hers. His blood looked shockingly bright in the stark light. As the trickle began to run down his finger, Isak flicked it in the face of the Wither Queen.

To Mihn's disgust she reacted like a dog snapping at a bone, her dead blue tongue flicking out to try and catch the drops.

"An acceptable covenant," she rasped.

Without sheathing his sword Isak pulled a small silver box from a pocket in his tunic and dropped it at the Wither Queen's feet. "The covenant is not yet complete," he warned. "Break one of your fingernails and put it in the box."

"You claim a piece of my body, boy?" the Wither Queen demanded with sudden fury, "a relic of the divine in the hands of a child?"

"Without it there is no bargain." Isak's voice was controlled and calm; his concentration absolute. The stubborn nature of a white-eye was to pursue every goal relentlessly; to be unshakable until success was won. Often it made them uncaring, even soulless, but, as the Gods had intended, they were more often than not the victors in any struggle.

The Wither Queen snarled and twisted from side to side, as though trying to shake off the bonds of the bargain, but it would be fruitless. Whatever the limitations, the power Isak offered was impossible to refuse. At last the Aspect of Death, hissing like an enraged cat, tore at one fingernail and threw a fragment into the box.

Isak nodded solemnly. "Then we have a covenant, my Lady," he said in a far more respectful voice. "The first prayer to your name shall be spoken at dawn on the steps of Death's temple. I will leave you to your work."

The Wither Queen stared at the Lord of the Farlan a long moment before whirling away and melting into the wind. The crawling sensation stayed on Mihn's skin until the wind carried it high over the city and away.

Mihn could barely move. He watched in stunned silence as Isak nudged the silver box closed with his boot and dropped a piece of cloth over it. He swiftly wrapped the box and tied it with some grey cord.

"You . . ." His voice trailed off. "That was . . ."

Isak looked up, his jaw tight with anger, but he couldn't hide the tear that fell. "It was necessary. They're our enemies."

"But—"

Isak cut him off. "I know. There's no hiding from it; I can't even count how many will die from this." He looked down. "It's genocide, and one more scrap of my soul withers to nothing."

Isak and Mihn didn't speak for the rest of the evening. Isak knew the condemnation he felt was his own, but he could not bear to look at Mihn, or look any other of his friends in the eye. He tried to lose himself in a book, but the effort increased his frustration and only Mihn's incredible reactions saved a rare work from the fire.

He felt sick to his stomach, and even his preferred option of drinking himself to sleep betrayed him as he retched up the first gulp of wine.

As a last resort he tried the forge, hoping to lose himself in the sweat and exertion of hammering, but when that failed he drifted back towards his rooms. As he passed through the Great Hall, something caught his eye. He stopped dead and stared at the heavy double doors that were the entrance to the Tower of Semar. They were framed by the wrought-iron wings and head of a dragon, a clear reminder of a task he had been avoiding for far too long.

"Now's as good a time as any," he said to himself. "I can hardly say I've got anything better to do."

From the stairway there came a cough and Tila moved into Isak's view. "Xeliath was asking for you," she said with a smile.

"Is it urgent?"

"I don't believe so—she wasn't swearing, anyway."

"Will you let her know I'll be there later—I've something that needs doing and I've put it off long enough." At Tila's quizzical look he added, "The dragon made a bargain with Lord Bahl, not the Farlan nation. I must try and strike the same bargain."

He wanted to get on with it now. Isak walked into the centre of the room and reached out a hand before stopping himself. Instinctively he had reached towards the symbol on the wall that would carry him up, but for only the second time in his life he needed to go down. He put his hand on the lowest of all the symbols and let it draw a little magic from his body. A torrent of ghostly wings burst into life all around him as he felt the floor rush downwards.

In a moment the swirl dissipated to nothing and Isak found himself in pitch-blackness. He recoiled automatically before creating a ball of light in his palm. Total darkness was a rare thing in his life; it unnerved him. Here in a small, crudely finished stone chamber that more than resembled a tomb, it was worse.

The only exit was a hole in the wall that led onto a long sloped tunnel. As he followed it, walking as quickly as he could without breaking into a run, he remembered the first time he'd walked this way, a little more than a year ago. He found it hard to recognise the youth he had been then: he had changed in every possible way; the snow white skin on his left arm and shoulder was far from the least welcome.

As he walked he began to detect the strange acrid smell he recalled from his previous visit, and listless threads of dormant magic in the air, drawn to the beast and the magical artefacts that had been entrusted to its care. He reached the cavern sooner than he'd expected and lingered a moment at the crudely cut archway that led in. He allowed the ball of pale blue light to dissipate, blinking to let his eyes adjust. There was the faintest of green tints outlining the room, tracing the flowing line of the ceiling and walls and producing a faint sparkle from the quartz nodules that studded the cavern's central pillars.

"*Welcome, Lord Isak,*" came the unexpected boom in his head.

He gave a start at the sheer volume and it took him a moment to gather his wits. He crossed the threshold and entered the cavern, peering around, trying to make out the shape in the gloom that was Genedel. The last time he had been here the dragon had been resting in the centre of the room, between the crystal-studded columns, but he could not see it there now.

"Ah, thank you," Isak said eventually.

"*What brings you to my cavern?*" There was a shuffling sound in some far distant corner of the cave which prompted Isak to peer forward.

"I—Where are you?"

"*Where I choose to be. The sound you heard was a gargoyle; there are a number of entrances to this cavern system and more than one sort of carrion-eater comes down here.*"

Isak froze. It was hard to tell whether there had been rebuke or insult there, but even so, Genedel's words had sounded less than friendly.

"Do they bother you?" he asked tentatively.

"*I am a dragon; do you think much bothers me for long?*"

He swallowed, remembering the sight of Genedel in battle. "No, no I suppose not. Why do they come down here then?"

"*They have their reasons. Some to pick over the bones of my prey, others to escape the dangers of the city. Your breed does not welcome others to its city and of late I have sensed even daemons walking the Land.*"

Isak nodded. "It's not been a lot of fun for anyone up there."

"*Yet you appear to have thrived. Why have you come down here, young lord?*"

Isak hesitated. He was growing increasingly nervous of the fact he still couldn't see the dragon anywhere. Since it was speaking directly into his mind the only source of echoes were his voice and whatever carrion-eaters were lurking in the dark.

"You had an agreement with Lord Bahl, one that appeared to benefit both the Farlan and yourself."

"*And you come to negotiate?*" The edge of hostility in Genedel's tone suddenly magnified. "*Bearing weapons that have killed Gods, you come to my cavern to strike a bargain?*"

"I—No! No, that wasn't the reason!" Isak blurted out in protest. He looked down. While he wasn't wearing Siulents, Eolis was buckled to his hip as always and fused around the guard was a Crystal Skull. "Gods, I didn't even—"

"Those objects have been used to kill and enslave my kind over the millennia," the dragon snarled, causing Isak to wince and clutch his head. The darkness above him suddenly changed into a swift flowing movement. Isak retreated a pace as the silent swirl of dark curved back on itself and a huge horned head appeared barely two yards away from his own.

"They are not welcome here, and neither are you," Genedel growled. *"Leave now or negotiations shall be swift!"*

Isak heard the low rushing sound of an enormous pair of lungs drawing in breath and took another step back.

"But I didn't—"

"Go!"

Isak stared a moment longer at the dragon's opening mouth and enormous teeth before his survival instinct kicked in and he threw himself to the right, barely managing to stay on his feet as he stumbled through the dark up the slope and back to the palace. As he ran, the roar of an enraged dragon rumbled down the tunnel after him.

CHAPTER 27

TOR SALAN WAS A CITY OF FOOTSTEPS; merchants, labourers, and clattering hooves. Within its borders there were two small rivers, but neither was big enough for much trade and the city existed solely on the happy coincidence of its location: it was the heart of the West, sitting at the centre of a web of trade routes that brought both wealth and diverse population.

As he sat in the darkened guardroom of Tor Salan's northern gate, Major Amber realised the city was as quiet as it had likely been in decades.

The city that never slept; the city that night never truly darkened—in one savage move the Menin had stripped away its names to leave just a collection of buildings and people, shocked into fearful silence. Without its thousand mages, Tor Salan cowered like a whipped dog anticipating the next blow. Without its mages, Tor Salan's streets remained dark and empty—the only light and movement Amber could see came from the massive oil lamps flanking the monument they'd built to Lord Styrax's victory. The squads of soldiers keeping curfew were barely necessary, but Lord Styrax used it to impose routine on his newest troops. Thus far the tachrenn of the Ten Thousand had reported no unrest. Amber knew that every day the Chetse soldiers patrolled the streets in Lord Styrax's name, wearing Lord Styrax's crest, was another day closer to winning their wholehearted loyalty.

We're a simple breed, he thought, running his tongue around his mouth for a last taste of the pale wine he'd been drinking. *Give us routine, food and women, and we'll bark on anyone's command.*

He had been sitting there concealed by shadow for half an hour, staring out through the open doorway at the empty street beyond, before anyone but the patrolling troops passed. When they did come it was in two groups. He could see each distinctly, despite the city's newfound gloom now that there were no mages to light its streets. The first looked little different to the Menin guards posted around the gate, unconsciously walking in time with each other, as soldiers always do. The second group came a few minutes later;

their furtive voices and glances were enough to arouse suspicion, if the patrols hadn't already received specific instructions.

Amber sighed. He was there as a nursemaid, to usher the groups quietly out of the gate and ensure there was no confusion between troops. When he walked out of the guardroom, the first group saluted as one. The second, four men and a woman, barely broke the flow of their conversation to give him a cursory inspection.

The big soldier didn't bother taking umbrage. He looked up and gave a short whistle which was swiftly echoed from the vantage point above the gate. A head appeared to look down at the men below, then disappeared again before the muffled clank of gears sounded and the gates began to open ponderously. As soon as they were wide enough, a small figure hopped through the gap and approached Amber.

"All ready?" she asked after offering a sloppy salute. Amber nodded to the woman. In the darkness he could just about make out the easy smile on Kirl's face, made lopsided by a broken jaw from years back. He'd realised one lazy evening that he'd known Kirl longer than any other woman in the Land. There had never been anything between them—a great shame, Amber thought every time he felt the years lift off his shoulders when he saw that smile, but she had been attached to the Cheme Third Legion for longer than he'd served in it.

"What do you call that?" spat one member of the second group. The rest of them fell silent and looked at Amber.

"I call her Horsemistress Kirl," Amber growled, "and I suggest you do too, or you might find yourself walking to the Circle City."

The man took a step towards Amber, close enough for his expression to darken the soldier's mood further. He was dressed in functional travelling robes of poorly cut hessian. "Just make sure she knows her place," he said, peering forward with unconcealed distaste at Kirl. His face was thin and pale, and there appeared to be no spare flesh on his body at all. As ordered, his hair and eyebrows had been shaved. The lack of hair made them look less Menin; it was as good as a disguise because they barely looked human without it. The man was probably younger than Amber, but there was an unnatural sense of age surrounding him that added to his otherworldly appearance.

"My place," Kirl replied in a level voice, "is giving you orders when and as I feel like it." There was no hostility in her tone; the veteran horsemistress had had a lifetime of dealing with soldiers and knew not to let the man rile her.

Amber bit back the words on his lips; Kirl was perfectly capable of handling this herself.

"You will find it different soon enough."

"No I won't," she said, bored now. "You hold no military rank and this is a military exercise. My job is to escort you to the border, then return. If I return early because you've decided to play your games on the way, you'll be jeopardising the operation."

"And then you'll find out that your master's position means nothing when it comes to punishing you," Amber added, turning to face the man head-on. He was big even for a Menin soldier, and powerfully built. Amber didn't want to try his luck in a fight, even though the man looked like a wimp, he and his colleagues were adepts of Larat, mages one and all. He would be quick enough to take their leader down, but the rest would surely kill him for it.

"Threatening a man of the cloth?" the adept said with a cruel smile. "That is as foolish as trying to deny my master." To emphasise the point he raised one hand, showing the black sleeve and silver ring on his middle finger that indicated he was a priest of Death.

"I know exactly what you are, and that you're in costume doesn't make any difference, mage." Amber leaned closer, using his bulk to force the man back. Adepts of Larat, the God of Magic, were not priests but mages, acolytes of the Chosen of Larat. Since Lord Larim had slaughtered his predecessor's closest followers, he had wasted no time in building a coterie of his own mages to extend his power base, each one young and ambitious, and as keen as Larim for power. However, it looked like they lacked the white-eye's sense of where to stop. They weren't unusual in disapproving of a woman holding military rank, but it surprised Amber since magery had always been open to both sexes.

"Keep your mouth shut and do what you're told," Amber warned the adept, looking past him to take in the other four as well. If anything, the female of the group was giving Kirl a more poisonous look than her colleagues. "You've got ten days' head start on us; once Horsemistress Kirl drops you off you're on foot so I suggest you enjoy the use of her horses while you can. Whether you're alone or have witnesses, make sure you act like the priests of Death you're supposed to be—and that includes whatever drugs you might be carrying. Take only those necessary for the mission, understand me?"

The adept looked sullen, but he didn't argue.

"Good, now go and get mounted up," he snapped.

The five adepts went without a further word, though they all glared at

Amber, but he was already beckoning forward the first group, who'd been watching the proceedings in silence.

"Same goes for you lot," Amber started, "but you're soldiers and I don't expect you need telling."

The men all nodded. They were dressed as novices of Death, and each was to act as servant to one of the adepts, or so they had been told. He didn't know which legion they were from, just that they were loyal, and they had not been given the full details of their mission. Loyalty would go only so far, even in the Menin Army.

The five men saluted and followed the adepts, leaving Amber and Kirl alone in the street.

"Poor bastards," he commented quietly as he watched them go.

"I don't want to know," Kirl said.

"True," Amber agreed, "you really don't. It's for the best though; it will save lives in the end. We've just got to stomach it."

She smiled that lovely lopsided smile again and saluted, already turning away from him. "See you at the border, my friend."

They sat on horseback, no one speaking. The silence was unnerving. Somewhere in the distance behind them came the mournful call of a lone kestrel, but from the ruin ahead there was nothing. Stones blackened by flame littered the ground, and dark grass grew over their edges, as though the Land was attempting to conceal this terrible folly.

"Not one building stands," Count Vesna breathed from Isak's side. "It was still burning when we left; the walls remained at least."

They were not far from what had once been the Autumn's Arch gate of Scree, the very place where the Farlan had entered the stricken city only a few months before. Now . . . Now it was only the road that told Isak where the gate had been. The only other traces of human endeavour were shattered beyond recognition.

"They kept the heat fierce," Isak said dully, as though repeating something learned long ago. "The walls stood until the fires went out, but as they cooled, so they weakened." He felt a stirring all around him, a rustle in the shadow of his cloak that had no natural origin. They were still with him, four of the Aspects he had somehow torn from their God's grasp in the shadow of His temple. The Reapers recognised this place—they remembered the slaughter done not so long ago on those very streets.

Up above, the sky was dark and threatening. The morning had started brightly, but before long thick banks of cloud had rolled across the sky from the north and now the air was cold, promising imminent rain.

"Now there is nothing," croaked High Cardinal Certinse. He was shocked by the sight of something that could never have been adequately described to him. He might be cold and calculating, but Certinse's reaction showed he was no monster. His link to Nartis had been severed years ago, so Certinse had not felt the Gods' savage backlash as they raged at having been rejected by the people of Scree. While the cadre of mage-priests included in his bodyguard still felt the echo of that fury in their bones, he felt only terror.

Certinse had stared at the devastation for almost an hour before he ordered a cairn be built in memory of the dead, ignoring the objections. Whatever their crimes, he knew the people of Scree had not been remarkable in their impiety. They had not deserved this. *No one* deserved this.

A city had been obliterated, and what few survivors there were had been slaughtered by the blood-crazed faithful. With the walls fallen, they could see into the ruined city itself: the piles of rubble devoid of life stretching into the distance. Not even Chief Steward Lesarl had anything more than a rough idea of how many had died there. Few cared to contemplate the toll.

"Has anyone gone inside?" Commander Jachen asked. He was lost in his own memories of that last night of fighting. Since that day he had withdrawn from Isak's inner circle. He still commanded the Lord of the Farlan's personal guard, but he had no interest in doing anything more than following orders. Isak didn't much blame the man; his shadow was a crowded place and since that last night in Scree the company there was increasingly unsavoury. The memory of their last stand at the Temple of Death, when the Reapers slaughtered their attackers, was far from glorious.

"Who would want to?" Certinse said, and no one could manage a response. There was a murmur from the assorted clerics in Certinse's retinue, none of whom Isak recognised. No one said anything loudly enough for Isak to catch, but he knew they were afraid of the ruined city. He guessed they did not feel the horror inflicted upon it had cleansed the heresy from its streets.

The High Cardinal had been accompanied by a retinue of clerics from a number of cults. They didn't trust each other—they'd all provided minders to report back—but the commander of the troops was Certinse's man. He had been introduced as Colonel Yeren, though there were only two regiments escorting Certinse rather than a full legion. Isak saw both Count Vesna and Commander Jachen stiffen at the man's name, and Yeren appeared pleased that his reputation, whatever it was, had preceded him.

Behind them Isak heard the horses growing restless. He turned in his saddle and looked at the column of troops stretching back. With the full deployment of the Palace Guard and the army he had a total of seven thousand cavalry with him, and five thousand infantrymen, who were already trailing behind—most likely too far to be of any use when they encountered the enemy. An advance guard, a thousand light cavalry under General Lahk's command, led the way ahead of the main group as they pushed hard to catch up with Suzerain Torl's force.

Isak was accompanied by Suzerains Fordan, Selsetin, Foleh, Lehm, and Nerlos, and Scions Tebran and Cormeh, while Saroc, Torl, and the newly raised teenager Suzerain Tildek were with the lead army. Each of the suzerains and scions had brought their hurscals as ordered, and at least a division of standing troops. Isak had stopped counting at three dozen wagons just for the heavy cavalry's armour.

Troops in red and yellow livery caught his eye: two regiments of light cavalry, flanking some two dozen mages from the College of Magic. Lesarl's special order had invoked standing agreements with the college, which had provided four of its most able scryers, sixteen battle-mages of varying power, and a pair of healers to aid the twenty-odd portly priests of Shotir riding at the back of the column.

And he was expecting more soldiers from Lomin, up to fifteen thousand men. They'd be coming through the only large pass through the mountains, on Lord Chalat's heels, collecting scouts on the way. The band of mountains between Lomin and Scree were home to a mass of small goat-herding villages hidden away in narrow, twisting valleys. The isolation and the savage creatures that roamed the mountain wilderness had made the villagers a tough breed—and the best scouts in Farlan lands.

"It's a good force," Isak said to himself, shaking off the oppressive mood, "and I've urgent matters to deal with. Where is the lead army?" he asked Certinse.

"At the Twins, we estimate, if he hasn't passed them by now," Certinse said, tearing his eyes away from the dead place ahead of them.

"The Twins? Torl must have been pushing them hard." Isak pictured the dead river channel he'd once travelled down with the wagon train. The two mountains were two-thirds of the way between Tirah and the Circle City, and no army from the south could stretch its supply lines further than that. There were only half a dozen towns of any significant size on the sparsely populated plains south of the Twins and north of the Circle City.

"It's the sensible thing to do," Vesna said. "Keep moving so fast the troops don't have time to think—and it'll allow the dross of peasants who've joined them to fall behind again. That sort of rabble of fanatics, madmen, and bandits won't stand in a fight; they'll just get in the way of his cavalry when they try to hide behind them. He knows they're not going to be attacked this side of the Twins, and a crusade runs on its own fire. If he's lucky he can force thirty miles a day out of them—even if it does kill some of the horses."

Isak nodded. The suzerain was a hard taskmaster, but every night he would walk the camp, talking to his men. A little consideration from the general went a long way in any army. While Suzerain Torl's battered armour and whitening head were not easy to pick out as he prowled the lines of tents, his gold earrings of title gleaming in the firelight marked him as he shared a joke or a drink with the soldiery.

"Every general has his way," Carel had told Isak. "You and General Lahk are the rocks they know they can depend on, powerful and unflinching. Vesna's the hero they all wanted to be as boys, and Torl's the father to every man-jack of them—and you better believe men will fight to the death for their father."

Isak had immediately bristled at the comment and Carel had spent the next five minutes persuading his lord the comment hadn't been a veiled rebuke. The memory of his frail ego almost put a smile on Isak's face, in spite of the sight of Scree.

"Might I ask why you summoned me back?" Certinse asked, breaking his thoughts.

"You may," Isak said slowly, dragging his thoughts to the present. "As you know, the situation has changed. I've decided to mobilise the army and—"

"Against whom?" one of Certinse's attending clerics broke in. The priest of Vasle was the smallest of the lot and had no sign of rank on his blue robes.

Isak had barely even registered the man's existence—and he certainly hadn't expected a lowly unmen to speak to him.

Commander Jachen gave a splutter at the interruption, but it was Suzerain Lehm who spoke first. "Who in Ghenna's festering depths are you?" he snarled, his hand automatically moving to his weapon and running his thumb along the curved spike on the reverse of his axe, shaped to resemble a thorn in deference to his rose petal crest.

"I am Unmen Eso Kass," the priest said, hunching his shoulders as he peered up at the suzerain, "and my question remains; against whom is the army mobilised exactly? I have not yet heard anything regarding the heretic of the Menin." His thin lips were so bright against his skin they could have been painted.

"Just an unmen?" Lehm said, his anger momentarily blunted by surprise. "A damn parish priest, and you presume to question the Lord of the Farlan? Get out of my sight before I have you whipped."

Isak kept silent, knowing he shouldn't even acknowledge the insult, but he felt his hand tighten all the same.

"Kass, you go too far," Certinse snapped at last. "Leave us."

"High Cardinal, this is a holy crusade; the troops must be under the command of the cults, and fighting to destroy the heretics! There is no place in a crusade for political concerns!" the unmen protested.

All around Isak there was an explosion of furious voices. Lehm was not the only one to spur his horse forward but Isak beat them all to it. Quick as a snake he drew a dagger from his belt and threw it straight. It pierced the unmen's eye and Kass's head snapped back, his jaw falling open in an expression of surprise before momentum took him out of the saddle.

The voices stopped as the corpse slid to the ground, slowly enough for Colonel Yeren, who was next to him, to reach out and pluck the knife from the wound. He ignored the blood that sprayed over his horse's flanks as he did so.

"Anyone else," Isak began quietly, "who suggests command of my soldiers be taken away from me will also find themselves paying the price for sedition. Is that clear?"

The arrayed clerics were still staring aghast at the twitching body with blood still pouring from the pierced eye. The High Cardinal managed a strangled whimper and a shudder that could have been intended as a nod.

Yeren, by contrast, carefully wiped clean the dagger, a broad smile on his face, as though murdering priests was a commonplace occurrence in his world. "Perfectly clear, my Lord," he said cheerfully, nudging his horse forwards as he held the dagger hilt-out towards Isak. "And might I compliment you on a fine throw?"

Isak ignored the man as Jachen moved to take the dagger from the mercenary. He passed the knife to his lord.

Show them the storm, let them fear its return, he thought, recalling Lord Bahl's words to him. Following the advice was harder; it called for restraint to follow anger, and Isak's temper did not cool so easily. But it was good advice. Fully aware that they were expecting a display of the normal white-eye temper, he kept his voice level.

"Playing games with Lesarl is one thing," he continued. "Your ridiculous Morality Tribunals, and whatever else has gone on in Tirah recently—it has all been tolerated. But we are in a state of war now, and any challenge to my authority will receive the same treatment.

"The Farlan are at war—a war you are part of—and you need to ensure your minions understand what this entails. If they interfere with military matters, if they do not show the proper respect, they will be flogged as a soldier would. If there is organised opposition to my command, I'll slaughter the whole damn lot of you."

In spite of himself Isak could hear the building anger in his voice and he took a deep breath and forced his muscles to relax a little.

"It—Yes, that is understood," Certinse managed, adding, "my Lord," hurriedly. "The recent laws are no excuse for breaches in protocol, and you remain the Chosen of my God. Unmen Kass did not speak for the cults."

Isak inclined his head to the High Cardinal and slid his dagger back into its sheath. "Good. I am glad we understand each other.

"Now back to the matter at hand. I summoned you here because I shall be joining the clerics' army as quickly as possible, but tensions remain in Tirah and I wish you to return and work with the Chief Steward to ensure the smooth administration of the city."

From the expressions on Certinse's retinue, Isak realised the ploy had worked. Inwardly he breathed a sigh of relief. They assumed they would be ruling the city in the absence of Isak—and his Palace Guard—but Certinse had been told exactly what powers he would have, and Lesarl was certain the High Cardinal would not overstep his bounds. It was a bit of a gamble, but Isak was sure Lesarl could handle it. And crucially, it meant the crusade would lose its most rabid of leaders, who would all be running back to the city.

"This is a letter for you to pass on to Lesarl," he continued, motioning to Jachen, who handed Certinse a sealed envelope. "The contents are a matter of national security; please read and reseal it without showing to anyone."

Certinse nodded, understanding Isak's meaning well enough. The letter detailed fully their collusion, and Certinse would have to keep it from his colleagues or be forced from his position. It also concerned matters of succession in the event of Isak's death, something he would need the High Cardinal's support for, because there was no clear successor. As head of the Synod, Certinse would be able to confirm a ruler—or spark a civil war. Isak hoped Lesarl had gone into sufficient detail when he'd explained to Certinse exactly how he would be killed if he reneged on his promise.

Too much gambling for my liking, Isak thought as Certinse tucked the letter away from the keen eyes of his entourage, *and not least because of my choice of heir*. With the barest amount of formality, he made his goodbyes and ordered the army to continue.

The priests started off just as quickly, all pointedly ignoring the unman's body lying in the dirt. Two penitents were left to dig a grave. As he rode away, Isak realised they weren't even bothering to find a river to bury the priest of Vasle beside. In their anxiety to leave Scree behind, they contrived to forget all semblance of custom.

Scree: our memorial to forgetting who we are, he thought bitterly.

CHAPTER 28

THE WIND ROARED PAST STYRAX as he led his army towards the Circle City. Ahead, Ismess, the southern quarter, stood out against the Land's winter livery of browns and greys. All that remained of the ancient city of the Litse was a dirty white half circle of ancient buildings surrounded by squalid shantytowns, all huddled against Blackfang Mountain. In the centre he could just make out the only impressive part left: the enormous stepped walkway leading up to the Library of Seasons.

Lord Styrax was joined by his son and his general. They gazed upon the city as the Menin warhorses, bred huge to bear the weight of white-eye soldiers, cropped the sparse winter grass. After weeks of marching, only a few miles of windswept pastureland and the arc of a river that ran off the mountain now separated them from Ismess.

"A perfect day for a battle," Kohrad commented. "Wind behind us, ground dry and firm."

Lord Styrax nodded. "A fine day," he agreed. "Shame about the view, though Ismess's glory was fading even in Deverk Grast's day."

"Can manage a lot more fading over a thousand years," General Gaur added from his usual position on Lord Styrax's right.

The Menin lord agreed. Ismess was a dump; the whole Land would benefit if he just rode in there and burned most of it to the ground, killing their incompetent rulers on the way. The last bastion of the Litse was crippled by religion and the rule of idiots, a miserable prison for Ilit's few remaining followers.

"Do you remember the intelligence report?" Styrax asked his bestial general.

Gaur gave a twitch of his shaggy head. "About conquering Ismess? Hah! Teach me for not believing someone when they're the expert."

Styrax smiled, causing tiny lines to appear around his eyes. Unlike most Menin white-eyes, he was a cultured man. Rather than the usual mess of wild curls prevalent in the Reavers, the white-eye regiment, his thick black hair was cut short. His face was clean shaven and unblemished—when he had served in the regiment he had avoided the traditional facial scarring many of

the Reavers sported, and his beard had always been neatly braided. His differences had sparked dozens of fights and it had taken eight deaths for them
to accept his dominance.

"'*Only distaste for slaughter and vague piety prevents any of the other quarters
from conquering Ismess,*'" he quoted. "'*While preserving the balance of power is the
reason given, it is an empty argument as the benefits to all quarters would be realised
within a few seasons.*'"

"'*Ultimately, all that prevents this,*'" Gaur finished, "'*is the sense that such an
act would be pathetic to behold; that the rulers feel it is beneath them.*'"

"'Beneath them?'" Kohrad echoed. "It's a good idea, but they would be
embarrassed?"

"Exactly so," said Styrax. "Deverk Grast was not the first to identify the
Litse's endemic problems; he was just the first to try to solve them by genocide. Sometimes a helping hand isn't so welcome."

"My Lord," called Major Amber from behind the three men. He spurred
his horse closer so that he wouldn't have to shout. "Lord Styrax, the messenger from Duke Vrill is here. The army is ready."

"Thank you. Signal the Arohat regiments and Lord Larim."

"Yes, my Lord," Amber replied, standing tall in his stirrups and gesturing to the three columns of soldiers behind him. Riding in the middle was
a brightly coloured figure that could only be the Chosen of Larat. The soldiers broke into a trot to overtake their generals. The officers were at the
front, also on foot, but unencumbered by packs or spears.

The Third Army had travelled at an unhurried pace from Tor Salan.
Styrax had taken half the men with him as he went from town to town
accepting surrenders and installing garrisons where necessary. The Second
Army and the bulk of their Chetse allies had remained in Tor Salan, where
they were enjoying the impounded wealth of the city's slaughtered mages.
Those few Chetse who had travelled north had joined the heavy infantry in
the Third Army. Once the Circle City had surrendered he would summon
what was left of the Ten Thousand and unleash them on Embere: conquering
other cities under his standard would tie them to it. Once they had seen
friends die in Styrax's name they wouldn't rebel without good cause, and he
had no intention of giving them that.

The Menin advance party covered the remaining distance to the city
quickly, barely slowing when they encountered an emissary sent to greet
them from Lord Celao. She was a young woman with pale skin and hair so
fair it was almost white, riding a dappled grey horse and looking suitably ter-

rified by the Menin force. On her tunic was the device of the Lords of the Air, the snow white wings that were the notable difference between Litse white-eyes and those of other tribes.

Kohrad moved out of the way so she could ride alongside Styrax, but it was a few minutes before she managed a coherent sentence, despite being herself proficient in the Menin dialect. Once she had presented Lord Celao's formal greetings Lord Styrax cut her speech short.

"I thank your lord for his greetings. Please offer him my compliments and inform him I am going to visit the Library of Seasons. I believe it is traditional to obstruct no one's passage to the library—I expect this gesture of respect to be extended to me irrespective of past crimes committed by members of our tribes."

Amber could see by the woman's face that she had grasped the full import of Lord Styrax's words: both distancing himself from the spectre Deverk Grast that would loom over any conversation between Litse and Menin, and the none-too-veiled threat.

"Yes, your Grace," she managed to gurgle in reply. "Lord Celao has invited you to be his guest tonight, however. It would be reassuring for the city to have you enjoy our hospitality, to prove to the people that your army poses them no risk."

"I'm quite sure that would be nice for them," Styrax said firmly, "but it's not going to happen. I would not enjoy Lord Celao's hospitality; the contrast between his half-starved subjects and that bloated warthog would interfere with my appetite."

If such a thing were possible, the woman's face became whiter.

"Furthermore," Styrax continued, his voice hardening, "I couldn't give a damn whether your citizens are reassured or not. The three regiments under the command of Lord Larim will encamp in the Garden of Lilies, at the foot of Ilit's Stair. My companions, bar two, will accompany me up into the mountain while the remaining two will deliver messages to Cardinal Sourl and Natai Escral, the Duchess of Byora.

"I have a message for Lord Celao as well, of course. He will attend me in the library tomorrow at noon to negotiate the surrender of the Circle City."

"Surrender?" the woman coughed, nearly falling off her horse in surprise.

"Your scryers and scouts must have told you that the rest of my army is close behind. If he fails to attend, I will take Ismess by force. I prefer not to have to do that, but if Lord Celao honestly believes he has a chance against my army he is free to test the theory."

The massive white-eye turned to look straight at her. "I have eight élite legions close enough to deal with any preemptive attack on my person. They are all bored, and they are all hoping that they will at last get a fight."

The young woman shrank back in her saddle, only too glad to jab her spurs into her horse's flanks and gallop ahead of the Menin.

"I think she'll remember the message well enough," Styrax laughed. "Major Amber? Messenger Karapin?"

"Yes, sir," they replied in almost unison. Amber glanced at Karapin out of the corner of his eye and felt a pang of sympathy for him. He was a humourless man of forty-odd summers who'd been wearing the brass vambraces of the messenger corps for almost thirty. It was unclear whether Karapin realised why he, rather than a soldier of Major Amber's stature, had been chosen to delivery the message to Cardinal Sourl. Unfortunately for Karapin, the Devoted had a history of executing emissaries conveying a threat. Since Sourl was using his religious rather than military title these days, a considered reaction might be too much to hope for.

"The same message to Akell and Byora. I will see you tomorrow."

The pair saluted and broke off from the small party. As they headed northwest, the clank of armour receded behind them. They rode together in silence.

Amber found he was having to make an effort to keep his eyes on the road. The closer they got, the more the mountain dominated the entire horizon, and the harder it became not to stop and stare at the monstrous blot on the landscape.

He could see why the mountain had got its name. Blackfang looked like a tooth of impossible size that had decayed and broken. It was an ugly stub, with a sliver of a peak, if you could even call it that, rising from behind the cliff wall Ismess backed onto. The rest of the mountain was a wildly jagged surface that supported so little life a desert might appear abundant in comparison.

Only behind Ismess was there anything other than dead black rock to look at: the single slender peak that at first glance could have been a tower of astonishing size overlooked the valley housing the Library of Seasons. Amber didn't know much about the library itself, only that it was reputed to house a scholarly collection unrivalled throughout the Land, one assembled when the Litse were still the power in the region.

"Karapin?" Amber said suddenly, startling the army messenger. "Did you see those troops with Lord Larim? Why do you think he ordered regiments from the Arohat Tenth to escort him?"

"I do not believe it is our place to question Lord Styrax's orders, Major," Karapin replied solemnly. His heavy accent was slightly reminiscent of Lord Styrax; they both came from the outer lands, outside the Ring of Fire that was the Menin heartland.

Mentally Amber apologised to Karapin. The man wasn't an idiot—he most likely knew he was on a suicide mission, but he'd do his job cheerfully—or whatever passed for cheerful—because men from Lord Styrax's home region possessed a loyalty even the devoted Major Amber could barely comprehend.

"I didn't mean to question them," he said, sounding conciliatory. "I was just trying to understand what he'll require of us. The Cheme legions have been his élite for years; he's always trusted them to keep him safe. I hadn't heard that had changed."

"Your point, Major?" Karapin's eyes were on the buildings ahead of them. They had passed the boundary marker that divided Ismess territory from Byora a few minutes before. There were farm houses now, clustered around a small square fort; no soldiers yet in sight, but they both knew they'd be challenged soon.

"My point is that our Lord does nothing without reason," Amber went on, working it out in his mind. "Not having his best regiment accompany him into an enemy city? There was a reason." Amber paused as he saw movement around the gate of the fort. "This trip into the Library of Seasons, he's not expecting it to go well. The Arohat Tenth are decent enough troops, but not so good that he'll lose sleep over their loss."

If Karapin had anything to add on the subject he failed to voice it and Amber didn't bother saying any more. He checked his weapons one last time, ensuring they would be ready at a moment's notice, and adjusted the black standard bearing Lord Styrax's insignia. After that there was nothing to do but ride and wait, so he started to whistle instead.

Karapin continued in silence, even when at last soldiers confronted them.

The soldiers sent to escort them looked young enough to be recruits. They travelled on a long curving road that appeared to skirt all the way around Byora, which was itself nestled between two jutting arms of what looked like impassable bare rock, riven with great crevasses.

As they marched over a wooden bridge crossing one small river, their escort split in half and Amber gave Karapin a comradely nod as the army messenger continued towards a second bridge.

The remainder turned right and led him down a busy road lined with large detached houses, on towards the city that rose in natural steps until it reached the base of Blackfang's jagged cliffs. Standing tall were vast towers that could have only been built with magic—anywhere else, Amber might have marvelled at the size of them, but the oppressive presence of Blackfang behind, at its lowest point still double the height of the tallest tower, rather diminished the effects.

The farms and small holdings had given way to the large detached houses; these in turn were replaced by closely packed cottages. To Amber it looked like they were all cowering away from the mountain. It took him a moment to realise why. He turned to look over the wide expanse of marshland fed by the river that cut the district in two before branching out in a dozen directions in the fens. He remembered that Byora suffered worst of all the quarters from rain washing off the mountain after a storm.

Here the tight knots of houses faced away from the city. Their rear walls were banked up with earth—though no more than half of those had grass growing on the banks, Amber noted to his surprise. The city had been carefully laid out, that was obvious from his position, with the main highways acting as long channels to carry the water swiftly away, but out here there was no real planning. The poor were on their own.

He continued through a wide gate, copying his companions and dismounting so he could lead his horse up the steep hill. The gates were manned by older guards, soldiers in wine-coloured livery, and the youths escorting him fled eagerly once they'd handed him over to the sergeant on the gate. Amber just continued on, ignoring his new companions. He had to trust to his own brutal appearance and the fact that the army was so near to avoid any casual intimidation.

Two of the soldiers were sent with him. They led Amber up a long, slightly curved avenue that took them straight towards a big gate, leading to the Eight Towers district, one of his guides informed him taciturnly when he asked. He could see a unit of the red-clad soldiers and disordered groups of what looked to be irregular troops dressed in brown and white.

Strange, the city is full of troops, Amber thought, noting knots of soldiers at every major junction on the avenue. *The duchess looks to be more worried about her own citizens than the approaching army.*

Amber realised it wasn't just the soldiers watching him; people were studying him from every alleyway and open door. He felt the suspicion and fear in their eyes, but what unnerved him most was the bubble of silence that accompanied him through the city, almost as though some sort of spell had been cast on him.

Just before he reached the gate a voice called out from one group of onlookers and the people all turned, then parted as a figure lurched forward. Amber slowed and stared at the figure dressed in rags heading towards him. One of the soldiers started towards it and the figure stopped, calling out again.

Amber blinked in surprise. He'd been expecting to hear the local dialect, but it was Menin the figure was speaking—moreover, it was his own name being called.

"Major Amber," the figure repeated, and slipped the hood off to reveal hair the colour of dirty straw and the hopeful grin of a hungry hound.

"Nai?" Amber said, incredulously. The soldier walking towards the ragged man stopped and looked back, uncertain, but Amber ignored him, still staring in shock at Nai, once manservant to Isherin Purn, a deceased necromancer formerly in the employ of the Menin Army.

The last time Amber had seen Nai, he had been off on some fool's errand in the unlikely company of King Emin and Zhia Vukotic, among others. Amber himself had barely escaped the massacre of refugees in the days following the fall of Scree, and he had assumed anyone unfortunate enough to not be immortal or have their own army could not possibly have survived.

"Nai? he repeated, before realising he was looking foolish. He gestured the man over.

"Good to see you too, Major," Nai said, trotting forward. As when they'd first met, in Scree, Nai was barefoot, as though proudly displaying his mis-shapen foot. Under his filthy rags he had a thicker, cleaner leather coat. *A subterfuge then, but who're you hiding from? Looks like your friends have turned on you.*

"I didn't say that," Amber snapped. "Fucking necromancers; you're like cockroaches crawling out of the woodwork."

If Nai took offence, he didn't show it. The grin stayed on his face as he made his way right up to Amber and squinted up at the big soldier. "Major, if your lord could train cockroaches to bring him information, the West would be conquered by now."

"You've got information?"

"Some." The necromancer made a dismissive gesture. "Not much—I've been keeping a low profile of late—but I can still be useful to Lord Styrax, if he's willing to extend his protection to me."

"Someone's trying to kill you? Zhia? That Farlan bitch?"

Nai grinned again, looking unperturbed. "Not just with a slipper either; there've been some very curious happenings in this city."

"Piss and daemons," Amber growled. "Considering our history, that's not a good sign." He sighed and gestured towards the gate. "Fine, come along then. Just stay downwind of me," he added, wrinkling his nose.

Gaining access to the duchess proved to be a remarkably simply affair. Amber and Nai were stopped at the gate of the Ruby Tower compound while the guards sent word of Amber's arrival. Within a minute or two a tall sergeant sauntered out to look them over. He stood there for a minute, scrutinising first Amber, then Nai, who scowled and looked at his feet under the weight of the man's gaze. Amber immediately noticed the change in demeanour among the other guards; suddenly they were all nervous, even the seasoned men. Amber blinked and had a sudden image of himself, as though standing before a mirror.

Strange, Amber thought suddenly, *he doesn't look anything like me. Something in the way he stands, perhaps, or maybe it's just the look of a veteran about him?*

"I'm Sergeant Kayel," the man declared eventually, flexing his fingers as if preparing for a fight. His stained steel vambraces were crisscrossed in twine, his only deviation from the standard uniform. There was no obvious point to the twine that Amber could see, but he guessed there'd be some significance to those who knew. Perhaps it was a reminder of an old regiment— Amber had seen enough small traditions, memories of the lost.

He dismissed the curious thoughts from his mind and leaned forward in his saddle. "I don't care who you are," he said quietly; "just take me to the duchess. I am on business of state."

They were of a similar size and age, both scarred veterans, neither men to mess with.

But there's at least one difference, Amber assured himself, *he's not a man likely to back down from a fight and that's something I grew out of years back.* Something about the man screamed for Amber's attention, but he couldn't place it. He's not a local, he judged, but that's not what's out of place . . .

Have we met already? No, surely I'd have remembered a man of his size who walks with the confidence of a king. And yet, there is something . . . Gods, maybe it is just that he's like me and you don't get men like me staying a sergeant.

"We'll see who pisses highest next time we meet," Kayel replied with a confident smile and gestured at one of the soldiers at Amber's side. "He'll look after your horse and weapons; the duchess is waiting for you."

Without waiting for a reply, Sergeant Kayel turned and headed for the main entrance. Amber remained where he was, puzzled, for a few more heartbeats before heaving himself gratefully out of the saddle. He handed the reins to the soldier and unbuckled his sword belt, catching Nai's eye as he did so. Understanding, the necromancer came closer.

"Why do I feel like I've seen that sergeant before?" he asked softly.

"Looked in a mirror recently?" Nai retorted. "For men who look nothing like each other, you're more than a little similar."

"What in Ghenna's name is that supposed to mean?"

"You carry yourselves in exactly the same way. There's the same look in your eyes, even if you're more careful about it than he, and—" Nai tailed off for a moment and gave Amber a quizzical look. Without explaining he passed his hand in front of Amber's face and muttered a few words under his breath.

"Be careful what sorcery you try on me," Amber growled. The soldiers nearby flinched, not understanding his words, though they could hear the tone of his voice.

"I was just seeing if someone else already had." Nai frowned. "And I think I was right—without looking alike beyond build and a certain brutish demeanour, he reminded me intensely of you at first glance. I need time to test the theory, but there's some sort of link between you two."

"How is that possible?" Amber asked, astonished.

"I have no idea." Nai pointed to where Kayel was waiting at the main door. "Presumably our answer lies that way."

As he entered the circular audience hall, Amber noticed that there were only noblewomen there to meet him. A pair of guards on either side of the door watched him intently and a quick scan of the room revealed crossbowmen perched on a gantry above the door, their weapons ready. There were servants, but no men of rank in sight at all. It made him think for a moment of the White Circle, despite the fact that Byora had always resisted the Sisterhood. Now that the White Circle had been revealed as a political front for the exiled Yeetatchen tribe, Amber guessed that the duchess was delighted she'd kept well clear of that particular can of worms.

Natai Escral, the Duchess of Byora, was easy to pick out. She was sitting on a throne, with a child with a piercing stare squeezed in beside her and a well-dressed woman standing on her right.

I thought she didn't have any children, and her main advisors were men? Our intelligence seems to be out of date, he thought.

Sergeant Kayel took up position to the left of the duchess, next to the child. Both women wore heavy gold jewellery and richly coloured dresses, one green, the other a deep pink. Oddly, the older duchess displayed far more cleavage than her advisor, who wore such a high neck it looked like her chin would be permanently tilted into a haughty poise.

In the shadows at the back of the room was a nursemaid, who stood with hands together and eyes on the ground, presumably there to step in if the child grew fractious. By her stood a functionary of some sort, trying to look impassive and reserved but succeeding only in looking constipated. Amber's gaze passed over the nurse without recognition, even as Nai beside him yelped as though stung. The Menin officer shot him a look and Nai took the hint.

The weight of their combined gazes was like a hot southern wind on Amber's face and cleared his throat nervously, feeling suddenly ill at ease. "Duchess, I bring a message from Kastan Styrax, Chosen of Karkarn and Lord of the Menin," he said, bowing low.

"You're an unusual sort of messenger," the haughty advisor commented, inexplicably giving Amber a broad grin. The woman looked genuinely pleased to see him, as though she and Amber were old friends.

"And you are, Madam?"

"Lady Kinna," she said, scratching at her neck through the material of her dress, "Principal of the Closed Council."

"What is your message?" the duchess interrupted softly, her fingers idly tousling the child's hair.

Amber hesitated before responding; he wasn't experienced with children but this one's unblinking stare was beginning to unnerve him. The duchess's calm detachment didn't surprise him at all, but weren't young children supposed to fidget and squirm rather than take an interest in politics?

"Lord Styrax sends you his greetings," Amber said at last, "and invites you to join him as his guest tomorrow for lunch in the Library of the Seasons to discuss terms."

"Lunch?" The hint of a smile appeared on the duchess's lips. Something about the expression transformed her face and Amber realised the duchess's age had not diminished her sexual allure a jot. Her knowing playfulness immediately brought Horsemistress Kirl to mind. "Your lord is sure of himself then."

Amber coughed and tried not to stare too hard at her. "With respect, your Grace, he's sure of his armies. We took Tor Salan in a day and its defences were greater than yours. The Circle City is divided and weak in comparison, but he does not wish undue bloodshed."

"Why come to us for talks?" Lady Kinna asked. "If he has so easily conquered Tor Salan, why bother to speak to us first? Surely if he could so easily prove his power he would have done so already, and imposed his terms afterwards."

"Tor Salan wouldn't have surrendered—the Mosaic Council was too sure of its defences. You have nothing comparable to be overconfident about."

"Or he has overextended and hopes to bluff," the duchess pointed out.

He inclined his head to accept the possibility. "Lord Styrax isn't a man in the habit of making threats he cannot carry through. If any of the three principal rulers do not attend, he will assume your quarter is hostile to his plans, but my lord hopes you will attend the meeting; it will lose you nothing."

The duchess leaned forward, her face betraying her curiosity. "Does your lord believe we will simply hand over our city to him?"

"I bring the message, nothing more. I'm empowered only to tell you that Lord Styrax intends you to remain as ruler of your city, with Fortinn under the command of an overseer appointed by him."

She sat back and thought for a long moment, all the while running her fingers through the child's curls. The distracted movement did nothing to interrupt the child's intent stare and it was Amber who felt the urge to squirm.

"Very well, tell your lord I shall attend."

Amber bowed. "I am instructed to accompany you."

"Out of the question," she snapped with unexpected anger.

"As you wish," he said bowing again. "With your permission I will instead spend the morning praying at the shrine to Kiyer of the Deluge located on the mountain side of this tower."

His words had the desired effect and the duchess, with a look over to Lady Kinna, shrugged and nodded. She stood, helping the child off the throne too with far more care than was required for a child that age.

"As you wish; Jato will show you and your servant to a room and see to your needs."

At the mention of his name the functionary hopped forward, bobbing his head like a starling. Without looking back the duchess headed for the main stairway, leading the strange child by the hand. Lady Kinna followed a few paces behind the pair, but paused long enough to smile at him again and add, "Don't oversleep."

Amber didn't move for a moment, trying to fathom whether the woman was insane or he had somehow met her before and forgotten. His train of thought was interrupted as Nai plucked his sleeve urgently.

"Come on, we need to talk."

Amber smiled grimly. "We really do."

CHAPTER 29

WAKING EARLY, Amber had scrubbed his body over the washbasin and was halfway though dressing when a servant knocked on the door. She was blonde and a bit too curvy for Amber's tastes, but she didn't once look him in the eye as she carried in a tray bearing porridge and wide bowls of black tea. The first was too bland, the second too bitter, but the room was a chilly place and he gulped both down eagerly. He was eyeing Nai's food when the portly necromancer emerged from the sleeping cell opposite his and gave a small cheer at what awaited him.

A tall window at one end of the thin room admitted the only light. The windowless bedroom had been an unnervingly dark place in which to sleep, so Amber, feeling foolish and cowardly, had gone to sleep with the candle stub still lit.

"Bit too much like prison cells for my liking," Nai said in between mouthfuls.

"At least they let us out this morning."

The night had been far from restful. Once Nai had warded the room against eavesdroppers they had talked for an hour or more, and Amber's head had been awhirl by the time he turned in. Nai had recognised the nursemaid at once, even if Amber hadn't—he could barely believe how much she had changed. But the necromancer had no explanation of how she had ended up in Byora—even Zhia Vukotic had presumed Haipar died in the fighting.

That hadn't been the only revelation of Nai's to stun Amber. That Zhia herself had been party to the conversation he'd had with the duchess, courtesy of Lady Kinna's eyes, had also come as something of a surprise. He didn't know who the child was, or the big sergeant, Kayel. All Nai could tell was that there was some link between the two of them—it was fading with time, but there was a clear residue of some magic that had been done. Similarly, the information that Legana, the Farlan spy, had killed Mikiss in their rented rooms was given without explanation. Nai had claimed the Lady herself had been present in their rooms, only a few days before she had been killed in the Temple District.

"I've been thinking," Amber began slowly. "This link, it's fading, right?" Nai looked up from his bowl of bitter tea and nodded. "Can you do anything to increase its strength?"

Nai pursed his lips in thought. "Mostly likely it would probably replicate the spell."

"Didn't seem to hurt the first time round," he said dismissively, "and I reckon this link might come in useful, so I don't want to lose it."

"It's not going to disappear any time in the next month," Nai said with a shake of the head. "The spell is ended and there's nothing draining the energy other than normal attrition."

"Good, Lord Styrax might be keen to keep track of that sergeant."

"Why?"

"Do you remember when we were taken by Zhia? When that lost lamb of hers, Doranei, came to visit he was looking for someone in particular, someone he was sure had been seen going into that house. I always thought it was just too convenient that we got hit the first night we were there."

"You don't think it was simply mistaken identity?"

"Who attacks a necromancer without making damn sure there's a good reason?"

Nai nodded. "And if you were leading someone to attack a necromancer—whether to set them against each other or just poke a stick in the hornet's nest—you'd not rely on a passing similarity, not if you had the skill to make sure."

"That King's Man always gave me a strange look when he thought I wasn't looking. Never liked to have me behind him. I noticed that. What if that was because of the link? What if he was reminded of Kayel every time he looked at me, and Kayel's someone he wants to kill?"

"So who is Kayel?"

"Haven't got that far," Amber admitted, "but according to Doranei, Azaer was behind everything in Scree. Not sure if I believe that, but he did."

"Kayel is a disciple of Azaer?" Nai mused. "Lord Styrax would certainly be interested to hear that whatever part the shadow is playing."

Amber's face became glum. "Let's hope Kayel don't find out in time. Gods, I hate having my swords out of reach."

The journey into the mountain turned out to be encouragingly uneventful. Amber and Nai went directly to Kiyer's shrine at the back of the Ruby Tower, then had to wait for over an hour before anyone else turned up. The two soldiers posted at their door had followed them, but made no attempt to restrict their movements. Nai was reluctant to enter at first. He told Amber that the shrine had been deconsecrated, that there was no fragment of the spirit of the Goddess residing there any longer. Unsure what to make of the information, Amber had ended up pacing the room and muttering to himself until the duchess and her small entourage arrived.

When she did finally appear, the duchess was resplendent in a riding dress of emerald and cream, and a glowing firegem the size of a quail's egg was hanging from her neck. Oddly, she wore a dirk at her hip, hanging alongside a green cloth bag of similar length.

"The guardians of the library demand you hand over your weapons before you enter the grounds," she explained, seeing Amber note the weapon. "The first time I went unarmed the poor fool looked like a lost puppy when I gave him nothing; it cheers them up to have something to be officious over."

"What about my weapons?" Amber asked as the little boy from the throne room trotted in. He was wearing a miniature guardsman uniform, and much to Amber's surprise he was gently ushered over to the duchess by the savage-looking Sergeant Kayel.

The duchess pointed to Kayel and Amber saw the man had a long wrapped bundle in one hand. "Kayel has them."

On cue Kayel slung the strap over his shoulder, all the while keeping his sword hand free and near the grip of his bastard sword. Keeping his eyes on Amber, the sergeant produced a key and locked the shrine door behind them, handing the key to the duchess. Now that Amber was paying attention he saw the sparkle of gems set into the hilt of Kayel's sword.

He wears that and still they think him a sergeant? What's wrong with these people?

"You're bringing your child? We'll be walking for miles."

"Ruhen comes with me," she replied fiercely, bring the boy chose to her side. "He is a perfect child, he will not complain."

Amber didn't push the matter, a little taken aback by the passion of her reaction. "No Lady Kinna?"

Her expression softened as soon as the subject was diverted. "Lady Kinna will not be necessary; we keep these trips to a minimum number. Sergeant Kayel will come along to keep an eye on you, and he will carry Ruhen, should he tire. Now, Major, if you please; that stone font should slide towards me quite easily."

The Menin soldier set to work, noting the grooved track in the floor. He gripped the ornate handles bolted into the font's sides. The font had a wide basin to catch the water Amber guessed was poured to accompany prayers. In keeping with the theme of lapsed piety, the silver jug he would have expected to see in the shrine had disappeared, doubtlessly stolen once the chapel had been deconsecrated.

The font's large square base concealed a wrought-iron spiral stair leading down to an unimpressive passageway. As the duchess walked to the top step she produced what looked like a small iron mace from the cloth bag, except bound within the head was a piece of cloudy quartz shaped like an egg. Extending past the egg were two steel prongs that appeared to be a tuning fork—and indeed, now the duchess was tapping the prongs delicately on the wall. As the note rang out the quartz began to cast a bright bluish light over the room. She handed the strange implement to Sergeant Kayal and produced another for herself.

"Far more practical than pitch-soaked torches," she said as she reached the bottom of the steps. "Do remember to keep up; you'll find it terribly dark by yourselves down there."

Amber didn't reply. He had a tinder kit and candles, in addition to Nai's magery—but there was only one passage leading to the library, so they didn't have much choice anyway. He quickly caught them up and moved ahead as Kayel stepped to one side and motioned him to pass so he could be watched.

The passage through the mountain, two yards wide and at least seven high at its peak, was so smooth it had to have been magically made. It sloped down for about fifty yards before turning sharply right, heading southeast towards the library, and beginning a long climb upwards. Setting a brisk pace and trying hard not to think about the countless tons of rock above, Amber headed into the darkness.

After an hour the passageway ended in a sharp left turn. Past the corner, Amber found a tall pair of doors secured by a brass latch. Opening them he found an identical pair five yards further on, except the second set didn't budge when he tried them.

"They're barred," the duchess told him as Kayel set Ruhen down on the ground and shut the first pair of doors behind them. "There is a chain by your servant's shoulder, pull it and you will signal our presence."

Amber did as he was told. A bell pealed solemnly from somewhere above the door and within a minute he heard the clunk of bolts being withdrawn. The door jerked open and light flooded the room. For a moment Amber couldn't see anything, then he made out an indistinct white shape standing in front of him.

Despite knowing what to expect he still gave a cough of surprise. The Litse white-eye was tall and slender, except for a chest deep enough to rival a Chetse's, and hair nearly as white as his skin—but that all paled into insignificance when set against the crucial difference between Litse white-eyes and all others: the pair of grey-speckled wings neatly folded on his back.

"Natai Escral, Duchess of Byora, welcome," the man intoned, his expression blank. "Please hand me your weapons."

"Good morning, Kiallas," the duchess replied breezily, unbuckling her dirk and handing it to him. "How fares life in the library?"

Kayel looked less than pleased as he handed over his weapons and the bundle containing Amber's scimitars, but the only reaction Kiallas gave was to frown when Amber had nothing to hand over.

"The library endures as it always has," Kiallas replied, disinterested. He didn't look like much of a scholar; his breastplate of shining steel had the rune of Ilit, God of the Wind, emblazoned upon it. Intricate scroll work detailed the edges of his breastplate, his vambraces and greaves, and the latter were topped with a small wing shape that protected his knees.

A quiver full of javelins hung from his belt, but Amber was more interested in the pole arm resting comfortably on his shoulder. Not as long as most spears, it had a curved head the length of a short-sword; the major, trained to fight with scimitars, could well imagine Kiallas in flight, this weapon slashing beneath him.

"Still as engaging as ever I see," the duchess said with forced cheer as she made her way around the white-eye and out into the daylight. "This view, however, more than makes up for the lack of conversation." She stretched her arms up and took in a deep breath before turning to look for Ruhen. "My dear, come and see the Library of the Seasons."

Amber and Kayel followed the boy out as Kiallas turned to descend the grey stone steps cut into the bedrock that led down to a stretch of meadow and a low-walled garden full of withered brown plants that a wingless boy was hoeing without apparent impact. Beyond that was the first of half a dozen enormous white-stone buildings that Amber now saw dotted the whole craterlike opening.

There were vertical cliffs on all sides, hemming in a space Amber guessed to be more than half a mile across—a valley like a dented bowl sheltered by the surrounding cliffs. Looking down on it all was the black dragon-tooth of Blackfang's single peak, rising from the apex of the valley's dented wall. He could hear falling water, and he saw the thin blade of a river flash behind the largest of the buildings, a huge six-sided construction with a green-furred copper dome and wings extending from three of the sides like a crippled insect.

None of the buildings were even remotely similar to each other. The nearest to the party was low and wide, with half of the second floor exposed to the elements. Furthest away, stepped levels crept up the cliff face beside the enormous double archway that led down into the Ismess quarter of the Circle City. There were dozens of figures in white visible, mostly without wings but all blonde—pure-blood Litse. Amber recalled his briefings; it was usually only the white-eyes who carried weapons, but clearly the presence of Lord Styrax and his attendants had stirred them up, for all the adult males nearby were armed, despite looking somewhat awkward.

"Remarkable," Nai said, moving up beside him. He held his hand out, fingers splayed, and moved it through the air as though dipping his fingers into a stream. "Nothing, nothing at all."

"Looks good to me," Kayel commented, grinning evilly at Ruhen as he spoke. "I'll take it."

"Nothing at all?" Amber echoed, ignoring Kayel's contribution. For a moment he didn't realise what Nai was talking about. "Oh, of course."

Some unknown quirk in the formation of the library exploited the fact that just as some places were high in background magic, others were starved. The Library of the Seasons was one such place; magic simply would not work there. Try as he might, Nai would find no energies to draw from the air around him.

"I hadn't realised it would be like this," he said, shivering. "The air's so dry it tastes like sand on the wind. It's like suddenly having the colour blue erased from your sight." Nai looked utterly bewildered; he didn't even notice the sharp look the duchess gave him.

"Well, get over it," Amber urged him, and forced himself to look away from the awe-inspiring sight. "There's work to do. Kiallas, can you tell me where I'll find Lord Styrax?"

"I am to escort you all to the Scholars' Palace so you may refresh yourselves," Kiallas said, pointing to the tall building hugging the cliff face, seven or eight storeys high with long balconies running the length of each floor. The white-eye looked at Amber with a mixture of disdain and faint contempt.

"I don't need an escort," Amber said, trying not to let the white-eye arrogance irritate him, "just point me in the right direction."

"Visitors must be escorted at all times."

"Fetch an escort then," Amber said shortly. He pointed towards the largest of the buildings, the copper-domed one. It was called the Fearen House, where the library's collection of grimoires and treatises on magic were housed. If Lord Styrax was anywhere he was most likely to be nosing around those. "We're going that way."

Amber set off down the steps with Nai trailing along behind. He heard a fluttering sound and another winged white-eye, of lower rank, judging by his armour, scampered over. With the sense of a weight lifting, Amber left the duchess and her bodyguard behind, their voices soon fading into the wind. He felt like shaking his body out like a dog, elated to be free of the oppressive tunnel and unpleasant company. It was hard to decide which one unnerved him most: Kayel, with his malevolent demeanour, or Ruhen, with the shadows in his eyes, but the fresh air was all the sweeter for being rid of the pair of them.

"What's that?" Nai asked when they reached the massive building, pointing at a dark stone monument at the base of the steps leading up to the portico. Beyond it was a crescent-shaped hump of ground twice the height of a man and more than twenty yards long.

"The Failed Argument," Amber said, "a monument to Kebren. The curved rock is called The Dragon, it's supposed to be the guardian spirit of the library."

Their guard sniffed in annoyance. "It is not called the Failed Argument," he said. The white-eye was young and, though still taller than Amber, lacking any of Kiallas's glowering presence. "It is the grave of an unknown Fysthrall who witnessed the death of Leitah, Goddess of Wisdom. The monument is to *her* memory, not to the patron God of the Fysthrall."

"A monument to the failure of reason over violence then," Nai mused. He walked around the oblong block of granite, looking for a seam in the rock and finding none. Unlike the buildings, the monument had been cut from the dark stone of Blackfang itself. Its surfaces had been smoothed and engraved with many lines of flowing script, but the dialect was too ancient for either of them to understand.

"Is he underneath?" Nai asked, looking at the paved ground at the base.

"Encased within the rock," the Litse replied, not trying to hide his annoyance. "Treat it with care, this library was founded according to his writings— my ancestors were charged by him with keeping the memory of Leitah alive."

"Encased within the rock?"

Amber could see Nai assessing the monument, trying to work out how it had been made. *He's not like Isherin Purn*, he realised, *necromancy isn't about power for this one. He's just so inquisitive he doesn't know when to stop!*

"It must have been done in the city then," Nai concluded. Without warning he reached up and hooked his fingers on the top of the monument. Their escort gave an indignant screech but Nai ignored him, pulling himself up so his head was above the level of the monument.

The white-eye pulled a javelin from his waist and raised it, ready to throw, until Amber grabbed his arm.

"Nai, get down," Amber ordered.

The white-eye tried to twist out of his grip, but flight required him to be slender and light boned, like a hawk, and Amber had the advantage of weight on his side. The Litse hissed in frustration and went for his dagger, at which point Amber gave him a hefty shove that sent the youth reeling backwards, wings unfurled and outstretched as he tried to regain his balance.

"Did you recognise the unknown soldier?" came a voice from the steps. Kastan Styrax stood there, in front of a mixed group.

Amber dropped to one knee.

"Well? I can see there's a face carved on the top, is it anyone you recognise?" Amber could hear the laughter in his lord's voice. Throughout history the Menin had never been able to resist bating the fussy, humourless Litse. For some reason it pleased Amber to realise his lord was not immune to that impulse, a rare glimpse of humanity in one normally remote and unknowable.

"Rings a bell, my Lord," Nai replied cheerfully, prompting Amber to wince at the necromancer's blithe irreverence. "I'm not saying I've got drunk with the man, but there's something about the eyes that's familiar."

Their guard gave another squawk of outrage but this time he only looked up at the steps for instruction. There was another Litse white-eye beside Lord Styrax, bigger than Kiallas, with flashes of gold on his ornate armour. He was watching the proceedings with a frown, but so far he had refrained from getting involved. Now, as he started down the steps, Lord Styrax said quietly, "Heel, Gesh."

It was the first time in a while Amber had seen his lord out of armour; even a white-eye as strong as Kastan Styrax would find a full suit tiring in this valley, so he had opted instead for something more suitable for a nobleman. He wore an expensively tailored cream tunic with red braiding, and red leather cavalry boots, as strange a sight on a white-eye as the rings he wore, diamonds and rubies flashing from his scarred left hand. Behind him walked General Gaur and Kohrad. The young white-eye looked less ostentatious than his father for once in a black brigandine. From the expression on Kohrad's face, he had more than baiting Litse on his mind as he stared with undisguised hostility at his father's escort. Amber could tell the slim, aloof Gesh was well aware of the scrutiny but did not deign to take note.

"Amber, what is your strange friend's name?"

"My name is Nai, my Lord," the necromancer said before Amber could reply, bowing briefly.

"I don't remember speaking to you," Lord Styrax said. "Remember your place or Major Amber will cut that lopsided grin off your face."

Nai's smile faltered as he realised there wasn't a trace of humour in Styrax's words.

"Now, Amber: talk."

Amber bowed to the correct depth. "The servant of Isherin Purn, my Lord—I mentioned him in my report, but clearly I was mistaken in my assumption he had died." He hesitated and looked Styrax direct in the eye. "My Lord, he has news you should hear."

Styrax nodded. "I understand." He glanced back up at the entrance to the Fearen House, set behind a colonnade of eight enormous pillars standing sixty feet high. The main entrance was a brass-fronted door some thirty feet high, polished to a shine at the expense of whatever image had once been imprinted onto the metal. "Come with me," he ordered.

They ascended the steps and entered, Amber checking his pace to glance at the bas-reliefs of winged warriors on each side of the door before following Lord Styrax in. The Fearen House had high windows of stained glass on each of the six walls: two thin windows alongside the entrances to each wing and three enormous ones on the other walls. They filled the massive central space with tinted light, adding colour to a drab day. Above the windows were drapes of richly coloured cloth, gold-edged flags of bright red punctuating long swathes of flowing blue.

The Menin weren't the only visitors to the library. A few scholars were leaning over some of the half dozen U-shaped desks below the dome, where lecterns on two sides were angled towards the scholar in the centre so he could study the enormous leather-bound books. Two men and a woman looked up at the sound of feet before averting their gaze quickly, at which Amber allowed himself a small smile.

The prohibition on weapons doesn't seem as effective in the presence of a man double the weight and a foot taller than a normal man.

Lord Styrax ignored the looks and continued on into the very centre of the room. Amber looked around at the huge room; he'd not before been in a temple as large as this and it was undoubtedly as magnificent as any room he'd ever seen, even if the dome above did lack the gold ornamentation he'd expect in a Temple of Death. There was the dry scent of book dust on the air, and solid blocks of bookcases protruded out into the room on all sides. Arcane symbols were carved into every available wooden surface of the bookcases and armed guards were posted at every door.

Lord Styrax had stopped in the very centre of the room. Amber caught him up and stood at his side.

"Do you know what that is?" Lord Styrax said in a soft voice. The Fearen House was as quiet as a temple at prayer, its few devotees bent silently over their icons of worship.

Amber looked at the object: a five-sided column of black granite, two feet high and one foot square, with the corners smoothed down and the whole thing polished to an almost mirror shine. In the centre of its flat top was a half sphere which, for no reason Amber could tell, appeared to be solid gold. A tiny script was etched into both stone and gold, so small Amber had to bend down before he realised it was not a language he could read. It took him a while to work out what the language was: single or grouped geometric runes cut at one depth, overlaid with a shallower, more flowing style, like scroll work on a picture frame—Elvish, the first mortal language, made up of a hundred and twenty-one angular core runes and five hundred and five lesser, to which the flowing script added detail, case, and tense.

"It's called the Heart of the Library," Lord Styrax said, anticipating the soldier's response.

Amber straightened again. "Does it do anything? That's Elvish, isn't it?"

"Not as far as I can tell, and of course no magic works here."

"Why write in Elvish then?" He frowned. "I thought folk only used the language for magic, that it was the best representation for channelling energy? You don't write secrets in it and leave them in a bloody library where there are the resources, and scholars, to translate it."

"The script is apparently a poem, one that is so obscure it most likely contains a code. They call it the puzzle of the heart."

Amber looked up at his lord. Without warning the hairs on his neck prickled, as they did when he suspected he was not in control of a situation.

What sort of a conqueror gets distracted in a library, however magnificent? Karkarn's horn, is conquest not your goal?

"Have you broken the code?" Amber asked in a hoarse whisper.

Lord Styrax smiled in a way he had never seen before: in genuine pleasure. The huge white-eye rarely showed his true emotions and Amber gave a cough of surprise as Styrax replied, "I will start today; none of my investigations have managed to procure a transcription. All I have heard is that the code is fiendishly difficult and reveals a surprising truth—the few individuals who have managed to decode it all refused to reveal the answer and destroyed their working."

"And you've come to test yourself against it?" Amber asked. Duke Vrill had said once that had Lord Styrax not been born a white-eye or a mage, he would have become a renowned scholar all the same.

Styrax inclined his head. "How could I resist such a challenge? Since I could not find a transcription, I spent my time researching the object itself. I suspect the code's creator never expected a more practical approach to the mystery."

Amber looked puzzled. Clearly Lord Styrax had a point, but he had no idea what it was. If he wanted Amber to work something out he'd need another scrap of information.

"I've been looking at their records," Styrax continued after a moment. "There is an allusion to the heart of your unknown soldier being encased within, but no explanation as to why he would donate his heart for this purpose. What's more, according to the ancient records, Deverk Grast spent a few days here after he sacked Ismess, during what he termed the grand finale of *the scouring*. One night he walked out of those doors, called off the slaughter, and began to draw up his plans for the Long March instead; the turning point in our tribe's history. All very strange, wouldn't you say?"

Amber gave a helpless shrug. "Ah, yes, sir, I suppose so."

Every Menin child learned about the Long March, the exodus of the Menin tribe to the Ring of Fire. Approximately half had died on the two-year journey across the Waste but there was only ever conjecture and propaganda given as Grast's reasoning.

Lord Styrax gave him a pat on the shoulder. "Don't worry, you won't have to sit here and help me with the code; just stay long enough to tell me what could not wait."

Amber glanced back. The winged white-eye, Gesh, was watching them impassively from beside one of the bookcases, his feathers brushing its shelves. He cleared his throat, trying to speak as quietly as possible in the echoing room.

"A few things of great importance. First of all; more people survived the fall of Scree than I had realised, Haipar the Shapeshifter for one. I was sure she'd died but now it appears she's a nursemaid in the employ of the duchess."

Lord Styrax gave a sharp bark of laughter. The sound echoed around the room but by the time faces looked up in surprise his face was blank again. Amber felt his cheeks colour as though he'd been the one to laugh. Despite being noble born he had never felt at ease in genteel surroundings.

"Are they all this surprising?" Styrax asked.

Amber nodded. "Secondly, Zhia Vukotic is in the city, or so Nai claims. Apparently she has some influence over the duchess's chief advisor and made sure he was aware of it."

"Hardly a surprise; you said Haipar was one of her agents in Scree, no? It's far from surprising the vampire has more than one in place."

"True, but I thought I should tell you she made the contact. The last thing is the strangest; I don't know whether what I've made of it is even correct."

Lord Styrax raised his eyebrows. "Your own puzzle of the heart?"

"The duchess has a bodyguard, a new sergeant in the Ruby Guard called Kayel. He bears a basic similarity to me, nothing more, and yet it even brought me up short. For a moment I thought I had looked into the mirror, and Nai felt the same. He didn't have time to investigate but he confirmed there was some sort of trace magic linking us."

"And you've not met him before?" Lord Styrax mused. "A pretty little puzzle indeed; do you have a solution to it?"

Amber shifted uneasily. "Perhaps. That is—I don't really know."

"Tell me."

"King Emin's agent, Doranei—he came to Zhia Vukotic to ask about the prisoners she'd taken after the fight at the necromancer's house: us. Afterwards, he kept a watch on me out of the corner of his eye, even though she'd proved it was impossible for him to have known anyone there."

"And so you are thinking, what if he was reminded of Kayel because of this link?" Lord Styrax continued. "A good deduction. You said the Farlan knew nothing of the necromancer, nor did Narkang?"

"Exactly, and Zhia wouldn't have been playing those games, which leaves only Azaer's disciples in my mind. They were the ones intent on stirring up chaos in Scree, after all, and to hear Doranei tell it, King Emin's been waging a silent war with the shadow for years."

"Azaer," Lord Styrax breathed, as though savouring the word. "That would make times interesting. You think the lovely duchess is under Azaer's control?"

"From what I saw, she's not all there these days. It's as if she's too wrapped up in that child she's adopted. She brought it with her today," he added.

"A child?"

"A boy, Ruhen she called him. About five winters, I'd guess. Haven't heard the brat say a word myself, it just stands there and watches in silence." Amber scowled. "Something not right with him either," he added. "Too quiet for a child, too still."

"A good vehicle for exerting influence over her," Lord Styrax mused, "but to what end?"

"Sounds like she's tearing apart the cults in Byora; the situation looked worse than even our reports had suggested. Folk are scared in that quarter, and her troops are on the street corners, not the walls."

Lord Styrax exhaled slowly, deep in thought. "It would then follow that Azaer's intent is to drive a wedge between the Gods and the masses. Perhaps it went too far in Scree and couldn't control the storm it had created, so it's trying again here, with a little more subtlety. My concern with that theory is that it's a time- and disciple-consuming process, considering what you said about the minstrel dying with the city. Does this shadow really have the power to run such an operation in every city of the Land?"

"Couldn't it be working one by one?" Amber asked. "The shadow seems to be immortal, so time isn't against it. Why doesn't it trot along quietly, running the operations and recruiting in parallel? Could that be the purpose of the Azaer cult they were talking about, a recruiting ground?"

"I think you're right there, yes. But King Emin is a mortal and running against the years," Lord Styrax pointed out. "Given the chance to tackle the same tactic from a different angle, the man would surely find a way—especially since Azaer is taking a rather prominent position in Byoran politics. Every report we've had from Narkang has stressed we do not underestimate King Emin's intellect, no matter how unlucky we were sending the White Circle after him."

Styrax looked thoughtful for a moment, the hint of a smile on his face. "I suspect this shadow has a little more imagination than to use the same trick twice, and it lacks the strength to risk being so predictable. The powerful man can batter down the doors of his enemies; the weak man must find a new ploy for each.

"I think we should go and meet this little scamp who looks like you." He clapped a massive hand onto Amber's armoured shoulder. "Time for lunch, Major."

CHAPTER 30

THE SCHOLARS' PALACE, more than fifty yards wide and eight storeys high, got even more impressive the closer Amber got. It was built of white limestone set against the black rock of Blackfang's cliffs. The upper six levels had open walkways at each end, connected by a communal balcony from which Amber could see more than a dozen men and women from different nations watching them approach. Dark-haired Farlan in traditional wide-sleeved shirts stood shoulder-to-shoulder with Chetse scholars wrapped in furs, but he couldn't identify more than half of those watching him. The few who were blond didn't look like Litse bloodstock; western states most likely. It appeared the tribe charged with protecting the library didn't much value its knowledge.

He walked in silence with Lord Styrax, their winged escorts trailing along behind. Other than the cries of birds high in the air above there were no sounds of life here. Looking around, Amber saw white specks, sheep or goats, maybe, in the furthest corner of the valley, and a double bank of what he guessed were chicken coops tucked into an overhang of the rock. With a few acres of land penned with lines of stone where crops would be grown, the Library of Seasons was more self-sufficient than he had expected.

Or perhaps they can't rely on Ismess to keep them fed.

The living quarters for guests of the library were in the upper six levels of the Scholars' Palace. Doors placed at short intervals opened onto each storey's balcony, indicating small, austere rooms for each visitor. The ground floor looked to be given over to kitchens; it was more than double the depth of the other floors and supported an enormous terrace which had been decked out in all the colours of those who would be attending the strange luncheon Lord Styrax had announced.

Surrounding the terrace was a balustrade made entirely of white stone, the pillars of which were all human or animal figures in a variety of actions. Death and Ilit were at the corners, their outstretched hands holding up a fat rail beneath which the mortals lived and died. Unlike most statues of the

God, which were either painted or carved from black rock, the cowled figure of Death was as white as the rest, something that looked oddly disconcerting to Amber.

The Fanged Skull of Lord Styrax presided over the centre of the balcony, facing into the valley, flanked on the left by Lord Celao's Bundled Arrows and on the right by the Ruby Tower that was Natai Escral's family crest. Opposite the Fanged Skull was the Runesword of the Knights of the Temples, unadorned by any personal symbols. Amber frowned when he saw that: did the Knights of the Temples not use personal crests, or had Cardinal Sourl's position changed recently?

Below each crest was a long table, forming a square that did not meet at the corners. Litse servants busied themselves setting the tables for a formal meal, and Amber's heart sank when he counted the number of places laid at Lord Styrax's. Unless Lord Larim joined them, something he doubted a mage would willingly do, Amber thought he knew who would be filling that seat.

As though reading the soldier's mind, Lord Styrax pointed towards the nearest of the open stairs, where a servant was watching them, long golden hair tied neatly back and a set expression of welcome on his face.

"Your clothes have been taken to a room; go and make yourself presentable for lunch. I don't believe Cardinal Sourl has arrived yet so you have a little time."

"Yes, my Lord," Amber said. He looked up at the sky, trying to discern the position of the sun.

"It is time, yes," Lord Styrax confirmed. "The army will have arrived by now."

Amber nodded. "Doesn't do a man's appetite much good," he muttered with a sour expression before bowing and trudging off.

"These are the sacrifices we make," Lord Styrax called after him. Amber didn't dare turn and show his expression to the lord he worshipped.

Put it out of your mind, he thought to himself, *there's a job to be done.*

A deep bellowing voice echoed through Fist, causing Major Teral to jump with alarm. He looked up from his soup, for a moment not hearing the words, as more voices took up the cry, confusing the message even further, but the urgency was unmistakable. Teral was on his feet and reaching for his sword belt before he translated the words in his head, "To arms, to arms!"

Major Teral was Farlan by birth, and had only just arrived in Akell two weeks ago with his legion—this was his first day as duty-commander. Once in the corridor he had to pause and wait for the calls to come again, panic clouding his memory as he tried to remember which way led to the upper station. Already he'd got lost three times in the rabbit warren of corridors filling the Fist, the enormous fortress that was Akell's forward defence.

"Major!" yelled a voice behind him. Teral whirled around to see Sergeant Jackler barrelling towards him. The bearded old sergeant had adopted him years ago as an officer in need of a guiding hand, to the profit of them both, and it had since grown into an unshakable loyalty. "Bloody Menin Army at the gates, sir!"

Jackler turned back the way he had come, Teral close on his heels as they headed for the upper station where they would be able to get a good view of them.

"Are they attacking?" he yelled as Jackler battered soldiers out of the way, clearing a path for Teral.

"No, bastards just sauntered into view!" Jackler called back. "Tells us why those scouts were late reporting back." He added with a pitiless laugh, "won't bother putting them on report now!"

Teral didn't reply as he followed up the stairs and out onto the upper station. The highest part of the Fist was half full of soldiers already and he had to fight his way forward to get a decent view.

"Jackler, get the enlisted to their stations," he shouted, roughly elbowing past men there to get a decent view. Leaving Jackler bellowing behind him, Teral reached the far edge and pushed his head cautiously through the crenellations.

"Piss and daemons," he whispered, eyes widening at the sight before him.

"Cocky bastards, ain't they, sir?" Jackler laughed behind him. "No urgency, no assault squads formed. Looks like they're expecting us to just open the gates right up!"

The force with the Menin standard at the front wasn't the biggest Teral had ever seen, but as he looked at the three groups forming up outside bow-shot range he realised it didn't need to be. There were at least two legions of heavy infantry standing in neat ranks, their long pikes waving in the air, with another two legions of lighter troops behind. The mass of cavalry on the left were led by the legendary Bloodsworn, all sporting the Fanged Skull of the lord they worshipped. But it was the right flank that frightened him most of all: a dark crowd of figures too large to be human lowed and roared, their noise louder than the hooves of the rest of the army combined, and beside them a regiment of heavy infantry screamed with manic delight, all the while waving enormous polished steel shields above their heads. Teral didn't have to be close enough to see the blades fixed on the edge of the shields, and he barely noticed the cadre of mages behind them.

"Oh Gods," he breathed, "the Reavers, and minotaurs too."

"Good thing they ain't attacked yet, then!" Jackler said cheerfully. He pointed at the infantry with the massive Menin standard. "Look, flags of parley. Probably come to surrender to us, sir!"

Three horsemen broke away and headed towards the Fist: two Blood-sworn, with the bloodred Fanged Skull painted onto their black breastplates and shields, and a nobleman between them, brandishing the white banner. He was taller than the knights escorting him.

Thank the Gods; someone I might actually be able to negotiate with, rather than that blasphemy of a creature that's Styrax's favourite general, he thought, thankful for small mercies.

"A white-eye?" Jackler asked, noticing the man in the middle was towering over his companions.

"That's ornate for a white-eye," Teral remarked. The red, white, and blue livery made a very obvious target, no matter who escorted him. He looked blurred, but Teral was Farlan and knew it wasn't his vision that was at fault. "The man's wearing ribbons," he exclaimed. "If he is a white-eye he's enough of a peacock to rival Suzerain Saroc."

"That'd be Duke Vrill then," Jackler advised. "They say he's Chief Steward to Lord Styrax." He paused and with a laugh added, "Imagine that: Chief Steward Lesarl with a white-eye's temper."

"Lesarl's viciousness surpasses that of any white-eye," Teral said sourly, "but you're right, that must be Vrill. What does he expect us to say? He must realise there's no man here ranked above colonel; all the commanders are meeting his lord!" He pushed away from the wall and headed for the stairs, Jackler on his heels. "There's no one here authorised to negotiate surrender, and why else bring an army here?"

"Talking would be better than attacking the Fist," Jackler pointed out.

He was right, Teral realised. Even with the terrifying troops the Menin had, the Fist was a hard place to take at the best of times—and reinforcements had just arrived for the Akellan defenders: four legions of Knights of the Temples from Canar Fell and Aroth, most of the Order living under Narkang's rule. The Order had considerable resources and much land at its disposal, and it ensured its troops were all well supplied and trained. Its armies were spread over a dozen or more city-states, in the charge of select generals, and they all maintained a reputation for martial excellence.

They had planned to resupply at the Fist and continue on to Raland, a key city-state controlled by the Order, but Sourl could not have been more delighted to receive them. The politics of the Order were complicated, but it never boded well whenever a general welcomed troops under his superior's colours.

"What's he going to say to persuade us to give in?" Teral yelled over his shoulder as they reached the bottom of the stairs and made for the fortified gatehouse, the only entrance on that side of the Fist.

An attack alarm was clanging above his head, and there was movement all around as men made for their battle stations. The Fist was a massive square building, the straight line of the walls broken only by a jutting gate-house on the northern face. The outer wall was ten feet thick with defensive walkways built within that, and served as a massive outer shell to the inner building, itself five storeys high and a maze of kitchens, storerooms, barracks, foundries, halls, offices, and stables.

The Fist would be hard to take. The outskirts of the city had crept ever closer, until now only five hundred paces separated the nearest dwellings from the massive walls, but the ground had been carefully planned to hinder any attacker, with piled earthworks and deep ditches close to the fort and enough open ground to leave anyone trying to slip past the Fist exposed and vulnerable for far too long for comfort.

Teral looked up; the sky above him was grey, making even the scarlet of their uniforms look faded and dull.

"Is Colonal Dake not here?" he snapped, watching the ordered chaos around him.

"Back in the city," Jackler replied. "I'll send a rider."

"Where in the name of the Dark Place is Major Sants, then?"

"I'm here, Teral," called a laconic voice from the shadows of the gate-house, "just waiting for you to show your face."

Teral bit down the curse that was on the tip of his tongue. Now was not the time to let Sants wind him up. "It looks as if their general, the white-eye Vrill, wants to parley. I don't think we can afford to wait for Colonel Dake to arrive, so we should go and hear what he has to say immediately."

As he took a step forward, Captain Shael and the rabid Chaplain Fell joined him. The chaplain was still wearing the bronze braiding on his half-black, half-red robe.

Gods, the Knight-Cardinal must have reversed his decision, all so a few chaplains can pretend they're Mystics of Karkarn, Teral thought, noting the chaplain's clothing.

Clerics had always been a driving force within the Knights of the Temples, but the recent fanaticism sweeping through the cults had taken that to an extreme. It might have been comical to watch formerly mild-mannered clerics assuming all the swagger and aggression of a Farlan regimental chaplain, if it hadn't been accompanied by savage fervour and increasingly brutal punishments for any man betraying the slightest disrespect towards a man of the cloth.

No doubt that priest of Belarannar whispered in the Knight-Cardinal's ear again; man's been closer than a flea and just as friendly. How long can I last without being assigned a "spiritual advisor" of my own? he wondered.

Major Sants pointed past Teral at four horses being brought around from the stables. "We were just waiting for you to catch up," he said with an infuriating smile.

Teral whipped the reins of his own horse from the groom, not caring how ungracious he appeared. The man didn't bother to look aggrieved, nor did he react when Sants accepted the reins of his own warhorse with exaggerated courtesy. As soon as they were mounted, Sants gave a cough. "Ahem, Major?"

The gates were shut; Teral was duty-commander, and only on his order would they be opened. The gates were twelve feet square, made of bog-oak from the marshes to the west, and reinforced with steel rods. Four men stared down at him from the gantry above the gate, waiting for his order.

He opened his mouth, about to speak, when a man stepped out in front of his horse and the creature shied. It took Teral a moment to regain control of the beast before he could look at the person blocking his path: a priest in black robes. The red stripe running down each voluminous sleeve and around his waist was unfamiliar to Teral, as was the small, curved dagger attached to his robe, clearly a ritual implement, though he couldn't place the cult that required such a thing.

"Major," the man called out in a strange accent, "Major, I must beg favour of you." He spoke the Farlan dialect, although with a strong accent.

"Your Reverence, now is not the time," Teral said, trying to keep his temper. "Please, whatever it is, make your request later."

"No, Major, it is time," the man replied loudly, his high foreign voice making it sound like a rebuke. As though to support his point, a small group shuffled closer: four more dressed in black and five in novice grey, though the colour of the stripes was different. It was hard to make out in the weak light.

What sort of priests are these? Is that stripe yellow or white? Some instinct made him wheel his horse away from the men. Jackler, seeing the movement, stepped directly between Teral and the priest, his hand on his hilt.

"What God do you serve?" Teral asked as the gatehouse troops stepped out of their guardrooms and surrounded the priests. "What could possibly be so important you need to speak to me now? You do realise there's a Menin army out there?"

"I hear alarm. Now is time," the priest insisted. He pushed back the hood of his robe to reveal a face of indeterminate age, entirely hairless and frighteningly white.

Teral wondered if the man came from the Waste; he'd heard many of the tribes there had strange-coloured skin, ranging from as grey as a corpse to red like a birthmark.

"We are priests of Death. When there is battle, we must pray."

"Pray then, dammit," roared Chaplain Fell, a priest of Karkarn, "but just get out of the damn way!"

Teral couldn't help but wince, fearing to find himself caught between feuding priests, but the strange man appeared to take no umbrage at Fell's belligerent tone.

"Well, Father?" he said. "You don't need my permission to pray."

"Apologies, we are—" The priest floundered for a moment, then turned to his colleagues for help.

"Aligned," one of the novices said quietly. He wasn't as young as most novices; though he was also hairless, he had the weather-beaten face of a penitent.

"Ah, yes." The priest gave a small bow to the novice and turned back to Teral. "We are aligned priests; we serve the Reapers."

Teral blinked in surprise. Aligned to the Reapers? He'd never heard of such a thing before—though it did explain the colours on each man's robe.

But Gods, what sort of madman would be a priest to any of the Reapers?

"You serve the Reapers?" he said, stunned. "What do you want with me?" Fear made his question harsh, but the priest didn't appear to notice.

Sweet Nartis, one of these men worships the Headsman?

The priest gave a bow. "All priests of Death must pray before battle; we must pray on site of battle."

"Out there?" Sants retorted, pointing towards the still-closed gate. "You want to walk out there to pray?"

The priest nodded.

Teral hesitated, trying to work out what to do. The Order bowed to religious authority; that was inbred, and of late that had been even more evident, yet something here felt wrong. He looked at each of the priests: all in black, each with a similar ageless face.

Gods, are they mages? he wondered. "Sergeant," he shouted in the general direction of the guardroom, "where's your witchfinder?"

"I'm here," came a shout from above before the sergeant of the gate could answer, and a pale-haired man with long limbs waved from his seat on one of the wall's walkways. He dangled a leg over the edge. Teral couldn't tell whether it was just a trick of the light, or if it was a combination of age and grubbiness that made the man's white hair and tunic both look grey. The witchfinders were the only people within the Order to wear white and black.

The man didn't bother saluting, but that didn't surprise Teral; witchfinders were a law unto themselves, and even the best were half mad.

"Name?"

"Islir," came the reply, followed eventually by "sir."

"You tested these priests?"

"'Course I did," floated down the mocking reply. "My job, ain't it?"

"They're mages?"

"Bugger me, yes, and strong'uns too!" Islir said with a laugh.

Jackler half drew his sword as Islir spoke, prompting the other soldiers to follow suit. Islir watched them with increasing amusement. "Hah, bloody knitting circle, the lot of you! They're safe; dosed 'em meself. Not going to be casting anything for another few days at least—I gave 'em enough to stop bloody Aryn Bwr himself in 'is tracks."

Teral winced at the mention of the great heretic's name, never spoken aloud within the Order.

"Get down here and check again," he ordered. With a theatrical sigh the witchfinder climbed to his feet and headed for the stair.

"What are you doing, Teral?" Sants said, the irritation plain in his voice.

"They're foreign priests, and mages," he explained, "and before I open the gate I want that lazy shit to double-check they're no threat, just as the Codex of Ordinance requires me to." He gave what he hoped was a suitably respectful nod of the head to the priest, who smiled and bowed again, making it clear he took no offence.

The Knights of the Temples did not use mages in battle, and despite their various factions, none disputed it was the province of the Gods alone. Mages were only accepted into their ranks if they foreswore use of their powers, except for witchfinders, whose meagre ability allowed them to do nothing more than sense power in others. Any mage not of the Order but in their midst was required to drink a concoction that suppressed all magical abilities. Teral wanted to ensure they had not found a way to negate the effects of the potion.

"This ain't necessary," grumbled Islir as he appeared from the stairway.

"Indulge me," Teral growled.

The witchfinder grabbed the first of the priests by the hand. He paused for a moment then moved closer to look the pale-skinned man in the eye. Teral could see his lips moving, probably chanting some sort of charm to Larat.

It would certainly explain the man's sense of humour, he thought darkly. *Let us hope the priest's own weathers it, otherwise I'm in deep, deep shit.*

"This one's fine," Islir announced. "I'm strong enough to sense power without needing to touch the rest of 'em—which is just as well, 'cause I'm not touching no bastard aligned to the Wither Queen. All their power's deep down and locked tight; they couldn't light a fire if their lives depended on it. The only magic they got is in those daggers, and that's latent."

"What do you mean, 'latent'?"

"Latent means it ain't doing nothing at the moment. It's a ritual weapon, so 'course there's going to be some trace o' power in it—but not enough to take on an army, so don't you worry 'bout that."

"You're certain?"

Islir squinted up at Major Teral. "Cardinal Sourl's orders are that any witchfinder who makes a mistake is to be executed as a traitor, no second chances. Believe me: I'm damn sure."

"Satisfied, Major?" the priest asked. "We are no threat. May we now go and pray, or must we dance for you next?"

There was an edge to the man's voice now, a note of warning that Teral had heard often enough over the last few months. Offending a priest with influence within the Order had become tantamount to heresy. Even this unknown wanderer could cause trouble for him.

Teral tried to look contrite. "Of course, Father. I apologise, but our regulations are quite clear and I must fulfil my obligations, which I have now done. Your request is granted." He looked up to the men hanging around on the gantry and shouted, "Open the gate!"

"What is this?"

Lord Styrax turned to his right with an expression of excessive innocence. "This, Lord Celao? It is called 'food.' I had not been aware that scarcity had turned to nonexistence so you no longer recognise it."

The Chosen of Ilit, unable to match Lord Styrax's gaze for long, scowled down at the bowl before him instead.

It took all Major Amber's efforts to not stare at the white-eye. He had an enormous, spherical head, currently red with fury, and Amber thought he looked more than ever like a red melon wearing a wig of straw.

Celao was nearly as tall as Lord Styrax, and he was one of the few men in the entire Land to outweigh the Menin lord. He was not just fat; he was a corpulent monstrosity who would not be able to walk were it not for his Gods-granted strength. The wings sprouting from his back were significantly larger than either Kiallas's or Gesh's, but there was no way they would lift Celao even an inch off the ground.

It would take a dragon to lift that body, Amber mused. *He'd probably make quite a snack for one too. If I were him, that's what my nightmares would be about.*

"Peasant food," Celao declared petulantly, shoving the bowl of mushroom soup away, slopping it onto the table. The Lord's companions leaned back from the table, unable to eat what their lord had rejected.

"You could usefully miss—" Kohrad started, but was cut off short by his father.

"A little civility over lunch, if you please," Lord Styrax said sharply before his belligerent son could say anything more. "Lord Celao, I apologise for my son's demeanour, and also the food. I am a man of simple needs; I have no taste for such delicacies as swan's liver pâté or white-thrush tongues."

Amber noted the differences between Styrax's perfect calm and the boiling bag of emotion that was his white-eye son. Lord Celao was a huffing whale wrapped in what looked like a tent of cloth-of-gold, and he betrayed his discomfort by a host of fussy mannerisms, but he at least was touched by a God's strength. Kohrad had only the frustrations of young manhood in the presence of at least two men above him in the food chain.

Gesh and Kiallas sat at either end of Lord Celao's table. The lord himself sat between golden-haired noblemen with androgynous faces who looked near identical, though their badges of nobility showed no family link. Both appeared unaware of either the Knights of the Temples or the Duchess of Byora; their attention was fixed on the Menin, their historical enemy.

Amber wondered what exactly they were expecting Lord Styrax to do, for they sat like rabbits just waiting for the dog to notice them and attack. *Do you think him Deverk Grast reborn? Has the Land changed so little for the Litse?*

"Your food and hospitality is ill fitting to a man of my position," Celao announced after a long moment.

Amber saw Kohrad's mouth open, the words "ill fitting" forming on his lips, but his father cut him off with a look.

"For my part, I am quite content," announced the man sitting opposite Lord Styrax. "I have spent too much of my life travelling to consider a fine soup anything less than a pleasure."

All eyes turned to the man at the centre of the Devoted table. Except for the High Priest of Belarannar, the men were dressed almost identically: scale-mail hauberks of black iron over red and blue tunics with red sashes bearing the white runesword of the Order. The speaker, who was half a hand taller than his companions, was clearly no local, his dark hair and elegant Farlan features marking him out from those around him. His expression was amiable and he ignored the scrutiny, supping a spoonful of soup, then helping himself to more bread as they stared.

"I am pleased we are of a similar mind," Lord Styrax said, picking up his own spoon, which looked tiny and fragile in his hand. "I hope that continues."

"Perhaps," the man said calmly. "It rather depends on whether you revise yesterday's threat." He gestured towards Messenger Karapin, who was standing stiffly at one side, a pair of Devoted officers on either side.

Amber had almost missed the man as the Devoted party approached the Scholars' Palace—until he realised Cardinal Sourl was walking half a pace behind him, not leading the group. When Lord Styrax had planned this meeting, he had not expected Knight-Cardinal Certinse, Supreme Commander of the Knights of the Temples, to be anywhere within a hundred miles—and yet here he was, making quiet inroads into his lunch while everyone else waited for Lord Celao to begin. Amber wondered what this unexpected turn of events would mean for their plans.

"Message," piped a child's voice. Amber looked past his lord to where Ruhen sat beside Natai Escral. The boy sat in the centre, between the big sergeant, Kayel, and the duchess, looking like a mismatched set of parents from some ridiculous romance story. Curiously enough, Sergeant Kayel—to whom Amber bore no similarity, now they were in the magic-deadened valley—was as attentive to the child's needs as the duchess. The man was a better actor than Amber would have given credit.

"Yes dear," the duchess said in a soothing voice as she gave Knight-Cardinal Certinse a sharp look, "the message. Lord Styrax, you wish our surrender. Now, while I may be a feeble woman, I cannot but remark that you are a long way from home. The dull little men I employ to pay attention to such matters, they tell me that in the business of war this is considered bad."

"Yours will not be the first army to have marched from Tor Salan," Lord Celao added bluntly.

"I have no desire to force anything on you, my honoured guests," Styrax said smoothly. "I wish only to present certain inescapable facts."

Amber recognised his lord's tone of voice; when he spoke in that overly polite way, Lord Styrax was not bluffing a weak hand, but was confident he could back up his threats. There was no need to force the issue, so he could be reasonable. This lunch was so he could look each of the Circle City's rulers in the face and tell them the plain truth: that he could crush them utterly.

Their intelligence had led them to believe that the duchess, a ruthlessly pragmatic woman, would accept her vassal status easily enough. Lord Celao was a coward without an army. The only problem was in Cardinal Sourl's quarter, and that problem was worsened by the presence of Knight-Cardinal Certinse and his army.

Ego, Amber thought, *that's what it'll come down to. They're too proud to accept the threat, and perhaps with good reason under normal circumstances—our supplies are limited, and Raland and Embere are still Devoted city-states; they may be squabbling for primacy within the Order, but that isn't going to stop them realising who'd be next. They'll prefer to march to Akell's aid than fight us one by one.*

"You have yet to present us with facts, my Lord," the duchess commented, her hand resting on Ruhen's shoulder. Here, in the presence of her peers, she had found some of the poise that had been missing from Amber's first meeting with her. The little boy was obviously still distracting her, but there was nothing wrong with her political senses. She was watching everything that was going on closely.

Lord Styrax inclined his head to the duchess. "The facts, your Grace, are that I will take the Circle City within the next few days. The only thing you can affect is the manner of that conquest."

"You're bluffing," snapped Celao. "You don't have the troops."

"I brought with me the tools I needed for the job," Styrax said mildly. "Why would I bluff on a poor hand when it would have been simple enough to bring the Second and Fourth Armies with me?"

"Because Tor Salan hasn't been the tea party you thought it would be,"

Certinse said. The Knight-Cardinal mopped up the last of his soup and looked up, his mild smile unwavering. "Without a strong garrison, you'll lose the city again. You need to recruit there before you can conquer the Circle City, and you've not had the time to build a force."

He broke off when the man beside him, the High Priest of Belarannar, judging by his robe, tapped him on the arm.

Cardinal Sourl, sitting on Certinse's other side, glared at the priest. He was obviously not enjoying his newfound subordinate rank. The cardinal wore military uniform, as befitted his rank of general, but it didn't appear to fit him very well and he looked uncomfortable. He lacked the martial or political power to challenge the Knight-Cardinal's authority, but he had to be irked by the fact his counsel was not even sought, so deeply did the high priest have his claws into Knight-Cardinal Certinse.

And Sourl had lost weight too, since he last wore that uniform. The Menin still knew very little about whatever had enraged the Gods so, but following that event Sourl had apparently taken to preaching to his troops every day, dressed as a priest of Nartis—he had been ordained as such when he joined the Order. The once-noted soldier had been eating like a monk and acting like a zealot, and was no longer the well-built man in his fifth decade they had expected to find.

After a few moments of whispering, Certinse looked up again. "My Brother-in-creed reminds me that you, Lord Styrax, have built monuments like shrines to your own glory, and you destroyed the Temple of the Sun in Thotel. Such desecration only clarifies our position: the Knights of the Temples cannot accept your rule."

Lord Styrax leaned forward, putting his elbows on the table. "Indulge me and listen a little longer. I will explain this fully, for your further consideration."

And all the while, Amber added to himself, *while you turn to your priests for advice, we're exploiting that trust you place in them—give it an hour or so and you won't be smiling so easily.*

The white-eye was looking pleased. Major Teral had always feared that.

"Gentlemen, greetings," he began. "My name is Anote, Duke Vrill, and in accordance with Menin tradition, I am here to offer you the chance to surrender."

The Devoted officers exchanged looks of amusement. Major Sants might be an arrogant shit, willing to undermine Teral's authority at every opportunity, but he knew how to keep his place when the enemy were watching.

"And what exactly makes you think we would want to surrender?" Teral asked. "The Fist has never been taken by enemy action, not once in three hundred years, and you've chosen a poor week to threaten us. Our reinforcements have made our biggest concern back there the lack of bunk space. So you are welcome to break your army on the Fist and distract the men for an hour or so."

Vrill gave a menacing laugh. He had removed his helm to receive the Devoted men and Teral could see his long dark-red hair fell past his shoulder—it was dyed, presumably, since the Menin were supposed to be as dark as Teral's own tribe. The snarling head of an animal Teral didn't recognise topped his helm and his armour was painted white, adorned with red and blue ribbons, and imbued with some magic that made the duke blur slightly when he moved. Teral had seen something like this before and he recognised how difficult it would be to fight a man wearing armour like this.

He was escorted by Bloodsworn, who stared straight ahead. Their lances were stowed and their right hands rested lightly on their saddles, inches from the handles of their long-handled crescent axes.

"Haven't you heard?" Vrill asked, looking in turn at each of the men facing him. "Lord Styrax took Tor Salan with ease, and their defences were greater than yours. My lord wishes the Circle City to accede to his rule without bloodshed."

"Your lord," spat Chaplain Fell, unable to contain himself any longer, "has abandoned the Gods. He desecrated the Temple of Tsatach and turned away from his Patron God, the Lord of Battle."

"My lord is fighting and winning battles," Vrill replied, "and what is that except serving Karkarn?"

"He shall burn in the black fires of Ghenna!" roared Fell, his hand instinctively going to his mace, but Sants anticipated it and grabbed the chaplain's arm. Fell struggled for a few moments, but he was a small man and couldn't break Sants's grip.

"Duke Vrill," Teral said in a loud voice, "I am the duty commander here, and I have neither the authority nor the desire to negotiate any surrender, unless I am receiving yours. You do not have the men to take us by force, so I am afraid you are wasting your breath."

"On the contrary," Vrill said, his smile widening, "it was hardly a waste."

"And why is that?" Teral asked, even as he finished the sentence in his mind: *to distract us.* He turned and looked back at the fortress. Nothing had changed, not yet.

I don't understand, he thought, puzzled. *They couldn't have sneaked troops around us, it's not possible.*

Even the five Reaper priests were doing nothing unusual, other than kneeling in the mud with their acolytes and praying—just as the priests of Death and Karkarn within the Fist would be doing.

"I wish to make it clear that any man who surrenders and throws down his weapon shall not be harmed," said the Menin white-eye. He raised his left hand and a monstrous roar cut through the air.

Teral almost jumped in surprise. The minotaurs were bellowing up to the sky as they headed off to the open ground to the right of the Fist.

"Your Western gate would be a good place to march your troops out of, once you surrender," the Menin general advised.

"Are you deaf, or just mad?" Major Sants demanded, though Teral knew Sants was just as worried as he. "We're not going to surrender the damn Fist just because you asked us nicely!"

"Oratory is not enough of a reason?" Vrill shrugged. "As you insist, I shall arrange a demonstration instead. Do not let me keep you, gentlemen."

He offered them a crisp salute and sat there beaming as the Devoted soldiers turned their horses and galloped back towards the half-open gate of the Fist. All four were dreading what they would find.

"Enough!" Lord Celao shouted, cutting Styrax off in midsentence. "Your administrative plans do not interest me, your trade strategies do not interest me, your political assessments do not interest me!" His face was red and his jowls were shaking with fury. "You insult my tribe by your very presence; you insult us further by suggesting we could ever accept Menin rule! The descendents of Grast will *never* rule Ismess!"

"Indeed," Certinse added levelly, "and might I also suggest you get a new chef—the eel was woefully bland." The Farlan powerbroker looked like he was enjoying himself, despite having listened to Lord Styrax talk for half an hour on matters they both knew were inconsequential. He knew this game, and was happy to listen to and watch the faces around him, making occasional comments and allowing the nameless priest in brown to whisper in his ear every few minutes. They would reach the meat of the conversation in due course, and then the game would really start.

The Duchess of Byora drummed her fingers on the table impatiently. Ruhen was staring in rapt fascination at Lord Celao and would not be dissuaded, no matter what she did. The sergeant, on the other side of the child, was causing her almost as much irritation: Kayel ignored her silent reproaches and not only joined in a conversation above his station but also encouraged the little boy's interest in the winged white-eyes.

"Lord Celao, you are here because you are the Chosen of Ilit and ruler of Ismess," Styrax said finally, "but you should not presume that means you can insult me any longer without Kohrad ripping your fat head from your body. Your army is a mockery; it befits the slob who is the Messenger God's Chosen. The shame your existence does Ilit must be testament to his diminished position."

The Litse white-eye screeched in protest, but looked even more put out when neither Gesh nor Kiallas leapt immediately to his defence. Though the winged men tensed, neither made a move to demand Styrax retract his statement.

"You *will* accept Menin rule; you cannot do otherwise," Lord Styrax continued gravely, placing a cautionary hand on Kohrad's arm, feeling his son quivering with aggression. "Your presence here is a courtesy; the only people I care to hear from are the duchess and Knight-Cardinal Certinse."

When he spoke again the hostility was gone. "Natai, if you will forgive my presumption I suggest your position is this: you do not have the troops to fight a war alone, especially now, when your quarter is beset by religious violence. You will support and provide troops in defence of the city, but you will defer to Akell.

"Knight-Cardinal, Cardinal Sourl—you will together decide to fight or to capitulate; the likely response from a martial order will obviously be to fight." He paused, making a show of looking at the sky, as if gauging the hour. The sun was hidden behind a thick blanket of cloud, but it was enough for the Menin lord. He knew he could trust Vrill's sense of timing.

"Gentlemen, I have brought you here today to tell you that option is no longer open to you."

Amber watched the smile waver on Certinse's face. "What do you mean?" he asked.

Lord Styrax stood and beckoned Messenger Karapin, who hurried forward with three rolled scrolls in his hand. "I mean, Knight-Cardinal, that I have just taken the Fist, your quarter's main defence. Unless you sign the peace treaty Messenger Karapin has here, I will not stop there."

He turned to walk away from the table. "You will be getting a runner from your city soon. Unless you wish my minotaurs to unleash havoc in your city, that would be a good time to kneel to me."

Teral spurred on his horse, determined to be first to face whatever had happened in the Fist. He saw the Reaper priests looking up in surprise, their prayers disturbed, and as he reached them the novices sprang to their feet, sensing trouble. It confirmed his suspicion that they were former soldiers, for who else would be drawn to the service of the Reapers?

They were now less than fifty yards from the walls of the Fist, close enough to make it back before the Menin cavalry could run them down, but the priests were ignoring their novices. They stared at the racing horsemen, then at the Menin army behind them.

"Run, you fools!" Major Sants called, sparking the group into action.

They turned and started moving towards the Fist, the smallest, a woman, Teral realised, half dragged by one of the novices. There was a sudden movement and the novice fell, sprawling on the ground.

"Gods, archers!" he shouted, and hunched low over his horse's neck, not slowing the beast until he was through the gate. He was sliding from his horse before a groom had even grabbed at the reins.

"Jackler!" he yelled, "get a squad and sweep the Fist, and double the guard on every entrance." He broke off as Major Sants and Captain Shael clattered in behind him, almost running him down in their haste.

"Sound the alarm!" Sants roared, "and look lively, you bastards!"

"Where's Fell?" Teral asked, fearing the worst.

Sants shook his head, his cheek purple with anger. "Idiot turned back to go after Vrill, I think." He ran back to the gate to look out. "Where are tho—?" The major froze.

Before Teral could speak a howl cut the air, like nothing he had ever heard: high and piercing, a shriek not of pain, but hatred. It stopped abruptly as a squat figure bounded into view and, without breaking stride, pushed Major Sants off his feet. It happened in the blink of an eye; Teral caught only the glimpse of long, misshapen fangs before they were buried in Sants's body.

He felt the ground under his feet shake, like the heavy footfalls of a giant, and he drew his sword as three guardsmen, their pikes levelled, ran past him to Sants's aid, and straight into a second dark shape. The first soldier, smashed off his feet by an enormous arm, collided with his comrades, knocking them to the ground.

Teral ran forward but before he could reach them a third figure darted through the air and stabbed down. He raised his sword, acting instinctively now, and caught the flash of a blade as it slashed across his face and knocked the sword from his hand. He staggered aside as the figure, its arms whirling like an enraged Mystic of Karkarn, pushed past him to attack the next man. He felt the blood splatter across his face as another creature leapt in through the gate, its blades flashing. Teral blinked, trying to make sense of what he was seeing. The first creature turned towards him, its red eyes burning through the gloom. He fell back as the creature shook itself like a dog and released a cloud of foul black smoke from its matted coat.

He gagged at the sudden stench of decay that filled the air and fell to his knees, retching. The largest of the creatures roared again, louder than the minotaurs, but with a more human voice. The beast was a dirty grey colour, with ragged scraps of cloth, or maybe feathers, hanging from its body. Its huge arms were almost as large as the rest of its body, and they were covered with shards of chitinous armour. It gripped one of the open gates and twisted it, snapping the thick, metal-reinforced beams like kindling. It bellowed as it tossed the pieces at Teral and knocked the major onto his back, then redoubled its assault on the gates.

The smoke grew thicker. He could hear the sounds of fighting behind him as the two beasts used swordlike forearms to tear through the gatehouse troops. The first of the monsters—daemons, he realised at last—had not followed them but stood just inside the gate, exuding a growing cloud of choking foulness that was borne into the Fist's interior by the wind. Teral could see its eyes as it watched with what he thought looked like terrible anticipation the death going on behind it.

Now a fifth figure came into view. It was quite unlike the rest and Teral scrabbled backwards in fear, ignoring the foul smoke that was filling his lungs and mouth. He was quite unable to face down the renewed fear he felt at the sight of the white hot, raging figure of flame.

The Burning Man, he thought through the whimpering fear, before realising it was not a man alight, but a figure of fire, comprised entirely of dancing flames: a daemon like the others. *Daemons, daemons all.*

He tried to run, but now smoke had filled the Fist. Screams came from every direction, as did the earsplitting roars of the largest daemon. All he could see were the burning red eyes and that terrible, shifting figure of fire. His eyes burned, his stomach heaved, his limbs were shaking uncontrollably as the infection of the smoke ran through his veins—

From nowhere a hand grabbed him and started dragging him away somewhere. He flailed at it, shrieking in fear, but in the next moment he felt himself being thrown. The sky lightened, the smoke receded, and suddenly there was cold dirt underneath him and cool air on his face. Teral rolled once, twice, before hitting something and coming to a stop. More hands grabbed him and pulled him upright, holding him as his legs wobbled under his weight.

"Getting the idea?" shouted someone in his ear and he felt himself shaken like a rat in a terrier's mouth. His hazy vision began to clear as a bright yellow light in front of him drove the smoke from his eyes. He blinked hard and saw the main entrance of the Fist, the splintered, ruined gates on fire and the fire-daemon reaching out to engulf the entire fortress.

At the side stood the largest of the daemons, propped on its gigantic arms and watching them, its jaw hanging slack. A dagger hilt protruded from the centre of its chest. He couldn't remember seeing anyone getting a blow in—then he recognised the knife.

Gods, it was the priests! The grey rags hanging from the daemon's body looked as if they were growing out of its flesh. *Their daggers turned their own novices into daemons!*

The revelation drove the last of Major Teral's strength from his body and he sagged, not caring when the grip on his arms became too painful to bear. He was hauled up once more and Duke Vrill's face came into focus. The white-eye was peering down at him, savage delight on his face.

"Ready to surrender yet?" Vrill pointed at the gate. "Or do you want the smoke and fire to take them all?"

Teral felt himself nodding as best he could, even as the tears streamed down his face. He was shoved forward and one of the men who had been holding him drove him on towards the burning, smoke-filled gateway.

"Go then," Vrill roared after them as the flames parted, "go and tell that to the rest of your soldiers!"

CHAPTER 31

"**T**HE GREAT AND GOOD, squabbling like spoilt children," Ilumene said with contempt as he glared back at the Scholars' Palace. At the duchess's request he had taken Ruhen for a walk, leaving her at the table, arguing with Styrax.

He turned his head to look up at the child now perched on his shoulders. "If they keep on like that, Lord Styrax will strike them down like the God of Vain Men."

His comment provoked no immediate response. Ilumene could feel the child watching the ongoing negotiations with his usual silent intensity. Evening had fallen with the stealth of a panther, suddenly sweeping down on the valley. When lanterns had been called for, the duchess had demanded a blanket for Ruhen as well.

Somewhat to Ilumene's chagrin, none of the Litse attendants had followed him when he left the terrace. Only the powerful and the scholars merited watching; apparently Ilumene wasn't considered either.

"Tell me," Ruhen said. His voice was soft and elusive to the ear, like the susurration of autumn leaves in the breeze.

"The story? Didn't you write it?" He chuckled and took the dirt path that followed the valley's perimeter. "In that case, there's a certain know-it-all king out west who owes me ten gold Emins!" He headed towards the tunnel entrance that would take them back to Byora once they had all capitulated. The Devoted, especially the Knight-Cardinal, had been thrown by the news, but had yet to actually surrender. What they were arguing about now was anyone's guess, but Ilumene didn't care. The first time he'd met Knight-Cardinal Certinse he'd been one of King Emin's faceless bodyguards; the intervening years had not diminished the Devoted leader's ability to waffle on endlessly whilst smiling all the while—but Ilumene was grateful that his natural Farlan arrogance meant the man hadn't bothered to remember the faces of the Narkang bodyguards.

He cleared his throat theatrically. "Right then, the story of the God of

Vain Men—you'll like this one. It's heretical, for a few reasons, which is why I'd thought it one of yours. There once was a rich man in the kingdom of Pelesei who found an old shrine on his land—"

"It's a lie," Ruhen interrupted.

"A lie? What's a lie?"

"Tell me about Pelesei."

"Pelesei?" Ilumene was struggling to keep up. "Pelesei was the Kingdom of the Crescent Peninsula, far to the south. It was destroyed by plague two millennia ago; now it's just a motley collection of fifteen-odd small city-states."

"Why's it remembered?" Ruhen asked.

He snorted. "Because of the stories based there, more than anything else." He paused. "Are you saying that every story about Pelesei was made up? But Rojak must have told me a dozen or more—"

"My herald knew."

"Knew what?" Ilumene asked. "Piss and daemons, *what*? That Pelesei never existed? Don't tell me that; it can't be true."

"It did exist, a long way south."

Ilumene didn't speak for a moment as he thought the matter through. "But the stories are fiction, so the only thing it was notable for was—existing a long way away? So no one much travelled there . . . it's a much more exciting setting for a story if it doesn't trade much, because it means anything might go on and no one's likely to correct you. No wonder Rojak used it as a setting. The minstrel loved his lies, but those that changed history were always his favourite!"

He laughed loudly, his voice echoing back from the wall of the valley. Here it was nearly vertical, but twenty yards ahead the slope became a little shallower; it would be possible to climb bits of the cliff there—not that there was anywhere to go or any sort of path to the top . . . As they approached, Ilumene saw futility hadn't stopped someone: a glow of light illuminated a figure slumped on a rock ledge with its bare feet hanging over the edge.

"Looks like he's dead or drunk," Ilumene commented, getting as near as he could without actually climbing himself. He peered forward. "It's that mage who popped up yesterday," he said to Ruhen. "Our friend in Scree's dog's body."

"Dog needs a master."

"So who's his master now?" Ilumene wondered aloud. "Might be he's a Menin man all the way through, but who'd trust a necromancer? Styrax wouldn't, so he knows he'll never reach an inner circle there. His best bet would be Lord Larim; don't all Chosen of Larat put together a coterie of acolytes?" He felt the little boy on his shoulder nod.

"So why isn't he down in Ismess trying to make nice to the new Lord of the Hidden Tower? He's adaptable, from what we saw in Scree. If I was Larim I'd want the odd-footed git in my coterie, to make the others second-guess themselves as much as anything else. There's nothing more likely to cause trouble than mages thinking they've got a secure position."

Ruhen pointed up at the figure on the ledge, which hadn't moved. Most of Nai's body was wrapped in the thick blanket against the evening chill; only his head stuck out. "Light," the little boy whispered.

"Fuck me," Ilumene exclaimed, "look at that!"

Nai flinched at the raised voice. He stared up at the cloud-covered sky for a moment before looking down at the pair watching him. He rubbed a hand over his face, brushing his hair out of his eyes, before pushing himself a little more upright. "Not good language for a little boy to hear," he said, with a slight slur to his voice. "What you want?"

"How about a light?" Ilumene called.

Nai flinched and cast a guilty look at the lamp beside him. Almost immediately the light dimmed considerably and began to flicker in the normal fashion.

"Fine spot you got there," Ilumene continued, grinning evilly. "Perfect for a quiet drink."

Nai raised the flagon beside him and saluted Ilumene. It looked as if the half-gallon flagon had very little left in it.

"There other spots like that?"

"Ah, no." Nai looked around at the valley, although there was little to see in the deepening gloom. "Well, maybe, don't know really."

"You just picked a ledge and got lucky?"

Nai nodded enthusiastically. "Figured I'd find a quiet corner to finish my beer. I didn't feel it till I got here. The dead area's about twice the height of a man." He laughed abruptly. "Sure I read somewhere magic was heavier than air."

Ilumene felt a tug on his ear; Ruhen wanted to move on. "I'll leave you to your beer then," he said, giving the necromancer an ostentatious salute. "Your lord's won back there, but you've got a few more hours until they admit it."

As Nai looked back at the Scholars' Palace, Ilumene continued down the path as quickly as he could, trying not to attract the necromancer's notice— he might be one of those drunks with the tendency to recall inconvenient details the next morning, and this was one crowd they didn't want to stand out in.

The path was stony underfoot, there was a smattering of gravel as much to mark the way as anything else, and it made enough noise for Ilumene to be able to talk without fear of Nai hearing them. "Didn't expect to see that," he said. "I'd heard the whole valley was a dead place."

"Palace," Ruhen contributed.

Ilumene stopped dead. "Scholars' Palace?" He pursed his lips. "You've got a point there; his explanation doesn't hold water, does it? The upper floors are much higher than where he was sitting."

He turned back to make sure: the ground sloped, but Nai's position was nowhere near the same height as the upper floors of the building he'd just left.

"So that just leaves us wondering if he knew about that place in advance, or was told to look for cracks in the glaze. Where's your money?"

Ruhen didn't answer. Ilumene guessed the child was thinking. He had a clump of Ilumene's hair bunched in his little fist. The boy was a strange one, displaying the traits of both a child and an immortal. He had noticed more than a few childish mannerisms slipping out unconsciously, which made him sure there was a trace of the mortal soul remaining. When Ruhen had ordered him to tell the story of the God of Vain Men, it hadn't been just a reassertion of dominance on the part of Azaer; just as the body the shadow wore needed clothes and food, so the sound of a voice telling a story satisfied some ill-defined need within the child.

So this is me playing Dad; didn't see that coming!

"Why choose?" Ruhen said eventually.

"You think they're both true?" Ilumene shrugged. "Could be right, I suppose. Lord Styrax sending him fishing is the simplest answer, but Nai was part of Zhia Vukotic's inner circle. No reason she's not still got her hooks into him—he plays the middle ground which is where she's happiest too." He started walking again, resolving to keep going for as long as he could, but juddered to a halt.

"What do you think Lord Styrax is up to here?" he asked abruptly. "If he's got Nai checking the boundary of the library, it must interest him more than we realised. What if he's got something up his sleeve?"

"Have faith."

"Hah. Emin always said, 'Better to have faith in your preparation.' If it's all right with you, I'll think it through a bit more."

"Good."

Ilumene waited, but there was no further advice forthcoming. *Damn it, do you deliberately act like Emin to goad me, or was Rojak right in saying you're defined by your enemies?*

"If he does have something planned, then it's a worry—it could pull everything here out of balance. Linking Lord Isak to Lord Styrax pits the two greatest powers against each other; the Farlan will only win a war on home soil, but they still have to last long enough. If Styrax gains a significant edge he might roll up the West too fast for us to exploit. The Devoted aren't ready for a saviour, the balance has to be maintained."

"And if it cannot?"

He slipped Ruhen from his shoulders and gently placed the little boy on the ground before kneeling before him. "You'd abandon your plans?" he asked, stunned. The shadow was patience itself, its steps slow, but played out over years, decades, even centuries. "I've never seen you step away from anything before."

"There was never need."

Slowly Ilumene nodded. "You can't control them; by your very design the players are beyond the playwright's power. What contingency plans can we prepare? We can't insert prophecies into the Menin history!"

"What am I?"

"A child," Ilumene began hesitantly, aware the obvious answers would direct him, however foolish they sounded. "A boy, a saviour, a mortal . . . a son."

"A son and a saviour."

"The Devoted are primed to worship a saviour," he breathed, realisation dawning, "while Styrax's only weakness is his son—but you can be both, and preserve the balance that way?"

He paused for a dozen heartbeats while he thought it through. Eventually he shook his head. "No, this goes against every instinct I have. No general abandons a successful tactic for the untried, let alone one his forces are ill suited for. Your disciples are all carefully positioned, your plans primed to bear fruit at specific times—how can we change now?

"Before offering battle a general must place himself beyond the possibility of defeat; it is a crucial precept of war. To throw away years of preparation flies in the face of everything I ever learned about warfare. And you have always told me to treat this as a campaign."

Ruhen was quiet for a while, long enough for Ilumene to wonder whether he had overstepped the mark. Rojak had told him many stories of those servants of Azaer who had incurred the shadow's wrath. King Emin's secret scribes wandered the Land, collecting tales of hauntings and horror, and Ilumene knew that not all of them were people who had opposed Azaer—some had merely failed him. Their endings were the worst.

"Even the most perfect fruit may decay," the child said at last. There was something in his voice that Ilumene had not heard before, and it made the hairs on his neck rise. With every passing day Ruhen grew faster and faster, growing into the powers he had possessed as a shadow, but it was in a very human manner. After countless centuries of incorporeal weakness, the shadow had grown impatient with its few months of helpless childhood. "Consider the forces we play our games with. Corruption is inevitable. We must not fear it."

Ilumene smiled. "So speaks the festering remains of Rojak's soul."

Ruhen nodded, shadows dancing in his eyes.

"Of all my curses, womanly and immortal, I reserve especial hatred for you."

Nai jerked awake again. He could see no one in the dark valley, but that was not necessarily a good sign.

"Ah, Mistress Zhia?" he ventured in a croak, his throat dry.

"Don't give me 'Mistress Zhia,' you stub-footed worm," came her velvety growl in his left ear.

Nai flinched, half falling off the ledge before his fingers found purchase on the stone. He turned all the way around, still seeing nothing more than black stone and the extinguished lantern beside him.

This time the voice sounded in his right ear. "Your idiocy is boundless; redeem yourself soon or I will pull out your intestines and hang you with them."

Nai was ready for it this time and managed not to shy away. In the alcoholic haze of his mind the necromancer reflected that it would be frighteningly easy for her to carry out the threat.

"I'm here as you told me to be."

"Did I tell you to announce it to the whole fucking valley?" Zhia snapped. "Forgive me for omitting the order to stay sober and not be seen doing something supposedly impossible!"

Nai glanced around guiltily. He couldn't see the empty flagon; he must have knocked it off the ledge as he dozed.

At least I didn't attract any guardians, he thought with a small sense of relief. *She really would have killed me then.* A gust of wind whistled over his body and he pulled his leather coat tighter around his body. He didn't respond to Zhia's words, knowing anything he said would only further enrage her.

"I didn't show you this spot just so you could announce it to everyone present; for your sake I hope you didn't risk it for no good reason."

"No Mistress," Nai said quickly, glad for the chance to change the subject. The snarl of an infuriated vampire had done wonders to clear his head. "There is news: Lord Styrax's men took the Fist this afternoon."

"I know that," she scoffed. "He does like to show off. The foolish boy has been playing with daemons again; he got five of them to incarnate and smoked the garrison out. I felt it happen all the way back to Byora. Tell me what he's doing in the library."

"The library?" Nai looked confused. "Negotiating the surrender of the quarters, you know that."

"So far from his troops, in a place where he can't use his greatest weapons? Don't be stupid. However wrecked it may be, the Litse Army in Ismess is far larger than the guard he brought—Styrax remains vulnerable all the time he is in here even if he does have his wyvern somewhere nearby. Is he planning on staying more than a day?"

"I believe so," Nai said hesitantly. "I overheard him talking to General Gaur earlier; I got the impression he had some research to do here. He was warning the general to keep an eye on Kohrad."

"Anything more?"

"He gave me a project: to walk the perimeter of the valley and mark the places where I could feel energies in the air."

There was silence for a few moments. Nai half turned to look up at the cliffs behind him and was rewarded with an icy blast of wind whipping past his eyes.

"If you find any, be sure to tell me also."

Nai nodded, though he was unsure what to make of the order. There was a trace of the vampire in the air: her delicate scent, so faint it could almost be a memory evoked by her voice. Zhia's understanding of magic far surpassed what Nai could learn in his lifetime—it might be that when he returned in the morning, this ledge would look just like the rest of the valley. Perhaps magic could be driven a little way into the perimeter from outside; or perhaps energy simply surrounded her like a diving beetle's bubble of air.

"Is there anything else, Mistress?"

"You're the one making the report," she said, drily.

"Ah yes, of course. Knight-Cardinal Certinse is giving the orders in Akell; he arrived a few weeks ago."

"Specifically here, or passing through to Embere?"

"I do not know."

Zhia paused. "I hear he's got four or five legions with him; that's more than he'd need to take over Akell; Sourl doesn't have the guts to rebel against his superior. I can't believe he'd pull so many troops out of Narkang lands just for that, and that man is ambitious. More likely he has some grander plan that requires actual tangible control over the Order, rather than just official control. The best way to do that is with Raland's gold mines, and Telith Vener is in control there these days. He'll have accepted Certinse's authority over the Order when Certinse was in distant parts and Duke Nemarse ruled Raland, but not now." She paused to think, but Nai could tell by her tone that Zhia was satisfied with her logic.

"Anything more?"

"There is some sort of magical link between the duchess's bodyguard, Sergeant Kayel, and our friend Major Amber."

"Curious, I saw nothing of that through Lady Kinna's eyes."

"It is very faint—it is like each carries an echo of the other in their shadow. You would only notice it in the presence of both."

"Kayel and Amber," Zhia mused. "That's an interesting twist."

"You know Kayel?"

"Only through Kinna's eyes—but clearly he's far more than a bullying sergeant. Keep your eyes and ears open. I want you to stay here as long as Styrax does. Make yourself useful in whatever manner you can, and report to me an hour after dusk each day—understand?"

"I do."

"Good." She hesitated a moment and her voice softened. "Nai, this is more important than you can begin to imagine. You will have to trust me that your safety is best served by keeping me informed. Now go, before you are missed."

Zhia released the stream of magic and sighed, feeling the energies dissipate into the night air. She sat, high up on the cliff, motionless, untouched by the howl of wind, almost as if she were encased in a glass bubble. The piece of rock she sat on was roughly oval, and some ten yards across, the only flat piece of ground in the desolate environment of Blackfang's upper reaches where it was impossible to travel even fifty feet in any direction without having to climb.

Nothing protruded above the outer ring of cliffs. Within, the surface of the mountain was a jagged wilderness protected from the worst of wind erosion. There were occasional small tufts of grass and patches of moss clinging precariously to the rock, but they were few and far between. Not many birds braved the treacherous gusts and lack of food to nest here; it was a desolate, inaccessible place.

It was a useful place to lurk unmolested.

"You heard?" she said after a long pause. She had abandoned her usual silk dress in favour of more practical hunting breeches and tunic, though they were decorated with embroidered sprays of blue flowers. Her long-handled sword was slung across her back, housed in a leather scabbard etched with a pattern that echoed that on her clothes. Furthering the image of martial readiness, her abundant hair was fastened back with long silver pins set with sapphires.

"I did," Koezh replied from the small cave behind her. "How far can you trust him?"

"Not at all." A small smile crept onto her lips and she turned to give her brother a look. "He's as honest a man as I know, but with no allegiance except to himself."

"So if he finds anything as he walks the perimeter, he'll tell Lord Styrax." Koezh sounded weary. "There can only be one reason why Styrax has given him such orders. Whether he knows exactly what he's looking for or not, he knows the dead space is not natural."

Zhia agreed, "He's guessed halfway, and he'll stumble upon the rest."

A light flared inside the cave, illuminating its cramped interior. Koezh sat upon one bedroll looking at the glass sphere which emitted the light. A small hamper and a few thick leather-bound books were piled beside it. Zhia's bedding was piled against the opposite wall.

The vampire looked grave. "So all we can do is wait." He gestured to the few belongings beside him. "It's been a long time since we played camp like this."

He was ready for battle, dressed in a full suit of ancient black armour, except for the helm and gauntlets, which lay on the rock floor next to him. His hate-filled sword was suspended on a pair of thick iron pins that he'd driven into the rock above his bedroll. Without the ward surrounding her, even Zhia would have found it uncomfortable to look at the weapon Aryn Bwr had instilled with the fury and grief of his heir's murder.

"It has been millennia," Zhia replied with a slight edge to her voice, "and I for one see no reason to repeat it now. It will take him days of research before he can make his move. If you wish to camp out, Prince Koezh, that is entirely your prerogative."

"We cannot know how long it will take," Koezh replied with a tone of infinite, infuriating patience. "You don't know how far along he starts, and we cannot take any risk. He is not a man we can buy off or threaten as we did Deverk Grast; even if he knew the whole story he would still go through with it. We cannot risk anyone taking possession and we cannot trust the guardian to stop him—quite aside from the destruction it would unleash upon the innocents of Ismess." He gestured towards her bedroll. "All this you know, so come and sit with me."

Zhia scowled, falling into long-abandoned habits of the younger sister but well aware that her brother was right.

"Even if we hand it to him later, we must be sure first," she admitted, joining him inside the cave. The icy gusts tore at her clothes for a brief moment while she exchanged one ward for the other. "I reserve the right to blame you for a poor night's sleep, however."

Koezh inclined his head. "Mother always said one must always accept a lady's blame. I believe the principle holds true even if one suspects it is misplaced anger."

"Your meaning?" Zhia asked coldly.

Her brother smiled. "Avoiding a certain young man seems to have put you on edge. It's all very sweet. Shall I sing to you to help you sleep?"

"If you do I'll cut my throat and you can wait by your damn self," she snapped, turning away from the laughter on his face.

"Suicide by petulance; a lesser-know joy of immortality."

CHAPTER 32

"**E**NJOYING THE MORNING AIR?"

Amber turned quickly at the sound of Lord Styrax's voice.

Gods, I didn't hear a thing, he thought, before replying, "Just so, my Lord. A night in Nai's company is enough to make a man appreciate a bracing breeze."

"The air was not fresh in your room?" Today Lord Styrax had selected the clothes of an officer at leisure: thick black linen tunic with no braids or badges of rank, black breeches, and tall riding boots polished to a high shine. The white-eye may not have been particularly handsome—indeed, people barely noticed his features, and few would be able to describe them. All folk remembered was the power he wore like a mantle.

"A little ripe, if you'll forgive the observation, my Lord."

"It was the pork—even my stomach thought it a trifle overspiced."

Even here in the library grounds where no magic could exist, Lord Styrax's presence was nearly overwhelming. He may have been one of the largest men in the Land, but he carried his size with ease, moving as deftly and neatly as a dancer. Amber believed the inscrutable giant to be something more than human: as if the Gods had finally perfected the model. Even Aryn Bwr could not have inspired more worship than Kastan Styrax.

Lord Styrax walked the few yards to stand beside the major. The Library of Seasons had only one exit, through an enormous gate. The gatehouse was set into the rock and jutted into the road, looking down the entire length of Ilit's Stair. The arch exploited a natural fissure in the cliff face, and square blocks the height of a man shored up the rock. Without gates the library looked remarkably vulnerable, but Ilit's Stair was two hundred yards of stepped slope more than twenty yards wide, offering no cover whatsoever to those ascending.

The guardians of the library had ensured it was no secret that there were enormous storerooms where, in addition to the weapons belonging to their current guests, there were whole rooms full of arrows—one for every man Deverk Grast had led into Ismess. Whether that was true or not, there were certainly a dozen or more ballistae kept for a similar purpose.

"Longing for freedom?" Lord Styrax said, gesturing towards the archway, through which they could see the sparsely wooded hills on the other side of the city and a clear, pale blue sky. It was still early; the sun had risen no more than half an hour ago and the valley remained in shadow. The air was cold and crisp.

It reminded Amber of winter mornings when he had gone hunting with his father and brothers.

"Just appreciating the view," he said eventually. "I get a little restless in these gentle surrounds, especially with my men out there without me."

"I will keep you busy then. I'll be in the Fearen House all day, and I shall need someone to attend me."

"Of course, my Lord." Amber hesitated for a moment, then asked, "My Lord, surely Nai would be a better aide? I'll only be able to contribute by carrying books."

Lord Styrax nodded. "Doubtless true—but never trust a necromancer. Folk might hate my kind for good reason, but we have nothing on the walkers in the dark." Styrax's words immediately reminded Amber of the conversation he'd overheard in Thotel, between the necromancer Isherin Purn, Nai's master, and Lord Styrax. Without understanding it, Amber had nevertheless recognised there was a subtext to each man's words, hinting at tensions and allegiances he knew nothing of.

They watched the heads of the guards at the gate turn their way: nervous Litse faces looking like deer that had sensed wolves. The white-eyes were slowest to react. Three of them were facing out towards Ismess, feeling the wind that rose up Ilit's Stair. One had his wings fully outstretched, though he would have to walk another ten yards or more to be able to fly. As large as they were, those wings would not be capable of lifting a man without magic.

"Caged birds," Styrax said, nodding towards the white-eyes as they finally turned towards them. He appeared to be enjoying their discomfort. "They're bound to this place; conditioned to stare past the bars but never slip through them."

Amber admitted, "I don't understand these people. Even their white-eyes seem alien to me, and I thought your kind at least would be the same the Land over."

"They are a broken tribe, unaware even of their past glories. Without a man or woman of vision, they will wallow another thousand years in this festering place, until inbreeding or war destroys them."

But which solution will we provide? Amber wondered as Styrax turned abruptly away, motioning for Amber to accompany him.

It had rained during the night and the ground was muddy, so they headed for the nearest gravel path. Gesh followed behind. The white-eye was dressed as he had been the day before, in formal white robes underneath ceremonial armour. It was strange to see so little colour in a man; with his pale skin, creamy yellow hair, and white eyes, Amber thought Gesh hardly looked alive. His slim build and ethereal appearance put Amber in mind of tales of Elves, and the contrasting bright red and green javelins held in an oversized quiver at his hip only added to that unreal image.

"He's got some spirit, that one," Lord Styrax commented, having followed Amber's line of sight. They continued down the gravel path as it meandered to follow a stream, then swung back towards the looming Fearen House.

"Give me some time and I'll find a way to get to him." At Amber's puzzled expression Styrax gave a laugh. "No, not like that! Lord Celao is an embarrassment and a fool; better he chokes on a fishbone and Gesh takes command of Ismess. I will not allow any vassal state to remain so weak."

"They'll never love you," Amber said, thinking aloud.

"True, but neither will they hate me, and their children will grow up knowing who restored their future to them. No, Ismess is a problem I need only time to solve—it is Byora that will require proper thought."

"The duchess, Natai Escral, or that bodyguard of hers?"

"Both of them. Your information reaffirms my belief that Byora is the Circle City's tipping point, and we're clearly not the only ones to think that."

"This is all beyond my comprehension," Amber sighed. "How do you second-guess immortals?"

"In some ways they are simpler to understand; their desires and fears are magnified to a far greater scale. I suspect Zhia is merely keeping herself in the game for the time being. She senses great things are afoot and she knows she must remain on the board if it is ever to be of use to her." Styrax clapped a massive hand onto Amber's shoulder. "You did much good in Scree, Major; you played the hand you were given well. Until then Azaer was nothing more than an obscure reference for me; now I see where its schemes have directly involved me. Zhia's legend also obscured the person behind it, but before the great traitor, before the monster, she remains a person, someone to be known, just like any other."

Amber nodded. The debriefing when he rejoined the army had been exhaustive and exhausting, at times verging on interrogation as Lord Styrax and General Gaur hungrily deliberated and debated over every conversation and action he could remember.

"All I heard of Azaer was its legend."

"One carefully fostered, but yes, it is Azaer I need to know better before I can understand it. The shadow warned me before I killed Lord Bahl that I would be facing rebellion when I returned. Why? Did it require my conquest to continue apace? Did it want me here as a witness, or had Salen betrayed it? What is it doing in Byora that may require a diversion? That will be your job in the months to come, to run a low-level observation of Byora and tell me what is happening there."

"I'm honoured, my Lord."

"I doubt you'll find much honour in it," Styrax said with a smile, "but you survived Scree and you know what you're looking for. Don't worry about your men; you'll be leading them next time they go into battle."

"Thank you, my Lord," Amber said, touched that his master understood his need to be with his men when they faced the enemy.

At the entrance to the Fearen House, Lord Styrax stood looking at the oblong monument again. "Mysteries upon mysteries," he said aloud. "However, the first business of the day is the puzzle of the heart. I take it your skills do not extend to cryptography, Amber?"

Amber shook his head and Lord Styrax clapped him on the back. "Never mind; let's see how fast you learn!" he said brightly, leading the way up the steps to the main entrance.

Sighing, Amber followed along behind.

Suzerain Torl left his tent when the dawn was still grey, the sun nothing more than a glimmer beyond the horizon. The camp was unnaturally quiet, even though it was early. As he looked around he saw a few fires being revived, but there were few men about. He had been pushing them hard for the last few weeks, but fatigue was not the only reason for the heavy silence. It was a good thing that Lord Isak had kept his distance, for there was quite enough death after nightfall already.

To his left Torl could see the fires of Lord Isak's army. One of his aides had jokingly described it as the Farlan's Temporal Army. Crusade was not a word the clerics had liked; for all their venom and spite, they had insisted on more palatable terms: Soldiers of the Gods, Defenders of the Faith, even Spiritual Envoys; every cult and faction had a different name, and each had a different idea of their goal. It left as bitter a taste in Torl's mouth as their insistence on consultation in everything, even logistics.

"My Lord Suzerain," called Lieutenant Zaler as he hurried over, "good morning, Sir."

"Is it?" Torl growled. "It's hard to tell."

Zaler hesitated. "Ah, which, my Lord?" He was a young man, the nephew of Torl's wife's cousin, and still oddly earnest despite having spent more than a year as Torl's aide. He was short and slim—he would never be much of a fighter—so Zaler tried to make up for it by being unfailingly helpful and efficient. Unfortunately, he lacked a soldier's common sense and had not yet developed a soldier's cynicism.

"Good or morning?" Zaler repeated anxiously.

"Don't be bloody stupid, Lieutenant," Torl said, exasperated.

"Sorry, sir. Shall I sound the reveille?"

Torl nodded, then realised from Zaler's expression he was once again screwing up his eyes and pinching the bridge of his nose. He guessed he was looking as washed out and old as he felt. A camp bed was no substitute for the huge feather mattress in the master bedroom of Koan Manor, his principal home. Though he was well used to campaigning, the years had suddenly caught up with him.

Zaler signalled the suzerain's bugler, who saluted sharply and raised his horn, producing a sharp flurry of notes that brought groans from all around even before the regimental buglers picked up the call and sounded it in all directions. Within seconds the notes echoed back from the other camp as General Lahk roused his own troops.

Torl looked down the rows of tents: his troops remained neat and disciplined, while the penitent legions were becoming increasingly ragged and disorganised. That meant the priests' men were not reaching camp before the light failed—but the only response the clerics had was to flog the slowest companies, which served only to make matters worse.

"Sir, should I fetch a healer? You look exhausted," Zaler asked, sounding worried.

Torl shook his head. "It's just fatigue. I can't have the men see the healer attend me two mornings in a row; it would send out the wrong message."

"My Lord, are you sure? Your face is awfully pale."

Torl saw the anxiety in Zaler's face and reconsidered for a moment; the young man was not one to push things unnecessarily, and in truth his hauberk felt as heavy as full armour this morning. "Men won't fight for a cosseted fool, Zaler," he said after a moment.

"Sir, no man in the army would ever think that way. The fact of the matter is that you're twenty summers older than most of us, and you've told me before that a general *is* more important than any of his troops. Your own words, sir; a general must look after himself. Illness or exhaustion means poor decisions and those cost lives."

Torl scowled at his aide. *Perhaps the boy's not entirely useless after all.* "This is the time you choose to demonstrate that you do listen? When you're contradicting a general in the field?"

Zaler winced, but he didn't back down. "You were most specific on the duties of a general's aide."

"If it means you leave me alone, fetch the damn healer—" Torl paused. "No, first tell me if there was trouble last night."

"I'm afraid so, but we appear to have come out on top again."

"Gods, we march to war while fighting with ourselves," Torl sighed, sinking down into his campaign chair and accepting a bowl of tea from his page. He cupped it in his hands and as he sipped the hot liquid, the furrows on his brow softened slightly. "Takes longer ever year to get the morning chill out of my bones," he said to himself before looking up. "Is Tiniq here?"

Zaler nodded and waved over General Lahk's twin brother. He was an Ascetite—a soldier whose latent magical abilities had never developed properly, but who was nevertheless gifted beyond normal standards. Lesarl had seconded him from Isak's personal guard to help Suzerain Torl deal with the more unfriendly clerics.

Thus far there had been two direct attempts on Torl's life, and most nights had seen violence of some sort, but the Chief Steward's agents were more than a match for the mercenaries trying to eliminate opposition to the cults' control. Tiniq himself now slept in the baggage carts during the day so he could be awake all night.

"Suzerain Torl," Tiniq acknowledged, walking over briskly. His left arm was bandaged, but it didn't seem to be bothering him much.

For the twin of a white-eye—an impossible feat, so every doctor would claim—Tiniq was far from remarkable to behold. The former ranger was of average height and build, and his eyes were normal. The only apparent skill he had was that of fading into the background wherever he went. Other differences became clear when one found out he was only five years younger than Torl, and saw his speed when a priest of Nartis had tried to murder the suzerain.

"What happened to your arm?" Torl asked, grumpily noting that one of them wasn't feeling his age that morning. There was an unnerving gleam in Tiniq's eye. For a man uncomfortable with being the centre of attention, he was unusually energised by the night's excitement.

"Assassins tried to take us out," he announced. "Nothing like a bit of recognition, eh? We picked up a team heading for the Saroc section; assumed they were looking to kill Colonel Medah."

"And they ambushed you?"

"Tried to, but they didn't notice Leshi and Shinir ghosting along behind us."

"Prisoners?"

Tiniq shifted his feet. "Ardela got a little overexcited."

"Ardela? The shaven-headed hellcat?"

"That's the one," Tiniq agreed, grinning wholeheartedly. "It turns out she's got a real problem with anyone attached to Nartis. Once she saw they were penitents of Nartis she just went berserk." He saw the expression on Suzerain Torl's face." My Lord, I'm sorry; I'd never met the woman until the day we left Tirah. I had no idea she was as mad as that."

Raised voices not far off interrupted their conversation and they all turned to watch a party of men approach. Suzerain Torl's hurscals reached for their weapons.

Torl looked past his men and spotted the massive figure swathed in white at the centre of the group of priests. "Gods, that's all I need," he muttered before raising his voice. "Sir Dahten, stand your men down."

A grey-haired hurscal turned to the suzerain and gave him a pained expression. Torl ignored it, so Sir Dahten growled an order to the rest of the bodyguard. None of them dropped their weapons, but they stood less belligerently as the breaking of camp went on around them.

"Chalat, good morning," Torl called out. The Chetse white-eye didn't immediately respond. His attention appeared to be focused on the other army's camp in the distance. Torl knelt and offered his sword hilt, the Farlan custom. He had not met the former ruler of the Chetse before this campaign, but there were stories aplenty. His appetites were legendary, as was his remarkable physical prowess, but it appeared some of the stories would have to be revised.

"Torl, your men are not performing the morning devotionals," Chalat said at last, his gaze moving over the assembled hurscals before settling on the suzerain. "Their lack of piety is a concern for us all. All success depends on the blessing of the Gods."

Chalat was as tall as General Lahk, but far more heavily built than any Farlan. His forearms were as thick as a man's thigh—his recent fasting had done little to reduce them—but where Chalat had once been famously barrel-shaped, now his belly had reduced and he tapered dramatically below his enormous rib cage, the new shape highlighted by the robe he wore tied at the waist by a length of rope. His face was gaunt, and he had dark rings under his eyes. His hair was silvery grey, rare for a white-eye. Though Chalat had lived far longer than a normal human, until the summer it had been the normal Chetse light brown.

"I do not question their piety, Chalat," Torl said in a strained voice, "which cannot be said for some of those who follow you like carrion crows."

The crows behind fluttered their feathers angrily, but Chalat stilled them with a raised finger. His face showed no emotion—he was at peace with the Land and secure in his purpose. For Suzerain Torl, father to a white-eye and Lord Bahl's confidant for many years, it was a worrying sight. No white-eye at the centre of an army should look that way; it went against everything that drove them.

"They are moths, not crows, and they are flocking to my light," Chalat intoned solemnly. On his back he still wore the great broadsword he had been given when he became the Fire God's Chosen all those years ago. The Blood-rose amulet that had accompanied it, however, he had given away before leaving Lomin. Torl had laughed when he first heard that, refusing to believe any white-eye would give away an artefact of such power, but Chalat really had: he had been irrevocably changed.

"*A white-eye no more,*" Torl remembered Chalat saying the day he joined them, "*a lord no more, but envoy of the Gods.*"

That's too close to "prophet" for my liking, and everyone knows they're all mad. Do you think faith will turn spears? he wondered to himself.

"Moths are brainless creatures, soon consumed by the flame," Torl responded.

Chalat nodded slowly, clearly interested only in the glory itself and not the effect it might have. "The army must perform the devotionals each morning, the officers alongside their men. The priests shall oversee them and instruct them in the ways of the Gods. There is talk of the godless among us, of creatures that sleep during the day and stalk the camp at night."

Instruct them in the ways of the Gods? I can just imagine what that will mean. Do they really think men will stand by and watch their friends be dragged off?

Torl looked at the priests lingering in the Chetse's shadow, seeing if he recognised any—they changed regularly, which pointed to a savage struggle for supremacy within the clerics of the crusade. Two were priests of Tsatach, still of fighting age, who Chalat had taken as his disciples. The rest were predominantly a mixture from the temples of Nartis and Death, although today there were representatives of Belarannar, Vrest, and Vasle in attendance.

"To make the men perform the devotionals en masse would delay us by an hour each day," Torl protested, "and that gives the enemy greater time to detect us and prepare."

"You claim your mages and scryers hide us from his sight. Is this not true?"

"I make no promises; the Chosen of Larat may prove too strong for our mages." *Now you have a use for them? Yesterday you wanted me to hang the lot as heretics, even as they told us where the Menin were!*

"In that case they are of no use to us," Chalat replied simply. "They shall stand before a Morality Tribunal and account for themselves."

Torl bowed in what he hoped would look conciliatory. "I'm afraid they cannot. Lord Isak has already ordered all mages to his army. After the deaths two nights past, he recalled all those with college contracts."

"They are under my command," Chalat said, for the first time actually focusing properly on Torl. A spark of the white-eye he had once been flickered in his eyes. "They are tools of the Gods, to do with as I see fit. Tell the boy to send them back."

"As you wish," Torl said, amazed at Chalat's behaviour. The white-eye could not conceive that his order would be refused. Presumably he expected Lord Isak would meekly comply.

The Morality Tribunals were becoming increasingly violent; men were being flogged, sometimes to death, before the sitting priests to obtain confessions, but it was those who survived Torl felt sorry for. Forced to admit their guilt, denounce their friends, and punish their comrades, then ordered to receive "correction"—Torl wasn't sure those sentenced to death weren't luckier. He had found himself ordering Tiniq to kill to save men from this madness, which was being repeated day after day.

"We are close to the enemy; I can smell their heresy on the wind," Chalat said, interrupting Torl's grim thoughts.

"We will ride in battle order this morning," Torl agreed. "In four days' hard ride we should have sight of Blackfang. My latest reports have Lord Styrax's forces to be encamped outside Akell."

"I must lead the army." Chalat looked over towards the other army, seeing the movement there as General Lahk was no doubt urging them to break camp first. "We will leave before Lord Isak; you may join me, Suzerain Torl." With that, he turned and left.

Torl watched the priests part to allow him through before neatly peeling around to follow him. Only one remained, a tall man of about thirty summers with a flattened nose, wearing the robes of Nartis. He appeared oblivious to the fact his comrades had already crossed the hurscal line, so intently was he observing Suzerain Torl. The older man didn't recognise him at all, but he guessed he was one of those with magical ability. From what Torl could fathom of the shifting alliances and allegiances within the cults, the prospect of battle had propelled the mages to the fore.

"The envoy of the Gods commands you. You will not need your hurscals. Leave them here." The priest gave Torl a crooked smile and pointed the way, intending Torl to follow Chalat. "It is felt you are in need of additional religious instruction."

"Fuck you and the rest of your zealot cronies!"

Torl blinked. For a moment he thought the words had come from his own mouth until he realised Tiniq had stepped forward, a look of undisguised loathing on his face.

The priest did not appear in the least intimidated. "Godless scum," he snarled. "For that insult to the cults you will face a tribunal, of that I assure you."

"Go ahead," Tiniq replied. "My name is Tiniq; I am brother to General Lahk and a sworn sword of Isak Stormcaller. If you think you can drag me before a tribunal, you are welcome to try."

The priest's head flicked around back to Torl. "You keep the company of heretics," he hissed. "Your education is in greater need than we had realised. Leave your weapons and follow me."

First he checked that the Lord Chalat had kept moving and was not there to witness, then he responded with a small hand gesture. At his signal every soldier watching—a full regiment of hurcals and sworn soldiers—drew his weapon,

"As a member of the Brethren of the Sacred Teachings for my entire adult life," he said softly, "I would love to come and be lectured by a man half my age on piety, but unfortunately I am bound by Special Order Seven and to contravene that would be treason."

"The Special Order does not overrule the word of the Gods!"

"Certainly not," Torl said, adding contemptuously, "but you are no God, you are a stupid little man drunk on power. Tell every other idiot sitting on your so-called Morality Tribunals that I have been instructed to carry out the details of Special Order Seven to the letter, and that means no military officer may be tried by any court but a military one, and no court-ranked man or commanding officer may travel unarmed or without the company of his hurscals. If you wish to educate me, you must first present your petition to the relevant Farlan military authority." He pointed in the direction of the other army, then at the head of his hurscals. "That would be Lord Isak, or, at a pinch, myself. Sir Dahten here is in charge of preliminary requests."

He turned away, signalling the end to the conversation. Behind him the priest spluttered with fury before Sir Dahten clapped a hand on the man's shoulder. The knight had a special knack; nine times out of ten he could get a finger in the soft hollow on top of a shoulder, hitting the sweet spot without trying. As he heard the soft thud of a man sinking to his knees, Torl knew Dahten had got it right again.

"Preliminary requests," Dahten began, a menacing tone to his voice. "They're not really of a discourse form, not at this stage of the proceedings. Now, hold your arms out wide—I'm sure your God will give you strength in this hour of need."

How long can we continue like this? Torl wondered, closing his eyes and listening to the squawk as a sword was placed in each of the priest's outstretched hands. *Five days until we reach the Circle City. Will we have torn each other apart by then?*

The following morning saw a storm break over the Circle City. The warning horn had sounded at the break of dawn, and its call had still been rolling over the city when the deluge came. In Burn, the scar surrounding the fissure they called Cambrey's Tongue was hidden by a thick cloud of stinking grey smoke.

Ruhen stood in his high room in the Ruby Tower and looked out over a city washed clean by floodwater. He was staring into the murky distance, a faint trace of worry in his ever-serious expression. In his hands was the slim book that had been his mother's only possession, one she no longer remembered; the journal of Vorizh Vukotic she had pulled from the ashes of Scree.

It amused him to have something so valuable, the contents of which would determine the course of the next year of war, as a child's plaything.

"Come away from the window, my dear," called the duchess, reaching a hand out towards him. "Come, Ruhen, sit with me." She massaged her temple, as she did almost constantly now, trying to rub away the dull ache from her head. The bags under her eyes indicated how badly she had been sleeping of late—Ruhen disliked sleeping in her room, preferring access to the tower's dark corridors whenever he wished, and without him the duchess found no rest. Each morning she looked a little more ragged, a little more nervous; she was wary of shadows.

"They are coming, lord," came a voice on the wind that no one but Ruhen heard, though Haipar flinched. The skeletal woman hunched a little lower and chewed harder at her lip, sensing Aracnan's presence in the room even if she couldn't hear him. Ilumene, nursing a hangover, was oblivious. He stared disconsolately down at the floor, occasionally swigging at a lukewarm jug of coffee.

"How long?"

"Perhaps four days if they leave the slowest behind; the whole army is made up of cavalry aside from a ragged swarm of peasants trailing after them. Five days if they wish to be in any shape to fight." Aracnan's voice was little more than a distant echo in Ruhen's head. The mercenary was somewhere in Wheel, hunting for the Farlan woman who had eluded him. His frustration at being unable to sniff her out was palpable. The mercenary's position in events had now changed. His allegiance was no longer secret, and so his usefulness was diminished.

"Ruhen, please, come and hold my hand, whisper my headache away," the duchess pleaded.

The little boy turned and offered her a smile, which was enough to smooth the cares from her face, at least until he returned to the window.

"The boy seeks to kill me. A strange choice to make—he knows the risk."

"One half is led by a Chetse white-eye."

"Lord Chalat? Excellent. Send dreams of daemons to him, fuel his fanaticism. He will bring this crusade racing on and give Lord Isak no time to treat with the Menin, nor to attack Byora. He cannot abandon the crusade."

"You will bargain with Lord Styrax?"

"He must not know me, not yet. Ilumene will offer him the duchess's army."

"You intend to wipe out the Farlan?"

"No, only to have both sides bloodied. Tell the Jesters to ensure Lord Isak can escape—this war must see no decisive action, but after the battle you must find a way to kill Kohrad Styrax."

"It will be done."

The contact broken, Ruhen stepped back from the window and turned to his adopted mother. She reached out again and he toddled over to her, allowing her to wrap her arms around him. A few kisses, a brush of her fingers through his soft brown hair, and Natai Escral, the Duchess of Byora, was soothed again.

"Ah, you're playing with your book again," she cooed at him. "Almost as much of a puzzle as my beautiful little boy! And what did you see out the window, little Ruhen?"

"Soldiers, Mother," Ruhen replied in voice full of innocence.

His words caused a beaming smile to spread over her face, then she glanced over at Haipar—but the tribeswoman from the Waste appeared not to have noticed that her position had been usurped.

Haipar would not have cared, even if she had realised; she was barely aware of anyone, for she was lost in her own sickness and misery, forever twitching and peering into corners. When she did notice Ruhen's presence, she always looked like a mouse startled by a cat.

"Yes, my sweet, the city is full of soldiers, but they are all under control. We would never let any of them hurt you."

"Not here, out there." He pointed towards the horizon and at last he felt the duchess tense. "Horsemen," he added, just to make sure.

She carried him to the window, but could see nothing beyond the city. Ruhen pointed northwest, but all she could see was mist and smoke. "They frighten me," he added for sport.

She put a protective arm around his shoulders. "No one could possibly hurt you," she said before turning to Ilumene. "Sergeant, have a servant run to the Vier Tower—Tell Mage Peness I wish him to scry to the northwest."

Ilumene grimaced and managed to heave himself to his feet.

The duchess smiled down at Ruhen. "Perhaps our prince is even more special than we had already thought?"

Ruhen returned to the window, his back to the duchess so she could not see the shadows dance in his eyes. Down below a crowd was gathering, beggars and other vagrants mainly. They had been encamped outside the gates for a few hours now, fleeing briefly when Kiyer of the Deluge swept the streets clean, creeping back when the water cleared. As he watched, more joined the throng, loitering in the shadow of the Ruby Tower.

Word was spreading, helped by Luerce and his little troupe of disciples. Empty temples and fighting on the streets meant many were searching for something—*anything*—to believe in. Only the most desperate were waiting outside the compound gate, hoping for a glimpse of Ruhen, but it was a start. Ruhen's patience was vast, and once word spread beyond the Circle City, it would meet those lost folk who had heard some new stories from the Harlequins.

"Can we go back to the valley?" Ruhen asked.

"Do you want to see the men with wings again?"

His solemn nod provoked another smile. "Very well, we will. Lord Styrax will be glad to see us; he wants us all to be friends—would you like that?"

Ruhen paused to think. "Friends are good."

"That they are, my dear." The duchess hugged him close again and he could hear the quick beat of her heart, quite unlike his own.

He took her hand and looked her directly in the eye. For a moment she froze, lost in the shadows, before the moment passed. "Allying ourselves with the Menin may prove the best course, but let us wait for what Mage Peness has to say. Becoming friends can always wait a day or so, and it is always preferable to bring a gift."

That evening Doranei and Sebe were eating in a small tavern on the outskirts of Breakale, just a short walk from the Beristole. Lell Derager, who continued to be their host, had suggested this as a good place to hear the gossip.

Wheel and Burn were increasingly unsafe these days, as the bartender had been quick to mention. She hadn't specified where the danger came from and the two men from Narkang were too experienced to show too much interest. They took their time over bowls of greasy mutton stew, alert to the chatter around them.

"—'eard she was going to sell the whole of Hale to the Menin—"

"—Devoted got what was comin' to 'em, just a bunch of priests with swords—"

"—mad enough ta think they can use daemons in battle!"

"—broke his curse just with a touch, I tell you—we all felt it!"

Doranei paused and cocked an ear. The room was full of quiet conversations overlaying each other, but that last had sounded different. It took him a moment to place it, but when he did, it was all he could do not to turn around and stare at the speaker. Something in the tone of voice reminded him of Parim, the demagogue King Emin had pressganged into the Brotherhood: it had that urgent honesty that Parim used so successfully to convince his listeners to shower him in gifts.

"Going for a piss," he muttered to Sebe, putting his drink down and tapping the bar twice with a spice-yellowed finger. He caught Sebe's arm as he was easing himself off his seat, so Sebe could turn a little and not draw attention to himself as he checked the room to see who noticed Doranei's departure. By the time he returned to his food he was sure there was no unwelcome notice being paid, just the usual raising of eyes as a big man with weapons approached, then passed. No one followed, no one stopped talking, so Sebe cheerfully finished his drink and waved for another.

When Doranei returned, he slapped Sebe on the shoulder, thanks for getting the drinks in, and whispered as he sat down, "Back corner, wearing white."

Sebe wiped up the last of his mutton with some gritty bread. "Looks out of place, doesn't he? Not a priest's robes, but no tradesman wears white like that."

Across the room came another snippet of conversation: "—no God ever did that for me, but you look into his eyes and it changes you. As noble as a prince and just a child—"

Doranei leaned over to Sebe. His friend smelled of damp wool and sweat, but Doranei didn't imagine he was any better. "Doesn't sound like he's talking about any friend of ours," he muttered. "What do you reckon?"

Sebe shrugged. "Dressed like that I'd say he's no innocent bystander. Don't think we'll get much out of him."

"Not the first one like that I've seen round these parts," Doranei agreed. "Looks like this is the next step, they're recruiting to spread the word. There's talk of beggars gathering at the gates of the Ruby Tower, of writing prayers to the Gods and fixing them to the wall. The desperate folk have given up on the cults, they're looking for something else to believe in—and the shadow's message is ready and waiting."

Sebe's expression mirrored Doranei's own. "It's your turn then."

Doranei sighed. "True, and it won't be the last either," he said grimly. "Let's hope he gives us something useful."

The pair finished their drinks and exited, quickly finding a dark corner of the street where they could wait unmolested for the hour until the man in white left the tavern and headed off alone through the night.

By the time General Lahk had asked him for permission to call a halt on the following day, Isak was already searching his memory for a secluded spot to carry out his unsavoury business. The route was one he knew well; past the Twins the road wound through rolling hills and across great stretches of grassland where once he would have stalked splay-toed geese and set traps for hares. Most of the game would have been frightened away by the approaching army, but the region itself was unchanged from the days when he'd crossed it in the wagon train.

As the order was given, Isak stayed in the saddle, watching the soldiers around him jump to Lahk's command. He pulled the blue silk hood from his face and let the blustering breeze run its chilly fingers over his cropped scalp as he stared into the advancing evening. The supply wagons had men swarming all over them, seeking tents, food, and firewood. The sight reminded him of army ants killing a praying mantis.

Isak had widened his eyes in disbelief when he'd seen how much baggage was to accompany the armies. Combined, they numbered more than fifteen thousand men, and the Quartermaster-General, a comical little man with stumpy arms and legs called Pelay Kervar, had another thousand under his command—as many in his charge as the colonels he screamed invective at on a daily basis. When the Farlan were at war, Kervar outranked both colonels and suzerains, and his bodyguard was nearly on a par with Lord Isak's own.

Isak dismounted and spent a few minutes seeing to Toramin, his warhorse, before allowing a hovering groom to take over. It was still habit for him to attend to his own horses before making camp, but he knew there was another reason he had busied himself there. Each evening he had a promise to keep, one that left him feeling sullied and, even worse, had not yet proved as necessary as he had hoped. Commander Jachen loitered nearby, carrying a canvas sack and a few lengths of black wood in a manner that made it clear he preferred not to touch any of them.

"Still no sign of more troops from Lomin?" he asked Count Vesna, knowing he would have been told as soon as they were sighted.

"No more, no. Looks like Suzerain Suil's optimism was ill founded; the Eastmen nobles will have been glad for any excuse to stay at home and watch the fanatics leave."

In their armour, they were a striking pair: Isak in Siulents, all in silver, and Vesna in black with his roaring lion's head crest in bright gold—they drew looks even from troops used to their presence. The magic imbued in Siulents demanded attention and that effect was magnified in the fading light, while Vesna's reputation made the hero almost as noticeable to the weary soldiers.

Isak had to agree with his friend. Duke Lomin had refused Isak's summons to provide troops, not believing in Isak's promise that the east would still be defended. That gave the suzerains of the east all the excuse they needed not to join a crusade they had no interest in.

"They would have given us the superiority we need. It cannot go unanswered," Isak said, though the words felt hollow as he spoke them.

"From what the scryers tell me, I believe we still have enough," Vesna assured him. "Lord Styrax brought only a small force: four legions of infantry, three of cavalry. It seems he is adept at taking cities without any large-scale engagement. He will not have had the time he needs to prepare for us. I doubt he is even looking this way."

Isak gave him a sceptical look.

"No, perhaps it won't be that simple," Vesna said, backtracking swiftly, "but just remember, Raland and Embere are his problem. How could he possibly expect a preemptive strike from the north?"

"So we stick to the plan?"

"Certainly. The scryers have his troops outside Akell at the moment, but I'm sure he'll retreat to the south of the Circle City so he's not watching his back."

Vesna retrieved a rolled map from his saddlebag and opened it up for Isak to look at as they walked. They headed for an outcrop, little more than a rise of rocky ground held together by the roots of an ancient oak, but it afforded a little shelter from the prying eyes of soldiers.

"The majority of the ground around the Circle City is pastureland, which favours us. A southern position offers good escape routes and to a degree constrains your attackers—they must come down the channel between the city and the fens, which means you can predict the route your enemy will take and most likely prepare a few surprises there. You can station archers and light cavalry to fight a running retreat and encourage pursuit, taking down the bridges over the rivers as you fall back. And you put mages on all sides to wear your attackers down further."

"Isn't it a bit obvious?"

"Yes—but we're the ones looking for battle. Chalat wants the ground to manoeuvre in and bring our force of numbers to bear and once past the two rivers he will have plenty of that. He has excessive confidence in the discipline of his troops. The enemy knows exactly what he's facing; scryers are not easily fooled by an army on the march."

Isak grimaced. "The more I hear, the more disastrous this all sounds. Talk to General Lahk, find me options." They reached the outcrop only a few paces behind Commander Jachen.

"The religious equivalent of pissing behind a tree," Isak sighed as Jachen pulled a square wooden panel from the sack and began fitting the wooden supports into it. On the panel was a painted icon of the Wither Queen, loaned with all possible grace from the Temple of Death, and hanging from it was a small iron incense burner. That Isak was praying to the Queen each evening was not a secret, but if he did so openly, he knew others would feel honour bound to follow suit.

"Better than nothing, my Lord," Vesna said as Jachen set down the makeshift shrine and retreated. "At least it's clear you don't expect every man in the army to pray to her; the note I found in my bedroll from Lesarl's man, Soldier, made that clear enough."

Isak wrinkled his nose at the thought. "She'd be the only one of the Gods growing in strength. I don't want to imagine how she might use her power." He waved a hand at the shrine and almost immediately a dirty-coloured smoke began to leak from it.

"Ah, my Lord?" Vesna prompted as Isak knelt down before the shrine. He picked up a broken piece of branch from the floor and held it out. "If you want something hot ready when you're finished . . ."

"I'm not a performing monkey you know," Isak growled. All the same he reached out a hand and strands of greenish light swirled briefly above his palm before erupting into foot-long flames.

"I would never make money from you in that manner," Vesna said with a smile.

Isak gave a noncommittal grunt; he got the joke, but it wasn't enough to lighten his mood.

The branch quickly caught and Vesna turned back towards the camp. As he walked away he caught the bitter scent of incense and heard Isak's voice, murmuring. He picked up his pace as a woman's purring laugh echoed distantly on the wind and a dead finger ran down his spine.

Not for the first time, Vesna pressed his fingers against his left forearm and traced the shape of the flat silver case that held Karkarn's tear. The action reminded him of when his father had died and he had inherited the two gold earrings of rank; he had been forever checking the heirlooms were securely fastened, and that reminder brought a renewed ache to his heart. He had been count for six months before he grew used to their presence, and only then did the guilt of inheritance start to ebb.

When do mortals deal with Gods and come away from it well? he asked himself for the hundredth time, looking back at Isak. *And still I keep Karkarn's tear close at hand. Still I have not refused him.*

CHAPTER 33

AI PAUSED AT THE ENTRANCE of the Fearen House and pulled his coat tighter around his body. He looked back the way he had come and saw Sergeant Kayel watching him in the distance. The other two soldiers the Duchess of Byora had brought with her were busy marvelling at their first sight of the valley. The sickly looking blond man from the Byoran Guard couldn't tear his eyes off the winged white-eye, Kiallas. The slim Ruby Tower major was more interested in the massive white buildings.

There was no respite from the icy wind, even in the portico of the Fearen House. It howled around the valley like a spiteful harpy. Nai worked the arm-thick brass latch and he found himself dragged in by the door as the gale caught it and pushed it open. He managed to stop it crashing against the wall, nearly pulling his arm out of its socket in the process, but still got a furious look from the guardian who'd had to jump out of the way.

He watched Nai struggle for a moment to close the tall door before reaching to help.

"Thank you," Nai growled in his native tongue as the guardian's efforts made no appreciable difference. "Nice to have a useless streak of piss getting in the way."

The guardian's expression made it clear Nai's tone had crossed the language barrier even if the words meant nothing. As the door clanged shut he gave the man an insincere grin and headed to the centre of the room where Lord Styrax had taken over the largest of the desks. Major Amber was there as well, sitting beside his lord and staring disconsolately down at a large book lying open in front of him.

Both men wore the formal grey uniforms of the Cheme Third Legion, and Lord Styrax's massive shoulders sported the gold epaulettes of a general. Nai suspected it amused Lord Styrax to conform to the library's rules one day and ignore them the next. Up above he could hear the wind rushing over the great dome. They had lit more lamps against the gloom of a day that had never properly brightened after dawn; midday approached and still heavy shadows lurked in every corner of the library.

"My Lord," Nai murmured when he reached the U-shaped desk.

Lord Styrax held up a hand to stop him. "Unless you're an expert in Elven cross-pentameter, I'm not interested."

"It is urgent."

Styrax opened his mouth, then shut it again in a rare moment of indecision. It was another few heartbeats before he spoke again. "Very well—but quickly."

Nai noticed a curious face that had also broken off from its work. Quickly the woman looked back down again, but still Nai walked around the desk and bent down so he could whisper directly into Styrax's ear.

"My Lord, I do not know what your intelligence tells you, so I will repeat everything. A Farlan army approaches from the north; it will reach the city within three days. The Duchess of Byora offers her troops to support your own men in battle."

"She said this to you herself?"

"Her man, Kayel, told me."

Lord Styrax was silent for a long while. Unable to read the man's expression, Nai had no idea if this was news to him or not.

"That was unexpected of them," he said at last, with the hint of a smile. "It's been a while since anyone surprised me." He pointed in the direction of the gate with his damaged left hand—the dark stain of blood underneath each fingernail looked almost glassy compared with the swirls of white scar tissue covering the rest of his hand. "Find General Gaur and repeat what you told me, then tell him I want the Third Army pulled back to the Ismess-Byora border."

Nai turned to leave when Lord Styrax grabbed his arm. "Once you have done that, go to Sergeant Kayel and tell him I accept his offer, then accompany him back to Byora. Larim knows your mind well enough to speak into it?"

The necromancer wavered a moment before saying, "I have probably spent enough time in his company, yes; I assume his technique will be very similar to Isherin Purn's."

"Go then."

Nai gave a short bow and hurried off.

Amber watched as the bare-footed man struggled to control the southern door, then turned to Styrax. "My Lord, do you have orders for me?" he asked, still wondering what it was Nai had revealed.

"That I do." Styrax smiled and pointed at the book in front of the major. "What have you learned so far?"

Amber glanced down. "Not a whole lot, my Lord. I'm afraid I don't understand a word—magical theory has never made any sense to me." He was beginning to fear he was going to be set another intellectual task.

"Time for a lesson on codes then," Styrax said, not appearing to care that Amber hadn't understood.

Amber suddenly remembered something he'd heard from Colonel Uresh, his commanding officer: he'd said that Lord Styrax was an unusual sort of genius and his preferred way to work things out was with a willing pupil rather than a quiet study. It was in the explanation to another that Lord Styrax found insight.

"My Lord, I am all yours," he said with a slight smile. If this was what it took . . .

Styrax looked at him quizzically, then began, "First of all, this is not a code—it is a hidden message. A code is something we would use in a dispatch to prevent it being read by anyone intercepting it—though our preferred method is to ensure the enemy doesn't get it in the first place. This tells us something about the message before we have even read the first line."

"That someone wants it to be read?" Amber said uncertainly. "Why put it in plain sight if you don't want people to try and read it?"

Lord Styrax nodded. "Exactly, and if someone wants it to be read, then the key must be available. Making it hard to read simply means they have some choice over who does so."

"A message for scholars only?"

"Of a fashion." Styrax said cryptically and pulled over the long sheet of parchment onto which he had painstakingly transcribed the entire text of the puzzle. "Here it is in full. I have copied it down so I can work on sections. I think in Menin, of course, but the more I work on this, the easier it becomes to use the original Elven."

"How does the magical theory fit in?" Amber interjected before Lord Styrax could get into full flow.

"Problems are best solved from a variety of directions. 'In warfare all approaches should be considered in the light of dawn, midday, and dusk.'"

Amber nodded, recognising the quote from a treatise on combat called *Principles of Warfare*. Every Menin officer read it, and the Mystics of Karkarn devoted years to its study, despite its heretical author.

"I believe I know what I am looking for," Styrax continued, "and have done ever since studying the Library of Seasons as I planned this campaign. The hunt becomes easier if one knows what one is looking for."

"But no magic works here," Amber said, "so what use is the study of—" He paused to check the book again and read, "field rigidity and the period petrification effect?"

"I wished to discover whether this deadened field had been created by magic in the first place—field rigidity and period petrification are ways to determine this, even when all trace evidence has long since disappeared." Styrax gestured to the page again. "So now we have an idea of what it might be talking about, and the hypothesis that this message is intended to be read by those with the right skills."

"Crossed pentameters," Amber said suddenly, remembering his lord's earlier words.

"Cross-pentameter," the white-eye agreed, "an obscure style, but one that has been revived by different generations of Elven poets. Deverk Grast was no poet himself, but his father was an academic and I would bet the man tried to instill an education in his son."

"So he recognised the style in this puzzle!"

"He did, although either my understanding of the style is flawed or the puzzle is."

"In what way?"

"The style dictates a certain rhythm to the lines, repeated in a pattern of fives, but here the pattern is not adhered to in every line."

Amber thought for a moment, but his expression of confusion only lifted when Lord Styrax reminded him gently, "Remember, the message is intended to be read."

"The mistakes are intentional?"

Styrax nodded and pointed to the first line. "The first mistake is an obvious one. The sentence is a mess structurally, but to read it in Menin would give you 'In combat a mirror to the heavens is raised, in struggle life flourishes.'"

"That sounds familiar," Amber mused. "Oh—it's an adapted version of the first line of *Principles of Warfare*." His eyes lit up. "The message uses a reference code! I know about those, where two men have identical copies of a book and then can use numbers to refer to pages and words. Even if the coded message is intercepted, it's useless without knowing what book is to be used."

"Exactly, and this message is written in reference to a work that was originally a collection of fifty-five scrolls—and that is exactly the number of lines written in correct cross-pentameter. But it's not a scholarly work, *Principles of Warfare*, not in the usual sense. The author wants a warrior to recognise Eraliave's great work, and a scholar to know how to use cross-pentameter."

"And the incorrect lines?"

"Dummies to throw off those who might guess the source work but do not understand cross-pentameter."

"Oh," Amber said, feeling a little deflated. "I'd have expected more to it than that. Whoever devised this was a genius and clearly wanted everyone to know it. I wouldn't expect them to be wasteful."

Styrax frowned down at the poem for a moment then reached for one of the pieces of parchment he had been working on. It was covered in tiny rows of precise handwriting. "Perhaps . . ." he said softly, failing to finish the sentence. "'The longest reach requires a second step.' Could it—?"

"Is there a problem?"

Styrax looked up distractedly. "Problem? No, not at all. Quite the opposite, in fact: I think you might have saved me from making a complete fool of myself."

Amber was too astonished even to look pleased. He had never in his life expected to hear those words from the Lord of the Menin. Styrax had returned to his page by the time Amber remembered to shut his mouth again.

"Ah, glad to have helped then, sir," he muttered in a daze, getting no response. "I'll go back to my book, shall I?"

Darkness fell and Byora was quiet. A lingering fear haunted its streets, keeping most people inside. Word of the Farlan Army's approach had spread through the city like a plague; those praying it was nothing more than fancy saw their hopes disappear as every soldier in the city was called to readiness. Companies of Byoran Guard stomped their way through every district, a warning to troublemakers, while mercenaries and household guards from Coin were drafted into the regiments. Any remaining penitents in Hale were disarmed on sight.

"Do you really think he's come for Ilumene?" Sebe whispered. He and Doranei were lurking in the deep portico of the Derager Wine Store, making sure the street beyond was clear before they risked leaving.

Doranei shrugged and continued squinting through the slit-window. "What else? Can't say whether he's sent an envoy on ahead to deal with Lord Styrax, but his timing's good. Whoever's calling the shots at the Ruby Tower,

they can't afford to flee right now, it'll all go to shit so fast . . ." Doranei tailed
off for a moment. When he spoke again his voice was harder, fiercer. "The
game's too far advanced now, there's nothing more they can do about it, and
I hope it's eating them up inside. They have to wait and watch how it plays
out, or tear up their plan."

"What can we do, then?"

"Shame that demagogue Parim isn't here," Doranei said. "I'd get the bastard to start the whisper that Sergeant Kayel is the reason the Farlan are
here—that he's the one who killed Lord Bahl, or something. You never know,
people might hang him for us."

"So what's Plan B then?" Sebe muttered, trying to conceal as much as
possible his weaponry, including the crossbows hanging under each arm.

"That *was* Plan B," Doranei said sourly. "Plan A was asking Zhia to help
us get in and kill them ourselves, but she's dropped out of sight and that
scares me all by itself. Nothing we can do about it now, though, so we're
down to second-guessing what might happen next."

"So if the Farlan attack?"

Doranei shrugged. "They defend the wall. Ilumene knows what he's
about; it's got to be worth trying to keep what they've got, especially with
Aracnan to back you up and no reason to give a damn about your losses.
You'd hold as long as you could."

"That Harlequin in the deck has already been uncovered," Sebe pointed
out. "Legana's still alive, so they've got to assume Lord Isak knows all about
Aracnan by now."

"Don't matter, the bastard's had too long to practise his art—as long as
he avoids a direct confrontation, he'll survive the battle."

"So what're we about then?"

"We fall back on what we are," Doranei said. "We revert to type. First
duty of a King's Man is to poke a stick in the spokes every chance we get,
whatever the risk."

Sebe nodded, fully aware that any action they took would effectively make
them hostiles in a besieged city. "Stories about Aracnan often have him turning
up in the hour of need, so it's fair to assume he'll stick with his usual routine."

"Exactly, so when the Farlan attack the city there's a good chance we'll
end up recognising someone heading for the outer wall—either Aracnan or
Ilumene." He paused. "We'll be noticed in Eight Towers, though, so we can't
risk going in there, and once you're out the gate there's a couple of roads you
could take."

"I reckon we spread our bets and take a fork each, find a room we can each hole up in. First target is Aracnan, next best is Ilumene, but chances are you only get one shot so take whichever looks best."

"See you when the killing's done," Sebe said in a gruff voice. Sir Creyl, the commander of the Brotherhood, had come up with the phrase; now it was their standard sign-off.

The Brothers looked grim as they set off in silence through the streets, their minds fixed on the task ahead. When the time came to part, they embraced tightly before going their separate ways. Above them, the clouds rumbled with the distant promise of violence.

CHAPTER 34

HE FELT THE DARKNESS ALL AROUND HIM, crawling over his skin, choking every breath he took. The air tasted of hot ash and tears. Every droplet of stinking, greasy sweat seemed to be scalding hot on his skin, but he could not move to wipe them away. His strength had been sapped by the heat radiating out from the rock and the searing chains that bound him. The pitted, ancient iron cut grooves in his flesh, tracing a pattern of bondage across his arms, neck, and waist.

In the distance there was sound. He tried to concentrate on the noise to block out the pain, but it was not enough. Sometimes he could hear faint screams, sometimes laughter. Often there was only the slither of scales and skin over stone, or a distant booming that he felt through the rock more than heard. Whatever the sound, it was always dull and indistinct, even when the claws clicked close enough to touch his body. Hot huffs of fetid breath came accompanied by guttural snorts. Their whispers produced images in his mind, horrors he had no name for, and the words themselves were unintelligible.

It was too dark to see, but on occasion flashes of vermilion-tinted light burst in his eyes. His prison was a forgotten fissure. His blood was a feast for his monstrous attendants who crawled up walls and along the roof; sometimes they fought desperate battles, tearing shreds from their enemies; greedily gulping down chunks of hard-won flesh before the battle was even over, or they got cast into the jagged pits and yawning chasms below.

His head sagged and he stared down into the emptiness beneath his feet, mindless of the cruelties inflicted upon him. His tongue was a lead weight that filled his mouth; he could no more gag than scream. For a moment he thought perhaps he had succeeded in howling, until the stench of putrefaction and heavy rasp of limbs told him there had been another victory on the walls around him. In the prison of his mind, his screams were deafening.

Isak wrenched himself awake with such force he fell from his camp bed. He moaned and dry-retched at the memory of the dream, shudders rattling down his spine. After a few moments he forced his head up and saw the grey light of dawn creeping through the entrance of his tent. He'd managed no more than two hours of sleep and his mouth felt like it was filled with sulphurous ash.

"No good reason it's today," he said hoarsely, and reached for the wine-skin hanging from the ridgepole. "Could be nothing but some damn shadow messing with my mind, or the Reapers giving Aryn Bwr a reminder of what's waiting for him."

The wine was sour and weak, but it took away the foul taste from his mouth. His tent was simple, barely long enough to fit the whole of his over-sized body, and far from the luxury some dukes went to war in. Isak was beginning to regret his decision to set an example. The fact that Chalat had burned or redistributed the finery some clerics had brought with them was small consolation on a cold, grey morning.

The bowl of water beside his bed was far from clean, but it was good enough. Isak plunged his hands in and started scrubbing roughly at his face, desperate to get rid of the hot, greasy feel of his dream that lingered still.

Afterwards, feeling a little refreshed, he struggled into his armour. The cold in his bones began to ease once Siulents touched his skin and he felt almost human again by the time he buckled Eolis around his waist and stepped out into the dawn light.

Two men were waiting for him under a sky of heavy black clouds: the implacable white-eye and the flamboyant hero. Count Vesna was resplendent in his legendary black-and-gold plate, while General Lahk wore the austere black-and-white livery of Lord Bahl over the lighter half-armour of the Ghosts. The sight of Lahk reminded Isak that one cleric had even gone so far as to demand command of the Ghosts be given over to the cult of Death, since they wore the livery of a dead man.

"Where the buggery is Torl?" Isak snapped.

"He presents his apologies," General Lahk replied in his usual flat voice, sounding almost disinterested. "Suzerain Torl says he cannot leave Chalat's army; that he must finish what he started."

"He does remember he started it because I ordered him to?"

"Isak, he's a proud man; a man of honour," Vesna said.

The hero of the Farlan Army somehow contrived to look fresh and awake, despite the fact dawn had not fully broken yet. His golden earrings of rank gleamed in his left ear and his shining hair was neatly tied back; he looked ready to attend a parade in his honour. The scattering of grey hairs among the black only added a certain sage dignity to his ever-handsome features. Isak glowered at him.

"He will not leave them now, not after he has force-marched them here."

"He'll bloody die!" Isak protested as loudly as he dared; he did not want to attract the attention of the entire legion of Ghosts surrounding them.

"I'm sure he understands that," Vesna hissed fiercely, "but it is his choice. Torl is not a man who walks away. He's sent Tiniq back, and all those seconded to him from your personal guard, but that's as far as he's going."

Isak scowled as a woman in the quartermaster's livery ran up to him with a steaming clay pot and a large hunk of bread. He accepted both with a grunt, and when the woman looked worried, fearing she'd offended him, he managed a small smile of thanks.

"What do the scryers say?" he asked through a mouthful of bread. "The enemy have held their position. There were a few probes in the night, but nothing serious, just scouts trying to draw us after them."

"And the reinforcements?"

"Theirs or ours?" Lahk asked.

Isak shook his head in irritation. "Theirs, of course—ours are so far behind we might as well have not even bothered calling them up. I doubt they'll be here in time to bury the dead!"

"Fifteen legions, no more than two days away. We could sacrifice our light cavalry to at least slow them down but only if we could get Chalat to hold off his assault long enough for us to outflank them."

"So he didn't bother bringing his full army to conquer the Circle City?"

"You are right to be suspicious, my Lord, but where the remaining troops are I cannot say. The scryers cannot find them anywhere."

"Let's count what blessings we do have," Vesna said firmly. "Chalat is determined to march straight into Styrax's men, making himself a damn big target for whatever Styrax intends. That saves our troops from the worst of their surprises, and gives us a chance to watch out for the rest of the Menin, whether they're behind the walls of Byora or elsewhere."

Isak nodded. "And also giving us the chance to not engage at all unless we really have to. The closer we can get to Byora, the better. With luck the

Ghosts can break through the gates and take the Ruby Tower. Either way, we don't want to give Azaer any space to intervene if we can help it."

"I doubt the opportunity will arise, my Lord," Lahk said. Everything I hear about Kastan Styrax makes me certain there *will* be a surprise waiting."

"I know, but it's still not why we're here. There's a fair chance he'll take Chalat out after the initial charge—if he does, those mercenaries will fall back. That's our opportunity to treat with Styrax—we can tell the clerics it's a ruse; if they do object, they'll be too disorganised to do anything about it in time."

Lahk bowed, his face expressionless. "As you wish, my Lord."

"How near ready are we?"

"Two legions mounted and formed up, plus the First Guardsmen to the east," Vesna said, pointing to Isak's left, "and the Fordan and Tebran divisions behind you."

As he spoke, an aide ran up with a scout in tow. The soldier was dressed more like a forester: his poorly fitting tunic had been reinforced with steel strips and he carried a light helmet. A long dagger was tucked into in his belt; if he had a bow, clearly he'd left it with his horse.

"Report," Lahk commanded as the pair saluted Isak.

"General," the aide began breathlessly, "Lord Chalat has given the order to advance." Isak guessed the youth to be a couple of years younger than he was himself, probably a noble son assigned to Lahk's command staff since it was deemed a relatively safe post.

"Disposition?" he asked.

"Wide advance, sir," the scout replied confidently. His accent marked him as a man of the mountains, despite the absence of any identifying badge. He was twice the age of Lahk's aide, and obviously experienced, if the scar on his face was anything to go by. "Divisions o' Knights o' the Temples and pen-itents, with Chalat and the Cardinal Paladins in the centre, Dark Monks on the left flank, and the rest o' the penitents on the right—penitents're in tight division blocks, though Suzerain Torl don't look like he 'eard the order quite right and chose to stay loose."

"Damn Chetse don't know anything about cavalry," Vesna muttered. "It's a wonder he's got them moving at all."

The scout wisely chose not to comment, but continued, "The Siul legions are clearing ahead; enemy's got archers and light cavalry stationed at each bridge. They'll have engaged by now."

"What state are the rivers in?"

"Look high to me, sir—the ground's soft, so I'd say there's been a fair amount of rain. Can still be crossed, but only slowly. I'd not want to be the one trying to outflank the enemy."

Lahk turned to Isak. "My Lord, we should have the Tirah cavalry standing ready as rearguard—if the enemy does have reserves hidden behind Byora's walls, we need to move now to ensure they're not exposed."

Isak sighed and looked up at the sky. *It's promising rain, and if it does, It'll be even harder going. The more bogged down the clerics get, the more likely it is we'll engage and I'll end up face to face with Lord Styrax.*

"Give the order," he said to the general. "It's going to be a long, hard day."

Dawn turned into morning with a sullen reluctance. Isak had a clear view of the battlefield from atop a small rise. In the east was the massive bulk of Blackfang, and in front was Byora. He had a fine view of the two levels which rose up from behind the main wall of the city. The quarter's unnaturally tall towers were dwarfed by the great black cliffs behind.

He couldn't see Akell; it was hidden by a sloping spur of rock that jutted out from the main bulk of Blackfang. *Pretty obvious the Circle City isn't really one continuous city,* he thought to himself. Outside the Byora city wall was a wide skirt of buildings that looked like shanties, getting progressively larger and nicer the further they were from the wall. Larger detached houses and farms dotted the land all the way to Ismess.

To the west were the mist-covered fens that spoiled the view from the Duchess of Byora's Ruby Tower. They looked closer to the city than Isak remembered. Even in his childhood when he was running wild, Isak had kept away from the fens: they were treacherous at the best of times. The wagon brat might not have been welcome on the streets of Burn or Wheel, but all the same he'd never wandered far from the city.

The waterlands were gateways to Death's realm, like ponds and lakes: still waters attracted all sorts of malign spirits and creatures, quite apart from whatever might come through those gateways. The fens were studded with copses of bent and twisted marsh-alder and silvery ghost willows, and they looked forbidding even in high summer. Isak had heard more stories of the

Coldhand Folk, will o' the wisps, Finntrail, and the like in Byora than anywhere else outside of Tirah. The hunting could be good in the fens, and the
willows from which the medicinal bark was harvested were plentiful, but no
one disputed the very real dangers either entailed.

"Shall I send the engineers now, my Lord?" said a voice from Isak's knee,
making him jump a little. He looked down to see Quartermaster-General
Kervar standing beside Isak's horse, looking out over the battlefield.

"The bridges? Aye, it's time."

After he'd carried out Isak's order, Kervar pulled his own mount away
from Toramin, Isak's massive charger. Bored of standing still, he'd decided to
investigate the horse next to him, and that was making Kervar's beast decidedly nervous.

Isak gave the reins a tug to quieten the fiery stallion and looked up. He
didn't need to see the Poacher's Moon, hidden by heavy clouds, to know it
was approaching midmorning. There was a stiff southwesterly breeze running across the plain, which would be enough to blunt the effect of the
enemy's strafing attacks.

Isak had studied the record books in Tirah Palace during the depths of
winter, and he had discovered that the Farlan heavy cavalry was always the
last weapon to be used in any battle. Most Farlan victories were because the
horse-archers were not only excellent marksmen—although that was part of
it—but they were so much more manoeuvrable than their enemies. The
classic Farlan tactic was to send the heavy cavalry in after the enemy had been
weakened by the others—which, Isak suspected, allowed them to sleep late
and enjoy a leisurely breakfast while the commoners did most of the work.

"Chalat is taking his time, I'm glad to see," Vesna said, breaking the con-
templative silence. They had an almost unrestricted view of the battlefield,
all the way to the ancient boundary wall three miles away. The Menin were
dug in behind that wall.

"At least he's not lost all his senses," agreed Lahk. "He's giving the skirmishers a chance to make a mistake before he fords that second river."

Isak managed a weak smile. The palace records had left one clear impression in his mind as he read them: most battles were lost because of one of
three factors: poor communication, bad luck, or stupidity.

Chalat's men were roughly halfway between Isak, at the rear of his own
men, and the Menin. It had taken them several hours to cross a mile of
ground and the first river. The bridges across the second river had been
destroyed by the retreating Menin, who now loitered just out of range, ready

to take out anyone who got within bowshot. The problem was simple: how to get across the river without losing hundreds of men.

"I'm bored," Isak announced. He pointed to the horsemen arrayed ahead of him. "Sound the advance," he ordered, gesturing towards Byora. The main gate lay between the rivers.

On the left flank were three divisions of the Palace Guard's heavy cavalry, with the College of Magic regiment nestled between them. The colourful centre consisted of various suzerains and their hurscals, a number of other noblemen, all in heavy armour, and two full legions of light cavalry. Next to them were two thousand more light cavalry in loose formation. The reserve troops, the last division of Ghosts and the remaining two cavalry legions, were on the far right.

General Lahk inclined his head. "Bugler, sound slow advance," he called, and behind him a set of three long notes sounded. The call was quickly taken up and Isak's army, looking like a great bloated beast heaving itself forward, began to advance.

Isak caught Count Vesna giving him a pointed look and he frowned for a moment, wondering what he'd forgotten. Then he got it and in a loud voice said, "Gentlemen, your helms." As he settled Siulents over his own head Isak caught a glimpse of Vesna touching his fingers to his left wrist. *Even our heroes need a lucky charm*, he thought with a sigh. *All I've got is a contingency plan that scares the shit out of me.*

In the distance he could just make out the black dot of Lord Styrax's enormous army standard. As though in response to his darkening mood he felt a tug at his mind from the Crystal Skull fused to his cuirass. The Reapers were stirring: they smelled death on the air. Up above him, clouds gathered, as though summoned by his call.

"Good to have you back, sir."

Amber looked up, his eyes widening. "Gods! What have I told you about taking your helm off, Deebek?"

The ageing sergeant grinned, showing an irregular set of broken teeth. "I weren't t'do it, sir. Said it pissed you off when I did that."

"Exactly," Amber agreed, thumping the man heavily on his armoured shoulder. Standing around Sergeant Deebek was his squad, all young men he didn't know, and all wearing expressions of relieved anxiety.

"I know we give you recruits to break them into the harsh realities of a soldier's life, but for pity's sake don't make them look at your face all the time as well!" he laughed.

There was no getting around the fact that Deebek was an ugly man— he'd not been a handsome child, what with arms looking too short for his stocky torso, but getting kicked in the face by a mule at the age of five hadn't helped. Then a warhammer crumpled the front of his helm and completed the job, leaving the tip of his nose sliced off by the torn metal. His cheek had shattered under the impact and his teeth and jaw were so ruined that it was a mercy Deebek had been knocked unconscious by the blow. There'd been no neat way of removing the embedded metal from his face, so it had been done quick and nasty, and that had woken him up quick enough.

"You really are a lucky bastard," Amber said, staring at the ruin of Deebek's face. Every time he returned from a mission and saw Deebek again, he was reminded of how close the man had come to an excruciatingly painful death—instead of the excruciatingly painful recovery that had left him looking like this. Amber was gripped with renewed fascination and revulsion, as usual.

"Don't I know it, sir," Deebek said, "and that's why I makes sure all m'boys gets themselves decent headgear."

Looking around him Amber realised it was true. Every one of the recruits had the top-of-the-range one-piece Y-faced helms. Normally any decent bit of armour got nicked off the recruits soon enough, but clearly Deebek had put a stop to that, at least where his boys were concerned. No one could fault him for that; if he'd been wearing anything less that day twenty years ago, Deebek would have been stone dead.

"How's it looking over there?" Amber looked out past the wall they were dug in behind. He could see the advancing Farlan well enough, but Deebek was one of the most experienced sergeants in Amber's division, and always worth sounding out.

Deebek's face went serious all of a sudden. "Goin' to be nasty, Major, that's for sure. Won't be long now. They're workin' their way over, and our horseboys ain't done much yet."

On the other side of the wall, six feet away from the base, they'd dug a foot-deep trench. They'd not had the time to prepare serious earthworks beyond a few pits a hundred and fifty paces from the wall, but the trench had been easy work, and at least it would give the Farlan horsemen pause for thought when they tried to leap the wall.

Amber looked at the crossbowmen bolstering the heavy infantry stationed along the wall. There were more companies waiting behind. Their bows might not be as good—or as plentiful—as the Farlan cavalry, but they'd blunt any charge.

The minotaurs, Bloodsworn knights, and a legion of light cavalry were covering the open ground on the right: they were all fast enough and dangerous enough to dissuade anyone from attempting to outflank them. On the left flank another legion of light cavalry were deployed behind a small wood, in which were two regiments of infantry and a spiderweb of cables strung between the trees, guaranteed to inconvenience anyone riding through. It was the weaker flank, but only time would tell whether the Farlan would take the bait.

"Going to get close and nasty," Amber pronounced, "just how we like it."

On the field ahead of them, two regiments of skirmishing cavalry moved into action, strafing the central part of the Farlan army. The colourful robes indicated priests, and there was a regiment of knights Amber couldn't identify. They wouldn't hold for long; the numbers bearing down on them were too great. In response to their arrows a lance of flame spat out from the advancing Farlan and engulfed the skirmishers nearest them.

"Karkarn be with us," Amber breathed, realising the fire was pinpointing Lord Chalat's position. The air shimmered above the white-eye and shapes began to appear in the sky. The archers immediately started to fall back, and he knew the cavalry would follow soon.

"Piss and daemons, what are they?" Deebek said, voicing everyone's thought.

Amber peered at the sky, then realised what he was seeing. "Gods," he muttered out loud, "they're actually bloody Gods! Those mad bastard priests have summoned their Aspect-Guides!"

As though in confirmation a figure of flame rose up from just ahead of the Farlan ranks, taller and broader than any mere human, even a white-eye. A deep roar echoed over the fields, causing one of Deebek's recruits to jump.

"Don't let that worry you, boys," Amber yelled cheerfully. "Stick those priests full of arrows and the Aspects'll be gone like piss in a river." He just hoped he was right about that.

He turned to leave for his own assigned command, fifty yards further on, where a beastmaster was standing holding Lord Styrax's hissing wyvern on a long rein. The blue-green beast was saddled and ready for battle. It sat up on its haunches and peered towards the enemy, half unfurling its pale blue wings until the beastmaster gave the reins another hard jerk and pulled the head down to his shoulder.

"Cover up that ugly mug, Sergeant, they're coming," he called over his shoulder. Deebek's laughter followed Amber as he pulled his scimitars from their sheaths and knocked the pommel of one against his own helm to ensure it was snug.

"Wouldn't want to frighten the bastards, eh, Major?" the sergeant called, and he raised his sword above his head in acknowledgement.

As the sound of hooves came closer he picked up the pace to reach his position, making sure he slapped his gloved hand on the helm of every man he passed. Captain Hain gave him a quick salute and looked nervously back at the snarling monster.

"Major," called a voice, and Amber spotted his commander, Colonel Uresh, riding towards him, with Army Messenger Karapin and a green-clad mage following close behind. "All done?" The old soldier looked invigorated by the coming fight, his lined face showing an energy at odds with his age— he and Amber's father were born in the same year. He might not be in the thick of battle himself, but still he wore heavy infantryman's armour.

"Aye, sir," Amber replied, saluting in turn. "Every officer's got his orders, every man knows his place." He pointed towards the Farlan centre. "Looks like Lord Chalat's leading the charge; we'll need an extra regiment or two to stop him breaking the line."

The colonel stood up in his stirrups to get a better view of the battlefield. "I'll give the order. Anything more, I'll be with the Reavers, waiting to signal our reserves. Good luck, Major,"

As soon as Amber returned the salute Uresh spurred his horse and was off again, leaving the two younger men behind pushing hard to keep up. The major took a quick look at the mist-covered fens, where Lord Styrax had stationed the rest of the Third Army—together with a pair of Adepts of the Hidden Tower, and six scryers who were most likely fainting with exhaustion as they continued to keep the presence of so many men hidden from the Farlan scryers. They had to be praying the Farlan hadn't started to wonder about the mist, which hadn't shifted at all. Luckily, the grim weather made it look much more natural. "Think our luck's going to hold, Hain?" he asked quietly.

The young captain grinned and he raised his long axe, the head painted with Lord Styrax's fanged skull emblem.

"Luck? You know we don't need that! We'll be building another monument to our lord's glory before the day is out."

Out of habit, Amber's finger went to the ceramic plaque fixed to his breastplate. Every soldier in the army had one, no matter what regiment he belonged to. "Aye, there'll be more skulls than Death himself knows what to do with," he said with a smile, while his mind conjured up the image of books on magical theory and theology piled on a desk in the Fearen House. For the first time he wondered whether there might be more to the monuments they had built in Kastan Styrax's honour.

Karkarn's horn, aren't I glad to be Menin? he thought with heartfelt sincerity. He turned to the beastmaster, who was still struggling to keep the wyvern under control. "Time for you to go; tell Lord Styrax he's got a good half hour before we'll need him."

The man saluted and yanked the reins hard, pulling the wyvern down far enough for it to let him scramble up into the saddle strapped to it. After a few eager hops the creature unfurled its wings and took off. Amber watched as the beastmaster directed an obscene gesture towards the advancing Farlan and then went to business.

"Archers ready!"

"Second group; attack!" Suzerain Torl yelled to his bugler and wrenched his horse around to head away from the enemy. Out of the corner of his eye he saw Count Macove lead out the second wave of Brethren knights, but he couldn't follow their progress until he'd gone another hundred yards and turned around and by then the men had switched from bows to engage with lances. With the Brethren and Bloodsworn both in dark uniforms it was hard to tell how they were faring at that distance, but he could hear the brutal crash of weapons.

"Bugler, tell the reserves to advance," he ordered.

The man sounded a flurry of notes, which were repeated back a few moments later. The division was arranged in three lines, bows at the ready, no more than a hundred yards from the fighting. Torl looked for the short figure of Suzerain Saroc, but he couldn't pick out his friend amongst the crowd. The only man not in a Brethren uniform was Chaplain Wain, who was standing up in his stirrups and waving his moon-glaive like a berserker.

Under Torl's commands his own division reordered itself and turned to face the enemy again, advancing to the right wing of the reserves with a clear gap between. They had the advantage of speed over the Bloodsworn and the minotaurs; as soon as they clashed, there'd be no avenue of escape and the Farlan men would likely be crushed.

On Torl's extreme left, a division of Farlan light cavalry were doing their best to distract the minotaurs and break up the Menin line, but their arrows didn't seem to be having much effect. The beasts had been making a terrible racket even before they took any casualties, and as Torl watched, they pulled further left, having seen their Menin counterparts creeping around behind the minotaurs, trying to outflank them. The Menin light cavalry were holding back, cautious of a head-on charge they wouldn't win. Although they'd really only drifted from one side of their lines to the other, looking for an opening, Torl knew he couldn't afford to let them get around.

"Call Macove back," he called, judging the benefits of his forward momentum to have finished now. As the bugler sounded the order, some of the soldiers began to peel away even before the order was repeated. "Come on," he said, gripping his reins, "you're hating this, so just fucking charge us!"

"Bastards aren't listening, sir," Brother-Captain Sheln said from beside him. He wore an open helm which had only a leaf-shaped noseguard to protect his face. For the first time that Torl could remember there was colour in Sheln's cheek—obviously leaving his lance-head in a knight's throat had a better effect on some than others.

"They won't," Torl predicted. "Looks like everything we've heard about the Bloodsworn is true. Bugler, tell the reserves to advance and fire on the minotaurs—let's see how much punishment they can take."

"Arrows!" called a man, pointing ahead as dark streaks began to slam into Macove's retreating division, courtesy of a group of crossbowmen who had appeared on the centre ground. There weren't that many men, but the crossbows were powerful weapons and it wouldn't take many volleys to leave the division disordered and vulnerable.

"Division advance at the canter," Torl roared, "bows ready! Close the range and fire as you go!"

As he urged his horse forward he saw the majority of the centre line had closed with the Menin line—a fine idea if one were leading the Ten Thousand, no doubt, but in this case it was a waste, using cavalry to fight on infantrymen's ground.

We're not going to break them on this flank. The minotaurs are their only weak point here and we can't bring a sustained attack to bear. If you do have a plan, Chulai, now's the time.

Amber swivelled and chopped down through the shaft, swinging up his shield as the Farlan passed him and smashing it into the man's side, almost knocking him from the saddle. Hain jumped forward and hacked into the man's back with his axe, he screamed as his horse carried him on past, and the two Menin were onto the next enemy soldier.

The stretch of wall they'd been defending had collapsed under the weight of a falling horse and the Farlan were piling towards the gap. Although they couldn't charge, they still had the advantage of height.

Amber chanced a step forward again and gasped as a spear missed his face by scant inches. The man who'd thrown it was already reaching for his mace when a crossbow bolt knocked him from the saddle, but a moment later he was replaced by another. They wore filthy robes over their mismatched armour and sported symbols of the Gods. Amber hadn't heard the Farlan cults had been recruiting, but that's what it looked like to him. Penitents of Karkarn were a common enough sight back home and he recognised the War God's black dragon's head symbol sewn over the man's heart.

The penitent was unable to get his horse past the wall, so he leaned over in his saddle and struck down at the shield of a private standing next to Amber. The blow sent the man to his knees, but it gave Amber the opening he needed. More spears were thrown; the Farlan charge had been halted for the moment, held by the Menin line of infantry. Amber bellowed words of encouragement which were taken up by the sergeants along the line.

The Farlan were unable to use the weight of their horses in a charge, so they were getting picked off one by one. It wasn't long before the recall was sounded.

"Hold the line!" Amber yelled at the top of his voice, but he needn't have worried. The Cheme troops were content to watch the Farlan retreat; only a few crossbow bolts and the odd boo followed the retreating Farlan. Then Amber saw a flowing white figure twice the height of a man flicker suddenly and vanish: someone had taken out a priest. The Aspect's disappearance was met with a renewed cheer. Judging by the bodies strewn on the ground and the horses milling around, the priests and their knights had put up quite a fight.

"They'll be back," Captain Hain commented, letting the axe handle slide through his hand until the butt hit the ground and he could rest his arm on the weapon, "but that could have gone worse!"

Amber nodded. "Took me by surprise, though. I was expecting something more than a straight charge."

"Maybe what we heard about Farlan cavalry is only rumour," Hain laughed. "Maybe they made it up themselves to make folk run away."

Amber took a quick count of their losses; it didn't take him long to confirm that the Farlan had been badly mauled. "Something's wrong sure enough," he said. "They're doing themselves no favours, fighting like this."

"We didn't get the worst of it," Hain said, pointing east.

"Aye, hope there's something left of Larim's coterie over there," Amber said. "Looked like they were having to deal with a whole lot of flames."

Lord Chalat might have been deposed and turned mad with fanaticism, but his power was undiminished. The Chosen of Tsatach was well known for walking into battle wreathed in flame and directing great torrents of fire towards the enemy. They couldn't match him for raw power, so three members of Larim's new coterie had been ordered to do nothing but deflect his attacks throughout the battle, blunting his efforts to break the line.

Amber breathed deeply. The air felt cold in his lungs, as though evening was drawing in, but he knew it was no later than midday. Assuming there were no breaks in the line, they'd be defending for another hour, he guessed. The Menin didn't have enough cavalry to countercharge, and they needed to wait for the right moment before committing their reserves.

The minotaurs and Bloodsworn had loaded the right flank specifically to encourage the Farlan to attack the left. The main bulk of reserves were infantry, so they needed the Farlan close. If Lord Chalat broke through the centre, they would have to deploy the reserves and hope their cavalry would be enough to screen five legions of infantry from the waiting Farlan behind.

"Come on, you bastards," he whispered, "take the bait."

"They're redeploying, my Lord," General Lahk said, standing up in his stirrups. "Going to turn to the right flank."

Isak looked back at the ongoing battle. His stomach was a tight ball of fear and nerves, and he knew he was clinging to the false hope that the departure of the wyvern meant Lord Styrax was absent. No plan, however brilliant, survived contact with the enemy, after all. The whole reason Isak had raced to the Circle City was to catch his enemies unaware—to act contrary to expectation.

"How can you tell?" Isak asked after a few moments. "You can't hear the orders from here."

"Look over there, to the extreme right," Vesna advised. He pointed past the copse of ash trees that was the only cover bigger than a house anywhere on the whole Menin line. "The cavalry units there; they're not penitents, they're the Siul legions."

"And they're engaging directly," Isak said, thinking aloud, "not trying to draw out pursuit."

"They would only do that if ordered," Lahk said, "which means Chalat wants to suck in some of the infantry units on that flank before he charges."

Isak couldn't help looking back at Byora; the Ruby Tower was easy to pick out at this distance. He had seen enough battles now to know that nothing would happen immediately—no matter how well trained the men, it takes time to react when the smallest unit involved is a division, five hundred men.

"Are you there, shadow?" he whispered to himself, "staring out of Ilumene's eyes—or that little boy, maybe? Are you afraid yet? You thought you were safe here, and now you realise it's luck, not artifice, that will keep you alive."

"Starting to move, my Lord," Lahk commented. "If the enemy has a trick up his sleeve, he'll use it now."

Isak turned back. "Torl's going to be damn lonely on that left flank, isn't he? He's got to hold, or they'll get rolled up by the minotaurs and Bloodsworn."

"Don't worry about Torl, my Lord," Vesna said. "They won't get around him, and they'll have a hard time catching him. Remember, he usually rides with the light cavalry. He knows their tactics better than any Farlan alive."

Isak suddenly went very still as a chill ran down his spine. For a moment his head swam, as if the Land had unexpectedly shifted around him, and nebulous grey swirls passed across his vision as the air went cold in his lungs. For a moment he thought it was Azaer's presence reaching out to him, but then he heard a familiar laboured breathing at the back of his mind. It was no shadow; it was the Soldier, Death's hand on the battlefield.

Now he could feel them at his sides, closer even than Vesna and Lahk. The Headsman was on his left, waiting with terrible patience; the Soldier on his right was so close the fingers of his sword hand ached for Eolis. In the shadows of his peripheral vision the Great Wolf took slow, stalking steps, while the Burning Man stared hungrily towards Lord Chalat.

"*Leave them, you cannot help them,*" came a whisper in his mind, a voice he had barely heard in months. Aryn Bwr, the last king of the Elves, had stayed hidden in the deepest recesses of Isak's soul, hemmed in by the Aspects of Death tied to Isak's shadow who so dearly wanted to claim him.

"*The moments slip by, one by one,*" replied the Headsman. Isak could feel the finality of each word like the vibrations of a tolling bell. "*Your time is coming. Your last refuge will soon be no more.*"

"*Turn to Byora,*" urged Aryn Bwr, desperation creeping into his voice. "*Forget the priests who would murder you in a heartbeat. You came for the shadow's disciples and now they are within your grasp.*"

"*The last grains are falling,*" the Headsman intoned, "*and we come for you, heretic.*"

Isak shook his head, trying to drive away the nagging voices. "Gods damn you all," he growled, one hand on Toramin's neck, aching to feel living flesh instead of dead souls. He blinked and the images of the Reapers faded away from his perception as they stepped back, content to wait once more.

"My Lord?" Vesna asked, trying not to sound concerned.

Isak looked at him. His friend again had his fingers pressed to his wrist, almost as though taking his own pulse—as though reminding himself he was still alive.

"I'm fine, it's just the voices in my head." He tried to sound amused, but it failed and he fell silent again. He rested his hand on the emerald pommel of Eolis for comfort.

"My Lord, the fens!" Lahk roared and as they turned, the mist over the fens was suddenly swept up and away and Isak felt an icy hand close around his heart. The fens were as they had been in his memory. There on the ground, about half a mile from the copse of tall ash trees, were dark blocks of soldiers rather than grass-choked patches of water. They were already marching, three legions of infantry advancing in a line as cavalrymen made their way around them to encircle the attacking Farlan.

"My Lord," General Lahk continued, "we have no choice now! They're outnumbered; if we sit and watch they'll be massacred and we'll be next."

"*The last grains are falling,*" came the mocking singsong whisper at the back of his mind.

Isak felt his body go rigid, every muscle tensing as the enormity of the decision crashed down on top of him. The clatter of voices and weapons faded to nothing and he was left in silence, staring out across the untended fields. All he was aware of were the heaving clouds above and the cold taste of mud on the breeze.

The scent of the grave filled his mind. His fists clenched so tightly that his hands shook like an old man's, but still Isak did nothing but stare over the drab fields where he would die.

Oh Gods, is it really true? I can't . . . The thought died unfinished. It wasn't that he couldn't believe it; the problem was that he could. What he couldn't do was *disbelieve*, though he had tried for months, hoping and praying, ignoring his instincts in favour of the preferable alternatives: possibilities that were all perfectly plausible, even likely . . .

It changed nothing, for the fact remained that he knew it was coming. The Reapers in his shadow could sense it; they were licking their lips in anticipation of the spirit that would be released when Isak died.

He could not escape it. He could not run, or pretend, or delay. The sands of time had run out; he could not abandon his fighting men and turn home again, for they would be slaughtered and that would give the enemy the reason to march north, confident that Isak would do nothing but cower at home.

The Farlan would be broken by a leader who betrayed the men he marched with. He had to give the order, and trust in a quiet little man to save him. He had to ignore the terror and pain and put his entire trust in a man whose whole life was centred on failure.

"Isak!" Vesna bellowed, grabbing his arm in a desperate attempt to get a reaction.

Isak flinched, staring wild-eyed at his friend for a moment before obeying the burn in his lungs and gasping for breath like a man emerging from deep water.

"Go," he said, his parched throat making the word an unintelligible mess. Isak coughed and swallowed his fear. "Sound the attack," he croaked.

I'm frightened.

CHAPTER 35

KASTAN STYRAX TURNED THE PAGE as his eyes drifted over the words without even registering their meaning. All around him a heavy silence reigned. There was only one other person in the Fearen House, an elderly woman who seemed oblivious of events beyond the library. The fact that Styrax was dressed in a full suit of armour had prompted a puzzled frown when he first entered the building, but it had been momentary.

Had she recalled the provenance of the armour—forged by Aryn Bwr, stripped from the corpse of Prince Koezh Vukotic—that might have sparked her interest, but he guessed she was not sufficiently engaged in the Land's events to make the connection. He'd discovered that even the sounds of a man moving in heavy armour were not enough to disturb a rather deaf academic.

A few minutes more, Styrax thought with anticipation, *and I might just capture your attention.*

Without warning the great doors of the main entrance crashed open. Styrax heard Kiallas gasp in shock, but he didn't look up. He knew who it would be, just as he knew what he was about to say. Brisk footsteps approached the desk, a man determined not to run for his lord, no matter how urgent the news might be.

"Lord Styrax," Larim said, in carefully measured tones. In the stillness the white-eye mage's deep voice carried all around the room, echoing up from the tiled floor.

"Lord Larim," Styrax acknowledged. At last he lifted his eyes from the book and looked directly at Larim. The man wore the patchwork robes of Larat's Chosen, but unlike his predecessor, he had no objects of power sewn into the cloth. Here and there were patches that were encased in silver frameworks, charms of all sorts, but they were all minor, defensive. "You bring news?"

"Your wyvern has been loaded and awaits your order."

"Excellent," Styrax said with a smile. "How fares the battle?"

Larim shrugged. "They attack, we defend."

Styrax could see the man was surreptitiously trying to identify the open book on the desk and he smiled inwardly. Clearly Larim hadn't realised they had been playing red herrings with him, carefully choosing which books he would see whenever he was in the room.

How disappointing of you, Larim. Even Amber caught on to that one. Today he had picked a book almost at random to read. He had finished his research and solved the puzzle of the heart, so now he was simply waiting for the rest of the Land to fall into place around him.

"A little more detail, if you please."

Larim's white eyes gleamed as he fought the urge to retort. The Chosen of Larat remained, at heart, as aggressive and argumentative as any white-eye. The more power they gathered, the less willing they were to accept the authority of any other man.

"My coterie tells me they have prevented Chalat from breaking the line. The reserves have joined the battle. Lord Isak's army has not yet engaged; they are stationed in battle order outside Byora."

"They will have to join the battle soon," Styrax said confidently. "Without them Chalat's troops will be slaughtered."

"Why would he hold back?"

"*Why indeed?*" *Because there's something in Byora he wants—that can be the only reason we've been promised support from the lovely duchess, and why she will provide it. Our friend the shadow feels the pinch.* "Go and join General Gaur," Strayx said after a moment of thought. "I will be along presently."

"As you command," Larim said icily. He bowed briefly and strode out through the still-open doors. Styrax looked out for a moment and saw the darkening colour of the clouds above the cliff wall.

"Isak Stormcaller," he said softly, "let me educate you on how a master does it."

He waited a few minutes to ensure Larim was well on his way out of the valley before closing the book. To his mage's senses the library felt dull and dormant; the air was so dry to the taste that there was barely even a flicker of anticipation in his stomach for what he was about to do.

Are the years catching up with me, or does this lack the sense of occasion I felt on Thotel's Temple Plain? he wondered. He stood and looked around the room, ignoring Kiallas's suspicion look. Gesh, the greatest of the winged white-eyes, had abandoned him for the first time since he had arrived at the library. He was busy overseeing their defences, Strayx imagined, leaving the older but no-less-haughty Kiallas as chaperone. So much the better; Kiallas was by far the stupider of the two.

"Kiallas," he began, noting the slight widening of the eyes, "have you ever wondered about the puzzle of the heart?"

The white-eye stared at Styrax for a time, then shook his head. "I do not waste my time with childish games."

"Of course you don't," Styrax agreed, "the duty of the guardians of the library is too solemn for that. I would appreciate it, however, if you would indulge me." He gestured towards the column in the centre of the library and as he did so, he saw the Litse's hand tighten on the shaft of his javelin.

With exaggerated care Styrax's hand went to a sheath on his belt and he pulled out a trio of stilettos, which he fanned out in front of him. Styrax watched the Litse's face; Kiallas obviously realised it would be foolish to raise the question of what was and wasn't allowed in the library in terms of weapons.

"Please take one," he said, offering them over hilt-first. Cautiously Kiallas did so, and Styrax walked over to the black stone column. The golden half-sphere at the top gleamed with a warm yellow light, attesting to the purity of the gold that had been used. Styrax knelt down and pointed with one armoured finger to a rune.

"Do you see this rune? Could you put the tip of that knife to the cross-piece?"

"What is all this?"

"I'm going to solve the puzzle, of course, but it requires three daggers to be used at once and I have only two hands. It would be a little undignified if I have to take my boot off," he said with an apologetic smile, pointing at his armoured foot.

Kiallas didn't share the humour, but it seemed to do the trick nonetheless. Javelin still at the ready, the Litse knelt and placed the stiletto at the appropriate spot, while still contriving to keep his spine as upright as possible. Styrax walked to the other side and took up position. He took a moment to identify the correct runes, then placed the knife points at the centre of each, one on a horizontal bar across the rune, the other vertical.

"On the count of three, push the stiletto into the stone," he said.

Kiallas peered around the monument at him. "In?"

"It will go easily enough. One, two, *three*."

The two men slid the stilettos forward in unison and both felt something inside give way under the pressure. The thin-bladed knives pushed smoothly into the rock until their hilts met the column.

"Now we will turn the whole column to the right," he said, "using the handles."

Kiallas, now intrigued, did as he was told and they found it turned with oiled ease until it came to an abrupt halt. Styrax smiled. "At this point, if it hadn't been for Major Amber, I might have looked a little silly." He drew one of the stilettos halfway out and turned the column an eighth of a circle back the way it had come. "Impatience will do that, I suppose," he added, watching the column rise very slightly as the base moved onto what looked like a sloped track.

Kiallas didn't reply. He was still staring in wonder at the column which had never moved an inch throughout his entire life. Styrax didn't take the lack of conversation to heart; that would be churlish under the circumstances.

Instead, he was still smiling amiably when he whipped one of the stilettos out of the column and into Kiallas's neck.

The razor-sharp blade slid into flesh and bone even more easily than it had into the stone. Kiallas continued to look surprised as his fingers loosened from the knife hilt and his corpse overbalanced. He sprawled untidily on the floor, trapping one elegant wing under his body.

"Interested yet, dear?" Styrax said quietly to the elderly scholar.

Her head remained bent over a parchment; she appeared to have noticed none of the drama being acted out ten yards from where she sat.

"No? Well, I shall not be deterred," he said and crouched a little lower. He placed his hands on either side of the column and tensed his massive shoulders. With one smooth movement he lifted the column up a good eight inches and let it fall to one side. The solid block hit the tiled floor with an enormous crash, shattering the tiles underneath and—finally—causing the old woman to shriek in alarm.

Styrax respectfully inclined his head to her before looking down into the hole in the ground. There, nestled in a close-fitting depression and surrounded by markings in the same script as those on the column, was a Crystal Skull.

"The Skull of Blood," he said to himself. "Three down, nine to go." He paused. "Two of which are about to be delivered to me."

He reached down and pulled the Skull free. He felt a shudder run through the building, followed by a sudden rushing sound that he sensed as much as heard. He stood, taking a deep breath and filling his lungs, and a gasp of pleasure grew into a great laugh as he felt magic flood through his body.

The cool air shimmered all around him as the spell was broken and magic returned to the valley, rolling down from the heavens to fill the parched ground with tang and fire, swirling around Styrax like a lightning-filled storm-cloud.

He blinked as the colours of the Fearen House blazed brighter and more brilliant, while the weight of his armour disappeared. In the grim winter light, tinted in Styrax's eyes by the aching absence of magic, the Fearen House had looked impressive, but soulless. Now he took a moment to admire the building anew, wondering at the glorious grandeur of the high walls and their vibrant, gold-edged flags, staring up at the intricate carvings on the dome's supporting beams.

A soft sound beyond normal hearing drifted through the room and broke his concentration. His quivering senses immediately snapped to attention as he became aware of a slow sense of vastness coming awake: a mind, huge and ancient, but not yet aware.

"Ah yes, the guardian," he said, looking down at the discarded stone column. With magic coursing through his body the gold looked dull, insignificant. "The threat that has stayed countless hands. Zhia Vukotic, let this be an object lesson; I am not like the rest of humanity."

Styrax pushed the Crystal Skull to his chest and held it there until the object melted into the black whorled metal. That done, he headed for the doorway, collecting his helm as he passed and giving the old woman another respectful nod. "You might want to stay there and keep quiet," he advised cheerily. "The librarian is in something of a mood."

As he walked outside and saw the first shocked faces, Styrax felt the awakening mind growing stronger and more distinct. Looking over towards the gate he saw more Litse guardians milling in disarray, their panicked voices lost on the wind. Through them raced his wyvern, its powerful legs driving it forward in leaping strides until it had the space to unfurl its wings and push up into the sky. It drove forward thirty yards towards its master, but instead of landing in front of him, the creature hung uncertainly in the air, sensing that strange mind.

"Come here," Styrax growled, letting a shred of magic roll out with his words, redoubling the charm placed on the creature many months ago. It obeyed without a second thought, darting forward so quickly the beastmaster on its back yelped in surprise.

It landed and dipped its head so low it ran its throat over the grass at Styrax's feet. He reached down and patted it, and the wyvern turned its sinuous neck to watch him mount while the beastmaster scrambled off the other side.

"Run," Styrax ordered the man, "run for the gate and try to catch up with Lord Larim. Everyone else is panicking, so don't worry about being stopped, just make sure you're not here in a minute's time."

"What's happening, my Lord?" the man yelled, and as though in reply the ground trembled and shuddered like an earthquake.

"Something even a lifetime in your profession could not hope to control," Styrax replied. "Now run, you damn fool!"

The man didn't wait any longer and scrambled back the way he had come, towards the gate leading to Ismess. Styrax checked his saddle and found Elements and Destruction, the two Skulls he had been made to leave in the guardhouse before he entered the library, along with Kobra, his massive fanged broadsword. Its black surface was dull and faded, for it had been starved of both blood and magic for weeks, but some of the lustre returned when he slipped Destruction over the sword's guard. The other he added to his chest as he clipped his dragon belt onto the wyvern's saddle. Above the valley, the air began to shimmer and tremble as the mountain itself heaved underfoot.

Styrax looked around at the library and gave a grunt of acknowledgement. "It appears everything has gone to plan," he commented to the wyvern as he gathered the reins that had been tied to the horn of the saddle.

A shadowy blur flashed past his eyes and his sword was drawn and raised in an instant—but the blur continued past him and stopped beside the monument to Leitah a dozen yards away. His mouth filled with the bitter, coppery tang of magic, but even as he drew on the Skulls fixed to his armour, the dark swirls evaporated to reveal a figure in armour very like his own. The ground shook once again, even harder than before, accompanied by the groan of tortured rock.

The figure turned to look at him. Styrax knew immediately who it was, and why the black whorl-patterned armour completely enclosed the body, hiding it from the weak sun. He looked back and saw another figure on the cliff behind. The distance was too great to make out much more than a black silhouette against the sky, but he did not need to guess its identity.

"Surely not here for revenge?" he murmured, readying his defences.

As though in response the armoured figure turned appraisingly to the great crescent-shaped mound of earth that sheltered the monument.

So, Zhia, what do you do now? Nai wasn't wrong when he said the face on the monument looked familiar, was he? You brought your father's corpse here for a final resting place and set a terrible guard—Styrax stopped dead. *Gods. Unless I've underestimated you . . .*

"Leave now," Zhia called over the sound of a mountain trembling, her voice rolling like thunder around the valley. "Leave, or we will kill you."

Styrax looked back at the other figure, who drew his sword to add weight to the point. *Both with Skulls, two immortals together? Not the best odds.*

Zhia did not wait for a reply but kicked the stone monument. The solid block tipped onto its side as easily as an upturned chair, but Styrax felt the heavy thump reverberate up through the wyvern's body as tons of stone were smashed asunder.

"Leave!" she commanded with bone-shaking volume. Styrax knew he wouldn't get another warning. He gave the reins a tug, but the wyvern had no wish to linger in the presence of these alarmingly powerful creatures and hurriedly began flexing its pale blue wings before leaping up into the sky. Three strong strokes took them to cliff level and into a rising thermal before Styrax wheeled the beast around so he could watch events unfold beneath him.

The sour taste of having been bested filled his mouth. He watched as Zhia looked once more at the mound of earth beside her, then she punched the underside of the monument with her mailed fist. The stone shattered under the impact and Styrax saw a momentary blaze of white light burst out.

If her father's grave was underneath the monument, she paid it no attention—but that hardly surprised Styrax as he realised what she was doing. She hit the underside of the stone again, and again, and as the shards of stone fell to the ground a massive pulse of energy was expelled.

Even up in the sky Styrax felt a wave of dizziness envelop him, but he still saw as Zhia collected a shining object.

She quickly wrapped it in a length of cloth, binding it tightly, before drawing her sword and stowing the wrapped object on her back instead. There was a strange ripping sound and she turned back as the ground split open like a gigantic chrysalis, ripping further and further along the spine of the mound as something pushed forward from underneath.

A massive soil-coated shape, still indistinct, lifted itself up, one foot, then two, three feet, before dropping again, and Styrax saw a gleam of emerald appear further along the mound as the earth fell away . . .

Then the mound burst open as the dragon inside drove up and twisted its body to free itself from the constricting earth. Its wings were tightly furled and coated in dirt still, but he could tell the beast was huge, even by the standards of dragons. Its movements were lazy, as to be expected after a magically induced sleep, but with every passing second Styrax felt its presence swell.

Unbidden, the wyvern climbed further up into the sky, desperate to be away from its vastly larger cousin. This time Styrax did not stop it. He was dazed by what he had just witnessed, but after a moment the instinct for self-preservation kicked in and he turned his creature west, towards his army. The puzzle of the heart had been clear: it kept a dragon sleeping, and that beast, if ever awakened, would turn on the one who solved it. There had been no mention of the Crystal Skull, but Styrax had guessed at the mechanism for keeping the dragon asleep and knew perfectly well a dragon's preference for mages. That was why he kept Lord Larim back; experience with the Skulls had shown Styrax they were almost impossible to sense when not being used so it was likely the dragon would go after the nearest powerful mage.

Now, with the Farlan army so close at hand, he had a distraction to serve several purposes.

Yet she fooled me still, he thought with growing wonder and disbelief. He was scarcely able to believe what he had seen—and he was relieved he had not thought to stay and fight Zhia. He had made that decision thinking two immortal vampires bearing Crystal Skulls would probably have proved too much, even for him. *But with one of them wielding Aenaris, the Key of Life itself? Not even the Gods could stop them!*

The cavalry smashed into the Menin lines and men and horses screamed and roared and fell. Amber found himself beside Captain Hain, huddled behind their shields, which were resting on the boundary wall. Behind him infantrymen filled the small patch of ground. The wall was little more than rubble for half of its length now, but that had been enough to blunt the worst of the Farlan charge and now the Menin crossbowmen were making their shots count.

Amber felt a spear bite into his shield and nearly rip it from his grasp. He lunged blindly forward and caught the horse in the throat. The beast reared and threw itself backwards, shrieking as it fell, trying to avoid its rider. The scimitar was torn from his grip, so Amber wrenched the spear out and brandished it at the next man who came for them. Behind him he heard the frantic shouts of the officer commanding the bowmen, and the heavy stamp of another infantry company moving up.

Half of the Farlan were now on foot, charging with remarkable fervour. Amber could see his men were easily getting the better of the ragged mercenaries, but among them were men of an entirely different calibre. A knot of knights smashed their way through the line where the wall had fallen, hacking their way through as their warhorses kicked and stamped a bloody path. Red and white ribbons fixed to their armour danced furiously in the breeze.

"Take them down!" Amber yelled to the arriving infantry. The men levelled spears and charged into the half dozen knights. The nearest was impaled, but he protected the rest, who turned straight into the company, driving into the ranks to get past the reach of their spears before chopping down on every available target. Two crossbow bolts slammed into the rearmost knight, throwing him from his saddle, but the others ignored him, intent on causing as much damage as possible. At last, enough of the pressing infantry managed to bring the knights down one by one, though taking heavy casualties right to the last moment.

Amber and Hain led the charge to close the gap, running forward with a squad close behind. More troops were running for the breach, led by an unnaturally tall figure swathed in shadows and carrying a pair of long scimitars.

"Piss and daemons, that looks like Haysh!" Amber shouted in shock. The figure was thinner and paler than the icon above the training ground of his youth, but that was no surprise—Haysh the Steel Dancer was a Menin Aspect of Karkarn after all. The Farlan version would reflect its own worshippers.

He threw the spear over-arm at the Aspect, but it slipped out of the way, turning the movement into an elegant double slash that cut away first shield, then arm, of the nearest man on the other side of the breach. Amber drew his remaining scimitar and swung it in a high circle as he closed on the Aspect.

"With me," he yelled to Hain, guessing the Aspect would recognise the style of fighting taught in its own temples and see him as its the greatest threat. "Stay tight and go low!"

The men rushed forward together. A sharp cold wind swept around them as they came within feet of the Aspect, but Amber didn't have time to worry about that. Keeping their momentum they charged the Aspect, which aimed a wide cut at Amber, momentarily stopping their run, and then gave ground. The squad rounded Hain, pikes levelled, and Amber lashed out twice, and was parried with ease each time. The squad charged, forcing the Aspect to turn and use both swords to drive them back. Amber struck out again, giving Hain the opening he needed to cut deep into the Aspect's left arm.

Black blood spurted out over the ground and the minor God gave a hiss of pain. Its left arm dropped under the sword's weight, but it didn't slow for even a moment as it cut down on Hain's raised shield. The captain fell, but

Amber was already stepping into the fight, cutting into the Aspect's neck, trying to bring it down. As the Aspect hit the ground he heard a scream in the background and glimpsed a priest reeling, then the body exploded into black flames.

Amber grabbed Hain and dragged the man back, letting the squad turn and lock shields as more Farlan soldiers attacked. Overhead the air was filled with a dozen golden arrows; one of Larim's battle-mages stood with hands outstretched, surrounded by a corona of painfully bright golden light.

Amber knelt down and rolled the man onto his back. "Hain, still with me?" he asked urgently.

"Bastard," coughed Hain, his face contorted with pain, "didn't have to drag my face over the ground!"

Amber grinned; swearing was a good sign for an injured man. He leaned over to get a better look at the wounded arm, but it looked as if the pauldron had taken the worst of the blow; the thick steel rim was cut all the way through, as was the shield that had been above it. Blood was running freely from Hain's shoulder.

"Gods, man, you bleed more easily than a virgin in a barracks," Amber joked. He got to his knees and started to haul the smaller man up. "You'll live, get that bound up."

"Aye—Shitfuckingdamn!" Hain gasped, his eyes widening.

Even before he turned, Amber could see the reflected yellow glow in Hain's eyes. A party of horsemen drove into the Menin line, knights and priests alike led by the enormous yellow-robed figure of Lord Chalat himself. The white-eye was silent and focused, striking left and right with a huge copper broadsword, a gauntlet of flame encasing his left hand. As Amber watched, the huge white-eye punched one Menin soldier and the man was thrown back nearly twenty feet, flames spreading over his body before he even hit the ground.

"Gods, where are the Reavers?" Amber called.

As if on cue a deranged shriek of fury and ecstasy cut the air and in the east he saw a large man crouched almost flat on an enormous blade-edged shield, two more following on in quick succession, but they disappeared behind the mass of cavalry swarming around the enemy lines.

"Shit, they're off target," Amber realised, looking around him to see what troops he had left to repel the attackers. The newly arrived reserves lost no time in heading towards the beleaguered line, but he realised they wouldn't be enough if there were any more Aspects or breaches. The battle-mage behind him had fallen silent, the golden corona replaced with a faint greenish glow, and his expression was one of total concentration as he focused entirely on the Chosen of Tsatach.

The major turned back to Chalat in time to see a crossbow bolt wing him in the fleshy part of his bicep. The wound wasn't deep, looking at the way he tossed his sword to his left hand, but perhaps it would be enough.

"You can defend against him?" Amber yelled to the battle-mage.

The man looked bewildered for a moment, then nodded. "Directly; only for a few seconds."

"Then defend me," Amber yelled, and without giving the mage a chance to reply he turned and snatched up Hain's long spike-tipped axe in his left hand. With his scimitar in his right Amber sprinted towards the huge white-eye cutting a bloody path through the defenders. Chalat had kicked a hole in the wall and pushed a few yards past his allies, fighting with all the skill of the Chosen, despite using his left hand. Amber had always been quick, especially for a big man, and now he ignored the fighting to put every last ounce of strength he had into the sprint.

Twelve yards to the breach, eight, five—a warm glow enveloped him as the mage wrapped a protective cloak over him. He saw Chalat glance around at the movement and flick a wrist in his direction. A lance of flame spat out just before he reached his target and was deflected by the battle-mage's protective wrap. Amber flinched, but kept running. One yard away and he launched himself towards Chalat with a scream of triumph, his scimitar whistling around towards Chalat's neck.

The white-eye moved faster than Amber could see and his vision went white as fire wrapped his body. Again it was deflected away, just in time for him to see Chalat had turned right around, his broadsword raised to catch Amber's sword. When the blades connected, with Amber's full weight behind the blow, he felt his body savagely jerked back as Chalat's arm didn't give an inch. Pain flared in his wrist as it snapped, but momentum carried him around. Now with no thought to his own survival Amber thrust the axe forward, slamming it into the centre of Chalat's body.

The spike drove in deep as Amber's face collided with the white-eye's. It felt like hitting an oak tree. He felt the axe head crunch against Chalat's breastbone, then the weapon was knocked from his grip and stars burst in his eyes as gravity embraced him once more. He fell back and the sky turned purple as the weight of his scimitar twisted his broken wrist around, then his head and shoulders hit the ground and sudden, shocking darkness enveloped him.

Advancing at a canter, the Farlan cavalry forded one river, then the next. Ahead of them were screens of light cavalry divisions, who had raced ahead to allow the heavier troops the ease of an uncontested crossing. He could feel a presence behind him, watching his back as they headed towards the battle. Byora had been so quiet all day that it fuelled his paranoia, but Isak knew he could spare no more than the legion of light cavalry he had stationed outside the quarter.

He fought the urge to squirm in his saddle, fearful of both what lay behind and what was ahead, and going against every instinct by marching between them. All around him fluttered the bright clashing colours of the Farlan nobility and their hurscals: six hundred heavy cavalrymen, the centre of the Farlan line. The men were hushed, apprehensive, the nerves wound taut. All around him men were gripping their weapons just a shade too tightly, even Count Vesna, and many were being a little too severe with their horses. The hero of the Farlan was silent, his attention fixed on some vague point in the distance and his visor down, so it fell to General Lahk to keep Isak informed. With every piece of news, and each word of advice, Isak's world grew darker.

On the left flank, Suzerain Torl was fighting a slow and controlled retreat; drawing back from the Menin lines, but taking heavy losses whenever they engaged with the minotaurs. In the centre and on the right flank chaos reigned; the Farlan were being driven back in on themselves by the steady push of the Menin reserves. Though he was being outflanked, Chalat was neither retreating nor regrouping.

The Menin centre had repelled several attacks and were refusing to be drawn off their positions, content to wait for their cavalry as they worked their way around. According to his scryers, without the heroics from the light cavalry, the entire crusade would have been wrapped up and slaughtered by now—but even so, they weren't going to last much longer.

"My Lord, may I order support to Suzerain Torl?" General Lahk asked.

Isak looked at the three divisions of Ghosts and one light cavalry legion. "You may—send the First Guardsmen and the Fordan-Tebran legion to Torl's command."

Lahk gave the order and soon troops were wheeling away, the light cavalry leaping ahead of the Ghosts to reinforce Torl's beleaguered troops as soon as possible. Isak was left with a division of Ghosts on his left flank and three legions of light cavalry on his right, with one of each as rearguard.

"Tirah legions advance to right flank attack?" asked General Lahk, sticking rigidly to protocol.

Isak repeated the command back and the order was sounded. The right-hand legions began to move ahead of the centre, peeling off to attack the rear of the Menin reserves. Isak couldn't see what was happening; he had to trust Lahk's experience, all the while his nerves were jangling like wind chimes in a gale.

Another hundred yards on, and the view opened out.

Parting before the steady advance, a straggly group of Farlan cavalry broke left as their assailants gave ground to the right. The battered regiments wore the dark robes of penitents, so Isak knew the ordered troops with white lances were Menin cavalry. They were retiring to ensure their infantry weren't encircled, not realising it was Farlan heavy cavalry facing them. As they moved, the Menin infantry units were revealed like the sun through parting clouds. Isak felt his heart quicken.

"Sound the advance!" he roared, not needing Lahk's prompting.

The pace of the heavy cavalry immediately quickened, every knight realising they could shatter the heart of the enemy's reserves. Two hundred yards, the gap closing fast. Some instinct made Isak look up and his heart lurched as he saw the winged shape of a wyvern passing high overhead.

The sands are falling, crooned the Headsman at the furthest recesses of Isak's mind; *the hunter is calling.*

Isak shook his head and drove the voice from his mind, flooding his body with the eager fire of magic from his Crystal Skulls. He felt his hands tremble momentarily as the intoxicating energy surged through his veins and wrapped him in a warm cocoon of power.

The enemy ahead snapped into focus and in the confines of his helm Isak heard his breathing turn to a growl and his muscles tighten with anticipation. His shoulders ached with power begging to be released and now he was only too glad to oblige. Raising Eolis he roared the order to charge that was echoed by every man with him, and he unleashed the fury of the storm.

A blinding burst of lightning flew from the tip of Eolis, forking in the air and lashing the ground once, twice, before snapping across the front rank of infantry in an explosion of sparks. Isak barely heard it, for he was near deafened by the hammer of hooves surrounding him, but it had the desired effect for he saw the bodies on the ground and the hole torn in the front rank for the Farlan to charge through.

Toramin barely slowed as they hit the enemy. Isak felt the impact as man after man was smashed to the ground by the huge charger's armoured chest. He cut left and right, shield held low, barely seeing the men he killed. Beside him he heard Vesna bellowing even more wildly as blood flew, weapons glanced off him, and men screamed and cried and died.

The Farlan cavalry battered a path into the heart of the enemy legion, leaving only crushed and broken bodies in their wake. As their momentum slowed many knights dropped their lances and grabbed the weapons hanging from their saddles. Only Vesna and Isak had swords in their hands; the rest hacked at the enemy with axes and maces—heavy, brutal blows that crushed skulls and removed heads. In the centre of it all, Isak roared, putting every ounce of unnatural strength into each cut and revelling in the jarring impacts. Eolis cut steel and bone with equal ease as Isak used his shield to batter weapons away and smash faces to pulp.

In moments or minutes, he could not tell which, the enemy fled under the onslaught. Many threw their weapons down and ran blindly, racing for the safety of the Menin line, which had now turned to face the Farlan. Isak screamed his frustration as he saw them run and drew on the Skull again.

He reached up and brandished Eolis above his head, and in the glittering blade's wake, so silvery threads appeared, and spun and spun at a blinding speed until Isak threw the swirl after the fleeing soldiers. Though it barely brushed the first, it ripped his arm and shoulder away, and streaked on past the shrieking man into the main bulk of soldiers. Everyone it touched was thrown to the ground, blood fountaining from a thousand cuts; those it engulfed simply disappeared in a crimson blur.

Isak released the stream of magic and panted for breath. The knights with him were cheering as they watched the enemy flee. He looked lower and saw the brutalised remains of the Menin infantry, a carpet of corpses spread out behind him.

"That's what it's about, my Lord!" yelled a man beside him, his voice ragged by heaving breaths and elation. Isak didn't recognise the crest for a moment before his memory kicked in: rose petals and a dagger; that's Suzerain Lehm.

"Showed the bastards what a heavy cavalry charge can do, eh?" Lehm gestured at the slaughter all around him and Isak realised he was right. Half of the dead would have been killed by the steel-shod, armoured horses.

"We've no time yet for celebration," General Lahk roared, his voice carrying over the clamour, "form up!" Men jumped to obey as the familiar repeating warble of the horns rang out. Light cavalrymen rode forward in pursuit of the routed troops, looking to cut them down before they reached safety.

As Isak watched, the Menin cavalry regained some semblance of order and started preparing to repel the Farlan soldiers—then a cry came from behind him as someone shouted, "Ware! Attack—attack from the city!" The alarm in his voice was plain for all to hear and Isak turned at once and began to force his way through the crowd, Vesna close behind him, leaving the general to berate hurscals and nobles alike for not reforming quickly enough. Somewhere near the back, a hurscal in Suzerain Foleh's colours called out, "Don't know how it happened, but judging by the way they're running, looks like someone's just torn through that legion." The man, who didn't appear much older than Isak himself, was standing in his stirrups, pointing back towards Byora. Despite his youth he sounded assured, like a veteran.

Isak could see the reserves were already turning; doubtless they'd heard the bugle calls from the legion guarding the entrance to Byora.

"There's never a bloody scryer when we need one," Isak growled. He closed his eyes and placed one hand over the Skull fused to his cuirass, drawing deeply on its energy again. A cold wave surged through his mind, making him gasp with shock. He centred himself, breathing slowly and deeply, and closed his mind off to everything but the steady rhythm of his beating heart for a moment before sending his senses soaring high up into the brooding sky. He ignored the angry swirl of clouds and concentrated instead on the Land below. The wind rising up off the ground carried the damp smell of earth and the tang of spilled blood. He could feel the remaining priests and Aspects as a gentle fizz at the back of his mind; Kastan Styrax was a bright burning beacon, his Crystal Skulls causing a spark of sharp pain until Isak managed to block him. He felt a sense of great age wash over him when he looked north: whatever was attacking them was old, very old. At the back of his mind a presence stirred, then all of a sudden there was a rushing sensation and he yelped, throwing up a hasty wall around his mind before realising he didn't need the defence because he wasn't under attack. Something had *left* him—maybe not entirely, for he thought he could still detect a thread of energy connecting them—but it had found the strength to cross the battlefield. *The Soldier*, he thought, *the Aspect of Death who is at his strongest on the battlefield—*

He paused, suddenly struck by something: the presences out on the field felt remarkably similar to the Soldier to him, more like divine than mortal. Before he could investigate further, a stirring in the east grabbed his attention. When he turned in its direction, a vast presence suddenly locked its gaze onto him and in that instant Isak sensed rage beyond anything he'd experienced before, even surpassing that fury that had almost consumed him in his first battle.

Isak didn't wait to find out any more but broke the flow of magic and forced his eyes open.

Vesna, his faceplate raised, was peering anxiously at him. "Gods, that's never a good sign," he said, not even trying to sound lighthearted as Isak pulled his helm from his head and tried desperately to suck in air.

Isak shook his whole body, like a wet dog. "Wasn't my fucking fault this time," he gasped, "but something's waking up on Blackfang."

"What do you mean, waking up?" Vesna said in dismay. "And *something*? Do you mean another water elemental?"

"No such luck—whatever it is, it's far bigger." He paused, trying to place the sensation, then a memory stirred in the back of his mind. "Gods," he breathed, "it reminded me of Genedel."

Vesna blanched. "There's a bloody dragon about to attack us?"

"Me," Isak corrected him; "it's about to attack *me*."

"What did you do to it?"

Isak snapped, roaring, "Nothing!" as he shoved Vesna with such force that he almost toppled from his saddle. "For once it's not my damn fault!" He looked back at the Menin line and snarled, "And it's not our only bloody problem either—whatever's attacking from Byora is kin to the Reapers."

"Kin?" Vesna thought for a moment. "Piss and daemons; those bastard sons of Death. It's the Jesters. We hoped they'd died in the fires of Scree, but looks like no such luck. Cockroaches always find a way to survive, don't they?"

"I doubt leaving Azaer's employ is an option either," Isak said grimly, "dead or alive. But more important: right now we're surrounded." Their plans hadn't included fighting their way out of a trap—none of the scryers had found enough troops to entrap a mounted army, and the legion stationed at Byora's gate should have been enough to stop any surprise sorties. "Suggestions?"

Vesna looked down at his wrist, then towards the Menin lines. His mouth opened a little, then closed again as indecision took over.

"Nothing?" Isak asked. "Do you think we might be able to rout the Menin with an all-out push?"

Vesna gave a helpless shrug. "I don't know. They're formed up now, so we won't catch anyone alone out in the open."

He looked around at the Farlan light cavalry regiments on either side of them. They were able to strafe the enemy lines, whilst remaining manoeuvrable enough to dodge any potential counterattacks. In the distance, the drums on the Menin lines beat out an ominous tattoo of orders he couldn't understand.

"We can't just stand here," Vesna muttered, thinking aloud. "If we call a full retreat we'll have them snapping at our heels, but as long as we can break through the Jesters, it should be manageable. If we push on—Well, I've no idea what we're going to meet. They know they only need to blunt our attack, and what with the Reavers, the minotaurs, and Lord Styrax himself, they've pretty much got the weapons to do it."

"Fuck," Isak breathed as he turned back to the eastern horizon, his mouth dropping open.

For a moment Vesna couldn't see what had attracted Isak's attention. He scanned the outline of Blackfang in vain before realising Isak was looking higher: at an indistinct black shape that was climbing, slowly, ponderously, into the sky.

"Gods . . ." Vesna stared at the shape, trying to gauge just how large it was, but he gave up. There was no point. "*That* is what's coming for you?"

Isak sighed. "I don't think it cares *who* I am, but it's angry, and I just waved a bloody great big red rag in front of it."

"Can you stop it?"

"How? With the Skulls? Give me a decade of training and maybe—but right now the only thing I know how to do that will stop something like that is to call down the storm, like I did in Narkang. If I do that, no one near me will survive."

"What about your companion?" Vesna asked, his voice lowered. He looked over his shoulder, checking no one was near enough to hear their conversation.

"If I gave him the control he needed, I'd never get it back," Isak admitted.

"*The last grains are falling,*" whispered a voice at the back of his mind, as if in response to Verna's question. It sounded gleeful and malevolent. "*The Master comes for you.*"

Isak froze. There was certainly in the Headsman's voice that he'd not heard before, like the finality of a tomb door slamming shut.

Gods, this is really it.

He tightened his grip on the reins as a wave of lightheadedness washed over him, making him sway. The clamour of battle seemed to fade away until all he could see was the naked blade of Eolis lying across his lap and the dark shape in the sky as it began to labour towards them.

"If we stay, we're all dead," Isak stated.

I feel it drawing me. My dreams have drawn me here. The threads that bind me—whether prophecy, fate or a shadow's scheme—have brought me to this place, and there will be no escape. They hold me too tight—

Vesna unknowingly interrupted Isak's dark thoughts. He raised his left hand and said clearly, "That might not be so, my Lord."

Isak looked at Vesna, who struggled with his vambrace as he continued, "There's something—I didn't want to tell you—I was frightened to tell you, but—"

"It doesn't matter," Isak said, cutting him off.

"It does!" Vesna insisted, giving up the struggle and using the edge of his sword to cut the vambrace away. "I can create a diversion for you: something that will give the Menin so much to think about that you'll be able to break through the Jesters."

"No, my friend, you couldn't," Isak said sadly. He watched as General Lahk rode through the knights, saluting his lord even now as the men fell silent. They surrounded Isak and Vesna with a ring of steel, and though they couldn't hear the conversation, they watched the two men, somehow aware that something momentous was unfolding.

"My Lord," Vesna yelled, trying to get Isak to pay attention, "listen to me!"

Finally Isak focused on his friend.

Vesna said out loud the words he had been repeating to himself, over and over again, for so long. "The night I was attacked in Tirah, Karkarn came to me and offered me the chance to become his Mortal-Aspect." He succeeded in pulling off his vambrace and tore off the bandage on his wrist. He pulled out a teardrop-shaped ruby and held it up. "He gave me this. All I need do to seal the bargain is to cut my cheek with it."

"And what would you do then?" Isak asked quietly. "Would you take on an entire army by yourself? Would you stand back to back with the God of War as the two of you fight his own Chosen and a dragon? You don't know if it'll even pay you any attention."

"It will give you a chance," Vesna insisted, emotion making his voice hoarse. "If we stay here and do nothing, then we are all dead!"

"I know." Isak let the words hang in the air for a moment.

He beckoned Lahk over and said, "General Lahk, I believe you to be a man who will follow orders, to your death if necessary; is that so?"

The general said nothing, but he inclined his head. His helm was still on, so Isak couldn't see any expression on his face, but he doubted the man was anything but his usual impassive self.

"Good. If you do not obey this order, I will kill you where you sit. Do you understand me?"

"Isak!" Vesna yelled desperately, but the white-eye raised a hand to stop him.

"General Lahk, sound the retreat," Isak continued. "Lead these men back the way we came. Do not—Do *not* stop, not for anything nor anyone. This battle is lost; all that remains is to salvage what is left. Do you understand?"

Lahk nodded again and turned to his bugler beside him. "General retreat to all legions," he repeated solemnly.

"Vesna, my friend," Isak continued while the order was being called, "no matter what you do, what bargain you make, you cannot buy the army the time it needs. I need you to lead this army from the front—or I will kill you too."

"But—"

"No more." Isak raised Eolis and took hold of the Skull that was fused around the guard like a coating of ice. "Take Hunting with you; there's no need for both of them to fall into enemy hands."

"You can't," Vesna said weakly.

"I can." Isak smiled as he felt the weight of the Land lift from his shoulders. In the distance the dragon was closing, but he still had time. "I never was much of a gambler—never had the patience for it—but it looks like I'm going to learn the hard way. Carel used to say a man was measured by the quality of his friends—I'm not sure what that says for my youth because I didn't have any friends, but now I hope he was right."

He slipped from his saddle and handed the reins to Vesna. "I'm about to take the greatest gamble of all, but at last I'm not afraid. I'll trust the quality of my friends to see it through."

Awkwardly, he held out an arm to Vesna, who stared at it in shock for a moment before taking it.

"Goodbye, my friend," Isak said simply. "Thank you."

And with that he turned around and walked towards the Menin line. The Farlan knights parted before him, some staring in bafflement, others saluting the silver-clad giant. He could hear the repeated orders being relayed throughout the legions, and the clamour as his men hurried to obey his last order.

Vesna too heard the sound of the general retreat, but he couldn't focus on it, not even when a hurscal grabbed his arm and yelled something in his face. He could make no sense of the man's words . . .

Then General Lahk roared, "Count Vesna, you have your orders! Lead the way, man!" and Vesna shook himself.

He looked up at the man who'd commanded him all the years he'd served in the Ghosts. His eyes inevitably fell to the ruby sitting in his palm, then he turned back to watch Isak as the white-eye walked calmly towards the enemy army, already wrapped in crackling coils of lightning.

Gods preserve you, my friend, he thought and raised the ruby to scratch the skin below his eye. An unusually sharp sting flared on his face and he instinctively jerked his hand out of the way—before realising that the ruby had stayed there. He tried to pull it away, but realised it was now fixed to his cheek—but that was the least of his concerns as he felt himself surrounded by shadows. He saw horror on the hurscal's face before the man was hidden from sight by a swirling funnel of darkness. A fire burst into life in his belly.

All at once he felt every injury he'd ever received, every battlefield scar, cut, and bruise, flared to life and Vesna howled at the excruciating pain, his head turned up towards the sky. He felt the shadows surge down his throat, driving him backwards, almost off his horse, before he caught his balance. His nerves burst into life, as if a map of sensation tracing every inch of his body. The screams and clamour of past battles echoed in his ears.

"My general," said Karkarn in his ear, so deafeningly loud that Vesna felt the words reverberate through his whole body and remain, shuddering, in his bones. All around him he suddenly felt raw power, both terrible and beautiful in its savagery, and his muscles flooded with inhuman strength. His vision cleared and the whole battlefield stretched out before him so he could see every curve and contour of the ground ahead. He could feel the fear in the eyes of his distant enemy, He tasted the blood on the wind.

"Raise your sword, my general," Karkarn cried, "we go to war!"

Isak felt the coursing power increase with every step he took as, unchecked, the magic from the Skull grew into a furious storm. The air shuddered under the assault and the ground beneath his feet trembled as the grass was slashed and torn by the lashing coils of energy. Up above clouds swirled closer, lowering and rumbling over the plain.

His senses were opened so wide to the Land around him that he could smell the dragon now; its presence was impossible to ignore. Isak was surrounded by a corona of blistering light as he walked towards the Menin troops. Behind him he sensed the sudden divine aura of Karkarn manifesting, but he forced himself to ignore it. He was close enough now that he could see the horror on the faces of his enemy, terrified by the gross display of unrestrained power.

Some nervous eyes began to turn east, to where the dragon was becoming clearer, but most remained on him as the raging corona surrounding him began to form into a cohesive mass. Distantly Isak felt magic striking his shell of translucent white fire, but it spluttered into nothing as it hit the raw power.

As he felt the dragon near him, he raised his shield above his head, sending a wavering column of light up into the massing clouds. The storm responded to him and Isak felt the earsplitting crash of lightning assail his protective cocoon. He looked up to see the enormous beast check its momentum, throwing its vast tail forward and its head back as another bolt of lightning split the air, then another.

Isak continued onwards; he knew he couldn't control such a monstrous amount of magic for long without burning his mind out. Fifty paces from the enemy line, a bolt struck the huddled troops, tearing a hole in the ranks. He added his own power to that and heard the screams as magic set a dozen or more alight.

More lightning fell, the frequency and intensity increasing with every strike. Hanging in the air the dragon wheeled and turned, searching for a safe path through the supernatural lightning to Isak. It roared in pain, its voice rivalling the thunder that boomed out over the plain. Its scaled body shone with emerald light as the lightning raced over its body.

Driven backwards, the dragon reeled from the blow, but not even the power of the storm was enough to knock the monster from the sky. It had enough height to recover, and it used its gigantic pale green wings to heave its way up again. Isak sensed the beast's shock, but its rage was undiminished. As best he could he directed the storm towards it and was rewarded by the sight of the dragon retreating another few hundred yards before it landed heavily.

With his shield and sword raised, Isak marched towards the Menin infantry, and they scattered before him, too scared to face the furious storm of energy surrounding him. A second line of troops lay behind: cavalry and pikemen packed in tightly. Isak didn't falter, but scanned the field urgently; he didn't have much time left. The Crystal Skull defended his mind while it fed it with power only the Gods could comprehend, but that torrent of power was too much for any mortal to handle for long—let alone a novice. Soon the weakest link in the chain would snap, and the riot of raw power would react like a whiplash.

Finally he spotted them: a beastman in armour and a large knight with Lord Styrax's emblem painted in white on his chest, sitting on horseback between the cavalry and infantry: General Gaur and Scion Kohrad, Styrax's son.

As he pressed on, each step required more and more effort as he felt his own awareness bleeding away. More magic struck him, but still to no effect; more lighting hammered down with the rage of Gods and tore men apart. He saw General Gaur point in his direction, though the words were lost in an ocean of noise, and saw crossbowmen level their weapons. With a sweep of his hand Isak tore a furrow through them, ripping the soldiers open three ranks deep, leaving only corpses behind.

Without warning, he broke into a run, intent on closing the ground while he still could. General Gaur spurred forward to meet him, but Isak swatted both the huge warhorse and its rider sprawling as he charged straight at Kohrad.

Kastan Styrax's son was no coward. The young white-eye roared a challenge, slipping from his horse, and swung both axe and sword at Isak, who lunged forward, using his own weapon to deflect Kohrad's. He hit Kohrad, only a glancing blow but it drove the smaller white-eye back, and a bolt of lightning crashed down between them. Kohrad howled and attacked again, feinting high then cutting at Isak's legs. He tried in vain to knock Eolis from Isak's grasp, but the Farlan lord dodged and smashed his shield into Kohrad's face. Kohrad rode the blow and slashed at Isak with both his weapons, bearing down so that Isak was forced backwards, but he caught the blows on his shield and lashed out with Eolis, a volley of cuts that had Kohrad defending desperately—

—until a blast of thunderous power gouged a great furrow in the ground between the two, forcing them apart.

Isak turned and saw a wyvern leap forward over the heads of the cavalrymen who had been watching the fight in stunned silence, too awed to intervene in this clash of giants. The storm suddenly focused and lightning began to target the black-armoured figure atop the winged beast, but Kastan Styrax held his white hand above his head, projecting a steel grey shield of magic. Though the lightning thrashed ferociously about the shield, it was to no avail—but it gave Isak all the time he needed.

He drew deeply on the Skull and sent wild tendrils of energy in all directions, before suddenly concentrating them on Styrax himself. Under the assault the air between them seemed to distort and rip. He heard the mocking, exultant laughter of the Reapers in his shadow, and the groan of the Land itself as he let loose more magic than he could ever have even conceived of.

Styrax twisted his shield down, somehow fending off the attack once again, and the wyvern disappeared behind a curtain of blinding sparks.

Now barely able to see, working entirely by instinct, Isak loosed his hold on the magic, tightened his grip on Eolis, and abruptly turned. He swept back the sword, and in one smooth motion, he threw Eolis . . .

. . . and the sword, moving as if in slow motion, pierced the incandescent chaos . . .

. . . and struck its target dead-centre . . .

Isak's legs gave away underneath him and he crumpled, falling almost simultaneously with Kohrad as the force of Eolis smashing into him made him stagger backwards before he fell to the ground.

In the next moment the storm of magic disappeared and pain engulfed his body. Isak forced himself to one knee, almost shrieking with pain. His lungs were wheezing agony, his throat a ball of flame inside his body.

Distantly he heard an animal cry of grief.

"Kohrad!" someone screamed, and a black-clad figure raced past. Isak lurched almost drunkenly, unable to focus his eyes, his body twitching in distress. He tried to turn his head, but his body refused to obey. More shouting, then a blow to the side of his head that laid him out, facedown in the ruined earth.

Hands grabbed him and dragged him upright, pulling the helm from his head. A face appeared, contorted with rage and hatred, shouting something, but he couldn't understand a word. Then he heard, in heavily accented Farlan, "You will *burn*! You will suffer agony with no end!"

Isak managed to choke out a laugh. "You think so? I'm dying," he whispered, the effort of speaking bringing tears to his eyes.

"Not before I'm finished with you!" Styrax roared. He knelt down next to Isak and smashed his mailed fist into the side of Isak's head.

Stars burst before his eyes as an explosion of pain overrode the previous agony, but Isak forced a smile onto his face. "Paradise awaits me," he wheezed. "I am one of the Chosen—and now I die."

A dark veil appeared around them all and through the one eye still working, Isak could see the Land suddenly appeared darker and colder. Death's hand rested on his shoulder.

"I will not allow it!" Styrax screamed in frustration and fury, smashing Isak once more to the ground.

At a signal, his men laid out the Farlan lord on his back, pinning down his arms and legs, though he was too weak even to stand.

Isak coughed torturously, trying to turn his head as he vomited up stinking black blood.

"You will never see the Land of No Time," Styrax snarled, digging his black iron–clad fingers into Isak's flesh, "you will see no Last Judgment!" He ripped the Crystal Skull from Isak's cuirass and tossed it aside almost carelessly, then punched Isak in the face, shattering his nose. With a thought he called his black sword and Kobra flew into his hand.

Isak felt the Menin lord open himself to the awesome power contained within his own Skulls, and a whirlwind of dark flames sprang up around them. His vision cleared a little as his body gratefully drank in the wild surging magic, but it did nothing to assuage the pain running through his blood and bones. His damaged eye bled freely down his cheek and the fire in his throat continued unabated.

He heard Styrax howling, words he didn't recognise, and he felt the earth writhing and shaking underneath him.

"Pain I promised you," Styrax spat, "and pain you will receive!" He lunged forward and the fanged sword split Isak's cuirass and drove deep into his stomach. Isak screamed hoarsely as the blade split his gut, both searing hot and burning cold. Styrax yanked the blade up and down, trying to make it as excruciating as he could, ripping Isak open from groin to sternum and driving the breath from his body. The air around them filled with a terrible chittering sound, the voices of daemons sweeping in.

The darkness grew thick and cold as Styrax gave Kobra one last twist. He was rewarded with another cry, and that won, he raised his boot and stamped down on Isak's broken face.

"Think of the life you took," he said, his own voice jagged with grief, "as your skin is torn from your body in Ghenna! The Dark Place welcomes you." He jerked out Kobra and Isak fell, feeling the earth give way beneath him as he plunged deeper and deeper. The darkness enveloped him and the cries of daemons became deafening.

He screamed.

ENDGAME

MIHN PULLED HIS TATTERED LEATHER COAT around him as he looked out over the lake, watching the raindrops form concentric circles on the otherwise still surface, trying to work out why he felt so uneasy. The rain had been falling steadily since early morning and the solid mass of slate grey clouds hid the sun so completely he could only guess the hour.

The only habitation in sight was a squat cottage in bad need of repair. A battered fishing boat had been dragged up the shore away from the water and left under a crude cover made of loosely woven branches covered with a ragged tarpaulin. The cottage had been abandoned for two seasons now, so Mihn had requisitioned it for himself. He valued solitude as much as the witch did, and had no intention of imposing on her hospitality for longer than absolutely necessary.

There was no sound other than the rain falling on water and ground. He looked back at the trees behind him, hoping to see gentry peering out from the shadows, but there were none. It looked like their curiosity had finally been appeased, and they had decided to accept the presence of a human as impossibly stealthy as they themselves were. Their absence made Mihn feel strangely alone.

He had been staring at the water for too long, lost in his disquietude, but nothing had changed. He was considering taking the little rowboat out so he could try his hand at fishing when a distant sound caught his ear—running footsteps, maybe?

Scarcely had he turned back to the forest when a girl of no more than twelve summers came careening down the path through the trees and stumbled to a halt in front of him. As she stared open-mouthed at the former Harlequin, he took note of her own appearance: bright blue eyes and a reddened nose peeking out from under a sandy mess of hair.

"Are you looking for me?" Mihn asked softly, trying hard to sound friendly and approachable, but the very act of speaking almost spooked the girl into scampering back the way she'd come.

"What's your name?" he tried again.

The girl swallowed. "Chera, sir."

Her faded dress had red flowers poorly embroidered along the hem. He guessed it had belonged to at least one older sibling before her. He gave a little bow. "Hello, Chera. I am Mihn ab Netren ab Felith. Have you been sent to find me?"

"Y—Yes, sir. She's screamin', sir, that brown girl, screamin' like the creatures of the Dark Place is after 'er."

Mihn frowned at the child's choice of words and she edged back a step, frightened by his expression.

He smoothed out his frown and asked gently, "Did the witch say I was to return with you?"

Chera shook her head. "Twilight, sir" she muttered. "She said to make yersel' ready and come at the ghost hour."

Mihn nodded gravely. "The ghost hour it is. Thank you, Chera."

He stood impassively, waiting until the child had disappeared back into the trees before he gave in to the overwhelming emotion that had hit him at her words.

His face drained of blood and he sank to his knees, his legs betraying him. Gasping like a drowning man, he allowed a single moan of sorrow to escape his lips before he buried his face in his tattooed palms.

"Isak," he whispered, choking on his own tears. "Merciful Gods, Isak, what have we done?"

ABOUT THE AUTHOR

TOM **L**LOYD is the author of *The Stormcaller* and *The Twilight Herald* (books one and two of the Twilight Reign). He was born in 1979 in Berkshire. After a degree in International Relations he went straight into publishing where he still works. He never received the memo about suitable jobs for writers and consequently has never been a kitchen-hand, hospital porter, pigeon hunter, or secret agent. He lives in South London, isn't one of those authors who gives a damn about the history of the font used in his books, and only believes in forms of exercise that allow him to hit something. Visit him online at www.tomlloyd.co.uk.

The story continues in

THE RAGGED MAN

OCTOBER 2009

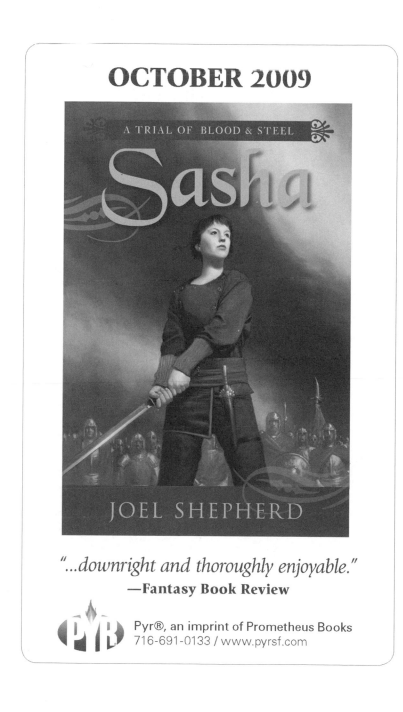

A TRIAL OF BLOOD & STEEL

Sasha

JOEL SHEPHERD

"...downright and thoroughly enjoyable."
—**Fantasy Book Review**

Pyr®, an imprint of Prometheus Books
716-691-0133 / www.pyrsf.com